LAO LANXANG

LAO
LANXANG
AND ITS LAST KING

XANOUVONG

UNICORN

Published in the UK by Unicorn
an imprint of Unicorn Publishing Group, 2023
Charleston Studio
Meadow Business Centre
Lewes BN8 5RW

www.unicornpublishing.org

ISBN 978-1-911397-40-3

10 9 8 7 6 5 4 3 -2 1

Cover by Unicorn
Typeset by Vivian Head

Printed in Malta by Gutenberg Press

Author's Note

I thought about Lao LanXang and Chao Anouvong when I was praying in the Emerald Buddha temple in Bangkok and have been intrigued by the true history of Siam and LanXang ever since. It fired my imagination. Two forces are influencing me: literature and the intellectual challenge on one hand, and the nobility of the truth on the other. If I've whetted the imagination of anyone with an interest in Chao Anouvong and the Lao nation, then I won't have written this in vain.

Lao LanXang and Its Last King is a historical story – part history and part novel. No attempt has been made to combine the two before. Of course, if you like, after you've read it you can call it anything you please. It shouldn't be taken as a full picture of King Anouvong's life. All records of him from the ViengChan court have vanished. We know little about his history beyond the fact that it happened. I've discovered no facts that aren't already in history books. This book is a serious effort, yet not a comprehensive account of the events. I wrote about what I've heard and read. It is to a large degree mere conjecture of what might have happened, or as much as a novel allows. Nothing exposes oneself more than a novel, because in a novel, one writes as one feels, or is capable of feeling. It's not meant to be controversial or contemptible and certainly not deliberately provocative.

It would be impossible for any one person to tell the whole truth about Chao Anouvong: nonetheless, I've written somewhat self-indulgently about the past because, like the present, it's made up of reasons and feelings and things seen. Some people will be unhappy about it, but I hope they don't take it too seriously. Bangkok might well take offence and even accuse me of lies and slander against Siam. Honestly, it's not intended to be disrespectful to anyone and neither is it an attempt to re-examine the well-established, glorified, impressive and romantic history of Rattanakosin Siam, firmly accepted by some Siamese scholars and academics, with Bangkok at the centre of the Siamese world.

The Lao people should take pride in Chao Anouvong's struggle against

Siam for LanXang. As for the exact thoughts in his noble mind, I have neither the ability nor the intention to guess them. But I think I can safely state that he wouldn't have been content until the Lao people of the ancient kingdom of LanXang, with the Mother Mekong (Mae Nam Kong) running through the middle, were united.

Many people have written Lao history as a tribute to the Lao nation. However, none, perhaps, have realised quite how terrible the events in Lao LanXang were between 1779 and 1829, up to Western colonisation. The Lao nation has miraculously survived, albeit with a fraction of its population and half the size of its former self because of the 1898 treaty between France and Siam. This book represents literature on Lao LanXang in history and memory. It should be educational, perhaps, and should be regarded as a lesson from the past. It's not designed to be the last word on the matter and I hope it might lead to a dialogue with those who've tried to colonise Laos and wipe it off the face of the Earth. The Lao people have tried to live with this. If you look at maps of the world, I warrant you will find comparisons between the Siamese and the Lao, but they are not entirely alike.

I am conscious of existing stories about the reason for and the timing of Chao Anouvong's war of independence: those from Siam are biased. So, I'm sure it's time for a new assessment that can be analysed and enjoyed by anyone interested in history. I'm not very far from thinking that most Lao and Siamese would like to know the truth. So, let's try to understand and agree why he did it.

As a precaution I will not name names, but to all concerned who assisted me with the book, I offer my sincere appreciation and thanks. My principal debt is to my close friend for supplying me with books, both in Lao and English, written by the most talented historian, Maha Sila Viravong – without his scholarship my endeavour would not have been possible. Friends read the manuscript and made many invaluable suggestions.

Books came and went as I continued to maintain my dignified silence, but this was a story I wanted to write. I have been helped through many solitary years by the thought of my motherland and Chao Anouvong, and in both respects I've been fortunate. LanXang is in the past, but I feel pain whenever I think of it, because there are Lao people on both sides of the Mekong, and they must have a shared future.

This book is a tribute not only to the greatness of the Lao nation, from the Ai-Lao of the NanChao kingdom (Land of Kings) in China to the Lao LanXang kingdom (Land of a Million Elephants) of Laos, but also to the last king of Lao LanXang ViengChan. Readers might be interested to know not only about Lao heritage, but also the pivotal and mercurial kingdom of modern Siam.

The abominably unwarranted and cruel invasions of LanXang and the sack of ViengChan by Siam are historical facts, attested to by the 'literary masterpiece' of the Chronicles of ViengChan (*Phuen Vieng*) that were discovered in the Ubon area of the Mun river before being copied and spread through word of mouth to various temples throughout LanXang. The Chronicles served both to maintain Lao traditions and to stir the hearts of Lao patriotism. Tradition maintains that the stories were passed down by word of mouth from one generation to the next, despite being heavily suppressed.

The identity of the Ai-Lao (Lao people) is attested to by Chinese history and the documents of the Legendary Khoun Borom. Sadly, many important manuscripts belonging to the Lao chronicles and archives vanished in the destruction of ViengChan and the general collapse of the entire Lao LanXang Kingdom.

While looking through the manuscript as I prepare for its publication, I began to doubt whether it could possibly be of interest to anyone but me. Then I thought, one doesn't have to be famous or a statesman to write a book: it is enough to be a simple human being. Life is always interesting, and one should always strive for truth, authenticity, empathy and justice. I don't expect this book to enhance my reputation.

I trust that readers will find the subject matter as appealing as I did. This book hopes to show not only what really happened in those days (and lead, I hope, to greater trust and transparency, and less hate), but also the character of the peace-loving Lao people. Through the story of Chao Anouvong, I hope to show how a man can become truly immortal. If, however, it proves an interesting and eye-opening read, then the Lao will no longer feel so alone. Besides, if it helps people – especially the Lao and Siamese – to love more and to think twice before airing their views, and if it shines a spotlight on the truth, then it will have played its part.

Writing this book has been one of the most personally fulfilling experiences of my life.

Xanouvong

Contents

Author's Note 5

Preface 10

I   Lao Consciousness 15

II   Talent Without Power or Wealth 39

III   Rite of Passage.. 54

IV   The Beginning 103

V   Quest for Wisdom 117

VI   Looking Back. 164

VII   Prophetic Vision 192

VIII   The Turning Point.. 203

VIX   The Dinner Party 233

X   A Fateful Encounter 248

XI   Farewell City of Angels 323

XII   Hopeful Return 343

XIII   Gathering Thoughts 382

XIV   Council of War 401

XV   The War 455

XVI   Catastrophe 537

Epilogue 581

Preface

After the complete annihilation of ViengChan (Vientiane), it is a well-known fact that, amongst other looted treasures such as the Emerald Buddha (*Phra Kaeo*), the majority of Lao palm-leaf manuscripts, chronicles and literature were burnt or spirited away from Lao LanXang during the Siamese invasions. As part of Siam's purging policies, they were hidden in various libraries in Bangkok. In fact, only literate Lao people (especially monks) could actually read the old Lao script, but Siamese officials and scholars could view them, even though they had no interest in them. The truth was that the Siamese tried to eradicate from the world anything to do with the Lao nation, but after nearly 200 years of isolation and neglect, the wisdom of Lao LanXang returned in triumph.

Fortunately, a well-educated Lao monk with a keen mind, Maha Sila Viravong from Roi-Et, discovered these palm-leaf chronicles and other literature in a Bangkok library in the 1940s. He didn't know which daemon told him to look at them. He threw himself into a chair, laid one on the desk and the dynamic story worked on him. He, like all his compatriots, placed a high value on Lao consciousness (*Khuam Penh Lao*). Discreetly, patiently and painstakingly, he copied some of them. It changed his life. He was an exceptional scholar who wrote, amongst other things, *The History of Laos*. Despite many difficulties, the fact remains that his discovery shed much light on the history of the Lao people and the reality of ViengChan.

Of all the Lao kings, Chao Anouvong exerted the greatest influence on Lao LanXang history. He came from a long line of Lao royals, a family that had played a prominent role in Lao conservative politics and promoted a peaceful relationship with neighbouring countries. It would have been natural for him to follow his ancestors' policies: to foster the love and unity of LanXang, to strengthen the kingdom by spreading knowledge of Lao history, culture, traditions and ideals, and keeping fresh the memory of those from all walks of life who'd served LanXang in the past to inspire leadership in the future.

Primarily, he saw moderation and consensus as more powerful in politics than ideological conviction. He maintained a core principle of patience and flexibility. However, he was disgusted by the injustice, cruelty and corruption of Siam's political life and was sickened by the suffering of his people: especially by the death (possibly execution) of his brother.

Chao Anouvong became concerned. He travelled extensively in search of a peaceful solution. Inspired by King Fah Ngum's unification of the LanXang kingdom, he sought to re-establish the political and philosophical power of the Lao nation. He arrived at a lasting conviction that the injustices inflicted on the Lao people would never cease until Lao LanXang regained its full independence, or if a philosopher or a just man became the Siamese ruler.

Nowhere was Chao Anouvong more reviled than in Siam, where Bangkok conceived a prejudice against this patriotic Lao man from ViengChan. They demanded his loyalty but offered nothing in return yet considered him ungrateful and accused him of being a traitor. Now we know that his only crime was to run out of patience. He was impatient to restore the identity and dignity of the Lao people, to take back their freedom and rights.

Many intriguing questions arise: why did Siam break the 1563 That Si-SongHuck treaty and invade LanXang in 1779? How was Chao Anouvong brought up and treated in Bangkok? Why was he allowed to return to rule ViengChan? Why did a man who grew up at the very heart of the Bangkok establishment seek to fight against Siam? How did he change the course of Lao LanXang history? Are there still further truths to be revealed?

It would be a mistake to provide answers before the questions are properly considered, but this is a complicated matter. It is an immense pity that to this day, no one has had the courage to condemn the royal Rattanakosin dynasty, or to accord Chao Anouvong the praise he deserves. He may well be hated by Bangkok and condemned as a traitor to Siam, but he's worth remembering as a man of justice and a true hero to the Lao.

Readers can discover for themselves why King Anouvong led his people against Siam. Perhaps the answers to these questions and many more can be found in this book, which I'm happy to dedicate not only to the Lao nation but also to anyone who recognises its value and believes in friendship, truth and justice. It should be everyone's duty to honour truth and praise its power and valour, both now and always.

Lao LanXang 1340–1779 in light purple and
Laos 1947 to today in dark purple

Chao Anouvong

ViengChan/LanXang	Reigns	Bangkok/Siam
(1) Bounyasan 1730–1781	–	TakSin 1767–1782
(2) Nanthasene 1781–1795	–	Chulaloke 1782–1809
(3) Inthavong 1795–1804	–	Naphalai 1809–1824
(4) Anouvong 1804–1829	–	Nangklao 1824–1851
		Chomklao 1851–1868

Lao Consciousness

'Khuam Penh Lao – ຄວາມເປັນລາວ'
Ai–Lao – Lao nation
My country is
LanXang – ລ້ານຊ້າງ
The Mekong flows north–south through the middle.

Friends,
Fellow countrymen,
Brothers and sisters,
Young and old,
In the Lao LanXang Kingdom and outside,
Whoever and wherever you are,
I have a story to tell,
Have no fear,
Lend me your ears,
I beseech you,
Please hear me and pass it on.
Tell the world!

My name is Jon, a descendant of the feudal lord Phommarath. But most of all I am a mortal belonging to Mother Earth, and a Lao. Wherever I reside I am as patriotic as the next Laoman and will always cherish the memories of my motherland. My most desired wish at this stage of my life is to write a story about the Lao LanXang kingdom and its last king, in the hope that it will bring about truth, reconciliation and peace and benefit future generations.

I was a courtier and private secretary (*Laykar* ເລຂາ) for over thirty years to the last king of ViengChan, LanXang. He and I seemed to share a single mind all those years, whether in public or private conversation. Officially he was *Phra Chao Anouruttharaja* (King Anouruttharath), *Phra Chao LanXang ViengChan* (King of LanXang ViengChan) or *Somdet Phra Chao Anouruttharaja* (His Majesty King Anouruttharath). The Lao people of LanXang fondly knew him as Chao Anou (Chao is the title of an aristocrat in Lao).

'An accomplishment for the benefit of society is more worthy than being a Chao,' he said judiciously. Lest anyone (the Siamese) should suppose he was just the son of a nobody, I can confirm he was of royal kin and the ViengChan royal family's bloodline ended with him.

Amusingly, once I accepted my appointment as his private secretary, he gave me the ancient noble title of a *Khoun* and addressed me as Khoun Jon. I grew to appreciate it in the end, somehow. Nine years later he unexpectedly granted me a peerage (*Phia*) in recognition of my service to LanXang. 'My dear Phia Jon,' he said occasionally with great affection. Mind you, he sometimes used my given name for introductions, when he demanded something, gave an order or teased me. Intriguingly he also gave me a codename, which he would only refer to when there was an important undertaking or a very urgent, serious and risky mission. The urgency of his voice galvanised me into action. I was overcome with awe and filled with spirit and daring.

From the beginning, Chao Anouvong and I were as trusting and affectionate as if we'd always known each other – our relationship was like that of father and son. I was touched by his charming, open manner, but the intensity of his ingenuity made me feel shy. I have to admit I was somewhat flattered by his attention. We were probably seeking each other before we met, and then found ourselves so taken with each other that our souls mingled and nothing afterwards came between us. We alone shared the privilege of our true friendship, which was perfectly private, though I regarded myself as one of the mandarins. The time spent with him was the best of my life. I believe our friendship was so strong because we appreciated the good in one another and my loyalty matched his.

If you want an honest answer, I only got the job because of serendipity and destiny. Working and living in the palace was a privilege but I abandoned power, wealth and politics for wisdom and philosophy, and committed myself solely to serve king and country: my only patriotic ambition. Like most proud Lao people, our patriotism was not boastful and showy but subtle and unassuming. We tend to be too bashful and awkward to say who we are. My choice of health over wealth led to a recompense reasonable enough to satisfy my modest needs, and I hoped for a modest pension. Alas, all my hopes ended with him.

I have always been susceptible to modest, dignified, decent and influential people, and Chao Anouvong's aristocracy and patriotism fascinated me. I was deeply mesmerised by his appearance, his elegance, intellectual brilliance, wisdom and apparent sophistication, mainly because I felt I was unsophisticated myself. My appointment was highly desirable even though I didn't have the complete run of the inner sanctum, although I thought I did. Naturally, it was a great honour to be given the job, and very exciting to serve and accompany him wherever he went. I spent most mornings being briefed on the events of the day or holding private discussions with him. I welcomed any instructions which helped me to be useful. Therefore, he admired me deeply and directed me to keep track of the kingdom's affairs. This highly rewarding task gradually became more dangerous and, finally, heart-breaking as I witnessed his ordeal: a great tragedy which left me in despair.

During those years, I probably spent more anxious hours with the king than with any other person. He recommended contemplation as a natural therapy for anxiety. I witnessed his private meetings and carried his innermost thoughts and plans. I eagerly took down his letters and his literary works, mostly in verse. Sometimes I had to trust my own memory to cope with the flow of words. You may ask what happened to all of them, but the Siamese came and did evil things in ViengChan. Sadly most, if not all, of his work, together with other historical records, were destroyed, burnt or illicitly taken away to Bangkok after the destruction of the ancient capital Chanthabury (ViengChan) in 1828. To have watched the city and the palace that I called home being ransacked and burnt to the ground and with it my life's work in the library – minutes, notes, archives – was truly and overwhelmingly upsetting.

Chao Anouvong advised me to repent and be humble and live my life as an ordinary free man in which Buddhism played a significant part. (Buddhism is not a religion: it doesn't prescribe a route to any god – that's up to you to discover if you wish. And it doesn't believe in indoctrination but allows the individual to make their own decisions). The king preferred a simple life, sleeping enough to feel more energetic, but not too much as to feel lethargic. He wished to relinquish attachment to physical satisfaction in order to eliminate ignorance, and anxiously wanted to free himself from the prison of Siam's political affairs in exchange for LanXang autonomy. A lavish lifestyle, he said, would inevitably lead to more desire, and one could easily become arrogant. To indulge oneself in satisfying one's palate would not only increase the burden on one's digestive system, but also one's sense of illusion and attachment. He was not pernickety about food but preferred less spicy or even plain dishes. He'd no desire for worldly goods and believed that material values were totally vain, preferring simple accommodation and clothing. This world is nothing but a temporary residence, after all. He sometimes wondered where all these worldly things came from. Intriguingly, we both had inquisitive minds.

Some people believe that money is essential to virtue, but Chao Anouvong said it depended on how it was acquired. Money is king but one should not assume it guarantees one's virtue: an opinion which seemed impossible to disagree with. In any case, moneymaking had never been on my mind, unlike those tiresome people who become devoted to money and have a good word for nothing else. I've tried without success to save or at least be careful with my expenditure, because I enjoy the power and usefulness of money – a hundred Lians to a Kip to provide me with security and freedom. Fortunately, living with nature was relatively reliable and the other essential ingredients of pleasure, however difficult, were not too expensive. I have been fortunate in my simple life, and within certain limits I wouldn't hesitate to continue to enjoy life the way I thought it should be enjoyed. The world is more flexible than it seems, and by simply determining what is right, life should be uncomplicated. Life is sweet for many but less so for others; it's certainly too short. I hope, therefore, that my savings, and a small grace and favour contribution, along with a few legacies perhaps, and kind friends, should be sufficient, if I live that long, to keep me in my retirement. With good natural local medicine and a healthy lifestyle, consuming mostly fruits, nuts, fish and vegetables, with all things in moderation, I shan't require much. But if it means I only eat occasionally or go hungry sometimes, well and good. Elderly people, they say, live on air!

One assumes that moral goodness is enough for a happy life. I personally didn't seek material comforts. Peace of mind and serenity were all I required. Perhaps knowledge is by itself sufficient to lead one to the virtues of honesty, truth and friendship, which should be placed above other kinds of morality. So, my real aim was to pursue a good life, hope to discover what virtue was, and maybe become a virtuous and knowledgeable person myself. Life is bewildering but I hoped the contemplation of justice and philosophy would keep me in a good state of mind and help me live properly. Some believe that pleasure's rightful place is at the beginning of life: having good health, good friends, the joy of giving, receiving, sharing fun, getting married and having children. But with sufficient wealth, the end of life should also be perfectly happy. Health is largely determined by one's state of bliss or the reverse, but what makes people happy is a matter of taste. Nevertheless, one ought to do everything to remain on reasonable terms with the troubled world and with good, reasonable people. These are the basic principles that apply to everyone; if only man would follow them, he might solve the world's problems so that conflict and war could be avoided.

All our dreams begin in youth. As a youngster with a natural curiosity about life, I was ready to learn. My father told me that education and nothing but education, is the only lasting path for the future. With a real love of learning and a yearning for the whole truth, I never wanted to miss my lessons. I strained every nerve to discover the truth out of sheer desire for knowledge, which I acquired to achieve my ambition. Basically, I had everything invested in myself. I have been and am self-sufficient and contented with what I have, although I like to converse with like-minded people. Friendship is very important, but one must recognise one's limitations and never envy the superior ability of others. One never wants to be without friends who know the way to one's heart, because a sympathetic friend can be quite as dear as one's parents. Life is far better with a cosy coterie of friends or someone to share a noggin or two at dinner, even though one can't always afford to keep up with them. Having Chao Anouvong as a dear friend was incredibly gratifying. Self-indulgence was never in my philosophy, but after serving him for many years, I understood that work in itself, together with relatives and friends, freedom, food, clothes and shelter, was one of the natural and necessary things that made life pleasurable. I have indeed lived a healthy and happy life.

I could only imagine myself trembling about on the floor as a toddler. I grew steadily, albeit a little slowly. I remember my father tossing me up like a toy, making me laugh. Later, my mother scolded me for glimpsing my face in her mirror, telling me I was still a boy. When my voice broke, she rushed me into her room and with an awe-inspiring voice amusingly told me I was a man. I realised instantly that my body had been going the way of all schoolboy bodies, making us blush and grope and unsure what we're supposed to do. Well, at my mother's words my fine baby face must have turned red with embarrassment. She flushed and her silky black hair seemed to stand on end and her small brown eyes widened. She promptly reminded me not to forget that it was she who bore, nursed, suckled me and lived her life for me. She started to cry, and after a shocked pause she laughed, dramatically collapsed into her chair and burst into a storm of tears, murmuring that she would not wish to see the light of day if I married a girl who would turn me against her. I embraced her affectionately and told her that I loved her best.

My looks changed a little, but I remained as slim as ever. I reached the age when boys start to think of love or fumble about and make mistakes and are laughed at by unkind, giggling girls. I blushed not only because of this strange sexual prowess, a new and welcome interpretation of my much-loathed weakness, but also because I was sad and ashamed, thinking that love was the stuff of fantasy. Perhaps my dreams of it were more innocent than the boys next door. I made a point of befriending everyone I could wherever I went, though I neither tried to seduce anyone or purposefully look for love – as perhaps most boys did – but resourcefully lived in hope of it. But I learnt why older boys were, or pretended to be, gripped by a paroxysm of sex, some without saying a word, others with grunts of delight, and without guilt-ridden after-effects. I was far too inhibited and refused to have anything to do with them!

I don't mind admitting that there had been several attempts by my understanding and sympathetic mother to distract me from my solitude by engaging me with beautiful and polite girls, with marriage in mind. She wanted me to marry young and to bring up an heir. I suppose all mothers are mad for grandchildren but never quite get on with their daughters-in-law. She was worried that I might die childless in battle if I joined the royal army. This was never going to be a problem, and a combination of Chao Anouvong's encouragement – and decent young girls of striking beauty – aroused desire in me. Nonetheless, I was content with my work at the palace and kept myself out of mischief.

When I was a teenager and growing up to be a merry young man, I always preferred to be meticulously clean. I was accustomed to long wallows in clear rivers or streams and being properly dressed before evening meals. I was not too fastidious about my looks, for this is only a phantasm, not a real self after all, nothing but a temporary and deceptive outer case which comes into being, bearing our own karma, and disappears again. Nevertheless, one tries to make the best use of one's own illusive body, because no one else faces the consequences for what one eats and does.

Laomen woo all year round but wed in winter (December and January). During my time, the custom was that older female family members watched closely over young, unmarried girls. This kind of security gave them a good name, as well as pleasing their parents and earning praise from elders who would condemn any girl who ran away to consort with men before she was properly married. Traditionally, women all over the kingdom enjoyed liberty but took little or no part in amusement, public life or politics. Their confinement to domestic affairs made them reserved in society and obedient companions, but not slaves, to their husbands, respectfully going to bed before their husbands and being the first to rise. Some Laomen had old-fashioned ideas about marriage. They oversaw their family with a proprietary air, expecting their wives to show deference and perform housework without complaint, even though both men and women worked hard all day and were too tired to quarrel. Most young people of the opposite sex rarely met, making romantic love impossible, and marriage would normally be merely a matter of arrangement irrespective of emotional compatibility. In the culture of wives and children it is generally accepted that the only difference between men and women is that one begets and the other bears – it is only in that moment of delight that they are truly united. Therefore, my aim was directed exclusively towards a suitable young girl; the object to produce children who will benefit society.

In fact, during our stay at Nakhorn Phanom, I told Chao Anouvong that I felt a sense of chivalry towards women, respecting rather than mistreating them. I was fond of the fair-minded, kind, intellectual men I became friends with in a sensible, not a thoughtless, sort of way. He said that sexuality should not be questioned because there are many different types of people on earth. But he personally believed that every man, wise or foolish, rich or poor, should take part in public service and social politics and fall in love. He grew more persistent and asked whether I would like to get married and procreate. Being a naturally sensitive and private person, I blushed and smiled silently. 'It is necessary,' he insisted mischievously.

'Marry? No. Not yet, Your Royal Highness,' I protested, rather too strongly perhaps. My instincts were against it and I couldn't possibly afford it. I also thought I was far too young to get married and emphatically believed that being unattached was far better than being married. Besides, I simply didn't want to become a son to my parents-in-law and then be forbidden from caring for my mother. 'I shall please myself when I have time to think and choose,' I added. 'It is presently not economical, and I have no plans to do so.'

He agreed entirely and warned that getting married was not for the faint-hearted, and that politics was not for an honest man. I've never been a political animal but neither do I have any aversion to politics. I'd long been interested in all that happened in the kingdom… and in the world. One had only to read a book to understand and know it by heart. I couldn't help learning anything from anyone, and I had high hopes. I simply preferred not to be famous or scrutinised at the epicentre of politics. At that time, I was still ruled by my emotions and probably thought I knew it all already. The king was not entirely disappointed with my political aims but readily suggested I should take one of his untouched, well-born concubines as a spouse. He even offered to pay the girl's huge dowry of land and money but promptly told me not to rush impetuously into it, for I might regret doing so. He roared with laughter when I said that I'd take the dowry first and the wife later. On reflection, I wish I'd taken his advice. Frankly, I thought married life would affect my work and that he was joking.

It is generally accepted that the desire to produce naturally beautiful and intelligent offspring drive most people towards others. In fact, for the sake of progress in civilisation, I was rather keen on having children. It is the simplest and surest way to achieve immortality. I personally believe children give life meaning, but they have to be psychologically and physically fit enough to survive in a dangerous world. Admittedly, having observed many young children dying at an early age and bringing grief to their parents, I wasn't too keen to suffer the same fate. Furthermore, I was put off by the difficult marriages of my friends. Finally, I failed miserably because I was mostly too preoccupied with my own freedom. My mastery of sensual appetites led me to resist girls' attempts to seduce me. I was tempted, of course, but set aside their charms as being of less value than the moral and intellectual beauty I was striving for. In fact, my main aim was to acquire knowledge, and to strive for truth and fulfilment. I had little time for pleasure. Unfortunately, none of the beautiful young girls my mother introduced to me shared my philosophy and wisdom, leaving me disappointed. Nevertheless, I tried to grasp what being human was all about. Perhaps physical pleasure and sleep make us all conscious that we are mortals. Mind you, whenever I met a decent girl by chance, I made sure she knew what she was doing.

Having discreet relationships with girls of various backgrounds was intriguing, but I established my own rule: there must not be any interference with my intellectual mind. I was fond of them only if they had the willpower to be with me. Alas, they simply didn't have the patience, and soon went off with someone else. Well, who could blame them? In silence, I felt sorry for myself. Privately, I gave them my personal blessing, while I pursued knowledge in the world. My one distinction was that I had the run of the royal library, full of volumes and bundles of philosophy, history, poetry, literature and Buddhist doctrine. Chao Anouvong had added plenty of his fine works and was very careful who he let loose inside.

You might have thought that being a bachelor would make me keen on company. Paradoxically, I was instinctively more solitary. Besides, as the king's unattached private secretary, I had been living part of my life in secret for so long I tended to fiercely guard my personal space. I sought no luxury but found true comfort in pursuing freedom from disturbance. I reminded myself constantly that no one could be completely self-sufficient but could perhaps try to be as little dependent on others as possible. I am not a man of genius so had to be sociable. So, as insurance against any mishap and loneliness in my old age, I hoped to cultivate enough friends and influence to obtain a source of social and cultural intelligence. Mind you, numerous people only appear very intelligent until they've had a few drinks; fortunately for me, too much alcohol merely sends me to sleep. One truly has to rely on the community for one's varied needs, such as food, shelter and clothing. Therefore, I spared no effort in avoiding arguments and unpleasantness of any sort. I preferred mainly to contemplate philosophy by day and dine by night with kind, knowledgeable, cultured and understanding friends and family members. I am baffled that all mankind doesn't have similar aims, but then again, everyone possesses different natural talents. In fact, since my youngest years, I'd never contemplated any undertaking as repulsive and upsetting or as dangerous as a political career. Naturally, one should learn how to make a living and enjoy one's life. My life is by no means different from my fellow human beings. Without wishing to complain, it has been a real struggle, spent largely on my own, but pleasant and satisfactory nevertheless.

It is the fate of man that not all mortal beings are born with influence and fortune to smooth their future path. In truth, we never bring material wealth into this world or take it with us when we die – perhaps only our karma will follow us through. I have been told that our last breath, the last snap of thought before we die, is of utmost importance. If our mind is completely pure, making no distinction between all forms of sentient life, we might be reborn with pure minds.

I happened to come into this world, so my father told me before he died, from what had once been a brave, reputable, feudal LanXang family. Lao LanXang was an ancient independent kingdom before the Siamese king, TakSin of Thonburi, invaded it during the reign of Chao Anouvong's father, King Bounyasan, in 1779. He said that few brave and patriotic families like ours were lucky enough to escape captivity after ViengChan fell. Thousands lost their lives, hundreds of thousands were made homeless and ViengChan was destroyed. It was a 'barbarous crime', symbolic of the sickness of a Siamese society that had become indifferent, egotistic and hateful. All the captured families were forced to migrate to Siam: nobles, artists, architects, intellectuals, traders, artisans and businesspeople ended up in Bangkok. However, the people who had helped defend the city, including peasants from the countryside – brave men, women and children – were forced to build new lives as slave labourers and farmers in various parts of Siam, some of them still in the flower of youth. They were made to settle in Saraburi where they bravely built new villages, naming them after those they'd left behind and declaring themselves as Lao ViengChan, Lao Krung and Lao Ngiao. The Lao Songdam people from the north-eastern mountains of LanXang were relocated to Phetchaburi. Despite settling close to Bangkok, they remarkably went from being dominated by the Siamese to being a primarily Lao-speaking unit preserving their Lao cultural heritage.

Well, my own background had no impact on the life that I led. It was clear to me that we were not too distant from the humble customs of our fellow Lao countrymen who, regardless of their classes, mostly worked in agriculture. They were the backbone of LanXang, highly family-orientated, living in houses on stilts that were spacious and open – like the minds of the people who built them – eating glutinous rice (*Khaow Neow*), and playing guitars (*Phin*) and bamboo pipes (*Khaen*). This *Khaen* was a quintessential musical instrument that had been invented centuries earlier and had long been part of the Lao people's nature and animistic culture. There was no shortage of talented balladeers. All types of song and music drifted out of the Lao villages. The *Khaen* music and folk ballads evoked memories of all the provinces of LanXang. It is known as *Kub* (singing) in the north – such as Luang Phrabang's

Kub Luang Phrabang and ViengChan's *Kub Ngum* – but *Lum* (singing) in the south, such as Khammouan's *Lum Mahaxay*, Salavanh's *Lum Salavanh* and the Khorat Plateau's *Lum Phern*. These melodies and verses became the signature moods of the people from that area. Besides, the Lao possess a degree of integrity, benevolence, open, honest candour and hospitality. When partying they are as fond of drinking, singing and dancing as any people on earth, and, as their lives depended on the land and nature, they respected everything – the elements that support life: earth (*Deen* ດິນ), water (*Nam* ນ້ຳ), air (*Akard/Lom* ລົມ) and fire (*Fai* ໄຟ).

Since the influence, power and wealth that had allowed my ancestors to live in luxury for centuries was no longer available I had to rely on my own talent and energy. My inspiration in life was beyond the realms of fulfilment. I had to forgo higher education and find work at the palace library instead, because supporting my mother came first. My only desire was to take care of her till the very last. Fortunately, with absolute single mindedness and determination, I managed to lead a moderately comfortable life as a servant to King Anouvong. I have been lucky and count my blessings. No, I have nothing to complain about. After many years devoted exclusively to administration, my face had become weathered, but my hands remained as soft as a maiden's. However, in time of trouble, I would have to depend on myself for protection. Admittedly, at the beginning, I rarely ventured outside the inner-city wall for fear of danger. I often enjoyed the privilege of accompanying the king on his engagements. I was secure – like a gold coin held in a strong hand.

In the decades after Chao Anouvong and his people's heroic struggle against Bangkok, I was often asked, usually in whispers, what he was truly like. 'Lao,' I said, always. Oh yes, he's fresh in my memory and how happy I could be if he were still alive. I often grieve for him as I sit alone disconsolate in my tumbledown small house, until my sorrow finds relief in tears. While I brooded over his loss, occasionally prey to melancholy, sleep and eating became unpleasant. My grief for him never faded from my mind, which often made it even more poignant whenever I thought of him and heard his name. When somebody mentioned anyone else, I paid no attention and couldn't make any worthwhile contribution. But whenever the king was mentioned at a dinner party, I was awake in a flash and very often my eyes were wet with tears, which one should never be ashamed of shedding. Make merry, they would say, but how could I be cheery or dispel the sorrows of my heart with a few drinks?

Anyway, I was all attention and used always to speak of him as the wisest and kindest of men. It really stirred the sediment of my memory. I wanted to know more, and I had a lot to say. I was modest, as it would have gone against the grain to thrust myself forward and reveal that I was his royal secretary (*Lasah Laykar*). However, I wanted to deliver a eulogy and tell everyone about him: his bravery, his indomitable energy, his abiding interest in glory, peace and stability – both for himself and for the Lao nation. He also had a deep sense of what was right and fitting for him to do. He was the incarnation of moral rectitude; he'd the courage to stand up to tyranny and yet remained good-natured, humane, fundamentally benign and Lao in his moderation. You may well ask if he was a nice person. Well, there is nothing more worth the wear of winning than the laughter and love of friends. He was part of my life: not just then and there but now and here. I miss him. As always, since I was sworn to secrecy, I have held my silence, because like all Lao we lived our lives in fear of persecution by the dominant Siamese officials. They were a ruthless lot, and without doubt they would repress us if we merely raised our voices in objection to their mistreatment. Any act of humiliation and frustration was quickly crushed before it set off a political storm. The Rattanakosins' critics were murdered; anyone showing any sign of dissent faced jail.

Chao Anouvong used to say that emotion is a sign of weakness. He told me to be phlegmatic. 'Control your mind,' he would say. He believed that people who did bad things weren't in control of themselves, unlike those who did good things. He complained that since 1779, the Siamese political establishment had been an out-of-touch elite who barely knew themselves, let alone their own people's interests and rights. They refused to accept that self-rule was the right thing for LanXang. They actively claimed that Lao LanXang and LanNa were part of Siam. Nothing was too deceitful for the Rattanakosins, the royal dynasty who ruled Siam. Their officials were monsters of iniquity who changed policy at will and treated the Lao as if they agreed with their ideas. Their objective was to bring about the destruction of LanXang – to see it disappear, in direct opposition to the 1563 That Si-SongHuck shrine treaty. They were shameless and thought everyone desired a 'Greater Siam'. 'If Siam has its way, it will be a catastrophe for LanXang – an end to our Lao nation,' Chao Anouvong would say with seriousness in his voice. 'But I have every confidence that our patience and our fight against a distant and unresponsive Bangkok will continue to withstand the worst. In the end, their success will be their undoing. Due to the changing political landscape, Siam will undergo a full-blown identity crisis, and then be consumed by the people and a dynastic power struggle.'

During our private conversations, Chao Anouvong said that Bangkok was a place of depravity. They focused on others' faults while brazenly singing their own praises. He acknowledged that they were obviously ambitious and resourceful. In plain and critical language, he noted that when faced with criticism, they were capable of being a petulant and thin-skinned people, as if they lacked the imagination to see through others' eyes. Like any aggressors and serial self-centred victors, they were terrible losers, hyper-sensitive to what the world thought or said of them, making them insecure and prone to violence: war first and talk later. They came across as condescending and arrogant to their neighbours. They liked to show off their talents and to seek advantage over others yet were totally ignorant of world history. They considered the ethnic Lao from north and north-east Siam as uneducated, like wild baboons, but they failed to see their own bald behinds as they laughed at the defects of others. Bangkok pursued a campaign of censorship that jeopardised other ethnic groups. They turned their backs on their Lao cousins simply because they thought they were cleverer and more capable, better educated, better off, better informed. In the end, their wealth, education and intelligence fostered arrogance of the most contemptible kind. They forgot that humility gains and conceit loses. They preferred to focus only on their own egos instead of working for the benefit of all.

The Rattanakosins clung on to their sense of self. They succumbed to their physical desires for a Greater Siam and insisted on ruling over the LanNa and LanXang territories, reflecting their government's devious mind and narcissism. Chao Anouvong believed that if they eliminated these attachments, their craving to dominate others would ease; they would become less overbearing and gradually embark on a path to liberation that made no distinction between Siamese and Lao. Their yearning to govern the Lao race went against the Buddhist doctrine based on respect, trust and mutual understanding. Unfortunately, the results of these attachments caused great distress among the Lao. Eventually, Chao Anouvong and his people fought back against Siam's domination.

No human race is perfect, but the influx of inconceivable wealth had made the Siamese in Bangkok even more arrogant. They could not reconcile themselves to the fact that they came from the same Ai-Lao race. Desperation was growing over Siam's fifty years of repression in Lao LanXang since 1779, becoming even more severe in the thirty-six years after King Anouvong's death. The Siamese authorities, I was informed, had set up an intelligence network to train agents and saboteurs in the art of spreading rumour and propaganda, aimed at demoralising and persecuting any Lao citizen who voiced an opposing view. There was no telling who was or was not a Siamese secret agent. However, since I knew for certain that King Nangklao had died fourteen years previously, I had no need to be too concerned. The present ruler, Mongkut, whom I caught a glimpse of as a fashionable young prince in the Bangkok palace in 1825, can't possibly remember who I was. Perhaps he was too wrapped up with his English teacher, the enchanting Ms Anna Leonowens, who taught the king's numerous children the philosophy of life. Nevertheless, I have been living in fear and expect to be purged at any moment. Perhaps they'll leave me alone to succumb to my silly, cynical old age. At least I hope so.

Whispered rumours spread like plague, a mixture of fact and supposition in the wake of Nangklao's death. Soon after he took the throne, he began to believe himself to be immortal, as did his imbecilic followers, who considered him a Buddha and a god. He commissioned a huge reclining Buddha at Wat Pho temple as a representation of himself entering nirvana, but it did not prove to be his redemption. He may well have styled himself the conqueror and destroyer of ViengChan, but surely the Sokhotai king Ramkhamhaeng would have disapproved. The horror of Nangklao's reign was probably best expressed in the form of the 'Rattanakosin Conquest' of LanXang, which endures in the public memory. Bangkok has never condemned or refuted these events but has shockingly and audaciously enshrined the Rattanakosins' ideology as the ultimate example of power; nevertheless, the shock of this crime must have echoed to the heavens.

Whatever the truth, Nangklao, staggered about like a drunkard and, supported by a consort, became irrational, stuffy and unapproachable; he was entirely alone in his anger and suffered from dementia towards the end of his life. Lord Buddha's anger and their victims' dying curse had fallen on the Rattanakosins and haunted people's imagination. Everything conceivable was done to keep the king alive; holy monks and medicine men all over the kingdom tried every kind of remedy. They even fed the revered king with cells from all types of living organisms hoping to produce a good outcome. Rumour has it that his body began to putrefy even before his death because of his sins. As a last resort, the palace turned to traditional practices, sending for a miracle healer and the most prominent oracles and saints with knowledge of ancient mysteries. They were convinced that by performing the prescribed rites they could charm his sickness into an effigy and throw it with great solemnity into the Chaophraya river, all to no avail. The palace oracle even hypnotised himself, crying out at the climax of his trance that the revered king was merely a dying mortal, not a god as he'd claimed, and deserved death for his sins. The royalists swiftly put him away for making such a statement.

It appeared that Nangklao had been condemned to a villainous death by divine intervention. He despised the Lao because they opposed Bangkok's ambition for a Greater Siam. He must have felt the pain of Chao Anouvong and the Lao people, however, and borne the misery of knowing that all the destruction, suffering and death for which he (and his grandfather) was responsible, was for the sake of a discredited cause. While lying for months on his deathbed, Nangklao must have been full of foreboding because of his own immorality, and for behaving like a cynical, snobbish brute. Such was his fate. His vanity and ambition had devoured his reason. Unsurprisingly, he suffered a protracted, agonising death. He was paying the price for all his sins. As he faced death, gasping for air, the thought of his own body in the infernal flame of the afterlife must have tormented him. When he finally died as a penitent sinner in 1851, his eyes were wide open, as if he were more alive than dead. This was the gods' doing and was marvellous in people's eyes. He'd been envied and revered by his admirers but was now utterly forgotten, as if he'd never lived at all, but the fear and pain he'd caused would linger. The same powerful Bangkok dynasty continued to rule Siam.

I've been blessed through all my life. I am now an octogenarian and a person of little consequence, ageing quietly, keeping myself to myself like a recluse, sheltering from the burning sun and the driving monsoon storm in a secluded little house next to the village temple. A town, I admitted, would have been a better place to live than the country for an old man, but the villagers have been my salvation. I've wandered far in the kingdom (and the world) and met numerous men of ability. I've examined many hearts and heard many truths from many dear friends and famous people. I've experienced the glorious satisfaction of contentment and success, but the experience of the indomitable Chao Anouvong's war of liberation and his demise truly traumatised me.

I have tended to be more contemplative since Chao Anouvong's death, examining the philosophy of growing old, assessing my life span in comparison to others and resisting mental and physical decay: the painful reminders of annihilation and mortality. One must accept that life is a loan, and that repayment could come at any time; one must try to accustom oneself to its inevitable arrival. The dread of death governs all thought. Sadly, people generally have no time for the old, who ironically need support more than ever before. Having a close, faithful, caring friend and companion is very comforting and can add years to a happy life. I unconsciously urged myself to be busy but couldn't be bothered to learn new things. Nevertheless, by keeping mentally and physically strong I hope to live to a hundred!

In my feeble old age, I cannot really keep in touch with the world anymore, but to have good health and live in peace is a rare fortune. I just potter around the house or sit in my chair dribbling most of the time, feeling my age, complaining about my hearing and eyesight, seeing the world full of wrongdoing. Sometimes I get headaches from reading and writing, but I'm determined not to become an old crock. I fully expect to survive for many more years. My way of life has become ascetic and deeply lonely. I have always remained collected and serious, for my entire being will always be linked with sticky rice and dear Lao LanXang. I occasionally fast and keep silence, thinking of loved ones and eating only one meal a day as if my body could barely be bothered to live. Like a misanthrope I visit no one and hardly have any visitors. Occasionally I feel sorry for myself and often recall being young and miss the 'City' life – ViengChan, friends and socialising – although I've become used to the ways of solitude. Overall, I like this way of life. I try to keep myself unmarked by wickedness and wonder whether my final destiny after death will match my life on earth.

I spend a lot of time giving advice to the younger generation, trying to inculcate them with a respect for Lao culture and history and for the world order, as is only right since I was once the king's private secretary. I find myself thinking of him most of the time. Our cordial friendship withstood all vicissitudes, and to the very day we parted for the last time, we had many good, interesting debates but never argued, or ever sustained even a casual chill from an unkind thought or word. We always respected each other. He allowed me to call on him and make myself at home with him. He took me into his confidence. However, since I was younger and rather inexperienced in most things, it was only right that I should listen to what he'd to say, sometimes not without considerable qualms, mind you. He shared his ideas and taught me everything. I learned a great deal from him.

We were close friends for thirty-three years, but since his death my life has been dark, dreary and insignificant, struck by occasional periods of grief. In my advanced age I sleep less but often dream he is still king of Lao LanXang. I see the palace hall once again filled with noblemen debating the future of the kingdom, and him leaning forward trying to explain why the Lao nation must not become part of Siam. 'LanXang was not and is not Siam,' he used to say, 'and without going back to the Rattanakosin version of history, Siam is in fact full of Lao people.' I can hear him now, brave, gentle and kind, sometimes firm, the wisest and most upright man I've ever served.

Human relationships are about teamwork. I worked in Chao Anouvong's administration and respected him from the day I first entered his life. We complemented each other: he, as a king, with his quick mindedness, deep interest in nature, politics, philosophy, ideas of justice and the welfare of his people; I, as a confidential secretary and confidant, with the willingness to serve loyally at the highest level. He'd a sense of proportion and breadth of vision. He was a guardian of truth, justice, courage and self-control that naturally led him to appreciate the real needs of the country. He was the ideal person to whom one could entrust the country. Most of all I remember my discussions with him and the touch of his reassuring hands. He was simply an amazing person. We had a real affinity from beginning to end.

Chao Anouvong not only made history for himself and the Lao people, but also provoked a rise in Lao nationalism without seeming to be aware of it. He really wanted the people to share everything – bravery, patriotism, conviction, his entire feelings for the Lao nation (*Zard Lao* ຊາດລາວ) and justice.

The Lao have been too sick at heart and too afraid to write this story, but events have prompted me to rise to the challenge. However, since my life is almost over, I no longer fear anything or care what people think and say. I have decided to offer this work as a contribution to LanXang, and to share my thoughts about Chao Anouvong's life, which is a great inspiration to me. The physical world has become rather a hostile and dangerous place for me, although my fear for the Lao nation and of this story not being told far exceeds my fear of the power of the Siamese establishment. Losing my anonymity would not be easy but, on balance, I think it's worth it.

So, I am sorry to be the one to tell you this story; perhaps others haven't had the stomach. Once you've heard it, you have a duty to tell this story to others. Your silence will make you complicit. I shall be frank. It is unlikely that the story will put me in an uncomfortable position mind-wise. But imagine living through a period in history when no one can utter a wrong word. How can telling the truth be an affront to anyone? The central point of my thesis is that history (and wisdom) is part of human progress. Whether my narrative turns out to be true or false, I hope it will have some effect on Siam, but it shouldn't cast a political cloud over anyone. I will try not to hold strong opinions and in the interest of justice, historical truth and posterity, I will do my best to oblige. Similarly, I strongly feel that it is my duty to raise the burning questions that Siam has yet to answer. If Bangkok decides to do so themselves, it will be a godsend. It will be quite interesting to see what they have to say.

Good people don't denounce their fellow human beings but show me one man on earth who is neither a denouncer nor denounced by others. Unjust decrees and unjustified deeds deserve criticism. One should perhaps not jump to condemn those whom others criticise, or fumble towards unjust conclusions from impulse and prejudice. Chao Anouvong said that to condemn other states for their atrocities would be pointless unless you yourself pursue what is right. Well, I'm not the only one prone to justifiably condemn evildoers, while singing my own and LanXang's praises. I don't mean to cause offence, but I understand that compliments bring delight and criticisms bring anger and distress. I believe our minds already contain enough bad thoughts without adding to them. On the contrary, I hope that any criticism, be it right or wrong, can truly help in the real world. In any case, one should be able to master one's own mind and make independent judgments. My mind was always vexed when I saw anything immoral and unjust. I hope this story about Siam and LanXang – the fate of ViengChan and Chao Anouvong – will not only liberate others but myself as well.

There ought to be a rational explanation for these events. Any institution making false claims should lose face as they howl their indignation around the world. Siamese officials are the best placed to tell the world the truth about the events and could redeem themselves by doing so. On the subject of redemption, the mood of the people in Siam did begin to change soon after Chao Anouvong's death. The Rattanakosins continued to enjoy public support in Bangkok, but the great majority of the Siamese people (and the Lao nationalists in Siam) quietly began to brim with resentment and indignation against the monarchy. Perhaps they wanted to get rid of it; change is more likely to come about if people's freedoms are threatened.

No one can overturn the truth of history. I am, of course, conscious of counterfactual history. I don't propose to make light of any serious issue. I shall base this story on my own and other people's memory as well as on important documents entrusted to my care, for my eyes and heart are fixed on justice. This is a world where good is the source of reality and truth, and it makes life worthwhile. I intend to tell it in my own style, with no wish to be seen as competing with anyone who may be obliged to give a differing point of view. Everyone is entitled to it, but opinion without knowledge is a poor thing. Even so, one can't control the opinions of others, but only live one's own life.

My final farewell with Chao Anouvong towards the end of my working life was very traumatic and I couldn't find the right words. It was the most upsetting time of my life. I saw him briefly on his final entry into ViengChan after over a year living in exile. We had no time to sit down and talk. He became more secretive, like a silent Buddha. He said very little, leaving everyone else unsure of his real thoughts and feelings. It was one of those moments when I knew he needed space. He spent some time living in solitude, sitting mostly alone in his tent or in the shade in the Emerald Buddha temple courtyard, not fully understanding why the viceroy (*Ouphahat*), Tissah, had betrayed LanXang. He also felt betrayed by Luang Phrabang, XiengKhuang and all the armies from LanNa for their failure to support him. It was not a scenario he'd envisaged.

Similarly, he was very disappointed with the Vietnamese king, Minh Mang, for not sending thousands of well-armed soldiers to fight the Siamese and expel them from Lao LanXang's territories. He'd reason to doubt the value and sincerity of Vietnam's friendship but had no choice but to continue to rely on them. 'We can count on Vietnamese support, although they did make use of our land as a base to protect their people and attack their enemy,' he said. 'But they'll have to respect our territory and do better than that if they want to be our good and reliable friend and neighbour in the future.'

Understandably, Chao Anouvong could never mend his relationship with the Rattanakosins of Bangkok, who brutally subjugated his people into slavery for political and economic gain. He believed that if LanXang were to have a special relationship with Siam, it was important to recognise the need for accountability to truth and justice, otherwise resentment and division would be never-ending. He therefore fiercely refused to accept their idea of domination, and the Bangkok political establishment reviled him for it. He said that they would fail in the end because they didn't understand Lao LanXang. Whatever fancy name they chose for Siam, he said, would exist only by definition, as the country would be in a state of perpetual insecurity due to territorial disputes with its neighbours. Seismic upheavals would take place. He aimed for reconciliation and wanted the Siamese and the Lao to remain close but bound by the 1563 That Si-SongHuck territorial agreement. He saw that Siam's hegemonic expansion had become a real threat to neighbouring countries, especially to the Lao nation, spelling the beginning of the end of Lao history in the Khorat Plateau. He and his people were determined to stop this at any cost.

Before 1779, LanXang benefitted from its rich natural resources and free trade. Bangkok then clearly wanted to grab more authority for Siam, and no longer confined themselves to necessities but embarked on the pursuit of unlimited material possessions, leading them to sacrifice public for personal interests. They greedily wanted to monopolise commerce in the area, but Chao Anouvong was a strict defender of the freedom of trade. Not everything about trade was glorious, but it did provide a foundation for LanXang to flourish, develop and prosper – enabling her easy-going stereotypical national character to connect with the outside world. But LanXang had been victimised by Siam's unfair trading practice, by which Lao goods – gold, silver, musk, frankincense, silk, ivory and rhino horn – were deliberately rerouted to Bangkok. The commodities were forcibly bought at a low price and resold as Siamese goods for export at a huge profit. Consequently, the Lao regarded the Siamese traders with great loathing and mistrust.

The Rattanakosins had shown disdain for the Lao through their determination to destroy and annex LanXang. Later, as we shall see, King Nangklao assumed that it was his right to barbarically enforce a census of ethnic Lao people by forcibly tattooing them. Human suffering meant nothing to him. Siam's restless jealousy and notorious ambition to enlarge at the expense of Lao national identity and territorial integrity could never be in the interest of the Lao people. The consequences were inevitable: war.

King Anouvong was meticulous about truthfulness and straightforward talk. His final words were a request to tell the world about himself and the critical events of Lao LanXang's history. I shall endeavour to achieve this to the best of my ability. I will try to create him on the page as he really was in my company. Many will say these events are past history and not worth talking about, but the Lao people believe in history because they have been victims of Siam's aggression and injustice, so have the right to comment on it and learn from their mistakes. History itself is a real nightmare from which those Lao who were forced to migrate to Siam are still trying to wake up from. Their fear and slavery forbade them to speak but could not ban them from singing and thinking. Truth forbade the Lao, including myself, to keep silent. I will sing it, chiefly for my own satisfaction, from the heart. One sings what one thinks. I would be very surprised if it changed anything, but who knows?

All stories need a hero and national stories are no exception. They are constantly rewritten as new evidence is unearthed. Basically, writing has been a public form of therapy. I will try not to honour Chao Anouvong any more than he deserved, but I truly want to restore him as a presiding figure who deserves the highest rank of humanity. The credit belongs not to me and my writing, but to him and all those who sacrificed themselves in a worthy cause. My story is based on historical facts so should not be regarded as a made-up tale of wickedness and depravity, but please allow me some leeway for recrimination, and make allowances if my narrative is not always entirely appropriate, both in my actions and my words. Examining the truth overwhelmed me. I may well have forgotten that I was amusing myself with this story, worked myself up and wandered beyond conscious thought. Besides, the devil gets into one at times when writing, though I put a note on my desk to remind myself that the Siamese rulers were great people. But as I was doing so, I had in mind that Bangkok believed that LanXang had no right to exist, and the unjust abuse that Chao Anouvong and the Lao people suffered annoyed me a great deal. I'm afraid that at times my mood was particularly dark and sarcastic, and full of pitiful laments. I might have become somewhat censorious, disingenuous and cynical, ferociously using inappropriate words and facetiously touching the most sensitive political issues that might disturb Bangkok and some of my readers.

Naturally, my indignation made me write more seriously and inappropriately than perhaps I should have, but I hope this story will resonate with many people. I have struggled to understand these events, but my real aim was to discover the truth in the hope of improving the future; I had no intention of bringing any historical figures into disrepute. My greatest motivation was to ensure that Chao Anouvong received the respect and recognition he deserves.

So please listen carefully to my humble thoughts and feelings on the past as well as the future. Please don't be surprised that in singing the praises of LanXang and King Anouvong, it may be that I've omitted several important points, got into a muddle or even misrepresented some facts because of the weakness of my understanding. If so, this has been done unwittingly, and it will be for someone with greater knowledge than I to fill in the gaps and make corrections. You don't have to like or believe in what I say, as long as you're emotionally true to yourself. It's better in principle to know the truth and to speak about it with laughter. Perhaps we should note in passing that history isn't worth arguing about. The past is an awful place but shifting through the dross in search of the truth is one way to right wrongs.

Siam had been waging indiscriminate war against the Lao people of LanNa and LanXang, using cruelly oppressive taxes, political indoctrination and the banning of freedom of expression. Bangkok was a cultural desert where only approved Siamese performers could be seen or heard. Culture enriches everyone, but a Lao man playing *Khaen* music that cheered up the streets of Bangkok was a bore to the snotty Siamese. Virtually anything to do with the Lao – history, language, culture, music and customs – was heavily suppressed. It was becoming a noose around our necks. Some customs, such as betel chewing, were banned. 'Only selfish fools,' Chao Anouvong said, 'would think of such prohibitions. We shouldn't mind what they think and say. Our primary task is to do what is right.'

The Rattanakosin Siamese political elite sought total domination. They were so desperate to try to hide from the world the existence of the Lao LanXang kingdom as a separate nation. Their purging policies were vindictive in nature and constituted a war against the entire Lao nation. The simplicity of the Lao ruling class – conservative but highly interested in people and world affairs and eager for knowledge and dialogue – was no match for the deceitful and naked greed of the Siamese establishment. While Bangkok was getting richer, the rest of the cities, towns and villages in the kingdom and vassal states were getting poorer, dividing the people into an idle rich and a long-suffering poor, highlighting the harrowing contrast between the comfortable lives of the unsympathetic Siamese in Bangkok and the hardships endured by people elsewhere. The Lao in the north and northeast of Siam had spent years wondering why they were being oppressed, so had every right to bewail the injustice of it all.

Since I have been provided with the necessities of life, I can now write merely for my own interest in the past. So, for the sake of argument, I will sing in Chao Anouvong's defence, which I hope my fellow countrymen, sympathetic neighbours and friends and just men will approve and pass on. On looking back through the aura of bravery and greatness that now surrounds him, it is easy to forget just how loathed he was by his Siamese opponents. King Nangklao and the Siamese political elite abhorred him. They despised what he'd tried to achieve because they wished to annex Lao LanXang, bitterly accusing him and his people of waging a war against Siam. In fact, Chao Anouvong was the beating heart of the Lao nation and a champion of liberty. If Bangkok believed that his voice would be silenced after his death, then we, the Lao people and I, believe we have a duty to keep him fresh in our memory and never forget the dark side of Bangkok's policy. We desire clarity – to understand not only why Siam wanted to eliminate Lao LanXang but also why Bangkok remains arrogance and dishonest on this subject.

The Lao wanted to express their grievances by writing about Chao Anouvong, not only portraying him in glowing terms as a hero in the eyes of men, but also to expose what happened to him during his struggle against Siam. It is their right to tell the world – and especially the Siamese – what they don't want to hear. However, Bangkok may painfully discover not only Chao Anouvong's virtue, but also their own guilt and shame, even if no proof exists. Considering Siam's track record as a proud country – invading, plundering and destroying its neighbours – it could hardly be expected to admit the truth.

After many years of pondering and avoiding asinine remarks, I decided it was my right and duty to put on paper historical facts, as well as the words and feelings of the Lao people, which should not become libellous. I reap the reward, not only in telling the story about Siam's illegitimate invasions of LanXang, but also about the Siamese oppression of the Lao. Some in Siam will no doubt deplore what I've said, but I only wish them to know the truth. And could anyone be blamed for wanting to know the truth? It's everyone's duty to act to reduce hate. Like any just man in the world, I personally believe in justice; whatever time is left to me will be devoted to the service of LanXang, to humanity and to saying no to oppression, killing and war.

I know life is too short and the time left to me is limited; I often feel it's not really worth the trouble. I've kept everything to myself until now because all I sought was harmony. I acted according to circumstances to enjoy peace of mind. However, while my brain is still active, I will have to write this story very carefully on a few dozen small packs of finest palm leaves (*Bai Larn* ໃບລານ) which I've collected for this very purpose. More haste less speed. I hope not to overlook too many important points and pray for forgiveness in advance for all my errors and lack of style. I have also presented a silver tray with five beeswax candles and flowers (*Khanh Hah*), made drink offerings, poured libations and prayed to the mythical great ancestors' (*Pu Nyeu's* and *Nya Nyeu's*) spirits, to King Anouvong's spirit and to the Theravada and other gods, that I may reach the end of the story before my own end overtakes me.

I really wanted to tell this story, to put the record straight and do justice to the reputation of a gallant king and a man of the highest integrity. The Lao would be traitors to their country if they didn't speak out. So, in homage to my ancestors, I will not be deterred, because pride and honour are at stake. It would otherwise be the greatest humiliation and betrayal of King Anouvong and the Lao people whose lives resemble the national flower *Dork Champa* (ດອກຈຳປາ) – as a new one comes to life, the old one dies away. Lao LanXang's traditional reconciliation policy since the reigns of Khoun Loh ຂຸນລໍ (757– 779), Fah Ngum ຟ້າງຸ່ມ (1352–1371), Xay-Setthathirath ໄຊເສຊຖາທິຣາຊ (1548– 1572) and Souriyavongsa ສຸຣິຍະວົງສາ (1633–1690) should not be blindly set aside to suit the vanity of the Bangkok Rattanakosin rulers of Siam. Some people are more resilient than anyone could imagine; there is more to the Lao people than the cream of the educated Siamese elite believe. Lao LanXang's painful past – the loss of her land and people – is tragic, but there can still be a happy future because of the people's ideals of peace, stability and prosperity.

Talent Without Power or Wealth

And it is of the Rattanakosin Siamese rulers' creeping power and Chao Anouvong's struggle for Lao LanXang that I should sing. He did not want conflict. He simply wanted to take back control – to save the Lao nation from Siam, though there was a real chance of Bangkok sending an army to invade without any provocation.

The truth was that the disapproving Bangkok dynastic ruler tried to control the leader of LanXang and his people, who were suffering severe economic, political and social decline. LanXang was under the intimidating weight of arrogant and reckless Siamese officials. Economic problems and Siamese oppression inevitably powered the Lao people's discontent, and their resentment surged to the surface. These reasonable, fair-minded people decided that the old certainties based on Bangkok's politics of repression had to go. The Lao LanXang wanted to be an equal member of the family of nations. They wanted to be Lao, not subjects of the rulers of Siam, whose behaviour and suppression suggested that Lao lives (and others) really did not matter.

The autocratic Rattanakosin rulers, in particular King Nangklao, imposed their superior power (*Amnard* ອำนาດ) over the occupied Lao LanXang lands. Since 1779, Siam had wielded the power of life and death over LanXang. Together with colonial powers and foreign arms traders, Bangkok was at the forefront of a policy that destroyed thousands of years of civilisation, splitting LanXang and the Lao people, who only wanted to be independent (*Ekhalath* ເອກຣาຊ).

Many kings and rulers have sought this power (*Amnard*), but Chao Anouvong was the greatest king in Lao history since the legendary Khoun Borom ຂຸນບູຣົມ in AD 750, ruler of Ai-Lao NongSae NanChao (Nanzhao), the ancient Lao kingdom based in China, in that he, after becoming king of Lao

LanXang 1,054 years later, pursued his policy with little resources to help him apart from his own talent.

King Xay-Setthathirath the First helped to put ViengChan (and the Mekong) at the centre of Lao culture in 1560. King Norkaeo Khumman (otherwise known as NorMueang) proclaimed independence from Burma in 1593. But most Lao will agree that Chao Anouvong was a true political pioneer with clear ambitions. He was one of the country's true advocates and, like a true Lao nationalist, he hated oppressors. He was a mortal with blood running through his body, seeking justice and willing to sacrifice anything and everything to preserve LanXang. He and his people refused to accept Siamese domination. He wanted justice and political freedom – as King Naresuan the Great of Ayutthaya did against Burma. The difference was that Siam was strong, while LanXang was weak.

Every nation is selective with its legends; the Ai-Lao people (*Lao*) introduced King Khoun Borom. Chao Anouvong clearly understood the significance of the kingdom of NanChao in the folklore of ancient Ai-Lao: The Tai Kadai ancestor. He identified Khoun Borom and King Fah Ngum as the great unifiers of the vast NanChao and LanXang kingdoms respectively. The Lao LanXang believed in the honourable and just society (*Heed Sipsong-Khong Sipsi*) of King Fah Ngum, based on the national enthusiasm for peace and dialogue; its respect for family and lineage; its undying respect for courage; and its conviction for justice and freedom. LanXang harboured such a realm and sought inspiration from its past.

'Unfortunately,' Chao Anouvong said during our first meeting while staring across the Mekong. 'We don't have what a king needs to run a country, and which three of our former kings did have.' I could feel his frustration. He suddenly turned to look at me. 'Firstly, Khoun Jon, we don't have a powerful army and national unity like Fah Ngum. Secondly, we don't have political power and respect, like Xay-Setthathirath. And thirdly, we don't have the wealth and popularity of Souriyavongsa. We are like a tiger without claws and teeth.'

He wasn't a man for excuses, and I could see what he meant at once. Chao Anouvong did not want sympathy. He'd to persevere because he'd no mighty army to back up his ambition, like King Fah Ngum. Khoun Loh (Goh Loh Feng) originally established LanXang at Mueang Swa (Luang Phrabang) in 757, but Fah Ngum was the founder of the united LanXang kingdom's vast empire. Chao Anouvong held Fah Ngum in veneration for unifying LanXang.

'One can safely say that Fah Ngum was undoubtedly the greatest warrior king of all the Tai Ai-Lao,' he said proudly. 'He owned a giant white elephant, which he always rode into battle during his campaigns.'

I listened silently and attentively.

In 1349, at the age of thirty-three, Fah Ngum returned to LanXang from the Khmer court of Angkor where he'd grown up, with the Khmer king's daughter Princess KaeoKengya as his queen, a golden Phrabang Buddha and a 10,000-strong army. Wherever he marched, he conquered. He was shrewd enough to realise that it would be difficult, almost impossible, to keep the land he'd conquered as a single, united kingdom unless the Lao and all other ethnic groups were granted equal rights and opportunities. Inter-ethnic solidarity was essential for maintaining LanXang autonomy and liberty. The Lao people live in village (*Ban*) communities which would normally link up to create a town or city (*Mueang*); many cities combined to become a province (*Khuaeng*), which were all ruled from the capital. Hereditary right was the custom. Fah Ngum understood that military power alone would not be sufficient to hold the kingdom together, but by controlling the cities, he commanded its rulers and people. He offered peace to each city that surrendered. He broke up oligarchies and set up social equality instead. His LanXang dictum was unity, freedom and justice for all. Therefore, based on religious and ethnic tolerance, he incorporated the cities with the surrounding towns and villages. He kept his word and allowed the people to retain their customs and get on with their lives, but in return he demanded the rulers and their peoples' allegiance, especially when tribute and manpower were needed in time of war.

Fah Ngum finally conquered all the Lao cities on both sides of the Mekong and brought governors (*Chaomueangs*), nobles and people from the mountains and the plains, from the far north to the far south, the far east to the far west, under his administration in 1352. He conquered them all and received their oaths of fealty. As he completed his gifts of land and power to his faithful followers, he told them that he personally had nothing to leave to LanXang but hope. Born in the Year of the Dragon in 1316, Fah Ngum finally declared a united Lao LanXang independent on May 1, 1353, and was enthroned in ViengChan under the name of 'Phraya Fah Lah Thorani Si-Sattanarkhanahout' (The Lord of Sky and Earth of Sacred LanXang).

During his conquests Fah Ngum almost went to war with a Sino-Siamese man from the city of Si-Ayutthaya who had married a Siamese princess and taken the name of Ramathibodi Uthong in 1350. After conquering ViengChan, Fah Ngum turned his attention to the west and the Khmer territories in the southwest, where Uthong was also trying to acquire more land. As the son-in-law of the Khmer king, Fah Ngum had the legitimate right to occupy the old Khmer territories. The Lao, who rightly claimed the lower Mekong River region for themselves, had been living on both banks for thousands of years. Fah Ngum didn't want war with Ayutthaya, but he wanted to make sure that his kingdom encompassed all Lao people. He was also aware that Ayutthaya might invade the kingdoms of Sukhothai and LanNa. After conquering the city of Roi-Et, Fah Ngum wanted to test Uthong, so he sent him a challenge:

'If not, you and Siam must always respect Khoun Borom's edict: truth, love and friendship.'

Fortunately, as Fah Ngum had expected, war was avoided because King Uthong declared that he and the Siamese were also descendants of the Ai-Lao, and brothers since the time of the legendary King Khoun Borom (729–750). Uthong agreed to Fah Ngum's territorial ambitions: from the Dong Phraya Fai range to the Chaophraya river was to be Siamese, and to the Mekong was to belong to LanXang. Uthong even offered his own daughter, Nang KaeoLotFah, together with a number of valuable gifts, to Fah Ngum, who was therefore obliged to pull his troops back to ViengChan. Uthong, as he'd promised, later sent fifty-one bulls, fifty female elephants, gold, silver, rare horns and hundreds of other valuable gifts. Obedience to Khoun Borom's edict prevailed, and the two brotherly kingdoms remained at peace until 1540 – when the Siamese first invaded ViengChan.

By now Fah Ngum had an army of 50,000 at his disposal and, before returning to the capital city of XiengThong (Luang Phrabang) from ViengChan in 1357, he famously laid down his strict policies for his subjects. His proclamations became the foundation of a traditional custom (*Papayny*) and a constitutional law (*Heed Sipsong-Khong Sipsi*) that taught people to improve themselves morally. These remain influential in the Lao LanXang kingdom to this day:

'There should be no stealing, or any acts of banditry, no fighting, or unnecessary bloodshed among all Lao. Any disputes should be examined and judged fairly, life sentences should be given as a last resort, prisoners should be released to *return to their normal lives after serving their terms, for there must be enough people to serve the land to produce commodities and the valuable things the Kingdom needs… All able Lao people should do their part to defend the territory against aggression from without. They should not make use of any of their own subjects against others for their own purposes nor commit acts of adultery; if found guilty, they should be liable to heavy fines.'*

Thus, a common peace was agreed among the Lao cities, and LanXang was united as a nation.

'During the peak of Fah Ngum's reign,' Chao Anouvong declared, 'a united Lao LanXang, with the mighty Mekong flowing through the middle, was within touching distance of the sea beyond Vietnam in the east; it bordered Khmer and Cham to the south and southeast, Ayutthaya (Siam) to the southwest, LanNa (and the Shan state) to the northwest, Tonkin to the northeast and Yunnan (China) to the north. The empire was large and powerful and had no need or desire to conquer its neighbouring countries – the Siamese kingdom of Ayutthaya in particular. Importantly, King Fah Ngum abolished slavery during his reign, a clear sign of his humility. He introduced Theravada Buddhism and encouraging the people to reject animism, the religion of spirit worship.'

Sadly, after his beloved queen died in 1368, his interest in the kingdom's affairs weakened; his supreme authority could not save him. Finally, his own mandarins forced his abdication and then deported him to the city of Nan in 1371. He found sanctuary in the Wat XiengNgam temple, self-exiled from his glory, and lived humbly as a monk. He died quietly two years later at the age of fifty-seven, with only a stupa (a Buddhist shrine) built in his memory and containing his ashes.

His son, Thao OunHeuan (1374–1487) took over the throne at the age of eighteen, with Nang NoiNonghiao as his queen. He was also popular with the neighbouring rulers and for that, LanNa sent him the princess Nang NoiOnsoh, Ayutthaya sent him the princess Nang KaeoYotFah and the Shan ruler of XiengHung sent him the princess Nang KaeoSida. From these three unions, a well-connected Lao royal bloodline was created, and the special relationships with neighbouring countries were sealed with royal marriages. During Thao OunHeuan's forty-three-year reign, Lao LanXang became an important trade centre: a census towards the end of his reign registered 700,000 fighting men, of whom 300,000 were of Tai Lao (lowland Lao) nationality.

The rest were of other ethnicities. He was ceremoniously crowned as 'Phraya SamSenTai Tayphouvanath Thipath Si-Sattanarkhanahout' but known simply as King SamSenTai. He ordered the transfer of his father's ashes from Nan city to Luang Phrabang, and they were laid to rest at the KuTay stupa.

Chao Anouvong also recognised that he'd inherited a vassal state that was still divided into three principalities. He didn't have the same political power and support to draw on in time of need as his predecessor, King Xay-Setthathirath the Great (1548–1572).

'We'll do our best, Khoun Jon,' he said optimistically.

'Without fear, Your Royal Highness, we can do no more than our best,' I said encouragingly.

He nodded his head and told me that when the ruler of LanNa, King Kethklao, who was Xay-Setthathirath's grandfather, died without a son in 1548, the people favoured a strong alliance with LanXang because Siam was their enemy. They asked King Phothisarath of Luang Phrabang to send his eldest son to take the throne. Phothisarath didn't waste any time, as he feared that the king of Si-Ayutthaya Siam, Chairacha, would invade; he'd successfully defended ViengChan when the Siamese invaded in 1540. Chairacha also invaded LanNa in 1545 and 1547, but King Phothisarath successfully defended XiengMai, saving it from destruction. He no longer trusted the Siamese after that.

King Phothisarath and his queen YotKhamtip (daughter of the late King Kethklao) promptly prepared their young prince Setthavangsoh, dressing him all in white with flowers and candles in his praying hands, with a procession of thousands of people and hundreds of elephants to accompany him. The convoy reached XiengSaen where the young prince became a monk on 15 July 1548. The procession arrived at XiengRai on 26 July and stayed there for nine days. Setthavangsoh, aged fourteen, finally entered XiengMai on 23 August 1548, and was ceremonially crowned two days later in front of the Emerald Buddha (the only king to receive this honour) as LanNa's king, under the name Xay-Setthathirath. (The Emerald Buddha statue itself had been hidden in the stupa in XiengRai's temple and forgotten about for many years. It re-emerged after lightning struck the stupa in 1434. It then found its way to the city of Lampang before being finally housed in XiengMai as intended in 1468.)

Meanwhile, the Burmese were also looking to expand their power. King Bayin Naung sent his envoys to meet King Phothisarath while he was still in

XiengMai to discuss an alliance against Ayutthaya. But Phothisarath did not trust the Burmese either. He rightly saw that it was more important to protect Ayutthaya. After his son's coronation he returned to XiengThong, but he sadly died two years later from an accident while demonstrating how to capture wild elephants for the benefit of foreign nobles and rulers.

The mandarins in XiengThong, thinking that Xay-Setthathirath would prefer to remain king of LanNa in XiengMai, promptly gave the throne to his younger brother, Chao Lanexang. Xay-Setthathirath overruled the decision and set out to claim the throne in 1550. He brought an army with him to LanXang and established a town opposite ViengChan, naming it Si-Xiengmai to honour the people of LanNa. He built the Wat SongNang temple in honour of his two queens, Nang Thip and Nang Thonkham from LanNa. Once his men were trained and ready, he sent a message to XiengThong demanding that he be recognised as the absolute ruler of LanXang. This was accepted and he ruled both LanNa and LanXang for two years.

It was in Xay-Setthathirath's interest to return to rule LanXang rather than remaining in LanNa to deter the Burmese invasion. Understandably, he did not like living in XiengThong: 'Not enough flat land for cultivation and too many mountains,' he declared when the mandarins begged him to return to Lao LanXang. 'However, if you could move the land of XiengMai to XiengThong, I will come to rule LanXang,' he famously said. He understood that he might never return to rule LanNa, but due to his royal family connections, he considered both kingdoms to be one and the same. Rightly regarding the Emerald Buddha as the palladium of the Lao kingdom, he decided to take it with him. He was the king of LanNa and therefore didn't need permission from anyone, least of all from the Siamese ruler who had removed it from ViengChan by deception. Chao Mekuti was ordered to look after LanNa's affairs in XiengMai and keep the Burmese out.

The royal barge floated down the Mekong, and upon disembarking at XiengThong, Xay-Setthathirath was told that XiengMai's earth had also come with him. Looking tired but relieved at the end of the long journey, the king thrusted his head forward in puzzlement.

'Your Majesty, the land of XiengMai has come with you,' the mandarins said joyfully.

'You are silly people. How is that possible?' he asked and stood up in amused curiosity.

'It is underneath Your Majesty's feet,' said the mandarins and begged him to step aside before removing the carpet to reveal soft, green grass underneath his seat. A piece of XiengMai turf had been cut and hidden under his chair. He sank back in his seat and gave a pleasant smile, drawing loud cheers and laughter.

King Xay-Setthathirath was crowned in 1550 in XiengThong as 'Phraya Uphaiyaphuthorn Bovon Xay-Settha Phuvanathathipa Si-Sattanarkhanahout' (Uphaiyaphuthorn signified a ruler of two kingdoms) but was commonly known as Chao Xay-Settha to the Lao of LanNa and LanXang. By 1551 he decided to inform XiengMai that he would not be returning to LanNa. He considered the city of XiengThong to be too small and too close for comfort to the Burmese, surrounded as it was by mountains and lying on an open invasion route.

ViengChan on the other hand was further away and much bigger, surrounded by fertile lands for stretching on both sides of the Mekong. To protect LanXang he'd to follow his father's wishes, and he finally decided to make ViengChan the Lao LanXang kingdom's capital in 1560. He moved both his followers and his property – including the sacred Emerald Buddha and the bronze statue of Phra SaekKham – down to the new capital, known officially as 'Chanthabury Si-Sattanarkhanahout Uttam Rajathani'. He subsequently changed XiengThong's name to Luang Phrabang in honour of the gold statue of the Phrabang Buddha he'd left behind.

Xay-Setthathirath was a quick learner and he realised that his father's refusal to cooperate with King Bayin Naung of Burma in 1548 in any invasion of Si-Ayutthaya made him a target. He quickly sealed an alliance with the ruler of Ayutthaya by jointly building That Si-SongHuck (the sacred shrine of two loves) at Dan Sai city in Loei province in 1563 to recognise the demarcation line – the Phetsabun Range – between the two kingdoms. The pact was of paramount importance and the two kings swore an oath during the ceremony, invoking Khoun Borom's doctrine:

'We, the two Royal kings, hereby declare that the people of our two kingdoms shall share the same destinies, there shall be no dispute between us, no aggression against each other, no attempt to take advantage of each other: we pledge friendship, and our love for each other until the sun disappears from our universe.'

They both called upon the gods of the sky and the earth as witnesses to their declaration.

After residing in ViengChan for two years, Xay-Setthathirath realised something was missing in his life. He sent a message to the Ayutthaya king Chakraphat requesting consent for a union with his daughter, Nang ThepKasatti the brave. After careful consideration, Chakraphat was happy to oblige, and the princess was escorted by a convoy of 1,000 attendants in 1563. King Xay-Setthathirath went to meet her at NongHan city, where he planned to hold a welcoming celebration. Unfortunately, Phraya Thammaracha of Phitsanulok ambushed the princess en route; she was captured but committed suicide on her way to Burma. Xay-Setthathirath did not have his queen and returned to find that ViengChan had unexpectedly been invaded by the Burmese. Successfully waging a guerrilla war, he drove out the invading army, saving his kingdom from Burmese domination; but they returned three years later.

During this invasion, it is said that Xay-Setthathirath, who was imbued with the power of the Buddha, entered the Burmese king Bayin Naung's camp outside the city while he was asleep. He could have killed him but left a white mark instead. At sunrise, he sent his envoy with a letter:

'Last night, I came to visit you, but you were sleeping. I did not want to disturb you but left a white mark on your neck. Now it is my pleasure to invite you to visit my palace for negotiations concerning our differences.'

Bayin Naung stared in the mirror and was most surprised to see white paint on his neck. He happily accepted the invitation and, after a friendly meeting, they erected a statue of the two queens at Wat Inpeng temple to seal their friendship.

But King Xay-Setthathirath kept his word to Ayutthaya,' Chao Anouvong claimed, 'and helped King Mahintharaja fight against an invading Burmese army in 1567 with 20,000 men and 200 elephants but failed to capture Phitsanuloke from the Burmese king Thammaraja. In 1569 Xay-Setthathirath raised 50,000 men, 300 elephants and 2,000 horses and commanded his forces to again rescue Ayutthaya. Both attempts to retake Phitsanuloke from the Burmese failed because of discord amongst the Siamese: Mahintharaja's commander Phraya Siharajteso betrayed him by siding with Thammaraja instead. Xay-Setthathirath returned to ViengChan having suffered heavy losses, severely weakening

Lao military power.' Chao Anouvong paused for thought and then said, 'The despicable Siamese rulers want to punish us for our generosity!'

And then, having succeeded in destroying Si-Ayutthaya a year earlier, and infuriated by Xay-Setthathirath's help in defending Phitsanuloke, King Bayin Naung decided to invade the Lao capital in 1571. He took command of a Burmese army consisting of 34,000 men, 1,800 horses and 180 elephants and marched on ViengChan.

This time, Xay-Setthathirath took no chances. He ordered the city's evacuation and scattered the people and his fighting units in the nearby forest (*pa*). The Burmese invaders arrived at a ghost city, and when their supplies ran low, they went outside in search of food and were ambushed by the Lao army. After more than six months of guerrilla warfare the Lao forces finally defeated the invaders. Bayin Naung's troops made a hasty retreat and were ambushed by Lao units during their journey home, suffering the greatest loss and humiliation in their history. Despite this, Xay-Setthathirath earned great respect and praise from the Burmese king, who proclaimed him as the 'King of Kings, and the only one who did not surrender to Bayin Naung.'

King Xay-Setthathirath's legacy in protecting LanXang was to build many temples and shrines. In 1563 he built Hor Phra Kaeo to house the revered Emerald Buddha statue, the pride of the Lao people. He also built That Si-SongHuck and renovated That Phanom. But the biggest and most famous monument of all was built on top of a structure first built by the resourceful Indian Emperor Ashoka, born in 304 BC, who, after many victories and killing many thousands during his reign (268–232 BC), suffered remorse and converted to Buddhism. His missionaries, Sona, Outala and five scholars were sent from India to ViengChan in the third century BC. It was believed they brought with them a piece of Lord Buddha's breastbone, which was then kept in the obelisk on That Luang hill. A few years later, Ashoka authorised the ViengChan ruler, Lord Chantabury Phasithisak, to build a stupa over the obelisk, and it was named Phra That Chedi. When King Xay-Setthathirath completed renovations in 1566, the stupa was named 'Phra That Chedi Loka Chulamany'. ViengChan was once only a small town on the Mekong plain, with marshland on the south side of That Luang hill. It was now a well-built, walled city with beautiful temples and houses, and the new stupa was known as 'That Luang' (Grand Stupa) by the Lao people and has famously remained the Lao national symbol ever since. Xay-Setthathirath mysteriously disappeared during a military

'That Luang' (Grand Stupa)

expedition into Ongkharn city in Atthapeu province in 1572, perhaps murdered by his commander-in-chief, Phraya Nakhorn, who wanted to dethrone him.

Xay-Setthathirath's son, NorMueang, who'd been held in captivity in Burma, survived him. He returned at the age of twenty to claim the throne in 1591 but died seven years later without a successor.

As if an omen of future struggle, Chao Anouvong, by any normal standard, was a poor king. He neither feared nor despised poverty but if the choice were offered, he would certainly have chosen wealth without assuming it would guarantee his virtue.

Unlike Prince Souriya Khumman, who at the age of twenty-five was enthroned as King Souriyavongsa Thammikarath (otherwise known as the Sun King, 1633–1690), Chao Anouvong simply didn't have the wealth, influence and good fortune that was needed to run the kingdom. The Sun King's reign was an era of trade, development and experimentation, and he was addicted to progress. He poured the vast amount of capital generated by trade into building projects, a powerful agent of social change in LanXang. He developed the kingdom to be the envy of her less happy neighbours, building grand palaces with lofty halls and opulent interiors, and many temples of imposing height in what became a golden age for ViengChan. He succeeded in making LanXang the most developed kingdom in the region. He encouraged the teaching of Buddhism, which was accepted as a religion. As a result, the kingdom produced scores of writers, poets, artists and philosophers; many outstanding poetic stories were written, such as *Sin-Xay* by the exceptional Thao Pangkham from NongBuaLamphu (Sin-Xay was a superhuman boy, who, with the help of his brothers Siho and Xangthong, succeeded in rescuing his abducted aunt Nang Simountha from the palace of a devil king, Khoumphan). The Sun King set up worthy legislation to benefit people of both high and low rank. He was the first LanXang king to receive a foreign commercial mission from Europe.

Unsurprisingly, landlocked Lao LanXang provoked much European curiosity but didn't do much to satisfy it. In fact, LanXang was not tempting for European trade, and merely kept herself in happy isolation. However, on 3 November 1641, after a long and relatively easy journey up the Mekong from Cambodia, a Dutchman, Gerrit van Wuysthoff encountered the raging and impassable waterfalls of Khone Phapheng on the southern borders of LanXang. His men had to unload and pull the boats upstream using ropes. They eventually made it through the dangerous Liphi falls and returned their boats to the water. LanXang came into the picture, and her veil of secrecy was lifted. The hospitable ruler of Champasak city welcomed Van Wuysthoff with curiosity and charm. The next morning, after a hearty breakfast, Van Wuysthoff's boats continued up the now tranquil and majestic river for a few days, before toiling their way through the hazardous Kemmarat rapids further upstream. Van Wuysthoff and his men then wearily paddled through gently meandering steep banks and meadows and stayed briefly at Nakhorn Phanom. From there onwards the mighty Mekong rewarded them with an area full of natural beauty and picturesque, hilly landscapes. The Dutchman finally arrived in ViengChan exhausted on 16 November 1641 with a letter from Governor General Van Diemen in Indonesia. Van Wuysthoff was ecstatic and highly impressed at the sight and scale of the dazzling ViengChan palaces reflected in the Mekong. It must have been the Dutchman's integrity that persuaded the Sun King to receive him during the annual That Luang stupa festival.

Van Wuysthoff was majestically paraded through the city on a gilded elephant howdah, joining the traditional wax castles (*Pasaatpheung*) procession led by thousands of monks and government officials from nine districts around ViengChan. He was astonished to see so many monks – more men in saffron robes in ViengChan than the whole army in the Netherlands, he was alleged to have said. He was ceremoniously welcomed in the royal tent on That Luang hill and watched with great interest a game of hockey (*Thiki*) between officials and commoners on the esplanade. During an audience with the king, followed by a banquet where the kingdom's wealth was proudly on display, King Souriyavongsa, clad in his ceremonial garments, unexpectedly invited (*Seurn*) Van Wuysthoff to sit on a mat beside him. Van Wuysthoff was not only taken aback but highly impressed by the king's liberalism. The king told him that his peaceful and vast Lao LanXang kingdom that almost touched Bangkok was trading with all her neighbours and was more than willing to trade with the rest of the world. He boasted that LanXang produced the finest lac, the best rice and many other commodities such as gold, silver, silk and spices for export. Before mounting his white elephant to return to the palace, the king wished Van Wuysthoff well and told him that his commercial dealings with Siam in the southwest were frustratingly unprofitable. He shrewdly suggested that the Siamese should be made to stop their unfair trading practices and refrain from monopolising the ancient trading route of Lao LanXang with the Khmer kingdom and Vietnam at Stung Treng.

Van Wuysthoff had discovered all he wanted to know about the independent Lao Kingdom of LanXang and wished to report back to the House of Orange in The Hague. He left a month later (20 December), taking with him a cargo of benzoin resin, musk, lac and many other commodities. He would have been convinced that LanXang was keen to cooperate with any other friendly nation, but it was unlikely that anyone, the Siamese establishment least of all, could alter the Lao character, such a curious blend of Buddhism and animism, of shrewdness and superstition, of integrity and humanity, of friendliness and generosity, of tolerance and diplomacy; and cheerfulness, never mind their laid-back attitude to life. Alas, LanXang was the envy of Siam, and her success soon attracted the attention of the Siamese ruler. Siam's political elite had long been secretly nursing malice against LanXang. Conflict was brewing; the special relationship hadn't always been harmonious since 1563: tempers had frayed but LanXang always chose to turn the other cheek, and life went on.

Chao Anouvong reminded me that King Souriyavongsa sent a good-will mission in 1670 to renew the special relationship. The ceremony took place at the That Si-SongHuck shrine and declarations 'taken on oath' were again made to respect the 1563 boundary agreement and to bring the Siamese and Lao together: it was emphasised that the two royal families should be considered as one, sharing their destinies with great affection. The two kings once more invoked the gods of the sky and the earth as their witnesses and swore on their lives that 'There should be no dispute, no aggression and no attempt at invasion by either side until the sun disappears from the universe.' Chao Anouvong looked at me in frustration and asked, 'Now, why did the Siamese invade us in 1779, Khoun Jon?' I replied that only they could tell us the truth. 'We became the victims of jealousy,' he said. 'They betrayed our friendship and trust by invading us. They destroyed our palaces and temples and looted our sacred Emerald Buddha that had been in our capital since 1560!' He turned to stare at the Mekong, shaking his head in disbelief.

King Souriyavongsa was apparently a man of honour. As a chief justice, he was determined to uphold the rule of law. He'd one son and two daughters, princesses Kummari and Sumangkala. When his first and only son, Chao Rathsabout, was found guilty of adultery, he'd him executed (Rathsabout had married the XiengHung princess Chanta Kummari and had two sons, Kingkitsarath and Inthasom, who later ruled Luang Phrabang). The Sun King, therefore, became highly feared and respected by neighbouring kingdoms. Born in 1608, he reigned uninterrupted for fifty-seven years and died at the ripe old age of eighty-two, leaving no clear heir to the throne. Internal wrangles began.

Internal strife, Chao Anouvong said, leads to external troubles, and so LanXang drifted towards calamity. By 1695, infighting began among the rival claimants for the throne. King Souriyavongsa's grandson, Kingkitsarath of Luang Phrabang, claimed the throne, only to be opposed by his cousin, Xay-OngVeh, a son of Souriyavongsa's older brother, Chao Somphou, who had been exiled to the imperial city of Hue in Vietnam. Xay-OngVeh reached for his sword, rode westward, captured ViengChan and executed its proxy ruler, King Nantharath. He took the throne and was crowned as King Xay-Setthathirath II in 1698 (he died in 1730). Distrust between the houses of ViengChan and Luang Phrabang now began in earnest.

Kingkitsarath marched south and attacked ViengChan in 1706, dismaying the population. Sensing defeat, Xay-Setthathirath II sent for help from Siam, whose opportunistic king, Chao Petharaja, was secretly delighted at the enmity between the two LanXang principalities. Seeing an opportunity to cause further friction, he arrived in ViengChan with a large army in 1707, but instead of promoting reconciliation between the two Lao royal houses, he wasted no time in stabbing Lao LanXang in the back. He cunningly brought about the partition of Luang Phrabang and ViengChan, and the devious Siamese policy of 'divide and rule' began. He was shrewd enough to see the outcome, and realised that by keeping LanXang divided, one side would eventually seek to dominate the other. Meanwhile the southern LanXang kingdom of Champasak declared self-rule in 1713; Lao LanXang seemed like the setting sun, barely clinging to life. Once the three sides had exhausted themselves in a power struggle, the path was clear for Siam to march in. With their brutality hidden beneath their charm, the Siamese seized LanXang by the throat in 1779, destroying ViengChan and removing the Emerald Buddha. Their power grew and their territory expanded. Siam was clearly in the wrong for wanting to exterminate LanXang: it was a serious breach of trust. This was how the antagonism between the two kingdoms began. Although time is a good healer, these events can be forgiven but not forgotten.

Chao Anouvong was frustrated and unhappy because all he'd was his own talent. Nevertheless, he was a wise man of courage and righteousness, who was prepared to stand up and fight for his principles. Whatever the obstacles, he was determined to persevere. He was born into the world, like all of us, with six senses: sight, sound, smell, taste, touch and ideas. He wanted to plant good seeds, and other people's welfare was always foremost in his mind, even at his own expense.

One could sense that, like King Fah Ngum before him, Chao Anouvong longed for LanXang sovereignty, and not even the fear of death, which was really just another part of life, could deter him from its pursuit. In the interest of the Lao nation, he resisted the kings of Siam all his political life. I feel bound to say in all honesty, though not without some trepidation, that a perfect country, society or individual cannot exist until rulers are inspired by a genuine love of true democracy and justice. It was not the will but the ability that Chao Anouvong lacked. He knew that all great undertakings were risky, and worthwhile ambitions were often achieved only with great difficulty.

Rite of Passage

I was born nine years after Chao Anouvong, to a feudal family in the strategic city of Mahaxay in the southeast of ViengChan, a year after King Bounyasan paid an emergency visit to the city to express his concern over King TakSin of Siam's invasion of LanNa in 1775, as near to a hostile act as a formal ally could commit. Due to his father's connection, it was natural for Bounyasan to seek a strong alliance with Vietnam – a major deterrent to Siamese attack. Three years later Siam declared war on LanXang, as Bounyasan had dreaded. Thus began a bloody period in Lao LanXang history.

I had never seen ViengChan nor even heard about Bangkok. Mahaxay city was a perfect gateway, used by many Lao kings to escape to Vietnam in wartime. Before that, my grandfather, a Lao Khorat nobleman, who held the uncompromising Lao values of King Fah Ngum, did not wish to be a Siamese subject. He saw that the Sino-Siamese king TakSin was a greedy and dangerous man, so he moved from Khorat city as soon as he could and settled with his family in the well-established old town of Cham on the Donh River in the southern principality of Champasak, and never looked back. They even migrated as far as the Kongtum area near Darlac in the southeast, then part of LanXang territory, but this felt uncomfortably close to Vietnam, whose culture was very different. They moved back to be closer to the Mekong for security and comfort in the early 1770s, where they quickly assimilated themselves into real Lao LanXang life. Mahaxay on the Xe Bangfai River was to be our sanctuary and my world until I was nine.

I was nineteen years old when I first entered Chao Anouvong's life and worked with him until 1828, after which my family was fortunate to escape forced migration by Siamese officials. I was quite small, still boy-shaped, and worried I would never grow to be a big, strong man. I considered myself a palace servant and had been working in the palace library since the beginning of 1794. Before that, I led a perfectly haphazard existence, and though I was now getting somewhere, I was in fact still the most wretched creature imaginable. Yet I firmly believed that the pursuit of wisdom was the only thing a man should devote himself to before passing on his experience to others.

Chao Anouvong was twelve, learning feudal rulers' and warriors' skills, when he was taken away as a hostage from the plains, forests, mountains and fresh, clean air of ViengChan to the dreary lowlands and smelly humid air of Bangkok. He was brought up among the Siamese under the watchful eye of King Chulaloke and his son, Prince Itsarasunthon, who was the same age as him. He was now a young man of twenty-eight; his knowledge of Siam was prodigious, and he was known everywhere as Itsarasunthon's friend. He returned to ViengChan with his younger brother, Phommavong (known as Phromvong in Bangkok), who was about my age, when his older brother Inthavong ascended the throne in 1795. At first, he appeared fresh, confident and happy, but he'd been suffering from nervous exhaustion and was struggling to overcome considerable anxiety. Valuable time had been wasted towing the line of the ruling house of Siam. They fed him strange, delicious food until one day he must have realised that it was high time for him to think of LanXang, for if he went on like that, he might never be a Lao or see ViengChan again.

Being back in ViengChan and living among his own people revived his self-esteem and enthusiasm. He'd longed for home and had returned to his kingdom, no longer at ease with the Bangkok dispensation and rule that he couldn't wait to get rid of. Here in the city of his birth he followed Lao traditions with gladness, finding comfort and enjoying high prestige where no one would look down on him. There was a gleam of happiness in his eyes as he searched for light to see into the future. He was no longer an over-privileged wastrel but the saviour of his kingdom. The thought grew in his mind to restore LanXang's dynastic rule. Few would have been brave enough to push, but Chao Anouvong had the knowledge and ambition.

I first learned about the history of the Lao LanXang kingdom through word of mouth: its people, its culture and its right to independence. It had been a Lao custom for educated or wise elders to pass stories on to the younger generations. Then, one bright and cool November morning in 1795, I was unexpectedly summoned to see Chao Anouvong, who had been appointed viceroy. Naturally, I was greatly excited by the prospect of appearing before him at the palace. My life changed forever.

I slept soundly and got up earlier than usual. It was indeed an exciting day for me. After carefully dressing, I made my way from my mother's house, heading straight for the palace. To make sure I arrived fresh and had time to cool down, I took a shorter route which I later took to work every day, directly through the southern inner-city gate before reaching the palace wall. At the main arched tower of the Luang (grand) gate of the palace where two uniformed armed guards stood on either side, I came across a very close friend. We addressed each other affectionately as *Sio* (best friend) in public. He was cultured, an excellent raconteur, courteous with an assuring manner, abounding in understanding and sympathy, patriotic and an admirer of Chao Anouvong; a good-natured intellectual with a quick sense of humour who enjoyed telling anecdotes and jokes and singing, and always went about with a book. He was sitting under a shady tree next to the gate when his eyes met mine. He sprang up in surprise and we greeted each other affably.

'Jon, *Sio*,' he cried, raised his hand in greeting and coming towards me. '*Sabaidee* (hello)! What brings you here and where are you going?'

'*Sene, Sio, Sabaidee*!' I said, adding that I was on my way to the palace. 'I'm doubly glad to see you. But how are you and what are you doing here?'

'I'm fine, thank you, *Sio*,' he said. 'Just taking a rest in the shade and reading one of my father's history books. We haven't seen each other for so long. Would you be good enough to stay and talk for a moment?'

'You know, I like listening and talking to you very much, *Sio*', I said, 'but I'm afraid I don't have any time at the moment.'

'Never mind about that, please come, *Sio*, we must talk,' he said, and grabbed me by the arm. 'I've plenty of new jokes to make you laugh, which can only be good for your health. More importantly, our meeting is a great opportunity for a chat.' He paused to catch his breath. 'I know some men are frightened of their passionate nature. Now tell me one thing, have you found your ideal good-mannered, beautiful young girl yet?' I blushed, as if I'd drunk some wine, at the question. 'You must lower your standards, or you'll never get married,' he exclaimed, and laughed teasingly. 'Come, *Sio*, you seem to me to be quite lonely, and this can't be allowed. You must find love; procreation is part of society.'

I chuckled and smiled broadly, telling him that I was being initiated into the mysteries of love. I now believe that any man who wishes to pursue love in the right way should begin by applying himself to the contemplation of all physical beauty, before falling in love with a particular person and producing noble feelings in partnership with them. However, if he is noble, he will soon realise that his passion for that person's physical beauty is of less value than the beauty of the soul and the knowledge and love of wisdom. He would probably wish to spend the rest of his life in the contemplation of absolute, true beauty, rather than a mere reflection of it.

He grinned at me and said, 'Ah, there's no need to teach crocodiles to swim. You don't have to tell me whether you're in love with someone. I can see for myself that you're far gone.'

Hearing this made me blush more than ever; he went on to say that though ignorant of many things, he could recognise a man in love in an instant. He wanted to know who the lucky girl was and whether I knew what to say to her. I smiled and jokingly told him that I knew only what the soldiers and guards in the palace claim to say in such situations: 'Come pretty girl, smile for me. I won't eat you.' We threw back our heads and roared with laughter.

'Seriously,' I said, catching my breath. 'I'm disciplined enough to overcome any sort of passion involving timidity and distrust. Most of us are instinctively against any woman being at ease with a man. I've learned that our body needs food to live, but love is the true food for the soul. Love makes us ashamed but hungry for glory; without it we wouldn't achieve anything great. However, any young man who knows what's what when it comes to love doesn't praise the girl he's in love with until he's caught her, for it would only make her proud and conceited.'

'That would be quite absurd,' he protested, looking overwhelmed.

'*Sio*, a girl being too frank is no compliment to a bloke,' I said. 'Do tell me precisely, since I'm taking you into my confidence, what a man ought to say and do to endear himself to his girl?'

'It's not easy to say, *Sio*,' he replied, 'but nevertheless, I hope you're in love with a nice person.' When I didn't reply, he said, 'We are friends aren't we? We've plenty in common and, if you wouldn't mind, tell me why you're going to the palace and what the girl's name is.'

I told him that he would always be a dear friend to me, but I couldn't possibly comment on my engagement at the palace, before suggesting he should start saving for my wedding gifts. We laughed and patted each other on the shoulders. He gripped me firmly by the arm; his palm and hands, like mine, were soft and smooth. It was obvious that I was eager to be off. He let go and wished me luck. I nodded, thanked him and we parted company.

I passed through the great main gate into the interior of the palace. I had arrived with only a small bag with a few belongings – I've never liked carrying things around. When I stepped through the inner gate and into the quiet palace courtyard, I calmly composed myself and walked slowly towards the main door. The multiple-tiered terracotta roofs of the palace and the Emerald Buddha temple glittered in the shimmering heat. The late morning sun beat down from a cloudless sky, but the heat was cooled by a welcome breeze. Nevertheless, anxious and excited, I still broke into a sweat. I fished in my pocket for a handkerchief to give my damp brow a wipe before cautiously approaching a large, glossy, black door. I jumped when it suddenly squeaked and sprang open. A glimpse of shade through the entrance was welcoming, and, slowly, an imposing, tall, slim man appeared. He was about fifty, with a touch of grey in his hair, dressed in a formal bright red *phasalong* (sarong) and light cream jacket that made him look like a nobleman.

'*Sabaidee*, and welcome,' he said warmly, with a gentle, friendly smile. 'Please come in.'

'*Sabaidee*,' I said and reverently greeted him with my praying hands. He gestured to me to enter, and I slowly stepped inside. I had arrived in good time, which was just as well because he remarked on it. He was a serious, unemotional type of a person with a strong body and a stern, pale face that looked untouched by the sun. I had the feeling he was a gentlemanly, well-mannered man before whom you should stand to attention. I stood on the shiny tiled floor and the cool pleasant air engulfed me. I welcomed it without any fear.

I looked up in amazement at the walls of the hall, the panels, the wooden beams and the soaring gilded pillars in the soft light. Everything that struck my eyes was unbelievable: never before had I seen such a place, full of priceless artefacts. The well-polished antique tables and chairs, all beautifully kept and correctly positioned, shone in the dim light. They looked as if they all possessed a soul that wanted to come alive and be stroked and admired. Had I touched any of them, the evidence of my crime would clearly be marked. The air in the hall felt damp and cool but here and there lay terracotta oil lamps and enough candles to light a temple. I stood motionless for a few seconds as I gazed at the portraits and landscape paintings hung on both sides of the stairway.

I paid particular attention to a large, stunning painting in a golden frame depicting a man commanding a huge white elephant into battle. It was hung prominently on the dark blue walls immediately in front of the entrance hall.

Like a guardian of the palace, it looked down with inquisitive eyes at every visitor who walked through the door, as if it wanted to introduce itself. After staring at it for a while, thinking that I heard a deep, authoritarian voice, my body started to quiver. With trembling legs I turned to look at the footman standing next to me.

'Yes, it is a fascinating portrait,' he said, politely allowing me to enjoy my encounter with the painting. 'That is our King Fah Ngum the conqueror in battle, trying to unify Lao LanXang,' he explained.

'Really? How amazing!' I exclaimed, fixing my stare at the painting.

'It is very impressive, indeed,' he said and turned his gaze at me. 'Chao Anouvong should be down in a few minutes. When he's ready, I will come back to lead you in. For now, enjoy the painting.'

'You are very kind, thank you,' I acknowledged with a smile.

He did not respond but stood silently for a few moments before discreetly disappearing through the dark hallway. I turned and slowly walked away from the portrait. The door shut behind me, the sound echoing through the still air, leaving me in a large, scented room filled with tables and chairs, anticipating my next encounter. The room seemed friendly and welcoming, but I felt rather unsure of myself, particularly since I realised how incorrect I had been about the place. Everything was beyond my comprehension. Before this I had only ever seen stacks and piles of books, papers and documents of importance in the palace's library where I spent most of my day working.

I sat on one of the soft, rectangular, high stools in the middle of the room, among lines of ancient steel drums along the walls, and waited. These types of seats were designed to make you sit upright with your feet on the floor and your open hands resting on your thighs, a posture difficult to maintain for any length of time. Since I was alone, I occupied myself by scanning the palace's ornate high ceilings, long beams and tall, rounded pillars, all beautifully decorated in gold leaf with a black or red lacquer background. Out of curiosity I peered through an open door into a succession of rooms. A sharp ray of light shone through the small, open windows. As the sun rose higher, the air became hotter, but the room remained cool. I returned to the stool, trying to keep calm, wishing I were outside basking in the sun like a lizard.

Suddenly the heavy teak door swung open outwards and I leapt to my feet. In came Chao Anouvong, looking informal but irritated. I was supposed to meet him in the other room but surprisingly he'd come to me instead. His son, Prince Suthisan Poh, around five years old, followed closely behind. My first impression of Chao Anouvong was very positive, as his imposing figure towered lovingly over the young prince. Seeing him in his casual outfit and silken slippers, one would never have thought he was a king in waiting: perhaps a schoolteacher or a philosopher instead. But it was clear he'd woken up in an edgy, preoccupied mood. Whatever had been going through his head the previous night had obviously disturbed his rest. He twitched irritably at his silk trousers (*phahthong*) that wrapped untidily round his waist. As if he'd never dressed himself before, I noticed that the cloth's flowing ends that were carried between his legs were not tucked in properly at the waistline at the back. The cloth should just fall neatly below the knees if dressed correctly, but it was too long. It brushed along the floor when he started to walk about. He was not pleased. 'This damned *phahthong*!' I heard him mutter to himself as he paused to adjust the cloth before looking in my direction.

'Poh, stop!' Chao Anouvong ordered. 'Please try not to walk in front of me.'

'Sorry, father,' said the prince and stopped dead.

'Didn't I tell you that it's not proper to do so?'

'Mother told me also. Why?' the prince said, with his head bowed and his hands behind his back.

'Well, you're not supposed to walk ahead of me. If you do that with the King of Siam, you'll be flogged!'

'Is that why we don't like the bossy Siamese, father?'

'Not all of them, so please don't be prejudiced,' Chao Anouvong reproved mildly, placing a finger on his lips to silence his son as he was about to speak.

He then came leisurely towards me. I was so tense that when our eyes met, I failed to smile properly, managing only a sheepish grin before lowering my head in reverence and waiting nervously for him to come closer. Despite his serious expression he seemed pleased to see me. It was an early November morning, but the cool palace waiting room seemed hotter than outside. I waited courteously for him to speak.

'*Sabaidee*. What's your name?' he said casually with a friendly smile.

'I pay my humble respects, Your Royal Highness. I'm honoured that you should condescend to welcome me,' I said ingratiatingly and bowed to him. One had to be obsequious when talking to royalty. I was calm but my voice and body were trembling with nerves. 'My name is Jon.'

'Jon?' he repeated and lifted his brows in surprise. 'I see. That's interesting,' he quipped, as if he were captivated by my name. 'I've never heard of a Lao name like that before. Are you Lao? You look like a Han if I may say so.'

'On a basic level, Your Royal Highness,' I said timorously, bowing again, 'I'm a human being and a Lao. I don't always think about my Laoishness, but I'm very Lao and proud of it. I was born to be nothing but a Lao.'

'Good! Very glad to hear it,' he said and chuckled pleasantly, adding that he too was glad to have been born Lao.

While trying to adjust his dress he told me to sit and relax. 'No need to stand to attention, Jon,' he said. At that moment I feared him and took him very seriously. I lowered my head to acknowledge his command but remained standing with my hands behind my back. 'Actually, let's go to my private room. It's more comfortable.' I drew a deep breath and followed him into his study, expecting him to deliver one of his witticisms, though I sensed he'd something important to say to me. He realised that both his son and I were looking at him. Suthisan Poh was inspecting his father's dress and giving him a funny smile. 'However hard I tried I just couldn't get myself dressed properly today,' he complained. It was clear that he preferred to do things his way.

'May I say something, Your Royal Highness?' I asked nervously.

'Go ahead, Jon.'

'You look perfectly dressed,' I said light-heartedly. My compliment pleased him.

'Come closer,' he said, asking me to stand beside him. I began to feel more confident.

'Father,' said Suthisan Poh, playfully clapping a hand over his mouth. 'Mother told me no one is properly dressed until he smiles.'

Chao Anouvong's head went back, and we all laughed out loud. He turned towards his loving son and ruffled his hair. 'Come, be a good boy. It's time for you to leave,' he said and started to walk him to the door. The prince obediently lifted his slight hands to his chest and bowed to his father. Then he made a friendly eye gesture at me and began to walk away slowly. Chao Anouvong raised his hand and said goodbye, telling the prince to be good, and closed the door gently.

He began to engage me in light and cheerful conversation after we'd exchanged the formal courtesies. He expressed himself with ease and wit on a wide range of subjects, but I struggled to sound confident and well informed. To my relief, he kindly said he'd heard many good things about me and that I could be the person he needed in the palace after all the time he'd spent in Bangkok. It certainly saved me from having to answer too many uncomfortable questions. It was friendship at first sight: the beginning of our close relationship. He studied my features with childish curiosity and teased me about my smooth, boyish, hairless face. 'Real men have facial hair, but you have none!' he said with a broad grin. With that remark, our conversation soon became unconstrained, and we both lost our shyness.

'I do have fine soft hair, Your Royal Highness,' I responded, stroking my face with a smile and wanting to look more mature and manly, hoping to impress the girls.

'Yes, but I can see that you'll never have whiskers like mine to twiddle with,' he said, stroking his moustache and smiling mischievously. Casual but conventional, it seemed, was his way of making people relax. He sat on a high teak chair with his feet on the floor, before commanding me to make myself comfortable on an identical chair opposite him. He fixed his gaze on me as if further seeking my trust. I tried to relax and placed my cold hands underneath my thighs for warmth. With a slightly shy manner but an air of quiet authority and a gentle, well-modulated voice, he began the conversation.

At the beginning, our meeting seemed so informal that I even swung my dangling legs about. He rambled on about many things – the country, the people and life in general. But our talk soon became so serious that one would think he'd marked me out as a genius since the cradle. Not so! I approached him with care, nervously fiddling with my long black hair before tucking it behind my ear with my index finger. You would be hard pressed to distinguish me from any other well-bred young Laoman, though there was one obvious big difference. Perhaps few respectable households could have been as poor as my family. Yet I was content with my unpretentious image. Chao Anouvong looked at me solicitously while drinking freshly made, fragrant jasmine cordial, put his cup down on the table and leant towards me conspiratorially. I straightened in anticipation.

'Jon,' he said. 'I presume your forbearance and attentiveness to the surroundings and your understanding of the world are all good. Now, everything has a beginning, though it's not important to go back too far in history, but do you know about our ancestry?'

I was honoured to have encountered such a heart-warming person but truly stumped by this question, which echoed round the room and weakened my composure.

'Your Royal Highness, I know very little, and virtually nothing at all about the world,' I replied cautiously, mumbling something about legendary Khoun Borom. With my head shaking gently I added, 'I must confess that my head is weak.'

'Good Lord. Don't you know where the Lao race come from?' he said, looking at me in astonishment.

'I'm afraid I don't, Your Royal Highness,' I said. 'But does it matter? We're all human beings.'

'It ought to, even so,' he said. 'The Chinese have a record of it, and it's not difficult to understand.'

'It is for me, I fear. Nevertheless, I am most interested and should like to know more if you would be so kind.'

He clicked his tongue, looked at me in disappointment and said that it would be a good investment to give me the benefit of his knowledge.

'Well, Jon, we, the Lao nation, are a distinct race,' he said proudly, in an awe-inspiring voice. 'In fact, we're the progenitors of the Ai-Lao: a non-Chinese people from whom we are directly descended. Our neighbours invaded us, looted our treasures and destroyed our cities, but we're still here. We will be Ai-Lao or Lao forever, but we mustn't take anything for granted.' He looked at me questioningly while taking a sip of his drink. 'Are you listening, Jon?'

'Yes, indeed I am, Your Royal Highness… with great interest,' I said. 'Do please go on.'

'Good! Now pay attention,' he said and paused for thought. 'Later, after the NanChao kingdom… in Yunnan that is,' he continued, 'we began to refer to the people from all the different places we come from as *Tai* – Tai Khorat, Tai XiengMai, Tai ViengChan, Tai Luang Phrabang, Tai Champasak, and so on. In general, we simply identify with each other as Tai Neau (north), Tai Tay (south). Historically, the Tai Ban Xieng (Ban Chiang in Siamese) who migrated from XiengKhuang are famous for making pots and have occupied this part of LanXang for thousands of years. And there are many other ethnic groups in the kingdom, such as Tai Dam, Tai Daeng, Tai Khmu, Tai Leu, Tai Nung and many more. They are all Lao citizens of Mother Mekong, where the people live together like one big, friendly family.'

He went on to say that the Ai-Lao race had come into existence in the universe at the same time as the Chinese. The Ai-Lao were a large group of people to whom the Lao, Shan, Zhuang, Siamese, Dai, Ahom, Li, Lue, Nung, Lolo and others are related. They were mostly an agricultural people, using oxen or buffalo to plough the fields and cultivating rice as a way of life. They also produced textiles of silk, hemp, wool and cotton; mined gold, silver, copper, iron, lead and tin ores; and made jewellery.

They first established themselves in the Yangtze valley in Sichuan province in mainland China more than 2,500 years ago. The first two main cities of the Ai-Lao were Mueang Lung (Loong) near the source of the Yangtze River to the north; but Mueang Pah (Ba), to the south of the river in the Erhai region of Sichuan, was bigger and more important. Later, Mueang Ngiao was built further south. Eventually, Mueang Lung and Mueang Pah were lost to the Chinese (who themselves had been invaded from the north by the Tatars in 843 BC). But those who remained in Mueang Pah fought back and regained their independence, at least until 338 BC, when they were again invaded. They gradually migrated southward to Yunnan, searching for freedom and a new kingdom. Their civilisation had been high in moral virtue since ancient times – equal to the Chinese civilisation of the Qin (221–206 BC) and the Han Dynasties (206 BC – AD 220).

In 246, Emperor Chin Tse Hon Teh, who built the Great Wall of China, invaded Mueang Ngiao. Most of the Ai-Lao migrated southwards in 215 BC where they united and built another city, called Mueang PayNgai, with Khoun Meng as king. When he refused permission for the ministers of the Chinese Emperor Wu Tee to cross his land to investigate Buddhism in India, war broke out. Khoun Meng fought valiantly but capitulated in 87 BC; the Ai-Lao kingdom became a vassal state.

Khoun Wang took over from Khoun Meng round AD 9 and maintained Mueang PayNgai's autonomy until AD 50, when the Chinese again invaded. Those who stayed put and fought on were to remain Ai-Lao, but those who migrated southwards were called Ngai-Lao. The Ai-Lao were slowly incorporated into the Han Empire, while Chinese settlers began to gradually colonise Yunnan.

In AD 57, Khoun Lee Mau (Li Mao) of Ngai-Lao accepted Mahayana Buddhism during the reign of Emperor Ming Tse of China. In AD 69, for fear of invasion, Lee Mau sent his son to the Han court, asking to be included among the imperial subjects, although Han control over the west and southwest wasn't particularly firm. Lee Mau died in AD 78, and his son, Khoun Lai Lao, took over. He refused to accept the high taxes that the Chinese had imposed; when Ming Tse sent his army to invade, the Lao people once again migrated southwards.

At this time the Chinese had split into three main groups: the Cao Cao of

Wei, Liu Pi of Shu and Sun Quan of Wu. The Ngai-Lao seized the opportunity to build six new cities along NongSae (Dali or Ta Lee Fu) Lake. NongSae was built as the kingdom's new capital and remained so for over 140 years (AD 78–225). Finally, after several years of defending NongSae, the Ai-Lao people surrendered to the Chinese general Kong Beng in AD 225. However, they fought back in AD 395 and remained as an independent kingdom until AD 649.

King Sihanara (Siu Nu Loh) 649–674) took over and united the six Ai-Lao cities as one prosperous kingdom and sent a goodwill mission to Tang China to maintain peace during his reign. He was succeeded by his son, Lo Seng (Luo Cheng). He also pursued friendly relations with the Chinese and even personally attended the Chinese Emperor Pu Sek Thein's daughter's wedding!

After Lo Seng died in 712, three confident kings followed, including his son, Seng Lo Pi, whose reign lasted until 728. Kingdoms were founded and new cities were built and lost, but the NongSae kingdom was in capable hands.

Chao Anouvong enthusiastically described the arrival of the legendary Khoun Borom (Pi Loh Goh), born in 697. At this time, Tang China was a prosperous and mighty polity, demanding tribute from neighbouring countries if they wanted to pursue political or commercial ties with the empire.

Khoun Borom succeeded to the throne in 729 at the age of thirty-two and has become known as the founding father and the first king of a unified Ai-Lao kingdom, combining the NongSae kingdom with vast areas of north-western Yunnan, known as NanChao. The incorporation of all NanChao's cities in the Erhai region can be attributed to his leadership. NanChao was an independent and vigorous political entity, and this was a period of peace and tranquillity for the six cities. However, the king was not satisfied with acting merely as the overlord of NanChao in western Yunnan. When eastern Yunnan, the Lui Pi of Shu, rebelled against Tang China's heavy taxation and levies, Khoun Borom took the opportunity to occupy the region piece by piece. He was a clever warlord, but also sent two goodwill missions to Tang China in 729 and 734. He never really trusted the Chinese, however, who always seemed intent on invading his kingdom. He built a new city further south on the west side of the Mekong in 731, calling it KaoLoang (JingHong). The area of the Mekong where the Ai-Lao had settled was known as Lancang to the Chinese (Kiu Lung Kiang: river of the nine dragons, referring to Khoun Borom's nine sons). Khoun Borom was recognised as king of Yunnan by the Tang court in 738 and died in 750 at the age of fifty-three.

King Khoun Borom had nine sons by two wives: the first was Nang Nhompala and the second, Nang Etkeng, but only seven became rulers. In the throne room the king ceremoniously plunged his right hand into a bowl of sacred water before flicking it on their heads and saying, 'Accept truth, seek no quarrel with your neighbour, be good to your people and do your best to earn their respect.' He presented each of them with a piece of elephant tusk as a reminder, telling them to honour the bond of brotherhood and never to invade or plunder each other's land. He made them solemnly swear never to take up arms against each other, even if their own kin were at war, by cutting the palms of their hands and collecting their blood in a gold cup. He then attributed magic properties to the crimson liquid, dipping his forefinger in and blessing them on their foreheads. Misfortune and long suffering, he said, would befall those who did not respect his laws. He made drink offerings to the gods and invoked the sun to shine on them and for their ancestors' spirits to protect them.

'Now go and rule (*Kin Mueang*) and remember you all come from the same father; never betray your Ai-Lao race!' he ordered. Then he sent them to rule seven different kingdoms in the Souvannaphum Phatet (the Lower Mekong region), thus beginning the long-lasting and equitable custom of dividing estates and even kingdoms equally amongst siblings rather than bestowing them on the first-born; this promoted stability and order, and, most importantly of all, allowed each kingdom to flourish.

His first son from his first wife (Nhompala), Khoun Loh, ruled Mueang Swa (XiengThong: LanXang).

His second son, Thao Phalanh, ruled Mueang TahHoh in Sipsong Panna (Xishuangbanna/Yunnan).

His third son, Thao ChuSong, ruled Mueang Tung Kea in Sipsong ChuTai (Huaphan to Tonkin).

His fourth son, Thao Khamphong, ruled Mueang YoNoke, XiengMai (LanNa).

His fifth son Thao Inh ruled Mueang Louva (LanPhya: Sukhotai/Ayutthaya/Siam).

His sixth son, Thao Khom, ruled Mueang Hongsa (Shan).

His seventh son, Thao Cheuang (Chuong), ruled Mueang Phuan (Prakan/XiengKhuang: LanXang).

'Remember this, Jon,' Chao Anouvong said assertively, gazing at me like a professor. 'Khoun Loh, who ruled from 757 to 779, known as Ge Luo Feng to the Chinese, was the founding father of LanXang.' I assured him that I wouldn't forget. 'During his reign, Khoun Loh sent his army from Mueang KaoLoang and defeated the Chong, the king of Khmer, in Mueang Swa (later known as Luang Phrabang) in 757. He made it his capital and became the first king of a newly founded kingdom: this was the birth of the Lao country that we called Mueang Lao.'

Khoun Loh was a great strategist. To prevent an insurgency in the central region of Yunnan, he depopulated the eastern area and forced hundreds of thousands of people to settle in the Erhai region. Facing attack, he sent a mission to Tang China to repair the relationship, telling them that if they didn't accept his goodwill, he would then turn to Tibet, and NanChao (Yunnan) would no longer belong to the Tang. The Tibetan ruler considered NanChao a 'fraternal state' and Khoun Loh was known as the Eastern Emperor.

The Tang in Sichuan carried out several unsuccessful campaigns in retaliation. They conducted more expeditions against NanChao and, in 754, they marched into the Dali Plain from the north with 100,000 men led by General Li Mi. The army was almost wiped out due to a combination of malaria, severe weather and difficult terrain. NanChao was safe from destruction and Tang China recognised its vast territory. By 779, under Khoun Loh's grandson Yi Mou Xun and a further seven rulers, NanChao had been devastated by years of warfare and came to an end in 902, becoming a vassal state of Tang China until 907. It was eventually lost to the Mongol leader Khublai Khan in 1254, leading to the mass southward migration of the Ai-Lao.

After Khoun Loh, there were twenty-one kings. Khoun Lang, crowned King Langthirath, was the last. So, after more than twenty-one kings and 624 years, it was Fah Ngum's turn. His grandfather, Chao Fah LuangNgom, sent his son, Chao Fah Ngio (otherwise known as Phi Fah: 'Spirit of Sky') – who had a taste for loose living – drifting down the Mekong into exile along with his son. The son – Fah Ngum – had been born in 1516 and arrived with companions and wet nurses at the Khmer court. He was carefully taught by a scholarly monk, Phra Pasman, and brought up under the strict guidance of the king, who gave his daughter, Nang KaeoKengya, to him in marriage when he was sixteen. He subsequently returned to Mueang Swa in 1349 after his grandfather died in 1343. Fah Ngum was a great conqueror and, with 10,000 soldiers at his disposal, he united the entire Lao country before taking the throne in 1353. He became the twenty-third king and named his kingdom LanXang: in the Lao language, 'lan' means 'million' or open or bare land, and 'xang' means elephant. In Sanskrit, LanXang is Sattanarkhanahout: Satta means 100, Narkha (Narkho) means elephant and Hout (Houta) means 10,000. It is 'the land of (a million) elephants'.

'Now, Jon, as far as LanXang is concerned,' Chao Anouvong said proudly, 'under King Fah Ngum, a united Lao LanXang reached the zenith of its political power and cultural creativity, which was enjoyed by the people and respected by neighbouring countries for 337 years… until King Souriyavongsa's death in 1690.' He paused briefly before explaining that the dignity of LanXang's king had undergone many changes – from the fearless doctrine of the legendary Khoun Borom to the patriotism and austere rule of law (*Heed Sipsong-Khong Sipsi*) of Fah Ngum, down to the self-destructive insignificance of Souriyavongsa. 'No king ever built a kingdom without turmoil, Jon,' he continued. 'Order and disorder are just a cycle of nature – one falls, the other rises. The decline of LanXang was regrettable, self-inflicted in many ways. The individualistic nature of its incompetent rulers and corrupt officials who thought more of themselves than of the Lao nation was the cause. Lao LanXang expected unity, but the kingdom faced a catastrophe from within.'

'By the way, Your Royal Highness,' I interposed when he paused for a drink. 'I'm proud to say that my grandfather was a *Tai* Khorat nobleman.'

'I'm delighted to hear it,' he said warmly. 'In fact, Jon, to give the Ai-Lao people who migrated southwards and settled on the central plain of the Chaophraya river their due, they share a similar fire and vigour of mind, despite choosing a different name. Basically, they speak a similar Tai-Kadai language to the rest of us because their language is Lao in origin – packed with ancient Lao words, flavoured with some others such as Khmer– and they know it. There are more Lao in Siam than they think. But some arrogant Siamese scholars foolishly claim that they're descended from the kingdom of Sukhotai because they don't want to be associated with us.'

He paused to pluck a white silk handkerchief from his waist, rolled it into a ball and wiped his lips. He went on to explain that the Sukothai rulers were the progenitors of Ai-Lao, beginning with Phor Khun Si Intratitya Phra Ruang (otherwise known as Thao Hung or Thao Cheuang in Lao) in the early thirteenth century, followed by King Ramkhamhaeng from 1277 to 1377, and lasted until the late fourteenth century. Meanwhile, King Uthong founded the

Ayutthaya kingdom further south in 1350, which lasted until 1750, when the Burmese destroyed the city of Si-Ayutthaya. Subsequently, it was a Chinese immigrant called Sin who founded Siam and became King TakSin of Thonburi in 1767. He was overthrown and executed by a usurper, Kasatseuk, who became King Chulaloke in 1782, established Ban MakKok (which means acidic fruit) as his capital and named it Bangkok – the birthplace and powerhouse of the Rattanakosin Siam kingdom. The real key to the kingly power of Siam since the reign of TakSin was the wealth that was plundered from neighbouring countries, as well as more legitimate overseas trading. Siam is governed by the wealthy.

'Therefore, since they're people from Siam,' he went on, 'we call them Tai Sayam (Siamese people) instead. Of course, we all have the blood of Ai-Lao in us, but we see ourselves as different from and senior to the Siamese. They regard what is merely a warlike concept as a coherent nationality, and it came to the fore when they invaded ViengChan in 1779, leading to conflict with other countries. Siam is now heavily involved in its neighbour's territories. The term *Tai* refers to a free-spirited and easy-going people. It doesn't mean 'free' as claimed by Bangkok… far from it, it's an absolute monarchy with a strict rule of law that merely protects a privileged few. If the general public complain, they are ruthlessly dealt with, only angering them further.'

'Aren't our rules the same as theirs, Your Royal Highness? Is strict law such a bad thing?' I asked naively, for I didn't know any better.

'Laws? Khoun Jon, humans make them, but don't follow them. Some take the law into their own hands. Siam is like a lawless country.' He paused. 'Our rules are comparable, that's true enough, but we value truthfulness more highly. Since King Fah Ngum's day it is our custom always to be true to each other and to speak the truth. It is our greatest proverb.' As if he were guided to rule, to reform and to modernise, he added, 'Besides, we intend to change them for the better. Our government should have no trace of snobbery or prejudice and be based not on class or money, but on reason, which is accessible to everybody. We're all human beings, as you rightly said. Prostration is for gods. I personally don't like it when people prostrate themselves, for instance. I'm quite happy to sit on mats with foreign envoys rather than on a throne.' He favoured saying 'ours' instead of 'yours and mine' so when he became king, no one would have to fall before him if they didn't want to. He wasn't used to it and didn't mind.

At this point I was getting rather tired and disinclined to listen further. It was all becoming a little too much for me to take in. Seeing that I was getting bored stiff, Chao Anouvong told me that to have the stamina to listen, even to boring subject matter, was the essence of learning.

'It is from bores that you really find things out,' he said, with severity in his voice.

'I'm sorry, Your Royal Highness, it must be the heat,' I said and immediately sat upright and paid more attention. A flood of anticipation rushed through my head. He sympathised with me because he'd had the same experience listening to the dreary routines of the Rattanakosin court in Bangkok. He said that trying to digest for sixteen years that you're just like the Siamese when you're in fact Lao, was a waste of time and difficult to take. He hated it.

'Did I hear that you're only nineteen?' he asked, taking me by complete surprise. 'You really look like a schoolboy,' he added.

'Am I, Your Royal Highness?' I said and blushed at the question.

Birthdays are unimportant dates in Lao LanXang and never celebrated. Personally, I didn't think or care about it and never have. I was astounded and honoured that he should know my age. I expected commands from him, not compliments.

'I found this out from one of the footmen who knows you well.' I could do nothing but thank him gracefully. 'You've done well. I wish you good health and luck.' He came closer to me and said, 'Here.' He took my hand and placed a small sandalwood box in my palm before folding it firmly into a fist. 'Goodness me, it's boiling hot outside, but your hand is cold!' He rubbed and squeezed it teasingly with both of his, before adding, 'Cold hands, warm heart, they say,' patting my hand gently before letting it go. I was so greatly touched that I could barely got the words out and had difficulty in accepting it. 'It's not a bribe so don't refuse anything from your future king,' he affirmed. I assumed that it was a present, but when I expressed my heartfelt thanks and appreciation, he told me to open it. Inside I found a gold coin. I was stunned by the gesture. 'I wish it were more and I hope it will help you.'

'I thank Your Royal Highness for your kindness, and I will be your humble servant and loyal subject,' I said with both knees on the floor, lifting my praying hands to my head.

'May the Lord Buddha preserve you and do what you have promised,' he said and bade me rise.

I graciously thanked him again and slipped the box into my shirt pocket.

He told me to look after it. Privately, I was pleased with myself for having the opportunity to serve him and to be given a special gift. At the same time, it was an unexpected honour. I couldn't help but turn over in my mind the fact that I'd touched a gold coin, something I never dreamed possible. He probably did it out of characteristic impulsiveness, generosity and downright sentimentality. Well, I swear that I kept it in my family's old steel drum for safety, but sadly, like Chao Anouvong, it was never to be seen again.

After a brief pause, he gathered his courage and swore me to secrecy about a story of his ancestors' past that had become lodged in his mind which he was most anxious to expel from his memory. He wished to correct the mistake and revive the kingdom's glorious past, intending to create history for generations to come. He spoke proudly of his thoughts and feelings in a low trembling voice because he found it unacceptable that LanXang was a vassal state of Siam.

'We don't like to live in the past,' he said, 'but there was a time when LanXang was powerful and respected. The people were united and we had a good king, but since 1779 it seems the Lord Buddha and the gods decided to make us suffer. There was to be no glorious end to my father and no great name for me to inherit. The whole kingdom has been in distress and the people have been left with nothing but sorrow and tears. On that account I'm anxious and unhappy, with problems piling on my head. In fact, I'll tell you my secret, Jon.'

'Which is, Your Royal Highness?' I asked quickly, rubbing my cold hand along my forehead and then combing my hair up and backward with my fingers. He jumped at my show of interest. The word 'secret' always makes me curious because, as a boy, my father had told me never to repeat anything beyond the walls of our family home, fearing the Siamese would take us away.

'What I'm about to tell you, Jon, is not to be repeated outside this room,' he said softly, warning me to guard my tongue like a spy. I promised: my boredom had vanished. 'You have my trust and I want you to know that my ancestors once ruled our beloved, independent LanXang Kingdom with the Mekong running through the middle,' he continued. 'Before I go on, do you know why and for how long LanXang has been a vassal state of Siam?'

'I'm afraid, I don't, Your Royal Highness,' I admitted.

The Lao are a highly homogeneous people; they all speak the same language, albeit with different dialects, and they respect and practise the same religion and customs. The male descendants of Khoun Loh have ruled LanXang, although not necessarily from father to first born son. To begin with, Chao Anouvong said that it was a grave mistake for King Souriyavongsa to judge and order the execution of his only son, Rathsabout, for adultery. Worse still was that the kingdom had no suitable royal heir to take the throne when he died in 1690. After thirty-two kings, the decline of Lao LanXang began in earnest. Infighting became intense and shameful. Consequently, the kingdom was divided into two, Luang Phrabang and ViengChan, in 1707. By then it was too late for reconciliation, leading to the drastic deterioration of LanXang.

Chao Anouvong blamed his grandfather, Xay-OngVeh, and his father, Maha Bounya Saya Setthathirath (otherwise known as King Bounyasan), who became king of ViengChan in 1730, for failing to patch up their differences with the other two main royal houses: King Suriyavong of Luang Phrabang and King Sayakhumman of Champasak. Khoun Borom's code of unity had been wrecked, broken by fear and greed. By 1713, the kingdom had been further broken up into three principalities (*Anachack*): Luang Phrabang with XiengKhuang in the north; ViengChan with most of the Khorat Plateau in the centre and Champasak with the Mun river valley in the south. LanXang was still considered a single geographical and moral entity, but Luang Phrabang and Champasak wanted to be different from ViengChan. The squabbling for overall control of LanXang between Luang Phrabang and ViengChan generated ill feeling, jealousy and distrust. Lao LanXang's independence, power and wealth finally fell to the opportunistic ruler of Siam.

Chao Anouvong said that educated people knew about well-published Siamese history, but the siege and fall of a peaceful but hugely powerful and sophisticated city like ViengChan would never be told by the Siamese. It was always tempting for Lao LanXang's ambitious neighbours to take advantage of the kingdom's weakness, but all were quite content to keep their distance: except one.

'The very "one" that LanXang never had to bow down to and least expected to invade us,' Chao Anouvong groaned, 'was our close Siamese brothers of Sukhotai, then of Ayutthaya Siam. Besides their abiding respect for Khoun Borom's laws and their close relationship with Lao LanXang, they had also sworn brotherly love and friendship. They had taken an oath agreeing the countries' boundaries during the celebration of the demarcation shrine of That Si-SongHuck (known as Si Song Ruck to the Siamese) in 1563 in Dan Sai. But they broke their vows. The invasion broke the Lao people's heart and

Siam could never again be trusted. It was the beginning of the Rattanakosin Siam's era of dominance, deceitfulness and broken promises.'

When Si-Ayutthaya fell to Burma in 1750, its population was scooped up and its riches looted. TakSin, a trader of Chinese descent, successfully escaped with 500 men from the destruction of the city before regrouping and kicked the Burmese out. But Ayutthaya Siam was left depopulated, without enough people to work the land. TakSin then seized power, declaring himself king of Siam in 1767 and establishing Thonburi on the west bank of the Chaophraya river as his new capital. The sun set on Ayutthaya and rose over newly founded Thonburi and Bangkok. The rise of this evil and power-mad ruler had begun. His successes made him even more ambitious, and he searched eagerly for opportunities to acquire manpower and new treasures for Siam.

TakSin saw a chance to increase his wealth and power and to expand his territories and, in 1775, made a calculated attack on the capital of the Lao kingdom of LanNa, XiengMai. The Burmese were too weak to resist the Siamese army; Lao LanNa was subdued and no longer able to assist their brethren in Lao LanXang. Encouraged by foreign advisers and arms traders, he turned his attention to the larger, more populous and wealthier, but weaker kingdom of LanXang.

Under TakSin, the Siamese did not seem to care nor have any regard for the fact that they were descendants of the same Ai-Lao people and were bound by a sworn territorial agreement. 'You should not invade your brother's land,' were the words of Khoun Borom that should have been respected by his seven sons, all of whom ruled seven different kingdoms in the region. TakSin planned for a full-scale invasion of the high-walled city of ViengChan. All he needed was a pretext.

Being a landlocked kingdom, LanXang was constantly being pulled and pushed about. To avoid tragedy, it had adopted a two-faced diplomacy, manipulating its relationships with its more powerful neighbours and managing to maintain its sovereignty. It was no mean achievement, considering that both Siam and Vietnam were the strongest powers at the time and had fierce ambitions to subjugate the region. So, for the sake of peace and friendship with its neighbours, the kingdom had to walk a tightrope. Moreover, in the process, LanXang had become a well-respected, sophisticated and powerful kingdom in its own right since the days of King Fah Ngum; it had a well-organised army to guard its borders; was well supplied with food and placed a high value on self-rule. Ruling both banks of the Mekong basin (and indeed the Khorat Plateau) had given LanXang immense power, but at a terrible price. Her success attracted jealousy, and she simply could not escape being influenced by her neighbouring countries' affairs, whatever they might be.

The weakness of the Lao LanXang dynasty provided the opportunity that the Siamese elite had been waiting for. They were still thirsting for revenge for their defeat by King Phothisarath in their first unprovoked invasion of ViengChan in 1540 and finally brought their feudal connection with LanXang to an end in early 1778. Their chauvinism, expansionism, brutalism, self-obsession and self-righteousness came to the fore.

Chao Anouvong's father, King Bounyasan, was conscious that Siam had been covertly making war on LanXang and LanNa for years. The real problems began when the oligarchies that ruled Siam sided with foreign powers and devious traders because they were jealous and obsessed with LanXang's wealth. Bounyasan knew that TakSin was extremely resourceful and a threat to LanXang and was looking for an opportunity to invade and obliterate ViengChan. Equally, he'd been aware of Siam's plans for the Khorat Plateau for some time and knew that something sinister was brewing in Thonburi. He also knew that TakSin wrongly suspected ViengChan of collusion with Burma, a pretext for hostilities which caused the gulf between Siam and LanXang to grow wider. Prospects for a compromise were not good.

Unfortunately, it was impossible to monitor Siam's preparations for invasion. TakSin's fevered imagination, which grew quickly and turned into an obsession, unnecessarily escalated tension between the two kingdoms. No one in his establishment dared to draw attention to his ignorance, mistrust and misunderstanding, and obedience was more powerful than common sense in the Siamese world. Therefore TakSin called for Siamese and Lao forces to combine in LanXang. Bounyasan was deeply alarmed by Siam's authoritarian style of government, which was completely at odds with LanXang's peaceful, liberal values and principles. As the hostile rhetoric intensified, he began to fear an open invasion and rightly refused to allow a foreign army in his capital, ViengChan: it was like inviting a wolf to one's home.

Despite the animosity from Thonburi towards his kingdom, Bounyasan wrote many letters to TakSin pleading for a cessation of hostilities. He categorically denied being in league with the Burmese and insisted that such an accusation was merely cynical propaganda aimed at damaging the traditional

Siamese–Lao special relationship. He wanted to stop the bickering, rivalry and suspicion, and work together for a peaceful co-existence. When TakSin finally acknowledged his letters, it was obvious that he was unwilling to accept that their peaceful relationship should remain unchanged. For LanXang to survive, Bounyasan had to avoid outright conflict; as a last resort he sent an urgent letter to TakSin, claiming that ViengChan was free from foreign influence and did not need to be liberated by or from anyone. Neither the Lao nor the Siamese would enjoy the days to come if it came to war, and he begged TakSin to see the bigger picture. In his desperation, on top of 500 ox carts of rice, he even offered TakSin his daughter, Princess Kanlayani, in a marriage alliance, though he disapproved of a young girl waiting on an old man. All to no avail: Thonburi pinned the blame on ViengChan. Bounyasan admitted failure in his efforts to convince TakSin and warned his people to prepare for the worst.

Truth did not matter in Siam; despite the lack of sufficient proof or any circumstantial evidence, ViengChan was still not safe because TakSin simply wanted a pretext for invasion. He became even more contemptuous towards Bounyasan, illustrating the absurdity of the Siamese ideology of domination. Rational people would feel incredulous and outraged but would go on to ignore the allegations. But TakSin had already decided to invade ViengChan, and nothing could stop him. He had his eyes firmly fixed on Lao LanXang's wealth and treasures. The consequence was outright war, and with it the brutal killing of the inhabitants and the shameless looting and destruction of ViengChan.

Whatever the truth, after an extensive discussion with his close Mon friend (Mon are native from western Siam) and the military commander of the northern provinces, Phrachao Chakri 'the warrior', TakSin promoted him to the highest rank of *Somdet Chaophraya Maha Kasatseuk* – 'the warlord' – making him quasi-royalty. In 1778, TakSin, intoxicated by the prospect of wealth, ordered this warlord, who had a propensity for violence, to take military command and attack LanXang, under the pretext that Bounyasan had sided with Siam's mortal enemy, the Burmese.

'It was utter nonsense,' Chao Anouvong said. 'The whole thing was just an excuse for them to attack ViengChan.'

At birth Kasatseuk was called Thong Duang: a golden grub. The king, originally of Chinese descent, was given the Siamese name *Sin*: a lender. He was appointed governor of the city of Tak; he was later awarded the title of *Phraya Tak* and then became King TakSin of Thonburi. King Boromakot's viceroy had adopted TakSin and Kasatseuk as small boys and sent them to be monks at the temple to learn Buddhist precepts, where they became friends and were known as Thong Dee and Thong Duang. Later, they were educated at the royal court and trained to follow the ways of the kingdom; they were both too ambitious to control themselves, however.

There are suspicions that it was Kasatseuk – a man of forty-one with a reputation for wildness and indiscipline – who personally talked TakSin into attacking Lao LanXang. As a warrior, he was cruel and bloodthirsty, with an appetite for killing. He was pumped up with rage and the need to destroy; death awaited anyone he met.

The situation became worse when King Suriyavong of LanXang Luang Phrabang, who blamed ViengChan for helping the Burmese to attack his city a year before, fed TakSin's suspicions that ViengChan and Burma were indeed allies. Open war was inevitable, but no one knew how and when it would begin.

Kasatseuk and his brother Surasiha, at the head of a 30,000-strong Siamese army that included well-trained mercenaries from overseas, marched out from Thonburi. They took the city of Khorat without much resistance, before marching eastward along the Mun river towards Champasak in the south of LanXang. They then turned north to capture the city of Nakhorn Phanom before reaching ViengChan. The Siamese troops penetrated deep into LanXang in the Khorat Plateau, catching Lao officials unawares. Without much warning, they attacked the Lao capital like the bubonic plague. Chao Anouvong said that Siamese aristocrats and political groups tended to be ambitious, greedy and violent. It seemed they saw war and death as luxuries. It was in the year of the dog and, like mad dogs with weapons in their hands, the two brothers and their soldiers drooled at the smell of blood and the sight of an easy prey.

'Even dogs,' Chao Anouvong said judiciously, 'have more sense than men. They do not rush to fight each other over territory. They often square up, respect each other's right and walk away. One should honour dogs, for they neither break faith, nor do they lie. Siam told outright lies, and its desire to invade LanXang and destroy ViengChan was an act of betrayal and barbarity.'

To the peace-loving and closely-knit world of Lao LanXang, which had been resilient in the face of adversity, the invasion was not just like a violent earthquake; it also made them feel angry and aggrieved. They used to respect and trust the Siamese establishment absolutely, but no more.

There was no hope of opposing the mighty Siamese army, but neither was surrendering an option. King Bounyasan called upon the people to resist. The citizens of ViengChan, a city central both geographically and culturally to ancient Lao, prided themselves on their heavily fortified outer and inner high brick walls with three gates: one gate to the north was close to the Mekong, with a footbridge over the Pasak stream; the other was just a kilometre away, where the KhuaLuang Bridge crossed the river in the direction of Luang Phrabang; the grand main gate opened directly towards the That Luang stupa leading to the south. Both walls were 2 to 2.5 metres wide and 5 metres high, but 20-metre-wide moats also surrounded the inner wall. Spaced out evenly on top of the inner wall were 80cm-thick, 1-metre-wide and 1.5-metres-high crenellations. Guard towers stood at 100-metre intervals along the wall. The outer wall also surrounded Mueang Si-Xiengmai, a suburb of ViengChan city on the right bank of the Mekong. The inner wall protected official residents and palaces within the inner city. King Souriyavongsa built ViengChan palaces to be impressive. Once a year the city was the scene of a grand occasion when provincial envoys from all over LanXang would arrive with presents for the That Luang festival of tribute to the king.

The main Lao lines of defence were on the right side of the Mekong, from Nakhorn Phanom up to Mueang Nongkhai, ViengKhuk and PhanPhao, all pillars of support for ViengChan. The invaders were successful at first, but still met strong resistance from the defenders and protectors of the cities. As the war intensified, Kasatseuk and his invading army became increasingly animalistic; they were on a mission to destroy life, to steal, to deceive, to become intoxicated and to perform ignoble deeds. The defenders held on for many months until Nongkhai fell. The Mekong ran red with blood during the horrifying slaughter of the battle, a massacre so enormous that most commanders would have flung away their bloodstained swords and ordered their men to return home. Not so Kasatseuk the warlord: he was far from being a wise and noble lord; he wanted more killing; he wanted to destroy ViengChan and seize the Emerald Buddha and other treasures for Siam. He deserved the sobriquet of the 'butcher and raider of ViengChan'; he'd truly given the Lao people cause to bear Siam ill will.

'Do you know what they did, Jon?' Chao Anouvong asked. I shook my head and stared silently across the Mekong. 'They decapitated a great number of the defenders of Nongkhai. They put the bloodied corpses on boats and forced the women survivors to paddle them up and down close to the riverbank for all to see. It is not hard to imagine how many heroes, warriors and unavenged souls were buried beneath the water. Severed heads, dripping blood, were impaled on poles and placed strategically along the outside of the city walls. After four months of fighting, the invaders captured ViengKhuk and PhanPhao, and then moved towards ViengChan.'

Kasatseuk wanted to walk straight through the gates and destroy the city, women and children included. He was beyond humanity. Some ordinary ViengChan citizens prostrated themselves before him and delivered themselves into his hands, pleading for the ancient sovereignty they'd enjoyed since the days of King Fah Ngum. Nevertheless, most of the nationalists and nobles fought on bitterly, until they themselves were slaughtered mercilessly. Only a few families managed to escape into the forest. Siamese troops were stationed by the city gates armed with bows and spears. A hue and cry soon echoed through the city, and the inhabitants roused themselves and sprang from their beds to fight the enemy. The defenders stood on top of the city walls and attacked the enemy by pouring red-hot sand and boiling oil on them and pelting those crouching under dense undergrowth with lumps of rock and bricks.

The Lao fight with pride in times of war. They fought courageously, putting up stiff resistance. King Bounyasan's son and viceroy, the admirable Prince Nanthasene, attempted several counterattacks. A pitched battle at the city gates ensued, and volleys of bronze-pointed spears, arrows and gunfire were exchanged. After raid after raid across the moat, many of the best Siamese warriors fell, and the groaning of dying men was horrendous. The Siamese toiled to bring the city down by every stratagem they could devise. In spite of the sight of the severed heads of their fallen brothers on spikes, more loved by the flies than by their families, the determined ViengChan defenders heroically held their ground and kept the main Siamese force at bay well into 1779.

Regrettably, on hearing of the Siamese advance, King Suriyavong of Luang Phrabang sent 3,000 men to help the invaders to attack ViengChan from the north. The city was surrounded: the situation was hopeless.

Sadly, over a year since the invasion began, sensing defeat, King Bounyasan fled secretly in the night, leaving his brave son to defend the city. His two other sons, Inthavong and Phommavong, escaped with him down the Mekong to Thakhek city in the south, and then on to Mahaxay. But both princes were later taken to the Siamese capital.

There are two morals to the story: the first is that Bangkok was greedy and villainous; the second is that ViengChan wanted to protect the interests of her people – the Lao nation. As Chao Anouvong said, Bangkok wanting to enlarge its territories but ViengChan valued Lao LanXang independence, albeit defended only by a small army. The result was inevitable.

'My brother, Nanthasene,' Chao Anouvong said disappointedly, 'became demoralised after our father escaped. The sight of the severed heads, more than all the other dreadful things that had happened, finally broke the spirit of our men. To prevent further loss of life and suffering, he called upon the people not to resist and ordered the city gates to be opened. ViengChan fell into the hands of a villain. I was twelve, and it was the most terrifying time of my life.'

Kasatseuk and his men were free to enter and do as they please. The city nobility and elders went to honour him with gifts: silver bowls full of gold necklaces thick with emeralds and rubies, and chests of rare wood filled with silk. Holding silver trays of candles and flowers in their hands, they threw themselves down before him and beseeched him not to destroy their city or take the Buddha statues. They begged him instead to cast a kind of spell on them and prove that he was a better man. But if he behaved like a victor, the Lao people would never forgive him or forget Siam's atrocities; he would be remembered as a warmonger and a looter (*Khon Jone*). Kasatseuk admired the gifts and put them in his war chests but refused to listen. He was an uncivilised man who didn't care; he'd never done an honest day's work but earned his keep by making war. Enraged by the nine-month siege, his army killed thousands of the male inhabitants. Those who survived were enslaved, including those who took sanctuary in the temples. It seemed that Kasatseuk had reverence neither for the dead nor for Lord Buddha. From Monday 3 October 1779, he sacked the city. ViengChan and its people felt the wrath of the Siamese conquerors. The women wept and threw their arms round the bodies of their beloved husbands and sons as they lay gasping in the throes of death and lifted their voices in lamentation. The invaders dragged them and their children off into slavery and a life of miserable toil in Siam.

Henceforth, Lao LanXang was an occupied country, and her freedom was over. The Siamese had demonstrated their insatiable plan for the creation of a Greater Siam and oppression and purges began. The Lao emphatically denounced the invasion. They always remembered this brutal attack on their peaceful country and their innocent people with burning and passionate hatred.

I was truly appalled, disgusted and upset to hear about this. Wouldn't you have been?

A truce was announced for Lao civilians who had taken refuge in the temples. Most were too stubborn to comply, but those who did were spared. The frenzied invaders then removed the sacred Emerald Buddha and the golden Phrabang Buddha, along with many other prized treasures. Kasatseuk set fire to some of the palaces and temples.

'As a security measure,' Chao Anouvong said, 'they forced us – Nanthasene, my sister Princess KaeoYhodFah Kanlayani and myself – to move to Siam. They arrested all royal family members, aristocrats, high-ranking officials and artisans, who were all taken to Thonburi and the newly founded city of Bangkok. But tens of thousands of Lao families were swept up and marched as captives along the Khorat plain and forced to settle in Saraburi and Suphanbury; some were sent further off, to Phetchaburi, Ratchaburi and Nakhorn Saisi in the southwest, and to Prachinburi and Chanthaburi in the southeast. ViengChan was littered with corpses. Kasatseuk showed no repentance; it is hard to equate him with the revered King Chulaloke of Siam, whom he later became.'

As rumour has it, one of the city's spirited elderly oracles, his skeletal body heavily tattooed, his powdered cheeks and red headband warding off evil, lit a sacrificial fire at the city gate. As carts stuffed with the Emerald Buddha and other plunder were approaching, this man raised his walking stick carved with a king cobra's head and said, 'Phraya Kasatseuk, if you are a Buddhist, nothing of Mother Earth belongs to you. Why come to ViengChan causing so much trouble?' Kasatseuk nodded slowly, laughed and then roared that he'd come to conquer. 'Have you fulfilled your destiny and enjoyed the fruits of it?' responded the oracle, stabbing his stick forcefully into the ground. 'Did you not know that Siamese and Lao are Ai-Lao Khoun Borom descendants? You have broken one of his sacred laws. You have betrayed us! Through you we have known only fear, anger, pride and desire. Your insatiable desires will soon consume you like a raging fire, burning you away. One day, your ruling house will come crashing down.' He seized a black chicken and cut its throat to propitiate the evil spirits and then threw incense onto the flames and poured libations. His white eyes staring, he scattered black rice over the path and called down curses on the Siamese for their illegal invasion, and upon the sinful and criminal removal of the sacred Emerald Buddha, mingling his incantations with the names of evil spirits and terrible deities. And he called for the 'five curses' that people had prophetically said would befall Siam if the Buddha was not returned.

At these words, the superstitious Siamese soldiers were entranced, as if they knew they were in the presence of evil, calling out to a red-faced Kasatseuk not to take the Emerald Buddha. Others took up the cry: 'We are cursed! We will be punished for our sins and wickedness.' But the greatest of ills, the one that surpassed all other vices, had seized Kasatseuk. Mounted on his black horse, he merely laughed at his men and bellowed, 'Since when were we afraid of curses?' With murder in his heart and white with rage, he cold-bloodedly gave an order for the elder to be killed. The half-naked oracle stood his ground, raised his stick and said that all he had was his body; if they killed him, they would be removing the last burden of his life. Before he died, he called a final curse down on Kasatseuk and all of Siam: they would share Lao LanXang's fate!

In late 1780, before leaving, the Siamese authorities left ViengChan in the hands of a Lao general, Phraya Soupho. King Bounyasan retook the city soon after but died in early 1781. He was the last king of an independent Lao LanXang, with ViengChan as its capital, for 219 years.

After the invasion, King Suriyavong of LanXang Luang Phrabang, despite helping the Siamese invaders, was nevertheless forced to surrender his kingdom. The kingdom of LanXang Champasak in the south went the same way. 1,022 years after her first king, Khoun Loh, the entire LanXang Kingdom fell under Siamese suzerainty – a tragedy of conflict and betrayal. These events brought the Lao community together; their shared sense of sorrow became embedded in LanXang's very roots.

'Nevertheless, Jon,' Chao Anouvong complained fiercely, 'Bangkok imposed their cruelty, inhumanity and savagery on us. They should instead have looked on LanXang as a country of the future and submitted to us as the chief repository of their religion and laws. They should have regarded us as their mother country.'

Kasatseuk triumphantly returned to Thonburi with all the loot, and a jubilant TakSin built the Wat Arun temple to house the Emerald Buddha. He persuaded the immigrant Chinese and the Siamese nobility in Siam – chiefly in Bangkok – to socialise and even marry in some cases. But it was not long before the old Siamese Ayutthaya elite, who wished to preserve traditional Siamese values, turned against him.

Men of heroic mettle in Siam were not in short supply, but some had lofty ambition. Perhaps the real embodiment of political nihilism was an aristocratic family of financiers of Persian origin. They converted from Islam to Buddhism and introduced excessive rituals of prostration. Their main ambitions were for more power and wealth; they bought their way into the Siamese elite and oversaw the country's finances. When they saw that TakSin represented a threat to their commercial and financial interests, they became jealous and resentful and proposed Kasatseuk as an alternative to the throne. Though there is no actual evidence, it can be assumed that the Persians, hated by the people for their lies and for the high taxes they levied, offered gold bribes to the Bangkok elites in an attempt to secure Kasatseuk's kingship. The bribe was as successful as if a rich man had thrown a few coins into a group of starving slaves. The elites conspired with the two power-drunk brothers, Kasatseuk and Surasiha, who were also resentful of TakSin. Kasatseuk probably felt the greatest resentment at the prospect of never becoming king and believed there was no happier life for a mortal than a wealthy one – for him, happiness did not involve doing good and being virtuous. In his eyes a king could do as he pleased: enslave his enemies, seize their property and execute them. Realising that he could not achieve power overtly, he chose a covert approach. Together with the old elite of Bangkok and other well-connected Ayutthaya court families, and supported by the wealthy Persian family, he plotted to overthrow King TakSin.

Meanwhile, on hearing of King Bounyasan's death in ViengChan, King TakSin promptly appointed the next oldest son, Nanthasene, to be the new ruler, and returned the golden Phrabang Buddha as a goodwill gesture. Nanthasene returned to rule ViengChan on 14 January 1781. His brother Inthavong was appointed as his viceroy and spent much of his time representing the interests of ViengChan in Bangkok. Princess Kanlayani, Prince Anouvong and Phommavong were detained as hostages at Bang Yi Khan.

In 1782, tortured by insecurity, TakSin went into the chapel in the Wat Arun temple to pray before the Emerald Buddha. Believing himself to be the incarnation of Buddha he declared himself a god: the power and glory had driven him mad. While he was pacing anxiously around the main palace (*Wang Derm*), news reached him that the two brothers had turned against him. The palace was in confusion, but he knew in advance who was part of the conspiracy. His enemies were out to get him, but he claimed he'd no fear of dying, because it was better to die once of disloyalty than to live in fear of it.

Whatever the truth, Kasatseuk, the leading conspirator and assassin, finally staged a military coup and put King TakSin to death. How he died is known only to god. In many eyes, Kasatseuk was a traitor and a usurper. He was crowned as King Yodfa Chulaloke – the father of the Siamese nation. He adopted the dynastic name of Chakri and saw great hopes for the future; according to him, the victory over ViengChan had been sacred, and because of the Emerald Buddha, he declared the birth of Rattanakosin Siam (*Rattana* means precious stone, *Kosin* means era). Success made him and his establishment insufferably smug and arrogant.

King Chulaloke presided over the kingdom's affairs from a new golden throne, and thereafter no one could enjoy constitutional freedom in Siam. A typical dictator, he only liked the rules he'd written himself. He epitomised Siamese chauvinism, fearing nothing and soon believing he was one of the gods, but he was also notoriously insecure. He absurdly assumed that he was the master of all men – another prerogative of royalty. He put the Lao people (and others) to work building his new capital on the eastern bank of the Chaophraya river opposite Thonburi. He ordered canals to be built to create an island, which was bordered by the Chaophraya river to the west, and the new canals to the east. The 'Rattanakosin Island' became an impregnable fortress, the representation of the kingdom and the centre of the Siamese world. Over 10,000 Khmer and Lao slaves worked on the stupendous Grand Palace complex, which was designed and built fit for the king, both to impress and intimidate the locals and to repel invaders. He encircled it with thicker and higher walls, inside which he and his associates remained cosseted out of sight. A new temple was also built within the walls to install the stolen Emerald Buddha, which he shamelessly proclaimed as the protector of his dynasty. His brother Surasiha became viceroy under the name Sura Singharat and died in 1803.

Chulaloke progressively abandoned the traditional Siamese rituals based on compassion, humility, self-control and maintaining order through a network of family ties. He took everything for granted and claimed to be able to divine the future in the palm of his hands. He imagined that running the kingdom was simply a matter of controlling the masses. He distrusted his friends and his mandarins, who ridiculously and ludicrously prostrated themselves before him like dogs. The idea of a self-made king who worshipped his creator was central to the Rattanakosin myth, embodying the Siamese ideal that an aristocratic and warrior hierarchy could live off the backs of the hard-working poor and an impoverished peasantry, and that society should not criticise the royals but be below them in the race of life: no one else could be better than the king. One could not conceive of a more powerful political engine to control the public mind in a Buddhist country than an institution that exalted itself over other nations. School children were taught to worship the king and were taught only about Siam's glorified history, shockingly ignoring the views and experiences of its neighbours. The people were tempted to believe in the idea of Siamese supremacy and virtue: a dangerous belief which bred arrogance and narcissism. And besides, human moral perfection is a myth.

But even in the relatively enlightened capital, people were far too slow to discover the absurdity of bigotry. Siam was always full of rumours and stories about the saintly king; most of his subjects were content with this and feared him as if he were a god. Those who weren't happy had no choice but to enter his service, because the only alternative was persecution. But good and reasonable people cannot exist without freedom. The Rattanakosins turned their own insanity and insecurity into Siam's ideological struggle, and there seemed no end in sight – Chulaloke's indoctrinated followers were blind to it all.

Having been transformed from a warrior into a warlord, and now into the powerful king of Siam, Chulaloke treated the Lao men and their families as if they were plants and animals, mere slaves to facilitate Siam's expansion. Even high-ranking Lao officials and princely families were forced to work either in the sugar plantations or rice fields. Chulaloke's men were extremely brutal, and their brutality had purpose. His government forced the conquered Lao citizens into slave labour, digging canals. These innocent people, the victims of calumny and oppression, were flogged mercilessly while labouring in Bangkok, their limbs dragged down by weighty chains. Your legs feel itchy at the very thought of such cruelty. From 1779 onwards, a dam at Ang Thong (built in 1813) and the Saen Saeb (Deep Pain) canal became reminders of the terrible cruelty that had been inflicted on the Lao people. One can imagine the shouting and the beatings when the canal was first being dug. Most of the slaves perished as a result of little food or rest. Those who lost their lives should never be forgotten. Even now you can sense their vexed ghosts as you sail through or stroll along the series of canals around the old part of Bangkok.

The court nobility of LanXang simply could not dispel their local animosities and, as usual, Siam cunningly played them off against each other. Siam had no intention of letting LanXang's princes settle their differences, and willingly set them at loggerheads once more. Consequently, Nanthasene of ViengChan, to gain favour, told King Chulaloke that Anouruth of Luang Phrabang was conspiring with the Burmese and the Shan ruler of XiengHung against Siam's interests. Chulaloke granted Nanthasene permission to attack, but not without the assistance of advanced Siamese contingents from Bangkok to operate their devious 'divide and rule' policy. The Lao elite and army had been destroyed methodically since 1779. Usually, wars between the two royal houses of LanXang were mere tribal skirmishes in the fields, where soldiers would fight each other in single combat and then negotiate. But the Siamese army spurred the two Lao princedoms to attack each other with the intention of further dividing LanXang, tearing it apart in a bid for total hegemony. King Anouruth and his family were captured and sent to Bangkok for indoctrination. Consequently, mistrust between ViengChan and Luang Phrabang grew and grew.

As the ruler of ViengChan, Nanthasene optimistically pursued self-rule for LanXang. He secured unity with the rulers of Nakhorn Phanom and XiengKhuang and actively communicated with the Vietnamese rulers, but they too were engaged in civil war, with the Nguyen in the north and the TaySon in the south fighting for supremacy. Nanthasene, against his will, but to please Bangkok, fought with the Siamese against the TaySon.

It is possible that Bangkok allowed the vindictive Anouruth to return to Luang Phrabang in 1793 on purpose, to get rid of Nanthasene and keep LanXang divided. Anouruth filed a complaint and Nanthasene was summoned back to the Siamese capital; he could have slipped away to Vietnam to save himself but that would have implicated his younger brothers, Inthavong and Anouvong. Nanthasene, together with his associate PhraBorom Souta, the ruler of Nakhorn Phanom, willingly travelled to Bangkok to prove his innocence. They were accused of treason for attempting to stage an uprising against Siam and put on trial, but no proof was found. Nevertheless, they were condemned by false and malicious accusations and locked away anyway.

Nanthasene was unfazed; he instructed Chao Anouvong to seek help by sending a secret message to the Vietnamese king of TaySon, requesting men and arms to be sent to push the Siamese army out of LanXang. The Vietnamese army finally arrived at Nakhorn Phanom and made their presence felt, warning Bangkok of serious consequences if they threatened the imperial city of Hue. This was perhaps why Nanthasene and PhraBorom were being kept in prison, Siam continuing their 'divide and rule' policy. When the conflict of interest between the Vietnamese and the Siamese began in earnest, it spelled the end of Nanthasene's reign.

In 1795, in spite of Chao Anouvong's appeal for them to be pardoned, Nanthasene and PhraBorom Souta were not included on the Siamese king's amnesty day, when it was traditional for thousands of prisoners to be released. They died, probably by secret execution, that same year. Bangkok would remorselessly put away any accused Lao ruler; they intended to place LanXang under their monstrous power.

The economic exchanges between Siam and LanXang took the form of tributes and rewards. ViengChan had no choice but to nurture friendly relations with Bangkok and tried very hard not to offend Chulaloke, who did whatever he pleased. However, when regaining sovereignty by peaceful means became an impossible task, the question arose whether there was a better way. Bangkok had adopted a policy of indirect rule over Lao LanXang by appointing hereditary local aristocrats as proxy rulers and granting them the titles of *Saenluang* or *Chaomueang* (ruler or chief) instead of king, and then removing them when convenient.

Chao Anouvong was determined to prove his worth in dealing with King Chulaloke's son and grandson. His brother's death had clearly upset him, but he was shrewd enough to realise it was part of a pattern of reckless behaviour by Bangkok rather than an isolated tragedy, a political crime and a blatant breach of civilised conduct. He was disgusted by it, but he made no attempt to avenge Nanthasene. He played it safe and did not want to waste time grieving; he was determined to move on – a sign of strength and vision – and the future of LanXang was never far from his thoughts. He was conscious of what had been lost and determined to act as his integrity compelled him and overcome the obstacles that life threw in his path.

Then it was Inthavong's turn (1795–1804). He was given a stern warning by Bangkok before he was allowed back to take over ViengChan. He appointed Chao Anouvong as his viceroy. So, here in the palace of Lao ViengChan LanXang in 1795, distant in terms of both time and geography from the Lao NongSae NanChao kingdom, it was such a privilege and an awe-inspiring experience to be sitting next to Chao Anouvong, and hearing about the ancestors and history of the Lao people.

I noted that Chao Anouvong's dreams were modest when he first returned; they grew more ambitious as time passed. His arrival was later acknowledged by some of the LanXang governors; they began to look upon him differently, though Luang Phrabang and XiengKhuang kept their distance. He was a respected figure, but understandably, only a few people knew who he was. He was just a viceroy, a new man – no one paid much heed. His opinions and points of view often counted for nothing, but he was determined to be heard. As a viceroy he'd more time to put his energy to good use in expanding his wisdom. He wanted a more adventurous life, even though he needed to represent ViengChan's interests in Bangkok from time to time.

It was clear to Chao Anouvong that Luang Phrabang would be the main obstacle to unity because of their differences with ViengChan. Nanthasene and Anouruth had barely communicated with each other and were guilty of not putting their own interests ahead of their country. Understandably, Luang Phrabang, whose rulers lost much of their power, became jealous of Viengchan when it was declared the capital in 1560. However, Chao Anouvong emphasised that King Phothisarath would have been very happy to know that his son, Xay-Setthathirath, had finally moved the kingdom's capital to ViengChan. Chao Anouvong, on the other hand, was more motivated by instinct and philosophy. He was the ideal man to emulate and revive the ethos of Fah Ngum, who had kept LanXang united for over four centuries before it had been ripped apart by internal feuding and ambition. He believed LanXang was a united country and should always be so. With his passionate ambition, he believed he could achieve what others deemed impossible. He was determined to follow in Fah Ngum's footsteps, and his immediate duty was to re-establish unity between the three divided Lao kingdoms and encourage co-operation between the governors (*Chaomueang*) of LanXang's cities, thereby empowering him to push for self-rule.

I profoundly shared Chao Anouvong's oft-expressed concern for the collapse of LanXang's unity. 'United we live, divided we die,' he would sometimes remind himself. True enough, he did not want to make matters worse, but life isn't worth living under foreign domination. As a vassal state, Lao pride and identity were at stake and Chao Anouvong could no longer tolerate ridicule and injustice at any cost. 'Without unity (*Khuam Samarki*), it would take the earth and the sky to convince Luang Phrabang to join us in the fight,' he often said while staring across the Mekong, locked in thought as if dwelling in another world. He must have had Bangkok firmly in his mind.

With his elegant, friendly face and luminous brown eyes, dominated by exceptional intelligence and the capacity to see things in advance, Chao Anouvong looked serious. He came across as an unassuming intellectual, but he was a very capable and dynamic ruler who became interested in politics, and even more so in philosophy. He had a fearsome voice to go with it: very often, the ideas and words teeming in his head exploded into a roar when he was stressed or fearful. His ideas were often too complicated for other city governors to grasp, but no one doubted his ambition to unify all Lao people. Despite some of his mandarins yawning and falling asleep, he made for an impressive site chairing his monthly palace meetings. His figure was of more than average size for a Lao: big and strong enough to house his ambitious mind. However, he was running a mere vassal state, with only a few friends to help. He fully realised that if he was to have a chance of achieving his goals, he'd need to become king in ViengChan. But the real power resided only in Bangkok, a city that gradually came to be known by its inhabitants as Krung Thep Maha Nakhorn: the great city of angels, built beneath a canopy of green trees and on a river of filth. There weren't actually any angels there, but all kinds of houses filled with undreamt-of delights: lovely, smiling girls, gentle conversation and delicious fruits.

Chao Anouvong needed help. He sought to convince all the provincial cities' rulers, especially those on the right bank of the Mekong, to support him and fight with him to the very end, but to be able to return to ViengChan with his brother Inthavong, he needed to earn Bangkok's trust. Chao Anouvong became close to King Chulaloke's son, who was the same age as him. Although he had to be careful because he was closely watched, he openly stated that to rule LanXang under Siamese domination was simply unacceptable: he would rather be a serf in the house of an honest man than king of a vassal state. Lao's sovereignty should not be surrendered to Siam, or anyone else for that matter. After many dreary years of Siam interfering in every corner of Lao society, it was rousing to hear him declare his commitment to save the Lao nation from being eaten up. He encouraged the people to recognise their own responsibilities in achieving an independent Lao nation: all must work together for the common good. In politics the buck stopped with him – in a feudal culture such as ours, the most important person took all the risks. He understood that negotiation and compromise were normally the correct path, but in this case confrontation and defiance were the only resources available to restore Lao national pride.

I was too young and inexperienced to feel the impact of the Siamese invasion in 1779. But now, at nineteen, after talking and listening to Chao Anouvong I was becoming more and more upset. I took pains to make a quick calculation: 1,045 years since the legendary Ai-Lao Khoun Borom of Lao NongSae; 1,038 years since his son Khoun Loh became the first king of Mueang Swa (Luang Phrabang); 442 years since King Fah Ngum united all the Lao LanXang territories. And here we were, a vassal state, just another Siamese province. It was unforgivable and undignified. A Disaster! It was unthinkable for the two of us to remain silent. Chao Anouvong had returned home not so much to make changes but to inherit, inspire and restore. He stood as a symbol of a new beginning, but he was in a more difficult position than his late father, because LanXang was not an independent country. It was clear to me that, at twenty-eight, he was destined to be king and to make history. I pledged to support him. He swallowed hard to clear his throat and his indignation rose.

'Remember this, Jon, our kingdom is very big, much bigger than what you can see. Lao people live in houses on stilts, eat sticky rice (*Khaow Neow* ເຂົ້າ ໜຽວ) and fermented fish paste or sauce (*Padaek* ປາແດກ), play the bamboo pipe (*Khaen* ແຄນ) and are dependent on the mighty Mekong. Our women style their long hair into tall buns, with a pendant or *Champa* flower, and wear the national dress of a high-necked silk shirt with matching woven shawl, a long cotton or silk skirt (*Sinh*) and a gold or silver belt. Unlike the Siamese from the Chaophraya river, the people living on the right side of the Mekong and beyond – right down to the ancient city of Khorakabora-Sima, otherwise known as Khorat – are Lao, and closely related to us. They are our close friends and true relatives. There are more Lao citizens living in fear of repression in Siam than Bangkok is prepared to admit.'

Well, one can identify a nation by its language, but you can tell a lot about a culture by its favourite food. The Lao have always been sticky-rice people. Sticky rice is quite simply the basis of the Lao diet. There are many types of nutritious rice in the world – thousands of varieties are found in Lao LanXang, including chick rice (*Khaow Gai noi* – named for its small grains), fragrant rice (*Khaow Horm*) and dark purple rice (*Khaow Kam*). The rice is traditionally pounded in a large mortar to remove the husk. After being soaked overnight, it's steamed in a cone-shaped steamer until ready. The soft, steamy stuff is then emptied onto a large bamboo tray and then transferred into several smaller bamboo containers. There you have it! Sticky rice: all ready to be eaten with the hand.

Good for dunking, dipping and dabbing. Rice is important because, unlike protein-rich meat and fish, it can be stored. Besides, it's cheap and adaptable. It can be cooked in many ways: flour, cakes, baby food, noodles, paper and more are only some of its by-products. Sticky rice is central to LanXang's sense of itself. No wonder Bangkok imposed heavy taxes on it.

I kept quiet while Chao Anouvong stared out the window, through a dramatic shaft of dazzling light across the reflecting mirror of the great Mekong. 'See, the land over the other side of the river,' he said, pointing his outstretched right hand. His eyes were as powerful as a hawk's. I turned and looked hard. 'That is part of our rightful kingdom, stretching to the west and to the southwest and almost touching Bangkok. We should have our own king and rule ourselves. We come and go as we please for now, but the shameful thing is that we're under the power of the shameless Rattanakosin king in Bangkok.' Before then, like many of our uneducated boys, I'd wondered whether anyone lived on the far side of the Mekong, and why we rarely went over. He answered my thought. I was saddened, and the thought of people not being able to cross whenever they pleased greatly disturbed me. 'It would be wrong to ask for permission to visit relatives in our own country in the future,' he complained. I didn't know what he meant by obtaining a permit but stared out the window and across the glittering river. I could see the golden sand and the houses on the green contour of the riverbank, but I could see no life. It was too far for my weak, untrained eyes. 'Too much self-interest among our own ruling circles brought real destruction to the kingdom,' he complained. He shook his head irritably, blaming those before him for the loss of tens of thousands of the educated ViengChan population. It was as though that old historical enemy, the Siamese ruling elite in Bangkok, were never far from his thoughts. Clearly, the flow of time had not washed past struggles from his memory and from the Lao people's minds.

At the mere mention of the names TakSin and Kasatseuk, he stiffened. It was TakSin the expansionist, he said, who had provided the excuses to invade LanNa in 1775, before presiding over the cruel death of the brave ViengChan people four years later. He'd only been twelve years old at the time; still with an innocent, fresh face, perhaps, but old enough to remember what had happened.

'Without any reason or warning,' he said abruptly, 'the Siamese came in droves. It was clear they intended to conquer us.' He frowned. 'Always beware, Jon, of people armed with guns, swords and sweet tongues, who say they come in peace and claim not to be seeking power for themselves: they are the most untrustworthy of the lot. Our people sought to flee the pillaging and looting of ViengChan and escaped to the forests. Most right-thinking people accept that civil society is damaged by war and its aftermath, but also believe that cultural property that has been uprooted should be restored to its rightful ownership. We realise now we stupidly let robbers and vandals into our kingdom.' Then, in a show of anger, he suddenly slammed his hand on the desk, making me jump. I turned to look at him. He was flushed; wagging his finger, he said, 'The people on either side of the Mekong were under our rule of law and had looked to us for protection since King Fah Ngum's day. Now we no longer have an army to defend them. They are incensed at Bangkok's indoctrination but powerless to prevent it happening. The Siamese plundered our land from end to end – taxed us, murdered us, stole our temple treasures.' He accused the Rattanakosins of being ungrateful since King Xay-Setthathirath helped them fight the Burmese. 'We went to their aid, but they never came to ours. They even sent their troops to LanNa in 1595 to stop King Norkaeo Khumman from rescuing Lao captives from Pegu in Burma. Like us, they're descendants of the great King Khoun Borom, or so they claim, and there hasn't been a decent king amongst them since they swore allegiance at That Si-SongHuck in 1563.'

He liked to get things off his chest. But his decision to tell me all of this was not born of some desire on his part, but purely as a matter of interest and to advise future generations on how to protect the country's security and freedom. He'd good foresight and I listened to him with great interest. Finally, he leaned towards me eagerly, expecting shock or surprise, But I listened to this sensational history as coolly as if I was being told about the weather. I was unconcerned. I hadn't the least idea what he was trying to tell me. Everything had seemed perfectly normal to me up to then, but I now felt lost in the cloud of history, both good and bad. All I was concerned about was having sufficient food to eat. LanXang had experienced a painful rite-of-passage up to that point and I abhorred colonialism; but the country's past simply couldn't be changed, and there was no telling what the future might be. I was more interested in getting on with my duty and my life; everything else was just rhetoric.

Since the past had meant little or nothing to me up to that moment, I felt neither the privilege nor the benefit of my work and behaved just like any normal person with a deep interest in learning, very serious and highly disciplined. Privately, I regarded everybody, rulers and commoners alike, as mere human beings with blood flowing through their veins. All human blood was red. And most blood was shed pointlessly because rulers and their officials, those with the nerve and the knowledge, decided that war was the correct medicine for curing disputes. Nevertheless I shook with anger that the Lao people were being victimised by the Siamese elite. I could imagine the sound of victory celebrations and the arrogant poses and self-congratulatory smiles of the Siamese people and their ruler. ViengChan, on the other hand, was in ruins and its people's freedom had been lost; this deep wound festered. Lao identity was at stake and their ruler was under Bangkok's control. Chao Anouvong appeared to take all the blame and felt it was his responsibility to give back what had been lost to the Lao people. My first impression of the Rattanakosin dynasty of its immorality; they were certainly not to be trusted. I agreed with him that the Siamese ruling class were a selfish and sinful group, like heads of state or politicians who say what people like to hear and make pledges, but ultimately use power for their own good.

I realised that the relationship between Bangkok and ViengChan had never been straightforward. Chao Anouvong explained that the conflict probably started in 1533, when King Phothisarath of LanXang moved his permanent residence from Luang Phrabang to ViengChan. At this time, Phra Chairacha (1534–1546), the king of Ayutthaya, had two sons, Athityarath and Sayarath. When a dispute arose between them, Chairacha supported Athityarath. Sayarath fled to ViengChan in 1539, where he successfully persuaded a reluctant King Phothisarath to invade Si-Ayutthaya city. Phothisarath was aware of King Khoun Borom's doctrine discouraging interference, but after much debate he considered it the right course of action to bring peace to the region. The Lao army marched out and camped for ten days outside the city. Having drafted a letter saying '*come out for talk or fight me. If not, please make peace with Prince Sayarath,*' he decided instead to sit and wait for Chairacha's reaction. Fortunately, Chairacha stayed inside the city and the inhabitants refused to take up the challenge. King Phothisarath saw no reason to attack people who were so closely related; he certainly didn't consider them enemies and promptly ordered his men to pull back. No blood was spilt, but it was probably the beginning of the bad blood between the two kingdoms.

The disgruntled warmonger King Chairacha sent his army to invade LanXang in revenge a year later. After a fierce battle the Siamese captured the city of ViengKhuk on the right side of the Mekong. After making offerings to the gods for victory, King Phothisarath ordered his people to fight. The invading army crossed the Mekong but were badly defeated during a vicious battle at Thong Salakham outside ViengChan. The inhabitants of the city celebrated while the Siamese army fled, leaving thousands of casualties and taking resentment, bitterness and animosity back with them. Moreover, had the Burmese persuaded Phothisarath to join in with the invasion and perhaps destroy the Ayutthaya kingdom in 1548, the Siamese would still have been suffering even now. And the voice of the victorious Lao, with thousands of captive prisoners at their disposal, would have been heard in ViengChan instead. However, King Phothisarath, who was ordained as a monk, was a devout Buddhist and a pacifist. He refused to cooperate with the Burmese and felt it more prudent to strengthen and protect the interests of both Siamese and Lao people.

The two unsuccessful campaigns by King Xay-Setthathirath to help the Siamese retake the city of Phitsanuloke from the Burmese in 1567 and 1569 was a turning point for LanXang; she became too weak to defend herself, let alone provide further military assistance to Ayutthaya Siam. LanXang then split into three principalities after King Souriyavongsa's death in 1690.

The Burmese eventually succeeded in destroying Si-Ayutthaya in 1750. Siam was depopulated and its treasures were looted: it became a bankrupt state. Could the Siamese ever forget what had happened to them, one may ask? As a result, Lao LanXang became Burma's next target.

With the benefit of hindsight, the Lao should have done things differently. Perhaps they could have conquered and dominated the Siamese of Ayutthaya, had King Phothisarath so desired. Even King Fah Ngum only stopped short in his conquest because he appreciated King Uthong's claim to be a descendant of Ai-Lao, like him. Both Fah Ngum and Phothisarath respected Khoun Borom's edict and held the Siamese people close to their hearts. Chao Anouvong stressed that one should recognise that the Lao had never sought domination over its neighbours or wanted to attack Tai-Kadai-speaking kingdoms – Siam in particular.

'Why?' he asked me. I gave him a blank look. 'Because we respect peace and want a good relationship with our neighbours and the world,' he said. 'We ended up as victims because of our respect for others. Perhaps we gave the Siamese too much respect.' I agreed with him, working my brain to the limit but finding no answer to the problem. 'And what did the ungrateful Siamese ever do for us?' he continued. 'They took full advantage of us by invading ViengChan – annihilation, forced migration, pillage and domination – that's what they've achieved. It was a disaster for us! Never before has such terror appeared in our country.'

'It's incredible! It should never have happened,' I muttered. 'It's in their interest and conscience to repent after their wrongdoing,' I added philosophically, attempting to calm him. He nodded in agreement, stood up and then walked towards the window. I followed and stood next to him.

'Nevertheless, Jon, no one in the whole of LanXang expected it... not for one moment,' he continued, looking across the Mekong with his hands clasped behind his back. 'They should have helped us to get things sorted. Not invaded us. All these killings, deeds of violence, the imprisoning of our people, none of it would have happened if they'd respected their vows – all would have been peace and friendship as before. Only the Siamese can honour you with one breath and take you for a fool the next.' He paused and sighed in despair. 'Since we're under our Siamese friends' domination, their power brings them many luxuries at our expense, but humanity and clean hands are seldom among them. History will tell, and the truth will prevail, Jon. One suspects that they aspire to rewrite history to conform to their own versions of reality. For certain, they will contemptuously downplay the importance of Lao LanXang. But surely they can't go on forever lying to their own people and the world. Let's hope someone will speak the truth eventually.'

'They betrayed us, Your Royal Highness, and that should surely be called to account.' I said, shaking my head in despair.

'Now,' he said firmly, turning towards me. 'We must believe that our territory and sovereignty can be regained. Not without a fight, I fear.'

'We simply cannot afford not to believe in ourselves,' I said. 'It's not in our character. And if we have to fight for it, so be it!' For a moment I stood motionless, my face grim. Chao Anouvong emphasised that Lao LanXang had to set specific goals of independence, peace, prosperity and democracy. Only then will we have an enlightened administration. I looked at him and said, 'Surely, Your Royal Highness, we must drive out the occupier.'

'Our wisdom is to know the proper and appropriate measure of all things,' he said, resting his hand on my shoulder. 'We must look to the future. First, we will slowly try to rebuild our country to boost our economy and the people's morale. Only then will our confidence return. We will be great again. But we have a great deal to do from now on.'

It was encouraging to hear him speak so knowingly. For LanXang to become a vassal state of Siam was too painful to bear. It got into our souls, making us angry and wondering whether there were other issues at play, or perhaps there was something wrong with Siam's royal bloodline. Even many days later, when I woke in the morning, these thoughts were still rankling in my mind. Chao Anouvong, on the other hand, wisely refused to dwell on it for he did not wish to become bitter: that would hurt no one but himself.

In silence we slowly came away from the window towards our chairs. He made himself comfortable in his seat and gestured for me to sit. I dreaded his superior status and cleverness, but sat nervously in anticipation, with an eye on the benefit to be gained from learning something. My ignorance quickly became evident whenever I met someone clever like Chao Anouvong, but my saving grace was that I was humble enough to listen attentively and learn, so I always liked to ask questions. Despite my limited ability, I never claimed knowledge I'd gained from another as my own discovery. After I had stubbornly begged him to cure my mind rather than my physical ailments, he concluded our discussion, announcing that he would do both.

'Very well, Jon,' he said keenly. 'You seem to me to be a thoroughly decent young man. You have a gargantuan appetite for knowledge. You have the brain and the energy for bravery and the ability to overcome difficulties. What else does one need? In fact, you are exactly the sort of son a father would want to have. But first, for your mind, I want to promote you to be my *Laykar* (secretary). This is an opportunity for you to open doors that have been both mentally and physically closed to you. I want you to work with me, to help me. That is the reason I summoned you. We will be benefitting each other and our country.'

I stood to attention instantly, feeling shocked, excited and pleased. In my mind I accepted the offer with alacrity and delight but instead stammered uncertainly. I hadn't seen it coming.

'There is no greater honour, nor can I imagine anything more important than to serve you, Your Royal Highness… and the country, of course,' I said, lowering my head in appreciation. 'I would be more than happy to serve, but may I please have your kind permission to think it over?'

'What, think about it?' he fumed, looking flushed. 'I order you to work with me.'

I had the boy's typical fear of his father, probably because he was bigger than me and seldom visible, spending much of his time on official duties, or going fishing or hunting in the forests. His words had always seemed firm, but on this occasion Chao Anouvong's voice and glare were shockingly powerful. I was stunned by his reaction. I glanced at him in astonishment and tried to explain. He wasn't concerned about my lack of experience, but my willingness to learn was important. He calmed down very quickly, and our exchange again became courteous and friendly. As an incentive, he suggested that I sleep in the palace.

'That is very tempting,' I said. 'Your Royal Highness is much too kind.'

'Apart from the library,' he said, 'I want you to take good care of the general confidential affairs of the kingdom. Your other role is as a liaison between the mandarins – who have grown in number since my return – and me in the main palace. You will fit in admirably. In fact, you'd better move in to one of the available rooms in the mandarins' quarters.'

It was uncomfortable at first, but we got on well throughout the rest of our conversation. It was a privilege in many ways, and I enjoyed that private moment with him. He'd acknowledged that my enquiring mind was worth the trouble and told me to relax in his company. He taught me about many things. Well, if knowledge was there to be acquired, I took every opportunity and thrived on his patience and generosity. Afterwards in my room I'd assess his wisdom and intellect and seek more at every opportunity. However, I was careful not to appear too enthusiastic, for fear of putting myself under unnecessary pressure. Besides, I was still troubled by the great respect I had for him as the future king of Lao LanXang. Although he was merely a viceroy under his brother, King Inthavong, I saw him as a royal personage with an air of superiority. I often felt nervous when I was close to him, but I was unfazed and shameless when it came to wisdom and knowledge and would suck the bones to get to the best part of the meat. I was seldom idle during my time with him; it reminded me of my school days, the bustle of the classroom, the lessons, the exams, the sports day and the school playground, all requiring my energy. The prospect of enormous hard work, however difficult, and with little chance for play, was a great opportunity for me.

Besides, I'd mainly committed myself to the huge job of looking after the library: keeping and archiving the historical records was not an easy task. Equally, it would have been quite fatuous to appear ungrateful and ignore the chance that he'd offered. Faced with such a dilemma, I did not want to be rejected by him, because his presence was always an inspiration.

I rose to the task with great enthusiasm and assured him that I relished the challenge and the extra energy that serving him would provide. The responsibility would drag me from my humble home outside the city walls into a room in the palace. My self-satisfied smile and embarrassed blushing were probably his first impression of me. Afterwards, I became more relaxed in his presence. There was no doubt that this promotion would change my life.

He looked pensive and, for a delirious moment, I thought he might be about to invite me to join him for dinner. At some stage our conversation grew more relaxed. I was a little cheeky with my remarks about his knowledge of LanXang's history. I put it to him that the Sun King Souriyavongsa was thoughtless, perhaps even guilty, because he'd ordered the execution of his only son; the infighting that followed divided LanXang. I complained that his own father, King Bounyasan, and his brother, Nanthasene, together with all responsible Lao people, should never have surrendered to the Siamese in 1779. He recognised that I had a point, but I thought to myself that I deserved at least some verbal retribution from him. There I remained seated, both excited and afraid, while the birds sang sweet songs outside and I could hear the tree branches shaking in the wind.

'Well, never mind about that,' he said. 'We can learn from our mistakes, but we can't change history. More importantly, what is your answer to my offer?'

My sweaty hands resting on my thighs, I immediately sat upright. I hesitated and anxiously looked at him.

'I can see nothing better than to serve you and the country,' I said softly. 'If Your Royal Highness is serious and with your kind permission, then I'm at your command.'

'Yes, of course I'm serious. Can't you see?' he said, looking at me impatiently.

I then revealed that I was worried about my poor mother and her house two miles outside the city walls. It wasn't far but would seem much more so as I moved from one world to another: from the palace to the village beyond That Luang stupa, through the rough, winding forest path that was dusty when dry and very muddy in the rainy season. It was quite impossible to neglect the woman who had borne me and brought me up. It could be weeks or months before I could visit her again, and her surroundings, as I remembered them, would certainly arouse strange feelings in me. I had always preferred the free open countryside to the packed town, and even less the confining walls of the palace. But it was an offer one simply could not refuse.

On hearing my thoughts, he lifted his eyes and looked at me sympathetically. He appeared to be a man with karma and unlimited patience. I realised that with clever, educated men of the ruling classes like him, it wasn't consistent boastfulness which made them wise and powerful, but rather the capacity, when necessary, to be unexpectedly, even extravagantly, kind and generous. In effect, he caught me off guard. My greatest worry had been whether my knowledge would be accepted as equal to a Siamese man in Bangkok, or whether I would be regarded as a backward Lao. He told me not to confuse education with intelligence; apart from their inferiority complex, the Lao in general are anything but dim witted. He said that one may often feel embarrassed but never need be shy; this stuck in my mind forever after, often providing solace in moments of spine-tingling inferiority. I said that I'd always been deeply interested in the lives of great men and wished to learn of their exploits, But his interest wasn't limited to kings. In realising that I was effectively being given the job of my dreams, an ambition I had never even dared voice in the presence of anyone for fear of making them jealous, I immediately used my charm to test his patience further.

'Your Royal Highness, you overwhelm me,' I said in a voice trembling with emotion. I had to cough before I could continue. 'Unfortunately, fate has decreed us to be on different levels. I am merely a dim star compared to your bright moon, with little learning and insight; I dare not accept such a responsibility.'

'Not necessarily,' he said, looking at me in amazement. 'I accept that I am on another level, but to achieve supreme wisdom is everyone's ambition. I believe some people are full of wisdom and better than others in most things – knowledge, perseverance and sophistication. Those who have exceptional knowledge and a good intellect tend to be more modest. The more intelligent someone is, the less they display it. I have come to realise that if we are to survive as a nation, we need wise men serving our country.' He paused and gazed at me. 'Khoun Jon, I know that you will never do anything unworthy of yourself. But you mustn't hide behind your true abilities or try to conceal your intelligence. I can tell you have great foresight, so let us share it for the sake of the future of our kingdom.'

Such encouraging words! I'd never seen myself in that light before. I knew that I couldn't live up to his high opinion, but I could at least try.

'Your Royal Highness, you are exaggerating, and I'm flattered. Don't most people think they're clever?' I responded. 'Overly intelligent people are often victims of their own ingenuity; perhaps I'm merely an ignorant but incorrupt candidate with inadequate skills. To accept this job is all very well, but any hint of lack of knowledge and moral backbone would be fatal.' I added that my mother might not be able to cope without me.

'I'm not exaggerating at all,' he said, adding that he considered me competent and erudite, and behaved impeccably. 'The task could be difficult and will certainly be complicated. I can reassure you that I don't mind providing moral support to allow you to excel. Regrettably we are a vassal state and our wealth is restricted. The truth is, I could find no one more capable or more suitable than you for this job: to build a bridge to link you, me and everyone in our country. That is why I want you to assist me as my private secretary, otherwise all your erudition will be lost. Don't you agree?'

It occurred to me that neither he nor I, in fact none of us, were born exactly alike. We had different natural aptitudes which fitted us for different tasks. But our perception of less fortunate people – the old and the young, the disadvantaged and the marginalised – was very similar: we wanted to help them all. He was a man of compassion and righteousness, and his virtue inspired the people: their hearts were with him. I saw that his ideas could be developed through discussion; my immediate task was to assist him, which in turn would profit all our lives. I looked at him in puzzlement, not understanding his surprising philosophical approach. It left me reeling, not least because what he was suggesting was both kind and sensible, with enormous responsibility attached. It was also an ideal solution for me, enabling me to pursue my ambition with him taking the lead. I gathered my nerves and tried to compose myself. Then, raising my praying hands to my head in submission and leaning forward a little, I spoke gently.

'Your Royal Highness, I shall be frank with you. I merely took the librarian job to support my mother but have set my heart on taking care of the library and furthering my education, knowledge and wisdom. It is my inspiration, and I have no other means of smoothing my way in life. The only lasting glory for anyone is an achievement of some sort. The truth is, I do want, more than anything, to serve and to achieve. As a mortal being, to achieve immortality would be a dream come true. Being a man of influence and authority, you accomplished so much in Bangkok. You know what it is like.'

'I certainly do. Too well in fact!' he said persuasively. 'The truth is, Jon, even in the Siamese capital, or anywhere else in the world for that matter, a man should never have his statue built just because he's a king, or because he is powerful, or, least of all, because he is wealthy. No benefit can be gained from knowing how to bestow immortality without the knowledge of how to use it. Only a few of our ancestors achieved immortality.' He paused for thought. 'I can name a few: Legendary King Khoun Borom most certainly, for he will always be remembered as the father of our Ai-Lao race. Khoun Loh the founder and King Fah Ngum the unifier of our LanXang kingdom certainly deserve it. In fact, without King Fah Ngum, we might not even have the concept of a nation and remained disparate tribesmen: Tai Neua in the north and Tai ViengChan and Tai Tay in the south.' He paused, before declaring that King Xay-Setthathirath's achievements also richly deserved immortality. 'Look at That Luang stupa,' he said, like a historian. 'That is his immortality, by which we will always remember him.' He also pointed out that That Si-SongHuck and other monuments would be the everlasting symbols of King Xay-Setthathirath. 'They are his architectural legacy.' Finally, he said, 'Surely you don't need any more persuading to accept this job. Do you, Jon?'

'Forgive me for asking. What about a man's wishes?' I said, knowing that I'd have to obey his every command if I became his private secretary. 'Surely that is his right? If a man wishes to be free and to preserve his identity, which would immortalise him, would you not permit him to do so?' I pressed on as he listened intently. 'King Fah Ngum, as you said, united Lao LanXang, but he allowed freedom for all people to be themselves as long as they obeyed his rule of law, which was designed to benefit people of all walks of life. He abolished slavery and eliminated cruelty and injustice. Why don't the Lao receive the same treatment from the Siamese government? It seems they treat us like slaves!'

He looked aggrieved at the lack of respect he'd received while living in Bangkok. I then pointed out that the Rattanakosins' perception of the Lao people while under Siam domination would never be fair, even though we shared a common link. The problem with the Siamese was that they failed to focus on what brings people together. Being wealthy, they tried to differentiate themselves from the Lao and other ethnic groups and to erase LanXang from the surface of the earth. This perpetual tendency to discriminate against the Lao manifested itself in a negative attitude that they wanted to pass down to their children. What was more, after Ayutthaya was destroyed by the Burmese, their history became riddled with falsehoods and they battled ceaselessly to control what the LanXang and LanNa people knew about their past. Bangkok wanted to create its own version of history in which the Rattanakosin regime was faultless. It became very unhelpful in its dealings with vassal states, seeing them as its inferiors; it is beyond dispute that Bangkok took advantage of Lao LanXang and LanNa in its pursuit of a Greater Siam.

Chao Anouvong sighed heavily, rose from his seat and turned his gaze towards me.

'Don't you want to serve your king and country?' he said sternly, as if his patience was beginning to run out. 'Your brilliant views are enlightening. The kingdom needs people like you!'

'Your Royal Highness, please understand that I greatly appreciate the offer,' I said submissively, shifting nervously in my seat and realising that my hesitation to accept the job was making me look ungrateful. I felt I would faint if he withdrew the offer altogether. I made obeisance, then, looking directly at him, said stubbornly, 'I beg you to allow me to think it over… please.'

'Yes of course you can think about it,' he said with a grin, looking straight into my eyes. 'We have plenty of time. In any case, your elderly mother comes first.' I felt calm air had engulfed us both and was lost for words for a few feverish moments. Like all Lao we had a unique bond of humility. He told me that he intended to get the best out of me; that I would be more than a mere private secretary and that we were quite similar in nature. 'Now, let me tell you, Jon,' he said briskly. 'This offer has no conditions attached to it. You have earned it, otherwise I wouldn't have offered you the post. You must decide what you think is best for you.'

As our conversation came to an end, the sun was going down and darkness was approaching. I enthusiastically stated that I, too, strange as it might seem, was comfortable in his company. He smiled warmly and dismissed me to ponder alone. I was about to leave when he suddenly called.

'Jon, tell me, is working in the library your first job or have you worked elsewhere?'

'Indeed, it is the only job I've ever had, Your Royal Highness.'

'There is another thing,' he said with a smile. 'Your given name is unusual.'

'Uncommon perhaps,' I said guardedly. 'But there isn't anything odd about it, and a name is unimportant.' I must confess I felt quite uncomfortable whenever someone asked that question, so hesitated to say more. He made me promise to tell him some other time.

'I assure you I'll reveal all my secrets another time,' I said and grinned cheerfully. 'I have no wish to deceive you or be evasive. On the contrary, I'll tell you everything, but I must warn you it's a long story.'

That was how our conversation went. We were congenial in each other's company, but sometimes I struggled to keep up with his smart repartee. He was genial and took pity on my lack of experience and learning; I expressed my gratitude and paid obeisance to him again, getting the impression he was very pleased with me. He came towards me, making me shift timidly from foot to foot. When I left him to his thoughts, he touched my arm tenderly.

The meeting was a success. It had been exhilarating because I was talking to a prince; and exhausting because of the intensity of the experience and the need to be on full alert. As I walked through the palace gate and looked back in a euphoric daze, I could barely believe I'd just spent nearly half a day in serious conversation with this most remarkable man, and that he'd offered to appoint me as his private secretary.

The Beginning…

Before the meeting, I had glimpsed Chao Anouvong many times after his return from Bangkok. He certainly appeared sophisticated and glamorous. In silence, I had been hoping for the honour of serving him. The meeting held great significance for me; I was much taken with everything about him, especially when I realised he was a kind, wise, intellectual. Nothing else was needed to make me his ardent admirer, and this really turned out to be the beginnings of our intimacy, although I always took care to show him the respect due to the future king of LanXang. Now he knew me well enough to put his trust in me, I relished the intellectual stimulus which would allow me to reinvent myself in his circle. I could sense that I was going to be working with a ruler who was benevolent and virtuous, and his fame spread far and wide. He thought that my forthright opinions were slightly alarming, but exciting nonetheless. We shared similar ambitions and ideas; we were both liberal-minded and held strongly sceptical views about the Rattanakosins' ideology. He was not just clever, kind and modest but also instinctively felt and thought as I did. Like him, I was able to compartmentalise my life. We had the same dogmatism and stubbornness, and the same desire to search out truth and justice. I really wanted to be of service to him.

Naturally, I yearned for honourable liberty; I wondered whether I was on the right path and what it would be like to live in the palace. What was I seeking and who was I? I saw myself growing up to be a new man in the world, no longer a dreamer. Henceforth, I worked in my own sphere, which made me healthy and happy. I cherished a secret desire to belong to the elite, but to be armed with the ultimate power of philosophical, not political, knowledge. I felt that I had a great future, not in the field of politics but in the more subtle world of diplomacy. But I barely noticed the larger world: I did not have overweening ambition or desire a ringside seat to history, but my confidence was unlimited.

The following day I had an audience with him in his study. He keenly demanded to know my decision. You might have guessed: I eagerly accepted the job, for nothing could be more agreeable to me.

'My humble respects Your Royal Highness. And your wish is my command. I will render whatever service I can,' I said, bowing my head.

'Excellent!' he said enthusiastically and heaved a euphoric sigh of relief, gazing at me. 'Now, Jon, allow me to tell you this. You are brimming with energy, enthusiasm, ideas and curiosity; you are a remarkable young man of the most outgoing and engaging appearance, elegant and interesting in your manners, with something of distinguished nobleness and dignity of deportment. You are blessed with ears and eyes that take in everything and give nothing away. You have demonstrated statesmanlike qualities and the quintessence of a gentleman. We know you have charisma, intellectual eagerness and an inclination to learn, listen and enquire – you have a mind that never shirks from mental hardship. Furthermore, you have a strong sense of patriotic rectitude and of doing things properly. You also have zeal and a thirst for knowledge, a prodigious memory that probably never forgets anything apart from injuries and insults; you are determined and fond of hard work.'

'Your Royal Highness is much too generous,' I said, feeling rather awkwardly flattered. Frankly, I never thought of myself in that way.

'How, otherwise, would you be able to behave and cope with such a demanding job?' he said. 'Besides, the protocol and the court language (*Lasa Sab*) are different here from the outside world. Personally speaking, I think it unnecessary and time-wasting, but observing the rules is important. Equally, it might be useful for you to take elocution lessons. It is important to never be at a loss. I find it helpful to bear three things in mind: hard work is rewarded with success; physical exercise is good for the body; but enforced learning rarely sticks in the mind.'

'I do understand and will bear that in mind, Your Royal Highness,' I said, 'and I'm humbly grateful for your kind words.' To my surprise, I also received a new outfit: trousers, shirts, white jacket, black shoes, all of which were a little bit too big… and a gold-thread sash – too pretty for a man, I should say.

'Good. Now, I'll be frank, and you must be discreet. As my private secretary, you must firstly promise never to reveal anything or mention what is being discussed between us to anyone else… not until I am gone. Is that understood?'

'Your Royal Highness, there is no need to suspect my loyalty and discretion,' I said. 'I shall not lack the dignity befitting a Lao official. Yes, I'm proud of my status, but it will not breed any sort of haughtiness or egotism in me. I am an unshakably discreet and unassuming sort of person, and very much prefer to do things diplomatically, behind the scenes. Besides, I am extremely reticent, and it's never been in my nature to talk about anyone, least of all myself. As one says, a wise bird chooses its branch for roosting and a sagacious man chooses his lord to serve. I'm ready to take an oath of silence and you will soon learn well enough how staunch I am. I will keep as silent as a block of stone.'

'Splendid! Glad to hear it,' he said pensively. '… And yes, indeed a wise lord always chooses someone he trusts as his confidant. If it's true that we have lived many lives before, you were once a king but now return to serve.'

We gazed at each other with a smile to signify our understanding.

He took a deep breath and said, 'Good! Excellent! From now on you are my private and confidential secretary, In fact, you are the royal secretary (*Phrarasa Laykar*),' he announced, 'and we will call you by your given name… wait, perhaps not. You may not like it.'

I made it clear that I would rather not be known by my given name. After a short pause he proposed that I should be given the ancient noble title of *Khoun*. Thus began our close relationship. I fervently expressed my appreciation and willingness. I was to be known formally as 'Khoun Jon', but Chao Anouvong toned it down and told me that ViengChan palace was not entirely the centre of the world. I hesitated to speak; I had pinned my hope on him to bring justice to the Lao nation.

The effect was instantaneous, I walked on air, heart thumping, mouth dry, retching with excitement. It all became clear what I was getting myself into. So, I earnestly took my oath of loyalty to minister to his needs with absolute confidence and great moral satisfaction. I intended to hold true to my belief that my main role was to support him in his onerous job and condemned myself to a life of confidentiality and deception. We were united in our love of LanXang, in truth, justice and freedom. From that instant, I was part of the establishment. I made sure his private affairs were kept private: secrecy is seductive, and I was ambitious. I also enjoyed the privileges, of course; I felt a flood of relief and a fluttering surge of adrenalin.

I met Chao Wang Nah, the senior security officer, the next day, as was customary for new arrivals. My role in the palace was entirely clear: my responsibilities concerned Anouvong's private affairs and on matters of secret intelligence. At first, I was oblivious to the fact that some of the mandarins and government officials were incompetent, lazy or corrupt – usually all three. They spent more time falsifying their expenses and partying than working. There were some 200 staff spread all over the four palaces: the Main Palace (*Wang Luang*) – supreme power; the Front Palace (*Wang Nah*) – security; the Rear Palace (*Wang Lhang*) – supply; and the Middle Palace (*Wang Kang*) – finance and welfare. Most of the important work was done in the Main Palace, in his study overlooking the Mekong, which proved to be the throne-room of judgement on the future, where we focused obsessively on LanXang affairs and the paranoid policies of Rattanakosin Siam. I preferred to pass my time in the library at the north end of the building: it boasted a splendid and unhampered view over the Mekong into infinity, which was truly magical.

My working life as Chao Anouvong's private secretary had begun a new phase. I rose early and worked late, but I did not neglect my other duties. I still cared for my mother and tended to the library. He valued me as an individual, not just as part of his staff, and was as trusting and affectionate as if he'd always known me. My enthusiasm probably prompted him to say that I had imagination, was full of plans and initiative and was not easily prone to panic or despair. I had little time for pleasures and hobbies for I had to be ready when needed. I would become used to analysing my relationships, always assessing my own actions and words and those of others. We spent a lot of time together, chatting, discussing the country's affairs, talking about literature, art, music and philosophy. To avoid awkward silences in his company, I chatted like mad. He took me seriously when I remarked that, under his guidance, the people would become more aware of how the country had suffered in the past. Political power in the regions was there for his taking. But I warned him that his friendship with the Siamese royal family was dragging LanXang under Siam's yoke, and he should make sure that politics was not merely a fight for justice. It is a profession for those who seek fame and power, and for those who want to retain power.

'Politics!' he snorted. 'I don't think much about it, but what do you know about politics?'

'Not enough, I'm afraid,' I said, and asked him whether he'd led an enjoyable life in Bangkok.

'Enjoyable?' he said, screwed up his eyes, sprang up from his seat and walked towards the window. After staring briefly across the Mekong, he swung round, fixed his gaze on me and said, 'It's a matter of life and death for us, Khoun Jon. It'd be fatal for us to allow our fellow countrymen, especially now, to suspect that we put the interests of Bangkok above them. We must lay this calumny to rest by protecting them.'

'May I speak frankly?' I said, bowing.

'Go ahead, speak.'

'In my humble opinion, Your Royal Highness, perhaps quiet contemplation is the way forward. The art of life, for the future, is perhaps to deal with problems as they arise, rather than destroy one's spirit by worrying about them too far in advance.'

'You have no experience and have achieved nothing yet!' he retorted. 'Khoun Jon, without freedom and identity none of us can achieve anything worthy in our lives.'

'I agree, but surely,' I interjected, 'one of the greatest pleasures in life is to be respected, but to be truly happy we should first respect ourselves before waiting for someone else to admire us. After all, before we can be judged by our achievements, we must first remember who we are. You and I are Lao and what we will have achieved by the end of our lives could be useful to the younger generation. As for regaining LanXang independence, this task awaits you. If you can't find a way, no one can. I'm convinced that you're the best person in the world to make it happen. It would be a history worth making.'

'You really think so, Khoun Jon?' he said with an expression of surprise. My compliment pleased him. 'Well then, we will settle for that, but should we fail, surely someone else, a hundred times better than me, will achieve our goal,' he added.

'Actually, Your Royal Highness, I thought of that,' I said cautiously, 'but the kingdom is fortunate to have you, and, for my part, I promise to do my utmost.'

He welcomed my pledge and said that if everybody in Lao LanXang were to make the same pledge, we would have a chance of surviving as a nation.

The seriousness of our conversation was surprisingly overwhelming. He stood still, with both hands clasped behind his back, staring contemplatively through the dusty windows into the gardens dense with vegetation, and the bougainvillea draped on the garden walls, defiantly shaking its multiple colours in the wind. He continued hesitantly, possibly with the weight of responsibility on his mind. After sixteen years of living under Siamese influence in Bangkok, it was obvious that he lacked confidence, but being positive was his strength. The kingdom's fate and destiny were within his grasp. The people, myself especially, had high expectations of him.

I had no business to feel upset when he told me that I was just a servant. Still, being a sensitive creature, I felt his words keenly. I wanted to walk away into the strong heat of the day, where the cicadas were singing, and pity myself. It would have felt like the longest backwards walk towards the door I had ever taken if that were to happen. I was determined to prove that he was the right man to be king. But I thought it best to discontinue our debate and promptly suggested that perhaps he wished to take a rest. I was just about to rise from my seat to take my leave when he beckoned me to stay.

'Very well, Khoun Jon, let's carry on with our conversation,' he said persuasively.

'Of course,' I said and sat back down, quietly heaving a sigh of relief.

'I'm satisfied, but let's put aside for now the question of whose thinking is most correct,' he said. 'If the premise is correct, the result will be in our favour.'

I stressed that the Lao had possessed their own identity, language, culture and customs since the days of the Ai Lao King Khoun Borom and earlier, all in the name of progress. Now more than ever they deserved a worthy king of their own, otherwise Lao LanXang might soon die forever. Believing in the argument that I was advancing, I looked at him and said beseechingly, 'You know that the liberty of the Lao nation rests on you, and for that, may I convince you with a single sacred word?

'And what would that be?' he said, leaning forward keenly.

'That word, Your Royal Highness,' I soberly replied, 'is "independence". We must be willing to sacrifice anything and everything to get it back. It will go down in history.'

'Yes, Khoun Jon, you're right, I agree with you entirely. Indeed, that very word is sacred to our nation. Our intention is to secure Lao LanXang dominion, and to do that we need unity. The true art of war is to win without having to fight, but also to go on the offensive if necessary. Presently, we have no power or wealth… and no army. Besides, our views would count for nothing without the support of the people. It would be impossible to achieve without them.'

His words were full of conviction and prophetic, as if he saw something that he believed in and knew that he had to take the lead. I observed his ideas with rising excitement. His answer to Siam domination had not been political, but economic. He added that if LanXang could regain autonomy, then LanNa would follow suit.

While I was immensely happy and excited with the idea of working with him, the thought turned into uncertainty and confusion. I was torn between my mother and him; to leave my mother at home alone outside the city walls troubled me, but on the other hand, it was necessary to be close to him: serving king and country and to improve people's lives was my ultimate dream. I'd convinced myself that if I worked hard and delivered, I could accomplish my duties: an ultimate accolade. After a short pause, he gave me a satisfied smile. I thought he was going to dismiss me.

'In fact, before you go,' he said suddenly. 'Since we are going to be working closely together, you'd better tell me more about yourself... that unusual name of yours for a start?'

I knew that I had to tell him at some point. Again I hesitated, but this time he persisted.

'Well, you may recall that I said it's a long story. I will tell with pleasure... if you insist.'

'I do. Time is on our side,' he said, and joked that he wouldn't go to sleep.

'Very well,' I said as I tried to gather my thoughts. He raised his brows attentively. After taking a sip of water and licking my lips, I began.

I was nine years old, and my father, a hard and imposing man, was about forty-five when he died. I was just a normal, small boy, born in the cold month of late January or early February, I'm not sure. Unfortunately, a well-respected senior monk from the temple borrowed and never returned the books containing my father's all-important archives. We were not amused. Alas, not even my mother, who had an impeccable memory, could remember the exact date of my birth. But she remembered vividly that it was on the cold night of a full moon, and my father made a fire to keep her warm.

So, according to my mother, I arrived discreetly in this world, with the help of my grandmother who acted as midwife and provided moral support in the private room of a house on the family estate that consisted of paddy fields and well-cultivated land. During my birth, it was said that my father waited, pacing back and forth outside the door, white with nerves, shock and alarm, for he'd been absent during my mother's previous labour. Nothing in his philosophical mind had prepared him for what was happening: the groans of pain and the deep breaths, and, most nerve-racking of all, the silence. Sometimes he stretched out on the floorboards and closed his eyes to calm himself. When he heard cries of pain, he jumped up, put his ear against the wall to listen and then paced some more. He smiled and sank to the floor with relief when I finally gave a gurgling cry, screaming and kicking. At the very beginning, all newly born babies, I am sure, give the same ear-shattering cry the moment cold air reaches their lungs – especially when being washed. But as soon as their mothers' warm milk touches their lips, they stop crying and fall asleep.

As part of the traditional convalescence, my mother was required to eat only hot, plain food, no chilli, drink hot herbal drinks and take a bearably hot shower. Once or twice a day, she would lay for ten minutes at a time on the planked wooden bed with steamy charcoal spread thinly underneath – a form of sauna or steam bath. If that weren't enough, it lasted for two weeks: it must have been like torture for her She firmly believed it helped to clean and refresh the body, and after giving to birth to each of her nine children, she always recovered her health and even looked younger. She claimed that I was a good, healthy baby.

Anyway, my father announced to his relatives and friends that he'd become the father of another son. A few days later, he carried me tenderly and proudly showed me off to the household and visiting dignitaries. Being wrapped in swaddling clothes, I imagine there couldn't have been much of me to see apart from a little, soft, red face and a lick of fine black hair. He would offer the bundle to elderly visitors who would hold me nervously, in the way that showed they had been out of practise for years; they were relieved when my mother took me back off them.

It was not surprising that the whole community liked to see and touch a new-born baby's soft and smooth body, but my mother was worried about infection. A few relatives got close of course, but she insisted they washed their hands properly before touching my delicate pink cheeks. I slept through all the fuss and attention. Fortunately I escaped any serious ill health, apart from an excruciating splitting headache after unavoidably contracting malaria at a later age. I managed to grow up with a most unusual name which I've since grown to appreciate and be happy with. I had no choice. What was more, I never even left home to become a novice monk, like other boys.

From the beginning, for some strange reason, my name provoked curiosity and fascination for a group of curious, white-haired and well-respected elders who brought gifts and gave me their blessing. 'Ah! Isn't he adorable? Look at that soft lovable pretty face,' I imagine they said, touching and stroking my soft cheeks with the backs of their fingers. Most of all, they wanted to know the given name of any new-born baby and made a frightful fuss about it.

Chao Anouvong looked at me with amused interest and smiled.

My father replied that he'd thought of a name for me while proudly watching me being breastfed. After a little hesitation, he lifted my delicate body to his bosom. My mother watched worriedly and told him to be careful. He gazed at me like I was a piece of gold and announced casually that my name was to be Thao NaGoh (*Thao* is a Lao word for male; *Nang* is female). Some of the elders were bemused by what they'd heard and, after a short pause, my father said jokingly that perhaps my name should be Jon. The elders looked on with amused curiosity, giggling and laughing a little.

'*Pa Ti Toh*! (Goodness me!),' one elder exclaimed. 'How odd! I know he was born in the year of the dragon (*Nark*), as was King Fah Ngum the Great. The word NaGoh is Sanskrit for Phraya Nark in our language, but why Jon for heaven's sake? I've never heard of it; surely it's not quite right?'

The room went quiet and the guests looked sideways at each other. In silence, my father lifted his eyes to heaven and worked his brain. Everyone looked on intriguingly and waited.

'I am grateful for your knowledge of words,' he thanked the elder. 'I was just thinking… I know,' he said slowly. His voice seemed to come from far away, as if he was waking from a dream. He concluded that with due humility my name should be Goh Jon – a name that had never before existed in the entire kingdom. This didn't go down well with tradition: there was a gasp and then total silence. At first the wise elders didn't think my father was serious, which gave them a fit of the giggles. Their jaws dropped; thinking they'd misheard, they asked him to repeat it, which he did in a firm voice. 'What's wrong with that?' he added, carefully balancing me on his shoulder.

Chao Anouvong gave a chuckle, trying not to laugh and saying nothing.

'*Phachao Euyh*! (Good god!). How did you think of such a name as that? And where on earth did you get it from?' one elder in her late eighties with no teeth cried out, bursting with laughter. My father put on a brave face and explained that it was about time someone had an unusual name. 'Ha! I am superstitious,' the elder said. 'I've never heard of such a Lao name like that before, not in my lifetime or a hundred years before me.' She threw back her head and laughed out loud, producing shock waves and ridges across her thin, wrinkled face. The cramped house was often packed with visitors; they happily joined in with the laughter, and such hilarity must have shaken off several roof tiles. I started crying and my father quickly handed me over to my mother. She recommended that I should simply be called Jon, but he insisted on naming me Goh Jon.

I looked at Chao Anouvong and said, 'Consequently, Your Royal Highness, that's how I got my name.' He just smiled a little and said nothing, but I knew he found it amusing. I told him that it had often been suggested that my name ought to be more conventional; that it should be changed to something less sophisticated that corresponded with the environment. My father was determined to be different and would have none of it.

'In some way, your father may have realised that you were indeed different,' Chao Anouvong said, adding that it was most unusual my father should think of such a name.

'No, not really, Your Royal Highness. It's just a name, no one cared. I'm just human,' I said, adding that my deeds were more important and, like all other mortals, I would become what I was born to be.

'Nevertheless, it is unique and I've never heard of a Lao name like yours before either,' he said, with a mischievous glint in his eyes. 'And I'm surprised that anyone would have been given a name like that… wait, I just thought of something.' He paused and thoughtfully lifted his index finger to his lips. 'I know… yes, that's it. I'll give you a codename: 'Anoujon'. What do you say to that?'

I gazed at him in puzzlement and was intrigued to know the significance of the codename and what it was supposed to mean.

'Fate is written on every man's forehead,' he said sternly. 'You are one of us… the real bearers of the Ring (*Thammalong*).' There was a short pause and, after taking a deep breath, he said, 'Anoujon means the one who follows and acts. It is your destiny, but let's keep this just between the two of us.'

I was honoured but I really didn't think he was that serious. When he enquired whether my father had explained the meaning of my name, I replied that if he'd, I'd forgotten. I vaguely remembered that my father mentioned something about the nine planets (*Noph-Phakhor*), and that one day, humans would be able to leave the earth for outer space.

Chao Anouvong immediately jumped at the idea and mischievously said,

'Well, Goh Jon, space traveller, to start with, I want you to accompany me on more earthbound journeys, both private and official.'

I smiled cheerfully and assured him that I loved travelling and looked forward to it very much. He liked to venture to every corner of LanXang, mostly for the sheer pleasure of being able to do so. I was an adventurous person by nature; thrilled at this prospect, I pledged myself to his service and swore I would willingly travel and stick by him as long as we both lived. My only hope was that my spirit would go to heaven when I died.

'Everyone has one aim,' he said. 'We all want to go to heaven. The truth is, Khoun Jon, we don't really need to travel anywhere; everything is here on our earth, especially hell. We are responsible for our actions.'

I told him that I was strong physically, due to my father's exercise regime. As part of my education, I was free to do what I liked when I was growing up, a real nightmare for my worrying mother. I was a fearless energy-packed little monkey who actively took on any challenge. I once climbed a tall cherry tree in the garden and swung from branch to branch in imitation of a gibbon, only without a tail as an extra arm for balancing and holding onto the branches. It was great fun, but it also taught me a painful lesson.

'Please don't do that or you'll fall down and hurt yourself,' my mother yelled in despair, anxiously watching me. 'Come down at once!' she ordered, screaming out her disapproval. From below, I could see that she'd cupped her hand above her eyes to shield them from the sun and was squinting up towards me. I took no notice and carried on being a monkey. Suddenly the branch snapped. I came crashing down and fell heavily to the ground. I broke my ribs and my elbow, but most of all I shattered my pride! I cried, not just with pain but with shame. I received no sympathy!

'Well, I'm not surprised,' said Chao Anouvong disapprovingly and added, 'We all have to learn from our mistakes, but you're never to climb trees again.'

I nodded and stated that had my father been alive, the sharp crack of his strong hand across my buttocks, or even a slap on my stubborn face, would have rung throughout the city. Then he might have pulled me by the ear into his study for more punishment. With no one to stop him, I could easily have ended up seriously harmed. My older brothers and sister were not so fortunate.

My mother gave me a colourful lesson, delivered in such a high-pitched voice, and at such a volume, that my father's body must surely have turned in his grave. 'And this...' she said, taking a deep breath and rounding on me, her cheeks flushed, her chignon undone, her body trembling, her small narrow bosom rising and falling rapidly. 'This is all because you didn't listen to me!' Then she went inside the house, leaving me to cry in pain alone. She was right. I deserved it but back then I didn't know it was my fault. I never let her see me doing monkey business again after that. Nevertheless, my persistence paid off: I grew up to have a good healthy body, with strong limbs and arms.

Chao Anouvong thought my story was stimulating, but, after giving me a good look, he suggested that I should get even stronger physically. He then asked me how I did at school.

Well, you'll forgive me, I'm sure, if I sound like a self-congratulatory clever person. An abiding memory from school was that we were told to be polite and never to forget to be kind. I was a fairly shy boy, which I think dated from my first attempt at singing, an experience marred by the fact that I had no voice. Much of my predicament was that I wasn't just a little boy, but a little boy with a strange name. When my name was announced at school assembly, the other boys gave me a funny look and a wry smile. I must confess it made me wiggle with unease and I found it hellishly embarrassing at first; I was equally glad, however, that my father hadn't changed my name. Like any schoolboy with an unusual name, I got teased, though not too badly and I somehow overcame the bullies by playing school politics and establishing my popularity in the school playground by standing up to any confrontation and breaking up fights. In those days, you didn't pay bribes to buy favours, but to make friends. I carried fruits and sweets for that reason and won many friends and favours.

Chao Anouvong congratulated me and disclosed that being a young Lao prince in Bangkok did not spare him from being sneered at and cruelly bullied. He wasn't happy about the experience but believed it had hardened him. 'We have to be proud of who we are,' he said, 'and proud of our motherland.' I nodded earnestly and reaffirmed my commitment and readiness for sacrifice when he asked again whether I was happy to serve him. 'Good, I am pleased,' he said. Then he jangled the bell loudly and dismissed me.

The footman promptly appeared and asked me to follow him. I bowed to Chao Anouvong and followed the footman out of the room with alacrity. We walked along a long, dark corridor and then up to the second floor. The wooden stairs were only partially covered with a strip of red carpet in the middle: it was quite impossible not to walk on the bare wooden edges of the stairs as we went up. Suddenly, a light brown cat appeared out of nowhere. I jumped sideways to get out of its way and it made a threatening noise at me before dashing down the stairs at great speed. I saw it jumping up high in mid-air, somersault, land on its back legs, lose its balance, roll down a few flights of steps and then stand up on all fours, determinedly and astonishingly carrying on with its nine lives. We carried on walking noisily up the stairs.

'He'll soon get used to you and probably sleep in your bed,' the footman said. 'Do you prefer to sleep in a normal bed or a four-poster?'

'Four-poster please,' I replied enthusiastically, telling him that I used to sleep in one as a little boy and that I had to use a step to climb up to it. I hadn't slept in one since moving to ViengChan and had been longing to do so again.

'Here is your room,' the footman said, as he pushed open a heavy, shiny, squeaky teak door. I followed him in as he opened the windows, and the faint sound of the sacred Bo trees' leaves shaking gently in the breeze outside could be heard.

We were in the middle of a large, high-ceilinged room with wardrobes, large and small teak tables and a porcelain water jug and bowl. The sight of the big bed left me momentarily speechless. The inspiring views of Hor Phra Kaeo temple across the city increased my enthusiasm. It was like a fantasy come true that I really was going to be sleeping in a four-poster bed in the palace. The sun was now high, but still hidden behind the surrounding treetops. The beautifully carved wooden wall panels depicted a way of life – a hunting scene of men with spears, trees, flocks of birds, herds of deer, groups of wild boar and dogs. They made the room look dark, creepy and haunted. I was sure there'd be ghosts at night.

'Well?' the footman said with a smile, telling me it was one of the most important rooms.

'Wonderful! Splendid! I'm honoured,' I said, smiling at him with delight.

The bed was truly grand: the headboard's central panel was elaborately carved – real imagination had been used to depict flowers of various kinds. The bed itself was firm and delicately covered with smooth, pure, white silk. It made me want to jump on it. A heavy, gold-embroidered material hung over it; the fabric opened like mosquito net curtains, draping gracefully at the top end of the bed, giving it an appealing and alluring look. I was daydreaming but managed to mutter a word of thanks as the footman made his excuses and left me to my thoughts.

At first, I pitied myself in my mother's small dwelling outside the city walls. I could not quite free myself of the image of my mother sleeping in her house; until then I couldn't have been happier: my appointment and my future seemed so full of possibilities. However, everything now seemed different. I've always felt lonely whenever my thoughts deepen.

The sun shone through the large south-facing windows overlooking a neatly cut green lawn. I gazed at the slightly damaged but imposing reddish-tiled roofs of the Hor Phra Kaeo – the Emerald Buddha temple, which rose like praying hands. Bushes between the courtyard and the wall had been cut into the shapes of horses, squirrels and birds, and, to my particular delight, an elephant. As in a dream I pictured Chao Anouvong, not as a gleaming king-to-be who would fight against Siam, but as a mere man of twenty-eight, lying sleepless at night, thinking about the fact that he, a true Lao royal of ViengChan, had been reduced to taking orders from the inferior ruler of Bangkok. His antipathy towards the Rattanakosins and their aristocrats was real; he viewed them as interlopers and impostors, who dedicated all their powers to destroying the Lao nation.

From then on, I devoted my life to the tasks that were given to me. My brain was active and subtle. Like poets who love their poems, parents who love their children and citizens who love their country, I had no greater honour than to pledge my service to Chao Anouvong and LanXang. I had made my vow.

Quest for Wisdom

I can now reveal that over a year later, in 1796, Chao Anouvong decided to spend some time away from ViengChan. He wanted to relinquish his attachment to physical gratification and live a simple life. He was a very unusual royal in that he was wise, steadfast and brave, and understood that corruption derives from temptation. He felt that the best way to enlighten himself and create a sense of trust was to engage people outside the palace walls. He preferred the idea of adventure to living a quiet life in the palace, worrying about the affairs of the kingdom, and wished to travel both to refresh his mind and to sound out the opinions of the leading nobility and all the able Lao population. He preferred a life of austere simplicity, without private property or family life, and wanted to ensure the happiness of his people as a whole, rather than any particular class. In this way he was similar to the Indian prince Gohtama, who left his palace, discovered Buddhism and became the Buddha himself. Chao Anouvong felt that he didn't really exist until he'd been seen by and established a genuine connection with his people; his words would have no meaning until they could understand them. He wished to study *Dhamma* (a universal truth proclaimed by the Buddha which governs how people should behave), but primarily he intended to consult the learned senior monks (*Phra Ajarn* or *Luang Phor*) on the west bank of the Mekong, for their rhetoric, philosophy and wisdom. Around this time some of the most distinguished monks resided in the That Phanom temple in the south.

I was responsible for the upkeep of the palace's small library, and had a decent knowledge of Sanskrit and Pali, which I had learned from monks in various temples. Chao Anouvong asked politely if he might take me away from my duty and family, as one might remove a manuscript on loan, to accompany him south of the Mekong. As I was his private secretary, he'd the right to demand it. My main task was to supervise arrangements for transport, find accommodation and so forth, and then he would return me to my old job at the palace. In the end, like many loyal and useful subjects, he demanded that I should be with him forever. Perhaps, in retrospect, my ability to remember things by heart made me his favourite servant. Perhaps he regarded me as arguably the brightest and most capable mandarin at that time. Naturally, I expressed great interest in education, and in many ways possessed a reasonably quick grasp of any unfamiliar topic. His assessment of my destiny was correct, and no one in the palace said he was wrong. At the beginning I lacked confidence, but he encouraged me to be brave and do my best.

The first thing I did that morning, just over a year after I'd become his private secretary, as I did every morning, was to dust and arrange everything in an orderly fashion in the library. For some reason, I paid more attention to how everything looked, especially the palm leaf folders (*Bai Larn*) containing archives and chronicles that I'd labelled and arranged in alphabetical order. I was working like stink to make them neat and tidy and was about to sit down with my back to the big window for a rest and a read. I was feeling lonely and in need of company, so when Chao Anouvong turned up unexpectedly, I jumped to my feet, nearly dropping the books I was carrying. I lowered my head in reverence to greet him.

'Just the person I wanted to see,' he said cheerfully and came briskly towards me.

'My respects to you, Your Royal Highness. What a pleasant surprise!' I said jumpily; I was rather pleased to see him. I quickly presented him with a chair so he could sit at the window overlooking the Mekong. A shadow moved across his face. 'And what can I have the pleasure of doing for you?'

He smiled and politely started to badger me.

'Well, actually, Khoun Jon,' he said, briskly. 'I came to see whether you would like to do something different for a change, so let us get to the most urgent and immediate point.'

'Yes, certainly,' I said, turning my attention to the urgent business of the day. 'Please tell me what's on your mind, and I shall gladly do what you ask of me, if it's within my power to do so.'

'I have divined a good omen and there is one thing I would like to ask of you,' he said. 'I wish to embark on a journey and would like you to accompany me to visit other provinces (*HuaMueang*), mostly those on the right side of the Mekong. We could make Nakhorn Phanom our base, discreetly, mind you.

We could pay homage at sacred stupas and famous temples and meet lots of important people. All Lao citizens, both ordinary and noble, are important to the kingdom. You'll learn something new and gain plenty of experience.'

'How are we to get there?' I enquired.

'Boat,' he said succinctly, looking rather relaxed about it. 'A good, strong one of course.'

'Is it going to be safe?' I said, with a hint of seriousness. The river could be treacherous. Besides, at least two armed guards normally escorted him wherever he went. My main concern was for his safety, as well for my own, so I told him that it might not be a wise thing for a future king to do. 'And may I ask, how many people are you planning to take?'

'It would be just you and me,' he said confidently, as if he'd already made his mind up.

He took me by surprise, and I didn't respond immediately, thinking hard about the implications. My immediate thought was again about my mother. I remained seated on the chair with my hands submissively but defiantly together before replying. One should never refuse or object to a future king's words, for they are absolute, but I was brave enough to ask for more time because I wanted to know what he was leading me into. He'd been aware of my obstinacy before my appointment as his private secretary.

'I know that you have an elderly mother at home and can't bear to leave her. I understand that anyone who has filial affection would rather see to one's parents needs for the rest of their lives. But it's difficult to fulfil both loyalty and filial piety.'

'Perhaps you would allow me to think it over,' I pleaded.

He hesitated, but seeing that I wasn't going to be shifted, he raised his masterful voice and reproved me for my indecisiveness.

'What is there to think about, Khoun Jon?' he said crossly. 'You're fortunate, and every young man of your age should be primed for physical activity rather than merely working in a library. You could learn more and do a lot to help your country. You might even make a name for yourself.' I smiled at this, but the thought vanished in a flash. I wanted to impress him but feared I would never succeed. 'We'll improve our physical and mental strength,' he went on. 'Come with me. You'll become wiser and better able to serve the kingdom with me – much better than most. It would please me very much if you did.'

He was very insistent and I saw his point. I had a notorious aversion to any kind of harsh punishment, physical or verbal, but I wasn't prone to nerves or squeamishness. I was shrewd enough to stand my ground because I wanted to discover more about how his mind operated: after all, he would soon be king. He was perhaps beginning to demand service of others rather than just taking orders from Bangkok, as he usually had to. He rightly reminded me of my pledge to go travelling with him.

'I have my poor widowed mother to consider, so please allow me to think about it,' I said defiantly.

In silence, he stood up, smiled and then turned away to take a brief look outside. There was a long, silent pause. I felt my hands beginning to sweat with nerves, yet I was determined to make him see that I wished to make my own decision. He flashed me his smile again, but, for once, I refused to part with mine as the thought of my mother's well-being came to mind. He was badgering me into going but it wouldn't be without any resistance from me. I also knew that I would never win and would eventually have to obey his order. On the other hand, a slight frame, a weak chest due to a nasty infection at an early age, poor digestion and poor eyesight added to my woes. I was quite unfit. Nevertheless, the idea of spending some time away from the comfort of the palace during the dry season, as well as going to a traditional Lao retreat in the temple, both to refresh my mind and to learn more philosophy from the scholarly monks, was something I'd always wanted to do. It would make a change. In appreciating the honour of being asked and recognising the significance of serving him and my country, I decided not to resist.

'Your Royal Highness, please forgive me for my indecision,' I said contritely. 'I'm ready to fulfil my pledge.'

'Excellent! You'll enjoy it,' he said, standing with his hands behind his back and staring across the Mekong like a man on a mission. 'By the way, Khoun Jon,' he said, coming away from the window towards me. 'Remember, this is top secret,' he added, gazing at me as if judging whether I could keep a secret. 'It's not to be revealed until I am gone… dead! You must guard your tongue.'

'Have no fear, Your Royal Highness. I promise to keep it a secret!'

'Good,' he said trustfully. 'You may go now.'

I rose, bowed and excited, silently walked backwards toward the door. 'Khoun Jon,' he called, as I was about to reach for the door. 'There should be no distinction between us. We should be like fellow countrymen during the journey and perhaps you should address me as 'Ai' or, if you like, 'Ai Anou', as the disrespectful Siamese do.'

'That is going to be the most difficult task of all,' I said with a smile and added that considering our differing ages, we should compromise. The Lao have respect for every human value and regard themselves as being related to each other (*Pheeh-Nong*). Therefore, those born within an appropriate period are brothers (*Ai-Nong*) and sisters (*Eua-Nong*). After careful consideration we decided that I should address him as 'Anou' or just 'Ai' (elder), while he should address me as 'Jon' or just 'Nong' (younger), a true Lao custom of addressing each other according to the age gap. Nevertheless, he was very direct in using my given name when issuing an order. He was full of ideas, and I was never short of energy in realising them. We were like friends, as if made for each other, but we were careful not to expose our true identities.

It was at the end of Buddhist Lent (*Khaow Phansa*) in 1796 (236 years after the foundation of ViengChan as the nation's capital); this was followed by the boat race, then the traditional That Luang stupa festival and finally the almsgiving, held to restore merit. During Lent, monks were confined to prayer and Buddhist teaching. Some took part in transcendental meditation in the temples, or in remote places where they sat as still as a Buddha statue with their feet folded on their thighs, hands laid in their laps and eyes cast down to their bellies, breathing gently.

After Lent (*Ork Phansa*) and three months of confinement, the monks became more relaxed and approachable. They started to travel, visiting friends and family. Some of the monks and laypeople travelled from as far away as Khorat to attend the That Luang and That Phanom festivals; those who remained in their temples were able to welcome visitors.

Before the break of dawn at the beginning of January (*Daeun Jiang*), we went to the sacred grounds of Wat Si-Mueang temple, just south of the ancient city pillar (*Luck Mueang*) that had been destroyed in 1779. The junior monks were reluctant to open the Ordination Hall's (*Sim*) door as it was still very early, but when I told them who we were, they hurriedly rushed for the key to let us in. There we prayed to Lord Buddha with six candles and flowers representing the six senses, asking for safe passage and protection.

At that time, Chao Anouvong was nothing like the commanding figure he later became, his features so well known by the people that he couldn't go about without being recognised and praised. On canvas he was a handsome man with a neat moustache, long thick brows and piercing brown eyes. His forehead was prominent; his nose was rather big and straight for a Lao, his short chin jutted slightly and his lips were somewhat curled. What has happened, one wonders, to all his portrait paintings, which once adorned so many public buildings and his subjects' houses?

In the Wat Si-Mueang temple grounds that cool January morning, Chao Anouvong looked like an ordinary young Laoman. To avoid too much attention, he'd dressed himself in clothes borrowed from one of the servants. He wore below-knee-length black trousers, a fine cotton blue-and-white check sash round his waist and a dark blue silk-and-cotton shirt. He looked strangely shabby and a little thin, round-shouldered, with a slightly long neck and a large Adam's apple which plunged up and down whenever he swallowed. He seemed oddly nervous as a commoner, but outside the palace wall amongst the poor, his common dress was an everyday sight. Nevertheless, he cut a solid figure: his complexion, like my own, was much lighter than the average Lao, but was sallow and dry, and his cheeks were sunken. In short, he was the picture of poor health. He'd a slight breathing problem due to a bout of ill health and an unhealthy lifestyle in Bangkok. His eyes were protuberant but shallow, as if he lacked sleep because he'd so much on his mind, but they were full of expression, charm and vivacity. His long ears stood out in a similar way to the Buddha's. He may have been thinking of himself as the Indian Prince Gohtama (Siddartha Gautama), who had for many nights dressed like a common man and left behind the comfort of his palace under the cover of darkness in search of truth. Indeed, like Gohtama, Chao Anouvong wished to discover for himself what was happening outside the palace, so he decided to leave his princely life behind in the hope of discovering something new. He also wished to understand the past.

Well, despite my own poor health, I remember thinking I should make the most of this expedition, because it might not last long. It was a great privilege to accompany him and, frankly, I was rather looking forward to it.

We aimed first for the important old city of Nakhorn Phanom on the right bank of the Mekong, which had a long-standing allegiance to ViengChan. He wanted to see it before he became king, but his real goal was further south: to study Dhamma and philosophy from the scholarly monks at the Wat MahaThat temple of the sacred That Phanom stupa, which was said to contain the Buddha's breastbone. Chao Anouvong also wished to pay homage to the

That Sikhottabong and That Inghang stupas on the left bank, both of which were built during the reign of King Soumittatham of the ancient Kingdom of Sikhottabong in the ninth century; the ruins of the sandstone Giant Wall can still be seen there today. King Xay-Setthathirath the First had restored both stupas in a similar style to the That Luang stupa in the sixteenth century.

I carried his bag, tucked my chin down onto my chest and climbed slowly down the banks of the Mekong, where a sturdy, decent-sized pirogue was waiting for us. I was no great judge of watercraft, but she looked safe enough to me. A mist was still floating above the river as I loaded the boat with various appetising provisions and a few belongings, and then carefully sat myself down at the stern. Before he got in the boat, Chao Anouvong gave me a determined look.

'Listen carefully, Jon,' he said. 'While we're paddling along, I'll navigate, but I trust you to steer. And between us, even if the boat is in danger of capsizing in rough water, it will not sink. Do you understand?'

'*Chaow* (Yes), Your Royal Highness… *Doy, doy* (Yes, yes) *Ai*,' I stammered.

'Good. We'd better get used to this familiar way of speaking,' he said.

'*Doy…*' I said submissively. We laughed at ourselves.

After he was certain that I'd understood his words, he carefully climbed aboard and sat down with his back towards me in the prow. As usual, no Laoman could be induced to begin a journey without making sacrifices or offerings to win the favour of the gods or the spirits. Buddhism is respected alongside the worship of ancestral guardian spirits (*Phi*) that were said to live in shrines and other sacred places, such as rivers, mountains, forests and trees. Once the boat was steady, Chao Anouvong dropped flowers and offerings and poured libations into the water, calling on the guardians of the river for protection. Then he turned to look at me, gently stabbed his oar into the bank and pushed the boat out onto the smooth, empty water. With his face tilted towards the cool wind we gently paddled downstream just before dawn touched the east with red, leaving behind the waking city. We could hear life high up behind the trees on the riverbank, but after the noise of the busy city, the silence of the river was profound. The sound of the water broken by the pull of our paddles reminded us to concentrate on our course. I was trusted to steer the boat while he navigated, his eyes watching the currents of the river. He was all navigation, subtlety and invention, directing our line with his hand, dodging rocks over the rapids but telling stories on smoother sections of the river. He could be resolute and fierce, but also clever, funny and loving when need be. There was no need to choose between these qualities; they were all available to him. Looking back, I still wonder why on earth he wanted to venture out of ViengChan without a bodyguard.

While Chao Anouvong admired and enjoyed the scenery, I carefully observed it. I felt my spirits rise to the skies as I studied and memorised everything I saw to the best of my ability. How I loved travelling along the river. Like an explorer, I will now describe it in some detail.

From its source in the Tibetan plateau the mighty Mother Mekong (*Mae Nam Kong*) flows all day, never waiting, but it gives everyone a share. It enters LanXang through a majestic canyon in Yunnan China and then broadens into a basin at Luang Phrabang, ViengChan, Savanaketh and Champasak. In some places, where the riverbanks aren't too steep, water buffaloes and wild elephants came down to drink and to bathe in the shallow water. While the elephants socialised amongst themselves, using their trunks to shower their bodies, the buffaloes, only their heads, ears and sharp horns above the water, lay quietly submerged close by. Further away, rhinos stood motionless under the tall trees, chewing in the shade. We steered our boat clear so as not to disturb them, but all life seemed to be enjoying its apparent loneliness under the burning sky. A group of white cranes flew overhead; a fish jumped to catch its prey, then another. A strong wind kept biting insects away. We grew sentimental and talked about our ancestors and our country. I got some pleasure from dropping bits of sticky rice over the side of the boat and watching small fish rush madly towards them. I asked Chao Anouvong's advice on the fish, birds and other things of interest that we came across. We expressed our desire for freedom, and afterwards to spend the rest of our lives in the temple: reading, writing, debating about the future of the world and eating just enough to live.

Technically, the ancient land of LanXang was in the hands of a few feudal princes and noblemen, but most of it, especially the marginal areas – uncultivated plains, forests, the banks of the rivers and streams – belonged to the people, or to anyone who cared to claim them. In truth, Lao LanXang was a diverse place because it had always been a nation of many ethnic groups, principalities and even kingdoms. One way or another, like other nations, it has always been divided between feudal princes and the ordinary people, between east and west, north and south, rich and poor.

The prevailing wisdom is that King Khoun Loh established LanXang in

757. But it really began in the fourteenth century, when King Fah Ngum grabbed the warring factions by the throat and united all their principalities into one Lao kingdom (*Anachack*) of LanXang, with the Mekong running north-south through the middle. The surrounding countries feared Fah Ngum and agreed to his demands. Thus, LanXang territory stretched as far as Siam in the southwest (along the Phetsabun range down to Dong Phraya Fai), to LanNa in the west, Shan state in the northwest, China in the north, Vietnam in the east along the Annamite range, where ethnic Lao built their houses on stilts, and Cambodia in the south. Chao Anouvong reminded me that timeless Lao LanXang had been bestowed by nature with the raw elements of sun, water and rich soil. It was big enough and had no desire to expand, but Siam was trampling all over it. The environment shaped the Lao people and they in turn shaped the environment. The kingdom was blessed with mountains; wild, deep valleys; rivers; fertile plains; forests, raw materials and many other resources, including the most crucial ingredient of all: water.

Although LanXang was spared nature's worst disasters, heavy rain sometimes leads to flooding. While it's hard to visualise what ancient LanXang felt like, one can perhaps attempt to do so: extensive paddy fields, a world of moonshine and flickering starry nights and bright mornings, spirit-haunted forbidden forests teeming with wildlife, elephant-roamed, tiger-stalked, the cries of the gibbons and the birds from ancient, giant trees, rivers of thundering rapids and falls gleaming with silvery water gushing down from the undisturbed mountains. These were as integral to the laid-back nature of Lao life as the houses on stilts, the sticky rice and the sound of the *Khaen* and the *Phin*. It was as if the whole kingdom was heaven on earth, making LanXang a country of peace and contentment: where peace is made, not war; where lovers love winter, youth love sunshine and clear streams, old age prefers tending to the shrine of the family guardian spirits and enjoying the cool shade of home or temple.

Lao LanXang is the ancestral home of sticky rice; it even spread to Siam, but soon lost its appeal to the Rattanakosin ruling class. Eating sticky rice with your hands became anti-social in Siamese high society, and they opted for normal rice. But there was no denying the pivotal role that Lao language and sticky rice played in Siam, where millions of Lao speakers bite into sticky rice and chew *Padaek* (fermented fish) without the least idea where it all began.

Push back a little; the natives of what became Ai-Lao have always been sticky rice people. But like most people, they also had a taste for something stronger. Rice wine was the by-product of sticky rice, conveniently left to be fermented in water in a big jar: a favourite tipple during festivals or at dinner parties. Not only did it quench the thirst, but it also provided calories and brought man out of gloom into jollity. There is no stopping them when the Lao are partying.

Most countries on earth have important rivers, including Lao LanXang. River basins allow people to enjoy busy commercial and agricultural lives, and they toil away under the burning sun during the monsoon. The mighty Mekong is the river of unity and the soul and lifeline of the land – Lao LanXang's natural north-south arterial passage. Naturally, the innumerable tributaries that wind their way to her through deep, wild valleys from east to west (the Rivers Ou, Khan, Ngum, Ngiap, Kading, Bangfai, Banghiang, Donh and many more) and through the Khorat plain from west to east (the Rivers Songkham, Chi, Mun and more) are the vital veins of LanXang. They never run dry, provide fresh water, a wonderful transport system and a means of communication. In addition to forming family bonds, the rivers have been a powerful presence in Lao people's lives. Not only have they formed a close-knit and effective network around the country, but the people are heavily influenced by their seasonal fluctuations. The landscape has played a crucial role in human (and indeed animal) affairs. The Lao have been a self-reliant, patient and tolerant people since their earliest days; their keen sense of self-sufficiency gave them many advantages for survival. Together with religion (Hinduism, Buddhism and animism combined), it equipped them with the enthusiasm needed to withstand hardship and gave them a long-term view of human endeavour. They became industrious and produced what they needed as far as nature allowed.

Anyone who lived on the riverbanks, as most Lao did, had a deep awareness of water; the Lao is king of the waters as he navigates his long boat, pirogue or canoe without fear through the seething foam of the rapids. The rivers, sticky rice and the *Khaen* were central to LanXang's sense of itself. Rice determined many aspects of national life, not least the balance between the ruling class and the peasants, but also between having something to eat and starvation. There were a few ways to become rich, but the country's greatest riches are its people: amiable, hospitable, always open hearted and ready to do their best.

The Lao are great travellers, but carts are likely to break down and no one wanted to walk or ride through the forests from Luang Phrabang in the far north to Champasak in the south. So the villages and towns along both banks of the Mekong became trading posts and places to eat and stay the night. In these settlements, centuries of small rural businesses reliant on natural resources had quietly fostered an immense number of talented individuals. The Lao culture rested on what lay beneath its feet; the ground contained ample amounts of metal (gold, silver, copper and others) and minerals; its resources represented a rich heritage of natural, cultural and economic value both at regional and global level. This natural wealth would remain the backbone, the sustainable economy, of the Lao nation for generations to come, but many of the people remained poor.

Alas, the villagers weren't the main beneficiaries; instead, city entrepreneurs and men of power developed a kind of self-confidence for LanXang that not everyone found likeable. Chao Anouvong said that LanXang mustn't become rich at the expense of the common people. He believed that the landlocked country should develop and utilise its natural resources to create wealth, overcome poverty and be recognised by its haughty neighbours and the world at large.

LanXang's location may have forged an enduring natural characteristic, allowing the Lao people to play a starring role in one of LanXang's pastimes: the contemplation of a healthy life. You shouldn't grumble about anything, but make offerings and pray to heaven instead, content in the knowledge that fate governs everything. Why should anyone not want to be healthy and happy? This made a deeper imprint on the Lao national personality than you might imagine. Far from being isolated, the picturesque environment had the power to inspire awe, and the ability to encourage peace and a carefree existence. A Buddhist people with sticky rice in their veins, as it were, became a laid-back, peace-loving nation with a total lack of interest in causing trouble to anyone else. They preferred to turn the other cheek and just grin and bear it, which became a Lao mantra: never mind, nothing matters, everything goes round full circle.

While the Mother Mekong played her part in the formation of the nation, most people in the far away hills and mountains had never even seen her. And if her immensity fed into centuries of LanXang's existence, she also nurtured the Lao fondness for simplicity, a natural paradise without the artifice of man, which they loved and tended with their hands. They saw minimalism and isolation as virtues as they drifted away from the world in search of peace. The Lao subconscious has always been heavily influenced by nature: even in the city they would fantasise about remote places in the country, a walk in the forests or on the river's bank, interspersed with picnic lunches beside the rapids or the waterfalls, eating, drinking and dancing to the tune of the *Khaen*.

This rich and luxurious land is so ancient, unique and peaceful that one cherishes the very roots of the gigantic forest trees, their intertwined flowering branches disappearing into the sky and their flowers infusing the air with a powerful scent. The rosewood, the mahogany and countless other trees large and small scramble for sunlight, forming a dark green ceiling high above while wild animals roam below, and fish swim in the clear water.

Our journey became more interesting. Along the green banks of the meandering Mekong, a flock of wild ducks settled along the river edges, busily preening themselves, some with their ducklings swimming behind them upstream. A few wagtails dashed along the narrow sandbanks catching insects, and cranes stood pensively with their necks poised ready to strike at the fish in the shallow water or minced around delicately on their slim legs in search of food. Bright blue-green kingfishers hovered above the calm water edges, then, wings pulled into their sides, dived like arrows, sliding into the smooth water with scarcely a splash, then reappeared with fishes wiggling in their beaks, taking off in a flurry of beating wings. A lone cormorant with perfect, shiny plumage swam about and then disappeared into the deep. I held my breath and waited in anticipation, looking around anxiously, guessing when and where it might emerge with its prey. Suddenly, I jumped to the sound of its wings beating harshly as it lifted itself out of the water, flew away and vanished from sight.

After many hours and days of paddling and wandering downriver like fish, we were rewarded for our efforts by a mysterious but splendid view of the river, winding its way along a range of mountains. We began to talk mysteriously about haunted places. A series of enormous chalk-coloured peaks rose their gentle spires to the skies; trees perched on the summits, their reflections in the deep, placid water looking like gigantic river monsters lurking below. This was like paradise, the most beautiful sight I'd ever seen, so pure and untouched by man. A supreme happiness seized us and took our breath away.

Chao Anouvong thought it a good idea to travel overland for the rest of our journey rather than landing at the pier at That Phanom. After a week's journey, zigzagging downstream, eating delicious and succulent fish cooked over the fire and sleeping on the riverbank, we finally nosed our boat into a small, sandy bank quite a way from our destination. We moored our boat on sand and rocks along the water's edge and tied it to a pole, out of sight. It was an ideal spot, which Chao Anouvong had discovered on previous journey.

Whenever I look back, it's as if all this happened yesterday. I watched him happily walk around the waterside with his trousers hitched up in search of flat stones. With all his strength he skimmed them across the surface of the water, occasionally jumping up and down with joy like a child at the sight of five bounces. He asked excitedly whether I'd seen it; I said I had and congratulated him. I challenged him, but after numerous tries and a sore arm, I managed only three bounces at the most.

We disembarked, unloaded all our belongings and proceeded to climb a rather steep bank used by the locals. There was no handrail to pull us upward. It soon became clear that Chao Anouvong had the right technique, as though he'd done it many times before. He was sure footed, but I picked my way up slowly in search of firm steps, often nearly slipping and sliding down the slope. I pushed my hand against my knee for strength and support while the late morning sun beat down on my back. He was much stronger and fitter than I and disappeared up into the shade without serious loss of breath before I'd even reached halfway. 'Come on Jon!' I heard him shout, but I was out of breath and didn't reply. I felt encouraged to push on. When I reached the top, I paused to regain my breath and wiped the sweat from my forehead with a sodden handkerchief. He looked at me, laughing mockingly at my lack of fitness: I'd learned my first lesson. I would never underestimate anything again. With a sword on his back in Samurai style, a long knife in my hand and a big shoulder bag over my shoulder, we marched on to a nearby village.

Behind the green banks and beyond the river cliffs were rows and rows of cultivated vegetation: forests and paddy fields stretched for miles over the flat, fertile land, but all was silent under the aching tropical heat.

I observed symmetrical rice fields in the thick jungle's hinterland: bright, rich and green under a thin coating of afternoon dust during the monsoon, but now just brown straw in the baking heat of the dry season. Beyond the fields, the hills climbed gently higher and higher with a succession of different types of cultivation: isolated patches of sweet potatoes, cane sugar, papaya trees, banana trees, huge varieties of citrus fruit and vegetables, and here and there coconut trees planted like columns. Shoulders of rock pierced the covering leaves and emerged into the daylight, standing up as if in defiance of the soil, the covering that had hidden them for so long. There was a sharp, rotten smell, the true scent of nature's life cycle, as though centuries of decay had not managed to suppress the ever-dropping leaves. Yet, amongst the rows of shade, where a lush copse of trees and rhododendrons sheltered the giant rocks, birds roosted. The wild and heavily scented fallen flowers colourfully painted the ground in the stillness of silence. Small birds of paradise with fluffy bright feathers of all colours danced purposefully, darting about the tangled profusion of the undergrowth. Where the wind blew gently through the treetops, one could hear them twittering in splendid chorus.

The most irresistible quality of the jungle must be the profound mixture of silence and frightening, mysterious noises. The rich, black-and-red earth – haunted ground – became restless with weird sounds; it was a place one normally avoided. The vast forest appeared to be spooky and chilly with decay, as if spirits were clearly present but could not quite be grasped; a strange sense of power lurked in the dark. The gigantic trees were believed to be the dwelling places of powerful demon spirits (*Phi*), the keepers of this place. When walking through, eerie echoes in the hollowness of the jungle whisper all around, orchestrating in confusion somewhere nearby. A shiver runs down your spine. Once under those giant trees you can barely see the sky, while the branches tremble and squeak as the wind rushes through them. Occasionally fruits drop, crashing through the thick leaves and landing heavily on the soft ground. The earth shudders and you stop to listen and look around, muttering to yourself nervously, feeling as if something was about to pull your body down into the soil and eat it.

For many generations our ancestors had lived through fast changing times. The people cultivated the land, grew the crops, fished in the streams, rivers, lakes and ponds and hunted wild animals in the forest for food. They worked habitually throughout the seasons and their lives went on unrecorded, but LanXang had changed rapidly for the worse since becoming a Siamese vassal state. The people hated oppression and became fearful but tried to keep going anyway.

As we got closer and closer to the village, the soothing sound of *Khaen* music got louder. We went through the gates, where two huge effigies of giants stood with horrified, staring eyes and large fangs, enormous swords raised threateningly to ward off evil. Intrigued, I ambled behind Chao Anouvong.

Soon we were in the middle of the village, an ancient settlement nestling in the forest surrounded by cultivated fields. The hamlet was comprised of around forty houses grouped about a temple. Some were surrounded by bamboo fences with trellises of green vine or shrouded in great cloaks of multicoloured bougainvillea. With the molten, golden sun flaring on their thin, thatched roofs, some village elders took shelter beneath their houses, happily snoring on the planked wooden beds or dozing in their chairs in the cool shade of the trees. On hearing and seeing the arrival of strangers, the dogs started from their sleep and snarled at us. The cats hissed and dashed madly away. The chickens and their chicks scattered and ran into the bushes to hide, as if we were hawks swooping down on them. The villagers turned and looked at us in dismay, as if they'd never seen strangers before. Soon the dogs calmed down and came towards us with tails wagging, and the chickens emerged from hiding and flapped their wings, squawking: cluuuuuuck… cluck-cluck-cluck, cluck, pecking on the ground, calling to their fluffy yellow chicks to come out.

A moment later a group of vociferous, eager children appeared, like ants attracted to sugar. We were certainly guilty of breaking the peace but needed transport, for which we would of course pay. They grabbed us excitedly by the arms and then marched us along, pointing at nothing.

We passed many houses with wooden columns resting on dark stones, granaries with vegetable and herb gardens beside them. Under these houses with their thatched or tiled roofs, young girls were focusing on their looms while the women spun the silk threads or kept flies away from their sleeping babies; old women were using small hand gins to separate the cotton from its seeds. The men were also busy with their work, smoking mild cheroots while sharpening knives or axes on whetstones, repairing their fishing nets and tools or making mats and bamboo baskets.

A genuine welcome is always extended to strangers and visitors in Lao homes. Some old people were taking a nap or sitting on the veranda, where a big, rounded terracotta water jar stood with a coconut dipper beside it, and pots of blooming orchids and other flowers hung. The elderly men with their impressively long, grey beards and wearing baggy shorts took a curious glance, smiled broadly and flashed their eyes in answer to our greeting but did not reply. They then genially and courteously invited us to have a drink and a rest. Some greeted us in complete silence, gazing at us as impassively as lizards, or paid no attention to our presence.

Chao Anouvong rightly reminded me to guard my tongue about who we really were. It was important that our expedition was kept secret so that Bangkok did not become suspicious. We were just ordinary people travelling around the country.

Our transport arrived – an elephant and its mahout, suitable for a two-day journey. We couldn't decide which was the beast and which was the beauty, but we needed them both. I remember thinking that at least the elephant had small, friendly eyes, large, thin ears and a soft heart. I got the impression that the mahout, with his heavily tattooed legs below the knee giving the impression of trousers, was kind and gentle. He moved his skinny body lazily, brushed his dusty backside and came towards us.

'*Sabaidee*. I am Morn,' he greeted us with a laid back voice before asking politely, 'Where have you come from? And where are you going?' Chao Anouvong told him where we wanted to go in a hoarse voice. 'My elephant is at your disposal,' replied the mahout, 'and I'm at your service to escort you to the holy That Phanom temple where Phra Ajarn Khoon lives.'

'Thank you. I'm sure you know the route well,' Chao Anouvong said.

In silence, the mahout looked at us with widening eyes and bowed reverently. He moved sluggishly and tended to the bull elephant that he called Siho, who was adorned with a bell and whose back was long and curved like a bow. Elephants can swim but can't jump and are afraid of mice, which can run up their trunks. Their sight is said to be dismally poor, but they have a good sense of smell and superb hearing. Siho stretched his big trunk towards us as we approached him. Chao Anouvong gave him a banana which he seized with his trunk; it quickly disappeared into his mouth. He was a giant beast and very intimidating at close quarters. His small, brown eyes seemed friendly enough, but I was rather frightened of him. I could easily have walked under him. Did I? No, I certainly did not! I didn't want to end up being squashed by him!

Before boarding and taking my very first elephant ride, the story of 'Nang Phomhom' came to mind and I wondered whether Siho would let me get on his back. (My grandmother had told me that Nang Phomhom was a girl with scented hair who believed that the Elephant king (*Kudsalo Xang*) was her father and only she was allowed to ride on his back; anyone else who tried would fall off and be killed.) Indeed, I was very nervous. Luckily, with the mahout safely in charge of Siho and with the help of the villagers pushing from below, we found ourselves on board. But in my panic, I embarrassingly managed to climb on the wrong way round and briefly sat on Siho's neck facing backwards, which produced roars of laughter. I quickly climbed up to join Chao Anouvong on the howdah. We set off immediately to great cheers, leaving the villagers to revert to their normal lives. I looked down anxiously at the long drop but as Siho gained momentum, I felt elated, blessed and rather smug. I smiled and whispered to Chao Anouvong, who looked comfortable, that I hoped I might enjoy this.

The howdah was made from rattan for strength and lightness; Siho was a massive, strong, mature, plodding bull with frighteningly long pointed shiny white tusks and a powerfully thick, strong trunk with which he gave an occasional ear-shattering trumpet. His head and neck were draped with red flowers to ward off evil. His broad ears moved back and forth gently like fans.

The rider was wearing shorts (*Phahthio*) and a slightly torn white shirt; his head was wrapped in a faded red cloth like a turban, the loose end of which he used to wipe the sweat from his face and neck. He sat firmly, his thin legs spreading right over the elephant's neck. He controlled the creature with his knees and feet behind the big flapping ears and used sharp commands. Siho was most obedient, but should he disobey, the quick-tempered mahout reprimanded him fiercely by rapping the sharp end of the instrument, his *ankus*, on top of his bony head. It drew some blood and Siho squeezed his eyes shut and trumpeted in objection. I felt his pain and Chao Anouvong told the mahout to be gentle.

I was glad I didn't have to walk, but the journey was a torment, attempting to keep one's body in the correct position in the rattling, creaking, lurching howdah high above ground. I was afraid of heights and felt unwell at first, thinking I was going to fall off when dizziness struck me, but slowly I got used to it and then loved it.

Our journey was slow and miserable. The ground was still partly wet after a prolonged rainy season; our path was often blocked by fallen trees which Siho threw aside like twigs. In places, along the narrow tracks, a tunnel of cobwebs filled with big, long-legged spiders confronted us. The mahout spent hours wielding a bamboo stick, breaking the webs out of the way. I often panicked when I felt something crawling down my neck. We were badly bogged down by late afternoon, and it would be impossible to find a place to stay before dusk. The sun was sinking fast in the west and darkness soon fell. With no settlement in sight, we built a simple shelter under the giant trees and the mahout put down flowers and offerings at its foot and poured libations, calling upon the guardians of the forest for protection. We slept there in discomfort through the wretched night, wondering which of us might make a decent meal for hungry beasts of prey.

When the tender dawn touched the east with red, I woke up shivering, my teeth chattering. The dawn chorus of birdsong, woodpeckers tapping on the trees and the call of gibbons had stirred me. Despite the morning sun shining through the leaves, I felt stiff and damp with cold from the dew. For a moment I had no idea where I was or how I'd got there. Trying to remember, I saw Siho standing behind the trees and realised we were under a giant tree in the forbidden forest (*Pa Himmapanh*). Chao Anouvong was sitting by the fire and eating. He looked at my grim face as he glanced across to the elephant. The mahout was already preparing him for the journey. I stayed silent but knew it was time to move on.

I peeled off my blanket to find my clothes wet with dew. I'd suffered nightmares and hadn't got much sleep; I wondered whether Siho had slept at all. He looked happy enough with a big stack of bamboo leaves for breakfast, while I made do with a handful of cold sticky rice and a banana. The treetops shook and the gibbons were looking down at my upturned face from high above. I put a banana on the ground, and they fought it out amongst themselves. When we had warmed ourselves at the fire and the day began to grow hot, we set off.

Chao Anouvong was anxious to reach our destination before nightfall. For a faster pace the mahout prodded the elephant behind the ears with his feet, or poked his head with the sharp *ankus*, causing blood to run down the side of his bony cheeks as if he were in *musth*. Siho kicked up a thick cloud of red dust and trumpeted in protest. I gave Chao Anouvong a look of disapproval but said nothing.

We approached the That Phanom temple before sunset. Streams of excited children followed us on both sides while passers-by stopped in amazement, staring open-mouthed. Our elephant reached the temple gate just before it was shut and Chao Anouvong told the mahout to stop and let us down so we could walk to the abbot's residence. He climbed down carefully and walked on while I jumped off Siho's back as he knelt on all four knees. I stretched my stiff limbs and followed him excitedly. It was wonderful to see That Phanom again – it was typical of the LanXang architectural style in that the main structure towards the summit was similar to That Luang in ViengChan. I'd first visited at the age of eight when my mother brought me there for the annual prayer festival. I quickened my stride towards the main gilded temple gate as if it were a homecoming.

'Slow down, Jon,' Chao Anouvong called me back. Realising I was ahead of him, when I should always keep my distance behind, I stopped to let him pass. 'The place isn't going to run away from you. Now, let's not draw too much attention to ourselves,' he whispered as he walked past me, discreetly putting his hand on my shoulder. He strode on ahead, swinging his arms gently. I noticed his once brilliant white shirt was stained with sweat. He seemed unconcerned.

That Luang and That Phanom are two of the holiest stupas in LanXang, which the pious wish to see at least once in their lives. They are sites of annual celebrations, meditation and the recital of poetic stories. During the festival, Lao people from all over LanNa and LanXang (but not the Siamese from Siam) come to pay homage, to celebrate and to honour the shrine. They dress in their finery, carry offerings, and parade along the wide avenue leading towards the gilded gate. Dancers and musicians perform before cheering and admiring crowds along the way. The procession ends at the temple grounds where monks chant prayers and the people gain merit by making offerings of food, money and flowers. And then, while the monks chant, worshippers pour libations in memory of their ancestors and loved ones. It was a spectacle I remembered well.

We entered the main gilded gate and walked through the temple (*Wat*) courtyard surrounded by high walls. Within was the Ordination Hall or Chapel (*Wihan* or *Sim*), its tiered roofs curving and rising upwards like praying hands to house the sacred idols for worship; the stupas (*Phrachedis* or *That*) contained relics or Buddhist images; the monks' dormitory (*Kuti*); the donation or eating hall (*Hor Chaek*); the monastic library (*Hor Tay*) to keep sacred books (*Bai Larn*); the Buddhist teaching library (*Hor Tay Pidok*); the school temple (*Hong Haen Wat*); the pavilion or rest house (*Sala*) for public use; and the drum and gong tower (*Hor Khong*). Scattered around were a shady banyan tree, letting down its branches and spreading like an entire wood, sacred Bo trees, frangipani blossoms (*Plumeria*), palms, mango trees and the red hibiscus (*Rosa-sinensis*) that attracts butterflies.

We reached the chief monk's residence as the sun was setting and climbed the stairs to a veranda where a cheerful novice monk (*nane*), about ten years old, greeted us. He told us that he hoped to be ordained as a monk at the age of twenty-one and experience nirvana. He offered us some very dusty old rattan chairs. I gently lowered my aching bottom to a soft seat which gave off a spray of dust, making me sneeze violently three times. Pigeons took off from the roof. It was a relief to be sitting still. We waited.

Chao Anouvong stood with his hands clasped behind his back in readiness to greet the chief monk, keeping his thoughts to himself, so preoccupied was he with what was about to happen. His eyes were red from tiredness, his hair also reddish with dust from the journey, but he still asked me how I was and expressed complete satisfaction when I replied that I was fine. He just smiled a little and winked when I asked how he was feeling.

I told him later that while waiting for the abbot to appear, I nearly fell into a deep sleep. In fact I think I did, for how long I could not tell, but it felt like hours, not minutes. Fortunately, I was saved from further embarrassment by the squeaking noise of the door. The novice had come to warn us that the venerable abbot would soon be with us. I awoke, quickly got out of the chair and slipped outside the veranda where a terracotta jar of clean water and a towel were kept for visitors. I used the smallest coconut shell ladle to pour the water into my cupped hand to rinse my face and neck and refresh myself.

Chao Anouvong on the other hand demonstrated those remarkable powers of recuperation which I've observed to be the distinguishing mark of a true leader. I noticed that he'd already washed, his hair was combed, and his blue-and-white check shawl was draped over his left shoulder. No one would have guessed he hadn't slept much for the past few nights. We sat close to each other and exchanged smiles to keep calm. He said I'd done well; at that moment I realised for the first time just how close we'd grown over just a few days. Although I'd begun as his private secretary, I was now a true travelling companion. When the abbot appeared, Chao Anouvong, as ever, was in his element as he immediately lifted his hands to greet him.

'*Sabaidee*, Phra Ajarn, please accept our respects,' he said, paying obeisance to the abbot and revealing himself as Anou. I followed suit by lifting my hands in supplication and introduced myself as Jon.

'*Sabaidee* and welcome,' the abbot said pleasantly. 'I am Phra Ajarn Khoon. Where have you two come from on this visit to our temple? Your looks and manners make me think you're both sons of noblemen, and your accent reminds me of ViengChan.'

'Yes, that's correct, from the festival of That Luang ViengChan,' Chao Anouvong replied gracefully.

'Very glad to see you both. Sadly I missed it this year, but never mind; and what's the purpose of your visit to us?' the abbot said.

Phra Ajarn Khoon was pleased and excited when Chao Anouvong said that he wanted to learn Dhamma and philosophy from him but expressed doubt as to whether he could really bring about the transformation that my master desired. He observed that Chao Anouvong seemed to possess moral integrity and toughness; his intellectual eagerness made him determined and fond of hard work. He was the right sort of man to absorb himself in philosophy.

He asked Chao Anouvong whether he knew of the sacred trinity – Buddha, Law and Monk (*Phuto*, *Thammo* and *Sangkho*) – as well as the five important precepts: not to kill, not to steal, not to lie, to abstain from impurity and from intoxicating drinks. He declared that he was and was comfortable with them. He said that he was a lover of wisdom, one of the most beautiful things in the world, and that his mind was in a state halfway between knowledge and ignorance. However, Phra Ajarn Khoon promptly told him that he probably had nothing to teach such a sensible-looking person.

'I don't wish to quibble, but if I can make someone wiser, then others might follow,' said Ajarn Khoon.

'I am still young and willing to take a chance,' Chao Anouvong responded, 'and put myself in your hands to use whatever means at your disposal to make me a better person.'

'Tell me, then,' Phra Ajarn Khoon said, 'do you really want to become wise, and then even wiser still? Not to be ignorant? Do you really mean it? Are you serious?'

Chao Anouvong confidently stated that he wished to change; that by studying Dhamma and philosophy, he might be able to learn how to wisely exercise wisdom and virtue. I listened very carefully to what the chief monk had to say next. I gazed at both, expecting to hear awe-inspiring stuff. Miraculously, after Chao Anouvong had established a moment of empathy, sufficient to leave the abbot feeling he'd been specially complimented, we were sent to bed exhausted in the guest quarter (*Sala*). I certainly was glad and slept like a log!

Next morning, I was pleasantly woken by the call of cockerels instead of guards, and we rose at dawn. After a light breakfast, I accompanied Chao Anouvong to the Grand Ordination Hall (*Sim*). We strode along and he whispered to me to stay close by and remain inconspicuous. I draped my small, colourful, woven-cotton shoulder bag containing books and writing materials across my thin chest. I thought the lecture was going to be on a one-to-one basis. As we approached the hall's entrance, I peeled off.

'Where do you think you're going, Jon?' he called. I replied that I was going to sit under the shady mango trees to read and write something, like a good and obedient person. 'No, you're not. You're coming with me!' he commanded. 'In order to acquire some knowledge that might be useful for you in the future, I've obtained permission for you to be with me. I wish you to learn a little philosophy, so I have someone clever to talk to during our long stay. Now come along.'

Therefore, to begin with, he and I lived like brothers. We dined together, slept in the same room and would often talk and laugh about everything and anything late into the night, the birds and the bees included. He taught me plenty: I learned that some plants have medicinal properties, that elephants never forget, that the Mekong contains huge catfish, stingrays and dolphins, that some snake bites can kill, that mosquito bites spread malaria, that the male camel, unlike other quadrupeds, pees in reverse because its operational tool points backwards instead of forwards, that some old men like to have young wives and that hedgehogs mate standing up. We sat long of an evening, examining and sharing our thoughts, talking quietly about art, history, nature, literature, justice and philosophy. But I was not over fond of discussing religion and politics because, without common sense, both were a source of disagreement. However, despite both of us thinking we were perfect, we clearly weren't – even gold can't be pure, and a diamond may have its flaws. At any rate I certainly wasn't perfect, although I was intrigued with science and maths and had an eye for detail. At that time, I wasn't really able to understand of the sort of serious discussion that always leads to a specific conclusion. It was a hard task listening to him lecturing me, with his wealth of important knowledge, as if he were preparing me for the battlefield or for running the kingdom, a matter of life and death. In the end I used to sulk in submission, my simple, weak head hanging low in defeat.

I obeyed him and, like an acolyte, followed him into the *Sim*. I couldn't very well refuse: it was a great privilege. At first I was in awe at the sight of the high-ceilinged, ornate hall. It was dim inside and the small, glassless windows on both sides didn't help. A strong aromatic smell choked my throat and almost punctured my lungs, causing me to hold my breath momentarily. A wisp of white smoke spiralled from a row of flickering beeswax candles and small bowls of burning minerals; large and small Buddha statues, all gazing spiritually downwards with pointed, spear-like extensions on top of their heads, either sat or stood. The biggest of the lot had shiny, black, stone eyes, sitting centrally with folded legs with his left arm resting across his lap, his right palm hung over his right leg, the fingers pointing delicately downwards. Phra Ajarn Khoon – in the posture of the Buddha, and Chao Anouvong – sitting cross-legged – faced each other on the cool and well-polished floor; several steps away, out of the Buddhas' gaze, I bent slightly forward, listening attentively and discreetly taking notes.

Phra Ajarn Khoon was a philosophical nobleman from Khorat city; he'd become a novice monk as a young boy and then been ordained to full monastic orders at the age of twenty-one, becoming deeply religious and moralistic and arriving to study at the That Phanom temple. He'd regularly entered a hermitage at Lent, living on nothing but boiled rice with vegetables and herb tea, becoming celebrated for his exemplary life and much respected. He was also hugely knowledgeable about plants and herbs with medicinal properties, which he grew around the temple. He sometimes collected rare specimens from the forest to be sorted and laid out to dry, which he then ground into powder and kept in airtight bamboo containers. He became a leading teacher and preacher of the temple, a title achieved only after years of dedication to hard learning and studying many old Buddhist texts. He'd a deep voice and took command at prayer time, giving an impression of quiet confidence and magical power. He was well built, with a lean, intelligent face, amused-looking brown eyes and a newly shaven head that shone in the sunlight. He was a foremost orator with vast wisdom and subtlety and could recite and chant every prayer and teach in many different styles. Now he was in his forties and had attained such an eminent position, a novice of his own choosing would tend to his needs, waiting on him and serving him at breakfast and lunchtime (only two main meals are allowed each day, which must be eaten before noon). Pious villagers and visitors brought food and also served the monks and novices. After lunch no more solid food is allowed, but water and fruit juice can be taken.

In general, novices aged between nine and twelve years old would perform the most menial tasks for the senior monks, as if they were apostles or servants.

They were bound by the strict law of the Buddha's doctrines, which may not be tempered with. Most formal education originated in the temple schools, as they were by far the most respected institutions in the country. Intelligent children learned how to read and write Sanskrit, studied the teachings of the Buddha and took part in religious discussion before being promoted to the higher monastic grade. For physical exercise, monks expended their energy tending to the medicinal plants and herb garden and keeping the temple buildings in good repair and the temple courtyard free from debris and weeds; they soon acquired athletic figures and toned muscles. Fully ordained monks would normally become Sanskrit and Pali scholars. The learned ones would always gladly talk about scholarly subjects as well as devoting themselves to meditation, study, reading and writing and teaching the younger generations. In addition to free food and lodging, the monks received money and gifts from merit-makers, devotees and pilgrims. Every monk rose at dawn for prayer; some would then collect alms from inhabitants outside the temple, after which they ate breakfast in the donation hall (*Hor Chaek*) before returning to their quarters or schools for study. They finished at sunset each day in communal religious exercises, chanting prayers facing the Buddha statues in the *Sim* before retiring early to their beds.

Phra Ajarn Khoon spent many hours each day in the temple's shady precinct or cloister, with Chao Anouvong and sometimes myself sitting close by. He turned out to be not only willing but even eager to answer questions. He dreamt and talked about enlightenment and the future reform of society but was clear-sighted enough not to offer false hope. He said a good, brave man should renounce nirvana to help his fellow citizens. He disliked loose ends and blurred edges, so his explanations were always rigorous. His style of teaching was quintessentially Lao, but also diverse: one was to get his students to read and learn by heart. He patiently taught Chao Anouvong Dhamma and philosophy, memorising methods and then how to deliver a speech.

Chao Anouvong welcomed the memory work because his eyesight was poor in dim light. He sat on the floor with folded legs and a straight back so as not to emphasise the superiority of his birth, while the abbot stood before him or paced around punctuating his questions with gestures. He'd to memorise texts, poems, verses and famous quotations, with flies and mosquitoes buzzing about and geckos scattering on the walls and ceilings in search of insects. It was clearly not just an opportunity for Chao Anouvong to show off his intelligence; he answered all the questions, and the abbot was hard put to hold his own. He seemed to enjoy listening to the abbot's expositions a great deal, until at last he felt more confident and was sure he had his teacher's measure. I was deeply impressed and felt genuine admiration for his presence of mind; if I truly believed in reincarnation, I would like to come back as him in my next life.

One day after lunch the abbot took Chao Anouvong out of the cool, sacred hall into the midday sun and told him to recite one of his speeches, his audience only dogs dozing in the shade, pigeons cooing and the cicadas droning on the fruit trees. Phra Ajarn Khoon spoke without any embarrassment and with the assurance of a knowledgeable holy man. He explained that speaking to a mass of important people was comparable to coming out from hiding: it required bravery and a show of confidence: that was how you gained an audience's sympathy. One could also command attention by one's ideas or arguments; it was easy to make people happy and laugh, but much more difficult to make them sad and cry. Then he joked, 'And the hardest job of all to silence the background mutters of a noisy Lao audience, who always seem to be chattering away!'

Chao Anouvong somehow thrived on memorising speeches and therefore had no need to read out a text or consult a sheaf of notes. He marvelled at the improvement in his health and appearance brought about by greater self-belief. While pacing around with his hands behind his back, Phra Ajarn Khoon told him that communication skills – body language, eye contact, voice projection, highlighting key points – could be learnt; the rules were simple, but you still needed a lot of practice. You should stand upright, keep your neck straight and your shoulders still, and don't twiddle your fingers. You should raise both palms of your hands, like the Phrabang Buddha statue, to call for attention and for calm, and of course keep looking in the same direction and never fumble for the right word. Chao Anouvong looked frightfully serious as he closely followed the abbot's instructions.

I acted as a kind of extension of him, like an extra hand and foot. I was indispensable to him partly because I was truly loyal and could run fast and fetch him whatever he wanted. Mind you, he sometimes seemed to test my loyalty by making unexpected requests of me, but it was all worth it.

I stood discreetly out of sight among the shadows under the shady trees and watched him being put through his paces with admiration. I glanced up at the blue sky, where the sun had passed its zenith. Chao Anouvong stole a glance at me as if to assure himself of my approval. Even now I can still picture the rapture of his confident face, flushed red and sweating in the glaring heat, turning towards his mentor. Then, like a performer, he raised both hands chest high and placed them naturally together with all his fingers extended; he told me afterwards this was a habit he'd acquired as a young boy when displaying submission to the king of Siam. Finally he bowed his head in reverence towards the seated Phra Ajarn Khoon, acting as his imaginary audience. I turned my gaze at the astonished abbot and held my breath in anticipation.

After a short silence, the abbot got to his feet and lavishly congratulated him in a hoarse voice. 'Well done, very good (*deelai*), I'm amazed at you. You've understood my teaching well. You are proficient in oratory and rhetoric, and you have become a wiser man.' Then, without any hesitation, he gestured with his outstretched finger across the blazing temple courtyard to the outside world and said, 'Now you can leave. Go and find your destiny, rule ViengChan, conquer Bangkok, bring back the sacred Emerald Buddha, restore LanXang and make your dreams come true.' He muttered some of the Lord Buddha's sacred words in blessing. 'Good luck (*Sokdee*),' he added, and smiled.

I'd never seen Chao Anouvong smile properly before, a big smile of self-gratification as if he'd found the solution to his ideas. On hearing Phra Ajarn Khoon's praises, he became a different man, a sincere, friendly, happy man with a soul, not the fearsome persona as heir to the throne that he'd learned from the Rattanakosin system. He'd tasted the respect and freedom denied to him in Bangkok. He'd started living. He heaved an ecstatic sigh of relief, his sunken cheeks filled out and his tired eyes brightened. His white teeth briefly flashed in the sunlight but vanished when he turned towards me: he was trying to control his emotions. I smiled at him but suspected he must have revealed his real identity to the monk. I asked him afterwards why Phra Ajarn Khoon had said, 'rule ViengChan' and 'conquer Bangkok'. He admitted that he'd told him everything in confidence, for he was a discreet man of Dhamma, happy to have him as a student and troubled by Siamese oppression. Even though monks weren't directly affected, the people were still suffering. 'We can trust him, Khoun Jon,' he whispered, 'but our lips must remain sealed to everyone else.'

All very well, but how could all this be achieved? How do you 'conquer Bangkok' and 'make your dreams come true' with no resource other than your own talent and wisdom? He'd been rooted up from ViengChan at the age of twelve and kept in Bangkok for many years under house arrest, an object of scorn and amusement, wasting away under the glaring eyes of the arrogant

Siamese, when he should have been learning how to run the affairs of his ancient LanXang kingdom in ViengChan. His beloved mother must have been longing to see him. He told me how from the very start he'd felt bored, lonely and resentful, growing up and playing war games in a secret garden with his boyhood friend Prince Itsarasunthon, who was at least civil to him. His friendship for the prince began straight away; they'd been born the same year, though Chao Anouvong was about nine months younger. Despite being a hostage, Itsarasunthon treated him as an equal. They were almost like one soul in two bodies and shared most things. Chao Anouvong wasn't a quarrelsome person and kept his misgivings to himself, but as expected, the Siamese prince could sometimes be a little aggressive.

They often observed the heavens at night. The stars were more divine than anything else the human eye could reach. Chao Anouvong told me he deliberately pointed at some bright stars in the northeast and told Itsarasunthon that he was feeling homesick. They were taught indoors when they needed to write or draw and there were lessons on protocol, economics and politics, as well as ideology tuition to reinforce the young students' commitment to 'Rattanakosinism'. Chao Anouvong dutifully learned all about Siam. He showed an early aptitude for Siamese language and history but nursed a secret contempt for the Rattanakosins' ideology and superiority complex. He concealed his inner self, being Siamese on the outside but someone quite different inside. Although part of the system, his feelings of disillusionment grew by the day. Chao Anouvong and Itsarasunthon walked in the secret gardens and talked of ethics, politics, justice, virtue, friendship and love. The Siamese prince was very knowledgeable about the birds and the bees and knew where babies came from, but I couldn't possibly comment on what he said to Chao Anouvong. They discussed friendship a lot, which they recognised as one of the most important things in life. They agreed there should be no discrimination between them; they thought deeply of the root causes of the many problems in their world. Itsarasunthon understood why Chao Anouvong was aggrieved by the Siamese invasion and the loss of the Emerald Buddha.

On one occasion, they were sitting in a secluded spot, out of view, eating cashew nuts. A young, intelligent, creamy-brown palace dog sitting close by pricked up its ears, watching and listening with its tongue hanging out and begging. Itsarasunthon shooed it off because it was after a nut he was holding. But Chao Anouvong was a tremendous animal lover: the sight of a gentle and humble dog always gave him pleasure and gladdened his heart. He considered dogs to be man's best and most faithful friend. When the dog started to nose him, he said, 'Down, boy. Sit!' and dropped one of his cashews on the ground for the dog to snatch up. He stroked the dog's head, and it raised its forelegs, pawing at him with much wagging of its long tail, fawning on him as if he were the master. Itsarasunthon suddenly stood up and said, 'Anouvong, listen, when we are big… when I am a man and a king… do you understand what I'm saying?'

'When your father the king dies you mean?' said Anouvong, smiling to himself and stroking the dog.

'Yes! That's right,' Itsarasunthon said courageously. 'Then, when I go to war, will you be my ally and bring your brave Lao men to fight my enemies alongside me?'

'We always have done. You shouldn't forget what our king Xay-Setthathirath has done for Ayutthaya Siam. But listen, please don't be angry, this is important,' Chao Anouvong continued softly. 'Do you know that it was wicked for Siam to invade LanXang? I dare say you know all about it, but did the king tell you about the sacking of ViengChan?'

'What… Oh yes. Yes, of course he did. For the glory of Siam, we all knew about it; we made an example of your father, as we do of anyone who doesn't obey us. Never mind.' After a short pause, Itsarasunthon said brusquely, 'Anouvong, you must pledge to me now!'

'And may I ask what is to become of me if I don't?' said Chao Anouvong defiantly.

'Don't be a fool; if you refuse, I'll make you sorry,' threatened the Siamese prince. 'I swear it by my father's head.'

Chao Anouvong told me he immediately knelt down, gently pushed away the young dog that was trying to lick his face, folded his hands and swore, 'Yes, of course I would. We're close friends; I would rush straight in front of you amongst the enemy.' And with his hands still clasped formally, he spoke eloquently, asking Itsarasunthon whether he would pledge himself too.

'I am the Siamese king's son and neither make vows nor keep them,' he answered, staring down at him. 'What do you want me to swear to?'

'Not to enslave my people and keep them in Siam against their will. Not to make LanXang part of Siam. To invoke the words sworn at the That Si-SongHuck shrine. To return the Emerald Buddha to ViengChan. Not to keep me in Bangkok. You must swear all that by your father's head and call down a death-curse on yourself and your family if you break your oath.'

'You could be killed for saying that!' Itsarasunthon asserted. He looked over his shoulders, then said softly, 'My father would slap my face if he heard I'd sworn an oath to you, but you're my friend. I feel sorry for you and want to do the right thing without anyone else knowing.'

Surprisingly, Chao Anouvong told me, Itsarasunthon stood before him with his hands folded, looked up to heaven and swore to keep faithful to his oath until the sky fell and crushed him, or the earth opened and swallowed him, or the sea and the Chaophraya river rose and submerged Bangkok and drowned him and his people.

Chao Anouvong told Itsarasunthon that his father, King Chulaloke, should not only be a truly better man than his subjects but should recognise and learn to pity Lao LanXang. He also told him that he (Chao Anouvong) was no longer a child who needed toys, but a man who needed to put his mind and body to better use. The Siamese prince put his arm around Chao Anouvong's shoulders and said sorry. They embraced and carried on being boys.

Chao Anouvong also revealed to me that he was tormented from dawn until dusk, scrubbing the floor in the morning and performing hard physical exercises in the evening, including running, lifting, press-ups, jumping and so on. If he said he was still hungry after dinner, he was mercilessly told to speak in the 'proper' Siamese language, using the word *Yi Sip*, not *Sao*, for twenty; *Mie*, not *Bor*, for no; *Aroy*, not *Saeb* for delicious; and *Ruck* not *Huck* for love. Asking for more was a punishable offence; anyway, too much food was bad for your health. Life in the Rattanakosin citadel was dreary: it was a prison, built by slaves to keep the royals penned in – a physical manifestation of their insecurity as much as their insanity. In the evening all the gates were closed well before nightfall, after which guards went through the whole palace to make sure everything was in order, their shouts ringing menacingly in the oppressive stillness. In contrast to the brisk, high life in the affluent city, nights within the palace enclosure seemed peaceful, but no one dared speak about what went on behind closed doors. A dim atmosphere of terror emanated from the shrines of the dynastic ancestors, making the whole place feel like an enormous medieval prison.

They started to poke fun at him because, by and large, he found it objectionable to adapt to Siamese customs. Despite his principles, however, he served the Siamese court contentedly, even though he was fiercely tenacious of his Lao habits: eating sticky rice, papaya salad and grilled chicken with his hands and pouring libations. He bluntly told them that they were *Tai Sayam* Bangkok while he was a *Tai Lao* ViengChan; he insisted the ancient Lao word for *Tai* was a generic term meaning people (*Khon*) and did not denote a specific *Tai* race, while the Lao word for January is *Jiang*, followed by *Yi* for February. Therefore *Yi* couldn't simply be claimed as a Siamese word. He rejected the stereotype of Lao people being rustic and backward. When he said, 'They're a sophisticated people with a talent for government and a sensitive relationship with the natural world,' he didn't get much more food that day.

Chao Anouvong enunciated and repeated the Siamese language briskly during lessons and was soon able to write it perfectly. But whenever he was with his compatriots (*Phuean HuamZard*) inside the Lao enclaves in Bang Yi Khan, Bang Khun Phrom, Ban Lao Phuan, Ban Lao, Ban Thi Kham, Ban Mo, Ban Kuai and even in the Grand Palace, he happily and proudly spoke in broad Lao. Despite his skill at speaking it, he disliked the Siamese tongue. His tutor thought this a disgrace, especially considering his older brothers spoke it like natives. He learnt many Siamese books by heart but longed to return to ViengChan. When he obeyed when asked to praise the Siamese King Naresuan the Great, he earned plenty of applause. However, if he disobeyed, he was called a stubborn country boy with the head of a buffalo, seized by the scruff of the neck and thrashed, drawing blood. He never cried or begged but prayed there was pity somewhere in the world. He learnt to conceal his emotions and to conform to Siamese ways; his ingrained common sense taught him that tittle-tattle could cost him his life. He became increasingly critical of the Rattanakosins' ideology, which he feared would destroy the love and affection between the two nations. He grew up around secrets, learning to keep his mouth shut and saying nothing to his older brothers. He managed to control himself doggedly, without complaint.

Wherever he went in Siam he took Lao LanXang with him and felt homesick and sad. Although he was fluent in the rather haughty and old-fashioned version of Siamese spoken in Bangkok, he felt himself hard done by because some of the palace staff, and many people around the city, openly spoke Lao to each other. On the other hand, to emphasise their dominance, the Siamese would deliberately pretend not to understand or to speak Lao. The Lao people had been skilfully spinning and weaving silk in their own homes for centuries, but Siamese homespun clothes were too harsh for his skin, despite being good enough for the king of Siam's sons. He was often sent out shirtless to pick up leaves around the palace courtyard, so his soft, pale skin would be hardened and darkened, but he refused to accept that the Lao people who'd been brought to Siam would ever resemble the natives there.

I imagined that Chao Anouvong probably quite enjoyed Bangkok without liking it or being aware of it. One would have assumed that he'd developed a lasting hatred of, and a fascination for, all things Siamese: pretentiousness, material possessions, boastfulness, haughtiness, a love of fashion and drama, high-society gossip, bitchy asides and revolting prejudices, but none of these had any effect on him; he simply reinvented himself when he was in Siamese company without forming any lasting emotional attachment. He'd been inducted into the deepest secrets of the Siamese ruling house, gaining a comprehensive insight into Siam's past, present and future. As a foretaste of what he might become if he joined the Rattanakosin set-up, he witnessed the great physical and symbolic divisions that split the country.

Chao Anouvong was a poor, clever boy from LanXang who was shaped, twisted, damaged and very nearly destroyed by the Siamese establishment. The enjoyment of traditional Siamese privileges could have become a badge of honour for him, but instead it made him sit up, view his wasted life in the mirror and swallow hard. Although immersed in culture, he clearly felt betrayed; the impact must have been considerable on a sensitive and independent-minded young boy far from home, who'd lost his father at fourteen and hadn't seen his broken-hearted mother for a very long time. He'd learned the hard way that everything can suddenly change for the worse, and he had to stay alert to the possibility of future conflict. Although he grew to despise the Rattanakosin establishment, this never extended to the entire Siamese nation: he acquired a taste for Siamese customs and a perfect command of the Siamese language. Most teenage boys are ready for rebellion given the right conditions: the Rattanakosins' ideology provided the seed, Bangkok the soil.

He was now a man of great wisdom, born in a small kingdom that he was trying to prevent from becoming part of Siam. Although he preferred philosophy to politics, he was shrewd enough to realise he would find no allies in his fight for justice in the fragile political life of a vassal state. What was more, if he was unable to fight Siamese savagery, he would surely perish amongst the wild beasts of Bangkok before achieving anything on behalf of his realm. When I reflected that perhaps no civilisation on earth was good enough for his philosophical nature, he gave me a hard look and said he knew exactly what Lao LanXang wanted. Would you agree?

We stayed over two weeks with the abbot in the That Phanom temple before heading further north to Nakhon Phanom city, where we were housed in an ancient, modest teak house where the timbers creaked when we walked about and shook when I rushed after flies or mosquitoes: one could hardly resist killing them. The house was conveniently just outside the Wat Si-Buabanh temple's perimeter and belonged to an elderly gentleman who'd become a monk at the That Phanom temple to seek solace after his wife died. He kindly offered the house to us in return for its upkeep and repairs. We borrowed mattresses and bedding from the temple. Like all Lao LanXang houses, it was built on stilts, with the pillars resting on thick slabs of stone. (In most houses the base of the pillars is sunk half a metre into the ground; this provides security against strong monsoon winds, but they do get rotten very quickly.) It stood on a high ridge facing the river, with a shady terrace where Chao Anouvong liked to sit and read, write and rehearse his speeches or just sit enthroned in a chair with his eyes closed to clear his mind.

A vegetable and herb garden at the back fell away into the woods, hemmed in by a thick wall of lush bamboo on one side and mature fruit trees on the other: coconuts, mangoes, palms, oranges, bananas, papayas, pomegranates, limes and countless others, all merging together with the massive forest trees. If one could be bothered to find a way of climbing up to the top of one of those trees, whose great long branches stretched high above, one would be rewarded with a panoramic view northeast across the Mekong to the vast, smoky mountains of XiengKhuang and Vietnam, and, to the southwest, the thick curtain of forests and rice fields of the Khorat Plateau.

I often complained about the house because it lacked privacy. The only furniture was a table, three chairs and two old, partly broken rattan stools. If you could see how primitively we were lodged there, you would be astonished that a member of royalty could lead such a simple life. I wanted us to stay in a bigger house with more room but Chao Anouvong wouldn't move: he wanted to live closer to the people. He liked to meet and be surrounded by them; in some ways he was a gregarious individual – an old-fashioned, cheerful and down-to-earth soul who enjoyed mucking about and was always ready for a joke. He put a great deal of effort into appearing to be a lot more stupid than he actually was. Therefore, the house went very well with our modest image; if anyone had suggested to us we were clever princes, we might have thought they were being deliberately offensive. We tried to veer away from conversations of a personal nature.

As was natural for a man of his birth, Chao Anouvong made friends not only amongst the aristocracy but also with ordinary people who looked back with nostalgia at the good old days. He opened himself up to win his people's hearts and minds wherever we went and to share the Lao's common desire of regaining power for LanXang. They deplored Siamese domination and cherished their own customs, culture and sovereignty. The feudal lords of Nakhon Phanom, Udon, Khon Kaen, Mukdahan, Ubon, Khorat and the other cities of the Khorat Plateau shared a common language and believed in King Fah Ngum's insistence on an honourable and just society. They hated Siamese rule. They were disciplined, hardy people; their young, who were respectful and did what they were told, had gradually lost their self-esteem and pride. However, Chao Anouvong believed that LanXang culture and Lao manners were bred in the bone and were here to stay; he hoped the Lao who'd been forced to emigrate to Siam would take their manners with them.

Chao Anouvong had convinced himself that he'd been a great success with Phra Ajarn Khoon in the monastery. He now wanted to tour the Khorat plain in search of allies who hadn't yet been swayed by Bangkok. He squared his shoulders in pleasurable expectation whenever he chatted with local dignitaries and commoners alike. I tried to hint that perhaps his appearance was not entirely all it should be, and he would often find himself staggering around drunk trying to find his way home after a truly Lao party, brushing me aside with a smile as if he'd finally found his inspiration.

Most days we went out to meet and address the people. He always rose before dawn, and we would visit temples near and far when festivals were held. We enjoyed these spectacles, and meeting people in nearby towns such as Mukdahan and Khemarat, thriving as our knowledge increased.

It was forbidden to light the resinous torches known as *Kabong* (made from a mixture of wood pulp and resin tightly rolled in palm leaves which gave off a black, smoky flame) inside our sleeping quarters before the break of dawn. I often stayed in bed, wrapped in my thin blanket, contemplating the future, although I knew that he'd been out of his bed for a while dutifully performing his morning routine. I lifted my head up from the pillow, pulled the mosquito net open and craned my neck to see whether he was outside somewhere. In the darkness, with a cold breeze lingering, I could see his ghostly, motionless shape meditating on the veranda. He occasionally practised transcendental meditation because it's such an effective antidote to stress and takes away the doom and gloom, refreshing and invigorating the mind and the body. In the crisp January dawn air, the mist gathered and quickly rose from the Mekong, rolling, swirling, creeping up the bank and lapping the house like the arrival of a phantom. Chao Anouvong's shoulders heaved as he took a deep breath, thinking about the day ahead.

I would normally lie wide awake with my eyes closed, listening for the thump of the hard floorboards and a commanding signal from his throat: a sort of big yawn and cough. It was time for me to get out of bed. I rolled off my blanket, fluffed up the pillows back into shape and, my eyes half shut, struggled to my feet and blearily staggered to the terracotta jar of cold water at the end of the veranda. I picked up the coconut dipper and, as was customary, rinsed my face and mouth, gargled and took a small draught. I sniffed the air at the smell of cooking bonfires from nearby houses, opening my bleary eyes and turning towards the aroma – a mixture of baked sweet potatoes, grilled sweetcorn and sticky rice. A pang of hunger erupted like a volcano in my stomach and, like a hungry animal, I sprang out of the house to face the day.

LanXang's climate was hot and dry for half the year, allowing us to chat with people at the temples during festival time. It was common to linger in the shady temple grounds and talk to strangers between the late afternoon and the anxiety of the night. Chao Anouvong soon became well known to shoppers, traders, stallholders and merchants, rich and poor, around the city.

He always liked to look good. His black hair was pomaded, shiny and slicked back; his white shirt and dark blue or purple silk *Phahthong* (trousers) were freshly laundered, and his brown leather sandals were brushed. His face was bronzed by weeks of being out in the sun ever since we'd left ViengChan, seeking popularity in the open air. He was looking lean and fit. He glowed in the bright promise of the morning as we strode along into the gathering clamour of the city, with me just a step behind him. We were like a professor (*Ajarn*) and his student (*Looksit*). I had difficulty keeping up whenever his stride quickened; he certainly kept me on my toes. He liked to do most of his thinking on the move and used to say that the real business of the kingdom wasn't done in the palace office, but outside in the cities, towns and villages, in public parks, market squares and temple courtyards, where people were obliged to wait, listen, learn and ask each other for advice. In that way, people would socialise, unite and bond as a society.

It was the nature of things that not all feudal rulers accomplish greatness. They pottered about and were of no use to their country because their people were too frightened to make any use of them; they focused on being important rather than actually achieving great things and were doomed never to have the genuine support of their citizens, because peasants and farmers were poor and cautious, while businessmen and landowners were financially comfortable: all were patriotic, but suspicious of the arrogance and pomp of the wealthy aristocrats and their associates, some of whom didn't seem to care about the people and had only risen to their positions because of incompetence. Chao Anouvong was different. He'd a capacity for comradeship and a sense of humour which enabled him to establish personal friendships, win other people's confidence and convince them to follow him. He was determined to be a mixture of all the different levels of society. Above all, he meant business by encouraging unity and amity; this was the pillar of his philosophy, and it bred patriotism.

Just before dawn one chilly morning during the festival in Nakhon Phanom, the traders were gathering outside the temple's perimeter; the usual sizeable crowd of vendors were already putting up their stalls, where fruit, flowers and vegetables were placed neatly, creating a sea of colour. The poorest of society gathered, jostling quietly around the smoky remains of a bonfire where only embers were left to provide warmth. I made mental notes of everyone as I walked past: I recognised most of them, but many had long hair, were unshaven and unwashed and dressed in dirty, torn clothes. Chao Anouvong was all affability, greeting everyone heartily, saying goodbye to everyone and wishing them good health and good luck. His undiscriminating friendliness made him popular and he talked to everyone as casually as a farmer leaning on a gate; his manner, like the house where we were staying, was unassuming. It gave him pleasure to pursue friendship; some might have suspected his motives weren't sincere, but it was always his policy never to make an enemy of anyone. Here and there small groups of people sheltered in makeshift shelters among the ruins left over from the 1779 invasion, huddled over smoking fires. They'd watched us walking past many times but didn't know who we were. He greeted them all politely, sometimes with his customary thundering, cheerful voice. His sharp brown eyes and his sensitive ears registered every wave and greeting. He acknowledged them all and won their admiration.

'*Sabaidee*. Good morning, everyone,' he often said, cheerfully practising his art. Despite their hardship, a few perked up and half-heartedly returned the compliment, without even turning their heads to see who he was. He behaved like this whenever we went out for a fresh supply of fruit for breakfast, or occasionally a bunch of flowers to brighten up the house.

'The first rule in seeking recognition and gaining support, Jon, is to remember names and never forget a face,' he told me in front of a curious crowd in the temple courtyard in Nakhon Phanom. I turned to look at the crowd's faces and they stared back at me. 'Gentlemen,' he said to the crowd, 'there is nothing that cannot be created, undone or repaired by words. We must share our ideas and knowledge; such is the tradition in Lao LanXang. In our case, we'll share with you who we are, where we come from, what has happened to our kingdom and, more importantly, what will happen to it in the future.' I nodded earnestly, and the crowd followed me. Then, without any show of nerves, he straightened his pose, lifted his chin and looked around. With his forefinger outstretched, he pointed to the southwest and shouted fiercely that the Rattanakosin Siamese had benefited from LanXang's past weakness and internal crises. This drew a few desultory claps, then loud cheers; the people were showing their indignation at being treated so unfairly by Bangkok. With an awe-inspiring voice he said that Bangkok should be ashamed for invading ViengChan in 1779; they had been devious and had destroyed the special relationship between the two countries. They should be reminded that the That Si-SongHuck stupa in Loei province, built in 1563, doesn't only mark the countries' border but stands as a reminder that oaths had been sworn to cement the sacred trust between the two nations. 'The past cannot be changed, but neither will it die!' he roared.

'Quite right,' I chipped in, doing my bit to encourage the crowd.

'Yes, quite right!' one said; 'Agreed!' shouted another, followed by a round of applause.

After that, Chao Anouvong gained the impression his canvassing was proving effective, and that when it came to history, rich and poor people alike should know who they are and make themselves fit to be citizens. I now see why he chose this approach: his greetings became a welcoming wake-up medicine which the crowd depended on to get their lives moving. They were in the palm of his hand; they didn't care who he was and what his name was, but they just wanted to see him and jostled to listen to what he'd to say. Some people began to talk to him, telling him of their grief and sadness that they were earning their living as bearers for the stallholders and fruit and vegetable sellers.

Surprisingly, one was even brave enough to come forward. I gave Chao Anouvong's arm a gentle tug when a frail, pale, dead-eyed, middle-aged man peered at us, his hands in the praying gesture. Then, holding his right elbow with his left hand as a sign of respect for his betters, he firmly gripped Chao Anouvong's hand and poured out his problems. He said that severe floods the year before had ruined his life and that he needed help; he'd lost all his crops and livestock and was unable to pay his taxes to Bangkok. We expressed our sympathy but didn't pay too much attention for we'd heard this sort of hard-luck story many times before. But this poverty-stricken fellow gave me a real fright; his unwashed animal stink lingered in my nostrils and in my mind. As he desperately droned on, pausing occasionally to draw breath, he almost sank to his knees to put his hands on Chao Anouvong's feet. My master caught my eye and I gestured to him that it was time to go. He quickly and sympathetically interrupted the man and, like a holy monk giving a blessing to calm a man in distress, he told him to be patient and have faith; his luck would turn.

As he turned away with great sorrow, my eyes glinted with tears. 'Poor people!' he muttered. 'They're not educated. No wonder they can be indoctrinated and bribed so easily by Bangkok.' With that, we left the crowd as dawn was breaking, filling the air with sunlight and heat. We walked away briskly but also with some discomfort because our breakfast was late. My stomach rumbled with hunger all the way back to the house. I tried to stay calm, but he sensed that I was a little edgy.

'What's troubling you, Jon?' he said when we got back home.

'Nothing important,' I responded and calmly went to get our breakfast ready.

With his good looks, he was a magnet for women. In repose, his expression tended to be stern but his face lit up when he smiled. In company he was very friendly, no question about that, but there always seemed to be something else lurking inside: a longing for self-improvement, perhaps, or his concern for his people.

I was too pre-occupied with breakfast but turned round, smiled and asked how long we were to remain in Nakhon Phanom. When he replied vaguely, I joked that he must have found a beautiful young concubine, for why else would we be staying? He gladly told me how much he enjoyed meeting followers, young and old, women and children, wherever he could, mostly in the temple courtyard during the festivals. He derived great pleasure from making his philosophical speeches, encouraging people to think and earning respect and recognition for himself in the meantime. This bothered me: I found it odd to see him spending so much time with all these ordinary citizens and no-hopers. It did seem to make him wiser, but when I mentioned it, he answered that philosophy was more important than just creating history. When I asked him why, he smiled, saying that philosophy can create empathy in an ever-changing world.

'No one person or nation can change history or invent it just to suit their purposes, for it would only reveal their self-serving nature,' he added. I struggled to understand this and ignored him instead. Much to my amusement, he calmly watched me eating my breakfast – without paying any attention to what I'd said – before turning his mind to his own food. 'All will be well, Jon' he reassured me, and praised me for getting his six-minute boiled egg ready. 'There is much to be said for a hearty breakfast.'

I responded with a thin smile, ignoring his charm and watching him humming through his breakfast and finishing it before me. Afterwards, I went outside to sit under the pomelo tree; clasping my knees and looking up at the heavens, I reminded myself to be forever humble in the face of my own mortality.

Then, one day, Chao Anouvong, his brows drawn together in thought, called me, gesturing with his outstretched hand the way he'd learned from the abbot. The sun was quickly setting, turning redder and bigger, painting the clear blue sky red and the silver river gold. A flock of parakeets gathered noisily on the sandbanks for their evening drink and a squadron of dragonflies fluttered, darting and skimming over the surface of the water before settling down for the evening. It was still hot. I'd been watching him for a while in expectation and dread. He was pacing about in the shaded courtyard with his head hunched forward, hands clasped behind his back, doing his thinking after his siesta. I knew he was brooding on something and didn't notice the black birds swooping past. I sensed my personal idyll was coming to an end.

'Jon! Please come here,' he commanded with severity in his voice, reminding me of my father, making me jump a little. I untangled and heaved myself out of the hammock and hastened towards him, my pulse quickening. When I was within reach, he suddenly drew back his arm and threw an orange at me. I caught it without thinking. He lunged forward, wrapped his right arm firmly around my neck and dragged my head down, so that I was bent double. I let out a muffled cry and my fingers clawed feebly at his arm.

'You're hurting me,' I protested stiffly. He started laughing, ruffled my dusty long hair and let me loose. I gave him an annoyed look and staggered about, coughing and massaging the side of my head and throat, but appreciating this was just his way of showing affection and playfulness, I soon laughed and straightened up. He quickly pulled me towards him and we wrestled mischievously.

Khem, a simple but very kind widow of good stock whose husband had died fighting the Siamese invaders seventeen years earlier, stood restlessly on her veranda fanning her face. Alas, she was neither young nor beautiful but sometimes she performed the role of a servant for us, collecting the water, cleaning the house, lighting the fire and cooking our meals. Seeing us messing around, she shot a disapproving glare at us; she was concerned for the best reasons but full of fun, nevertheless. With her motherly smile and laughter, she yelled, 'What a pair you two are!' Her lips were slightly red from chewing betel and tree bark, a practice the Siamese government was trying to ban. She told us to stop behaving like children and when we ignored her, she threw a jug of water at us from above like a true expert. A lot of it went over me. She flashed her rotten teeth and gums in a fit of giggles. We quickly pulled apart in laughter and wiped our faces. 'Serves you right!' she said, giggling loudly.

'Human beings are born, not made,' he said as he put his right arm round my shoulder, and we walked towards the shady seats. 'We must prepare ourselves for the fast-approaching future. We ought to be fit, strong and healthy: both physically and mentally.'

I asked him what he meant by this, butterflies fluttering in my stomach. My languid demeanour was more suited to thinking than doing, and my physique was certainly not that of a fighting man. He said that being away from the palace's routine had improved his mental faculties; I told him that being with him had educated my mind too. He looked at me, then gently jabbed my soft belly with his strong fingers and suggested that we should get into shape before it was too late, even though we were past the time when our bodies can be more easily moulded.

'You may remember I once said that compulsory exercise does no harm to our bodies,' he reminded me.

'Yes, I do rather,' I said.

'We must be lean and keen, otherwise our superfluous flesh will make us puff and blow and we would be unable to cope,' he said. 'Now, I suggest it's high time for me to cure your physical ailments as I said I would; and mine too. Would that be agreeable to you?'

'I'm at your disposal,' I said, almost indolently. I dreaded having to train hard like a soldier but accepted it was good to get sweaty and stir one's blood rather than becoming flabby by being inactive.

'Physical exercise is necessary for our health,' he explained. 'As you know, we're mere mortals. Our true ancestor is the earth. Our bodies grow and decay; nothing is indestructible, and most things are subject to their own specific form of deterioration. For example, the body gives way to illness, bronze to rust, timber to rot, grain to mildew and so on. We must try to eat well but in moderation, exercise to stay healthy and laugh to be happy. Firstly, you must eat more: you need the right nourishment. Like knowledge,' he went on, 'if your body is properly taught, it will improve in the same way as the mind.' Well, I instantly thought to myself, this was going to be easy. 'I'll give you some of my food if you want more.' My appetite was stirred by his bribery. I was still growing and therefore eagerly and gladly welcomed any extra food; eating more was never an issue for my ever-hungry, greedy soul. However, he made it clear that this was a form of reward and that I must work hard to earn it. 'No such thing as a free lunch,' he warned, looking at me severely. I smiled and nodded gently.

It was around mid-January. That evening we were alone; the moon and the stars were shining. After making drink offerings to our ancestors, our meal began with two large, hard-boiled duck eggs with a heap of steamed vegetables. When I'd finished, Chao Anouvong made me eat a lump of partially cooked buffalo meat which I'd seared over hot charcoal under his supervision. How I disliked it! I couldn't possibly eat it without my favourite sweet and sour chilli sauce to dip it in, or hot and spicy papaya salad (*Tum Mak Houng* ຕຳໝາກ ຮຸ່ງ) and rice noodles (*Khaow Poon* ເຂົ້າປຸ້ນ) to accompany it. It also needed plenty of vegetables and fresh herbs: spring onion, mint, coriander and others. He seemed to enjoy his seared meat well enough, but after living on Siamese food for so many years, he also couldn't do without freshly steamed sticky rice. I must confess we both loved to eat the rice that had been steamed at the bottom of a bamboo basket.

'You need bulking up,' he insisted, patting his own broad chest. I gave him a rebellious look but dutifully finished my plate. He smiled and as promised tested my sensual desire by offering me his food.

'Oh, no, thank you, I'm satisfied,' I said courteously, patting my enlarged belly. 'No, I simply can't eat anything more but your words,' I added, turning my face away.

'Really, you've had enough?' he said; he leaned towards me and whispered, 'I know you're not an epicure, but food and alcoholic drink are fine in themselves, although overindulgence in sensual desires provokes greed.'

I took his words very seriously and have stuck with moderation ever since. Chao Anouvong believed it irresponsible to consume alcohol in the throes of a national crisis. After dinner we went straight to bed, although I don't believe he slept much. I heard him in the middle of the night, pacing about in his room. I was concerned for him but, my stomach full of food, I felt much too tired and lazy to get up. I slept soundly and barely heard the dawn chorus. When I woke up, I was startled to find him in my bedroom; when he opened my window and the sharp morning light blinded me, I put my hand up to protect my eyes. He playfully pulled me out of bed while I clung on to my dear, warm blanket like a little boy. I resisted but it was no use.

'Come on, sleepyhead, time to wake up,' he said, 'and bid your pleasant dreams farewell. You have work to do.'

Like a half-comatose drunk, I crawled out of bed and groggily went outside to empty my bladder beside the bamboo bush. Then, with my eyes half closed, I splashed and rinsed my face with cold water, waking myself up slowly and dreading the tasks that lay ahead. In the early morning the grass was wet with dew and it was refreshingly cold. When the sun rose and the red dawn light appeared over the distant mountains in the east, the river was smooth and glittering. Still feeling full of food from the night before, I sat and tilted my face towards the sun for warmth and skipped breakfast. I didn't have time to anticipate what was to happen next. I jumped when he called, pulled on my shoes and went towards him.

'Come quickly, Jon!' he said, hurrying me along.

As the sun was rising, the physical exercises began. 'Strengthening your body,' he said, 'requires effort, energy, determination and stamina.' Without warning he threw a weak, fake punch at me and I let out a loud 'oof', holding my tummy with a grin on my face. He promptly showed me how exercise should be done and then took his turn.

At the beginning, we flung our limbs about and leapt up with as much agility as we could muster. I soon broke into a sweat but my hands remained cold. He then made me stand with my legs apart, knees rigid, then bend from the waist ten times to touch my feet on either side. He did the same. After that, we did ten sit-ups by lying on our backs on the ground with our hands across our chests without shifting our bent legs or moving our feet, followed by press-ups. Then he made me sit on a wooden bench with my legs apart, feet in front of my body, and he dumped a pair of big green coconuts in my hands. 'Now, push your right arm up slowly above your head,' he said, 'and then your left arm while lowering your right. Yes, that's good, up and down, good, excellent.' After doing it himself he punished me even more. 'Keep your back straight,' he called, willing me on. The effort of pushing tired out my delicate arms and hands, and before my turn was over I dropped the coconuts to the ground. They rolled toward his feet and he jumped backwards to save his toes from being crushed. I flushed with a smile of revenge, clutching my arms in pain; he brought them back to life by massaging my shoulders. We repeated these exercises but took a light lunch break when the mid-day sun became too hot.

Before sunset, after some stretches, he made me run; slowly at first, and then at speed for the last five laps along the shady path around the garden. The sunlight was coming in rods, lighting up the branches of the fruit trees high above; between the shafts of light the air was soft and grey, yet the heat was feeling its way between the leaves to my skin. Eventually my exhausted body was covered in sweat; it ran down my legs and my sandals gave a strange, squelching, wet noise. He ran alongside me, urging my near collapsing body on, placing an encouraging hand on my arm. 'Come on, you've nearly finished,' he said, cheering me on to the finishing line. My shoulders heaved as I panted. Once I got my breath back, he raised his eyebrows and promised to tell me something. I looked at him, breathing heavily. 'Catch me if you can!' he yelled; then he was gone, leaving his voice hanging in the air. I sprang after him like a lion chasing its prey. We chased the sun's shadow down to the river for a cool swim and washed ourselves in the clear water. After we'd scrubbed the dirt and dust from our bodies we returned home in partial darkness for a hearty dinner.

That was the order of the day; each day more exercises were added, and their duration increased. Our bodies gradually changed: our thighs thickened, our shoulders and chests broadened, the muscles in our arms became so toned that anyone would think twice before taking us on. Exhausted at the end of the day, I slept soundly and had no trouble eating medium-rare buffalo meat, even without spicy sauce and freshly steamed sticky rice.

When he offered me his portion, I suggested we donate it to the two underfed children of the widow who lived next door. 'I'm quite sure they have plenty,' he assured me, emptying his plate instead. He revealed that in Bangkok, mealtimes were unpleasant because he didn't like the company of the other diners. 'Remember, Jon, when you grow old and become wiser,' he said, like a father teaching a son, 'it's not the quality of the food and drink that should matter to you, but the company and the conversation.'

I looked at him with mock displeasure and, exhausted, replied, 'That's true enough, Your Royal Highness. But aren't we tired of talking politics and philosophy?'

'But when we were out talking to people in the temple,' he responded, looking at me in astonishment, 'you performed well with your customary charisma and charm.'

'Thank you, Your Royal Highness,' I said. 'I apologise, but may I say that politics is so dull sometimes, and there must be more to life than that. Could we perhaps talk about something else next time we eat?'

Our eyes met and he gave a barely perceptible shake of his head, as if to say I was being silly and it wasn't worth arguing over. Nevertheless, he added that politics was like history on the move, unfolding before our very eyes, vividly exposing man's strengths and weaknesses. Life would be very boring without it. Well, I had no choice but to agree with him. Occasionally we would wind each other up like that for fun. I sometimes wondered whether he got pleasure out of it. I think he knew I enjoyed it too.

'Very well Jon, enough politics,' he conceded. 'For now, I propose a toast.' After pouring libations to the ancestors he said, 'Here's to LanXang, and may this day be the beginning of a more successful future for her.' Amazingly, not only did he have detailed knowledge of every province, but he also knew every governor by name. This erudition was not lightly acquired, and I was so impressed my eyes became wet with tears. We raised our glasses and took our drink. 'To our country!' he said, raising his voice and glass in salutation before poetically and enthusiastically reciting all the names of the provinces like a sentimental poem he'd composed himself. Impressively, he also included every province of LanNa. 'It's impossible,' he said, 'to keep LanNa out of LanXang's history. After all, King Xay-Setthathirath the Great ruled both kingdoms for two years. We are strongly connected.'

'Here's to us!' I said, reminding him not to forget our own family. My eyes brightened with homesickness over the rim of my drink.

'Yes, of course, our family,' he said. 'Here's to your mother!'

'Thank you, Your Royal Highness. And here's to your family and your future,' I responded.

'My future depends on the unity of LanXang and the support of the people.'

'You love LanXang and the people love you. You can at least always count on my loyalty and support.'

'And I shall not forget it,' he said. After a moment of silence he said, 'All right, Jon, I understand. When we are older, we can spend the bulk of our time on philosophy and the weary business of politics, not for the sake of honour but for the benefit of society and as a matter of necessity.' He then quietly asked whether he could get me to agree on something we'd discussed before.

'Certainly, but I can't remember,' I said. 'What is it, Your Royal Highness?'

'Well, it's about righteousness being the best policy. I think it's a good idea to discover how justice and injustice manifest themselves in society.'

'Please go ahead,' I said.

'We must, however, be careful to distinguish between justice and injustice when discussing all human virtues, such as kindness, loyalty, integrity, courage and discipline.'

'Indeed, we must. It would be unreasonable to do otherwise,' I said.

'Now, tell me something. Would you concur that justice and injustice are opposites?'

'Definitely… of course they are, but justice is of paramount importance.'

'Very good. Do you think then that just people live better and happier lives than unjust people?

'I do, most certainly,' I replied.

'Would you agree that we can't see with anything but our eyes nor hear with anything but our ears?'

'Yes. As they say, seeing is believing.'

'Good,' he said cheerfully. 'We know that the power of our eyes and ears can be improved with training when we're young, but still fall far short of perfection. Nevertheless, they would be useless without the mind, wouldn't they, Jon?'

'Most certainly. The mind's in control, isn't it?' I responded.

'I agree. So, therefore, do you believe that life is a function of the mind… or the brain, if you like?'

'Very much so,' I said, 'and the mind is incapable of performing properly without its own excellence. You could find this distinction amongst people anywhere in the world.'

'In that case, Jon, a good mind is just and a bad mind is unjust.'

'That is true… I suppose,' I said, feeling confused.

'Should the just man be happy and the unjust man miserable then?'

'As a rule, unjust people with guilty consciences can't be happy, surely. There's no need for an honest person to dissemble,' I said cautiously.

'Excellent!' he cried. 'Remember this, Jon, the desire to be happy is common to all men. It never pays to be miserable, only to be healthy and happy. Injustice, both of the individual and of the state, is beneficial to a privileged few but is never in the interests of the majority.'

'Of course, Your Royal Highness, but never mind,' I agreed, attempting to stop the debate as my brain had become deluged with words. I couldn't possibly respond to his insatiable philosophy, and he must have thought I was too stupid to do so. All I could see was that justice and injustice were opposites and that they both had their advantages. A very keen mind was required for this debate; mine was far from that. It was simply too huge a task for me to undertake without having thought about it deeply beforehand. 'As a human being I find this intriguing, but I promise I'm not being deliberately obtuse,' I said. 'Haven't we become used to suffering from injustice? We're only people so let's just be happy and enjoy our lives.'

He shot a satisfied look at me and said, 'Well, then, if we do enjoy it, it's thanks to both of us, and I must say that since you've stopped being so emotional, I am indeed happy. Now, please remember that justice is the best thing, both in this life and in the next. We have in fact been acting justly, despite our humiliation at the hands of the Rattanakosins. So, if Bangkok changes its behaviour and leaves us alone, we would be happy.'

'Your Royal Highness, it's my fault,' I conceded, 'and I humbly apologise.'

He promptly slapped me gently on my shoulder and blamed himself also for talking so greedily about politics. I was fond of turning in early and said it was time for a certain tired, keen-minded person to go to bed. When he consented, I reaffirmed my apology and my pledge, bowed to him and wished him a pleasant sleep. I slowly and exhaustedly dragged myself to bed with a small candle and a book of philosophy, which I was too tired to read.

We'd been away from ViengChan for nearly a month. I'd long since taken to sleeping in a different room to avoid being disturbed by him when he rose before dawn. Later, I heard the bolts slam shut on the front door and then he tiptoed across the floorboards and went to his bedroom. The air was getting cool. I partly covered myself with a thin blanket and rested my head on the pillow with my right arm across my forehead, thinking. I sank deep into my own family's past: my mother was back in ViengChan alone. I blew out my nearly burned-out candle and surrendered myself to sleep.

Next morning, I woke up with a slightly troubled mind because of disturbing dreams about my poor lonely mother. When Chao Anouvong realised this he decided to act. In many ways, I owed him much for having taken a shine to me, for sharing his wisdom and knowledge with me and giving me the opportunity to live and travel with him. As I looked at him, I felt a strong pull towards my birthplace, where I would settle down, marry some girl of equal status and have plenty of children of my own as insurance.

'Jon,' he said to me in the cool, breezy morning, sipping a small cup of his usual strong, warm mint herbal brew, 'I believe we've had enough of this small, perfumed, dark house, and I think we've overstayed our welcome in this area. We'll leave on the full moon in two days' time, cross the Mekong to Thakhek city, head to Mahaxay and then back again before returning to ViengChan.'

'That's a very good idea,' I cut in excitedly. He said that he wanted to pay a visit to the governor and nobles in the area and sound out their thoughts and feelings. I sensed he'd a plan in mind.

He later told me the real reason for visiting and being seen in Mahaxay – a city of strategic importance halfway between Vietnam and the Mekong – was to pass on news of the impending conflict with Bangkok to the governor in person and to urge him to be prepared and to gather support from Vietnam.

Having sorted out all our affairs, we conveniently slipped away before dawn, whilst most of the inhabitants were just about to stir from their beds, although many of the women was already preparing to steam the sticky rice to give as alms (*Tuckbadh*) to the monks. Alas, having crossed the Mekong, we were informed that the ruler of Mahaxay was on official leave in a town near the Vietnamese border. Realising our effort was wasted, we decided to cross back to Nakhon Phanom before taking a long overland detour back to ViengChan.

We first went to Sakon Nakhon. Armed with our newly acquired knowledge and desiring to see our families, we anxiously headed back north to ViengChan. During our journey, which was rather slow in coming to an end, I got rather tired; our horses too were slowing down. We fought our way through rough paths and crossed many streams and rivers. Chao Anouvong's calmness allowed me to relax and reflect on happy memories throughout our long passage home. He kept me talking so that he could stay quietly awake and told me many funny stories which made us laugh. Most of the time, however, I left him to contemplate. My nerves were shredded, and it was quite a relief when we reached ViengChan.

VI

Looking Back

On reflection, during our stay in Nakhorn Phanom, I was able to satisfy Chao Anouvong's interests by telling him about me and my family. I think listening to it was his way of relaxing; it helped to take his mind off the issues that were troubling him. Some of our conversations were a little too serious, but occasionally we had a small drink which added to the jollity of our meals, and we entertained each other with jokes and amusing chats.

'You must have been quite a small boy when you left your hometown,' he said during one evening meal. 'Won't you tell me what happened?' I went quiet because I never liked to talk about myself, though I did promise to tell him everything eventually. When he sensed my reluctance, he insisted.

'Very well, Your Royal Highness,' I said, 'give me your ear and I hope you enjoy the tale, but please keep it to yourself.'

'I'm listening,' he said eagerly and smiled.

I took a deep breath and began by revealing that my mother's mother had passed away three years before my father died: she caught malaria at the age of sixty-two. My mother blamed my father for her death because of his lack of care and attention. I was just six, barely knowing what life and death were, but I remember her well. She was a great person, kind-hearted and happy, who always found time to support me. My mother fell into a state of shock at losing her and lost her way for a few months. She hardly spoke and blamed herself for not caring for her mother until the end.

After my grandmother's death, my mother said she would never marry another man if she outlived my father, for the love of her children. I'm number six; there were nine of us but only eight survived into adulthood. The last one, poor boy, suffered ill health from birth and died at the age of three.

Chao Anouvong then revealed to me that he loved his sister, Princess

KaeoYhodFah Kanlayani, and missed her very much. He was upset he'd failed to bring her back from Bangkok. He was very interested in my mother's vow never to marry again.

'Really? But why?' my father had said, looking surprised but pleased she'd remain faithful to him, even after his death.

Their startled eyes met with a smile.

'Because, as far as I am concerned, none of them would be a gentleman like you,' she said thoughtfully.

He was uncharacteristically touched by her devotion and wept in gratitude. He toyed with his drink before taking a sip to restore his self-control. There was no escaping the fact that he was under a heavy obligation to be faithful and to bring up and protect his children, otherwise he risked losing face and suffering humiliation. 'I would rather kill myself than risk my children's safety with another man,' she added, giving my father a hard look. 'What do you advise?'

'Suicide?!' he said, letting out a terrible groan. 'Surely, my dear, you can't be serious. If you fall in love with another man, he might well provide security and happiness for you.'

'No thank you,' said my mother, cutting him off quickly before he'd the opportunity to press his argument. 'I've suffered enough torments, and our children's well-being must come first.' They looked at each other with understanding.

'I'm very sorry to hear that, my dear, but as you wish,' he said softly, with relief, but he persisted in his argument. 'Please remember my dear, although remarrying can be risky and might stir up a bit of gossip, on balance it's probably worth it.'

She sat in silent contemplation. With that, they made their peace. She'd plenty of suitors but refused them all; she hated the idea of remarrying.

Chao Anouvong found it fascinating how my mother had sacrificed herself for the love of her children. He emphasised that if all Lao were so dedicated to their motherland, then the struggle against Bangkok would be victorious. He wanted to find out as quickly as possible all about the kingdom and the people before he acceded to the throne.

I explained to him that in Lao LanXang, dawn comes early for keen minds. I just couldn't wait to get up in those days. It was the most perfect time of day, when the sun touched the east with pink. Winter was the most perfect time of the year – warm enough to bathe in the milky river, but cool enough for the air to be refreshing. The young, fresh, green leaves of the mango shook gently like papers in the breeze. The big, black sandstone rocks across the river gleamed in the first light of the sun. Meditating on how the LanXang kingdom had fallen into decay and ruin, my thoughts turned to death: something that comes to us all in the end.

Perhaps every individual's fate is destined by heaven. The search for my destiny began darkly and dramatically and when my father died, our family struggled for many years. Armed with humility, wisdom, patience and faith, I put my trust in optimism, my own talent and fate. I cured my health with laughter.

Memories of LanXang before the days of King Fah Ngum lingered on in the minds of the Lao, in the knowledge that they were not one people, but many different ethnic groups, living in towns (*Mueang*) and villages (*Ban*), stitched together and speaking a similar language. The sea was alien to them; they preferred the jungle that rose among the beautiful eastern mountains and drifted high into the cloud, where they could hide and where wild animals roamed. They nurtured the soft landscape of the fertile Mekong flood plain, where herds of cattle and buffaloes grazed, rice grew and frogs croaked in the wide paddy fields that extended in all directions. It was a peaceful country of deep valleys and rivers; elephants, rhinos, deer, tigers, black bears, boars, wild buffalo and dogs prowled in the jungle. Birds, gibbons, monkeys and other strange and rare animals also made their homes there.

At the time of my birth, LanXang seemed a land of impossible contrasts, but it was a place that people travelled far to visit because of its natural beauty. The highlands to the east of the great Mekong were a mixture of mountains and plains; a land of dense forests and high mountains, the people had worked hard to cultivate the flood plains. Each day, there was only one clock: the sun, accompanied by the sound of the temple's drum welcoming the break of dawn at 6 a.m., and then to signal nightfall at 6 p.m. Every day there was a race to get back home before total darkness fell. It was unwise to take short cuts through scrubland or along remote tracks for fear of poisonous snakes. Even armed with a stick, the prospect was none too pleasing.

Furthermore, leeches infested some of the ponds and forests, hundreds of them, swarming all over the place. They fell from the trees onto men and animals; they would creep through all the openings in your clothes and coil onto your skin, sucking blood from a vein. You would lose more blood if you tore them off before they'd had their fill. When shocked with a tobacco light or rubbed with a pinch of salt, they would tremble and turn over onto their backs, wriggling in protest before dropping to the ground and slithering away. I gave myself a little shake to put them out of my mind. I wish I were less of a cissy, but I simply can't bear to even look at them, far less touch them.

Surprisingly, despite his daring, Chao Anouvong gave a quiet murmur and a look of discomfort at the thought. I quickly changed the subject.

On a few occasions, I remember sitting on the bare sandstone rocks that bridged the rapids to watch the fish. Their silver bodies curiously reflected through the sparkling clear water that flowed endlessly, breaking and rushing around the rocks. How strangely the water frothed away and then quickly healed up behind them, becoming smooth again. It was peaceful to rest close to the cool water; the sound as it beat against the rocks made me feel serenely relaxed. When you closed your eyes, it relaxed your mind. You felt it spin away as you trailed your feet or hands in it and it flung up a fine spray when a strong wind blew. I smiled whenever the blending of colours burst upon my sight like stars and vanished in the clearness of the water. How swiftly it rushed; if you stared too long, you became giddy, as if falling under a hypnotic spell. Closing your eyes only made it worse and you would whirl around in a chaotic darkness, punctuated by sharp, bright sunlight before feeling left you. I would look around, scanning the distance, taking a deep breath to clear my head. The sun was still very hot, though it was fading away below the treetops. The redness of the sky had turned the sandy island into gold. I threw small white pebbles as far away as possible to test my strength, watching them drop deep into the heart of the placid water.

During the rainy season (May to September), thin white clouds abruptly turned dark, showing their black teeth. Lightning flashed and thunder roared. The monsoon rain came down in torrents, the hard ground soon turning to sticky, slippery mud. My feet slid about under me. Too much rain was a little depressing for both man and beast, but a shower was cool and refreshing after the heat. I would slow down and plod aimlessly through the mud, enjoying my surroundings. Then the cloud dispersed to reveal blue sky and the sun would quickly evaporate the water into humid air.

I often passed under the shadow of the cloud when the low, pale evening sun was sinking to give way to dusk. The rivers and streams twinkled in the soft, green, shadowy carpet of the rice fields. The vegetation was green and shining; the rusty treetops glowed. In thick forests higher up in the mountains, gigantic trees perched precipitously. Below, on the ground, the colour of the forest floor changed from green to grey, then grey to silver, until the first webs of darkness blurred the outline of the surroundings. In the diffuse half-light, the trees glittered and changed shape and position, the rocks receded slowly into the earth and the thundering of the white water became more subdued and echoed monotonously. The wind sent a fleet of high, thick, white clouds sailing across the patches of blue sky before transforming them into dark cumulus on the horizon. In the immense skies, giant birds flew high and played, toying effortlessly with the wind as if chasing the rain clouds away. I enjoyed sitting on high ground under the shade of tall trees, looking out towards the wide, deep valley as the crimson sun went down. Crickets rose, singing and chirping to greet the fast-approaching darkness.

Some early evenings during the dry summer season (October to April), you could sit on high ground and admire the big red sun when it was just beginning to set behind the distant treetops, throwing a huge shadow across my trail. When the red sky turned the river and the gentle, undulating plateau into enormous fields of gold, it was the grandest spectacle of all, but the atmosphere quickly transformed into a soft, pink glow. On such occasions you could really appreciate the subtle power of twilight – neither the strength of the day nor yet the mystery of the night. As I was a lover of nature, I would fall prey to its charm. When the sun dropped into the river valley, I knew the day had gone and another would begin in the same way. As evening gave way to the shadows of night which fell almost jet-black, the villagers chopped wood for cooking fires and lit beacons. The whiff of grilled meat and fish and spicy foods stirred the hot air, provoking my hunger. I descended carefully, navigating the slopes and contours towards home.

Before dusk, young girls and boys made their way bare footed down to the river for their evening swim and wash, tiptoeing along the narrow path, feeling the still warm, dusty ground under them. Girls bathed separately from boys, but they all gave loud shrieks of laughter. They walked gracefully into the shallow pool, swimming naked in the flowing water and sitting on partially submerged rocks. After washed and rubbing themselves clean, some returned home with bucketfuls of water hanging from yokes on their shoulders. The sound of the villages – blasts of laughter across the dim roofs, the cry of babies in their bamboo cots and the noisy clatter of the elderly in their houses – mingled with the approaching dusk. Fishermen, hunters and women out searching for food had to race home before it became too dark to see.

I came out from the wood into the open field and followed the rough, narrow footpath home, where I entered the holy ground where rock incense was burning and candles were flickering outside. The monks had convened inside the Ordination Hall at nightfall for their evening prayers in front of the Buddha statues. I walked through the temple courtyards, where pigeons called to one another in the dusk, flying squirrels glided from one tree to the next and bats swooped and dived in the still air, catching insects. I felt drowsy from the scented air and the weight of my tiredness from the heat. The sound of chanting monks soothed my mind; my mood became separated from real life and its concerns. I remember thinking that whatever happened, the sun would always shine, and during the monsoon it would always rain.

When night fell, the surrounding sounds became dulled and deadened. It was a strange illusion: as the enveloping darkness took over, the forest softly absorbed all noise, giving the fireflies, as green as emeralds, and the flickering of the oil lamps, a unique quality. Under the moonlight the stillness of objects was reflected in the mirror of the rivers, the lakes and the flooded paddy fields – a mirror that was always ever so slightly swaying in the gentle wind or broken by the slightest movement of fish, tadpoles and insects. The orchestrated sound of the flute, the *Phin* (guitar) and the *Khaen* slid smoothly across the thin roofs, soothing the sleeping world – the dogs in their owners' homes, the birds in their nests, the babies in their cots and the old people in their beds. Out on the veranda, wrapped by the cool night air, I was disturbed by the change of light as a ghostly white moon appeared, transforming the water into a sheet of silver coins. I listened: other than night noises the silence was deep, as if the earth and all its living creatures were breathing in sleep.

I paused and looked at Chao Anouvong who didn't share these experiences with me and seemed lost in thought. After so much self-sacrifice, I said to him, one wondered what it would be like not to have so many interests, but to live a simple life in the shade. In theory, he said, one longed to live the life of a wealthy man or a prince, doing next to nothing, but in practice it would be a recipe for madness. Nevertheless, I told him that was what I planned to do when I was free from work... and old. My idea of heaven, perhaps, was to sit under a large, shady tree on the bank of the river and read, write, eat the fruit and vegetables I grew and have someone wait on me. I would shut my eyes at night, detached from all my dreams, and never worry about anything ever again. I emphasised that we should be proud of our land and our nation.

'Yes,' he said, staring into the beyond, 'but first, LanXang must become independent so we can be free to enjoy our own country.'

He was happily surprised when I further revealed that both my father and one of my brothers saw King Fah Ngum as a true patriot. They were brave warriors and fervent supporters of his father, King Bounyasan; both made sacrifices to defend the LanXang kingdom. When news of the Siamese invasion came in 1778, my father voluntarily made the journey from Mahaxay city to ViengChan, as did my brother a little later. I hesitated to go on, but Chao Anouvong insisted.

'Remember, Khoun Jon, I was only twelve at the time,' he said. 'We, my sister included, took refuge in a dark corner of Hor Phra Kaeo chapel. When ViengChan fell, we were taken away as hostages. It was a frightening time. Besides, I wasn't fortunate enough to be with my father when he died.'

After a few moments of silence, he pleaded with me to continue my story. Although it wasn't in my nature to dwell on private matters, I couldn't possibly refuse. I decided to tell him in the hope it might lessen his sorrow.

I felt rather choked up as I explained how my father suffered a gunshot wound during a battle with the Siamese invaders just outside the outer city wall. He survived and returned home in 1780, when I was just four years old. The bullet had lodged in his stomach causing an infection and he never really healed properly. The infection gradually got worse and slowly sucked every drop of fluid out of his defenceless body, leaving his slim body like a dying skeleton. Five years later, he suddenly fell ill during the hot summer month of March.

One morning, despite late nights caring for my father, I rose at dawn. After breakfast I went to inspect him in his sickbed. He asked me in a croaking voice for a glass of water. I turned away to fetch it, heard a groan and then a thump. When I looked round, he'd dropped heavily backwards, knocking his head on the pillows. He was howling in pain and his face had turned white. I dropped my shoulder bag, quickly went to his side and pulled him up gently.

'Where are you going?' he asked in a weak, breathless voice.

His sharp brown eyes had sunk deep into their sockets, barely open. His cheeks were grey with white patches and his dried mouth hung slackly open.

I propped him back up on the pillows, hearing the rasp of his breath, before hurriedly fetching water from the veranda. He revived a little and gestured for more, gazing at me like a man clinging to life, as if he'd been pondering much on his deathbed. I told him softly that I was just about to leave for school; although I was reluctant to leave him, I emphasised that I loved going there and never wanted to miss my lessons for fear the other boys might get ahead of me. It gave me a chance to play games with other boys too. I loved long-distance running; there was something about its solitary nature that was a form of character building. I would run alone with my thoughts through forest paths and paddy fields, in competition with myself, testing my own limits.

My father drew breath to speak but coughed instead and brought up blood. In severe pain, he pressed his hand to his side and asked me to stay.

'No, please don't go, I beseech you. I need you by my side,' he said. I nodded and gave him more water to soothe his dry throat. He took a deep breath to regain his strength. 'Listen, son,' he continued. 'I'm on the verge of dying and aren't long for this world. Take care of your mother.' With a shaking voice and an air of certainty he added, 'You'd better miss your lessons if you wish to witness a dying man taking his last breath.' I promptly sat down on one side of him on the hard floorboards. My mother returned from a brief nature call, looking tired and concerned. She looked at me sadly as she sat on his right-hand side, vigorously waving a fan to cool his face and soothing him with a wet towel on his forehead. In the meantime I clung on to his cold hand, comforting him for as long as I could. We laid him gently down on the pillows. My mother felt for his pulse and listened to his chest. He watched us as we looked at each other.

'Please don't go yet,' my mother said. 'You have young children to bring up – please make it.' He mumbled something in reply. His eyes were closed and his head dropped forward, knocking his bony chin on his thin chest. My mother stared straight down at him and said, 'No,' as if she'd seen his end. This was all she said for a long time: 'No, no.' She didn't even blink. Her mind seemed blocked.

I watched over my father's drained body in shock, overwhelmed and confused but praying for the gods to spare him. We lifted his head up gently and I tried to keep him alive a little longer by dripping water into his dry mouth. He licked his cracked lips in silence, desperately clinging to life. I put my cold hand on his chest and voicelessly uttered the Lord Buddha's sacred words: 'Phuto, Thammo, Sangkho' (Lord Buddha, hear my prayer). I then added a spell that I'd heard from a holy man before blowing gently on his forehead. It was worth a try, but I knew deep down it was all hopeless: the end was near.

Eventually, although I couldn't persuade him to take any more water, he knew I was by his side and put out his hand and held my arm. I saw his lips move so I leaned forward to listen. Through his laboured breathing, he muttered that I was dependable and told me he loved me. It was such a pitiful sight – a once healthy and strong man now departing this world, leaving me with such a sudden responsibility. I held on to his hand as his breathing became shallow and rapid and then began to slow. I drew close and whispered that I loved him and bade him farewell. I watched intensely as he took a last gasp of air, followed by a long sigh and a slight tremor along his body. His breath ceased. I listened to his heart in vain, thinking that his soul must be preparing to depart. My mother flung herself on him, crying aloud. For a moment I just sat there, bewildered. Suddenly, emotion overwhelmed me; I got up hurriedly and walked away in silence, leaving my poor mother to mourn over his lifeless body. I couldn't think of anywhere else to be but paced about in the garden, my body weighed down with his death. I started to cry at the sound of my mother's wailing.

In Buddhist LanXang the dead enter nirvana – a better existence than our mortal one on earth – so the former abode of the deceased should be a happy home (*Heuan Dee*). That night, while the monks recited the praying words of the Buddha and the mourners kept vigil, I sat in mourning alone in his study and paid tribute to the affection in his noble heart. I left his chair untouched, out of respect.

Due to the circumstances of his death, the body had to be buried quickly. After his face was washed with pure green coconut water, his body was cleaned, anointed, dressed in his finest traditional official white jacket and sky-blue silk *phasalong* (sarong) and laid in a simple coffin, his skinny feet pointed towards the door. I clutched my mother's hand in grief as she was weeping so hard she could hardly catch her breath. For such a private, philosophical man, a surprising number of friends and neighbours came to pay their respects. I was unable to collect myself sufficiently to watch, but I can still vaguely remember the sad and respectful glances of people at the funeral procession. His body was laid in the burial ground in the forest, among the shady trees by day and under the stars by night. I had lost a father, a friend.

Grief kills time and memory: I remember only fragments of that morning and afternoon and of the days that followed, like hallucinations left behind after a malarial fever. I recalled how thin and wasted my father's body had been, lying on his back with his legs outstretched, and how my mother wiggled his hand in grief, calling him back to life; she shunned all human contact for weeks. My father's death was a huge loss to me both in my public and private life; to this day I still miss his kindness and affection. I walked aimlessly in the garden and the forest, sniffing the flowers, hoping to drown my sorrow. I heard his voice in my head: 'Listen, son,' it said, 'now it's all yours. You're the strongest; please see to it.'

I glanced at Chao Anouvong again. He was deep in thought and looking rather sad, prompting me to stop and quickly say to him, 'So, Your Royal Highness; with the sudden loss of my childhood, I became a man of responsibility and master of my own thoughts.'

There was silence for a while before Chao Anouvong told me he was moved by my story, because when his father died in ViengChan in 1781, he was only fourteen years old and living far away from home in Bangkok. He was very sad he was unable to attend his father's death bed. In philosophical terms, he added, the world goes on forever, but only the gods know where our existence continues after death. Meanwhile, we must live as if every moment might be our last; we must remember we were born mortal.

'But what happened to your brother?' he asked. I was surprised he wished to hear more.

I told him that time passed quickly, and I was left to fend for myself. There was barely time to think, but much to do and so many decisions to be made. The house had to be kept in good condition during the dry season: it would be too late for any repair work by the time the monsoon arrived. My father had always been too preoccupied with socialising amongst his fellow countrymen to manage the house properly and had slowly let it go to ruin. The terracotta roof was old and some of the tiles were cracked. The entire house had the air of a hard-up landowner who had allowed it to fall into disrepair. That way, he used to claim, it drew more attention from passers-by. Keeping it smart, in the way he assiduously attended to his own appearance, was never important. No sooner had one repair ended than it was time to start the next. As the new head of the family, the responsibility for running the estate fell to me.

A few months after my father's death, something happened which was to entirely change my life and the future of our family, although I didn't realise it at the time. One late afternoon, I tried to be a handyman and took to the roof to replace the broken roof tiles, which were still hot from the baking sun. I kept watch on my mother busying herself in the herb garden below, weeding the plants. When I realised how old, worn and sad she looked, I halted and sat down on the roof with tears in my eyes. Everything there bore the imprint of her hard work: especially the orchard, where the orange, pomegranate, papaya and mango trees hung their greenery on high, their fruits never failing or running short. They always came in their due season; I picked them every morning for our meals.

Suddenly, from the direction of the river where the boat was moored, came a huge gathering, with children scampering excitedly and the inspiring sound of thundering drums. The air was hazy. I wiped away my tears, yet I still couldn't see well in the glaring heat. A small, thin boy suddenly appeared, running ahead of the main crowd. He arrived in a sweat with a message and asked my mother to accompany him. He kept pulling her arm and pointing in the direction of the noise. There was a sudden cry of excitement.

'What?' she cried out euphorically. The boy pointed frantically towards the crowd. 'Dear boy, don't make fun of my distress. Are you telling me the truth?' she said, her body trembling.

When the boy told her that her son Boon had come home, she came alive like a wilted wildflower in the forest after a sprinkle of rain. Her heart leapt in excitement as she clung to his bony arm with tears streaming from her eyes. The words were barely out of his mouth before she, unladylike, turned on her heel, slightly lifted her long, silky skirt and walked briskly ahead, bouncing along, holding onto her dress. The bun on top of her head came undone and her shiny black hair flew after her like waves of silk threads.

I quickly slid down the ladder, jumping the last few steps and ran after her. 'What's happening, mother?' I called out as I caught up with her. She took no notice; she just kept striding along, churning up clouds of dust with her little feet, with me keeping pace alongside her. Seeing what was happening, a stampede of people set off in pursuit, dogs jumping up and down barking excitedly, the elders watching from their verandas in bewilderment. Soon we were swept along in the rush from the house into what felt like a solid wall of bodies, noise, heat and dust.

Out of the crowd, a lone figure in army uniform dashed towards us. My mother slowed down and stopped momentarily until they both met. With trembling knees and a bursting heart, she flung her arms round his neck, and he caught her, fainting, to his chest. She pressed her face against his and showered him with kisses, as though he'd just escaped from the jaws of death. She sobbed as their arms folded round each other. 'My son, my son,' she said, letting tears roll down her soft cheeks. He hugged her tight, pressing his body against hers; his eyes, too, were wet with tears and he sank to his knees and placed his hands on my mother's feet. The crowd circling round shared this moment of happiness and delight; most of the children had snaked their way to the front and curious onlookers stood back, feet eagerly scrabbling in the dust, watching silently. The hope that my mother had cherished so long had been fulfilled. With tears in her eyes and a voice filled with emotion, she said, 'Thank the Lord Buddha, you are alive. Once you volunteered to defend the kingdom, I thought I would never see you again.' She wiped away her tears and took a step back. 'Now, let me feast my eyes on you.'

I stood amused, my tall arms folded across my chest, my heart hammering, watching the scene nervously. I appreciated what a naturally well-bred man my brother was: his uniform gave him an air of importance and solidity; his gaze was steady as he turned. I could tell by the way he moved and his air of detachment that he came bearing much news. He heaved himself up and basked in the surge of applause, turning his beaming face this way and that, like a tiger in the early morning sunshine. His chin was held slightly high as he smiled broadly, his eyes seemingly directed towards some glorious point of his happy return. I continued to watch, my arms still folded, waiting patiently for his attention. I permitted myself only the most fleeting of smiles and then composed my features into a dignified expression appropriate for a younger brother. When he turned his gaze on me, it was with such intensity that I felt certain he was going to say something and touch me. I lifted my shoulders slightly and took a deep breath, never taking my eyes off him. The entire crowd seemed to hold their breath too.

'You must be my little brother, Jon?' he said with a big smile. I replied in a firm voice that I'd never seen him before, but should he think so, then I most certainly was. He pinched my cheeks and ruffled my hair. Then he stooped down, pulled me into his arms and gave me a brotherly hug, smelling rather disgustingly of dried sweat and leather. You might have thought somebody had farted given the exquisite expression of distaste that spread across the spectators' faces. Some children even held their noses. I politely held my breath for as long as I could!

The cheering crowd acknowledged my brother's action and praised him fulsomely. There he was among us, a fully-grown man, grinning, touching, clapping backs and touching shoulders and hands in friendship. My mother smiled happily and proudly took hold of his arm.

The curious sound of thundering drums and gongs came from the temple. Soon, a senior monk in saffron robes turned up to chant a welcoming prayer. The oracle also appeared to make offerings and mutter a traditional spell to ward off evil. The monk dipped a jasmine branch into a large, silver bowl of holy water, generously flicking it all over my brother before aiming it at everybody else. The crowd wiped their faces and hair and prayed. Distinguished elders clamoured for my brother to make a speech, at which my mother said apologetically that her son wouldn't do so until he'd settled down at home with some food and drink. Just for a moment I saw a shadow pass across my brother's face, but the crowd's laughter came to the rescue, and they parted to let us through. We walked slowly towards the house, the crowd following. I clung on to my mother's hand and mischievously looked up at my brother's face. 'You look just like our father, only a little less severe,' I said. He threw his head back and laughed.

My second brother, Boon, I reminded Chao Anouvong, presumed dead in front-line fighting against the Siamese in 1779, had turned up unexpectedly. His unit had refused to surrender and had been hiding deep in the forest to evade capture after the fall of ViengChan. They'd been on the run, surviving on food left for them at secret locations and engaging in skirmishes and guerrilla warfare. The main Siamese army had left the city, but large groups of Lao troops continued to resist the occupiers. We'd received no news of him for many years. Refusing to believe any rumours, my mother sought advice from the diviners, but without success. Nevertheless, without fail, she dutifully made drink offerings and prayed every day for his safety in the temple and in the ancestral house of worship.

After my father died, she sent a grieving message to ViengChan, where my elder brother, Khamfai, had lived since becoming a civilian after twenty years as a monk. Once he received the news, he managed to find Boon, whose initial request for compassionate leave was refused. In distress, Boon then fired his gun into the air to draw attention. In desperation, he went straight to his commander's house with a letter that said, 'If you don't let me go home, you'll see a dead soldier at your door.' He refused to leave until he'd received a reply, a straight answer as a reward for his absolute loyalty. His eyes red and wet with tears of anguish, he fired a second shot into the clear blue sky. The commander's assistant promptly appeared, asking him to calm down and return to his quarters. Pre-occupied with his dead father, his grieving mother and his wish to go home, he isolated himself in his room and refused to either eat or speak to anyone for a whole day.

As far as the respected and considerate commander was concerned, the war was still going on and he didn't wish to lose one of his most trusted men. Boon had been under the commander's watchful eyes and he'd marked him out for promotion. Finally, conceding he couldn't refuse Boon's request, because it would be interpreted as an insult, he ordered, 'Give some money to the poor boy and let him go.' Lack of transport badly delayed his journey, which was by ox cart, elephant's back and on foot. It took him nearly a month and he was utterly exhausted when he finally reached us.

Anyway, the news spread fast and the crowds had grown larger and larger as we strode excitedly towards the house. Soon, more elders and distinguished guests in traditional semi-formal clothes joined us, all to see and greet the homecoming of a lost son and receive him properly. By sunset the courtyard was jammed with people helping to prepare meals. As night fell, intrigue had worked its usual magic and I should think that at least a hundred had crammed themselves in the brilliantly illuminated courtyard to welcome him, waiting eagerly to hear his story. There was that thick atmosphere of oil lamps, food and drink and noisy, joyful conversation that often follows the release of anxiety and tension. All the important guests were present, but the young girls and boys outnumbered them. I couldn't remember all their names, but the most enthusiastic learners and listeners made themselves at home.

My brother hadn't yet made a formal speech, only a few protestations of humble gratitude and modesty and an appeal for calm. He didn't have to say much, for his presence alone had made the peaceful community come alive, such was the enthusiasm he inspired. Nevertheless, once everyone had eaten and drunk their fill and settled down, he sat up and spoke with a theatrical flourish.

'Ladies and gentlemen, I'm glad to see you all,' he began, telling them to make themselves comfortable. 'I left this house as a teenager, with a profound memory of my father's land that will always be dear to me. Now I return a wiser man, to pay respect and remember my life here.' He raised his hands in a gesture of gratitude and applause erupted from the excited crowd. As people went wild with enthusiasm, I glanced across to my mother. Her expression was one of enraptured happiness and pride, as if she were glimpsing her future.

'What news has a noble son brought to his ancestor's land?' said a large, impatient man at the back.

The crowd began to stir. My brother smiled, turning to acknowledge the elder with a slight bow. 'I'm afraid I have no good news as such for the kingdom,' he said, looking straight ahead, 'but plenty to keep everyone here awake into the night.' The crowd smiled, looked at each other and nodded their heads approvingly. The children grinned and waited eagerly for the real story to begin.

'Quiet everyone! Let's hear what he has to say,' a man in the crowd said abruptly. 'We heard that nasty man Kasatseuk and his men broke through the city gates and captured ViengChan, killing people, burning temples and raiding our treasures. Surely it means we've lost the war and our livelihoods.'

The crowd looked worried and disturbed, but their morale was lifted when Boon explained that for many months, fierce Lao resistance had prevented the invaders from entering the city. 'I can assure you the city gates weren't broken by the enemy,' he said. 'They were opened to save lives when a heartbroken Chao Nanthasene learned that his father, King Bounyasan, had fled in the night. I fear the royal army cannot win a war of this magnitude. We are under-armed and heavily outnumbered. We may win a few hearts and minds for our bravery, but that won't be enough to safeguard our way of life.'

There was an air of despondency amongst the crowd. They sat patiently, waiting for the story to begin. Boon raised his hand for calm and, after licking his lips, he began slowly by saying that he was overwhelmed by everyone's presence. After pouring a libation and taking a sip of warm tea, he seemed to come alive and said, 'I just have one really good story to tell you.' His audience were mostly boys of my age, jostling for position with gathering excitement to see him and be close to him. The older ones spread around at the back, chatting quietly amongst themselves. Acknowledging the crowd's encouragement, Boon scanned the audience like a lecturer checking how many students were present before starting. He raised his hands for silence again. The noise quickly died down and the crowd breathed gently. There was a sudden quietness, a silent quiver of anticipation in the still air. He straightened his posture and lifted his head high. After a quick glance around, he cleared his throat, then sat back into his chair. Like an assistant, I proudly stationed myself pensively beside him and listened. That evening, my brother poured out tales of his dangerous experiences in the army.

'During the war, my regiment,' he began, 'was set up and stationed in the forested area of Tha Duea, south of ViengChan, to intercept the invading enemy. We'd dug in on the edge of the paddy fields and, camouflaging ourselves using thick-leaved branches, we waited in ambush. We knew the Siamese army would head in our direction once they'd crossed the Mekong. We were on full alert.' He paused. The air had turned dead still.

'It was night!' he continued, pointing his outstretched finger into the dark sky. 'Under the ghostly moonlight, deep in the desolate forest, the fighting started. We ambushed them as they approached our position and many of their men were killed. We came under heavy fire but fought with endless determination throughout. By morning we found ourselves surrounded by the enemy and completely cut off. There was no help, no food, no medical supplies, but we were able to hold onto our position. Fortunately, it poured with rain during the night.'

He paused again to regroup his thoughts. No one made a noise but waited anxiously for him to continue. 'Then, before a gleam of light touched the treetops the following morning, the attack came,' he continued. 'We were ready for it of course and when it began, I realised this could be the moment of my death. I was terrified but managed to pull myself together. The Siamese were like phantoms, darting from side to side across the paddy fields with their guns, swords and knives flashing in the moonlight as they advanced closer. We were outnumbered and they were better equipped than us – most of our guns were home-made and out of date – but we shot them down; many of us died too.'

There was a groan of horror amongst the crowd.

'How many did you shoot?' asked one boy in the audience before yelling 'Ouch!'; another boy sitting next to him had pinched him and told him not to interrupt.

'I don't know the exact number; I couldn't see well enough to count. Five perhaps, maybe more.' He shrugged his shoulders. 'Fortunately, this furious battle went on for about twenty minutes or so, charging back and forth as we fought. The sound of guns firing, the crashing of swords and the roaring of the brave warriors, the screams of resentment, the shouts of killing and revenge and the groaning of injured fighters rang through the air. Then, there was complete silence. Dawn was breaking and I found myself alone, shaken but not frightened.'

The crowd became tense again; they moved about a little, but no one spoke.

'I waited and listened for the noise to start again,' he continued, 'but there was nothing – not even a breath of wind. I kept myself still, hiding inside my dugout under the bush. The silence made me restless and eventually I dared to emerge from the bunker. The air was hot and humid but I felt stiff and cold. I hadn't eaten properly for a few days, though I had drunk some rainwater which I'd managed to scoop up with leaves, but I was feeling weak and lacking in energy.'

After a short pause, my brother took a sip of water to refresh his memory. There were plenty of throat clearings and swallowing noises and shifting legs from the audience.

'What happened then?' asked one boy impatiently.

'Well, hostile darkness soon gave way to early morning light,' said Boon and took a deep breath. 'I could smell blood in the muddy water and gunpowder in the air. I sat motionlessly and looked across the bunker, my heart beating so fast I thought it was going to burst out of my chest. There were dead bodies scattered here there and everywhere, their lifeless limbs twisted and bent. Then, suddenly, I saw movement from small figure about twenty meters away from me. I shrunk back in shock, but my tired eyes remained fixed on him: a little man with a muddy face was lying on his back next to a small, leafy plant. His head had fallen to one side as though his neck was broken. Whenever he tried to lift it, it dropped back helplessly on his half-bent arm; his other arm was resting on his blood-spattered chest.'

Chao Anouvong glanced at me sorrowfully. I told him I'd been in a state of shock and awe when I heard Boon's story. I was very uncomfortable at the thought of blood; I've never even liked red or half-cooked meat, but sometimes forced myself to eat it when my father insisted. I probably went white, for I was squeamish about pain and death, even when inflicted on animals. I'd always avoided hunting: fighting your way through dangerous forests for deer or boar never sounded much like fun to me. Boars are terribly dangerous: they can charge at you with their tusked snouts, knocking you over and ripping you open as you fall. I tried to forget one rare occasion when I'd gone hunting: the frightening, staring eyes of a wild boar as it was caught in the hunter's net; its furious, grunting squeals as it fiercely fought back; a terrible moment when the air seemed to tremble with stabbing sounds, deafening screams of pain and the sudden buzzing of flies in a thick swarm. Trust me, you'd rather be somewhere else. But there I was with my philosophical mind, listening to the story of a dying man by the flickering light of oil lamps and moonshine. I caught my brother's eyes and asked him, 'You hadn't shot or stabbed him, had you?'

'I couldn't tell whether I had or not, I'm afraid,' he replied softly and took another sip of water. 'We fired our bullets everywhere during the fighting,' he explained, drawing the attention of the tired crowd; when he brandished his arms in imitation of a gun and made a firing sound with his tongue, the crowd jumped. 'I thought I could see his soul trying to leave his body. Then, suddenly, he groaned and tried to raise his head.'

Killing just seemed a waste of life to me; Boon's answer pleased me, but I still felt sick. I readjusted my tired, numb legs, stretched my sore neck, took a deep breath and remembered my father's last moments; I was convinced that souls leave the dead bodies of their former hosts in search of new resting places. I opened my tired eyes and listened to more of Boon's story.

'For a moment, the man's groans became louder, then his head sank back upon his arm,' he went on.

'So he was badly injured but not dead!' said a slightly chubby, middle-aged man squatting with both hands resting on his knees. His voice sounded familiar, but I couldn't quite place him.

'Correct, the man wasn't yet dead,' Boon declared. 'I gathered my strength and stood up. I started to walk but, probably because of my nervousness and fatigue, I found myself staggering about like a drunk before collapsing to my knees. I slowly dragged myself towards him, hesitating, supporting myself on my weak hands. I crept a little further and rested to recover some energy.' He demonstrated by making dragging movements with his hands. 'It was really terribly tiring.'

'Were you frightened?' asked a little, skinny boy with a squeaky voice next to me. He'd forgotten to return home for a wash and eat his supper and had been playing games with his friends all afternoon. His body smelt of dried sweat and his tummy rumbled with hunger. I turned my nose away and held my breath but inhaled heavily when Boon spoke again.

'I was nervous, well, a little frightened, perhaps,' he said. 'In fact, I was a bit worried he might not actually be dying at all. But I couldn't bring myself to kill him even though I knew he could easily have picked up the gun next to him and shot me.' After a brief pause, he shouted, 'Bang, bang, bang!'

This startled the skinny boy and he seized my arm tightly with shaking hands. Being a sensitive boy myself, my heart leapt at Boon's loud imitation of a gunshot. It was an unnerving experience for everyone. Soon the boy's anxious grip loosened, and he turned to me and laughed sheepishly. The crowd started to shift about and look around nervously, before smiling and laughing noisily at each other in good humour. One elderly woman complained jokingly that it had nearly made her wet herself, and the gathering erupted in a fit of giggles. The whole courtyard rang with such a shout of laughter that pigeons roosting on the mango trees took off and flew overhead in a great cloud of poo and feathers. I couldn't see the people's faces, but I could guess what some of them were thinking; someone said it was good luck to have bird droppings land on your head, which drew yet more laughter. My brother put on a brave face, sitting there smiling before raising an arm apologetically before continuing. After a moment of silence, the crowd, chins propped on hands, again listened quietly.

'Eventually, I got close to the man, exhausted,' he went on, reminding the audience he hadn't eaten for three days and was feeling extremely tired. 'As I sat on my heels and stared at him, I began to see him in a different way. He looked just like us; his skin was a little darker, perhaps. Aware of my presence, his sunken little brownish eyes slowly opened but were blinded by the bright morning sunlight. His expression suddenly changed from one of dignity to a stare of utter terror, even though his body, clothed in baggy, dirty green trousers and a brown shirt, lay perfectly still. He looked so frightened! I froze in anticipation, wondering whether I should strike first.'

He paused briefly. The crowd waited in silence and I feared what he was about to tell us.

'What happened next?' the wide-eyed, tiresome, skinny boy said. I pulled out a sweet from my shirt pocket and gave it to him in the hope he would shut up and his tummy would go to sleep. It didn't work!

'At first,' my brother continued, 'I thought all the life in him was gathering itself for one tremendous effort to flee – terrified of dying, terrified of me. I forced myself to stand up and walk but my tired legs almost gave way after a few steps. I dropped to my knees and elbows beside him, gasping for breath and trying to speak. 'No, no,' was all I could manage.'

'Poor man!' the crowd cried out in great sympathy.

My brother glanced in the direction of the voices, then continued. 'His eyes red and tearful, the man followed me, begging for mercy. I tried to look at him in a friendly manner and he responded with a gleam of hope in his muddy face, before his hand slipped from his blood-soaked chest to reveal the state of his wound. It was such a pitiful sight. What would you have done if you'd been in my position?'

The crowd perked up, heaved a sigh of understanding, coughed gently and looked at each other in puzzlement. No one spoke. Biting his dry lower lip, Boon went on to express his pain and despair. He was clearly in a state of emotional exhaustion but wanted to go on with the story.

'His shirt was soaked in blood,' he continued solemnly. 'The moment his wet, staring eyes closed, intense horror and pain followed. He groaned loudly and fainted, and his body stretched out on the damp ground. I leaned forward, shaking my head hopelessly. 'No, no, it's all right,' I whispered to him, quickly raising my hand to show that I wanted to help. I stroked his forehead and rubbed the sticky black mud off his face. 'This is an enemy', I said to myself, 'but a dying one.' I could feel his pain.

'That was very decent of you to help him!' complimented the pot-bellied, chubby-faced elderly man. The crowd murmured their approval. 'We congratulate you for your truly noble deed,' he added.

I instantly lifted my eyes and directed my attention to this elder. It turned out he used to be fit and lean, a well-known local intellectual who'd just returned home from a two-month religious seminar in the capital. He'd put on weight there. He was never short of an opinion and readily expressed it given the opportunity. The more I looked at him and listened to him, the more I liked him. He was in many respects very similar to my father – almost the same age, clever, amusing and knowledgeable. They had often sat in the shade and chatted together for hours.

'You see,' my brother responded, 'for more than a year, since I'd volunteered to join the army at the age of seventeen, I'd never convinced myself that killing other people was a good thing. The enemy that I'd tried to teach myself to hate was a fellow human being. I didn't find him repulsive. I carefully examined his hairless, bony face, wrinkled from dehydration: he'd a strong chin and he appeared toothless because his cheeks had sunk into his mouth. His short, thin hair was pasted with mud, making what was left of it look spiky. His eyes shrank back as I pressed my hand gently against his forehead. Then they lost their stare, his eyelids drooped lower and the moment of tension had passed. I rolled up some clothes and placed them behind his head to make him more comfortable. When I gently loosened his collar, he looked at me with an expression of gratitude; his mouth opened slowly as he tried to form words that seemed to jam in his throat. His lips were dried and cracked like mud that's been baked for days by the sun. He was breathing with great difficulty and blood was running out of his nose and mouth. I wiped them gently and he gave a dry, choking cough: he was obviously very thirsty.

'Alas, I didn't have my small, pumpkin hip flask: I must have left it in my shell-hole. Fortunately there was some water in the potholes. I peeled off my red bandanna, unknotted it, spread it out over the muddy water and pushed it under for the fluid to filter through. I then scooped up the yellowish water with a cup that I'd fashioned from a leaf, poured it into the hollow of my shaky hand and carefully drained the water into his gaping mouth. He gulped it down thirstily and appeared to come alive. I gave him some more. When he showed even more signs of life, I asked him not to move (*ya ting*) as it would make his wounds bleed even more. I knew they needed to be properly bandaged and carefully unbuttoned his shirt. He groaned loudly and tried to resist but was too weak. His tearful eyes lifted once more when I began to remove the outer layer of his blood-soaked clothes, most of which had dried up and become slightly crusty and sticky. He groaned louder and severe pain flickered crossed his face. "Oh, no," I said to myself when I saw the state of his wounds. Softly and repeatedly I whispered to him that I wanted to help; he seemed to understand and calmed down.'

'What was the nature of his injuries?' I asked while my brother paused for thought. I sensed the end was approaching.

'There were two stab wounds,' he said, 'and, to my horror, they were very bad ones. I used a spare field dressing to cover them and pressed gently to stop the bleeding. It was no use: the blood ran out and spread over his chest. I pressed the dressing down slightly harder and he cried out in pain. That was all I could do. After a while I forced myself to stand up; I staggered about and waited for help to come.'

After a long silence the crowd began to shift in their seats and whisper. But there was intense interest in how the story would end, for Boon had been away fighting for nearly six years. Some were surprised how much he'd changed; others, young boys like me, had never set eyes on him at all. Even my parents had thought he must be dead because they'd heard nothing of him for so long. He'd a broad face, high cheekbones and thick, long, straight hair that floated in the wind like black threads. His face conveyed confidence and command and he'd the body to go with it – wide shoulders and a strong, thick chest.

Help failed to arrive, and the man died. His unit scattered. He survived to tell the story. The events had clearly filled him with rage, for he couldn't believe why the Siamese ruler had embarked on this war. The end of the story pleased the crowd but they were sorry the man didn't survive. Some mild-mannered seniors expressed their dismay and disbelief at the invasion and the loss of the Emerald Buddha. Their trust in the Rattanakosins had vanished and they sat in silence, barely able to speak, shaking their heads in contempt. They got up, dusted themselves down, thanked my brother fulsomely for entertaining them with such a gripping story and then dispersed quickly to their houses.

I was glad when he finished A light breeze had sprung up, blowing in from the river. I instinctively turned my face to it and gratefully drank in the taste of the fresh, clean air.

'May I say something,' I said to my brother when we were alone.

'Of course,' he replied.

'Promise me,' I said, 'that if you ever achieve the rank of commander or anything else you desire, you'll never preside over cruelty and injustice to your fellow human beings.' He looked at me and said that he would do his level best not to but added it was a soldier's duty to defend his kingdom against aggressors: to kill or be killed. 'But good, honourable men,' I countered, 'shouldn't abandon their philosophy for the sake of political influence and power. Kings, rulers and politicians make history for themselves at the expense of other people.' When he agreed, I pledged in return to remember what I'd heard that evening and to avoid the pursuit of fame and power. I admit, however, that I too wanted to play my part in defending my country after that. I went to bed with a troubled mind, wondering why men hated and killed each other, especially when both the Siamese and the Lao are descended from the same people.

Chao Anouvong was proud to hear about the kingdom's brave defenders, but he'd been just a small, frightened boy at the time. He told me he shared my thoughts and feelings about war and loss of life but he'd a duty to put things right. He knew that when he became king, he would have to make many sacrifices for the sake of the kingdom and would need to keep closely in contact with ordinary people. He believed that a king should be a public, not a private person. I told him he could count on me.

'Good. I certainly will,' he said. 'But first let's hear more about yourself.' I looked at him, hesitating, reminding him that I disliked talking about myself. He smiled and nodded at me. 'Go on, I want to hear, and I won't tell anyone else.'

I went on to tell him how, the following morning after breakfast, my brother casually suggested I would be better off in ViengChan where he could enrol me at one of the leading temple schools to advance my education. A full-scale argument arose between him and my mother, who was most upset.

'But surely it's for Jon to decide?' she said.

'He has, mother,' Boon responded. 'I believe he's keen to come with me.'

'Ah,' said my mother, sitting back in her chair. 'In that case, it will be easier for you. Presumably if he goes, he must have the full support of a guardian.'

'You're right to be concerned, mother, but that would have to be me and Khamfai.'

My mother shot a disapproving look at my brother then rested her chin on the back of her hand and appraised him carefully – he was young soldier, single, full of fighting talk, and would most certainly be tortured and killed by the Siamese if he were caught.

'You know, Boon,' she said, 'I've suffered so much hardship and I'm still grieving my own mother and your father, yet I steel myself to continue to live. So, what do you want me to do?'

'Mother, perhaps you should tell him that his future lies away from here.'

The suggestion seemed to soften her a little as she toyed pensively with her earrings. 'In my opinion,' she said cautiously, 'you and your older brother's ability to care for him is as limited as my faith in the law of possibility is boundless. Don't you think he's too young? I doubt very much the best thing for him is to take him away from me.' Saddened, she looked away.

'His future!' repeated my brother. 'This has everything to do with the future. If you love him then you must let him go.' With a gleam in his eye Boon leapt to his feet. 'You must be strong, mother. If we can't cope, we'll find someone else to sponsor him.'

'What do you want to make of him?' she asked. 'A clerk, a scientist, a doctor, a merchant, a trader, a lawyer, a civil servant… a diplomat? He should do what he wants to do. You would make him a soldier like yourself, perhaps. He is fearless. Three years ago he even caught a small falcon with his bare hands when it swooped on our chicken hiding in the bush.' After a short pause she looked at him disapprovingly. 'I suppose you'll put him in the temple as a senior monk's helper (*Sangkali*), she added sarcastically, 'and his soul will have scarcely an hour to breathe from his rising to his sleeping.'

My brother waited until he thought she was prepared to listen and then said, 'He's not a *Sangkali* type, mother. I would be sorry to see it too. I'll make sure he has a tutor instead.'

My mother sensed she couldn't win the argument and asked Boon to calm down and take a seat. He hesitated, frowned, then sat on the edge of his chair, ready to leap up again at the first hint he might have to back down. 'Of course you may take him,' she said, accepting defeat, 'but isn't ViengChan in ruins? They even took our sacred Emerald Buddha. Did they really destroy the That Luang stupa and force thousands of people to leave their homes?'

'I'm afraid so, mother. ViengChan is in a sorry state.'

'These Rattanakosin Siamese are so thoughtless and so un-Buddhist like. Shame on them! It's all to do with their ruthless ruler's dreams of a Greater Siam. I don't think anybody in LanXang can trust Bangkok now. They've betrayed our trust. And they may have ruined ViengChan forever.'

Boon said, 'It's true The Siamese have destroyed part of the city, looting and burning and forcing people to migrate to Siam. But people will flood into the city and rebuild it. We'll never let our capital die; like our national *Dork Champa* (plumeria) flower, a new one will always replace the old.'

'I'm sure we can rebuild it,' she said, 'but it will take time and we must be patient.'

'The people who fled for safety into the forest have already started to return, mother. Our capital will soon find its feet again. We won't let the Siamese, or anyone else, destroy us. We will be strong again.'

'I'm sure we will,' she said, pausing and lowering her eyes in thought. 'I don't have enough power or wealth to keep Jon here with me. Your father believed everything depends on a good education and gave me clear instructions before he died. He was convinced your brother has what it takes to further his ambitions; he didn't want Jon to leave one ounce of talent unspent or a mile of energy left in his legs. It's his destiny to go with you to the capital now... and to travel further.' She paused to wipe away her tears. 'He can't be spared to count animals or tend to fruit trees in our ancestors' land in the back of beyond,' she continued. 'Most of our young children are naturally clever but lack a decent education, so they remain backward and poor, hindering our nation's development. I wonder if Jon's future isn't even in this country but in a foreign land perhaps. Perhaps that's why your father chose such a strange name for him. It would be wrong to keep him here. So, let's have no more foolish talk.'

I sensed they were both anxious, but also relieved their tense argument was coming to an end. There was an air of expectation.

'You will let me take him then, mother?' he said, holding onto his chair. 'Is the answer yes?' he insisted when she didn't respond immediately.

'Yes, of course, he can go,' she said. Then, with severity in her voice she added, 'Take him!'

The room went silent for a while. A moment later, I appeared from the next room where my brother had told me to hide and listen. The door was ajar and I couldn't help taking a peep while they were arguing. I moved anxiously toward my mother and knelt down; when she reached out for my praying hands, I slipped them into hers. She gave me a loving, firm hug, as it was the last ever. I said nothing but wondered what the future had in store for me. I'd always preferred the country to the town; nature is where your memories reside and the cradle in which you grow. The wild mountains, the dark caves, the deep lakes, the rivers and forests were unsettling places that filled me with anxiety and dread. The tiny, sun-soaked sandy island in the middle of the sparkling river where I used to swim to and run around on, bare as a fish, had been the limit of my world. Leaving the place of my birth aroused strange feelings in me. I could hear the river's white water and smell the wildflowers. This was the place to live, I thought to myself; all I needed was a shady garden to read in, a wild forest to walk in to search for food and listen to birdsong in and a clean river to bathe in.

As I bent in reverence and pressed my face against her, I felt a strong sense of returning home; then, the idea came to me that perhaps I could remain there. I ached to imagine that I might depart from the earth never again seeing the place of my birth. Could anywhere else in the kingdom or in the whole world be more beautiful than this, I murmured to myself, I took a deep breath and shook my head as if dispelling a nightmare, then turned my attention to my impending departure.

There was to be a celebration to welcome my brother. According to tradition, beeswax candles were lit and saffron and dried herbs were burnt on sacrificial fires. The smell of spice oozing out of the crackling, bright yellow flames, the shiny clarity of the air at sunset and the two massive, plodding, spotted pigs destined for sacrifice all made an unforgettable impression on me.

In the early evening, monks in simple saffron robes recited passages from the sacred Dhamma – the Buddhist law – and prayed. They blessed the pigs, begging them for forgiveness and for their spirits to rest in peace. Then, at sunset, the poor unfortunate animals were slaughtered. I was desperately upset when I heard them screaming in the distance, at the first thrust of a knife entering their bodies, a sharp cut at their throats. They squealed piteously as they bled to death. This was all in my head as I spared myself the horrible sight and hung around instead amongst the dwindling crowd in the courtyard. Most people hunted for their meat but on this special occasion the two sacrificed pigs were a luxury to be enjoyed by everyone there.

The daylight quickly faded into a pink glow before the purple twilight ripened into darkness and the stars began to appear in clusters above the roofs. My mother and brother and I waited to greet the guests in the large sitting room. Relatives and invited guests, dressed in formal clothes that rarely saw the daylight, came in waves, queueing up and slowly and patiently crawling forward on their hands and knees until they reached the hosts. With tears of joy and sadness in their eyes they greeted my brother and expressed their heartfelt sympathy for the loss of our father. They showered Boon with praise and tied a white cotton thread around his wrists as a symbol of welcoming him back and recalling his soul. He thanked them generously and in return entertained them with more of his life story.

The community prepared food and guests were invited to help themselves, eating and drinking in true Lao style with uninhibited gratification. While some guests enjoyed their food and drink, bursting with laughter, I followed my mother closely behind, greeting the guests as if I hadn't a care in the world while she looked on. The most important guests poured libations, took sacred drinks together and talked about honour. The destruction of ViengChan and the loss of the Emerald Buddha had struck them dumb with horror. 'Bangkok has betrayed us!' they cried and agreed to fight for LanXang against Siam. The time will come, they said, when one must stand up for the truth. I peered at some of them closely, detecting the strong, stale smell of un-distilled rice wine, hot on their breath, taken with a long bamboo straw straight from the jar. I'd become quite familiar with the sophisticated ways of adults and longed to join them one day. Later, I paced up and down in the courtyard and leaned against the coconut tree, wondering what life would be like away from the comforts of home.

I was glad when all the guests, having made their libations and drunk their fill, finally reeled out from the house; some had clearly had too much to drink but were harmless and delightful. They staggered to their feet and drunkenly disappeared through the lit courtyard into the darkness, zigzagging and swaying a little as they dispersed to their own homes for the night. Soon, all the smoky, flickering torch lights went out and the night fell silent. I bade my mother good night and went to my bed but lay awake long into the night, pondering the present and feeling increasingly anxious about the future. My brother didn't sleep much either; I could hear the creaking of floorboards as he moved about in his room. When sleep finally came to me, it was restless and full of disturbing dreams.

At dawn next day, I jumped from my bed at the sound of a cough. I quickly went outside and found my brother on the balcony, looking impatient. In panic I washed my face in cold water to revive myself and went up to him uncertainly. He put his hand on my shoulder. I welcomed it.

'We must leave soon and not linger about for any more drama,' he said. 'Now, please go and bid farewell to our mother.'

I walked away reluctantly and went up to my mother, who was sitting on a couch. She'd been crying and looked lost and empty. She swivelled round and stretched out her arms the moment she saw me; we hugged and held each other tightly a little longer. Neither of us wanted to let go. I certainly wanted it to go on forever. After we loosened our embrace, she held on to my hands.

'What I'm doing is for the sake of your own future and the survival of our family,' she said, with utmost sadness in her eyes. 'Your father would have done the same. It was his wish.' Then her emotion took over again; she shed tears, constantly wiping her damp eyes with a white sodden handkerchief in her trembling hands. I tried to calm her down by telling her how I felt and how grateful I was to her.

'My respects to you, mother,' I said. 'I know that by going away I carry the hopes of our entire future. I'll try to learn as much as possible. I love you and will never let you down.'

She nodded with a smile and tears rained down her soft cheeks. Then, very reluctantly, she rose, put her arm over my shoulder and walked me out of her room. I swung round and flung my arms round her, making her once again break down and sob aloud. She took my hand, propelled me through the door and guided me towards my brother. 'Now go!' she said tearfully, wishing us good luck and a safe journey.

I was the centre of attention up to the moment I parted from my mother and my village. No one knew I was leaving for good but they still wished me well. I looked at them but didn't really see them; I seemed to be playing out some inner drama in my mind, the story of a lone traveller heading out into the world, armed only with his talent and ambition. I left my mother behind with a very heavy heart; it must have been a great sorrow to her to see me go. My brother clung on to my hand and walked me away in silence. After a few more steps from the house that felt like a world away, I looked back. There was no sign of my mother on the veranda; she'd presumably gone inside to her room for a quiet cry.

It was getting late. At the sound of the usual hooting owl, I looked at Chao Anouvong and found him deep in thought. 'I'm afraid that's the end of the story,' I said softly, my eyes downcast. He sighed and looked at me. 'So, here I am, Your Royal Highness. My childhood is truly a thing of the past. I've learnt to use my brain and to know right from wrong. I'm the luckiest person in the world to have crossed your path. It's the greatest honour of my life to have the privilege of meeting you and serving you… the future king of LanXang.'

'Well, yes, Khoun Jon,' he said. 'I'm very glad to hear it. I firmly believe we were destined to meet, but there's no telling how it all might end. I hope we'll be blessed with a bright future, not doomed to an inglorious one.' With a firm grip on my shoulder, he reassured me: 'Frankly, no one could top the anecdotes you've told me. I congratulate you. It's gratifying to hear you tell your stories so vividly and I'm deeply moved by your pledge of loyalty. You were at least fortunate your mother allowed you to leave home; as you know, I was man-handled and forced to go to Bangkok against my will!'

It was clear he was still traumatised by these experiences, but he realised his turn to take responsibility as king was fast approaching. 'But from now on, Khoun Jon, we have work to do.' I nodded in puzzlement, wondering what I was supposed to do. I decided not to ask but to await his command. I made my excuses and left him to his thoughts. It was past midnight and I was very pleased to go to bed. Outside, beneath the dark sky flickering with stars, the temples, houses and forest stood ghostly in the moonlight. Before surrendering to sleep, I lay on my back in bed listening to the mysterious night-time noises, thinking that if man were to travel into space, he would at some point hit a star or planet. It was not long before dawn began to break.

VII

Prophetic Vision

L et's get back to the subject in hand – Chao Anouvong – before I stray too far. I apologise if I have done so. After our return from his Dhamma and his philosophical studies at the That Phanom temple, he certainly became calmer. He was happy meeting people of all ranks and used his experience to encourage them to work together in pursuit of national unity. He was also by now much fitter, stronger and wiser; he continued to practise his oratory and his physical exercises, and he urged me to maintain my discipline to stay fit and healthy. I did my best but found that contemplating or reading and writing in the cool shade suited me best.

As commander in chief of the Lao army he'd to be strong to earn the respect he badly needed from Bangkok. I spent the next year or so catching up with my own work in the library while he went to war in LanNa. It was a dangerous task, but he'd no choice and had serious and difficult decisions to make. As usual, I was at the centre of it all.

Before sunset one cool, breezy evening, I found him sitting outside on the veranda looking very pensive. I slipped out unobtrusively behind him, leaning on the handrail while observing the fast-setting sun. Its red glow had turned the Mekong into a mirror of gold. He sprang up suddenly, his fists clenched on his hips and leant forward with his strong chin jutting out as he told me how he could restore LanXang to her former glory. To promote unity and stability, he wanted to distribute power and wealth amongst the people. The country, he said, was trembling on the brink of total collapse. He argued that increased stability would bring increased wealth, allowing for increased taxation to fund the rebuilding of the kingdom and divert more funds to the people, who had to be weaned away from corruption and taught to love their country and recognise their duty in its redevelopment. While he fixed his stare across to sandy Donchan Island, he stressed that King Fah Ngum was right:

people are power and the country could never develop without their support. Unfortunately for him, the kingdom had lost most of its population to Siam, and worse, real power lay on Rattanakosin Island; the crocodile of Bangkok had swallowed half of his body and his people were being suppressed.

'Is there any country in the world more peaceful, friendly and beautiful than Lao LanXang?' he murmured, taking a deep breath. I knew what he was really thinking as we both watched the setting sun: that it must have been a great relief for him to escape the enfolding gloom of Bangkok. He felt ecstatic to be back amongst his own Lao race, to be back in his home country, for he was descended from legendary Khoun Borom, a member of the very ancient (*Duekdamban*) royal family of the Ai-Lao NanChao kingdom. Then he returned to his seat and, with downcast eyes, sat still, like a meditating monk. I observed him closely. He took a deep long breath: in long and out long, in long and out short, his breath flowing freely to soothe his body and mind, directing and evaluating his thoughts. With his eyes shut he looked full and refreshed as if completely at rest, in a state of rapture, serenity and pleasure, preoccupied with a single, noble goal: the path to independence rather than nirvana.

Suddenly, like a visionary, he looked at me and said, 'Well, for the sake of LanXang, I do not intend to die leaving any little bit of talent unspent. And you too, Khoun Jon, must be willing to upset Bangkok. It is your destiny to travel this path with me.' He got up and stood next to me, giving my thin ribcage a gentle prod with his fingers. 'Come on, let's make a move. We've got plenty to do, and, together with the Lao people, we have far to go.' In silence we retreated inside from the darkness. I sensed something important was on his mind. We settled down: he, on his usual couch in his study, and I, on my normal chair facing him. He lay back on the sofa with his hands clasped behind his head, staring at the ceiling, stirring up some ideas.

After a long silence, he spoke so softly that his voice seemed to come from afar, as if he were waking from a dream. 'I was just thinking,' he said slowly. 'Do you know that water is the basis of all things, and do you know how important sticky rice is to us?' I didn't answer but pretended to read something and waited. After a long pause he said excitedly, 'In fact, Khoun Jon, rice is not a luxury.' I glanced at him and mumbled my understanding. 'It's a staple food which unites our people. Don't you think that if you enjoy eating this rice, then it's only right you should join the farmers and peasants and work in the paddy fields, or at least treat them fairly and have respect for the hand that feeds you?' I gestured my approval with a slight nod. 'We must show them we place more confidence in the ability of our fellow countrymen than in outsiders, and that we have a greater regard for the welfare of our own citizens than for the demands of our foes in Bangkok.' I could think of no sensible response, but again nodded and murmured my agreement. For a member of the royal family, his views were quite liberal; he disapproved of aristocratic or political privilege and believed sincerely in education for all and that the country should be run as a meritocracy. 'An absolute monarchy will soon be treated with contempt because it's prejudiced against the common people,' he said. 'I can see the end of the feudal system. The aristocracy is declining. People from all over the world will strive for freedom from tyranny in the pursuit of enlightened government. It's the beginning of the end for monarchy, not only in our kingdom but around the whole world; just mark my words.'

I was completely mystified by his self-depreciation, but it was an awe-inspiring comment, and his foresight seemed almost surreal to me. Although wise and full of ideas, he seemed more of a philosopher than a man of politics, or an opportunist who spied opportunity in difficult times. He was a rational man, without the usual aristocratic contempt for manual labour, and he wanted LanXang to prosper. He was prepared to live an ordinary life because he knew the aristocratic world, with all its grandeur and heroic values, was vanishing. I stated firmly that no one should rule unjustly over anyone else, be they natives or foreigners.

'Khoun Jon,' he said. 'If there is such a thing as reincarnation, I don't wish to be reborn into the royal family, and neither should you. But if that is what fate decrees for you, you should still try to be an ordinary, humble person.' I said I couldn't agree with him more. 'Of human relationships, that between father and son comes first; of social bonds, that between liege and liegeman is most important,' he went on. 'I lived in Bangkok amongst arrogant feudalists for much longer than I wanted to. I know what it's like; I've witnessed many unpleasant things. I can tell you bluntly they're rotten from the head down. It always starts at the top. The Rattanakosins' rule by decree created a divide in Siamese society; you can't blame people for wanting to denounce it and get rid of a tyrant.'

His words stirred my thoughts. To free LanXang from occupation by Bangkok, Chao Anouvong had to get involved in politics for the right reasons, not merely to receive awards or praise. He wanted to change society for the better and was willing to sacrifice his life to save the Lao nation.

'We want to take back control of our territory,' he went on, adding that the time would come when he would have to take the lead. He saw an equilibrium had to be established to achieve peace and stability in the kingdom. He would rather not be king, but neither was he prepared to bargain with Lao sovereignty: the most important mission of his life. 'The trouble with our past rulers,' he reminisced, criticising his family's past, 'is that we underestimated humility and simplicity. We have a tendency, it seems, to complicate and forget what's really important in our lives. We've focused on the process rather than the result. That's why LanXang is divided.'

He recommended that, as the pace of life continues to race along in the outside world, we mustn't forget to change our way of life to keep up. He also said that as sunshine is important to all living things, so is a kind heart and good humour to humanity. The Lao, therefore, shouldn't wait for ideal circumstances to fight for their freedom, because they might never arrive. I wasn't sure whether I completely understood him but murmured and nodded in agreement.

'But be warned. There is a price to pay,' he said knowingly.

'What would that be, Your Royal Highness?' I asked, hoping for a more detailed explanation.

He emphasised that the Lao people could not afford to be racist, because LanXang is home to many different ethnic minorities whose help they needed to administer the kingdom. In dealing with national minorities and tribal politics, the kingdom's policy should be Buddhist, socialist in content and national in form. King Fah Ngum managed to unite all of Lao LanXang because he was a noble ruler who cared about the well-being of his people. A happy community is a diverse community. LanXang had so much – culture and learning, laws (*Heed Sipson-Kong Sipsi*) and immense natural beauty – that needed to be protected and nurtured with care. But to forge a successful life in the future, you must lose sight of the old, learning from the past and looking to the future.

This sounded all very enterprising but somewhat confusing, I have to tell you. I remember thinking to myself: was this the end of the monarchy? Being conservative, I didn't necessary share his view that the country could exist without a king, but I did agree that a talented man could govern as well as a king, if not better. Rule merely by strict decree would severely damage the people's self-regard and force them to flee. Rule by morality, on the other hand, would allow the people to retain their self-respect; they would turn to their ruler of their own accord. All that bowing and scraping would be a thing of the past: all men are mortal, not gods. The three prevailing forms of government: nation, religion and king, would create patriotism amongst the people inspired by the geography and culture of their nation rather than towards their king. Therefore, the country would exist perfectly well without a monarch. Unfortunately, at that time, the dynastic king was a Siamese in Bangkok rather than a Lao in ViengChan.

I have to admit I heaved a sigh of relief when he finally stopped talking. Nevertheless, it was all very compelling and thought-provoking. He suddenly asked what I thought of the idea of a republic, which he said would suit the self-reliant and peaceful nature of the Lao. I was stunned but I realised that like Fah Ngum before him, he was desperate to unite his people in the fight for independence, and this was just another example of his desire for simplicity and humility. He was anti-pomp in style and chose to eschew the luxuries of the palace. Our expedition to the That Phanom temple and time spent living as commoners had been a wonderful experience for this humble man, and for me.

You might be surprised how much he confided in me, a lowly confidential secretary. It was always an honour, but trepidation was never far away: I sat still, my hands clenched, white with nerves, searching for the right answers. What was I to say to this man who so richly deserved to be my king? I calmly turned to him with downcast eyes, gathering my nerves and thoughts. And then, with a quick lick of my lips, I looked at him and replied.

'Very well Your Royal Highness, hear what I think,' I said confidently. 'Every country, independent or otherwise, needs a strong, clever, honest leader. This is even more urgent for us, a vassal state (*Phateth Salath*): we're fighting against time. Bangkok's dynasty is spreading like rabbits and is here to stay. They'll be a force to be reckoned with in Siamese politics in years to come. We mustn't let the people down and do nothing. In fact, I will be blunt. Of all the creatures that breathe and walk about on earth, man is more helpless than most. If he's prosperous and enjoys good health, he takes everything for granted, as if hard times will never come again. Yet when misfortune falls upon him, he must simply steel himself and bear it, like us.'

He gave me an understanding gaze. I went on to say that feudal rule of law risked something even more important – the freedom and unity of our people and society. It had become a matter of survival for the Lao nation. The truth is that feudal rulers were often incompetent, often their own kingdom's weak link. Kings weren't supposed to be political, but nevertheless actively interfered behind the scenes. Their flirtation with power and wealth, their unfair behaviour, their excess and irresponsibility, always generates public and social resentment. They should be made to see sense by being threatened with exile and humiliation.

'Well, Your Royal Highness,' I said purposefully, 'I know we're conservative and resistant to change, but we should try to run with purpose instead of walking. I entirely agree we should make a decisive shift for the sake of LanXang's future. I understand that our future as a monarchy might well be at stake, along with our honour and dignity. But we shouldn't care what Bangkok thinks and says but pursue what is right for our country. Nothing stays the same in this world. It could be a risk worth taking.'

He'd seemed uncertain and dejected but my answer pleased him and he smiled. He came forward and playfully flung his long arms around me. I was now strong enough to fight back, but I appreciated the gesture. Fortunately, he soon let go and took a step back.

'Thank you for your words, Khoun Jon,' he said, looking at me appreciatively. 'I can tell you have the right sort of blood in your veins.' This pleased me immensely. Unexpectedly he then placed his hands on my head. Normally in LanXang, you shouldn't touch someone else's head, unless they're a child: the head is regarded as the most spiritual part of a human being. I didn't mind of course because I knew my place and it was a tender gesture. I felt quite embarrassed but welcomed it: this was probably the first time he'd ever troubled himself to thank me properly. 'Sometimes,' he said, summing up his ideas, 'if you find yourself stuck trying to come to a decision, you should just go ahead and do it, even if you can't foresee the consequences. Only then can see your way through.'

'Yes, we must change,' he muttered, looking sideways at me, '…but slowly.' I nodded. The sun was setting and I was thinking of leaving when he said, 'Khoun Jon, do stay for dinner. It's only family,' he said casually. 'My brother Phommavong will join us too. I would like you to meet him.'

I was intrigued and excited by the prospect of finding out whether there was anything else he wanted to discuss. It was also a chance to get to know his brother better. Outwardly they seemed close, although perhaps Phommavong was a little more reserved. He was charismatic and said to be charming and very popular amongst fair-minded people in Bangkok – especially in the Bang

Khun Phrom area which had been named in his honour, where he'd supervised the building of temples.

The evening began with delicious food and jollity. Chao Anouvong's amusing stories and jokes produced roars of laughter, which he said was good for our health. I couldn't help laughing until my belly ached, I tell you. Later, as the meal was ending, he asked me to stay a while longer. It was late at night, without a flicker of wind to disturb the candles and oil lamps. Swarms of insects gathered, darting back and forth around the lights. Many accidentally flew straight into the flames, dropping to the floor. The monsoon mingled with the smell of the burning insects in the hot June air.

The two princes, Rathsabud Yoh and Suthisan Poh were sitting and looking relaxed as they enjoyed their freshly picked fruit and coconut juice after dinner. Nevertheless, they were observant, their eyes never far from their father.

The Queen, Nang Khampong, like a goddess, distilled charm and gentleness round her. She'd no formal constitutional role, but the king relied on her for emotional support. So, as usual, she made her excuses and went off to have a chat with her ladies in waiting and her servants.

Chao Phommavong, a very private man who preferred to keep his thoughts to himself, made himself comfortable in his chair, looking regal and dapper and very much a noble. I suspected that both brothers might have had just a little too much to drink as the soft glow of the light illuminated their faces. Suddenly, Chao Anouvong heaved himself to his feet, went over to the window and briefly scrutinised the moonlight outside. His serious face glowed as he came back to us.

'Gentlemen,' he said, perhaps just a touch too loud, 'may I have your attention please. I would like to make a little declaration. I thought it appropriate that Khoun Jon, who shares my thoughts and feelings, should hear it in person too. He is one of us.' Chao Phommavong turned to give me a quiet smile of consent. 'Now, as times are changing,' he continued, leaning slightly toward me. I sat nervously, twiddling my fingers. The princes became alert and sat up in their chairs. 'I believe we must seize the initiative. I propose we should transform our nation from a feudal state run by a privileged few, to a democratic state run by ordinary, free, wise people.'

'Oh, very good,' Phommavong said in his somewhat high-pitched Siamese accent, thinking it was part of his brother's usual banter. Chao Anouvong looked down at his brother; sensing the gathering excitement, Phommavong turned to look at the two princes and realised that Chao Anouvong was quite serious. 'But that's not funny,' he said, confused. The two young princes looked lost, their faces frozen, their jaws dropped.

I joined in at this point and asked Chao Anouvong whether he was serious.

'No fun and games. I'm perfectly serious, Khoun Jon,' he said, turning sharply towards me. 'We may suffer humiliation; worse, we may all end up dead.'

I was puzzled for a moment before realising that 'we' meant all the Lao people. It wasn't the royal 'we'.

'But you can't do that, Your Royal Highness,' I responded quickly, squaring up to him. 'What would our friends say? Who would the ordinary Lao look up to? They would think we'd betrayed them.'

He was taken aback and looked at me sternly, digesting the wisdom of my rebuke.

'Khoun Jon, it's not for others, especially our friends, to decide what we should do,' he countered, looking down at me before turning towards his sons who were gazing down at their drinks submissively. He raised his deep, probing voice, like a teacher struggling to help his students understand him. 'I know what you mean, and to a degree I share your concern and unease, but we're in a desperate struggle. We'll soon be obliged to take some risks. Ninety-nine per cent of Lao people think they're free to do what they want, but they're wrong. We really should have the freedom to make our own choices. I want to be myself, to live my life as an ordinary, free Lao citizen. There's absolutely no sense in preserving a feudal, authoritarian regime like that of Siam.'

'But surely we can't just change our constitution against so much opposition,' I persisted. Phommavong, who didn't like to argue, occasionally nodded in agreement with me. 'LanXang needs a leader of royal blood, a strong king, especially now. Your Royal Highness, what's the point of angering our closest friends in ViengChan?'

'After witnessing first-hand what the ruling classes have been up to in Bangkok for generations,' Chao Anouvong retorted, 'what's the point of trying to keep friends like these? Their pomposity and arrogance will destroy us all if we don't change. The Rattanakosin ruling dynasty is opportunistic and far from noble; since the day they came to power they've behaved as though they were gods… insecure and arrogant gods!' After a short pause he stabbed the table with his finger and said, 'Khoun Jon, we would be doomed if we were to follow that route. Mark my words.' I sat upright and trembled in disbelief, and he asked me if I had a better idea.

'Your Royal Highness, I doubt anyone has that foresight. But I do believe you're right,' I replied diplomatically. 'Our moment could pass before we even know it and we would have nothing left to bargain with. We must act now if we're to survive as a nation. But how do you think this can be accomplished?' He looked astonished. I reminded him that to fight for independence, the country needed a leader, a dynamic and capable king who understands the plight of the lowly poor and the wealthy privileged. And to run the country properly, the king needs officers, an army, architects, artists, writers, workers and farmers: all capable and enterprising people important to the kingdom's future. He, on the other hand, had a unique insight into the mind of the people and commanded their loyalty. 'Your Royal Highness, the people need you as their leader, their king.' I said vehemently. 'Freeing ourselves from our feudal system isn't going to solve anything, especially not our immediate problem. It might dull our thinking. We are under Bangkok's domination, after all.'

'Hear, hear!' Chao Phommavong said and nodded his assent.

'Father, please hear what I think.' Prince Yoh jumped in, putting his view forward in a forthright manner. 'Our identity as a nation is at stake. You must see to it that we have the courage to fight for it, I beg you.'

In support of his brother, Prince Poh asserted that his father must take the lead when the time came. Both princes were ambitious but lacked experience.

This all made me wonder whether acquiring philosophy from Phra Ajarn Khoon had made Chao Anouvong soft. Nevertheless, he was determined on principle to see these changes through.

'Come on! Why look so shocked and sad, Khoun Jon, and you too Phommavong, and both of you, Poh and Yoh? I'm not dead yet!' he said with a smile. 'These changes are a long way off; I doubt they'll happen in my lifetime, but talking about it won't do any harm, so no more long faces please! In the end, we'll have placed ourselves so firmly under the gaze of the ordinary people that we'll have no choice but to make the right decision before anyone forces us into it.'

'Bangkok is persecuting its own people and dominating Lao LanXang. One day they'll make enemies of their own people, you'll see. For now, they're our enemies because they want to deprive us of our freedom. They'll have a fight on their hands. It's time we became the defenders of the people and made friends rather than enemies. Then we can become a nation filled with good, ordinary citizens… but with one exception.' There was a long pause as he tried to gather his thoughts. Eventually he pointed his forefinger in the air and said, 'May the strongest, cleverest and most honest man lead our nation.'

On that evening, I couldn't think of anyone more suitable than Chao Anouvong himself.

Chao Phommavong made it very clear he wasn't in the least interested in political power. However, he agreed with his brother and told him that being a king in a vassal state was unbearable and he would rather live a simple life away from the palace. The two princes remained quiet at the end of our discussion. They had a lot on their minds. We were all tired. All three made their excuses and left the room.

As I was getting ready to go, Chao Anouvong looked at me with a slight smile, raised his finger gently to his lips and told me not to reveal our discussion to anyone else. As I didn't really understand everything he'd said, there was hardly any danger of me revealing anything important. Besides, I felt as though I were part of his family, and it touched my heart that night to hear him mention the word 'free' (*Issara*). He stressed that King Fah Ngum had abolished slavery in 1353. The noble Lao families were ordered to free their slaves and had to pay them handsomely for their services if they wished to retain them.

'All mortal beings should be free and equal in the name of humanity,' he said. 'And there should be no limits on this, since our brains can take us anywhere we want, in the world and in the whole universe. Any law that takes away freedom is deplorable. The Rattanakosins' laws are designed to suppress and persecute the Lao citizens in north and north-east Siam.'

Well, who could blame him for wanting to get rid of the Siamese? For a moment, I glimpsed the brilliant, starry future through his eyes, and I saw that he was right: that if we changed, we could be free and survive as a nation. Whenever I picture the word free, Chao Anouvong always comes into my mind. For all my working life I was a mandarin, a servant. I didn't think about my own worth. My services and sacrifice went together. That night he hovered over his ancestors' history, proclaiming himself mortal, an ordinary human being.

It was getting late. The two princes, I imagine, had already gone to bed, their minds full of their father's ideas. Seeing that the debate was ending, I got up abruptly, steadied my nerves and went over to him. I lifted my praying hands and he took them. Then he warmly squeezed my arms to show his appreciation.

'You're not leaving me already, Khoun Jon!' he said smilingly as I was returning to my seat. After a short pause and a sigh of relief he added, 'That went well.' But I noticed that his hand and voice were trembling slightly, for it was plain that his life, and the life of his nation, faced imminent change. There was no going back for fear of losing face. 'If you seek change,' he went on, almost to himself, 'and if you're directly descended from a feudal lord, no matter what happens, the people will still look up to you and respect you, but they will judge you for *what* you are, not *who* you are, because when it comes down to it, you're no better than them.'

'That would be correct, Your Royal Highness,' I said.

He looked at me out of the corner of his eye, gently nodded and smiled but almost immediately sank back into deep thought

At first, I must also confess I had some doubts: I couldn't see what he could possibly hope to achieve, except humiliate himself. In any case, people were too busy living their lives and were never going to pass judgement on him. If he managed to free LanXang from Siam, I suggested, we should then adopt a kind of quiet decency to avoid harsh comment and criticism. We would then simply melt into the life of ordinary, free citizens.

He threw himself into his chair with a gasp of relief, kicked off his slippers and closed his eyes. The tension in his face seemed to have eased. I realised his strategy was brilliant, but I felt for him; I was lucky in that I'd been brought up as an ordinary and free person, able to behave as I wanted, living my life without scrutiny of any form. I told Chao Anouvong that if something must be done, it must be done wholeheartedly, with no room for timidity. He lifted his tired eyes and turned slowly towards me.

'Well, Khoun Jon,' he said as he dragged his gaze away from the cobwebbed ceilings and their beams of red lacquer and gold leaf, 'to us and future generations falls a great test. We must have courage to free ourselves. And now,' – he sighed and calmly raised his hand – 'let us begin.' After a short pause, during which I lost myself in thought, he said, 'But first, as a nation we must be whole-hearted and win back our independence.'

In silence, we fixed our gaze on each other as if we'd discovered something special. And with that began a new era for Lao LanXang.

VIII

The Turning Point

You may remember that in 1795, Chao Inthavong became the ruler of
ViengChan. Chao Anouvong was appointed viceroy and subsequently
I became his private secretary (*Laykar*); the following year we embarked
on our trip down the Mekong to That Phanom.

Siamese oppression in the Khorat Plateau had polarised opinion in the
ViengChan palace and Chao Anouvong's arrival had transformed the Lao
movement. He injected a new sense of purpose and called for collective action
to be taken by the Lao people to protect their national identity and put an
end to Bangkok's ambition for a Greater Siam. He energetically combined
Buddhism and liberal politics to create a popular front against Siam, uniting
even ethnic groups in the most remote areas of the kingdom, long pre-occupied
with the cares of daily life to have any interest in politics.

I never forgot what Phra Ajarn Khoon had said to Chao Anouvong under
that hot midday sun at That Phanom temple. It often resonates in my head
like a temple drum: 'Go, rule ViengChan, conquer Bangkok, bring back the
Emerald Buddha and make your dreams come true.'

This was easy enough to say, but how do you achieve your goals with no
resources other than your own will power and determination? But Chao
Anouvong realised the only thing standing between him and the fulfilment of
his dreams was merely the will to give it a go and the faith to believe anything
was possible. He never shied away from challenges just because they were
difficult: he was an optimist who saw opportunities in everything. The ultimate
prize was within reach but he knew he'd to work for it. The first step was
obvious: he'd to become king in ViengChan. The throne was rightly his for the
taking and it was his duty to restore self-rule for LanXang.

He knew that to enter the corridors of power in Bangkok, he'd to be seen
to be trustworthy, to be prepared to take orders for Bangkok to allow him

to return to ViengChan and run his kingdom. He would then become well known and esteemed by his own people and the Siamese. He needed to put on a show, but where was he supposed to find the money? He'd no inheritance, only boldness and resourcefulness. His kingdom's wealth had been bled dry, its freedom stolen by Siam. He was a poor man by Lao aristocratic standards and lived in want. Allowances from Bangkok were grudgingly and deliberately small in terms of money and heavily monitored in terms of power, without a shadow of a doubt all designed to harm Lao LanXang.

Chao Anouvong faced, therefore, three difficult options: to develop LanXang and create wealth, which would take too long; to refuse to show allegiance to Bangkok, which would risk retaliation; or the middle path: patience. Predictably, soon after our return from Nakhorn Phanom at the beginning of February (*Deuan Yi*) 1796, he chose the third option. He really had no other choice because, as viceroy, he'd to report annually to Bangkok on LanXang's affairs, an occasion he considered a demeaning waste of time. But he'd to be very careful because the Siamese could easily make him disappear on the slightest pretext.

'Do you have a better idea, Khoun Jon?' he asked optimistically. My hands pressed against my mouth, I gave him a blank look and gently shook my head in silence. So, patience it was.

1797 was an uneventful year, but in 1798 he contributed to the Siamese war effort by going to war with Burma in LanNa. Bangkok was very satisfied by the viceroy's remarkable all-round performance.

In 1799, King Inthavong again ordered him to take the fight to the Burmese in LanNa, alongside the Siamese army led by the commanders Luang Thepharirack and Phraya Yommarath. His successes won him Bangkok's trust and he was appointed field commander of the Lao army.

In 1802 the Burmese army launched an offensive and captured XiengSaen before surrounding XiengMai. Luang Thepharirack and Phraya Yommarath were particularly hard-pressed, but during the dry season of 1803, from November onwards, Chao Anouvong was again sent by King Inthavong to help them defend XiengMai. Unfortunately the Lao army arrived seven days after the Burmese army had been defeated. Chao Anouvong had two options: to fight on or withdraw before the monsoon began. He favoured the former and prepared to march north-eastwards with 20,000 fighting men from six cities (ViengChan, Lampang, Prae, Nan, XiengMai and Luang Phrabang) to retake XiengSaen.

The beleaguered Siamese army apparently decided to return home during the rainy season of 1804 but Chao Anouvong insisted on retaking XiengSaen and succeeded in liberating LanNa from Burma. The wars were won with Lao blood and Siamese money, some of which came from selling off LanXang's riches. The war might have been lost without Chao Anouvong, and the two Siamese commanders were demoted and imprisoned by their commander in chief, Bovon Sathanmongkhol.

Bangkok showered Chao Anouvong with respect and honour for his bravery and a true friendship developed between him and the heir to the throne, Prince Itsarasunthon, who publicly praised him. This did not go down well, however, with Itsarasunthon's son, Prince Chetsadabodin. Chao Anouvong was shrewd enough not to revel in his popularity but had to work even harder to gain more respect and trust from Bangkok.

If Chao Anouvong had been killed in LanNa, history would have had very little to say about him.

After the victory at XiengSaen, he marched his army to XiengMai. He reported that the LanNa princes and people, who'd previously loved and revered King Xay-Setthathirath I as their ruler, extended the same courtesy to him. They held a grand *Baci* ceremony, and a lavish banquet (*Phasaveuy*) fit for a king to welcome him, and then again on his departure. He reminded them the people of Lao XiengMai LanNa (*Lao Xieng*) and Lao ViengChan LanXang (*Lao Vieng*) were brothers and pleaded with them to preserve Lao culture and traditions.

In the same year (1804), Chao Anouvong and his Lao army went on to help the Siamese army capture XiengHung, effectively expelling the Burmese from LanNa for good. He overcame every challenge, then relaxed and laughed at his own success. Prince Itsarasunthon not only greatly admired his bravery but also appreciated his many successful campaigns against the Burmese. But Chao Anouvong realised that even though these events had drawn him closer to the Rattanakosins, they also distanced him from some of his loyal supporters at home. He often flushed with anger when recalling his victories for Siam and cursed Bangkok for its unbelievable ingratitude. Nevertheless, this was the start of an even closer friendship between him and Itsarasunthon: they'd known each other for nearly twenty-four years but had always had their differences.

Although Chao Anouvong grew up in Siam with Prince Itsarasunthon, he remained a true Lao throughout. They both served as royal pages and often dined and listened at the king's joyful dinner table, sharing plenty of secrets. The whiff of Siamese superiority, however, was never far from the surface. Itsarasunthon, like his father before him, had one secret he never shared with Chao Anouvong: he was covertly working towards the annexation of LanXang and LanNa and also craved pieces of Cambodia, Malaya and Burma. Chao Anouvong knew the game, for he himself had been playing it diplomatically since 1795. Itsarasunthon guarded his secrets and Chao Anouvong, increasingly, guarded his. Their friendship was challenging one: in fact, they became the most intimate of enemies. It was inevitable their loyalties would conflict. Itsarasunthon had the ability to inspire awe, loyalty and affection and a wore a heavily embroidered gold cloak to emphasise his power. Chao Anouvong cherished his simple royal blue or purple-red robe.

As opposed to LanXang, which was of course ruled by a king but where the advisors were at least chosen on merit, in Siam the king's mandarins, enjoying the perquisites of their titles, were selected by birth alone. All power rested with the king, a figure of superhuman majesty, a god. This was the lasting principle in Siam, where intelligent, successful and knowledgeable Lao citizens such as politicians, lawyers, doctors, students, artisans and labourers were purged or prevented from attaining high positions.

Admittedly, while I concentrated on Chao Anouvong's affairs and my own, I quite forgot what had happened to his brother, the introverted Chao Phommavong, who refused to be involved in politics. He was a man of dignity and integrity who'd built many temples for the Lao community in Bangkok. Politics, as he saw it in Siam, was a dirty word. He said it destroyed humanity and added that Siam, like any selfish nation with an autocratic ruler, would end up destroying itself. I saw him only occasionally and the one time I ever got close to him was during that family dinner in 1799 when Chao Anouvong suggested the kingdom should relinquish its feudal mentality. Soon afterwards he went down to the south of the kingdom to avoid politics – possibly to Savanaketh or Champasak province. Mysteriously, he was never heard of again; not even Chao Anouvong knew where he was. I'm sure he and his family survived, but where could they have gone? Were they living in Bangkok? Somehow, I couldn't imagine that. I wish someone knew what had happened to him.

After Chao Anouvong's departure to LanNa, I was permitted time away from my duties. I'd been serving him for nearly nine years, working mostly in his study and travelling with him. Although I felt more motivated in his presence, it was exhausting at times. I was delighted to have time to myself or to spend with my mother. Like an introverted and eccentric individual, I silently separated myself from everyday life and enjoyed contemplation, breathing fresh air in the shade and thinking my own thoughts. I thought that life was but a dream, simplicity was purity and modesty was freedom from greed. I intended to live a solitary life, as simply as possible. I kept a low profile and was completely unmoved by fame or fortune. Like a misanthropist, I often avoided socialising because I didn't want to discuss anything hush-hush as my work was rather confidential. I lived in an atmosphere of perpetual peace for the sake of my soul, caring for my mother, dividing my time between the country and the palace, swanning around or sitting in comfort to read and write, expelling erroneous thoughts and relinquishing all aspirations and attachments. I became languid and apathetic. But I made a point of keeping in touch with a few kind and dear friends and meeting up involved much overindulging in eating and drinking. Consequently I began to put on weight. Fat once put on is never shed easily.

The benefit of being indolent was that I had time to think, in the shade of the day and the dark of the night. It was a halcyon period for me: I discovered that wisdom was a powerful inner light shining on the essence of everything and helping to eliminate the worries generated by one's own ignorance. Such was my life at this time: privately despairing of the future of the kingdom but praying for better times. I really took advantage of the spare time available to me to reflect, and reflection led to action. I even thought of writing a book, extolling LanXang and Chao Anouvong's merits and refuting Siam's claims. I'd gathered enough material and had even gallantly worked through quite a few chapters until I was on the very edge of slumber. I wanted to explain how wonderful Lao LanXang would have been if it hadn't been carved up by Siam. I prayed for my pen to strike more fiercely than the sword.

When I informed Chao Anouvong about this later, he took a great interest in my idle thoughts, telling me not to be too prejudiced against the Siamese, but he did agree with me about the Rattanakosins. The people of Lao LanXang, he said, had an issue with the Bangkok regime, but not with the Siamese people as a whole. He warned me it was too dangerous at that time to air my grievances and told me to wait until LanXang had achieved her independence and was strong enough to defend herself. This concerned me: it seemed the prospect of putting his principles into practice was even more remote. So I told him that if I outlived him, I would instead write a historical novel about him and LanXang. He gave me a worried look.

'I wish I could give you plenty to live on,' he said, 'for if there was a man who deserved security and care, it's you, Khoun Jon. The Lao people's lives are too hectic to spend time reading, or they're too busy partying, as if there's no greater goal than the pursuit of enjoyment. Besides, there's no money in books. Also, the Siamese government is far too thin-skinned to put up with opposing views, even when disguised as a work of fiction. I'm afraid your book might be banned, or even burnt. They'll be quick to denounce you and might whip you for it.'

'Nevertheless, I'm certain you would provide some eye-popping anecdotes about how the Rattanakosins conduct their cunning tricks (*Xiengmieng*) on us. I know you intend to fight them with the truths and expect to be heard in good faith. Your contempt will take you to some strange places, but don't be too specific and too incriminating: that might provoke criticism. On the other hand, your denunciation might shake heaven and earth and could well have a powerful effect on the people, especially the Lao. Your book will be incendiary, providing thought-provoking and highly detailed versions of events; it could well be a window into what people actually think. However, Bangkok will not fall by mere denouncing alone. Knowing the Siamese, especially the royalists, they would likely respond with hatred towards you and might even want to silence you. They might well mount a full-throated defence of the Rattanakosins' policy and scream with fury!'

'Equally, they might well become more understanding and come to their senses,' he continued after a short pause. 'Your portrayal of the Rattanakosins shouldn't really provoke controversy because it's based on history, a plain narrative backed by undeniable historical events. If they don't enjoy reading it, well, they can always just stop. They might admire and congratulate you; you might even become celebrated and end up friends with some of them. I'm sure your powers of recall are as prodigious as if my soul was reincarnate in you, Phia Jon. Your book will be too good to be true and a pleasure to read: as excruciating as it will be delightful. No one in their right mind could therefore challenge such an excellent account of our past. I know you're extremely sensitive about it and perhaps we shouldn't tell anyone else what you're writing about. But I hope,' he half-whispered and gazed at me, 'what you write about me will be worth reading; please don't forget to let me peruse it. I would like to be the first to enjoy it.'

'My main purpose in writing it isn't really to undermine the Siamese version of history,' I said. 'It's our right to take liberties in the interests of literacy. I'm prepared to take a risk in pursuit of the truth. Besides, the book shouldn't be considered incriminating evidence, but a useful lesson from the past that every educational institution should hold dear. You will be the first to read it.'

'Thank you and I agree, entirely,' he said. 'There has been little genuine teaching of history in Siam, but the regime is far too delicate to risk publication at this stage. The way out for Bangkok is honesty, but in my experience they've never been honest about their own history; all they do is exult themselves. They're congenital liars and would never tell the truth for fear of incriminating themselves.'

'Your Royal Highness, I'll try to be subtle, but it could become quite a sensation!' I added with a deprecatory smile, chuckling before revealing that I wasn't really equipped with the nerves for public life. I didn't want to be a target or stared at, and thus had no wish to be famous. I was very content in Chao Anouvong's company and in doing my best for LanXang. I seldom feared loneliness and dying alone, leaving behind no trace of my existence. It was an unsettling time and I talked to him of leading a more conventional life with a wife and children. I was fond of children because I often felt as if I were a child myself. Admittedly, in moments of solitude I often played with the idea, but I simply couldn't make up my mind to do so.

'A man without a wife or companion is like a house without beams,' he said astutely and suggested that, for LanXang's sake, it was necessary for me to procreate. He insisted on paying my bride's dowry of land and money so I could get married, have children, keep chickens and pigs and grow my own fruit and vegetables.

'Actually, Your Royal Highness, I could see myself calling out "chickens!" to my feathered friends at feeding time and when they go to their roost at dusk.' He laughed jovially. I thanked him and added that I was obliged to him, as always. He proposed two possible brides and he assured me he could obtain their parents' consent. One was his half-brother Phraya Tissah's young daughter Nang Angkham. She was a very sociable, endearingly loquacious, incorrigibly name-dropping, bubbly, slim, wealthy but unworldly girl who laughed loudly and infectiously, and goodness me she was incredibly ugly (to me at least). She was also an arrogant snob who was determined to marry a rich lord. When she finally did, she was miserable ever after.

The other was Phraya Sanon's only daughter, Nang Duangmala. She behaved like a lady with exquisite taste and manners. She was civilised, highly articulate, polite and devoted to clean living. She was two years my senior but looked remarkably young and angelic. Unfortunately she bore a remarkably strong facial likeness to her father, and, worse, I heard she snored. Well, could you imagine me coming home to a hideous wife or sleeping next to Phraya Sanon every night? It was no laughing matter, I tell you. In truth, because of his charisma and intimate friendship with Chao Anouvong, I would have liked to have known Phraya Sanon better. For that reason, I was more inclined to the idea of him as a father-in law, but then again, I would rather he was just a friend, and then his daughter wouldn't be my wife. Frankly, I simply didn't fancy either of the ladies. The poor women were probably as horrified by the whole idea as I was! There were plenty of other decent beautiful girls available, but my morals forbade me from fathering illegitimate children.

'There are plenty of lucky bastards in the world,' Chao Anouvong said jokingly, and we laughed. 'Anyway, Khoun Jon, Nang Angkham is all right for partying with, but marrying, never! If I were you, I would go for Nang Duangmala and then your children would be related to me.' He looked me in the face and said, 'Well, the choice is yours.' With a cheeky wink he added that both would provide me with plenty of children.

'Your Royal Highness!' I exclaimed and blushed. We laughed raucously and heartily. 'Actually, this is a dream of mine,' I declared, catching my breath, 'but the only girl I would wish to share my life with is quick, amusing, a good conversationalist, understanding, with all the virtues I so love in life; sadly she got married to a very rich man who was old enough to be her father before I had a chance of developing a relationship. How would you feel about me stealing the old man's wife?'

'Really!' he groaned, looking pleased. 'Oh, poor you, Khoun Jon. What can I say? Never mind.' He paused for thought. 'I'm sure she's a very nice girl but I think you'd better leave her well alone.' He looked rather relieved, as though he were worried my marriage might disrupt our friendship. As an attempt to discourage me, he didn't even bother to ask who the girl was. When I told him her name was Nang Sousada, he just winked and said, 'Yes, nice name, I suppose.'

Well, I knew he didn't want to lose me or my loyalty. I plotted for LanXang independence on his behalf more than I was prepared to admit. I think he knew it. Even so, I kept an eye out for Nang Sousada whenever I attended almsgiving at the temple or went about the city. My life was a little vacant, but I was contented enough. The thought of losing my freedom repulsed me. Perhaps the gods destined me to be alone and therefore denied me children with all the women I'd ever lain with. My liberty was very useful as his private secretary. Time sped by as I occupied my time with reading, writing, socialising and travelling. But most of all, I devoted my time to serving him; I never allowed myself to be influenced by fashion or following the common herd, but I just enjoyed my simple bachelor existence, preferring to live with nature and books rather than a spouse. However, I liked flirting at dinner parties with clever, amusing and pretty women, and loved good conversation and sharing jokes with influential, knowledgeable and fair-minded friends.

'So, Your Royal Highness,' I said dejectedly, 'may I tell you in confidence that I think I'll be living alone; from now on. I've decided to leave my hopes for the future in the hands of Lord Buddha and the gods.'

'I know you'll keep yourself happily busy,' he said, awe-inspiring severity in his voice. 'I tell you what, when I'm gone, why not write about our wit and wisdom instead?'

'I'll try,' I said. He was right in saying I was impassive and both mentally and physically strong, but he was worried my head was almost empty of religion or politics but full to the brim with wisdom and philosophy: I'd been educated out of my wits. But we both agreed that self-rule was the only way forward for LanXang and that eating less, exercising and laughing were all good for our health.

Anyhow, I'm delighted and proud to say again that Chao Anouvong exceeded all expectations. I think he was pleased to find me waiting at the palace when he returned from LanNa. I was very glad to welcome him, to renew our friendship and serve him again. He'd lost weight and looked ten years younger than when he'd left ViengChan. He was surprised to see my thick neck, chubby face and the solid flesh on my small frame. He ordered me to exercise and to get fit. Did I? I certainly did. Not only exercising – walking, jogging and gardening – but I also ate less and kept off alcohol to slim down.

The war effort had clearly exhausted him. Bangkok had promised him triumphs in return for his loyalty and military support but had done nothing about it. He'd been treading water, carrying out his military duties and nursing his secret antipathy to the Rattanakosins. He angrily told me how he felt betrayed by Siam.

'Life is unfair,' he said. 'After shedding so much blood and sweat for Siam, what do we get in return for our loyalty and bravery? They talk the talk as if they were successful businessmen, but we invested more than they did in terms of equipment, provisions and men. Therefore, in accordance with business principles, we should receive more dividends. No land's been returned to us; on the contrast they never stop grabbing more.' He paused; he was really angry. 'We'll have to demand all our land back even if they don't want to return it,' he continued. 'Bangkok should take a long, hard look at itself. How dare they want to dominate us? It's not just and it contradicts the compassion and morality they so often claim to promote. They've betrayed us! It's high time someone faced up to that impudent gang in Bangkok. For now, I'm afraid, we're in the hands of Theravada and the gods.'

He was right. To understand his fury, it was important to delve into the past. LanNa and LanXang were separate kingdoms, but the Rattanakosin kings wanted to annex both. The war campaign had been a great success but Chao Anouvong's conscience was now at a crossroads. But he still hadn't decided how to proceed: declaring LanXang autonomy wasn't yet possible but he wondered whether he might be able to persuade Bangkok to grant it. The most lasting consequence of the war, however, was not the defeat of the Burmese, but the opportunity it created for Bangkok to occupy LanNa and become too powerful for LanXang to oppose.

'Your Royal Highness, nothing wrong with anger against injustice, but we mustn't be bothered by trivial matters,' I reasoned, 'and get ourselves worked up, otherwise we'll be consumed by our own anger and fall ill. We must discover the enemy's strengths and weaknesses. We cannot act impulsively: for now, we must seek peace not war, and focus on development. We have time to work out our tactics and stratagems to prevent the creation of a Greater Siam, which is a conspiracy to erase LanXang and LanNa from the earth.'

'Khoun Jon, you're absolutely right. Well said.' He closed his eyes to calm himself down and then said, 'What would you suggest?'

'I have surmised Your Royal Highness's thoughts,' I said. 'We aren't powerful enough to prevent them taking LanNa. Perhaps we should gift it to them out of loyalty, to trick them into believing we desire to co-operate with them. They might then not bother about annexing LanXang, but they're so greedy for power I have my doubts.'

'Precisely, Khoun Jon; you're most perceptive. I'm impressed,' he said.

After his successful war against the Burmese in LanNa, Chao Anouvong had at least earned some respect and gathered a decent crowd about him. He was now in the ascendant: his image was everywhere, even in Bangkok, resplendent and popular.

When he returned from LanNa to ViengChan in 1804, Chao Anouvong began to feel more confident as his influence spread. He enthusiastically participated in festivals where poems, speeches and patriotic songs addressed the theme of national rejuvenation. He personally encouraged people to take part in literature, music and the performing arts to inspire a rejuvenation of Lao cultural heritage. He took a voracious interest in writing new poems and verses to spread his vision of LanXang's future. He'd an admirable writing style, beautiful and neat, as shown on an inscription on the black marble in Wat Sisaketh. However, most of the time he didn't actually write himself but dictated to me. He would gather his thoughts and, when he was ready, signal to me while pacing the dark, shiny teak floorboards of his study, reading or reciting his poetry with enthusiasm. I was not a trained amanuensis and occasionally struggled to keep up, having to store some of his writings in the depths of my memory. Sometimes he took me to his austere, simple bedroom in the palace, and then, while I blushed and tried not to look, he would unashamedly get undressed and continue to dictate. His speeches had both a sorrowful and a rhetorical tone, expressing his very personal desire for national reunion and his deep-felt antipathy towards Bangkok's domineering policies (as shown in his poem *San Leub-Phasoun*). The Lao population began to feel closer together; he still wasn't that powerful, but they respected him as his words and actions exuded kingliness. The governors of the major cities of LanXang, especially on the Khorat Plateau, turned to ViengChan for protection. Whenever they attended the half-yearly meetings in the palace hall, they all wanted to meet him and pledge their allegiance to him. He advised them to prepare the people for the liberation of LanXang from Siamese domination.

The more energetic and daring Chao Anouvong appeared, the greater his chances of earning respect and trust. King Chulaloke and Prince Itsarasunthon appreciated his loyalty and had no qualms in allowing him to rule ViengChan. His efforts to penetrate the Bangkok establishment had at last succeeded. He'd won his first battle – the political mind game – but more patience was needed.

King Inthavong ruled ViengChan until the end of 1803, but soon after Chao Anouvong's triumphant return from LanNa, he died suddenly. I longed to know what had become of his two daughters who he left in Bangkok, the Princesses Thongsouk and Kounthon. It is said the former became Chulaloke's consort and the latter became one of Naphalai's queens. Thus, Lao royal blood continued to be revered in Bangkok by the proud Siamese.

Finally, the ViengChan court officials asked Chao Anouvong to ascend to the throne, arguing it was his destiny and time waits for no man. It was a brilliant move but sadly the real power rested in Bangkok: they had to approve his accession. I also pleaded with him not to entertain any notions of a transition into a republic. The circumstances were right for him to be king and save LanXang. There was no alternative. Besides, I really approved of it in my heart: I wished the royal ViengChan line to continue.

He willingly accepted the duties and responsibilities of being king of LanXang because he honestly believed that the timing was auspicious. He wasn't lusting for power but heeding the will of heaven. He continued to wage war for Siam with one hand while keeping his eyes and ears open for the opportunity to rebel against them.

His ascension was not a particularly magnificent affair for he didn't believe in wasting time, and the resources available to him were limited. He never relished personal attention or sentiment, so insisted on a low-key ceremony with the absolute minimum of fuss. During the ceremony he proclaimed that he owed his kingship not to family, to military success or to Bangkok, but to the Lao people. He declared he would perform his duty with dignity and expressed his determination to protect Lao LanXang's honour and advance the happiness and prosperity of her people. He did not intend to merely fill the office of king, but to protect LanXang passionately and vigorously from the wicked desires of outsiders. This drew plenty of loud cheers from the crowd who wished most ardently to be liberated. He was truly the people's king in his own right and was given the kingly name of Xay-Setthathirath III.

'As a patriotic king, I owe it to the Lao people,' he declared. 'All of us must be prepared to serve the country. Let's get to work!' he added, gave a nod of thanks and waved his farewell to the cheering crowd.

'Long live the king and Lao LanXang!' the people waved back, shouting and applauding with joy before dispersing

The following morning, while I was working in the library and keeping an eye and ear out for his sudden appearances, it began to rain rather heavily – one of those showers you expect to see during the monsoon season. It was a phenomenon: it washed everything clean throughout the city and the air felt much cooler than usual, which I thought must surely be a good omen. I mentioned this when Chao Anouvong unexpectedly turned up with his son, Rathsavong Ngao. He merely shrugged at my credulity, saying that given their powers, the immortals should have bestowed independence on LanXang, not rain.

'Please don't eat too much of that mango,' said Chao Anouvong to his son and continued walking.

'I like it very much. W-h-y?' said the young prince.

'I told you you'll get tummy ache. Remember?'

'I remember you also said you're my father,' Rathsavong Ngao said confidently, taking a small bite from the yellowish-green mango in his hand. He didn't want his mouth full.

'Yes I did and of course I am,' Chao Anouvong said pleasantly, gazing at his son's upturned face, 'and a father should teach his children.'

'W-h-y?'

'Because children have to learn. You have to be educated to become a man.'

'And one day you will be king?' the young prince said and swallowed.

'But I *am* the king! Now, you must listen, learn and obey me… and be loyal to me.'

'I will, father,' said the prince and bowed in puzzlement. After a short pause he said, 'I am only small, father, and I don't know much yet, do I?'

'That's correct. You're just a boy and therefore you must be willing to learn.'

'W-h-y?' asked the prince without thinking and said, 'I'm not clever because I'm not big like you.'

'Of course not. And at your age, if you're not clever, you must be ignorant, mustn't you?'

'Yes, father, I suppose so,' said the prince, returning to his thoughts.

'So you're learning new things from me because you're ignorant.'

'Is it only ignorant people who learn, and not clever ones?' the confused-looking prince asked.

'No, clever ones also.'

'So, am I a clever one because I'm learning from you, father?'

'I jolly well hope so, and I think that's enough for now,' Chao Anouvong said, turning to me. I bowed to him.

'Father, when can I go to school?' the prince said. 'When I'm older?'

'When you are six, ask me again. Four is too young.'

'W-h-y? I shall be five in *Deuan Yi* (February) next year,' he said, but he could feel his father's silent laughter through his hand. 'Can't I start then?' He bit sparingly at his fruit, trying to think of more questions.

'Perhaps, if you're good,' said Chao Anouvong.

'I am good!' exclaimed the prince. 'If you promise me, I'll show you something, father.'

'Oh, tyrant! What can it be?'

They stood still. The prince told his father to look away, then carefully brought something out from his shirt pocket with his right hand, quickly covering it with the palm of his left.

'Look!' he said proudly, slowly opening his dirty, childish hands to reveal a bright, sparkling, green beetle the size of a thumb, tied by a thread around its neck. 'I caught it in the garden while playing with the puppy.'

'What is that?' said Chao Anouvong, as though he'd never seen one before, and his eyes widened. 'Ah, it's very beautiful, but if you let it go, I'll consider letting you start school next year.' The green beetle took off suddenly, but it could only fly around in a circle because the prince was holding the other end of the long thread.

'Please promise you'll let me go to school next year, father?' persisted the prince.

'Oh, very well then, I promise!' said Chao Anouvong, putting his hands up.

'Thank you, father.' The prince dashed to the windows, untied the thread and threw the insect out high into the air where it flew away. 'I've done it. He's gone,' announced the prince, and hurried back.

'Good,' Chao Anouvong said, giving his son a serious look. 'From now on, please remember that every living creature on earth, especially man, likes to be free. And we Lao don't want to be slaves. We want to be free.'

The prince nodded, like one to whom all has been made clear, but he longed to know more. He suddenly pulled his father's arm and asked yet another of his stored-up questions.

'Can I ask you something, father?'

'Of course you can.'

'You often say the Siamese boss us about. Is that why we don't like them?'

The question took Chao Anouvong by surprise. He stopped to think about it and looked down at his son.

'You'll soon learn all about it and then you can make up your own mind,' he said, and carried on walking. 'But please don't ask them to their face.'

'W-h-y not, father?'

'Because it's bad manners… and you'll upset them.'

'If they look down on us, why do we have to be polite to them, then?' said the prince, in anger.

'Well, it helps to have good manners and we're civilised and respectful people,' said Chao Anouvong as he walked towards me, 'especially towards those we don't like.'

The prince listened alertly, his eyes turned up to show the whites, then moving and focusing. 'When I'm big…' he said, then paused and silently counted up to ten on his fingers. 'When I'm big, I will fight them.'

Chao Anouvong's head went back and he gave a great belly laugh. He turned towards his adorable son, ruffled his hair with a grin and started to walk him to the door. 'Come,' he said, grinning and showing his strong, white teeth. 'I think it's time for you to leave us.'

The prince stood biting his lower lip, gazing up to his father. He said, 'I shall be five next year!' He bit liberally at the mango until he'd finished it.

Chao Anouvong paused, holding the door handle. 'Yes, alright you little monkey, but please don't go catching anything out there,' he said and then opened the door leading into the garden.

I must confess that when he spent more time with his son in the garden than he did with me, I felt oddly jealous. He often sat there in front of a lily pond, composing a poem or a speech while the goldfish somnolently swam about.

'I won't, father.' The prince turned and walked out of the room, smiling. 'I'll plant the mango seed in the garden for it to grow.'

'Very good. Excellent idea! But don't forget to water it,' said Chao Anouvong and dismissed his son with a wave of the hand.

The young prince turned round, raised his little hands to his chest, bowed to his father, bade goodbye and began to skip away. 'I'll water it,' the prince said and his voice rang faintly through the hallway as he disappeared into the secluded, high-walled, shady garden of tranquillity, where the trickling water of various bamboo fountains combined with the birdsong to make a soft, soothing, murmuring concert, and the sweet aroma of *Dork Champa* flowers and jasmine mingled in the still air. Chao Anouvong didn't shut the door until he'd seen that all was well but the prince didn't know he was being watched and relieved himself on the ground where he'd just planted the mango seed.

'Never mind,' muttered Chao Anouvong. 'It might germinate, I suppose.' He closed the door quietly and quickly came toward me. I prostrated myself before him as my new king. Finding this amusing, he ordered me to stand up instantly. As I heaved myself to my feet, he looked at me and said, 'Now, Khoun Jon, a wise lord recognises and honours greatness of heart. I want you to be the first to know that I wish to award you with a higher rank... and there's no question of you thinking about it.'

Overwhelmed by gratitude, I was speechless and respectfully dropped to my knees. I could hardly refuse. He touched both my shoulders in turn and told me to rise.

Henceforth I became a courtier: a member of the nobility with the title of *Phia*. Unlike the other courtiers in the palace, I became even closer to Chao Anouvong and from then onwards I reverently addressed him as 'Your Majesty' in public, and I was known as 'Phia Jon'. Unlike the kings who came before him, who styled themselves 'Lord of Lives' (*Chao Sivid*), he was quite a contrast, a down-to-earth, decent fellow who was capable of errors and unintentional misdeeds. More importantly, he couldn't just sit idly by while his people were suffering and understood he'd to deliver. 'Phia Jon, we're fine if we make ourselves useful in some way, but shameful if we're useless in the eyes of the people,' he said.

Prince Khi, one of his sons, became viceroy and represented LanXang affairs in Bangkok, enjoying an affluent lifestyle amongst his Siamese friends. Later, the viceroyship passed to Phraya Tissah in ViengChan.

Chao Anouvong surprised everyone by his wisdom, far-sightedness and cleverness in opposing Bangkok's domineering policies. Siam, he said, mustn't be allowed to annex Lao territory. I was more than happy in the duties that had fallen to me and it was incredibly worthwhile to be working so closely with him.

He understood that the loss of his brother Nanthasene was a merely private grief, but the enmity with Bangkok was a public affair. In 1806 his campaign to unite the kingdom gathered momentum. He travelled to the That Phanom shrine to pray with the leaders of the towns of Nakhorn Phanom and Mukdahan. As a sign of unity, they paved a path – known as the 'Bridge' – all the way from the Mekong to the temple. Chao Anouvong increased the height of the That Phanom spire and built an attractive sanctuary in the temple courtyard. He also sent many friendly letters and gifts to the king of Luang Phrabang as an attempt to secure unity, which he badly needed.

Now he was king, he bore his humiliation quietly and focused on restoring the people's trust. LanXang had been in decline but new life and ambition was beginning to stir. He set out energetically to increase his influence. The future of LanXang was never far from his mind and his commitment to bring justice to the kingdom was so unwavering that he began planning for ViengChan's reconstruction. He became a real working king, a true ruler of men, and promptly set his sights on restoring the kingdom to its former glory. He invoked King Fah Ngum's basic laws of honesty, love and leniency to reassure the people, albeit combined with the strict and clear understanding that right and wrong, reward and punishment, would be meted out appropriately. He focused his efforts on nurturing his people and asked them to cultivate more wastelands for growing rice on the Khorat plain so they could fill their granaries before taxes and levies were imposed. His other goal was to put an end to the futile dispute with Luang Phrabang. Over the next few years, he devoted himself entirely to the rebuilding of the capital and gathering support and trust, especially from the provincial governors along the right bank of the Mekong and the cities on the Khorat Plateau who were indispensable to his new alliance.

Chao Anouvong's time had finally arrived. King Chulaloke died unexpectedly in September 1809. His son, Prince Itsarasunthon, took the Siamese throne under the name Phra Phutta Loetla Naphalai (henceforth referred to as Naphalai), and became the second Rattanakosin king. He kept his pledge not to keep Chao Anouvong in Bangkok and allowed him to continue to rule ViengChan.

This move, however, provoked the jealousy of King Naphalai's first son, Prince Chetsadabodin, born of a common concubine in 1788. At a young age he'd been a bully, fond of sport and swordplay, and he liked to hang around with the officers of the guard. He saw Chao Anouvong as his rival, a thorn in his flesh and a threat to Siam, not so much because Chao Anouvong had become such a close friend to Naphalai, but because he was so much more respected in Bangkok than Chetsadabodin. The rivalry between them intensified when King Naphalai told Chetsadabodin that Lao soldiers had won the war for Siam in LanNa in 1804, not men from Bangkok. Naphalai even bragged of Chao Anouvong's military achievements and showed favouritism toward him. Chetsadabodin sulked in anger and became even more vindictive and jealous towards Chao Anouvong.

Presumably, some of the more impartial Siamese elite saw that Chao Anouvong cared more for friendship with Naphalai than political ambition and behaved in a manner that greatly profited Siam. There was a resurgence of interest him and he was often invited to their houses. Whenever he rose to speak at dinner parties, they listened respectfully. He never missed a chance to remind them that Siamese and Lao are Ai-Lao brothers. They praised him fulsomely, but he knew that deep down, some of them were envious of him.

In recognition of his bravery and in honour of their friendship, King Naphalai diverted his power and talents into creating an elaborate pleasure lake full of sacred lotus flowers and exotic fish. Although Chao Anouvong was presented with money and gifts, the Siamese were simply unable to win his heart, nor could the threat of death hinder his noble desires for LanXang. He was shrewd enough to realise that popularity and power are two separate things and tried to turn his good reputation in Bangkok into political influence. He worked hard to win more friends through diligence and panache; his status was on the rise because, after all, more people worship the rising than the setting sun. He was probably at the height of his popularity in Siam but he knew this put him on a collision course with the silver-tongued men of Bangkok who vied for Chetsadabodin's patronage with their petty minds and beguiled him with their smooth words.

Thus Chao Anouvong, at thirty-seven, fully approved by King Naphalai, continued to be king of ViengChan LanXang while his citizens actively opposed the Rattanakosin political establishment. Bangkok didn't resist and granted him the title 'The King of LanXang', allowing him considerably more political and cultural autonomy. Naphalai's approval was a popular move but Bangkok's suspicion of Chao Anouvong was far from over and the Siamese king's actions weren't welcomed by his entire elite, who wielded their power so aggressively against LanNa and LanXang.

Chao Anouvong insisted he wouldn't have become king if Chetsadabodin were in charge. But even though he was still only king of a vassal state, he was partly free from the confinement of Siamese rule and able to strengthen his kingdom's internal development and increase confidence amongst its people. He sought to enhance Lao, not Siamese, prestige and to dissolve the twenty-five years of Siamese domination into a single national consciousness. Some Lao nobles, especially those on the Khorat Plateau, spoke Siamese and even had Siamese names, but they increasingly viewed Siam as Lao LanXang's principal enemy. Chao Anouvong's patriotism struck an extraordinary chord: he stood as the embodiment of Lao – a true Lao nationalist.

Chao Anouvong was the catalyst for the re-emergence of Lao consciousness (*Khuam Penh Lao*) and desire for self-rule. Unity and independence were the way forward. His words were his weapons; he advocated a self-reliant and self-respecting ethos and promoted LanXang's position in the region. Luck may have played some part in his life but it wasn't luck that allowed him to remain as king. His extraordinary devotion to his duties had made his political ascendancy possible. By this time you could feel the weight of history was in his hands and he knew what LanXang had to do. He'd provided his people with hope and believed they would give him the support he needed in his fight against Bangkok.

The cities of Nongkhai, ViengKhuk and PhanPhao on the right bank of the Mekong were strategically important to ViengChan. Therefore he built the Wat Sibounheang temple in Nongkhai in 1808, followed by the smaller Wat Phra Kaeo temple in Si-Xiengmai, opposite ViengChan. He was very concerned about the dilapidated state of the original Hor Phra Kaeo temple – the Royal Chapel since 1566 – and ordered its complete renovation.

In 1812, to strengthen ties with the ruler of Nakhorn Phanom, he presided over the alms-giving ceremony at the That Phanom temple. Many governors from various cities along the Mekong also attended to pay their respects to him.

After several smooth and untroubled years, he'd brought his kingdom up to scratch, earning the complete trust and respect of the people. Gifts and donations soon began flowing in such abundance that he was able to build more new temples and repair old ones. With surprising proficiency he transformed the wreck of ViengChan into a proper capital city. Like King Fah Ngum before him, he imposed a code of moral standards that he'd always tried to base his own behaviour on. He channelled his energy almost entirely into rebuilding the country and, in almost no time, ViengChan became a magical place again.

King Anouvong ruled LanXang for twelve difficult, but successful and peaceful years. Happy, then, was he in the rainy season of his forty-ninth year: popular, well rested after the dry winter and ready to celebrate what had been accomplished. It was the most creative and contented period of his life. He'd performed incredible deeds, his intellect inspired awe and his merits were known all over the kingdom. The people had all they needed; he'd brought them hope, joy and happiness. He became the pillar of the nation. A tremor of confidence and excitement ran through LanXang and the people worshipped him and hastened to confer every possible honour on him. He was at his zenith.

Then, in 1816, he officially opened the Emerald Buddha Chapel (*Hor Phra Kaeo*) after its restoration. The raised foundations made the temple look strikingly imposing and celebrations went on for fifteen days and nights, despite the sacred Emerald Buddha still being far away in the Siamese capital.

Hor Phra Kaeo

'One day,' he announced at the ceremony, lifting his outstretched forefinger, 'I have no doubt the Emerald Buddha will return to our capital city.' The old fire came back as he reminisced about the Siamese invasion of ViengChan in 1779, how they looted and pillaged their way to a fortune and laid waste with cruel efficiency. The surprised and bewildered crowd looked at each other and then turned their gaze on him. He lifted his shoulders and stared back at them. He reminded them that King Xay-Setthathirath was the only monarch who'd been crowned in front of the sacred Emerald Buddha; he'd ruled both LanXang and LanNa and brought the Buddha from Lao LanNa to Lao LanXang, where it had stayed in ViengChan since 1560. The sad truth, he said, was that the Siamese had removed it using a monstrous deception; they ought to be ashamed of their rapacious past and atone for their sins by repatriating it to ViengChan.

'Let me repeat what the Siamese did and said,' he continued, looking up at the cloudy sky. 'Before removing the Emerald Buddha, they eyed it with jealousy and fingered it with covetous hands. They prayed and vowed they would only take it away on loan and return it when 'peace' returns to our capital. King Khoun Borom said that if something is borrowed or stolen, it should always be returned. As you know, we're a peaceful people and due to our strategic location, our kingdom has always been at peace. We've always had to tread with care with our powerful neighbours, minding our own business. The Siamese were the ones who brought war to us. We know what kind of people they are. Time will tell whether they'll repent of their deeds. If not, we'll neither forgive nor forget.'

A tremendous cheer erupted from the kneeling crowd. Suddenly the clouds lifted and ViengChan was bathed in rays of sunlight, as if the gods were presiding over the event.

'Let it be true! (*Sathu Anumothami*)' the people said in prayer.

Chao Anouvong also reminded them of the five curses predicted to fall on the Siamese if the Emerald Buddha wasn't returned.

1: The rivers and the seas would flood their land.
2: Political unrest amongst its people would bring chaos to their kingdom.
3: Siam would fall into turmoil and split into many parts.
4: Their monarchy would be abolished.
5: Bangkok would sink and some of their land would disappear into the sea.

Then he lifted his gaze to heaven.

'May what you say prove true? *Sathu, Sathu, Sathu Anumothami!*' the people said and prayed in chorus.

Empathy was the essence of Chao Anouvong's art. He was impressed. I glanced around and saw some people, mostly elders and women, with tears running down their cheeks, perhaps tears of bitterness. I felt a shiver had gone down the Rattanakosins' spine and would continue to do so. The Siamese dared not speak about their atrocities and the theft of the Emerald Buddha.

Chao Anouvong told me later that as a man of karma, he'd hoped the Emerald Buddha would return one day, otherwise it would only ever exist in the national memory. 'We must have faith,' he said, 'that what has been taken away from us, our lands and people included, will always return to us in the end.' I was immensely proud of his achievements. As for his faith, the Lao people had to remain peaceful, be optimistic and have patience – their karma.

The building of the new library in the palace was also finished. I was very happy to work in it: it gave me a new lease of life and my enthusiasm was limitless. The kingdom had never had a truer ruler than Chao Anouvong since 1779 and no one could reproach him for abandoning his people. He wished to undo Siam's crimes and restore LanXang to her former glory.

Then, during 1818 and 1819, the ruler of the southern principality of Champasak, Chao Manoi, got into trouble. Phraya Kai Songkram, the ruler of Mueang Khukan, complained to Bangkok about crimes committed by the Siamese governor against the Lao people there. King Naphalai dispatched his chief councillor (*Sena-amat*) to bring the commissioner of Khorat, ThongInh, a fraudster and restless predator known unofficially as Yokkhabud (*Yok* means authorised, *Khabud* means to defraud), who was on a mission in Mueang Khong in Champasak province, back to Bangkok for questioning. It was no use. The councillor was heavily bribed and, instead of obeying the king's orders, stayed on at Mueang Khong to enjoy Yokkhabud's lavish hospitality. While the people were paying heavy taxes, the king's councillor was being entertained in grand style. When both men failed to return, Naphalai sent his mandarin Phraya Kaisorn Khamdaeng to bring them back without fail.

Upon their return to Bangkok, they showered Naphalai with treasures – gold, silver, rare rhinoceros's horns, ivory and much more – all collected as a form of tax, cheated or looted from the people. They also brought hundreds of slaves with them. Naphalai was no different from his predecessors, blinded by his wealthy and opulent lifestyle. Instead of punishing him, he gave Yokkhabud even more power and authority.

Chao Anouvong knew that Yokkhabud was just one of many officials responsible for Siam's systematic and ruthless conquest. Siam had long been undermining Lao LanXang's autonomy and power, flooding the kingdom with Siamese immigrants and alienating the Lao ruling elite in the Khorat Plateau against ViengChan. The principality of Souvannaphum was the first victim of this policy: when the city's walls were destroyed, the inhabitants were forbidden to rebuild them and were forced to pay a yearly tribute to Bangkok. The city's population was resettled in the country, but only in small villages so they were unable to fortify and become strong again.

Despite being an evil man consumed by greed and power, Naphalai granted Yokkhabud the title of Phraya (Lord) Phromphakdy (a man who was obedient (*Phakdy*) to his creator (*Phrom*)) and then appointed him governor of Khorat when the ageing Phraya Boonchan died. Phromphakdy, with even more power at his disposal, was determined to acquire the power needed to rule the Champasak principality.

Phromphakdy, who thought himself better regarded than Chao Anouvong, acclaimed a local holy man, SaKietNgong, for his high reputation and magical power. By promising him control of Champasak, Phromphakdy succeeded in enticing him and his 8,000 ethnic highland (*Lao Theung*) followers to attack and burn the city. Champasak's ruler, Chao Manoi, was blamed for his failure to defend the city and taken to Bangkok where he later died, purged for being a Lao ruler.

On hearing of the destruction of Champasak, Chao Anouvong instructed Rathsabud Yoh and his men to paddle down the Mekong at speed and suppress the rebellion. SaKietNgong soon surrendered and confessed. Yoh suspected who the real culprit was and SaKietNgong's confession didn't surprise him. He sent for Phromphakdy who arrived looking worried, breathing heavily and shifting about in his seat when asked for his views on the revolt. He went on to provide an alibi.

'It was SaKietNgong who enticed the Lao Theung followers to rebel and destroy Champasak,' he said. 'I only heard about it by hearsay.'

Yoh didn't have the authority to pass judgement and didn't want to upset Naphalai in Bangkok. He hastily returned to ViengChan and reported the incident to Chao Anouvong. The Lao king decided to confront Naphalai directly, although he knew he would be treading on dangerous ground. He hastily set off for Bangkok – without dragging me along, I'm glad to say. He didn't really have to go; he was the king of LanXang and the incident had taken place in his kingdom. But because of his respect for Naphalai, he did the honourable thing. He knew that Phromphakdy was wielding power on Bangkok's behalf but he wished to air his grievances in person, to prove that Naphalai's governor was in the wrong. He fiercely complained to the Siamese king, expressing his deep concern over the injustices done to the Lao.

He returned beaming with satisfaction and told me in confidence that while it hadn't been necessary to go to Bangkok, it had been beneficial; he'd courageously and justifiably remonstrated in private with Naphalai and criticised Siam's oppression, which was proving so harmful to Lao-Siamese relations.

'Your Majesty, I pay my respects, but I beg you, please hear me.' Chao Anouvong had said in a low voice to the sleepy-eyed and partly bald Naphalai, who wasn't a talker and never smiled. 'Since we were boys, an understanding, a trust, has existed between us. We are now officially lord and vassal but in private we're still brothers and friends, though each of us is loyal to his own country. Besides, you're a great benefactor of mine and I'm very moved by your kindness. I don't know how to predict the future, nor do I know the secrets of providence. I don't count on the heavens, but perhaps my fate is tied to them. With a sober mind I seek peace and truth. I know my place. Everything I've done is by the grace of Your Majesty. I've served Siam loyally and my conviction remains solid, constant and true. With my heartfelt admiration for you, I neither boast nor look for merit. It's such a joy to see you, but may I take this opportunity to use our friendship to bring LanXang's troubles to your notice, in the hope it will help resolve our differences and benefit both our kingdoms?'

With little courtesy, Naphalai grudgingly looked at Chao Anouvong and nodded his consent. 'On our friendship, let's hear it,' he snorted.

'On our friendship,' repeated Chao Anouvong, looking directly at Naphalai, 'please hear me. You're a thoughtful lord and must realise we strongly disapprove of Siamese domination. I must tell you of my concerns. The facts, as witnessed by my son Yoh, should be brought to your attention so those responsible might be dealt with; you have the power to command it. I'm afraid to say your governor's repressive methods and unfair trading practices in the south of LanXang have created much resentment. Here are the written testimonies of monks whose temples have been robbed of priceless bronze Buddha statues, silver bowls and other treasures that have been there for hundreds of years. Here is the evidence of village officials in Mueang Khong and Ubon, who were threatened with death unless they paid money to Phraya Phromphakdy's agents. And here is the story of the wretched people of Mueang Khukan, Ubon, Souvannaphum, Roi-Et and elsewhere, seized by your governor's men, bound to coconut trees and tortured with hot iron rods.'

'Is that all?' the hard-faced Naphalai interposed when Chao Anouvong paused.

'No, there is more… much more,' he said. His voice was still low, but he was struggling to control it. 'Your Majesty, I have some words I would ask you and your people to keep in mind. We are both descendants of the royal Ai-Lao house of the legendary King Khoun Borom. Quite frankly, Siam's invasion of ViengChan in 1779 betrayed his doctrine. As you know, we've been of great help to Siam. Why sin against us when we've committed no offence against you? It was totally wrong and has damaged the bond between us. You have ruled over the central plain of the Chaophraya river since the reign of Khoun Borom's fifth son, Thao Inh. We represent LanXang and have ruled over the Mekong since his first son, Khoun Loh. You are Siamese and I am Lao, but we shouldn't fall out over territory. We're both steadfast in our principles. Under no account should our alliance be broken. Subjugating LanNa is one thing, but if Siam insists LanXang also belongs to her, there'll be trouble. Relations between our kingdoms will always be strained by the legacy of the Rattanakosins' domination. Please examine your hearts… ask your people and tell me. Are you being reasonable to us? You surely can't expect us to be happy. If the idea of a Greater Siam persists, the alliance between Siam and LanXang will be over.'

Naphalai was stunned and speechless as he gazed into the distance; perhaps he was pondering Khoun Borom's law – '…*respect the bond of brotherhood and never to invade or plunder each other's land*' – which must have made him feel ashamed.

'Your Majesty, the stability of Siam and LanXang concerns both nations,' Chao Anouvong went on. 'Before we do ourselves more damage, we must open a dialogue with each other. We must refrain from strife and quarrelling. Lao citizens shouldn't be subject to a census and the land where they bury their dead and which they call home shouldn't be robbed. Our people's respect for each other is lifelong. We should embrace what brings us together. You must understand we are the same Ai-Lao race. There is absolutely no need to marginalise the Lao people. It will only set us against each other; anger will melt into hatred and our two kingdoms will tear themselves apart. It will be a stain on Siam's honour. Our children should be taught the truth; they should know how important it is for us to love each other. You can tell how different we are by the way our people speak and the food they eat. The Lao people speak Lao; they prefer to eat Lao food and respect their ancient laws (*Heed Yi Khong Jiang*). They have their own customs based on the twelve months of the year (*Heed Sipsong*) and have followed the fourteen constitutional laws (*Khong Sipsi*) since Fah Ngum's day in 1352. Lao culture is distinct from Siamese culture. The deep-rooted Lao character, of individualism and self-reliance, of mysticism and jollity, of tolerance and strict convention, will never be changed!'

Then he said, 'It's clear in the eyes of humanity that your governors and their men have committed criminal acts. They'll lead to distrust and fear, prejudice and hate. They'll open a festering wound that may well turn poisonous!'

'All right, Anouvong, your feelings are profound, and your words are sincere,' said Naphalai, weighing Chao Anouvong up. 'But how should this problem be resolved?'

'Well, given our close friendship, that's a question I should be asking instead,' replied Chao Anouvong, fixing his dark brown eyes on Naphalai. 'You fear nothing, so please allow me to speak frankly. You know very well that the Mekong is the lifeline of the Lao people, on both its banks. Furthermore, if you force Lao citizens to the northeast of Bangkok – our very backyard – to migrate, it would be as if you were also taking our food away from us. Lao nationalism is rising. I used to think there were no heroes in Siam, but perhaps you alone can fulfil the dream of a restored LanXang. I would always respect you and you would forever be a hero to the Lao people.'

Chao Anouvong paused to take a sip of water. Naphalai shifted in his seat but said nothing.

'Your Majesty, Siam is powerful and the fate of LanXang is in your hands,' Chao Anouvong continued. 'You do not need to annex LanXang and LanNa to achieve hegemony; there is no need to hold rigidly to power. If we're to dispel mistrust and jealousy and maintain the strength and intimacy of our alliance, Siam must respect the That Si-SongHuck demarcation treaty and get out of LanXang without delay to preserve the balance of power. I believe the way of persuasion is greater than the way of power. LanXang may be under Siamese domination, but she will prevail. I have some questions for you, and I implore you to answer me honestly.' Naphalai looked as if his mind was troubled by many thoughts. 'The Lao are valiant, steadfast and unyielding in their quest for LanXang unification,' said Chao Anouvong. 'If you force them into submission, would they really accept you? Will they give up everything they've been striving for? We seek no quarrel and although we know our necks are made only of flesh, we have no fear. But we respect truth and do not mince words. LanXang simply wants the special brotherly relationship with Siam back but not the institution. Everything I've said is for the sake of our lifelong friendship, for the love of our people and for the greater good. Today, I call on Lord Buddha and the gods to bear witness to my sincerity. What would Your Majesty say?'

Unsurprisingly, Naphalai's expression was blank. He was unsure how to reply;

he could neither accept nor reject Chao Anouvong's words. After a while, the Lao king warned him further that Phromphakdy's instigation of SaKietNgong's rebellion had increased the Lao people's hatred for the Rattanakosins. He begged Naphalai to show more consideration. The Siamese king, stiff in his manner and coldly commanding in his tone, refused to condemn his governor's actions but bragged that Siam had the authority to do as she pleased and refused to give any consideration to Chao Anouvong's pleas.

Phraya Phromphakdy seized the opportunity and continued with his crimes. With the SaKietNgong uprising crushed, he was free to cross the Mekong. His men captured more ethnic Lao Theung from Saravanh and Attapeu provinces and forced them to extract more gold in the region. The Siamese soldiers burnt down many villages and killed those who resisted or tried to escape, thousands of people, a terrible massacre. Chao Anouvong was adamant that Siamese plans to annex both LanNa and LanXang had to be thwarted.

The Lao LanXang territories were important both strategically and in terms of resources. During the forty years of Siamese occupation, the kingdom had been progressively destroyed, its people enslaved. Phromphakdy's policy was now to fulfil Bangkok's objectives: to weaken and alienate the Lao people before annexing their country. It was therefore no wonder that Chao Anouvong's petition to Naphalai not only failed but led to open hostility between the two royal families and fuelled the drive for LanXang independence.

Unfortunately, Siam wasn't interested in compromise, reconciliation and mutual respect for the sake of peace. Phromphakdy, knowing that corruption was rife in Bangkok, went about boasting openly that he'd the immunity to do as he pleased.

King Naphalai showed some sympathy but, despite their supposedly close friendship, didn't take Chao Anouvong seriously. However, before leaving Bangkok for ViengChan, he made a final request to Naphalai that only he should be allowed to rule Champasak. Naphalai, ashamed of the truth, found it appropriate to try to calm Chao Anouvong. His request to appoint his son Rathsabud Yoh, who put down the rebellion, was agreed to, but not without strong opposition from Bangkok's privileged elite. While Naphalai put on an act of benevolence and righteousness towards the people, pretending to be a man who disapproved of injustice, in truth he permitted his men to carry out his cruel policies, using every stratagem to dominate the ethnic Lao in the Khorat Plateau.

It had been a very difficult and risky mission for Chao Anouvong, but once he was back in ViengChan, he issued an immediate order to rebuild Champasak to its former glory: a major city fit for the principality. He was naturally delighted in 1821 when Naphalai finally gave his consent for Rathsabud Yoh, now in his thirties, to be the new ruler of Champasak, with Chao Khampom as his chief minister. LanXang was now united, except for Luang Phrabang. XiengKhuang, on the other hand, was unsure of its allegiance. Chao Anouvong worked hard to convince them.

Although Chao Anouvong was unable to convince himself he was running the affairs of his country honourably, his plans were coming together as he'd expected. Meanwhile, the governor of Khorat remained free to plunder LanXang for its wealth. Phromphakdy demanded bribes, telling his victims to borrow the necessary money from his own tax officer, who acted as a banker and charged an extortionate rate of interest. Then he reinvested the bribe with the banker, not only protecting his capital and enriching the Rattanakosins in Bangkok but earning a hefty share of the profit himself.

Under the Rattanakosin king's decree, Phromphakdy ordered a census of the Lao population to be carried out. By force, he authorised that all Lao citizens should have numbers marked on their arms, in some cases burned on with hot irons. Rumours of this provoked unrest across the Khorat Plateau. The inhabitants of Yasothon, Roi-Et, Souvannaphum, Kalasin, Ubon, Khemarat, Mukdahan and Nakhorn Phanom on the right bank of the Mekong were all registered. None of the main Lao cities escaped this atrocity. Many Lao nobles led the exodus to ViengChan and asked Chao Anouvong for help. Phraya Phasombophit fled with his followers from Kalasin to NongHan in Sakon Nakhorn; the governor there sought refuge in Nakhorn Phanom, which in turn sought protection from ViengChan.

These areas were plundered and devastated. Siam was eager to improve the quality and quantity of its supply of slaves: thousands of Lao craftsmen were forced to migrate to Bangkok. Siam extended its aggression to other areas in the northeast and the cities along the Mekong. It was all too easy for Bangkok to turn a blind eye to the repression and brutality because they'd sanctioned it in the first place. Victims were sent to grim prisons to be interrogated and tortured. If they wanted someone to disappear, they would do so. No questions asked.

This was the most frustrating time for Chao Anouvong; he was full of anger but powerless, though he knew the time for the Lao insurrection would come.

Meanwhile, conditions grew ever more serious in the south and southwest of LanXang. News came from Champasak that Phromphakdy was preparing to pursue his ambitions to become governor there by using the Lao Theung's refusal to pay him tribute as a pretext to cross the Mekong. But the city's ruler, Rathsabud Yoh, who argued that he alone had the authority to exercise power in the region, categorically refused. He went quickly to inform his father in ViengChan, who found it difficult to remain calm. One couldn't blame him: he was a dignified man of high morals. He almost went to war then and there but was shrewd enough to know that he was far from prepared. He stuck to his plans and remained in ViengChan, his heart loaded with pain and sympathy for those Lao families who had been branded in XiengTeng, Khukan, Sisaketh, Ubon and Attapeu. He told Rathsabud Yoh to prepare his army before sending him back to Champasak.

'Go back to your city,' he told his son. 'And recruit the toughest and the best fighting men who share our dream and our determination for justice, who fear slavery more than death and who would fight for us heart and soul.'

A year later, in 1822, Chao Anouvong secretly travelled south to visit his son in Champasak. He wanted to give Rathsabud Yoh a message in person and to see how well his son was managing to inspire allegiance and unity amongst the nobles there. More importantly, he wanted to re-establish contact with the people before the rainy season started. He reminded me of my pledge to travel with him and asked me to accompany him.

'I've also noticed you're losing interest in your routine work in the library and the palace,' he reasoned, as though he were making an excuse for my inactivity. 'I too have had enough of this literary work: all this elaborate flowery poetry and these pompous phrases. Let's make our lives more useful and interesting. It's about time we shared food and conversed in plain Lao with our people, like we did twenty-six years ago.'

It was clear he needed a change of scenery. I agreed willingly. Thus, one mid-February morning, just before the sun rose to hasten dawn to break, before the rising heat disturbed our temper and while the river was not too low and still as misty and milky as a pearl, our company of three plain boats paddled downstream. Since I didn't have to steer, I basked in the spectacular views of the river and absorbed the pleasures of the journey. Chao Anouvong was right: by changing the scenery and our routine, our interest was renewed and our boredom dispersed. But he remained in deep thought, saying that as none of us were as morally perfect as we liked to think, then perfection is dull: it's best to learn things from one's mistakes. However, he appreciated that ideology would inevitably be hampered by pragmatism. There was an odd hesitation in the way he muttered to himself; I wondered if he'd just then glimpsed the whole extraordinary set of possibilities and consequences in his mind. If this were so he never told me; his words were mostly in the form of poetic verses, difficult to understand and often dying on his lips. Nevertheless, as we sailed slowly down the Mekong, discreetly stopping at various places along the way, I could vouch that the future of Lao LanXang and her people were always on his mind. He was the king, so it was his right and responsibility to act.

In the heat and humidity of a late March morning, we disembarked inconspicuously in Champasak. It was entirely Chao Anouvong's idea to keep the visit a secret; besides, pomposity was never his way. He'd no wish to upset Naphalai or arouse Bangkok's suspicions. The annual Wat Phou festival had just finished but the offerings of the pious were evident on the ground. The steep, stone stairway was ablaze with the white blossom of the *Dork Champa* trees, giving out its tantalising fragrance, while the phallic-shaped mountain rose sharply into the sky.

In Champasak we learned how all the main cities along the valley of the Mun river had suffered. Rathsabud Yoh was on his guard and had done well in rebuilding the city. The people had slowly regained their confidence but were still nervous of Phromphakdy's ambitions to become the city's governor. Chao Anouvong ordered his son to keep a close watch on Siamese activities before quietly returning to ViengChan to concentrate on building the Wat Sisaketh temple and running his kingdom.

Despite LanXang's economic problems, Chao Anouvong found himself in a more secure position than ever. With Rathsabud Yoh installed as ruler of Champasak, he was more powerful. However, things were far from peaceful on the Khorat Plateau. Phromphakdy, his subordinate officer Suriyaphakdy and their men, were on the rampage with the census. The Lao citizens were being brutally mistreated. Chao Anouvong barely had any friends in Bangkok and was considering turning to the neighbouring countries to the north, east and south for support. In the end, he decided against it on principle: the Lao people and the Lao people alone bore responsibility for protecting their national identity.

IX

The Dinner Party

At the beginning of the dry season of 1824, the building of the Wat Sisaketh temple was completed. Construction had begun in the first week of March 1818. A lavish ceremony was held over nine days and nights to mark the achievement along with a national celebration. Rousing themselves from their usual somnolence, thousands of people from near and far turned up. Colourful processions around the palace and pagoda went on for three days and nights, nobles and important officials slowly streaming into the temple courtyard in the early hours of the last morning, where they sat under the warm January sun in front of the four 55-metre cloisters (*Kommalien*). Inside were long rows of gilded, meditating Buddha statues, hundreds if not thousands in number. Important monks invited from all over the city sat at the very front. Along the cloisters' walls were 3,420 triangular niches in the shape of Bo leaves, each containing two miniature Buddha statues.

At the centre of the temple courtyard was the Grand Ordination Hall (*Wihan* or *Sim*) with a splendid façade and many-tiered roof; unlike other temples it had only one golden spire (*Yot Sorfah*) pointing defiantly to heaven, which Chao Anouvong purposely installed to signify LanXang resilience. The *Sim*'s door, facing the right bank of the Mekong towards the Khorat Plateau (and ultimately all the way to Bangkok) was also deliberately built to symbolise Lao LanXang unification. The entire interior of the *Sim* was decorated with one million sheets of gold leaf and the high walls featured rows of 1,026 slightly larger triangular niches, each also housing two small bronze Buddha statues. The *Sim* was similar to that of Wat Saketh in Bangkok, a mere gesture rather than a genuine attempt to curry favour with Bangkok. The lower section of its exterior wall was decorated with the Rattanakosins' royal emblem, the mythical eagle (*Garuda/Khoud*). Further inside the *Sim*, large and small gilded

Buddha statues were bathed in the glow of candlelight from a magnificent gilded wooden candleholder which Chao Anouvong had commissioned. The motif of the candleholder – two dragons with tails intertwined in the middle – signified peace and unity, their heads raised in a gesture of defiance. Chao Anouvong and other important dignitaries went inside the chapel to pray while the monks sat lined up in their best saffron robes below the Buddha statues chanting religious mantras in a monotone.

It was very moving. The people, full of devotion and joy, brought offerings to acknowledge Chao Anouvong's achievements. The almsgiving ceremony was held outside in the temple courtyard: money, fruit, food, flowers and so on were dropped gently into black offertory bowls; soon, ninety-six were overflowing. The people then lined up and gave more offerings to gain merit, amounting to 2,940 suits of saffron robes, 753 reed mattresses and 648 pillows. Finally, 642 rattan trays of various kinds of food were presented to the monks for the only main meal they were allowed to take before noon.

Meanwhile, enterprising vendors outside the temple perimeter piled their stalls with all kinds of goods: fruit, herbs and vegetables. Food of all kinds, such as newly harvested sticky rice slowly grilled over charcoal in a bamboo tube (*Khaow Laam*), barbecued chicken and Lao spicy papaya salad, all freshly prepared to order, triggered such hunger that they just had to be bought and eaten. Other traders stocked their stalls with traditional handicrafts and local products such as parasols, paper lanterns, bamboo baskets, stools, reed handbags, straw hats, silk garments, ivory, rhinos' horns and everything else necessary for a fruitful and joyful celebration.

At night all kinds of traditional music and dance was performed late into the night for the happy spectators – many of them took to the dancing floor. It was a moving spectacle for everybody involved and was staged so beautifully that it gave an impression of absolute authority rather than a mere cultural revival. It embodied the marvellous impulse of the Lao people who dwelt between the mountain ranges on the border with Vietnam to the east and the Khorat plain on the border with Siam to the southwest. Their spirit had truly been sparked into life during the uncomfortable forty-five years of Siamese rule. It was a true representation of the Lao Kingdom of LanXang and her people's dignity and freedom, away from the darkness of brutish subservience. It was what they had lost, a true expression of their culture as it had been practised for thousands of years. No Lao citizen that day would have dreamt that he or she would live to see it taken away again.

Before sunset a few days later, Chao Anouvong returned from evening ritual in the *Sim* of Wat Sisaketh. He saw me walking though the palace courtyard carrying a fresh new pack of palm leaves (*Bai Larn*) that I'd put out to dry. He raised his hand to attract my attention.

'Phia Jon!' he called and came towards me. I straightened myself, bowed in reverence and ran towards him. He complained about the heat but looked happy and cheerful. One could see his day had been exciting. 'You've come just in time to join us for dinner,' he cried out excitedly, beaming with pride. 'If you have anything else to do, put it off for the moment. Where have you been? Yesterday I missed you at dinner and tried to find you to invite you, but couldn't see you anywhere.'

'Your Majesty, my respects to you. I beg you to pardon me for having distressed you,' I said and accepted the invitation with alacrity. 'Yesterday, I went past the royal paddy fields (*Na Luang*) to a village beyond the outer city wall to gather more palm leaves for my writing. I didn't return until after dark. We're a little short of them.'

'Excellent! They look fine,' he said and praised me. 'Have you seen Prince Ngao, by any chance?'

'As a matter of fact, I saw the prince coming this way from the city gate,' I said.

'Splendid... but where is he? We need him,' he said, mopping his brow and looking towards the gate.

'The prince was following me just now,' I said, puzzled. 'I can't think what has become of him. He must have abandoned himself to his thoughts and gone somewhere else.' We turned to look around but couldn't see him anywhere.

'Go and look,' he ordered the palace guard, 'and fetch him in. He must be found. And you, Phia Jon, give the palm leaves to the servant for safekeeping. Now, please go and make yourself at home and sit anywhere you like.'

The dutiful palace servant soon brought me a silver bowl of limewater to wash my hands, which I then dried with a white cotton towel. I thanked the attendant, who bowed and quickly disappeared. I didn't want to be the first to sit down so stood in the corner and waited for the others to turn up.

Chao Anouvong had invited his Chief Registrar, Phraya Sanon, the viceroy Tissah and a few loyal friends to an informal dinner outside in the garden. The servants arrived with towels and a handsome silver jug of water which they poured into a silver basin for the guests to rinse their hands. I made obeisance to all the guests when they came swaggering in.

The guard returned to say that Prince Ngao was sitting under the white, cascading flowers of the *Dork Champa* trees in the garden, deep in contemplation, deaf to the guard's entreaties to come in. Although thoughtful and clever, the prince wasn't really a scholar. He preferred to practise his sword-fighting skills under that shady mango tree he'd planted in the courtyard back in 1804. He did his thinking quietly, in private and out of sight.

'Go and call him again,' Chao Anouvong ordered the guard, 'and please don't take no for an answer.' He hesitated and then said, 'No, wait, on second thoughts, we better leave him alone. He goes away sometimes and sits still to do his thinking. Don't bother him. Let him be. He'll come presently, I'm sure.' The subdued-looking Phraya Sanon gave a quiet murmur of assent. Then Chao Anouvong, casually, in true Lao style, ordered the food and drink to be served. 'You have complete liberty to serve what you please,' he told the servants. 'And treat us as your guests, myself as much as the others. We'll make sure your service is worthy of our praise.' They bowed and smiled, hiding their true pleasure, carrying on with their duty, placing lavish portions of various kinds of food and a small bamboo box of freshly steamed sticky rice for each of us on the table, and filling the silver cups to the brim with water.

To begin with, it was indeed a casual affair and I felt honoured to be part of the gathering. Chao Anouvong told the guests that the company and the conversation, not the food, was more important. After a while, he beckoned us to sit and promptly made himself comfortable in his seat. I respectfully bowed to him and all the other guests as they sat down and was the last to take my place. Chao Anouvong looked a little worried and, on several occasions, seemed to want to send for Prince Ngao again. But his good friend Phraya Sanon, who was slouching sleepily and saying little, stopped him, and murmured, 'Let him be, as you said. Meanwhile, if it isn't too much trouble, may we have a brief summary of what we intend to discuss today?'

'You may, but not just now,' replied Chao Anouvong. 'You should relax, enjoy my hospitality and not chat about anything too serious. I hope you have some new anecdotes to amuse us. I'm on my best behaviour and very much looking forward to discussing important business with you.'

We made offerings and invoked the spirits of the mythical ancestors (*Pu Nyeu* and *Nya Nyeu*) before taking our meal. We marked the occasion with a toast to Chao Anouvong and began our dinner but still Prince Ngao hadn't arrived. We normally ate with our hands but used a silver or coconut spoon to drink soup. We helped ourselves to the tasty fare spread out before us and light and cheerful conversation flowed. Some ate greedily, talking and laughing jovially between mouthfuls. I found myself observing them; I hardly uttered a word during dinner and was, as usual, sparing in my consumption. While helping myself mostly to steamed vegetables, fresh herbs and sticky rice, I kept looking at the door hoping the prince would turn up.

I should mention that I'd known Prince Ngao all my life. Ever since being able to run about, he'd sat on Chao Anouvong's knees listening to his stories or watching the guards walking, their swords clanking at their hips. As promised in 1804, Chao Anouvong did allow him to attend school in the palace at the age of five and had made a true Laoman of him since he left the care of his mother at the tender age of six. From the age of nine he was busy from dawn to dusk. Every morning before sunrise at the sound of the temple drum, he exercised with the guards, running along a narrow, twisting track around the palace, darting, leaping, hurling, lifting, doing press-ups and sit-ups, climbing and swinging on the roots of the banyan trees and doing stretches afterwards. After washing, combing his hair and dressing, he looked princely, healthy, alert and no doubt teachable. He listened well to his father who treated everyone in the palace well with rarely a harsh word for anyone. When breakfast at last arrived, it was never enough. He ate plenty at lunch and dinner. Unsurprisingly, he was not only big for his age but also ahead in everything else.

Prince Ngao knew a great deal about the officers, mostly those within the palace. He even learned the peasant dialect from the soldiers of the guard who came from various parts of the kingdom; what else, one can only guess. He liked sports and made a point of always keeping fit and never lacked strenuous occupation. His bodily toughness was due to the hard work that he genuinely enjoyed. He even helped in the royal paddy fields, planting the rice or taking part in threshing during the harvest. He was also addicted to competitive sports: I contributed to the enjoyment by competing against him in a running race. I almost won, having led for most of the way, but slowed down to allow him to catch up. I was aware he was hot on my heels but hadn't reckoned with his methods. In the last steep climb, he grabbed me by the seat of my trousers, and I was so surprised that I stopped dead and looked round. The young rascal passed me to claim victory. Amidst general laughter and applause, he smiled and raised his arm triumphantly. I laughed to conceal my dejection and congratulated him. The king commiserated with a gentle pat on the back.

It occurred to me that rulers must be trained for war when they're young. Prince Rathsavong Ngao didn't usually like to fritter away his free time on other activities, preferring to study military stratagems and practising his sword-fighting skills instead. He enjoyed martial arts and training in the use of military equipment. He became highly disciplined because one day he might have to fight man to man, either chasing and attacking an enemy or retreating and warding off an attack. He believed a good grasp of discipline would help him survive if he'd only one opponent to deal with; it would give him the edge even over multiple opponents. Chao Anouvong taught him strategy and the deployment of troops and was extremely proud of him.

It was still early but, as my evening meal was ending, Chao Anouvong unexpectedly asked me to stay. I would usually slip away to rest my head. It was a convivial party, so I quietly settled myself in the corner to take notes while everybody else was in full spate: joking, laughing and talking together.

Prince Suthisan Poh, Phraya Sanon and Tissah were laughing at each other's jokes. Even Chao Anouvong couldn't hide his amusement. He would put on the best face he could for his guests. But where was Rathsavong Ngao? The night-time sounds of ViengChan outside the inner-city walls mingled with the cool January air: voices, the barking of dogs, the mating cries of cats, the crying of babies, the laughing of young people, the call of the guards and the symphony of the *Khaen* music vibrating mournfully. I sat, alert, quietly observing and taking notes in the shadows of the candlelight, keeping a subtle distance between myself and the other guests. The sound of crashing swords outside in the courtyard had died down. Chao Anouvong looked rather anxious; he kept glancing across the table to check the entrance and I thought the prince would turn up at any moment.

Finally the prince – a steady and good-looking man with high moral integrity – appeared. They were about halfway through their dinner, laughing at one of Phraya Sanon's anecdotes, when suddenly the tall doors opened as if at the sudden appearance of a ghost. The mature yet youthful prince, now in his twenties, of great intelligence and charm, to whom everyone, young and old, men and women, took an instant liking, appeared from the dark room beyond. He'd grown up to be a very handsome and robust man with a well-developed torso but the well-drilled posture of a modest Laoman. I could detect some anxiety in his freshly washed face which was strikingly angular and lean; it was flushed and shiny with sweat from. His brown, penetrating eyes, lightened by the sun, dominated the overall effect, suggesting great intellectual power and a strong will. He still appeared somewhat absorbed in thought. He bowed, lowered his body and cast his eyes down until spoken to as he came forwards. Everyone turned to look at him. With his praying hands he cordially greeted his father and the other guests as if he was eager to open his mind.

'Ah! Ngao my prince, we've been waiting anxiously for you,' Chao Anouvong cried out with delight, pushing away his plate and meeting his son's steady eyes. 'You've come at last. Come, come and join us and please do tell us what you've been doing. Let me be the first, by touching you, to enjoy the discoveries you've made in the quiet of the garden.'

Rathsavong Ngao gave an appreciative smile and went straight over to his father.

'I pay my respects to you, father... and to everyone,' he said, glancing at the guests before sitting straight-backed on a cushion. He told us he'd been practising his sword fighting and contemplating under the mango tree.

'Mango tree! Yes, of course, your mango tree,' Chao Anouvong said, looking at me before teasingly revealing that twenty years ago, the young prince had sowed the seed and urinated on it. He'd also urinated many times afterwards on the young mango plant! We all smiled and chuckled. 'And now,' he went on and laughed, 'there are more mangos for all the girls in the city!'

'Father, please. You're embarrassing me,' Prince Ngao exclaimed; he smiled and his face flushed redder. The guests exchanged looks and smiled.

'Did you know, Ngao,' Chao Anouvong pressed on, trying not to laugh, 'that any girl who eats your mango will get pregnant?'

'Really?' the unmarried prince said in surprise, looking concerned. Everyone, myself included, started to chuckle and the room vibrated with happy laughter.

'Gentlemen, gentlemen, please.' Chao Anouvong called for calm, catching his breath. 'Now, let's be serious.' The room soon went quiet. 'First of all, Ngao, I apologise if I've embarrassed you, but you're a man of good heart with a good sense of humour. Now, my prince, I believe you must have found the answer to your problems in the quiet garden.'

Holding his praying hands out for his father to touch, he calmly said, 'It would be very good if wisdom flowed with contact, like water. I value the benefit of sitting beside you as you always fill me with your insight. I'm not very wise but I'm always ready to learn. I'm pleased to say that during the ceremony at your beautiful Wat Sisaketh temple, I had the privilege of sharing your wisdom with thousands of other happy Lao people. It was a great achievement, and your speech was magnificent.'

'Thank you, Ngao. We will decide which of us is wiser a little later,' Chao Anouvong responded, looking lovingly at his son. 'Our great ancestors shall judge between us. For the moment, devote your attention to your dinner. You must be hungry after so much exercise and thinking.' Ngao thanked his father and obeyed, settling down to eat like the rest. Chao Anouvong made offerings and poured libations to the mythical old couple.

'We all know there was once an old couple (*Pu Nyeu* and *Nya Nyeu*) he said respectfully, 'loyal followers of legendary King Khoun Borom, who sacrificed their lives in cutting down a giant gourd which had entwined itself around a gigantic fig tree and was blocking the sunlight. Because of them, sunlight and warmth returned to the earth. I think we should make the same sacrifice to safeguard our country. Our survival as a nation is vital. May our great ancestors' spirits protect us and help us on our way.'

We all performed customary offerings and libations and began to drink and nibble at the food. I normally assumed the role of butler or bar boy during Chao Anouvong's private dinner parties, obligingly filling everyone's empty glasses except my own, because I didn't want to get drunk: I disliked hangovers. This time, as I was about to perform my usual duties, he raised his hand to stop me.

Then Phraya Sanon, the raconteur who was always in the habit of taking Chao Anouvong's advice, especially when it came to health, asked him light-heartedly about the benefits or otherwise of drinking alcohol. He apologised for not feeling entirely sober but was very honoured to be in the company of friends. He was a well-bred, fine-boned fellow, but on that occasion, he looked like a complete dipsomaniac and a ruin, having had far too much drink the previous day. I could smell his horrible breath from where I sat, like fruit rotting in a bucket. 'In fact, gentlemen,' he announced humorously, 'I'm still feeling a bit queer even now.' Everyone smiled and chuckled. He admitted that his drinking bout the night before had left him in a poor way and in need of a break from the booze. He was worried his violent hiccups might return and apologised in advance should they do so.

'You're quite correct, Phraya Sanon,' said Chao Anouvong, dabbing carefully at his mouth with his red napkin before continuing. 'I know too well, of course, that we like to have a bit of distilled rice wine (*Lauw Satho*) and it's our custom and way of life to enjoy ourselves with uninhibited delight at dinner parties. Nothing makes us happier than sitting down to a table loaded with food and drink, surrounded by friends who can just drop by whenever they're in the neighbourhood and join in with the singalong. However, the effect of alcohol, as we all know, is a crazy thing. It makes you lose your inhibitions, your intelligence and your dignity. Worse, it can cause accidents and loss of life. It makes a wise man sing, dance and giggle like a girl, and divulge in an ungentlemanly manner what would have been better left unsaid. So, Phraya Sanon, if you're still not sober and not entirely yourself from yesterday's dinner party, a bit of detoxification would do no harm.'

Phraya Sanon wisely gave his seal of approval.

'Nevertheless,' Chao Anouvong continued, 'personally, I'm weak, very weak indeed, especially with the pleasure of good conversation and in your company. All of you, I may add. In fact, for our country's (*PathetZard BanMueang*) sake, we must be strong and stay in control.' He paused and looked at the guests. 'Drinking too much and getting drunk,' he continued, pushing his glass away, 'is bad for people of great responsibility: kings, rulers, politicians and soldiers alike. We must set an example to our fighting men and the younger generation. I'm sure you would all agree it wouldn't be sensible to get intoxicated on this occasion. We should drink merely as we feel inclined, without any compulsion. The definition of self-control is mastery over our pleasures and desires. Lao alcohol (*Lauw Lao*) would merely blur our thinking and weaken our judgement: very dangerous under the present circumstances. We shall instead entertain ourselves with worthy conversation. Besides, I have a very serious and important matter to discuss with you.'

At this point all the guests stiffened and turned towards Chao Anouvong, who paused to take a sip of water. They looked at their drinks, nodded slightly and listened.

'As for your hiccups,' Chao Anouvong continued, turning his gaze to Phraya Sanon, 'may I suggest you hold your breath for some time; if that doesn't cure it, then gargle with warm lime and salt water. If that still doesn't work, put a teaspoonful of sugar in your mouth and let it slowly dissolve before swallowing it.' There was a short pause. 'And yes, if that also fails, tickle your nose with a feather. You will sneeze once or twice, even three times, but that will stop them, however bad they are.'

In good humour, a subdued Phraya Sanon thanked Chao Anouvong for his advice and promptly asked one of the servants to fetch a fine, clean feather just in case, amidst much laughter.

After we'd satisfied our hunger and thirst, Chao Anouvong kept us in discussion far into the night. I happened to be sitting some distance from him but his conversation was much too interesting not to engage the attention of everyone present. When he came to the incident of our 'Quest for Wisdom' – our clandestine journey down the Mekong to That Phanom that only he and I knew about – he gave me a discreet, laughing glance followed by a wink. His poetic narrative of the significance of the mighty Mekong to LanXang charmed all the guests. He emphasised the importance of the That Luang and That Phanom stupas to the Lao people and mentioned Pu Chan, who was a visionary and a passionate ViengChan nobleman who'd taught the people on both sides of the Mekong to love each other and to unite as one. Traditionally, the people of Lao LanNa and LanXang gathered at the two stupas for annual celebrations. Young lovers from Khorat and ViengChan usually arranged to meet on the full moon to prayer during the That Luang festival. Some of them even ended up falling in love and making pledges of marriage!

Exhausted by this intellectual yet light-hearted exchange, some of the guests, lacking sparkle in their conversation, filled their glasses and listened quietly and diligently. Red ants with their behinds cocked up and green flies with their sucking mouthparts were foraging over the remains of the food. Phraya Sanon turned his thoughts to entertainment: 'LanXang is a beautiful country of poetry where love brings happiness. We don't need much to be content.' He added that he wished to summon the palace's favourite bard (*morlum*) and the *Khaen* player, for no Lao dinner was complete without music and song, he argued. The glorious bard who could improvise song (*Lum or Kub*) from his (or her) lips in every style in the kingdom would certainly make everyone merry. I have to confess I was thinking of slinking off to bed and some of the other guests also wanted to leave. Chao Anouvong compelled them to stay, telling them that what he was about to say was vital to LanXang's future. Everyone sat up and looked at him, desperate to know what he was planning to discuss. He raised his hands and asked them to be patient. They took a sip of their drinks, mused in silence and waited anxiously for him to go on.

'Gentlemen,' he said, heaving himself to his feet. 'Thank you for being here. Now, I beg your attention, for there is an important matter I wish to discuss with you and you must give me your frank opinion. All of us are loyal to our motherland, so please take care that none of this goes beyond these walls.' He paused and looked around. 'First, now that your cups are filled, may I propose, in accordance with our custom, that we again make a drink offering to our ancestors' spirits (*Phi Fah* ຜີຟ້າ), who watch over us and deserve respect.' He poured libations from a silver cup and prayed in silence. We all did the same, drank a little more and sat up in our seats.

'Now, please concentrate and I will come straight to the point,' he said. 'Gentlemen, we must look to the past to change the future. The topic for this conversation is Lao consciousness (*Khuam Penh Lao*) – our nation's future. I've been thinking, as I'm sure have some of you, that waging a war against Bangkok could be the only way forward for us. I'm frightened we're losing our identity. We're a peaceful people, but if we don't stand up to Rattanakosin Siam, it could be the end of the Lao nation state, and this cycle of pain and hatred will only continue. We no longer trust Bangkok, even when they give us their solemn word, because we know how treacherous they are. We may well end up seeing them as enemies or foreigners rather than fellow descendants of Ai-Lao Khoun Borom. Our peoples are surely too close for such animosity.'

'Oh, excellent!' said Phraya Sanon casually, laughing a little, thinking it was just another political joke. He then asked, somewhat more seriously, 'Are you trying to provoke a reaction or just being funny?' I should mention that his hiccups did briefly return; having a sweet tooth, he opted to dissolve a tablespoonful of sugar in his mouth, which was successful.

'I know this is a casual evening but perhaps I haven't expressed myself well enough,' said Chao Anouvong. 'On the contrary, I'm very serious. I can tell you, there won't be a Lao nation at all if we don't win back our liberty. Do any of you wish to be under the rule of Bangkok?'

Everyone looked at Chao Anouvong and shook their heads.

'I do apologise, Your Majesty. We definitely don't want to be Siamese!' Phraya Sanon said. 'But it would be very difficult for us to win if we go to war. Those villains in Bangkok will oppress us even more severely if we lose.'

'They most certainly would, but it is not for them to decide our future. We are a peaceful, culturally diverse people and quite capable of arranging our lives as we please. My friend King Naphalai, whom I admire dearly, will never grant us our rights. Bangkok is fixated on Siamese expansion. So far, we've been patiently countering their anger, resentment and jealousy with peace, contentment and generosity.' He paused. 'You know of course gentlemen that Siam is sparsely populated, not big enough to support its fast-growing economy. Bangkok wants to enlarge it. They don't just want a slice of our land but they intend to annex LanXang entirely, to capture more manpower for the multitude of works they're planning. We've never wanted to slice off any of their territory, but we do have the right to protect what we already have. We're Lao citizens, free to make our own choices and to be ourselves in a world that is constantly trying to make us something else. For that reason, I believe we should stand up and fight for our independence, just as that exceptionally courageous man from Sukhotai, King Naresuan, did for Ayutthaya against Burma. Well, if we can't reach a peaceful settlement with Bangkok, I'm afraid the consequences are inevitable – war. Am I right?'

'You most certainly are,' Prince Ngao cut in, his serious face flushed with excitement. 'If I may express my opinion here, I totally agree with you that we must fight and win this war.'

'For us to have any chance of winning,' said Chao Anouvong, 'I believe LanXang must unite and we must try to choose men with suitable abilities for the defence of our country, because soldiering is a profession that requires a high degree of skill, practice and sacrifice. We need men who share our dream!'

'All very well, but surely,' viceroy Tissah casually interrupted, 'there's no sense in going to war and losing. It would be a heroic, yet pointless dream.'

Ngao, not a man for small talk, his face reddened, went straight to the point. 'Let's drink to pointless heroism,' he said, raising his glass towards his father and his brother before shooting a disappointed glance at Tissah. 'I would rather be dead than a slave of Siam.'

'Yes, let's have a toast to that,' said Suthisan Poh, raising his glass towards Ngao and nodding his head. They poured libations and raised their glasses to their father approvingly.

'May I remind Your Majesty that we first need unity amongst ourselves,' said Phraya Sanon, raising his glass to Tissah. 'It's all well and good our people are so diverse, but we must urge them to find a way of ridding our country of the oppressors. If the Siamese refuse to head off to their own country, which they most certainly will, then we must be brave and cudgel our brains, either by cunning or in open battle. We must win. How otherwise can we be Lao and have our freedom?'

'With respect, a war against Rattanakosin Siam will be very difficult,' persisted Tissah. 'They have wealth, power and foreign aid. And what about those Lao noblemen on the Khorat Plain who are heavily influenced by Bangkok? They might well oppose us. To incur Naphalai's enmity is dangerous enough in my view.'

'There's no point fostering Bangkok's friendship unless you want to live under their rule,' retorted Chao Anouvong. 'I would rather abdicate now than let the Siamese rule over us. If we want to remain Lao this could be the right time to take our country back. Alternatively, we could go off to the country and the jungle and fight a guerrilla war, as our King Xay-Setthathirath did against the Burmese.'

'But the real question is, how can we win the war?' asked Ngao.

Chao Anouvong jumped in, gazing at his son. 'Bangkok's oppression and expansion has to be stopped. And don't forget that Siam's next ruler, Chetsadabodin, could be even worse for us.'

Everyone shifted a little in their seats. So, there it was. This casual discussion had finally brought together all the disparate dreams of Chao Anouvong's life. He looked like a man who believed the flow of history was rushing through him. The guests poured libations, took their drinks and swallowed hard, but no one spoke for a while.

'Come on! We haven't lost yet!' Chao Anouvong said with a grin. 'If we remain united by our love of LanXang and everything goes according to plan, I don't believe we can lose. Our principal aim is, of course, to bring the suffering people of Saraburi and the other cities back to ViengChan. They are with us and desperately want to come home.' He'd drummed up support in Khorat on the way back from his visit to confront Naphalai in Bangkok over Phromphakdy's crimes. Damning reports about the brutality of the Siamese officials there had convinced him that the Lao people from Khorat to ViengChan were all on his side. All of those who'd been forcibly removed to Siam were ready to return home.

'But what if we lose?' said Tissah, finding his voice again.

'We will unite to defend the people,' Ngao cut in swiftly. 'The Siamese officials are persecuting our people. We – the defenders – make friends, while they – the persecutors – make enemies. If we don't fight now, we may well end up losing our Lao identity forever.'

'In the name of the Lord Buddha and our ancestors, how gladly I would undertake the campaign,' Chao Anouvong said and nodded appreciatively.

'But first we should pray for guidance at this difficult time. It would give our nation a sure hope that if we conduct ourselves well in the sight of our ancestors' spirits, they will bless us by restoring Lao LanXang to its former glory and healing our wounds.'

With that, he brought the evening to a close. After strong murmurs of assent, the guests slunk off or quietly left, sober. I was glad I'd stayed put to hear everything.

This was the first time I'd heard Chao Anouvong mention his dreams so openly: a measure of his increasing confidence. To unite his people and fight for independence was a king's greatest responsibility the nearest step to heaven to achieving immortality; 999 of the 1,000 steps to heaven. He must have been nursing these dreams for years, ever since he was taken far, far away from his kingdom and separated from his parents and his people. He'd been teased and bullied in Bangkok, with no one to advise him or to protect him from injustice. But he was strong and his hatred kept him fighting. After years of physical and emotional abuse, he must have realised that even if the Siamese took everything from him, he would always have control over his heart and mind. He kept his dreams to himself until that night and speaking it out loud made them seem possible, even plausible. When he said the word 'independence', which was precious – sacred even – to him, he planted a banner in the ground for all the Lao LanXang people to rally around. For a moment I glimpsed the brilliant, starry future through his eyes. He really wanted to give ViengChan and the country back to the people, a completely unselfish pledge we could all admire. The Lao people began to believe that if they pulled together, they really could unify LanXang.

If Siam's actions had been worthy and just, there would have been no need for war. On the other hand, it would have been wrong for Chao Anouvong to stand idly by in the face of Bangkok's domineering policies. He simply had to act against such injustice, even though the Lao people desired only a simple, peaceful life.

It seemed reasonable enough to suppose that as Siam was prospering more than LanXang, then the Lord Buddha and the gods cared more for the Rattanakosins than for a just man in ViengChan. Obviously, if the warlord Phraya Kasatseuk hadn't been so arrogant, reckless and ambitious, he wouldn't have become Chulaloke, the first Rattanakosin king of Siam. Nevertheless, his dynasty never seemed at peace with itself, always craving more power. The dynasty would continue to use oppression as a means of staying in power. This would remain so without any genuine opposition from the people.

Chao Anouvong always emphasised that politics is ever changing, following a perpetual cycle of growth and decay, like nature. As soon as the power that most rulers obsess about begins to fade, they too pass away and all their promises count for nothing. No dynasty, however powerful and cunning, can be eternal. Surely, like nature, the Bangkok dynasty would one day expire amidst bloodshed and excess. Lao LanXang's golden age had ended in 1779 but the bad times in turn would also come to an end. If the time wasn't right for Chao Anouvong's plans, then he would be invoking fortune in vain.

A Fateful Encounter

Uring the rainy season of the south-west monsoons (May–August) in 1824, there were severe, heavy rainstorms. In ViengChan, a mighty tropical storm destroyed trees, houses and temples. The palace sustained serious damage. Many senior monks, astronomers and oracles saw these natural disasters as clear warnings of worse things to come.

In early May, gale-force winds unexpectedly blew down the building housing the gold Phrabang Buddha. Then, in June, a ferocious typhoon broke Hor Phra Kaeo's spire (*Sorfah*), and parts of the palace roof were blown off. A howling gale blew up and lightning struck the sacred That Phanom stupa in the south. But earthquakes concerned Chao Anouvong far more than thunder and lightning. One shook the city; large craters opened within the palace grounds, terrifying the people. The monks, oracles and elders, who had the country's welfare at heart, staggered about in shock, asking themselves what was to come of such a portent. They prophesied a great calamity was approaching for the people living under the clear skies of ViengChan. Chao Anouvong paid no attention: he refused to be deterred by the elements and stuck to the task in hand. The Lao people had learned to smile or shrug in the face of life's adversities, he said; being hit by earthquakes was no laughing matter, but a typhoon that blew away roofs was nothing to worry about and being caught in a downpour was just a joke. What could anyone do about it? He calmly ordered repairs to be made. These were natural events, he said, not omens from the gods.

By October, most of the rain clouds had been swept away by the wind. The downpour finally stopped and the winds died down. The paddy fields quickly turned golden. By late November, fragrant new rice had been harvested: reward for the people's hard labour. They then turned their minds to festivity and relaxation throughout the dry season: three months of ideal weather between

December and February, hot during the day but cool and breezy at night.

Then, in December, the sad news of King Loetla Naphalai's death in Bangkok on 21 July reached ViengChan. Chao Anouvong was taken entirely by surprise and much aggrieved. He wilted and sank to his seat as he read the dispatch. He thought he'd planted the seed of reconciliation in Bangkok and had witnessed it flowering with Naphalai, only to see it plucked away in front of his eyes. It was the end of an era and a dramatically sad turning-point for him, leaving him full of foreboding for what happen next. He'd befriended Naphalai, a kind-hearted man; in some respects they were fond of each other, sharing a mutual admiration and warm feelings. Chao Anouvong had done all he could to avoid upsetting Naphalai; after his sudden death, he seemed unsure of himself, but was anxious to find out what the new Rattanakosin ruler would be like and how he might behave towards LanXang.

Chao Anouvong hastily ordered his mandarins to select the finest elephants and horses and to organise an official trip to Bangkok to show his allegiance: he wanted to be among the first to offer his condolences. Nevertheless, his long-brewing rebellion against the Siamese repression of LanXang and LanNa never left his mind. If anything, his conviction for LanXang, mingled with a desire for survival, became more firmly rooted and stronger day by day.

Some officials and members of the royal household staff were excited at the prospect of seeing Bangkok and had wangled their way in to join him. The king insisted I saw the Chaophraya river and Bangkok. Frankly, I wasn't all that keen to go, but being a lover of marvels, I had a longing to see the whole world, including Bangkok. Most of all, I had a yearning to see the Emerald Buddha.

With much to turn over in my mind on the evening before the journey, I retired early to my comfortable bedroom, a small room in the north wing of the palace with a clear view over the Mekong. I sat on the firm bed and took off my soft shirt and trousers (*Pha Thio*). After folding them I hung them on a peg by the wooden bedstead. I lay late into the night on top of my bed, brushing up on my Siamese, imagining the trip and dreaming about Bangkok, which was much more developed than ViengChan. Besides, I longed to travel abroad before age overtook me and journeys became a burden. But the world beyond LanXang seemed tantalisingly out of reach. I imagined it would be an unpleasant journey, with few comforts other than a bed, clean food, water and fresh air. But I had to go.

So, at the beginning of January 1825, I accompanied Chao Anouvong to Bangkok to attend Naphalai's funeral. He expected it to be a dreary and unpleasant occasion as he was fully aware how strongly he was disliked there, particularly by the Rattanakosins' mandarins.

Naphalai's first son Chetsadabodin was technically first in line, but he was the son of the Princess Consort Sri Sulalai, rather than Queen Sri Suryendra, the mother of his half-brother, Prince Mongkut. Besides, Chetsadabodin was despised by many of his courtiers, both for his character and his low birth. Nevertheless, he took the throne as King Phra Nangklao, which made him even more conceited. He felt threatened by Chao Anouvong: a descendant of Khoun Loh, a genuinely royal-blooded monarch of the ancient Lao LanXang Kingdom. Moreover, he was respected by the Lao people, especially those on the Khorat Plateau, who looked to ViengChan for guidance rather than to Siam's powerhouse in Bangkok.

After assembling a large entourage, including over 100 members of the palace alone, we marched off from ViengChan, crossing the Mekong like a great armada, leaving the city in the care of Chao Anouvong's half-brother, Tissah. The king was in official mourning, and I left him well alone. He hardly spoke at all, but Prince Ngao became concerned and questioned him about the new king in Bangkok.

'During my younger days in Bangkok,' Chao Anouvong said, turning to his son, 'Chetsadabodin was simply known as Thap. He was a vile bully who seemed to enjoy handing out injuries. He's certainly not to be trusted.' He paused and sighed heavily. 'Personally, Ngao,' he continued, 'I don't mind Chetsadabodin being given the pompous name "Nangklao" when he's crowned king. He will rise to the status of a god in Bangkok, but like his grandfather and father before him, the only thing he has in common with the almighty is his taste for women. Quite frankly, I don't care where Nangklao takes his seat, as long as it isn't on top of our heads. The truth is that the Lao race (*SaeuZard Lao*) in the Lao country (*Mueang Lao*) want to live in a Lao state (*Pathet Lao*) as a Lao nation (*Zard Lao*). We simply don't want to be part of Siam. Nangklao and his men are selfish, lacking in empathy and unfit to govern. He's manipulative, an expansionist of the most insatiable kind. His reputation far exceeds his talent. In my opinion he's the nastiest person ever to hold power. There's now little chance of the reforms we crave. He's a Buddhist but has little respect for the five precepts; he's incapable of controlling himself and has no idea what justice is. He's just another tyrant in the making. I dread what he might do next. To tell you bluntly, Ngao, this could be a disaster for us. We must be on our guard and be very careful what we say.'

We all groaned in anxiety, and he reminded us to watch our conduct in Bangkok.

Once we were on our way, we rested before nightfall. Chao Anouvong was anxious to get to Bangkok well before the funeral. We took the usual direct route amidst great cheers and urged the mahouts to spur the elephants on. Some of us travelled in horse carriages or ox carts.

Over a month after leaving the luxuriant banks of the Mekong, we finally reached the outskirts of the Siamese capital at sunset. We were tired but relieved and went to bed early and slept soundly. Upon awaking before dawn, it was not without regret that I observed we were completely out of sight of the north-easternmost point of the Phetsabun Mountains, which terminated on the southern tip of the hotly contested Dong Phraya Fai range we'd left two days before. We were utterly out of LanXang and deep inside Siamese land. Our apprehension and excitement seemed to make the air much hotter than it really was. Bangkok lay ahead in the gloom as we moved slowly forward before sunrise. The hot sun soon emerged and when its fierce hear rapidly increased, we put up our umbrellas. As we were approaching Bangkok, a thick cloud of smoke hung over the houses and a succession of temple roofs and spires sparkling in the sunshine came into view.

On that very morning of our arrival I felt a greater buzz of excitement and anticipation that I'd ever experienced before. Chao Anouvong looked relieved, sitting aloft his elephant howdah and straining his eyes in the dazzling sunlight. He'd a beard and a longer moustache by this time. He was probably quite pleased to be back in his old stamping ground and he squared his shoulders in pleasurable anticipation.

One did what one could to be noticed. With a confident expression on my face, I proudly posed in a dignified manner but was longing to take leave of the elephant's back for a comfortable couch. I didn't observe anything spectacular as we passed along, except a great number of temples with their multi-coloured roofs and spires; they were very similar to those in LanXang, I should add. I was exhausted, but the distant view of Bangkok exceeded my expectations and sent jolts of adrenaline through me like magic. When we reached the bright, wide space of the Sanamluang Field where many people were assembled, my curiosity was aroused by the imposing Grand Palace complex, where the

Emerald Buddha temple and a range of other colourful, magnificent religious buildings stood. I thought of all the questions I would ask the Siamese who'd thoughtlessly invaded and pillaged ViengChan.

From a distance we must have made the onlookers shiver: perhaps our one hundred elephants and fifty horses reminded them of the terrifying Burmese invasion that had haunted their land in earlier times. We received no official welcome, but as soon as the crowds caught sight of our party, they seemed to move in our direction, but they only happened to be in the area for the market. A group of odious boys screamed abuse and threw things at each other; dogs barked; women with chicken or fruit and vegetables in baskets came hurriedly towards our colourful procession, gathering in large numbers at the sight of our marching horses and elephants. Chao Anouvong sat on the largest, a glittering image in his gilded howdah.

The more I observed the Siamese, the harder I found it to believe that we were all descended from the ancient Ai-Lao. I tried not to narrow my eyes at them as they waved their hands in greeting. They looked at us in awe or just stared, open-mouthed. Several of them, judging by the clothes they were wearing, looked Chinese. A group of no-hopers and beggars amongst the stream of milling spectators looked dishonest and greedy. I imagine they were no happier to see us than we them.

'Where have you all come from?' the pale-faced crowd called to us, while continuing to chatter amongst themselves. I wondered if the pale-skinned ones amongst them were Chinese.

At first, I just lifted my head a little, smiled and looked ahead. I knew that the Siamese had inherited much of our Ai-Lao culture and traditions, but they didn't quite accept that language was one of them. I refused on principle to speak their language because I was sure that if I could understand them, then they could surely understand me. I looked down on their upturned faces, gaping in surprise when I politely replied in my best Lao: 'We come from ViengChan on the mighty Mekong and it's nice to meet you.'

'From where?' the crowd responded dismissively, as though they didn't understand what I'd said.

'From the Lao ViengChan LanXang,' I repeated slowly, almost scolding them. I felt wonderful satisfaction merely from being able to speak Lao in the very heart of Bangkok.

'Lao ViengChan? Really!' said someone at the back.

'Yes, my good fellow. Our capital ViengChan is far away from Siam and has always been on the Mekong!' I exclaimed, keeping calm. To tell them anything else was a waste of breath.

'They are Lao (*Khon Lao*),' others mocked, followed by a snort of violent laughter which would normally have invited retaliation. I glared at them and they waddled off laughing; most of the crowd began drifting away once they realised there was nothing of real interest to be seen. A moment later, some sort of official on horseback arrived and escorted us to our quarters in the Bang Yi Khan district, not far from the palace. We were all very glad to settle down and rest our tired bodies. That night we slept in decent beds for the first time in weeks.

I enjoyed travelling, even with all its attendant worries. Fretting was never any use, however disagreeably things turned out. Besides, the pleasure I feel in occasionally recalling memories of the journey makes me forget how awkward things actually were at the time. In my fervid imagination, Bangkok (*Krung Thep*) possessed an aura of glamour and sophistication. I'd pictured wide streets and fine, gilded temples filled with elegant and cultured people. Some of us were entranced by the unfamiliar surroundings but I felt an unexpected pang of disappointment. I found instead filth; bumpy, narrow, muddy roads; the poverty and exhaustion of the common people (more Lao than Siamese); flies; dusty, humid heat; and the sharp stink of sewage and cow and buffalo dung. I couldn't possibly envy Bangkok's inhabitants, who seemed to tolerate the stench. The vile reek filled my dreams with a store of unpleasant fancies. Just like in ViengChan, I saw many simple stalls and carts in the streets outside the smarter shops, piled with wares. Some were stacked with fruit, roast sweetcorn, spicy papaya salad (*Som Tam* to the Siamese) and grilled chicken. I found it highly amusing to walk the streets and observe the riches of Bangkok, which I could only attribute to their successful dealings with foreign traders. The ruling class claimed to be compassionate and decent, yet they behaved like businessmen only pretending to be heads of state. They'd enriched themselves by selling Siam to foreigners. This combination of inconceivable wealth and a powerful military was bound to one day erode their people's freedom.

Bangkok city – the commercial centre and the beating heart of Rattanakosin Siam – seemed its usual self: sprawling, chaotic, noisy, dirty and smelly. Everything in Bangkok seemed to have come from somewhere else. The shops sold a bewildering array of goods, yet i there was nothing sophisticated about any of it. It was a very busy city that never seemed to go to sleep, full of strange-looking people I didn't dare approach. The city was probably best known for its beautiful temples and young men and women of easy virtue, creating vast wealth for the country and its rulers. The poorest citizens, young and old, including children pot-bellied with hunger, leaned against the temples or palace walls or watched lifelessly from their broken huts. There were an awful lot of them, living a semblance of a life in such unpromising and immoral circumstances. They raised their heads as we went by, casting melancholy looks of want and despondency. It sounds ridiculous, but the sight of those poor people silently reproached me. I prayed for someone to come along and relieve their suffering.

I would have hated to have been stuck in Bangkok. You could end up in prison merely for expressing controversial views about the royals or die from some unspeakable disease for mixing with loose women, who looked rather well off and elegant compared to the common folk.

Meanwhile, LanXang quietly went its way, in no rush to move with the times, probably because she saw and heard things differently, respecting nature and following not where the path may lead her, but going where there was no path and leaving her own trail. ViengChan could be forgiven for not being like Bangkok: it didn't have as many visitors to impress.

Once out of LanXang, some rustic Lao were like fish out of water. On the contrary, we weren't bored in the least and or reliant on others. We certainly didn't lack courage. Most days we trooped off on sightseeing expeditions. Strolling along the filthy and smelly streets in the sweltering heat wasn't particularly pleasurable, but most of us, myself included, wanted to explore the city further, to learn more about its history and politics, and the lives of these people who seemed so similar to those back in LanXang. We hoped to discover there was far more to Siam than its ruthless Rattanakosin government. Personally speaking, I wanted to see if there was anything the Siamese world could teach us. We set out merrily to explore the scenery in a most enjoyable manner.

It was our first visit and we needed guides. Officials offered their services but as we preferred the company of expatriates, the task fell to Lao citizens who'd been forcibly moved (*kwoad*) from the north-eastern provinces in 1779 and had settled in Bang Khun Phrom, Ban Lao and other districts. Several noble Bangkok families claimed to be of direct descent from the great ViengChan families of ancient LanXang, but in reality, the Lao are the true ancestors (*Banphaburuth*) of the Siamese. Bangkok seemed full of them, slaving away to make a living, happily eating and celebrating in Lao style, both openly and behind closed doors. Some of them knew the city and the Siamese more intimately than their own towns and people. They undertook to be our guides, mostly to prevent new arrivals like us – who were still young and energetic – falling prey to criminals, running into drunks or getting into fights. The prospect of walking about in the teeth of danger made me edgy: Siam seemed more of an alien world. Bangkok people had become arrogant and hard to place since the advent of the Rattanakosins.

Even in daylight we took care not to stray into any unfrequented lanes or to wander from our base at night. Armed ruffians were often on the prowl in search of prey. We constantly had to remind ourselves that we were in Bangkok, refraining from provoking brawls or wrangling with the hostile locals. By being so difficult to please, we didn't make things easy for ourselves. We were more active and adventurous than most and very curious to know more about the Siamese mentality, which we discovered was very different from ours. We encountered agents provocateurs and outright bullies who had provocative manners and were quick to strike. They couldn't cope with any criticism and were always bothering us or trying to sell stuff to us wherever we went. Some were anxious to help in an unctuous kind of way.

Sensibly, we stayed out of trouble. We were awestruck by how long the streets were. 'Bangkok! Bangkok!' one of our men hummed as we gazed in wonder at the colourful temples and the size of the palace compound. It was extraordinary how far some of the new buildings towering into the sky: it was a really frightening novelty when you looked up. They seemed to coalesce to form one huge structure, too immense to be compared with the Grand Palace itself.

We flitted around Bangkok and made clandestine contacts with possible supporters. Furthermore, with a sense of boyish insouciance, we also tried to befriend some slightly creepy but decent-looking inhabitants, although we didn't really want to fraternise with them. 'Hey brothers! You lost?' they called. We were aware of the hostility, but we responded by glancing and smiling at them, holding our noses and piling on the sycophancy. But we made sure not to let ourselves be badgered, conned or ordered about like idiots. One of our number accompanied a lyricist with his *Khaen*, bringing life to the busy streets.

It was a bit of turn-off to some of the snooty inhabitants, however, who merely sneered at us. But we didn't care: our main purpose was to arouse curiosity, to spread our culture and to cheer people up.

Apparently, Mongkut's younger brother Pinklao – an admirer of all things Lao who loved to show off to European visitors – played the *Khaen*, expertly fingering it as the air passes through the pipes while he breathed in and out. Surprisingly he even sang '*Lum*' in Lao and danced to the joyful sound of the *Khaen* like a true Laoman! He couldn't really have performed any other way as it would have made him look silly if he'd tried to sing in Siamese. Alas, it was said that on his brother's orders, Pinklao grabbed his *Khaen* and smashed it on the floor, denouncing it as inappropriate and shameful, citing the threat it supposedly posed to Siamese culture and, worse, its alleged role in bringing ill omen and causing natural disasters like flood and drought. This hypocrisy was too much to bear for us. Funnily enough, even though the snooty Siamese looked down on the Lao, the Europeans looked down even further on the Siamese. Some high-minded foreigners in the audience called out to Pinklao, 'But you sang and danced to the *Khaen* music just now.' Other diplomats cheered the remark. They all turned to look at Mongkut and one boldly said. 'Your Majesty, we never see you smile. You looked so unhappy until your brother started playing that instrument; the celestial tune it plays made us want to dance and helps to cool the rage in men's heart. Besides, music brings people together.' Amidst a chorus of jeers, the Siamese audience gave deprecatory smiles and looked sheepish, flushed and speechless.

Whilst we admired the beauty and charm of the temples, we found the great sprawling mass of Bangkok deeply unpleasant. Chao Anouvong only went out when he'd to for he never ever blurred the line between fun and formality. I took care to do the same. After chatting with various men in authority and some of our informants, I began to understand the realities of life in Siam, which I was pleased to inform Chao Anouvong about. He consumed my reports avidly and peered through them with fascination as if they were a window into the Rattanakosins' thinking. Siam's economic model rested on trade, wealth and the king's rule by decree. The main palace (a gilded prison to some) was the main power in the realm but the influence of foreigners – especially European traders – was striking: they played a decisive role in the country's wealth. You could clearly see a new society emerging, its growing prosperity heavily dependent on hospitality. The sense of belonging to an influential and powerful foreign power gave the Bangkok elites a sense of superiority over their own people. Naturally, we were less impressed with the inhabitants than with the smart-looking foreigners. The monotony of Siamese life was enlivened by the visits of important functionaries, European envoys and trade commissioners. The whole of Bangkok, it seemed, crowded to see their arrival.

The imposing sight of the tall, sophisticated European gentlemen with their clean, milky complexions overwhelmed me. My first impression of them had been correct. Some had paunches, soft golden hair and carefully tended or long moustaches or their faces were covered with bushy and fearful beards and whiskers, ridiculous to look at but oddly nice. Their perpetually astonished bright blue or onyx-green eyes were full of life; their hawk-like or large, long straight noses attracted the attention of the snub-nosed inhabitants. Some wore monocles and, often walking in the sun without a hat or umbrella, had been burnt and turned a pinkish red – a tint not favoured amongst locals. Some had caught colds and looked pale and queasy: eyes running, noses squelching and moustaches damply drooping rather than firmly upright. Those standing tall and straight and looking immensely proud of themselves made me wonder what their secret was. Some looked soft, with chubby, florid faces; they probably had breasts like women. Their ladies, with their graceful, corseted waists, honey-blonde hair, fashionable hats and big, full skirts down to the floor looked very beautiful. But perhaps they had slightly overdone the powder and lipstick. Some, perhaps, were over-painted and ultra-refined. Remarkably, both men and women exhaled freshness and cleanliness and, in their individual ways, had rather attractive, innocent faces. It was an awe-inspiring sight.

To show support, sympathy and respect to the Siamese court, Chao Anouvong took over 100 mandarins with him: high-ranking officials, important loyalists and other able people. He also took many costly offerings to dedicate to his dead friend Naphalai. He was clear and precise in everything, a godsend for the Siam-LanXang special relationship. But sadly, his dedication, seductive performance and sensitivity to the occasion didn't make any deep impression or help to end Siam's domination. In fact, it had opposite effect.

Although deeply saddened at Naphalai's death, he decided not to follow the usual custom of becoming a Buddhist monk and donning saffron robes for a few days as a formal way of showing his loyalty and respect. The state funeral was rather a subdued affair but at least went smoothly for us. It was a very elaborate, moving occasion, something I'd never experienced before. Chao Anouvong, clad in his elegant white official dress, remained solemn throughout. The procession involved thousands of people – officials, soldiers, musicians and dancers – and hundreds of animals. Elephants and horses were dressed for mourning and festooned with precious brocade. Some of the Siamese officials wore black in the European style to mourn their king, while others followed more local traditions and wore white and walked behind the immense cortège. Bangkok was full of rumour: most of the unwilling population had been forced into mourning and were extremely careful what they said about the late and the new king. The hand-picked mourners lining the streets, brought in from the countryside by the authorities to bolster the numbers, were in tears, prostrating themselves and weeping as the solemn procession went by. Spectators clustered at the back along the route gazed at the cortège, bidding farewell to their mild-mannered king who lay in a gilded coffin. They exchanged looks as if they hated, envied and feared his successor, but to be safe they praised both monarchs. Hundreds of monks with newly shaved heads and wearing brand new or freshly laundered saffron robes walked in the procession. King Manthathurath from LanXang Luang Phrabang, now a monk at the Emerald Buddha temple, was among them and remained there a year to emphasise his loyalty to the new king.

Evidently, the princes of LanNa who had always allied themselves with LanXang had refused to attend. Consequently, they were made to disappear soon after Nangklao's succession, a way of erasing the vestiges of Lao LanNa autonomy.

It is not my intention to dwell on personal gossip: such matters fell beneath my dignity. But I couldn't help noticing that many European representatives and traders, mostly in black, attended the cremation to express their grief and praise the dead king. According to the palace inner circle, most of the overseas traders had arrived in shiploads for their share of the spoils, forsaking the comfort and security of their homes and risking their lives to amass more wealth and whatever else they could find in the 'capital of fun'.

The highly elaborate, impressive and no doubt very expensive royal golden pyre, fit for a god not a king, was a representation of heaven; it looked like a newly built temple or a monstrous misuse of splendour towering into the sky. Within it lay the king's golden coffin. Torch bearers lit the kindling and, as the flames leaped, the officers yelled and the mahouts called to the elephants, who lifted and curled back their trunks, trumpeting their salute. The blaze rose, roaring and spiralling upward to the upper tiers and bursting in a great peak of flames against the firmament: not so much a moment of bathos as an amazing spectacle presented to the whole world. The king's faithful followers, mourning under the hot white Bangkok sky, believed the inferno was godlike. But on earth, so to speak, it burnt like hell – there can be no fire without ash. It fired my imagination but also filled me with apprehension and fear. Chao Anouvong lowered his head in sorrow throughout.

The occasion was seen by many (especially by the Lao) as nothing more than an opportunity for the overindulged Siamese elite to spend their ill-gotten wealth. Some of the decent, old aristocrats, the supposed pillars of Siamese society, had become increasingly out of touch and almost certifiably incompetent. They had no responsibility to explain themselves to the public. The elite of Bangkok had become increasingly partisan, their supposedly diverse, forward-looking and superior mentality based largely on fantasy. But from the perspective of the less fortunate citizens in the north and northeast, they came across as haughty: a self-perpetuating aristocracy with condescending airs and graces who intimately embraced foreign favour. Attempts to make them see the truth and earn the lasting appreciation of their people hit a brick wall. They seemed to have forgotten that Siam was the land of their Lao ancestors who, unlike them, had showed devotion to the past to secure the future.

The newly anointed king, Nangklao, looked very distinguished in his official attire. He was like a whirlpool on the Chaophraya river, sucking men in by the sheer force of his power. Although the whole of Bangkok became mesmerised by him, beneath the glamour he was just another progenitor of this disreputable and ruthless dynasty, crushing his enemies and frightening the nation. From the very start the new regime tried to impress its guests and the world with pomp, pageantry, protocol, banquets, royalty and ceremony to demonstrate its power and wealth, but the overriding impression was that Rattanakosin Siam remained an abusive institution. At the top of the pile, the royals looked the part, elevated high above their subjects and displaying all the earthly power at their disposal. Meanwhile Siam maintained its treacherous, avaricious and shameless policies towards Lao LanXang.

It was the beginning of a new era where most people had the chance to forge their own destiny and corruption and intrigue grew. Nangklao acquired a growing reputation as a powerful king with a tendency for overindulgence which he could never quite suppress. In this 'capital of envy', local aphrodisiacs were popular, and citizens and foreigners alike soon felt free to indulge in lust, drinking and sexual excess. Brothel sprang up everywhere. It was disgusting: how could anyone in their right mind encourage it?

The kingdom was often devastated by drought or flood. Landowners, farmers and peasants blamed Bangkok for stealing their crops but no one dared utter a word. At a time of hardship, when the people were hungry for rice, the ruling classes hosted lavish banquets for overseas envoys, friends and honoured guests who'd go anywhere for a free meal and a bit of gossip. How shocking it must have been to see these snobbish people brazenly indulged themselves, as if poverty didn't exist. They cosseted themselves quietly in their palatial homes during the day but went into the city at night to gamble and whore. The Bangkok establishment allowed this to happen in the knowledge it was far too grand and powerful to worry about any resulting scandal, striking a horribly vulgar and decadent note.

Perhaps some of the wealthy and privileged visitors had a great capacity for enjoyment, were used to weaker drink or were accustomed to doing as they pleased. They seemed extremely keen and enthusiastic to participate in matters that concerned them. They'd probably never seen so much beauty and were induced by hand-picked royal attendants to flirt more than they ought to. Their conversation was laced with naughty jokes and disrespectful language, their lives consumed by affluent living. Despite appearances, they were very witty and sagacious. Usually in fear of the king, they often let their guard down at his banquet table. Noble, well-informed and clever until they'd tossed down a few strong alcoholic drinks, they ended up reclining around the table. Their tongues loosened and their glances became more direct. They shamelessly asked where the royal ladies were – saying it was the custom in their homeland for the ladies to attend the feasts and share the drinking – so that they could flirt with them and lay their hands on them. They probably wanted to test how far they dared go. But these ladies, of great beauty with their small dark eyes that could invite intimacy as well as resentment, ignored the foreigners' lecherous gazes or flashed glares of undiluted disapproval at them. Disgusted at the sight of such unseemly behaviour, they threw down their napkins, stamped their feet and rose from the table in a state of high dudgeon. This merely provoked laughter while the host, who loved to show off their charms, just looked on. Some ladies, of course, used their beauty as an advancement in life.

An alternative to these noble ladies was, of course, the beautiful female court dancers in their costumes, or retinues of well-selected boy and girl slaves in their respective white and crimson livery, stationed around the table waving large fans of peacock feathers or gilded palm leaves; there were also the waiters and waitresses who hurried in and out of the banquet room. Some of the guests, their voices cutting noisily across the table, winked and gestured with their eyes, watching them hungrily but cheerfully accepting rejection when their amorous advances were turned down. They obviously wanted to test the waters but were happy in the knowledge their misdemeanours would be readily forgiven. Such luxury was the norm for the elite and the nouveau riche, especially those in Nangklao's service. But things were very different for farmers, the peasants and the urban poor: they were forced into slavery but also had to pay taxes and often died of poverty at an early age.

Unfortunately, relations between Siam and LanXang had been progressively deteriorating during Naphalai's reign. Once he died, LanXang fell into Nangklao's hands, a pushy and intensely ambitious character who took as much satisfaction in humiliating Chao Anouvong as he did in proclaiming himself a god. ViengChan exercised restraint in the wake of Naphalai's death but became sickened by Bangkok's arrogant and insatiable appetite for a Greater Siam. The ideological conflict between the two kingdoms gave way to resentment, which in turn deepened into outright hostility. Bangkok, as usual, was full of jealousy and suspicion; if Nangklao accidentally stepped in dog mess outside his own palace, they would have suspected Chao Anouvong had put it there. This grieved my master deeply and he realised that if the special relationship was somehow to survive, then Siam must withdraw from LanXang and LanNa.

A few days after the funeral, Bangkok was jittery and awash with speculation about a British invasion and a plot by Mongkut's supporters to remove Nangklao. Undercover agents – the 'living ghosts' – routinely tailed us wherever we went, people who remained loyal to king and country, inspiring fear and submission and rooting out any internal dissent. They cowed their people – the urban masses and country folk – into abject obedience, forcing them to believe only in the glory of Siam while they lived in poverty like slaves.

Tragically, most of us were cooped up in our guest houses, waiting for news, tipped off by our contacts around the city (and in the palace) about Nangklao's intentions. There were rumours of our being rounded up for hard labour: quite enough to provoke a nasty shiver of fear. Some started to panic like chickens when a fox or a snake is around. Once I'd absorbed the situation and had done some serious thinking, I went to Chao Anouvong and found him reading on his couch in the sitting room.

'My apologies for disturbing you, Your Majesty,' I said and bowed, moving closer to him. As usual he told me to relax. I calmly whispered the news in his ear. I sensed he was very upset yet seemed somehow far too calm for my liking. He swallowed hard and rubbed his forehead with the palm of his hand, trying to collect his thoughts. Eventually he heaved himself to his feet. I muttered that if the reports were true, our immediate priority must be to protect our people.

'Of course we must try,' he said, 'but what are we to do?' He looked at me sharply and told me to think of a way. I held my tongue, gave him an urgent nod, made my excuses and left him to his own thoughts. I retreated to the quiet of my room for a serious think and a bit of a rest before preparing for the evening. But for a while my mind was like a ravine shrouded with dense patches of fog. I became muddled and even wondered if I was somehow mentally deficient.

When I appeared for a light evening meal before nightfall, I was none the wiser. I found him sitting at the dining table, his head bowed, his knuckles pressed hard against his temples.

'We're trapped, Your Majesty,' I cried and shook my head when he suddenly turned and asked whether I had any clever ideas. 'We can hide them in a safe house but we're in Bangkok and there's no royal road to safety. There's nothing we can do and the Siamese will do their worst. We're doomed!'

'Nonsense, Phia Jon,' he said indignantly, turning from his food. 'We must try to save our people.' He paused for thought then looked at me with his exhausted eyes. 'We must work out… a way to help them,' he added, his words slowing as if he was coming to a decision.

'Of course we have to, Your Majesty,' I said, working my brain to find a solution.

We deliberately veered our conversation towards more cheerful matters, but I could see that his mind, too, was working out a rescue mission. After we'd satisfied our appetite and thirst, we prayed and poured libations to the immortals before retiring to our own beds for the night. I lay in bed worrying, my heart thumping.

Five hours later, I was roused by an urgent knocking on my bedroom door.

I was just about to go to sleep. 'Please come now, the king summons you to a meeting. It's urgent,' the servant at the door said. I leapt out of bed, quickly dressed and staggered bleary-eyed to the sitting room where Chao Anouvong was waiting. He came away from the window as I entered and urgently made his wishes known. While we were deep in conversation about the plan, Prince Rathsavong Ngao came rushing in and offered to help. He'd heard the rumours. We decided that the task was too hazardous for him. Chao Anouvong turned to look at me urgently and, for the first time, used my code name. I'd almost forgotten about it. I was stunned but realised I was being entrusted with a serious and risky mission.

'Are you ready to get to work, Anoujon?' he said anxiously.

'With pleasure, Your Majesty,' I responded and bowed.

'Anoujon?' said Prince Ngao, glancing at both of us, intrigued.

I was no coward and needed very little prompting. It was my plain and sworn duty and my spirits were never dashed by any fear of death. Although I'd never felt more ready, I was uncertain what I was actually supposed to do. When I hesitated (I was thinking of telling Prince Ngao why his father called me Anoujon), Chao Anouvong shot a frustrated look at me and ordered me to hurry.

'Come on, Anoujon. Let's be going before it's too late. It's dangerous work but we must do what we can to save our people. You know what to do. Now please hurry... and be careful!'

I headed out on my mission, which I was still unsure of, in the dead of night, out into a Bangkok which was far from stable. With my mounting excitement competing with rising dread, I got into a frightful flap thinking how best to go about it. I wished I could select our best men but I took two robust, brave characters with me instead. Straining our eyes into the darkness, we ventured out into the night where the houses lining the streets silently flickered under a white moon racing through motionless silver cloud. We took a circuitous route in case we were being followed, something we'd been trained to do. Despite our hearts being oppressed by so many apprehensions, we went on our way through the unknown, moonlit streets of Bangkok, all utterly alien to me.

Like a group of light-footed hunters under the cover of darkness, we stealthily slipped past unseen. Like stalking tigers, we sometimes crawled on our hands and knees and dashed along the edges of the streets, lit by a half moon illuminating the kingdom's decay and stagnation. It was one of those areas that changes character at nightfall, from innocent street food stalls to seedy bordellos. We shrank into the shadows when we saw anyone coming towards us. We crept along winding narrow lanes where women's clothes hung on lines from precarious first-floor balconies, ducking to avoid the low beams which jutted over walkways that were only just wide enough to walk through. Towards the end of the lanes, we sneaked past a group of loitering men and painted women. Red light, candlelight and the heat of alcohol flushed their pale faces. Touts stood in front of doors, looking tough and drawing extra attention to what couldn't possibly be overlooked. Rough, scruffy and frustrated men were propped up against the wall waiting their turn. To capture men's attention, tarts wriggled about on a chaise longue, stretching out their legs and lifting their skirts as an inducement. I watched agog. I'd never seen women so expertly enticing in sexual peccadillos.

We couldn't resist peeping in through the wide-open window where we saw wide-eyed girls with painted eyebrows and eyelids, bright red pouty lips, low-cut blouses and raised skirts sitting on stools with their legs apart. Some had beautiful faces and were lounging on a settee, lustfully revealing their white teeth and mischievous pink tongues as they gave primal grunts and sighs, flicking flirtatious smiles at the eager men standing at the bar who gazed back with lascivious interest. I noticed an absurdly large gold chain round the neck of one of the voluptuous girls and a strange-looking watch on her wrist. Her pouting, glossy pink lips were slightly agape, as if she were inviting intimacy. I considered knocking at the door and asking her for the time but we were in a hurry, so I pulled my two wide-eyed young men away and wondered if we had such a place in ViengChan! We pressed on, while from an upstairs floor a man cried in ecstasy. The passage stank of sweat and human waste. Late-night tipsy stragglers' voices rose here and there. We heard male laughter and female squeals. The sound of dogs barking and howling like wolves setting off others in the distance was menacing.

We moved silently like ghosts towards where our people were sheltering, mostly in houses on stilts. At each building I climbed the stairs first and entered a large open-plan sleeping room that was not sufficiently spacious to accommodate twenty people in any comfort. We tried not to tread on anyone or stumble against anything in the darkness. Most of them had long gone to bed and were fast asleep on their backs and sides, their thin chests giving gentle resonance to their snores. We woke them up one by one. Most of them began to stir slowly but some rose with a start from their sleep. I whispered my name and they recognised my voice. A candle was lit and sleepy faces flushed in panic. Knowing nowhere else safe for them to hide, I ordered them in the name of Chao Anouvong to take some provisions and leave before daybreak. We wasted no time in hastening back, expecting Chao Anouvong to have gone to bed. I returned to my bedroom in a muck sweat of fear and excitement, hoping that no one followed and wondering what might happen next. The chance of them fleeing safely was infinitesimal – only prayer might see them through. I don't think I slept at all.

At breakfast I reported to Chao Anouvong that although our mission had been a success, our people still weren't safe. There was no chance of fleeing. He praised me but looked very worried.

At first, most of them managed to scatter and evade captivity. They tried to flit around the city inconspicuously, but the Lao out in the open in broad daylight were easily identifiable. Unlike the short-haired and more masculine Siamese, our graceful and demure women kept their traditional style, wearing nothing but ankle-length Lao skirts (*Sinh*), their long, heavy hair coiled upon their shapely heads. Some of our men had intricately tattooed legs as a symbol of respectability and manhood. They also spoke Siamese with a Lao accent! Inevitably some of them weren't so lucky. One of the mandarins had brought his nine-year-old son with him to give him a taste of what lay in store in Bangkok. Both boy and father disappeared. Most of Chao Anouvong's followers got rounded up by palace guards and crazy royalists and ended up digging canals and cutting down palm trees to build forts. Some were beaten up very badly for resisting, escaping with broken noses and jaws and black eyes, unable to speak, tears of anger pouring down their cheeks. Many of them looked like beaten-down kick boxers and had only survived by pretending to be dead. I could see bitterness in their eyes. Chao Anouvong was extremely upset but powerless to prevent any of it. The incident was a terrible shock and a most distressing time for us.

Bangkok had been doing and saying what it liked without contradiction. Although we knew we couldn't count on aid from outside, we never resigned ourselves to losing LanXang. We realised that isolation spelt grave danger and wanted to establish diplomatic relations with foreign states and tell the whole world that Lao LanXang wished to unite and become an independent nation.

In his bold attempt to save the Lao nation, Chao Anouvong revealed to me that after paying a visit and reporting on LanXang's affairs to his friend King

Naphalai in Bangkok in May 1822, he'd sought help from an unlikely source. He was aware that the Bangkok palace was a profoundly paranoid place, an enclosed world of mistrust, intrigues, petty jealousies and vicious thinking, the guards keeping a sharp lookout for any intruders that might be lurking. They watched his every move and their snouts twitched with hostility. But despite all of this, he secretly and daringly went alone to appeal for help from Lord John Crawfurd, the cultured British trade envoy whose residence was near the palace.

After making obeisance by lowering his head three times to Crawfurd, Chao Anouvong explained as best as he could and begged the British Government to understand that his country on both banks of the Mekong, though so little known to the Europeans, was not a new state but had been an entirely independent kingdom until 1779 and was in desperate need of support to break away from Siam. He gave a damning report of Bangkok's atrocities in LanXang. He pleaded with him on moral and humanitarian grounds to reject the arms deals with Siam and cancel sales of weapons and ammunition. The British lord nodded politely but offered no reassurances. The Siamese were desperate to close the deal with the British. They were in constant competition with their neighbours and itching for a fight over territory. They needed British weapons to ensure success.

The situation was hopeless: Crawfurd was a mere bystander who chose to turn a blind eye for the sake of national self-interest. It was not surprising that Britain preferred to ignore the truth: its prime concern was for its own economic advantage and to that end it sought to expand its trade with Siam, signing off deals without properly assessing the risks. This, Chao Anouvong said, highlighted the hypocrisy of the British relationship with Bangkok. A strong Siam was in Britain's interests. They were keen to complete the colonisation of Burma and Malaya, and, more importantly, to secure the safety of the East India Company, which kept the British Empire wealthy. Therefore, with foreign money and weapons, Bangkok was able to terrorise a defenceless Lao LanXang.

Chao Anouvong's efforts to save his followers went unrecognised by Nangklao. Instead, all able people were sentenced to fearsomely hard labour. His son Rathsavong Ngao was made to supervise the construction work. Some of the poor conscripted Lao were forced to dig canals; others were sent to cut down palm trees in Suphanbury and then drag the logs to Samud Pakan at the mouth of the Chaophraya river, creating deep furrows to build a fort.

Named the 'Lao fortress', it was designed to prevent any attack by the enemy from the sea. The Lao slave labourers had to find their own food and water, but often there was no rice to eat and not even bones to chew, and most perished through exhaustion. It was an unimaginable injustice and yet, amongst his inner circle, his senior adviser Phraya Aphaiphuthon praised Nangklao for these 'achievements'. They flattered the king to curry favour but jeered at the quality of the Lao engineering work.

Choked with indignation, covered in mud and in a hurry to report to his father, Prince Ngao, the supervisor, slipped and fell at the Khong Saen Saeb canal; the spot was thereafter named Phalat Lom. This incident certainly upset Chao Anouvong, but he managed to keep his son's and his own anger in check and remarked sarcastically that the given name of Krung Thep – City of Angels – was not worthy. 'This accursed city,' he said, 'has become a source of unjustifiable and heinous crimes! It is forbidden to leave and impossible to escape. We'll be harassed to death by these "angels" unless we act now.'

I shared his pain, for he'd brought these people with him, only for them to end up forced into slave labour, digging canals that glorified Bangkok. I was becoming increasingly concerned, and even feared that Chao Anouvong's mind would never return from its wanderings. Staring out of the window, he said in a grim voice, 'We have to request an audience with the new king before we go back to ViengChan.' When I hesitated to acknowledge this, wondering if it was a bad idea, he glared at me and said that he was old enough to be Nangklao's father and wanted to gently inform him that he was completely lacking in empathy, before telling him outright that the Rattanakosin royal institution must change, otherwise the Lao people would not shy away from confrontation. He wanted to give him a forthright lecture about the forced removal of the Lao population from ViengChan, the branding with numbers during the census and the need to allow the Lao people in Saraburi and other cities to return to their homes in ViengChan. Most important of all, he urgently wanted to negotiate for LanXang autonomy.

Nangklao didn't seem to understand whether Lao LanXang's desires were admirable or shameful, right or wrong, but he simply whatever pleased him was good, and whatever annoyed him was bad: the characteristic of a neurotic oppressor and the privileged few in Siam. The senseless ostentation and inane pride of his admirers was there for all to see in their overbearing protocol and officious language.

Chao Anouvong opposed Siam's hegemonic expansion and felt that change was needed in Bangkok, but the question was how best to achieve it. As things stood, the current policy of humiliating him and his people would only destroy the long-standing special relationship between Siam and the Lao strengthened by bonds of history, kinship and common interest since Ai-Lao Khoun Borom's time. He saw Bangkok's vicious policies, including the use of death squads, as inhuman and absurd; the people they discriminated against most were the very Lao nobles and elite on whom LanXang's future depended. He was convinced that Siam deliberately sought a further escalation of tension; Phromphakdy and Suriyaphakdy and their men, he said, had been allowed to commit crimes against LanXang sovereignty for far too long. These problems had to be tackled at their source – the Rattanakosin king himself. But how was he going to charm Nangklao into agreeing with him? He shook his head. Nangklao was not only irascible and spoilt but a bully: the absolute ringleader of this deceitful and arrogant culture.

Our informants confirmed during one of our social engagements in Bangkok what we had long suspected. It was alleged that Naphalai's sudden death at the age of fifty-seven was due to poisoning; he'd favoured Mongkut as his successor, and Mongkut's relationship with his half-brother, Nangklao, had never been easy. They both eyed the throne and fiercely lobbied for their rights: a typical dynastic power struggle. Being Naphalai's second son, albeit born to the queen, made Mongkut the legitimate successor. But Nangklao emerged victorious; the mandarins who supported him failed to see beyond his successful suppression of the rebellion of King TakSin's only son, Prince Khatnachit, who'd plotted to claim the throne

Mongkut certainly had more right to the throne than any heir of Nangklao's, and when his half-brother died in 1851, the seal of power rightly went to him. Subsequently, without a hint of romance or any concerns about the dangers of inbreeding, he took Nangklao's granddaughter Thepsiri into his harem. She probably called him uncle in private. This was nothing new, as he'd already dallied with many concubines of various ranks. Later, one of Chao Anouvong's granddaughters, Princess Duangkham, became Mongkut's consort.

Incidentally, I also picked up priceless snippets of news in Bangkok from a popular teahouse and restaurant on the riverbank close to the Grand Palace, which was always full of smart, sophisticated customers who usually had a great deal of gossip to impart. Like an arch-deceiver with a hankering for intrigue, I kept my eyes and ears open there. Being an inquisitive person, I loved to hear what the Siamese thought about the neighbouring countries… and the world. I often found myself shaking my head in dismay at the Siamese insistence they were better than their neighbours, probably because they were born into a society that promoted this superiority complex. The opening up of trade with the outside world had clearly improved the people's standard of life in Bangkok but not necessarily for those in the rest of Siam. Alas, men don't seem to realise until it's too late how well off they are.

On the other hand, the peaceful, laid-back way of life in LanXang had existed for thousands of years. Would LanXang be happier as part of Siam? The Lao would be robbed of their rights and freedom. There was no end to the progress and chaos that reigned in Bangkok while, in contrast, the Lao stood back and watched, contentedly nurturing their dream of a better life.

One tiring afternoon I went alone into the teahouse, where smart locals and foreigners freely intermingled, to have a pick-me-up drink and on the off chance of finding some sensible people whom god respected. It was the sort of place that dispensed tea, coffee and foodstuffs, as well as gossip and slander in equal quantities. There was no problem in communicating: most Lao spoke Siamese fluently but never quite lost their accent, providing much amusement for the snooty, sophisticated people of Bangkok. The Siamese refused to speak Lao through pride and ignorance and failed to understand why the people in the northeast of Siam spoke it in the first place. In return, I refused to speak their puerile language because, quite frankly, we could already understand each other. But I found it tiresome and challenging to follow the highly modified and exaggerated Siamese pronunciation – a combination of the excessive rolling of the Khmer tongue and the high-pitched tones of the Vietnamese; it made them sound as if they were suffering from a permanent spasm of displeasure.

I took the liberty of sitting at a table for two in the middle of the room, next to a group of extroverts: frolicsome, bombastic, loquacious, aloof, handsome figures, yet pleasant, scholarly-looking young bloods. I gave them that, but appearances can be deceptive. On second thoughts, they seemed more like a band of affluent, superior youths with mouthy, greedy faces. They gobbled and shared titillating details about themselves. They'd probably been steeped in the Rattanakosins' ideology from childhood; they were vacuous, loyal admirers of their autocratic ruler, poor chaps. I sat cross-legged, stealing a friendly glance at people and eavesdropping with interest, looking at the sky with its wheeling gulls. Some saturnine faces and watchful, inimical eyes fastened on me. I could hear dimly, far away, the put-put-put or chug-chug-chug of the Chinese junks and all kinds of boats chugging their way across or up and down the river.

A few minutes later, a waiter came hurriedly and plonked a pot of fresh ginger and mint tea on my table and expertly poured from on high, visibly steaming. The men became aware of my presence, the only person in the teahouse wearing a dark purple silk shirt. I often felt ill-at-ease amongst Siamese highbrows and royalists – every word they uttered seemed imbued with some important meaning known only to themselves – but curiosity compelled me to look and listen. In fact my eyes and ears were riveted on them while they unguardedly burbled on about their and other people's social lives; perhaps they were concealing their own insecurity, or perhaps they just loved to gossip. Most of the other tables, I am certain, were listening to their conversation with bated breath. So a perfect opportunity presented itself for me to surprise the locals and put my knowledge of the Siamese language to good use. I wanted to cautiously probe their minds without raising a flicker of suspicion. My intention was – in my best Siamese of course, though with a hint of a Lao accent – to befriend these local partisans, introduce carefully planned questions and then gauge their reactions. Perhaps I could even persuade them to be sympathetic towards the Lao. I lifted my eyes and deliberately took a noisy slurp of my lukewarm tea. They turned and, catching my eye, gave a snide look and gazed at me quizzically as if I were an idiot. I gave them an apologetic smile which seemed to do the trick. 'Rather hot tea, sorry,' I said and smiled broadly.

'You got nice pale royal complexion,' said one with a switched-on smile, a sarcastic voice and a cynical grin: defence mechanisms perhaps, against an inquisitive stranger. With my face distorted into a grinning mask, I nodded and thanked him. With no intention to deceive them, I revealed where I came from, which caused some surprise. I tried to neither hide nor promote the fact that I was a Lao; I didn't give a fig that they knew. In fact I rather revelled in it. I replied that the sun in ViengChan doesn't burn or darken one's skin. It was an off-the-cuff comment which I thought sounded very friendly. They were amazed and green with envy. 'Really!' they all said in unison.

'Is that true?' said a tall, dark-skinned man with glossy hair and they gazed at me in awe. With my open face and jaunty manner, I gave them an encouraging smile. We anxiously fell into a fractured and twitchy conversation about language, culture and history. At the beginning it was a pleasure to meet them and I was impressed by their friendliness; they spoke with ready smiles and humorous faces and the sternness soon disappeared. Much hearty laughter at my feeble jokes created a pleasant atmosphere. I suspected they weren't prepared to open their hearts to anyone: a common sign of insecurity.

I was aware of their ingrained attitude towards the Ai-Lao and the crass assumptions and egregious comments they habitually made about the Lao people as a whole. Based on all of that, they probably thought I was dense and raving. They didn't conceal their surprise that I was Lao and seemed alive with anticipation as I tried to talk to them about significant matters. Once they'd relaxed, I tactfully explained LanXang's case to them in all its details and they listened to me with suspicion but also interest. As expected, their response was not wholly truthful and non-committal, and they couldn't refrain from laughing out loud at my defective Siamese. However, a slight tremor in their voices betrayed them. I knew they weren't sincere, though to be fair they seemed genuinely amused by life.

Siam might have been experiencing something of a heyday and looked down on its neighbours, who often describe the Siamese as egotistical, untrustworthy, treacherous, fickle and selfish. They could also be remarkably conceited, incurable as a nation though incredibly charming as individuals. You couldn't really imagine them being sensibly governed by anyone.

It wasn't necessarily curiosity that led me on. It was a dangerous approach, but if it led to friendship, then so much the better. It did not. As I'd predicted, because of their inconsiderate and parochial attitudes, they were unapproachable – historically, socially and politically. I found it very hard to hide my contempt for all they stood for: their blind obedience to the Rattanakosins' ideology – the cowardice of the masses living under an authoritarian regime – but I also couldn't help respecting them for their ignorance and obstinacy. They didn't bother to hide how superior they felt. I egged them on, eager to hear more. But alas I was overpowered by their eagerness to convince me of the superiority of the Siamese nation over every neighbouring country and even others further afield. I disabused them of that misconception. In fact, LanXang and Siam are all but indistinguishable in terms of population, language, culture, wealth and influence, which ironically leads to a greater emphasis on the differences between the two nations. I was really startled by the vehemence of their backing for their monarchy and Siam's domination; it struck me as a kind of national self-delusion. They knew nothing about Siam's invasion of LanNa and LanXang. They ignorantly insisted that the two kingdoms didn't even exist, and, worse, that all Lao land belonged to Siam. They implied that the word 'Lao' meant 'rustic buffalo', a euphemism for inferiority. How could such a civilised society display such rudeness?

I was much struck and truly tested by their profound naivety, ignorance and arrogance. I draw no parallel with their government's atrocious invasion of 1779, but their obsession with the glory of Siam along with the horrendous deeds perpetrated during the annihilation of ViengChan made me think that Bangkok, despite shamelessly portraying itself as righteous, actually led the field in arrogance, denouncing anyone who disagreed with them and refusing to admit their wrongs. Given that hundreds of Lao civilians died and thousands were displaced, it was remarkable how little hostility had been expressed in LanXang, although the older generation could be forgiven for recalling the callous indifference of the Siamese government. For certain, this group of men were inflated with self-praise. It was enough to make anyone cringe but I repaid their time, company and lack of civility with polite praise, a pot of coffee and cake. There was an 'ah' of delight mixed with sugary insecurity and incomprehension at my generosity.

'Ah, brother (*Khun Phee*)! Thank you (*Kob Khun khap*),' they all said, looking surprised at me – the uncivilised, rustic Lao man. They suggested we go to a bar or a massage parlour. 'The girls will add extras!' they whispered mischievously. It was highly entertaining. Calm and unperturbed, I politely declined their offer because I didn't want to be seduced, swindled, led astray or falsely arrested. In fact I felt uneasy, fearing a trap and that they might pounce on me. I made my excuses, got to my feet, apologised for disturbing them, thanked them for their time, bade farewell and calmly walked away. I was mightily relieved to disappear into the anonymity of the crowds outside. I skipped down a few steps at the next corner, sidestepped the throng and swerved past carts pushed along by Chinese hawkers and mongers, touting and shouting, selling fruit, fish and a variety of goods. After looking round to check no one was following me, I stealthily sneaked into a general shop. I had no idea about wine but bought an interesting bottle before safely hurrying back to my room, absorbed in thought.

It seemed the Siamese public, with all their sophistication and pontificating about their glorious past (the only light that would shine on them over the following years), had no knowledge of their neighbours' versions of history. I was dumbfounded that Siam, with all its power and wealth, could allow its people to be so ignorant about the rest of the world. It was as if they had no human cognition; they probably knew the truth perfectly well, but because they felt so insecure, they paid no attention to it. Every unkind word seemed to really upset them but they never wondered why the criticism had been made in the first place. Although they intrigued me, I took an instant dislike to some of them.

In general, it seemed that Bangkok had an animus against the Lao world. If only the just men of Siam realised this, they could have shown the courage of their convictions to put the Rattanakosins right. But, on the contrary, an anti-Lao crusade was in full swing in Bangkok, and nothing was being done to prevent it. Chao Anouvong, I'm sure, wasn't the only one to be dismayed at how far Siam had strayed from a compassionate Buddhist country. He was aware that any appeal to Nangklao would fall on deaf ears: their relationship had become one of mutual hate. However, he wasn't afraid to speak his mind.

Under Bangkok's dark influence, most of the Siamese thought of nothing but the splendour of Siam and had a completely distorted idea of what their country was really like. They showed a violent antipathy to anyone who criticised them or their royal family. 'Don't be ignorant, buffalo head,' they would mutter under his breath. You pretended not to hear it but they complained and lamented at the slightest provocation. Everyone was under constant surveillance and encouraged to inform on everyone else, everywhere, all the time. The people were permanently afraid during the night but showed feverish enthusiasm for the law by day. You could be denounced and lynched for any incautious word.

When questioned whether they genuinely respected their autocratic king, they would lapse into a long, impressive silence and stare at you coldly. Worshipping their king as a god, they could do no more than gaze from afar, avoiding the slightest contact with him. Others became scared, as if suffering from an atavistic and visceral fear of the royals, some of whom – they said – suffered from atrocious personal vanity. I detected no pride in themselves as they parried my questions. Perhaps they had already started to question what their country had done for them but struggled to perceive reality due to ignorance. They disapproved of the royal constitution but were forced to hide their feelings and were too frightened to oppose the power of the Rattanakosins' ideology, which they nevertheless believed destructive to humanity and obstructive to progress. Informers were much to be feared, especially those from within a group of friends. They would startle me by the vehemence of their response, saying they trusted foreigners far more than they trusted each other. The plain-clothes royal police and informers were ubiquitous, spying on people; rewards were paid to anyone who reported 'traitors' to the authorities. They really were terrified of their own kind. Despite their friendship and the fact they were all fellow Buddhists, they could betray each other at any moment. As for the Emerald Buddha being returned to ViengChan, they refused to accept it had been stolen in the first place and had been brainwashed into believing it had always belonged to Siam. You can understand how all of this nonsense would make any man of justice apoplectic with exasperation. You didn't pry any further in case you were arrested and thrown into prison, never to see daylight again. It was exhausting and nerve-shredding.

I really felt I'd gained a genuine insight into Siamese internal and foreign policy and what Bangkok was up to. In his pride, Nangklao couldn't cope with criticism so didn't like having people around him who were cleverer than he. He reportedly bullied his sycophantic staff, aides and advisers, ultimate yes men who obediently catered to his ignorance. They were discouraged to tell the truth to the world but rallied behind his desire for wealth and power. They were caught between a dysfunctional administration and a king who would blame or punish them if anything went wrong or if he didn't get what he wanted. This immature, unethical and unpredictable dynasty that treated its people with shrill contempt governed the supposedly most smiley nation in the world. Nangklao was influenced by mysticism and believed that he could see visions, like the Lord Buddha, through contemplation and meditation. He walked in the shadow of his predecessors and, like them, enjoyed an almost iconic status amongst the Siamese people, who naively spoke of him with reverence and awe. Some loathed him, however.

Most countries love pontificating and Siam was no exception. Bangkok was thriving and lively, but Siam was persistently waging a war of words with its neighbours. In their arrogance and egotism, Bangkok underestimated Chao Anouvong. They had no respect for him and bad mouthed him to curry favour with the colonial powers. It was symptomatic of their tactlessness that they treated their neighbours as ignorant rustics who didn't understand the ways of the world. To crack the arrogance of Siam's repressive regime or to rattle the Rattanakosin regime seemed an impossible task.

I later enjoyed a sober discussion over dinner with Chao Anouvong. I gave him my impressions of Siam in a concise, judicious way. He was pleased with my intelligence briefings and the horror he displayed at the news was no pretence. He felt it was time for him to try to make a difference, as if he saw the future of LanXang in black and white. 'We're all human beings,' he said, 'but while it's possible for us Lao to act as if we're Siamese, surely we can never actually become Siamese?' I said nothing but he knew my answer, in one sacred word, well enough.

We knew that Bangkok had issued a series of threats designed to force the Lao people to conform to its policies. Nangklao appeared to be too self-interested, too wrapped up in himself, to be properly human. He was not only vehemently anti-Lao but also decreed a horrible law that criminalised all Lao activities, tearing the two kingdoms apart. Even some of his loyal elite realised that the policy of branding the Lao population amounted to a crime against humanity. Furthermore, he used his executive powers to seize enough rice throughout the kingdom and vassal states to secure a plentiful supply for Bangkok as well as for export. Rice was one of Siam's major commodities, bringing Nangklao great riches.

'I simply can't believe there was such a serious shortage of rice in Bangkok, Phia Jon, that a new law was required,' Chao Anouvong said, his words slowing as he realised where his suspicion was leading him. 'I suspect they locked it away somewhere to push up the price.'

'Maybe it's true,' I said. 'Perhaps there isn't enough rice to go round and prices have risen extortionately.' He nodded thoughtfully.

I added that it was unprecedented for power over the kingdom's rice supply to be bestowed upon one man. It went without saying that as one of Siam's governors and commissioners, Phraya Phromphakdy must have rubbed his hands together in glee over the wealth he was accumulating under these circumstances.

Chao Anouvong remarked that the general dislike of Siam in Lao LanXang was due to a set of selfish, disorderly people in Bangkok. If the Bangkok public discovered that the Lao-speaking people were a genuinely separate ethnic nation, and Siam would find peace and stability impossible to achieve until it was ruled by men of knowledge and integrity, then the regime would find it very difficult to brush off any criticism of its behaviour. Its policies would need to change for it to become acceptable to its public and the wider world. Chao

Anouvong asked whether he would be able to persuade Bangkok to totally drop the idea of a Greater Siam. He didn't really need my advice but I replied that it would only be possible if Bangkok came to its senses, otherwise there'd be no end to the troubles of Siamese society. I said that his proposals for an independent Lao LanXang, though difficult, were not impossible to achieve. A chasm would form between the Siamese and the Lao. Otherwise Siam would forever suffer from political instability and teeter on the verge of civil war.

'Your Majesty, we must forget our ideological differences,' I reasoned. 'This isn't the time for it. We've travelled the length and breadth of the land to discover the fate of LanXang and her people. We've been patient and courageous. Our aspiration is to revive LanXang, so now isn't the time to be timorous. Perhaps this isn't the most propitious time to meet Nangklao, but we're in Bangkok so let's not worry about offending the Rattanakosins' sensibilities. It's time to summon all our strength and courage. We should go straight to him and wring his thoughts from him. We must be shrewd and frank if we want the truth from his lips. Not that I think we'll get anything out of him, mind you.'

'Heaven forbid, Phia Jon. I would never choose a tyrant for a bedfellow,' he cried. 'How can we meet and wring the truth from the heart of such a man?' He paused and his shoulders sagged. 'It'll be impossible to cajole him into granting us our wishes. But if we're lucky, we might be able to find out his secret, what makes him tick.'

'First we must get acquainted with him,' I said. 'Let's pretend we want his advice on how to run LanXang. Rhetoric and eloquence are our forte and we can speak the truth in his presence. Perhaps we'll enjoy a good reception for respecting a man of talent. I might be wrong but Nangklao seem to have lofty ambitions. He'll stir us into a fury, no doubt. But we come from Lao LanXang royalty and are by nature imbued with wisdom and statesmanship. We count ourselves amongst the noble-minded. There's more to us than Nangklao and his men think. We'll probably get absolutely nowhere with them, but if our wits fail us, let's hope heaven will inspire us.'

'Phia Jon, you must steel your heart for our mistreatment... even if they call me, us, names, you'll have to look on. The caprices of the Siamese aristocracy can surpass anything. We should be quick to hear but slow to speak. Remember, anger lowers one's intelligence and hatefulness make one lose one's good judgement. Our meeting with them will be belligerent but we will face them at the highest rank of serenity. You may of course bow to them most deeply and beg them to behave more sensibly. I must steel my heart not to bandy words with Nangklao, who likes nothing better than to stir a man's passion with his wicked tongue. He may be high-born, but believe me, he's a street fighter. There's never been anything noble about his behaviour or speech.'

Devoid of any trace of pomposity, Chao Anouvong was cordial and composed and always focused on his ideas. His art of war was to know both himself and his enemies. He knew that anger didn't achieve anything but dealing with Nangklao was never going to be easy.

He abhorred violence but the thought of his son Rathsavong Ngao and his loyal followers being forced into hard labour made him snarl with repressed fury and he growled to himself. Nangklao's conduct added fuel to his anger. He looked at me with concern. In the end, he managed to steel his heart to endure, shaking his head with a groan. He knew he would be condemned and humiliated but he'd to persuade Nangklao to change his attitude towards LanXang. He momentarily pressed the heels of his hands against his eyes. Coming out of the sparkling darkness, he blinked his eyes and turned to me.

'I believe you're right, Phia Jon,' he said. 'I agree with you and recognise sense when I hear it. We have no choice and we have nothing to lose. For the sake of LanXang and her people, let's get it over with. Let's make a start.' He added that he would dispatch a few mandarins with a short letter begging for a private audience with Nangklao. I smiled and nodded. Thinking it better to leave him alone, for he'd a huge decision to make, I told him I would be available if required. He raised his eyebrows but said nothing. I bowed and crept off.

I went straight to my room but kept my trousers on in case he called for me. I couldn't sleep but lay on the bed with mounting excitement and concern, thinking hard and hoping that Lord Buddha and the other gods might someday repay the Siamese villains for their insolence and their intolerable behaviour. How I wished I had magical powers to make Bangkok do what Chao Anouvong wanted for the Lao nation! I closed my eyes in silence, but my heart was seething with evil thoughts before I surrendered myself to sleep.

At dawn three days later I went for my daily briefing with Chao Anouvong over our customary herbal drink. The door was open but I gave it a gentle tap. He was standing in the middle of the room, as he normally did, looking out the windows. It was quite early. He was fresh from the shower and was being robed in his freshly laundered clothes while squeezing a newly acquired leather ball – an exercise to strengthen his hands and to help him de-stress. As I entered his room he turned round, said good morning and threw the ball at me. Luckily, I caught it without thinking, just as I'd done with the orange he threw at me at Nakhorn Phanom twenty-nine years earlier. 'Well done!' he congratulated me. I smiled alertly and made my reverence. He was no longer in his prime but still charismatic, with thick, silky, black locks on his head. He was looking good, physically impressive and well built, tall and quite imposing: every inch the noble who turns heads, the centre of attention. He was dressed in a royal blue *Phahthong* (trousers), a formal upright collar and a white jacket, with highly polished black shoes on his feet – most unusual for him this early in the morning.

'Good morning, Your Majesty. I pay my respects.' I said cordially, put the leather ball on the table and asked him whether he'd slept well and if he was going anywhere. 'And who's the lucky lady?' I added.

'One should be so lucky!' he said cheerfully and complained that he hadn't slept well for the past few nights, blaming Bangkok's filthy air.

'There are enough beautiful Siamese ladies with breathy voices in Bangkok for everyone,' I declared with much merriment, even though I didn't know whether it was true or not. 'There seem to be a preponderance of them; some look serene but they're quite without shame!' I then told him about the pink-lipped girl with the strange-looking watch I'd seen in the brothel. He peered at me and asked in disbelief if I really went to such a place, before bursting out laughing at my scarlet face. I assured him I only happened to be passing the place.

'I'm jealous, all the same,' he mused. 'No such luck for poor me, I fear.' He told me not to indulge in worldly pleasures and dream one's life away. 'Phia Jon, we mustn't allow Siam's beauty to entrap us. Now, the good news is that we're going to have a meeting with the new king,' he said excitedly, holding up a piece of paper. 'The message only arrived last night.' He paused to read the message again. 'We're in luck. Phra Nangklao has granted us an audience… isn't it wonderful? As for my finery, one must look one's best when one's going to see a revered and powerful new king. Mind you, I suspect the meeting won't be on equal terms. He'll treat me as a subject rather than a reputable ruler from another kingdom.'

During our stay in Bangkok, Chao Anouvong wasn't considered an important guest. If anything, he was ignored and made to feel unwelcome. By contrast, Nangklao had transformed himself into a great admirer of overseas envoys and traders and delighted in showing off his treasure-filled palace to them. In return, they showered him with condolences, congratulations and gifts that made him feel highly revered. The presence of the Europeans was most unusual in Siamese society, yet Nangklao engaged many of them in his public works department. He began wearing European-style clothes and to behave in an un-Siamese way. Sometimes he looked like he'd been bewitched. The expensive gifts easily bought his loyalty. This didn't bother Chao Anouvong at all, however, for he was a man of humility. He saw Nangklao as a despot and the Siamese king's flaws were obvious to him even before the meeting. He was more concerned about LanXang's future and the plight of his people. Since becoming LanXang's king, he valued righteousness over honour and even over his own life, so he put up with being vilified by Bangkok.

I told him the thought of meeting Nangklao had greatly disturbed my peace of mind but agreed that it was a marvellous opportunity to get inside his mind and find a way to end their dominion. However, I wasn't sure why Chao Anouvong seemed so enthusiastic when Nangklao, despite being a king, was a very irascible and difficult man completely lacking any emotional intelligence. I may lack wisdom when it comes to judging people, but I was certain the meeting would prove frustrating. The odds of it ending in disappointment were high. I urged Chao Anouvong to remain calm and affable and warned him that Nangklao would be touchy and truculent. I briefed him on LanXang's demands and explained how the discussions might proceed. 'Why is Nangklao so popular and revered?' I asked, intrigued.

'Thank you for these most sobering briefings, Phia Jon.' He paused. 'Why indeed is the Siamese king revered?' he muttered, turning to look at me. 'Now, hear what I think. In general, the Siamese monarchy shouldn't exist according to the republicans; the middle classes don't care; but it is popular amongst the wealthy upper classes and the poor lower classes. A popular and revered man can be dangerous and always attracts a following, although that is not what concerns me. As a new king he'll want to stamp his authority, and the people will have to obey him. As usual with such men, he'll then become corrupt and pay the price for his loneliness, vulnerability and insecurity. He's a dynastic leader who dresses well and looks respectable; he pretends to be a well-meaning reformer but he actually represents all that's bad in his kingdom, a ruthless and manipulative tyrant who wields power like a whip, not a shield and demands absolute obedience. He has widespread support from his own elite and his overseas alliances: a potent combination in politics. Furthermore, Siamese schoolchildren are being indoctrinated into believing he's a god. He claims the kingdom's wealth as his own when it should be held for the benefit of the whole nation. He is a most feared man.'

He paused while his valet adjusted his gold embroidered collar, shoulder bands and jacket sleeves. 'Anyway, let's not worry too much about him. You're looking dapper in that white silk shirt. How do you feel about coming along with me?' I said that I was at his disposal but should wear my white court jacket, because I didn't want to look like a peasant. 'Come on then, Phia Jon,' he said. 'We need you. You'll never outdo their glittering golden dresses so there's no point getting changed, but you can put on that smart gold chain that I gave you.'

'Forgive me, Your Majesty, only women wear jewels,' I countered. 'I would rather put on the mystical signet ring carved with a dragon's head that you awarded to me. I'll wear it until the end of my life to remind me of you, and as a remedy against illness and to protect me from all evil.' He looked at me pleasantly. 'Besides, if I come along, you must also think of some way of introducing me,' I added. I even considered suggesting a bogus Siamese name.

'Let's be going, Phia Jon,' he commanded and the valet hurriedly buckled an embroidered gold belt round his high-waisted jacket and, as a final touch, slipped an embroidered gold sash diagonally over his left shoulder. At fifty-eight, it was as if the gods had touched him with a magic wand. He really looked very elegant in his official robes. He picked up his ceremonial sword and told me not to be touchy and worried like a girl; he needed me with him. 'Two heads will be better than one to identify this two-faced ruler. We might see the real one: the kind and friendly version rather than the god if we're lucky.'

I dashed back and grabbed my official jacket (which I felt leant me a noble air) from my room, quickly put the signet ring on my little left finger and followed him. A number of well-dressed, high-ranking officials hastily followed behind us. I felt keyed up and confident about meeting Nangklao, though I had no desire to meet any other Siamese royalty.

With a few other high-ranking mandarins in their sparkling white official uniforms, we climbed into two horse-drawn carriages and speedily made our way in the morning heat through the narrow lanes (*Soi*), where small, muddy streams carried filth and garbage down to the canals or the Chaophraya river. I silently rubbed the signet ring in the hope it might protect all of us. Chao

Anouvong was unusually quiet; no doubt he was aware the future of LanXang might hang on this meeting.

The horses trotted along and, as we got closer, I stuck my head out to see the palace, which was nowhere near as grand as the former palace in ViengChan. I realised why Bangkok was jealous of the Lao capital: it was 222 years ahead in architectural grandeur, even though it had been rebuilt after being partly destroyed by Nangklao's grandfather during the 1779 invasion.

Finally, Chao Anouvong had his meeting with Nangklao. On arriving at the Grand Palace, hidden behind thick, high walls, its gates guarded by day and night, footmen dressed in bright uniforms came running to open our carriage doors. They led the horses sweating from the yoke and tied them up under shady trees on long ropes so they could graze in the fields. The paved court was scattered with windblown leaves and twigs, but dust and cobwebs had gathered at the edges. The gardeners with dirty feet in sweat-stained shirts sat idly on benches in the shade, yawning their head off, while birds flew, twittering, to perch on the nearby trees. It was a very hot day. I gazed around at the grandiosity of the complex with great curiosity. The palace and the multi-coloured tiled roofs of the surrounding religious buildings and various Siamese-style rounded stupas shimmered in the sun. In the distance, the steep, many-tiered yellow pagoda roofs glowed golden. But there was nothing magical about the place at close quarters: you could smell the blood and sweat of the people who'd been forced to build it. The Emerald Buddha Temple itself looked utterly unexceptional and unworthy of praise, a poor imitation of the original in ViengChan. I gazed at it with nostalgia.

The guards ushered us into the royal buildings. The rest was easy, until we got to a small court from where a stairway ascended to the guest room, between walls painted with scenes of dense forests, birds and strange protecting deities. Sentries were doing their rounds on a large landing at the top, standing easy as if it were their off day or they had sore feet, holding their long, bronze-pointed spears on either side of a polished door. I opened my eyes in wonder at all I saw as we passed through from one lofty room to another; the sight overwhelmed me and I felt a little nervous. When I'd feasted my eyes, Chao Anouvong told me to compose myself. The guards made us sit and wait in the lobby. Late morning sun streamed through the windows, painting the white marble floor with the shadows of the trees' branches. He sat calmly with both his hands on his thighs and signalled to me to keep calm by raising his hands slightly. The doormen watched our every move. It was all rather uncomfortable under the circumstances. Soon we were asked to follow a doorman and passed through various rooms stuffed with chattels.

Siamese culture had grown spectacularly, Chao Anouvong later told me, as wartime loot flowed into the various rooms where immense treasures had been accumulated and inherited by one ruler after another. It seems they liked to flaunt their wealth as they filled their palaces with plunder. 'People normally respect men for their decency and moderation, but it appears the Rattanakosins aren't haunted by any fear of retribution,' he murmured. He told me some of the riches had come from ViengChan.

A moment later we came to a great chamber with huge pillars where a group of very young girls in their finery were talking and giggling with a young man. The ladies, perhaps members of the harem or even princesses, stopped prancing about and stood in the corner, laughing at some remark. When the originator of the witticism turned at the sound of our footsteps, I espied a fresh-looking young face. Chao Anouvong had described Prince Mongkut to me before so I instantly thought it was him. The conversation stopped. They looked at us out of the corners of their eyes. 'Who are they?' I heard them whisper as we passed them. Chao Anouvong was well composed. He didn't look at them directly as I did but glanced discreetly as we followed the doorman. He muttered that any one of the girls had as much chance of becoming 'Queen' as being demoted. One of them, I noticed, looked rather pale and thin, as if she'd had a miscarriage – poor thing! They were gracious enough to give us a polite bow.

I think the incident startled Chao Anouvong a little because we hadn't expected to see Mongkut. We thought he'd entered the monkhood to pay respects to his dead father, Naphalai. But there he was, at about twenty, looking very flamboyant in impeccably swanky European-style dress, slim and quite well built., His presence was a little overwhelming. With his puffy fresh-faced schoolboy looks, amused twinkling brown eyes, dark shadow of a beard and neat, manly, moustache perched like a butterfly on his upper lip, he looked intelligent and very distinguished. His round head was covered with the sort of well-oiled backward-combed black hair he and his fashionable friends liked to sport. He was the most handsome man in Bangkok. Though still unmarried, he was several times a father, with no sense of duty to his scattered offspring.

Chao Anouvong rightly thought that Mongkut blamed Nangklao for the stagnation of his career. He even hoped he was a Lao sympathiser. Mongkut hadn't acquiesced to Nangklao's accession and had done LanXang a great service by strongly condemning Nangklao's policies towards our kingdom. We believed Nangklao had risen to the throne not because he would make a better ruler, but because he hated the Lao more than Mongkut. Our agents also reported that Mongkut privately acknowledged his nation's cruelty in its 1778–1779 invasion of ViengChan. Most pious Siamese had been horrified by the carnage inflicted on the Lao and appalled by the booty brought back to Bangkok. They believed the removal of Buddha statues from ViengChan temples to be a wicked deed and that forcing people to leave their homes was as cruel as taking chicks from their nests. Mongkut was said to have tried to persuade Naphalai to put a halt to the injustices committed against the Lao people.

Chao Anouvong agreed with my analysis that the Rattanakosins appeared sensitive, liberal and benevolent but were grudging at heart. Their real aim was to create an empire stretching from the Andaman to the South China Seas; even the relatively friendly Mongkut probably had some ulterior motive.

Anyway, not long after passing Prince Mongkut, we walked through a whispering group of servants who took no notice of us. At the head of the Grand Staircase, a doorman greeted us and showed us through a large ornate door where two fierce and savage-looking sentries, the faithful royal guards, were standing to attention with drawn swords. They were more muscular and a great deal more alert than the others; their heads cocked the moment they saw us. They didn't sheath their swords until their king went to bed.

Passing into an impressive anteroom with its grand door leading to the main chamber, I gazed in awe at the wall mural *The Sack of Pegu*. The figures were almost life size. King Naresuan the Great rode a long-tusked elephant which towered in the background. The king was plunging his sword into his enemy, also mounted on an elephant. On the ground, Siamese and Burmese soldiers with screaming mouths rushed at each other with spears and swords and some warriors floundered in their own blood. Satisfied, I turned away and steeled myself to face Nangklao. In that cold, haughty palace, my heart warmed at the thought of ViengChan, worth more than ten Bangkoks. The sense of being Lao, inferior to no other race on earth, the Siamese least of all, always sustained me.

As we were sitting there waiting in silence and anticipation to meet

Nangklao, a giggling and whispering group of high-born young girls came trooping past with many a laugh and exchange of pleasantries. Chao Anouvong swivelled round and whispered to me to keep calm. A moment later, the guards signalled to us and opened the door silently. A mandarin in a pristine white uniform conducted us in. Chao Anouvong braced himself before entering the grand audience chamber, as if he were about to shoulder a great weight. He was probably as tense as I was at the prospect of confronting Nangklao face to face. He knew that to negotiate with his enemy was one thing, but to fail to win any concessions would be an outright humiliation. He gestured to me to stay close by and I instantly slipped in unobtrusively to his right, carrying a white shoulder bag full of documents that I hoped cast a cloak of anonymity around me. I did my best to remain inconspicuous, pacing respectfully behind him. Our mandarins shuffled like dancers and followed closely behind me.

When we walked silently through the grand door, the chatter faded away at once and everyone turned towards us with leering eyes. We proceeded into a heavily scented and cool, shiny, white-marble-floored grand chamber where Nangklao was waiting with his mandarins beside him. You couldn't help but stretch your eyes up in awe at the lofty, treasure-filled Hall of Audience.

At the centre, not too far away for me to make out his impressive profile, sat an unsmiling and well-fed King Phra Nangklao, a man I so earnestly desired not to meet. A feeling of intense awe washed over me on seeing him clad in his elaborate garments. He was seated amongst golden cushions on a throne-like chair placed higher than anyone else's. He was robed in a heavily embroidered golden cloak that he alone could wear, as if he were openly pursuing immortality under the sacred garb of religion. It was so bright it even sparkled in that dim light. Black velvet slippers embroidered with sequins adorned his feet. One glance at him was enough to fill me with fright, and his presence made the room feel oppressive. You got the sense that anyone who crossed him would pay for it. It was scary. He certainly looked like an autocratic king: hard and smug. All that was missing were his ceremonial sword and tall, jewel-encrusted crown of victory.

I was very unsure how to approach Nangklao, whether to prostrate myself or stand and bow deeply. With downcast eyes and almost paralysed with fear, I lost my nerve and quickly made the prostration with as much care as if it were for the first time, but without any loyalty in my heart. I then rose gracefully and tucked myself closely behind Chao Anouvong, directing my gaze to the floor.

You weren't supposed to look up at the king. Our retinue of mandarins peeled off to one side and nervously prostrated themselves before Nangklao, like squatting frogs in a pond. He looked down at them as if they were alien beggars.

From the shadows and the aura of power around him, Phra Nangklao's identity was immediately obvious. Even the air seemed to crackle when he moved and spoke. It was said he'd no fear of dying because he believed he'd an immortal soul. I wondered whether all that power and glory had driven him and his people mad. He thought he'd no enemies but still went everywhere with a large bodyguard because he knew he was disliked intensely by his people. He'd no compunction or any real warmth of character. Where on earth had he learned his manners? Perhaps he'd been conceived in a horse carriage or against the palace garden wall.

He seemed a little shorter than Chao Anouvong. He'd a broad, flat head covered in shiny, well-combed black hair, with large but slender ears and flat cheekbones. Unlike some of his dark-complexioned courtiers, his pale skin and eyes suggested a foreign ancestry; he didn't look entirely Siamese, nothing like his father or grandfather. His shiny, perfumed, crafty face seemed full of arrogance, yet his body diminished the effect. He'd a long, fat nose that twitched as if he could smell everything, especially power and money. His wide, greedy mouth with its thin, mean lips seemed set in a thin, cynical grin, as if forever saying, 'Know that I am the king.' He'd rounded shoulders and a weak chest: the torso of a meditating monk. Festooned with one large golden chain on his neck and another across his chest, he appeared to have been spoilt from birth and wore a permanently ruthless look. His chin was held so high, his brows furled and furrowed through constant denunciation of others. Like a predator, his eyes were directed towards some imaginary paradise in the distance. The great hall made him look even smaller. He hardly ever smiled, at least genuinely, but his yellowish teeth flashed like gold in the dim light whenever he talked. From where I was standing with downcast eyes – close enough to detect the strong whiff of his strange perfume – I noticed his crafty brown eyes studying each of us in turn in a rather hostile and superior way. Although his somewhat diminutive stature failed to match the wickedness of his actions, I still didn't dare to look at him directly.

I have always taken an interest in the vagaries of human nature and have often wondered about the origins of kings and heroes. But I have observed that kings – good and bad – interact with one another differently than with ordinary people. They mostly discuss politics and warfare and what goes on in the palaces, cities and villages with each other. On this occasion, I knew exactly what Chao Anouvong was going to talk about. I took out his formal letter of appeal and handed it over to him so he would be ready.

At first, Chao Anouvong caught Nangklao's eye and bowed to him before moving closer and courteously offered his formal greetings and condolences. 'I, Anouvong, pay my respects to Your Majesty,' he said confidently and bowed more reverently than if he were worshipping the bodhisattva, or as if Nangklao were a wise scholar or sage.

With a leaden look, Nangklao, who was twenty-one years younger, grinned deprecatingly like a schoolboy who desperately needed to feel loved. It was clear he was a villain who hated all Lao, but he hated Chao Anouvong, who represented everything that he despised, most of all. He even pretended to check his fingernails and then gazed lovingly at the rings on his fingers as if he didn't care about the loss of his father. Perhaps he was trying to use his charm to conceal his cold nature. Perhaps he avoided confronting Chao Anouvong head on because, beneath all his finery, he was actually afraid of him. I suspected he'd a mediocre brain yet vast reserves of low cunning and deceit, and at that very moment he was probably thinking of new ways to undermine his adversary. He made a show of respect but a shadow of scorn and mistrust lurked in his eyes. With pursed lips he looked superciliously at Chao Anouvong, who mouthed 'Your Majesty' when he gestured for him to sit down. Nangklao exercised his privilege of speaking first but his voice was devoid of any warmth or enthusiasm.

'Nice of you to have attended my father's funeral,' he said.

'Your Majesty, it would have been wrong not to,' responded Chao Anouvong, smiling weakly. 'We all belong to Khoun Borom's Ai-Lao family, after all,' he added, at which Nangklao became pensive.

'Yes, we're one and the same family, I suppose,' he drawled in an unfriendly way. 'And how was your journey?'

'It was good, and we're glad to have arrived, Your Majesty, thank you.'

'Are you pleased with your accommodation? And are you being looked after well?'

'Very good and we are indeed, thank you,' Chao Anouvong said, as though he wanted to get to the point and get out of that place as quickly as possible.

It seemed that the room had suddenly turned cold. You could see that Chao

Anouvong hadn't warmed to Nangklao; although he lowered his eyes and showed a respectful demeanour, he disliked Nangklao's authoritarian mindset. He went on to express his appreciation for the palace's hospitality and gave a courteous nod to the high-ranking mandarins seated near Nangklao, who merely blinked disrespectfully and failed to acknowledge him. They probably went out of their way to be as unpleasant as possible, abusing him to anyone who cared to listen.

Such was the hostility between Chao Anouvong and these aristocrats – who regarded him as a mere prince of ViengChan, not a king – that they never once invited him to their homes. This petty jealousy smelt nastier than sour grapes. Rather than disturbing him, this in fact amused him, for he knew how much it must have irritated Nangklao and his cronies to have to accept he was a true Lao royal from LanXang.

It was quite the opposite of the treatment he'd enjoyed from the late Naphalai, who'd always made sure he felt welcome, receiving him in a gilded boat and ensuring he was carried in a gilded sedan chair.

During our journey to the palace, Chao Anouvong told me that the real centre of power behind Nangklao wasn't his private army – which performed ceremonial functions as well as issuing orders to the rest of the army – but a shadowy umbrella organisation: the nobility. They were supposedly wealthy, healthy, capable and intelligent, but clucked around the king like chickens, intensely tribal and fiercely loyal to the court. They controlled the king rather than being controlled by him and operated behind a shroud of secrecy, seeing themselves as the anointed custodians of the Rattanakosins' power. They believed their own destinies were inextricably linked to the glory of the kingdom. They used their influence with the king to ensure they maintained their grip on power and passed edicts outlawing the writing or speaking of any unflattering comments about the monarchy. Nangklao knew that power was sacred but was unable to live without the flattery and fear of his subjects. Cowed by his might, the people obeyed, hating him in silence.

Now, much to my discomfort, when Nangklao had finished his formal greeting with Chao Anouvong, he turned to me deprecatingly, as if he'd just only noticed me. I felt so shy and inferior in his presence that I couldn't think of anything to say. Having been taught to think for oneself, I was normally able to nerve myself to maintain my dignity, but when Nangklao glared at me with his sharp eyes, I nervously made a deep obeisance to him to indicate my inferiority, leaving me with a sense of the futility and insignificance of life. However I, a humble servant, a royal secretary, but a mere Lao rustic to the Siamese, still youthful looking at the age of forty-nine and soon to be fifty, could now boast that I'd met the intimidating King Phra Nangklao, the mightiest of all the Siamese aristocracy, a man who thought he was a god. I could hardly believe it. It was unreal to see him there, just an ordinary, breathing mortal. My face flushed under his glare and I couldn't miss the spite in his glance. I wasn't entirely inconspicuous after all and braced myself for an unpleasant encounter. I didn't want any trouble but I appeared to have bothered him a great deal. He seemed to hate the look of me. I tried to show grace and not look up, but, like a schoolboy, I couldn't resist taking surreptitious peeks, which probably prompted him to ask Chao Anouvong who I was.

'And who is that rustic halfwit-looking creature behind you?' he said, staring and pointing his knife-like finger at me.

I was startled into looking up and saw his eyes had grown cold; it was almost enough to make my heart stop beating. He gave me a really foul look and went for me like a drunkard. The tone of his voice became overbearingly loud and menacing, I can tell you. I suffered a jolt of fear which I struggled to disguise. With trembling hands and knees I exchanged a concerned glance with Chao Anouvong; this was the moment I'd been dreading. I felt as if I'd just been stabbed in the chest, my insides turned to liquid and my poor knees shook beneath me! I began to wilt and struggled to stand while the Siamese officials looked at me smugly. I knew at once that Chao Anouvong was going to give my name away; there was no telling which one, but I prayed it wouldn't be my given name. I told myself to keep calm and held my breath. Chao Anouvong bowed to Nangklao.

'I beg your pardon, Your Majesty. This is my private and confidential secretary,' he announced pleasantly. He turned to give me an affectionate look, as if there were no one more important in his life than me and discreetly winked at me. Then, like a proud owner, just a touch louder perhaps and much to my relief, he said, 'His name is Jon… Phia Jon. He is ebullient, simple, very modest, outstandingly clever and witty… and completely truthful and faithful.'

These were his words, but even so they did nothing for my morale.

'Jon?' Nangklao repeated at once in awestruck tones, but then giggled. 'What sort of a name is that? Is he a Lao or what?' he sneered.

For a terrible moment I wished I could make myself vanish. My eyes fixed on the floor I instantaneously made more obeisance to Nangklao. Without thinking, I rubbed my signet ring and tried to invoke its magical power, but to no avail.

Nangklao's companions – advisers, aides and mandarins, the cream of the high-born and over-privileged Siamese elite – cut contemptible figures and seemed scandalised that Chao Anouvong wasn't ashamed of me. They smugly swivelled their eyes towards me as if I were a dog. Perhaps to compensate for their humble beginnings they'd become obsessed with Siamese history but lacked the intellect to draw any lessons from it. Despite their advantaged position in society, they lacked a formal education and were wholly obedient to the tribalistic culture of the Siamese court. They had no official function other than to prance about in an exaggerated swagger. They spent their time on slandering or fiddling their expenses and won swift promotion by playing brutal politics and being sycophantic towards the king. They greeted you with cruel snarls and warm, kindly words on their lips, but with cold brewing in their hearts. They pouted and leered at me and the room shook with laughter. I blushed in embarrassment and fear.

Nangklao glanced at me suspiciously again. I stood rooted to the spot, thinking he was about to order his guards to remove me, but then, to my relief, he shrugged and sarcastically asked whether I had a proper Lao name. Chao Anouvong politely replied that I did. Nangklao then tutted at him and said, 'I see,' before looking at me again. 'Despite his ridiculous name, you're lucky to have such a loyal slave. He's not only handsome and clever – unusual for a Lao rustic – but he seems to be able to do everything!'

I could see that Chao Anouvong was as offended as I, but he didn't let it show and merely acknowledged Nangklao's words with a polite nod. I was badly disturbed; in my fear and nervousness I forgot how to bear myself and quickly moved nearer to him for comfort, like a frightened child. I was in a daze, looking at my feet, thinking. Even though 'Siamese' was hardly a byword for discretion and etiquette, I'd never thought anyone, least of all a king, could be so outrageously indiscreet.

'Your Majesty, I beg you, there's no need to ridicule him,' Chao Anouvong said, looking at me. 'He's civilised and quite harmless, and I certainly won't be allowing him to retire just yet. He fully deserves his peerage,' he added and boldly requested I stood by his side.

'Even so, we believe no one, we suspect the worst in people and we certainly don't want him anywhere near us,' Nangklao snapped, with a sideways glance. 'We object to him listening to every word we say, whether he's a peer or not,' he continued, pointing his finger at me again. 'Whatever passes between us today must never be divulged, or else I'll have him skinned alive.'

My knees shook and my spirit quailed at his heartless words. I was left in no doubt that he meant every one of them. His mandarins murmured in assent, nodded at each other and chuckled at their own humour.

Chao Anouvong was not an envious person; he didn't even envy Nangklao, despite his riches and his many other advantages. They meant nothing to him. He must have realised that Nangklao wanted to pick a fight with him. He permitted himself only the most fleeting of smiles and then composed his features into an expression of dignity and authority appropriate for a Lao king. He hesitated and turned to give me an apologetic look. I smiled nervously and gestured to him not to take any notice.

'Please allow me put your mind at ease,' said Chao Anouvong calmly. 'My secretary is utterly trustworthy. I shall do nothing to jeopardise our special bond, which I hope is as precious to you as it is to me.'

Suddenly Nangklao looked up, turned and clicked his fingers at two of his sentries. They rushed at me. I was in terror of being tortured as they took me unawares and grabbed me by both arms. Rigid with shock and fury and gaping with fright, I could do nothing to help myself. I truly thought the two guards were going to take me away for interrogation as they marched me off towards the door but Nangklao called them back. They made me sit by a large, gilded pillar well out of Nangklao's sight but close enough for me to hear everything. I felt badly humiliated but quickly moved sideways where Chao Anouvong could see me. With my eyes fixed on him, I sat there on my heels in silence, like a useless companion. I nodded to him that I was all right. His impenetrable eyes and inscrutable countenance gave little away, but he looked visibly upset and no doubt felt as humiliated as I. The thought of what they might do to him made me tremble. I could only steal a look as I craned forward to catch every word. As if under the influence of his mentor Phra Ajarn Khoon's spell, he'd calmly transformed into an actor and orator.

The meeting began.

As a token of his respect and loyalty, Chao Anouvong had brought Nangklao a magnificent pair of large elephant tusks, about three and a half elbows (1.65 metres) along their natural curve, covered with original carvings and gilded with remarkable skill by Lao LanXang craftsmen. The most significant gift, however, were two of his own gold handwritten manuscripts. One contained a quotation from the legendary Khoun Borom: 'Remember you are Ai-Lao, and you all come from the same father,' the original copy of which, he said, was the only precious thing left in LanXang and was kept safely in a treasure chest in ViengChan. The other contained the oath: 'Our two royal families should love each other until the sun disappears from our universe.' The original inscription, he said, was on a stone tablet at the That Si-SongHuck shrine in Dan Sai. By presenting these gifts, he hoped he could at least begin to suggest to Bangkok some understanding of the Lao people's most desired wish. Instead, Nangklao was scornful of the tusks and barely glanced at the red-silk-wrapped manuscripts before handing them to one of his mandarins.

How we wished we could retrieve them. We were worried they would be destroyed or used by one of the servants to light a fire in the kitchen. Anything to do with LanXang was of no importance in Bangkok.

In Siam, licentiousness was the most important pleasure and infidelity the norm. They probably thought women were only put on earth to please men. The common folk generally accepted their king's licentious life, unlike the ruling classes, who were sexually prurient snobs.

Nangklao, meanwhile, looked a little jaded, but his eyes lit up at the sight of the customary gift of a silver rhino horn containing a very bitter-tasting crimson liquor: a Lao aphrodisiac made from creepers (*Khuea Kaow Horh*) and pieces of rutting deer's horn fermented in strong Lao alcohol (*Lauw Lao*). Purely for Nangklao's pleasure, there was also a small silver cup containing the bile of a black bear, to be mixed in drinks. Nangklao smiled expansively and chuckled with delight. As the hall vibrated with lascivious laughter, I began to hope the meeting might become friendlier.

This aphrodisiac had been popular with Nangklao's grandfather Chulaloke (1782–1809), who'd possessed a large harem and fathered forty-two children before he died at the age of seventy-two. His late father Naphalai (1809–1825) was also fond of the stuff and managed to father seventy-three children. Nangklao himself (1825–1851) produced fifty-one children. Mongkut (1851–1868) was even more prolific, fathering eighty-two children with thirty-five wives!

The Rattanakosin kings were money-seeking bounders, adulterous cads, congenital megalomaniacs and womanisers; hardly surprising given their young and beautiful harems. To convince themselves they were real men, they fathered countless bastards with young, gorgeous girls who were fated not to last, and made no apology for it. Gossip about their feudal infidelity, which allowed them to ennoble and legitimise all their children, swirled around all Bangkok. you wondered how they managed it all. Then again, they really believed they were gods.

Chao Anouvong joked that the Bangkok accent made Siamese men speak with slightly high-pitched and effeminate voices. He'd told me earlier on that Nangklao was softly spoken but there was nothing quiet about him that day. The discussion gradually veered towards LanXang's wishes but Siam's domineering attitude was the real problem. Nangklao looked extremely malevolent, and I became convinced the meeting was part of a devious plot to poison us. He enjoyed taunting people. He aggressively asked Chao Anouvong to state his request.

'I know exactly what you are going to say, etc, etc, but tell me the truth. What's the real reason you came to Bangkok to beg me for this meeting?'

'Your Majesty, I, Anouvong,' he answered, 'am here to alleviate the grief in my heart, to pay my humble respects to you and also to plead with you to allow some of my people to return to their homes in ViengChan. I implore Your Majesty to let them go.'

'Do you, indeed!' said Nangklao sternly, turning to mutter to one of his aides. 'It took you nearly a month to get here. There must be something else on your mind. Speak!'

'Your Majesty, you are too clever for me! I must confess that I dearly wished to have a genuine discussion about various matters with you,' said Chao Anouvong, probably grinding his teeth in anger behind his fixed smile and calmly placed these formal and highly important written requests on a silver tray. He called it 'presenting everything on the tray to see if Nangklao was a reasonable man'.

Nangklao peered at the document suspiciously before handing it over to one of his mandarins, who broke the seal and nervously read it out, quietly and slowly. Nangklao cocked his head this way and that like a bird of prey searching for something stirring below. He heard it out, stroking his chin, looking at Chao Anouvong with crafty eyes. Suddenly he began to move about in his seat while the document was still being read out. He must have been listening keenly, for he then stood up and paced about with his hands behind his back. It was clear he wasn't remotely interested in any meaningful discussion.

Chao Anouvong asked if he could take his sister, Princess Kanlayani, who'd been forcibly abducted in her teens, back with him to ViengChan. She'd been meant for King TakSin but had been raped on the way back to Thonburi by Nangklao's grandfather Kasatseuk in 1779. He also wanted to take back to ViengChan the female court dancers, actresses and singers who'd accompanied him to celebrate the opening of the pleasure lake in 1820, but who were kept on as a harem by Nangklao's late father, as well as around 30,000 Lao people in Saraburi. Chao Anouvong called for greater freedom for his people, pinning his hope on a gentleman's agreement; he bitterly regretted not asking for written confirmation before King Naphalai died. Furthermore, after he'd fought the Burmese in LanNa and triumphantly retaken XiengSaen in 1804, Naphalai had showed him the highest esteem by ordering Phraya Chakki to design and build a pleasure lake in his honour. Bangkok had already authorised the repatriation of the princes of Lao LanNa. Chao Anouvong was convinced the granting of this request by Nangklao would at least safeguard his people's freedom.

He turned and again bowed in reverence to Nangklao and proceeded to plead his case. His face radiated gentleness, decency, sincerity and kindness – the very embodiment of Lao values – and he firmly but courteously repeated his written request in greater detail. He informed Nangklao that his sister and the Lao Vieng people of Saraburi begged him for permission to leave. They wished to return to live and die in ViengChan.

Having been with him for thirty years, I had grown more accustomed to his extreme magnanimity, his remarkable eloquence and his ability to surprise than to his whimsical liveliness. And much to my surprise, on the pretext that LanXang was a land of peace, he daringly asked that the Emerald Buddha might also be returned to ViengChan. I couldn't quite believe what I'd just heard but I admired him enormously for his courage. I peeped at Nangklao who flinched, became jittery and looked uncomfortable, gulping down his guilt but not his anger. Perhaps he began to realise just how wicked his grandfather's invasion of LanXang had been. Bangkok could never live down the sack of ViengChan and the scale of the ensuing human tragedy. He then breathed deeply to check his temper and played dumb, pretending he hadn't heard anything before lapsing into sullen silence. He was in complete denial.

Bangkok has vehemently maintained the same shameless, blank-faced denial ever since, ensuring bitter enmity between Siam and LanXang for years to come. But instead of eliminating LanXang and dehumanising the Lao, Bangkok had brought them to the very heart of Siam and they preserved their Lao consciousness and heritage.

'There is one sure way to show kindness and that is for Your Majesty to set them free,' Chao Anouvong beseeched, 'and allow them to return home. Instead of mistreating them, you should be gentle with them and show them compassion.'

On hearing this, Nangklao began to pace about as if he were alone with his thoughts. His murmuring, snooty mandarins looked sideways at each other. Chao Anouvong told me later that he caught what they were saying but decided not to interpose. 'What does he mean by mistreating them?' one of them muttered suspiciously. After a while, the frowning and pensive Nangklao returned to his chair and turned to one of his men, who leaned forward and whispered something in his ear. When he didn't quite get it. Nangklao cupped his ear and the mandarin repeated himself, shielding his mouth with his hand. 'What shall we do, Your Majesty? Shall we let him take them?' Nangklao whispered back, '*Mie. Miedai* (No, Never).' He then scrawled something on the document, blew on the wet ink, folded it up and gave it back to the courtier who then returned it to Chao Anouvong. My master gave a polite nod of thanks and put it away in his jacket.

'Take your sister back with you?' said Nangklao aloud as he rose from his chair. With his head back and his hands clenched into fists on his hips, he thrust his groin forward like a man in possession of a beautiful wife. He stared at the ceiling as though his mind were on higher matters and contempt seemed to ooze from every pore. He'd no time for justice and scowled derisively at Chao Anouvong. Overflowing with loathing, his language vibrated with violence. This was his real self, with no attempt at concealment: a true Rattanakosin. He scoffed at the very idea. 'So, you want to take them back by challenging me? That's very naughty!' he snarled, wagging his finger in reproach.

I couldn't believe what I was seeing and hearing. The meeting had rapidly turned sour. Chao Anouvong had tried very hard to avoid a shouting match with Nangklao, but the Siamese king's aggression exasperated him and made him more determined than ever to fight for LanXang. He was taken aback but managed to stay unruffled.

'Only for their sakes. I beg you,' he said nimbly. 'Besides, if you saw their sad and homesick faces, I believe you'd want to restore their happiness. I will always be obliged to you for your kindness.'

'So you should,' Nangklao roared, a devious expression on his face. His mandarins glanced sideways at one another and nodded. 'Take them back?' he repeated. 'No. I definitely will not allow this! Your Lao people migrated to Siam as refugees... do you know how many of them there are and where they're now living?'

'Not too many, Your Majesty, only about thirty million in twenty provinces in the northeast of your capital and other parts of Siam,' Chao Anouvong countered. He told me later that Nangklao's pale face went the colour of an over-ripe tomato. 'Please, Your Majesty, I beg you. Let's be honest,' he continued quickly. 'The truth is that some ethnics Lao were forcibly removed from ViengChan in 1779 and made to settle and work, building canals here in Bangkok and elsewhere all over your kingdom. There's no place like home and their most desired wish is to return there.'

The room went quiet momentarily for Nangklao and his men could only bite their lips. There was an oppressive stillness, a heaving silence of simmering antipathy.

'As for your pretty sister,' Nangklao fumed with sudden savagery, 'we have plans for her. We can always find a use for a beautiful princess like her. And the Lao people in Saraburi must stay to grow rice for us!'

Clearly, Nangklao had no idea he was committing crimes against humanity. Chao Anouvong must have felt sick, wanting to hide his face to conceal the fact he'd gone white with disappointment.

'But come now, Your Majesty. We Siamese and Lao are Ai-Lao descendants,' he responded, before straightening himself and looking directly at Nangklao. 'Besides, we must not forget our beginnings, especially when we represent the pillars of our respective nations. Right now, you know Siam and the Chaophraya river better than anyone. I implore you. For the honour of our ancestors, let's put our heads together for the sake of future generations and find a way of resolving our differences. I'm not saying this merely because of our friendship, but also to ensure peaceful lives for all of us. We should care for and be kind to each other while there's still time, otherwise our people will have more than harsh words for each other.' He bowed and continued. 'I beseech you, please don't disregard our shared Ai-Lao ancestry... don't seek to destroy ViengChan for the glory of Siam.' He paused for a sip of water and to mop the sweat from his forehead.

The lofty hall fell silent. Nangklao looked on in irritation and his mandarins shifted in their seats, pursed their lips, took deep breaths and glanced at each other in wonder.

Chao Anouvong continued. 'We must first remind ourselves that over 1,000 years have elapsed since the declaration of Ai-Lao brotherhood under the sacred laws of our legendary King Khoun Borom, who allocated similar plots of land to each of us – Thao Inh of Siam and Khoun Loh of LanXang. We've been settled in our respective territories peacefully ever since. As brothers, we share a common character and pursue the same ends. In LanXang, however, we have ruled peacefully along with other ethnic groups under a perfect political system: what we now call *Heed Sipsong-Khong Sipsi*. We've produced a decent society full of decent people and have happily devoted ourselves to preserving the ancient Ai-Lao name. We're proud to be known as Lao. In the meantime you've chosen to drop the name and become Siamese instead; we respect that. Now, I must remind you that 265 years have passed since the declaration of love and friendship at the That Si-SongHuck shrine, a treaty sworn by our two royal families to mark the boundary between LanXang and Siam. It would be wrong for Your Majesty to think that we, the Lao of LanXang, don't know what's good for us. It's wrong of Siam to want to annex our land. More importantly, in your omniscience, I must now beg you to tell me what is to become of LanXang. I'm sure you're fully aware that LanXang unity and autonomy is vital to us. Siam cannot possibly hold out against the united will of the Lao people. Our people – Lao and Siamese – shouldn't turn their backs on each other; we're virtually the same. We should live as one, albeit in different countries, and meet regularly. Nothing should spoil our joy in each other's love until the sun disappears from the universe.' There was another pause. No one spoke.

Nangklao and his men could have viciously attacked Chao Anouvong, but they just sat with their arms folded and frowned. They couldn't very well do or say anything, for he'd only told the truth.

To gather his thoughts, Chao Anouvong lifted his right hand to cover his mouth, then stroked his ear before resting it back on his thigh. He stared down at the floor in bitter disappointment. One could see by the way his shoulders slumped slightly that the confidence had gone out of him. Nonetheless, as a last resort, he suggested that the late King Naphalai himself might have mentioned Chao Anouvong's request to his son, but he realised even this wouldn't make his submission acceptable to Nangklao. The request for Siam to return the Emerald Buddha was totally ignored, as it had been when Chao Anouvong's brother Nanthasene made the same request in 1792. It's a fair supposition that Bangkok wanted to keep silent. Nangklao was obdurate or perhaps simply had no regard for the truth; he refused to even acknowledge the problem. No surprise there! Chao Anouvong was shrewd enough to realise that further adulation was required; it was an opportune moment to use flattery and witticism to reduce the tension. Leaning forward slightly he went for it, his voice devoid of emotion.

'Your Majesty, my humble respects. You are King of Kings, the son of my dear friend, your late father, for whom my love and respect were unshakable. I salute you whom the people love to honour.' On hearing this, Nangklao sat back in his chair and beamed with pleasure. 'I beseech you,' he continued, 'do not begrudge us the fulfilment of our wishes and grant that we may fruitfully accomplish the duty that has brought us to your capital on our elephants and horses and let us return home safely. Please, let me tell my people you have granted them leave to return home. I shall then personally escort them back to their beloved homes in ViengChan. What's more, you're undoubtedly without rival in terms of virtue and renown. I believe that virtue is a wiser policy than vice. My experience of beautiful young girls is very limited but even I doubt whether the best way to my sister's heart is through force and intimidation.'

Nangklao hesitated. He'd seemed so sure of himself until Chao Anouvong had confronted him, but the situation had now become a bit of a nightmare for him.

Chao Anouvong was a tough, fearless man with the courage to openly condemn Bangkok for its brutality. He was happy to share every hardship and liked to be seen working hard amongst his people. He was not only shrewd but generous and expected others to show the same spirit he asked of himself. During the meeting, however, he showed he was not a man to be crossed; he'd always held firm views on justice and knew exactly what he wanted for LanXang. With a gleam in his eye, he would have liked to have accused Nangklao of breaching the gentlemanly agreement he'd made with his late father, even though no documentary evidence existed. Naphalai had foreseen that the wounds inflicted on the Lao in 1779 must be healed before they became infected. Some discussion had surely taken place, some sort of agreement between father and son. If he could prove this, it would mean that Nangklao – who'd been jealous of Chao Anouvong's relationship with Naphalai – was a double dealer and a cheat. Therefore, the only assumption remaining was that Bangkok hated Chao Anouvong and intended to erase LanXang.

The meeting wore on tensely. It was impossible to question Nangklao; no one was able to speak the truth in Siam for fear of repercussions. Chao Anouvong tried to find the right words and arguments, using all his persuasive skills on his host. He was only looking for one tiny bit of empathy, some sort of assurance he could take his beloved sister back to ViengChan with him. Alas, his charm failed to disarm Nangklao and the Siamese king's sanctimonious refusals hurt him deeply. His heart might be able to forgive and forget but his soul never could. Had Nangklao possessed any statesmanship he might have sanctioned Chao Anouvong's requests, and the applause and praise of the Lao people would have rung throughout LanXang.

Unfortunately, Nangklao's obduracy was etched into his hard, unforgiving features. It seemed that however hard Chao Anouvong tried to please him, it made no difference. Nangklao was prepared to listen to only one man in Bangkok and the whole of Siam, indeed the world, and that was himself. I doubt acceding to Chao Anouvong's requests even crossed his mind for an instant. Hosting lavish banquets attended by overseas emissaries and tradesmen was more important than the welfare of his people.

Chao Anouvong did his best to win some concessions but in truth he was wasting his time burbling about love, friendship and sworn treaties. It was a real setback and a massive price to pay for his sister, the dancers and the Lao people in Saraburi. Even if he'd won the argument, one could imagine that if Princess Kanlayani had still been young, Nangklao would still have dragged her kicking and screaming from her room and done what he liked with her, as he would have behaved with any of the young, desirable beauties of the kingdom. No one would have dared speak of it for fear of persecution under constitution. Siam's laws were widely used to restrict its subjects' freedoms.

Chao Anouvong interpreted the situation well. He tried to convince Nangklao that Siam could easily grant LanXang her independence, but he wasn't the sort of man to test his principles by getting drunk in order to pick a fight. He'd no other choice but to remain composed, though I could see anger and frustration in his eyes. I knew he would calm down before long, he was all too aware that he simply didn't have the power to demand even respect from

Nangklao. It would simply risk more humiliation, already an inevitability.

There was a moment of levity when Nangklao looked in my direction again with his mean eyes and cheekily asked whether he could keep me in his palace. I blushed with embarrassment and fright: I really thought he was going to order his guards to take me away. To my horror he said, 'Can you leave that rustic wily man of yours behind when you go? We like him.' I thought he was making fun of me, but always with a nose for deception he made a cunning offer: 'We'd pay a good price for a loyal servant.' He paused before coldly adding, 'What about… 100 bars of gold?'

My heart sank and I froze with fear like a child, I can tell you. Whatever the amount, I honestly never thought of my own worth, but the proposal did seem too good to turn down. For one terrible moment, I was struck by a sense of dread that I'd be stuck in Bangkok. Perhaps the offer would be accepted or I might become a pawn in the negotiations and lose my freedom and my place in Chao Anouvong's life. I found it stressful being out of my comfort zone, completely banished from my beloved country, unable to live amongst my Lao people, eating my favourite Lao food and living instead amongst the arrogant Siamese in Bangkok. I really couldn't imagine anything worse. The heat under my collar made me feel faint! Fortunately Chao Anouvong was not easily intimidated. I was forever grateful to him for standing up for me. His reply, much to my relief, was business-like but light-hearted.

'Your Majesty is too generous, but you would be surprised to know I've already turned down an enormous offer from your predecessor, who didn't even see him,' replied the quick-witted Chao Anouvong with humour in his voice. 'He's too valuable and no one's going to pinch him from me,' he added and proudly glanced in my direction. Saddened, I lowered my head further. He turned to look directly at Nangklao and said prophetically, 'Your Majesty must understand that my secretary has been with me for the past thirty years. He is very loyal and shall always be so, to me and even more to his country. The day he's parted from us will be the day I'll part from this corrupted earth.'

These were his words and they lifted my morale to a new level.

'That makes us even more determined to have him… and we'll double the price for a loyal slave!' said Nangklao scornfully and laughed. His mandarins burst into sarcastic laughter.

There was terrible menace in Nangklao's voice. I almost fainted with terror. I was as frozen as if I'd been turned to stone but I also wanted to flee. However,

Chao Anouvong's safety was on my mind: he was being intimidated, but despite being clearly upset, he remained composed. On reflection, I thought this was exactly the moment he could have spoken his mind if he was as powerful as Nangklao. The bitterness with which the Siamese king assailed him for being Lao infuriated him. He must have wished he could have told Nangklao to show some respect or, failing that, shut him up and give him a good whipping. My legs were numb, but I sat still, stuck to the floor, my cold hands clasped together in prayer and trembling with fear.

'Your Majesty, please hear me,' Chao Anouvong said in a hoarse voice, shifting in his chair a little. 'To avoid any misunderstanding, I believe I should tell you outright that Phia Jon is my private secretary. He's not a slave and is not for sale at any price. We believe it to be the height of cruelty to make anyone work like a slave. Our King Fah Ngum abolished slavery in 1353, 472 years ago. We've had no slaves in LanXang ever since.'

At Chao Anouvong's comments, the new Rattanakosin king, for all his power and arrogance, drew back his head a little. One could see his anger rising: he looked furiously jealous, sitting with his arms folded and slipping into a gloomy reverie like a spoilt teenager. Suddenly he smacked both hands upon the chair-arms.

'Let's get to the point, shall we?' he roared abruptly, too agitated to sit still and jumping to his feet. He raised his forefinger for the footman and rapped out an order for fresh coconut juice to be served at once. He asked Chao Anouvong whether he would like some too before settling himself down on a different, larger throne-like couch with big golden cushions. 'If you want to keep your loyal slave,' he said persistently, 'there are two things we want from you. The first is your continuing support in our military campaign against the enemy. The second is your allegiance, your loyalty to my throne. If you agree to both, I am then prepared to consider some of your requests. You should be pleased with that!'

Chao Anouvong immediately saw his opportunity and said, 'And may I ask, what's in it for us?'

'Well, normally,' said Nangklao, turning to look at him, 'I'd insist on an exclusive pact, but given your prior commitments in ViengChan, I'm willing to let you return and I'll double LanXang's financial aid, something you so often asked for from my late father... and you're free to raise taxes and spend them how you wish.'

I knew Nangklao was trying to ease Chao Anouvong's mind, but to no avail.

'That is flattering,' Chao Anouvong responded quickly, letting out a long breath, lowering his head a little and bridling at the choice of words. 'Your Majesty's magnanimity is most exemplary, and your kindness is greatly appreciated. Unfortunately, my private secretary is a man of his word. He has pledged to serve me for life and cannot be bought at any price. But it seems that I can, is that so? To be honest, the size of the reward for my military support and personal loyalty should be proportionate to the degree of hardships my people endure.' He paused. 'Please don't misunderstand me. I'm a loyal citizen and I know that Bangkok must be protected. But I must beg you to let me think about your first condition, because I have to assess the strength of the Lao army.'

'There is nothing to think about!' Nangklao said, clenching his jaws and showing his teeth as if intending to kill. 'For all your eloquent sophistry, your attempts to wheedle your way into my heart will not work. We are decided that we will not let you return to ViengChan until you've pledged your loyalty. You must swear allegiance to us… and every Lao citizen must obey me from now on. I can perceive both loyalty and untrustworthiness in all men. I can discern their innermost thoughts. Any traitorous thoughts will be punished with execution. Make sure your Lao people all follow your example.' He reached for the silver mug that had been placed next to him. 'This coconut juice,' he said, looking down at Chao Anouvong with satisfaction, 'comes from the people you brought down from ViengChan. We ordered them to cut down the palm trees in Suphanbury it was produced from to build our fort at the mouth of the Chaophraya river.' He took a sip and then boasted, 'This land produces excellent coconut juice, the best medicine for anxiety.'

Nangklao was powerful and could afford to put on such airs. He was jealous of Chao Anouvong's talent and hated him to the bone, but most of all, he was obsessed by using his power as a cloak, behind which he could pursue his ambition at the expense of others, profiting himself and his family. What a bitter irony for ordinary Siamese to see their rights being trampled upon by his unholy policies. His arrogance was breath-taking.

Chao Anouvong was far from perplexed by Nangklao's mercurial temperament and deliberate antagonism. After letting him have his say, he made no immediate response and simply gazed disapprovingly at the coconut juice. You could sense he felt annoyed and humiliated, blaming himself for being unable to protect the people who'd accompanied him to Bangkok. He stuck to his seat and gritted his teeth. A moment later, he calmly said that his father descended from King Khoun Borom's son, Khoun Loh, and his mother from the ruling house of NongBuaLamphu, and as descendant of Ai-Lao, his blood ran true. He reminded Nangklao that he'd been taken from his homeland as a boy of twelve and had grown up with Nangklao's father and been immersed in Siamese culture for sixteen years. He was as much Siamese as Lao. Furthermore, he said that he'd led several military campaigns and fought for Siam in LanNa. He'd gained the respect and friendship of the late King Naphalai, Siamese nobles and commoners alike. Even some of the courtiers had learnt to admire him; he got on well with both Lao and Siamese.

A bemused Nangklao then sarcastically asked him to try the drink. He hesitated and one could see his brain was working through the consequences of both refusal and acceptance; but really, he'd no choice.

'Your Majesty, could any honest man in my position,' Chao Anouvong said, his voice breaking, 'bear to taste food and drink while my people are being forced into slave labour by building canals and cutting down palm trees? But I like coconut juice and feel thirsty. I can think of nothing nicer on such a hot day. I shall certainly take it with pleasure, in the hope that you'll grant them their liberty.' I took a brave glance from the corner of my eyes at Chao Anouvong's face. Simplicity and humility were his strengths in diplomacy. There was silence as he lifted his glass. 'This drink is in Your Majesty's honour and I pray to the Lord Buddha for your health,' he said, calmly pouring a libation into an empty silver cup before taking a sip of the juice. I could tell by his expression that the juice was not to his taste but he pretended to find it satisfying. I was glad he took his drink politely as it dissipated the tension of this difficult meeting.

'Why waste such a healthy drink?' Nangklao interrupted, confused by Chao Anouvong's actions. He asked snappily, 'What's the meaning of this ritual?'

'Forgive me, I'll explain,' Chao Anouvong said. 'The native peoples of LanXang consisted mostly of Lao and around fifty other ethnic groups but our social customs, such as the Baci welcoming ceremony, help us coexist. Making a libation is indeed one of our rites. It gives us a sense of identity and helps us to mourn the dead, celebrate festivals, conduct family meals, remember and honour our ancestors and so on. The Lao believe they come from the stars (*Dao*). Most of us, of course, believe in and worship the ancestral spirits (*Phi*

Fah or Phi Thaen) who protect us and plead for us with the gods in heaven. It's therefore our custom to set aside food and drink as an offering to them. We normally pour libations to our mythical great ancestors' spirits (*Pu Nyeu and Nya Nyeu*) before or after we eat or drink.'

After a short pause he said, 'I can assure Your Majesty this libation doesn't symbolise a declaration of LanXang independence, but I pray you'll grant it sooner rather than later.' I could tell at once he was referring to King Naresuan the Great of Siam, who poured water in Ayutthaya city in 1584 as a symbol to denounce Burmese domination, but I doubted Nangklao would have realised this. Chao Anouvong drank the juice more enthusiastically and spoke warmly of Nangklao's enlightened views about commissioning a giant reclining Buddha in Wat Pho. Still holding his drink, he said, 'Yes, indeed, this coconut juice tastes refreshingly healthy, but my Lao followers shouldn't be forced into producing it for you. Then again, we're also concerned for Your Majesty's safety and are pleased to know that the fortress at the mouth of the river, built by our citizens, will offer Bangkok some protection from foreign invaders. Free from such worries, Your Majesty will be calm and serene.'

Nangklao looked pleased but still somewhat unimpressed.

A little later, Chao Anouvong recited an extract from Khoun Borom's doctrine, which he'd memorised, reminding Nangklao of the special relationship and its origins in the bonds of history, kinship and common interest since the Ai-Lao of the kingdom of NanChao. 'Personally,' he continued, putting his drink down on the silver tray and leaning forward a little, 'may it please Your Majesty, I have neither eye to see nor tongue to speak in this palace, but as this court is pleased to direct me, I believe Your Majesty has earned your mandarins' confidence and loyalty. By coming here today I hope I've also have earned your trust and I pray that you honour kindness and friendship. As for my loyalty, it's at your disposal.'

'Excellent,' beamed Nangklao, but he still looked unconvinced.

Chao Anouvong was aware that negotiations were a process of give and take but at no point did Nangklao suggest that Bangkok would give anything away. It was all absurd political posturing, in which Nangklao, with his sense of entitlement, his inability to accept criticism or even to smile, his smallness, his petty furies and his self-absorption, demanded loyalty but offered nothing in return. He was an absolute curse on earth and on LanXang in particular. If Nangklao had behaved in a more gentlemanly manner, engaged in genuine dialogue and spoken the truth, Chao Anouvong, I'm sure, would have been more respectful. But with Nangklao in charge LanXang would never be treated fairly; on the contrary, she would be deliberately humiliated. Even so, Chao Anouvong had been right to err on the side of diplomacy rather than using sharp-tongued retorts. He was courteous, even charming to Nangklao. He was able to maintain his composure and integrity and remained gracious, a quality deeply rooted in the Lao character. He'd been careful not to make any gaffes, listening carefully and trying not to let anything upset him. He recommended free movement between the two kingdoms. The Lao of the lower Mekong and the Siamese of the Chaophraya river, he said, would be better off if they retained their own independent kingdoms rather than fomenting trouble against each other.

However, when Nangklao claimed that Siamese rule was superior, boasted about his triumphs and raved that Rattanakosin Siam existed only to wield power, Chao Anouvong punctured his exuberance with a sharp rebuke, for he was determined to speak his mind. When forced into it, he was quite prepared for a scrap over the fate of LanXang and her people. He lowered his head slightly but looked directly at Nangklao before continuing in a more severe tone of voice, abandoning his usual affability. These were words only Chao Anouvong dared to speak. I must say I froze when he lectured his host on the merits of self-rule and freedom and advised him to look no further than the truth.

'There's no guarantee of loyalty from every corner of Siam, let alone from the vassal states of LanNa and LanXang,' Chao Anouvong said. 'For example, our King Xay-Setthathirath ruled over both LanNa and LanXang as one kingdom. He saved ViengChan twice from Burmese domination because he managed to capture the citizens' hearts and minds – their very loyalty. Any Siam-educated elite will tell you that he allied with Ayutthaya to fight the Burmese, arriving with his Lao army not once but twice, because of his loyalty to King Phra Maha Intharaja of Ayutthaya and his love for the Siamese people. Unfortunately, despite his cleverness in warfare, he was unable to defeat Phra Maha Thamaraja of Pitsanouloke only because of the traitorous Siamese general Phraya Siharajteso. May I remind Your Majesty that the Lao exhausted their strength helping Siam, paying dearly in equipment, provisions and lives. As a result of these two heavy losses, King Xay-Setthathirath returned to ViengChan with his military greatly weakened. He was almost a broken man and Lao LanXang became a weaker kingdom. We were too weak to provide any support to Ayutthaya thereafter. Consequently, the Burmese destroyed Ayutthaya in 1750 because its king failed to win the loyalty of his own citizens. Ayutthaya completely ceased to exist after 1767.'

I was frightened but steeled myself to look. Nangklao was taken aback by Chao Anouvong's directness; it got under his skin and must have been painful for him to listen to. He just sat motionless while his mandarins shifted nervously in their seats. There was a slight chill in the air, another period of oppressive silence. I wondered how Chao Anouvong could extricate himself from this situation. I held my breath in anticipation. Hours seemed to pass while I waited for him to continue. When he did, pointing in the direction of the Emerald Buddha temple built by Lao architects in imitation of the original in ViengChan he said, 'I believe you have made the Emerald Buddha temple a symbol of Siam's conquest, and your triumph.'

'Preposterous!' Nangklao said and shifted in his seat as if in a temper. He turned to look at the temple before staring back at Chao Anouvong, who bowed in reverence.

'Pray don't be angry and please forgive me if I've misspoken,' he stammered. 'We Lao appreciate straight talking. We should really only speak honestly on such an occasion as this. The Emerald Buddha Temple has lost its true significance since you looted the sacred statue from ViengChan. If their land is annexed and the Emerald Buddha is not returned, the Lao people, as long as they have tongues to speak with, will remember the name of your grandfather Kasatseuk, who invaded ViengChan in 1779 and killed thousands, forced many others to leave their homes, looted our treasures and destroyed our temples and cities. I believe any true descendant of Ai-Lao Khoun Borom would never even think of behaving like this. Remember our King Fah Ngum and your King Uthong: they saw sense and never invaded each other's land.'

Well, I tell you, I felt immensely proud and couldn't help but raise my head in astonishment. It must have amazed Nangklao and his men that a Laoman had the audacity to adopt such a tone. A hiss of insults, derision and sneering laughter greeted Chao Anouvong's rhetoric. Nangklao's men murmured angrily that he should be punished for such comments. He was fully aware how much they detested him.

Nangklao's mouth fell open as he perceived the truth. Suddenly, he sprang from his seat and stood with arms apart, staring at his adversary with a hard, frozen expression on his face. Unable to believe what was happening, I could just make out Nangklao's profile. There was nothing he could say: he knew Chao Anouvong had spoken the truth. He checked his temper, returned to his seat and sat down heavily. The pride had entirely drained from his imposing frame. Slumped in his throne-like chair, he reminded me of some great beast that had been captured, shackled and taunted in the arena by a creature weaker than itself. He imploded amidst Chao Anouvong's reproach – utterly speechless, utterly defeated. He looked like a man who'd been strolling in the palace courtyard amongst his sentries, thinking himself invincible and above everyone else on earth, who'd then suddenly seen a ghost and stopped dead in alarm as if he'd been turned to stone.

Chao Anouvong lifted his head to show his seniority and, like a kick boxer, went for the knockout blow.

'These are all historical facts,' he continued confidently. 'And let's not also forget that our King Phothisarath took steps to prevent anybody else setting LanXang and Siam against each other. He refused to cooperate with the Burmese to spare the destruction of Si-Ayutthaya. I recall very clearly that our two royal houses swore friendship and fraternal love during the ceremony at the That Si-SongHuck shrine. I'm only telling you the truth; I mean no offence.'

There was another pause. I shifted sideways to see Chao Anouvong better but sat nervously out of Nangklao's direct view. I felt myself beginning to sweat. Of all Chao Anouvong's triumphs, I should say that telling Nangklao to do what was right was the sweetest, especially considering it was technically a defeat, not a victory. It was impossible for him to win and he now had to show some submission to escape alive.

I had long become used to Chao Anouvong's way of thinking: he was always capable of springing a surprise. To my amazement, he took evasive action: he hung his head and put on such feigned dejection that I found it hard to keep a straight face. Although he appeared to have retained his confidence and his faith, the laughter and jeering must have made him panic and wonder whether he was in the wrong. I sensed he saw no point in further argument and didn't want to further exacerbate the ill-feeling. He would now capitulate to Nangklao. He glanced around, took a sip of his drink and cleared his throat, as if trying to buy time. He lowered his noble head slightly and sank lower in his seat. At last, he went down on one knee in reverence, holding onto his seat. He was contrite and said that he was at fault, offering Nangklao his humble apologies. He begged for forgiveness and promised he would fight for Siam.

It was all a damage limitation exercise to reassure Nangklao, but he managed to ask the Siamese king to stop the Khorat governor Phromphakdy and his officials from carrying out the census. If it became known that Bangkok was behind the policy, the relationship between the two countries would be devastated for years to come.

To my surprise, he didn't ask Nangklao whether Phromphakdy was guilty but merely presented the problem from the point of view of a man who simply wanted justice for his kingdom. He paused for thought and then said he wanted to clear up a few other small points. He hoped Nangklao would answer truthfully.

'Your Majesty, your knowledge of men's ways and thoughts is unrivalled. I am also here to plead with you in the hope you'll tell me the truth about my brother's unhappy end. There's no need to soften your words out of concern for my feelings. So, please enlighten me, how did my dear brother Nanthasene meet his death in Bangkok in 1795? I dare say there's no evidence of any crime. And why were his remains not honoured?' He paused.

'I'm also troubled by certain reports,' he went on, 'and must now appeal to your discretion, in the name of Buddhist precepts and peace, to revoke the tattooing decree. I truly beg you to be persuaded by me, since I take no delight in seeing my people being harmed and humiliated. Otherwise, be under no illusion that you'll be committing a grave offence against our special relationship.' After another short pause during which Nangklao remained silent, Chao Anouvong said, 'Furthermore, what's the true reason for the order given to the governor of Khorat?' He also pointed out the suffering inflicted by Phromphakdy's chief officer Suriyaphakdy and his men while taking the census. In a puzzled manner, as if it were all a mystery far beyond his comprehension, he then asked how Phromphakdy had managed to bring so much wealth and valuable treasure to Bangkok.

Nangklao, who'd revived a little, suddenly looked like a man struck in the chest by an arrow at close range. He did not react to the question about Nanthasene's death, but the suggestion of a palace connection to Phromphakdy's crimes brought him to his feet again. He grew angry, standing rooted, mouth and eyes gaping, like a man clubbed on the head. His ruthless gaze fell upon his adversary, a contemptuous smile flashing across his face. Chao Anouvong was entirely lost for words, a rare event indeed. I couldn't see Nangklao's face from where I was sitting, but Chao Anouvong told me in delight afterwards that it became suffused with blood. The question had been aimed directly at him.

Eventually, the annoyed Nangklao turned towards his antagonist, dramatically sweeping off his magnificent royal gold silk cloak and revealing the foul body beneath. He seemed totally at odds with the rest of the world, a man stubbornly clinging to his outdated precepts. The Bangkok authorities constantly evaded the truth and found fault with others, this making their mission to cement a place in Siam's history even harder. Their greedy pursuit of power had made them arrogant. Perhaps due to earlier hardship, Nangklao had become even more immature and addicted to physical satisfaction; as his addiction grew, so did his yearning for greater power. He pumped himself up so everyone could get a good view of him as if he was advertising himself. He stood with legs apart and arms akimbo, speaking loudly, narrowing and rolling his eyes. He struggled for words but haughtily lifted his face like a spoilt child. I have to say he did look impressive as he towered over the people around him. He pointed at Chao Anouvong and roared that he would act only for his own advantage, not for the LanXang king. This drew disdainful smiles and loud cheers from his own mandarins.

Chao Anouvong, a strident opponent of the Rattanakosins' ideology, was in a terribly delicate situation, taunted and surrounded by foes. As expected, his questions about his brother's demise and the royal household treasures had fallen on deaf ears and I wondered what he would say next. I don't think he wished to further upset his host and create even more enmity before our departure for ViengChan; but despite being an excellent diplomat, he was a fighter at heart, prepared to stand firm when necessary. He left Nangklao in no doubt he was completely loyal to LanXang.

'We welcome your generous offer to tackle corruption in your kingdom,' Chao Anouvong continued. 'This will strike terror in the hearts of those guilty of it. They must be reminded that your command is sacred. We are, of course, at your disposal in this matter.'

Nangklao shot a sideways glance at his mandarins. After a moment's silence, a great hubbub of displeasure, derision and antagonism poured out from them. They trembled from head to foot. Nangklao wasn't a man much used to facing honest questions. Chao Anouvong's directness made him flustered, but he kept his silence. No doubt he was a great actor who'd cast himself as a glamorous figure. There seemed no end to their trickery yet, once their magic had dwindled, it proved as much a weakness as a strength. Nangklao stood still, legs parted, arms unfolded and hanging tightly by his sides, like an animal preparing to fight a rival, about to jump at Chao Anouvong and strangle him. There was no friendship here, just enmity.

I was too frightened to move, and the room was hushed. However hard he tried to persuade him, Chao Anouvong knew that Nangklao was so besotted with amassing wealth and dealing with overseas traders that he would never lift a finger to help the victims of Bangkok's institutional racism. Chao Anouvong, by contrast, never discriminated against anyone and never acted through ignorance and delusion, constantly questioning his motives to ensure they remained pure. He looked solemn and dignified as if he were laughing it all off. He gazed downwards and silently sipped his drink. Despite Nangklao's admonishment, he preferred to be guided by his own convictions. He then spoke of karma: he would rather not be enemies with anyone but was prepared to endure it if necessary.

He later told me that perhaps he'd once failed to foster a good relationship with Nangklao in a previous life. He added that he didn't mind Nangklao hating him as long as he also feared him.

'You can say whatever you like, but this is preposterous. How dare you!' Nangklao roared, staring down at Chao Anouvong in puzzlement. With his head tilted sideways and his face upturned, he rudely and sarcastically added, 'You Laosy people spend your time in ViengChan looking at the past and talking to your buffaloes. I know far more about Bangkok and the rest of the world than you lot. Your constant pontificating about the past will achieve nothing. It's our privilege to do as we please. We don't need to be reminded about the northeast (*Monthon Tawan Ork Sieng Neua*) and all that nonsense about the That Si-SongHuck ceremony. It's a version of history we don't care for, and we don't give a fig about you and the rest of the world.' A moment later Nangklao, who'd been roaring like a lion, snarling like a tiger, hissing like a snake and screeching like an eagle, checked his temper again, as if he'd grown tired of this latest repertoire. Having returned to his seat and consulted with his aides, as a sign for the meeting to end, he abruptly announced, 'Well, I suppose we must let you Lao, you sticky rice-eaters ploughing your elephant-infested lands, go back to ViengChan... to your jungle, your paddy fields and those buffaloes of yours!' He glowered and fell silent, his cheeks flushed with fury.

Well, without interference from Bangkok, our natural assets – mountains, rivers, forests, wildlife, fertile plains – were enough for the Lao people to live on. Water and rice were the lifeblood of the community. There were indeed herds of elephants and buffaloes in LanXang, but they were hardly novelties since they'd long since been tamed. It was hard to think of more useful domesticated animals. The elephants, most of which had been taken away to Siam after the 1779 invasion, carried men and goods and helped to build houses, palaces and temples. The buffaloes pulled the ploughs for growing rice (buffaloes plus rice equal gold). Nangklao certainly wasn't speaking from the point of view of a mere rice-eating mortal!

'Your Majesty, please allow me to take my leave,' said Chao Anouvong. 'I beseech you to send me safely home to my animals. I'm eager to be gone and so are my people. It will genuinely grieve me to leave Bangkok, but ViengChan needs me. However, I assure you that you have my support and that of my sons. If you wish, you can call on the whole of my household in LanXang. In fact, the Lao people would be delighted if Your Majesty would pay ViengChan a visit one day. We'll pull out all the stops to welcome you.'

Nangklao seemed unconvinced but at least looked a little less red. He remained in his chair and looked around with an expression of great displeasure. The remainder of the meeting passed off calmly, albeit in an atmosphere of suspicion. Neither king had any appetite left for further conversation. As time went on, the room began to fill with a strange perfume and the scent of incense became rather oppressive. I was more than happy for the summit to end. Not long after, Nangklao slapped his hands on the armrests to signal that the audience was over. He then leant forward, stared at his foe and said, 'Now, get out!' in a voice so lethal it cut through everything. There was no disguising the fact that the supposedly friendly encounter had not been a success. They seemed to have turned their backs on each other.

In silence, Chao Anouvong kept his head down and gazed at his drink. He'd showed commendable valour in facing Nangklao, but he probably felt quite shaken as he folded his long, aristocratic hands in an attitude of peace. Then he shrugged, coughed politely into his hand and articulated his thanks with a nod. He didn't care what the palace circle would say about him. He knew they would slander him: proof that truth and despotism can never coexist. He hated to be mocked but at that moment he seemed entirely unconcerned. He wanted only to return to his kingdom, his queen and his people. He'd long tired of Bangkok, as had I.

Realising the meeting had ended abruptly, I remember saying to myself that Chao Anouvong had made his peace but I was unsure of the price he would have to pay. He must have realised he'd lost face, but even with the wisdom of hindsight, what else could he have done? Nangklao's rebuke had been very nasty but in his desperation Chao Anouvong had lost control and made his feelings quite clear by demanding more respect for his people's rights and freedoms. He was saddened, but before departing, keen to end on a friendly note, he lowered his eyes and performed obeisance. He then bade farewell, expressed his appreciation for the audience and beseeched Nangklao to examine the gold, hand-written manuscripts, begging him to excuse his poor handwriting. He hoped that the meeting and the manuscripts would help him understand ViengChan a little better. He picked up his drink and raised it to Nangklao.

'Your Majesty, here's fortune to you,' Chao Anouvong said as he rose. 'I take my leave of you now. May you be happy and may your palace be blessed.' He put his drink down, bowed his head then walked backwards a few paces, trying not to look at Nangklao, who said nothing and looked oddly confused.

I sat motionless like a bronze Buddha, holding my breath. The sentry came forward, gave me a quizzical look, touched my shoulder, nodded and pointed towards the exit. I gave him a sullen, resentful look and quickly found my feet. As I stooped and backed out of Nangklao's presence with downcast eyes, I smiled beguilingly and made obeisance to him before tiptoeing behind Chao Anouvong amidst a faint stir and sarcastic laughter amongst the golden cushions. With our mandarins shuffling behind like frightened children, we made swiftly for the door, which swung open as we approached. As it was closing behind us, I thought how easily one of Nangklao's sentries could have ended our lives. My heart was racing as if I were recovering from a bad fall. Leaving Nangklao in his cold palace, we went out into the late afternoon heat. I breathed a sigh of relief. There was no doubt the meeting had proved an unhappy one. No emotional bond had been formed between the two rulers. Chao Anouvong had been given his first real taste of wealth and power, and it had been made clear that Bangkok was never going to play fair.

While we were walking away from the palace and looking down the stairway, I felt dizzy, tinged with excitement and a queasy unease. I was in a state of befuddlement. My head was still reeling from the scene and from Nangklao's words. It was difficult to believe that only a little earlier, I'd been sitting in a room with the high and mighty. Nangklao's lack of respect had demonstrated a disturbing degree of insolence. He'd behaved like a god amongst men, yet at the same time seemed to me a sad and insecure soul. Perhaps he was jealous of those more talented than himself. I knew I'd heard most of the meeting quite clearly because the moment our carriages started to move out of the palace courtyard, I reconstructed it while still fresh in my memory.

We left empty-handed and crestfallen, but I was rather anxious to get away from the palace. Our carriages cautiously moved through the gate and once we were outside the palace walls we hurried along the streets. The sun had just gone below the treetops but it was still swelteringly hot and humid, with a torpid breeze wafting gently from the south. It was the worst possible combination in late March because it carried the stench of the drowned bodies of dogs, cats, horses, buffaloes and cows, and probably everything else not worthy of a proper burial, all mixed up with household refuse, floating and rotting together on the Chaophraya river at high tide. The canals and the Chaophraya river that supported life also carried filth and discharged a pernicious stench. Noxious fumes played at our nostrils from every direction, sometimes with hardly a breath of wind to purify the nauseous atmosphere. I couldn't imagine anything worse than being condemned to breathe this insufferable stink, which drew great flocks of crying sea gulls from the sea at Pataya, flapping their wings over the floating remains. The reek was especially acute that evening and you could even taste it on your tongue. It must have been even worse during the cholera outbreak of 1820 that killed thousands of people.

We had become acclimatised, but the greatest difficulty was the heat. I don't mind being hot but I hated getting hot and sweaty. The salty sweat ran into my eyes and the perspiration from my neck trickled down my back like raindrops. It was so hot, as if there were two suns glaring over Bangkok, that even the earth gave off the aroma of humid, menacing air, making it difficult to breathe. I gritted my teeth against the sun burning my cheeks and squinted at the sky to see whether the clouds might be blocking it. I took a quick glance back at Nangklao's multi-coloured palace compound. To anyone who cared to look closely, the contrast between the myth and reality of the Rattanakosin Island fortress was self-evident. The palace was grand, colourful and spotlessly clean, with great attention to detail. On the other hand, it was an unapologetically unprincipled, repressive, paranoid and ruthless place, where policies of political warfare, intimidation, disinformation and forgery were bred.

I contemplated Siam's history with mixed feelings. Perhaps it had always suffered from a split personality, its friendly manners contrasting with shocking cruelty when branding the Lao people like slaves and working them to an early grave. I tried to imagine things as they used to be there but couldn't help wondering at the unpleasantness of Nangklao, a dynastic ruler who'd emerged from the shadow of an ambitious family and become a brute, a total degenerate. The plush palaces were built with ill-gotten gains: impressive buildings, temples, stupas and living quarters, surrounded by canals and bougainvillea-clad high walls, along with calm pools to reflect the floating clouds. Yet the complex seemed stained by its ruler's cruel power and sucked the life out of its subjects. Groans of violence lurked beneath smiles and courtly manners. Bangkok was in a climate of fear, trembling with uncertainty. Although Nangklao's immediate environment was calm, the rest of Siam most certainly was not. In such a divisive political environment, a ruler like him always tends to ignite controversy and conspiracy in equal measure.

A party of diehard northern and north-eastern Lao noblemen were in rebellious mood, stirred up by Bangkok's haphazard approach to justice, extortionate taxes and objectionable personality. They wanted to bring Bangkok to heel and felt strongly they had the right to revolt against Siam. Bangkok's failure to respect the 1563 That Si-SongHuck treaty also stirred up trouble; it had not only established the border between the two countries but also covered feudal tax, fairness, love and friendship, and guaranteed special privileges for the two royal families. Alas, Siam had no wish to abide by its terms and would not tolerate the presumption of its vassal states of LanNa and LanXang in threatening to proclaim autonomy.

The air was stinking beneath the white sky of Bangkok and Nangklao's reign brought fear to every citizen. A symptom of his insecurity, insanity and ego was that he placed more emphasis on being a king than on simply being a human being, a Buddhist and a Siamese. The meeting could have far-reaching consequences. It had been clear from the beginning that Chao Anouvong's requests wouldn't be accepted, but his brave performance showed he didn't intend to remain a mere instrument of Siam. LanXang's destiny was as an independent nation. For one delirious moment I wanted to compliment him on his success in persuading Nangklao to allow us to return to ViengChan, but it wasn't the appropriate time to do so. He was fully aware that Nangklao and his men despised him and everything he stood for. They wished to exterminate not only him – a true Lao royal descendant of Khoun Loh – but they wanted to wipe LanXang from the earth. When I looked back at the palace once more, I realised the enormity of the risk he'd taken. I could hear Nangklao's menacing voice in my mind. In silence, I looked up to heaven, prayed and breathed a sigh of relief again.

'That went well,' I said but my hands and voice were shaking. It was clear Chao Anouvong was in the gravest peril. He must have felt it too but calmly said he was relieved when the encounter was over. I congratulated him on his performance and for getting us out of the palace alive. All through the meeting I'd been discreetly watching the faces of Nangklao's men as they exchanged looks and carefully watched my master. I remarked that Nangklao, descended from a family of usurpers, should have shown better manners towards Chao Anouvong, whose title derived from the time of legendary Khoun Borom. I'd been tempted to tell him so.

'I'm glad you didn't,' he said.

I've never craved power. I'm certain Chao Anouvong understood how it could be used. If ViengChan had possessed it, Nangklao would have bowed to him, renounced his ambitions on pain of death and returned to LanNa and LanXang what was rightfully theirs. Bangkok and ViengChan would have treated each other as brothers and equals.

He was in a preoccupied mood and didn't talk as we headed back to our residence; he was probably trying to relax after the spiralling tensions of the meeting. Whatever had been agreed with Nangklao troubled him. The daylight was fading fast but the air was still baking hot, intensifying an aroma of highly spiced food wafting up from the street, joined by the poisonous stench of human waste and rotting death. Chao Anouvong kept his sleeve pressed to his mouth and nose to ward off the smell. I handed him a small white towel and he mopped his face, wiped his neck and dried his sweaty hands. I was aware of the stench but there was a sudden foul odour I didn't recognise, something rotten and decaying, a stink of such potency I was nearly gassed. I blew my cheeks out in disgust.

'Your Majesty, please bring your wits to the rescue,' I said cheerfully. 'We might be dead men soon. This disgusting smell is killing me!'. On hearing this, he laughed at my ignorance. He whispered that it was the smell of human effluent from the intricate network of canals. 'I'm afraid I feel like throwing up,' I whispered back to him miserably. Thinking I really was going to be sick,

I shuddered and leaned forwards. He kept his sleeve firmly pressed to his mouth. Occasionally, when the locals opened their doors, we could hear the muffled sounds of voices, often in Lao, and laughter. I was quite aware of the distinctive strong smell of raw, fermented fish (*Padaek*), so familiar to Lao people but often intolerable to others. With this indescribable stink all around, one wondered how anyone could possibly find the stomach for food. I longed to be back in ViengChan and far away from the hostility of Bangkok. The whole place stank in every respect. As we drew closer to our lodgings, I asked him if he wanted anything.

'Yes, Phia Jon, fresh air and a quiet life in ViengChan,' he replied. I wanted it badly too. I chatted away in an attempt to cheer him up. The smell didn't help.

We returned to our quarters, disappointed that things hadn't gone well. Chao Anouvong kept his hand up to his nose for neither the heat nor the smell had diminished much. I kept quiet but as soon as we stopped at our residence, I ran towards the foot of the coconut tree and was sick. I must have looked as pale as a corpse and to save further embarrassment I dashed upstairs, slipped into my little room and sluiced my head, neck and face with cold water from the jug. That evening I felt as though I'd turned into a monk for I couldn't face any food. I stayed in my room for a while and the thought of coconut drink made me thirst for revenge instead.

Although I didn't really want to think about it, the incident prompted me to stay awake into the night writing up everything I could remember from the meeting. I expected Chao Anouvong to ask about it later, but more importantly I wanted to preserve the events for future generations.

Chao Anouvong's arrival in Bangkok for King Naphalai's funeral is a historical fact. It's also true they were both friends and implacable opponents. Bangkok's highest ambition was to create an empire while the prospect of losing its statehood was a matter of the highest national concern for ViengChan. He'd attended the funeral to show the new king his loyalty, yet he was even denied friendship. He was a patriotic and sensible man but felt that Bangkok had taken him for a ride; his requests had been made in a spirit of goodwill, but Nangklao's arrogance and inflexibility had thwarted all attempts at reconciliation. Instead of admitting Siam's misrule of LanXang, Nangklao had even rejected Chao Anouvong's more modest requests and demanded his and the Lao people's loyalty by menacing him in a most unacceptable way. It had clearly been a frustrating encounter for Chao Anouvong, but he respected his rank and managed to remain calm.

It would have pleased Chao Anouvong enormously had Nangklao at least understood the depth of anti-Siamese feeling that he was trying to contain with his ill-fated request. He – Nangklao – should have consented to the repatriation of the Lao people. Equally, had he not opted to humiliate Chao Anouvong, there would have been at least a chance of reconciliation, but his behaviour had demonstrated an unbelievable degree of egotism and incompetence. His point-blank refusal was perhaps born of the glaring disconnect between the arrogance of the wealthy Siamese in leafy Bangkok and the humble, patriotic people of Lao LanXang. There were many good reasons for ViengChan to maintain a good relationship with Bangkok but sadly LanXang unification would not be one of them.

It was hardly a surprise to discover that certain people – emperors, kings, rulers, statesmen and politicians – can't bear to be in the same room together, even if the strong tide of national interest dictated they should at least try. Clearly Nangklao and Chao Anouvong were among them: they had nothing in common and didn't care for each other. They couldn't coexist any more than fire and water. Chao Anouvong desired freedom for LanXang and its people. Nangklao wanted to destroy them. With his absurd sense of entitlement and pomposity, Nangklao refused to honour Chao Anouvong's desire for respect and justice and the Lao King struggled to rid himself of the disgrace that Nangklao had poured upon him. Reason would never rule the heart of such a king and it was impossible for the two of them to be reconciled.

Although Chao Anouvong's requests had come to nothing, he was a master of rhetoric and had scored a massive victory over Nangklao, no doubt about that. Nonetheless, I think he was aware his behaviour had been a mistake. He might have enjoyed his momentary triumph over Nangklao, but he must have realised he'd made himself a powerful enemy. It had without doubt been the most nerve-racking ordeal he'd ever endured, and it was vital he'd at least attempted to establish a friendly rapport with Nangklao. However, the result was never in doubt from the moment Nangklao spoke – the whole room had turned cold to the bone and everyone, the sentries at the doors included, had stiffened. Knowing his regal status, Chao Anouvong had managed to stay composed, not even stirring at the Siamese officials' smirks. But it had become clear to him that Bangkok simply wanted to wipe out the Lao nation and intended to annex LanXang and claim all aspects of Lao culture – food, customs, art, literature, history – and appropriate them as their own. Moreover, Bangkok had lost touch with reality even while Nangklao's reign was still young. Bangkok had become the pawn of overseas traders and a vital cog in the colonial powers' machinations but was earning a handsome income from financial aid and gifts.

An hour after sunset Chao Anouvong sent a servant to fetch me from my room. I took the liberty of taking a bottle of red wine with me. He sat silently at the sitting-room window, brooding, frustrated, gazing into space. He gave the impression of thinking of nothing else but freedom and glory for his nation. Looking back, I now understand why he looked so grim when we'd left the palace: the meeting had been a complete failure. He said that although he didn't really fancy any food, he would settle down for a quiet and simple meal and we could talk. He told me I was his boon companion, and I returned the compliment. I had no heart for eating either so fed my own thoughts instead of helping myself to the food. Our schedule had been so hectic and we'd barely slept. When I mentioned this, he told me there'd be plenty of time to sleep when we were dead.

'I can hardly breathe,' I grumbled, 'and feel as if I'm dying in this disgusting place. Let's have a drink.'

'Phia Jon, we must stay alive,' he said, watching me opening the bottle, 'and treat every day like it's our last, because one day it will be. We better eat something to keep up our energy. We have work to do to win back our rights.'

'Of course,' I responded, holding my breath while I pulled the cork. When it popped, I said, while pouring the wine, 'I must say, we should be proud of ourselves today. If I'm right, you've proved we're neither cowards nor fools. Let's pour libations, raise our glasses and drink to that.' I presented him with a glass of ruby liquid. 'For now, we must put Nangklao and his plots out of our minds. The Rattanakosins have no sense of honour or any inkling that Bangkok is doomed to an inglorious future.'

Chao Anouvong believed that Nangklao had permitted him to return to ViengChan only because he'd promised to personally lead his brave men to fight against Siam's enemies: the victory would then be Nangklao's, not his. There was no choice but to take an oath of allegiance even though he clearly perceived the malice hidden behind Bangkok's policies; all that wealth hadn't been acquired without intimidation and hard bargaining. However, all Chao

Anouvong had asked of Siam, really, was to restore LanXang's right to self-rule, his main goal in life.

'But why did you agree to help them?' I asked softly, raising my glass to him and sipping at my wine. I had no appetite but to keep him company nibbled at my food, mostly nuts and vegetables.

'Because, Phia Jon, we need to get back to ViengChan and fight another day,' he said. He took a sip of his wine and commented that the first drink of the evening is always the most enjoyable; after that, you're simply chasing that same feeling it gave you.

In silence I took another sip, my thoughts dwelling on its taste but more than ever on home. I could hardly wait for daylight to arrive, longing to get away from the fetid air of Bangkok.

We normally led a teetotal lifestyle or insisted on a period of abstinence but sometimes we took a drink as a pick-me-up. That night in Bangkok, however, for the very first time in all the years I spent with him, we both had a little too much. At least I think *I* did. We sat at table and drank and talked. Usually we talked more than we drank. He remarked that my hairless, boyish face had turned very red: no wonder, what with the heat and the wine. We drank a bit more and then mused in silence for a while.

'This is a nice wine, Phia Jon,' he said pleasantly and held his glass up to the light to admire the rich ruby liquid. 'Where did you get it?'

'From a little Chinese man's shop in one of those alleyways near the palace,' I said, holding the glass up to the light so that it glowed. 'I'm glad you like it,' I added.

'Very nice wine indeed. It's far better than that coconut juice I had earlier!' he said derisively.

Exhausted by our thoughts, we filled our glasses and lapsed into silence again. The houseflies and black ants were helping themselves to the remains of our food. Suddenly, Chao Anouvong called for a toast to our health and commended my faithful service. Under the influence of a little alcohol he could be dazzlingly brilliant, but a little too much drink had loosened our tongues and fuddled our wits. It was probably my fault for expressing my doubt about the promises he'd made to Nangklao. He veered morosely from Lao to Siamese and complained about the iniquity of the Rattanakosins and how much he hated their domineering policies. He believed that Nangklao had a personal animus against him and was very upset that his son, Rathsavong

Ngao, was going to be kept as a virtual slave, supervising the canal-digging to connect Tachin to Bangkok and not returning to ViengChan with us. It was very frustrating for all of us.

It wasn't until we'd eaten and drunk our fill that he thought of checking what Nangklao had scrawled on the document. 'Something contemptuous, I'm sure,' he said bitterly as he took it out of his pocket. I waited anxiously as he unfolded it. He held it in his hands and read it in silence at first before reading it out to me. '"Permission? No. Never!" What do you think of that?' he said and handed it to me. 'That revered man isn't a Buddhist; he's a tyrant, a despicable schoolboy bully. If we'd have known, nothing would have induced us to come to Bangkok. No one plays dirtier in politics than people in Siam. Is he entirely lacking in sense or compassion? Doesn't he see that his refusal is unethical, unreasonable and unkind? His policy of burning numbers into our people as if they're Siamese property is a lunatic system of totalitarianism: moronic and downright wicked. It's quite unbelievable!' He sat slumped in his chair in despair. 'We're foolish, Phia Jon,' he went on, 'to be in Bangkok begging for our future. But let's face it, every man has his moment. Our time will come.'

The scrawling was on the margin where Chao Anouvong had written, '*I beg Your Majesty's permission to take my beloved sister... and the Lao people in Saraburi back to ViengChan.*' I looked at him in concern. He urged me to be extra careful because he thought Nangklao might decide to stop us leaving Bangkok and we might well get assassinated. I quickly briefed him on our well-prepared escape plans. But there was nothing we could do at that moment but pray.

Later, Chao Anouvong was pacing about the room, looking calm but stern. He paused when the creaky door flew open and Rathsavong Ngao burst in and then stood breathless, looking upset. He told his son to get a grip. I offered the prince a glass of wine, but he politely declined. He bowed to his father, swallowed and reported that the Siamese had rewarded his engineering efforts with mockery, kicking and flogging. He didn't wish to be a slave to the ungrateful Siamese any longer and urged his father to act. I commented that I couldn't possibly agree with him more. Chao Anouvong ignored my interruption and reminded his son that over eagerness could prove fatal: it was better to exercise restraint. He looked at me for support and I nodded, not forgetting we were still in Bangkok. Father and son looked at each other and, without another word, Prince Ngao bowed and left. I could tell his fury would last.

Anyway, it was probably the drink in us that made us have a small disagreement over our meal rather than our usual ebullient, courteous philosophical disputes. The drink not only brought rest to our minds but also revealed many hidden things: anger was never normally one of them. I didn't take it to heart because I knew he didn't mean it. He was simply berating his own ignorance and stupidity, the result of misplaced loyalty and lack of judgement in ever trusting such an obviously dishonourable, nasty bunch of people. He said that he'd lost the argument because his opinions commanded no respect. He lamented that Nangklao was a self-important, snobbish individual who lacked humanity and moral understanding. 'That was why that wretched man ordered coconut drink,' he muttered furiously, 'to intimidate me by mocking me with the suffering of our poor people.' He was very red, helpless before the power of Nangklao's intimidation and ridicule. 'I doubt whether any Lao, once they hear of this, won't feel hurt and will rise against Bangkok. Would you, Phia Jon, for example?'

I quickly reflected on a means of retaliation. When I replied as angrily as an injured lion that I most certainly would, his eyes lit up and he placed his hands firmly on my shoulders. His touch made my blood flare up in a fire of patriotism. He said the time would come when the Rattanakosin king, whoever that might be, would be unable to stop the power of the people. I realised this was an extremely testing moment, even for someone with his equanimity. I turned away and kicked the dusty air after he told me to be patient.

'But then of course,' he said bitterly, 'this new king is neither a reasonable man, a compassionate Buddhist nor a gentleman.' He really felt he'd been tricked and that Nangklao had played him for a fool. 'What a ghastly person. He's not even a proper aristocrat, let alone royalty.' This was a dig at Nangklao's mother, who was of lowly, provincial origins. 'I dislike the Siamese aristos,' he said, before reminding me that the true nobles, who ruled Sukhotai and then Ayutthaya, were Ai-Lao descendants until the Burmese destroyed their capital city of Si-Ayutthaya in 1750.

'Your Majesty,' I said, 'forget what happened earlier. Let's make libations to our ancestors and the other gods before we think of sleeping. It's bedtime: the sun has long disappeared into the Chaophraya river and beyond the western gloom.' He said nothing. We made offerings, poured libations and drank to quench our thirst. The air was heavy and gloomy. Fearing for our safety, I considered keeping him company for longer but thought it best to leave him.

I tossed my drink down, bade him goodnight and retired to my room, leaving him looking tired and thoughtful.

Bangkok in the heat: mosquitoes, midges and other insects buzzing about in thick clouds and biting you; geckos scuttling on the walls for flies; mice running along the skirting board and the beams; the bathroom alive with cockroaches and humid air reeking from the stench of the canals. Hell on earth. It was the dead of night and since there was no breath of a breeze to stir the trees, the air was suffocating. While lying inside the mosquito net, damp from the sweat beneath my back, I felt like a roasting pig. My rest was spoilt by the fog of fear that we might be pounced on, but above all by vindictive feelings against Bangkok. I tried to sleep but, as the minutes passed, I was awakened by a noise. I thought I was dreaming at first when I heard the shouting – 'No!' – and then a crash. I jumped from my bed thinking only of Chao Anouvong. The first hard, clear thought that came to my mind was that he'd been assassinated, and I wanted to kill the first man who'd touched him. My second thought was that he'd been poisoned by the coconut drink or the hellish Bangkok water. As I went to him he was groaning with pain as if struck through the hand with a spear and was swaying about on his feet. When I saw the broken glass and his shirt stained with blood, I thought he was a doomed man.

'Phia Jon,' he called out the moment I appeared. 'I'm glad you came. I'm afraid I don't feel very well.' He looked rather green. He had me worried but nevertheless I was deeply relieved. The blood came from a gash on his hand. I rushed to him, hooked his arm over my shoulder and clucked and muttered as if to an upset child, not holding him too hard but letting him feel my firm hands. He clung to me. I got most of his weight on my legs, finding him heavier than I'd supposed, but I managed to get him to his room and laid him down on his bed. 'Rebellion… war… independence,' he mumbled into his pillows as I took off his shoes. 'Rebellion, that would be the way out, Phia Jon, and if we have to die because we lost the fight – well so what? There'll always be someone else to fight for our nation and our freedom.' Suddenly he sat up and I thought he was going to be sick. Like a helper (*Sangkali*) tending to a monk in the temple, I placed a chamber pot in front of him. 'We'll return to ViengChan,' he mumbled, 'to indulge our appetite for virtue and noble deeds and embrace philosophy in our newly built Wat Sisaketh temple.' I fetched another pillow for his head and gently dropped him back onto them as he muttered self-pitying, burbling words. I put a glass of clean water on his bedside table then sat on the chair beside his bed and carefully tended to the small cut on his hand. His eyes were closed. He breathed heavily and seemed aware of my presence, so I vowed not to tell anyone about the incident and asked permission to leave. I rested his bandaged hand on his chest and pressed it reassuringly. It didn't move. I sighed with relief then blew out the candles. He was snoring even before I reached the squeaky door; even the sound of the latch didn't rouse him.

I summoned a guard to watch outside his door, went back to my room and propped myself up with pillows. While resting with my eyes shut, I could hear a faint, distant snore. I was drained by what we'd endured and longed for a good sleep. I eased my head down on the pillows and lay awake long into the night, shivering with fear, listening for more disturbances, pondering all possibilities and feeling very anxious for the future. When sleep did come to me, it was restless and full of omens of grave portent for LanXang.

XI

Farewell City of Angels

I slept on and off throughout the night worrying about our long journey back to ViengChan until the dawn chorus started up outside. In fact, because of my restlessness and tiredness, I thought I'd overslept and woke up in a panic at the sound of Chao Anouvong's usual pre-dawn exercises in the sitting room, performed just a little more slowly than usual, perhaps. He woke uncalled, though he could only have slept a few hours. It was still too dark to see much when I opened my eyes, yet some of the cocks were already crowing. I stayed in bed thinking and waiting for the daylight to break.

When the new dawn touched the east with red, I jumped out of bed and rushed to open the window. The sharp morning sunlight blinded my eyes for a few seconds. The daybreak over the eastern horizon was stunning and I experienced a calm, transcendent moment. It was difficult to imagine that such immoral and iniquitous policies could be created on Rattanakosin Island, a place of religion and worship. I stuck my head outside and took a deep breath of fresh air. A soothing symphony of invisible birdsong from the nearby trees greeted the breaking dawn. They entertained me in my loneliness, and I wanted them to linger so I could enjoy the pleasure of their song. The people were beginning to come alive. Nearby rose the smell of cooking fires and the sharp cries of babies. I heard the distant screams of pigs and the bleating of livestock as farmers drove their herds out into the fields for feeding. The sound of soft, sleepy conversation broke out here and there; the noise of housewives' kitchen chores, the loud cry of the roosters and the barking of dogs vibrated in the bright, breezy morning.

I marvelled at the surrounding landscape struggling against the desecration of man. Developers were tearing up acres of forests but amidst the chaos and the mangled and bulldozed earth, a few ancient trees and plants – a form of life devoid of evil – survived. Not far away, coconut trees leaned over the riverbank, their delicate leaves waving like brooms, were reflected in the river that mirrored a deep blue sky, dazzling to the eye. All kinds of boats – tiny canoes and long boats; Lao passenger boats with cabins and uplifted tails propelled by women with oars or men with long bamboo poles – were bobbing about. Large steamers and Chinese junks were tearing up and down the river, while a few people were squatting beside the bushes. As I gazed from the window towards the cloudy Chaophraya river at high tide, the water faintly reflected the sky in a greenish blue, sparkling brightly like crusted diamonds. I stared in a daze to where the waters crashed and foamed against the bank. The wind had created small, undulating waves which broke along the edge of the slightly raised ground, as if the water was rising. I thought Bangkok was sinking and the flood waters would one day destroy it – an omen of grave prophecy.

By recalling the image of myself reflected in the clear, glittering Mekong, I felt as thrilled as a little boy. The sky was cloudless; on impulse I wanted to touch and stroke the water and then jump in for a swim. How odd that such experiences lodge in one's mind. I well remembered the sweet smell of the air, the taste of fresh, cold spray on my lips, the warm sun on my cheeks and the thundering of the white water rushing over the rocks.

I wiped my sticky eyelids with the back of my hand and, with half opened eyes, glared into the sunlight and tried to get Bangkok into focus. I smiled gently and spontaneously yawned. A gulp of humid air rushed in to fill my lungs, almost bursting my fully expanded chest. I thought with pleasure that it seemed a lovely day for the journey back to ViengChan, although it was to be a very long passage home. Next, I gave myself a good stretch to ease my stiffness. I touched my feet then raised both hands into the air, up then down repeatedly, until I felt my heart pumping the sleepy blood through my body, an exercise taught by my father when I was a young boy and later by Chao Anouvong during our stay at Nakhorn Phanom in 1796. I was soon awake but still felt a little tired. I sleepily undressed and went half naked into the bathroom. For some strange reason I stood in front of the mirror, staring at my own reflection. I saw so many different faces: the face of a child, a boy, a young man and a gentleman half a century old – too short for many, too slim for most and no longer much in demand sexually, all there together, preserved in superimposed layers, like fossils. I treated myself to a quick cold shower which made me shiver but was refreshingly reinvigorating. Unsurprisingly, the sticky feeling returned soon before I'd got dressed. Finally I brushed my hair and settled down on my soft rattan chair for a quiet cup of lemon tea to gather my thoughts for the day ahead. Once I was satisfied I was ready, I sipped a cool drink and thought about the interesting journey ahead. A thought struck me suddenly as a surge of energy hit my memory cells and reminded me that I needed to see whether Chao Anouvong was all right and in good spirits. I heaved myself to my feet, put on my shoes and went to him.

The door was ajar, but I gave it a gentle knock. He was writing at his desk but quickly put everything aside. He looked rather pale. After returning his morning greeting and paying him my respects, I asked if he'd slept well. 'Like a log,' he replied and sat down on his couch. No mention was ever made of what had happened the previous night. I served him a strong herbal brew with a fresh piece of lime thrown in. He screwed up his eyes to take a sip of his drink, smacking his lips in pleasure. Soon, his bleary brown eyes began to clear as he contemplated the bright sunshine of the day. His brows drew together in thought.

The privileged elite of Siam arrogantly compared the Lao to buffalo and failed to respect Chao Anouvong's unbroken royal bloodline. He was ridiculed as a mere country buffoon from the northeast, humiliated and frustrated when his pleas for his people not to be forced into manual labour had fallen on deaf ears. He was greatly upset when his son Prince Rathsavong Ngao had been forced to work as a supervisor. More humiliation followed when his requests for the return of the Emerald Buddha and to take his sister and the Lao people in Saraburi back with him had been refused. His ability to run LanXang's financial affairs had been drastically reduced by Bangkok's insistence on imposing higher taxes on the kingdom. He'd also been offended when his request for one of his female relatives to be cremated in the royal crematorium temple had been turned down. Nangklao deliberately had his dog Yaleh lavishly cremated there instead. Chao Anouvong had suffered intimidation, hostility, and humiliation while in Bangkok. It was an absurd situation.

Chao Anouvong was also affronted when told that the Lao national flower (*Dork Champa*) wasn't fit for ceremonial purposes, but only for the dead. For all their snobbery, he said, the Siamese would soon grow *Dork Champa* trees in their gardens. Whenever they sniffed at the flower, they would detect not only its unique fragrance but also the virtue of the Lao ancestors they'd so condescendingly sneered at. But it was quite remarkable how easily he could detach himself from these insults, as if they'd never happened. Outwardly, he remained calm and careful. He sometimes gave people too much respect, the late King Naphalai for example.

Nangklao's offhand treatment of Chao Anouvong and the humiliations he'd felt must have fanned the fire of his ambition. It gave him momentum. Far from deterring him, his meeting with Nangklao had convinced him he'd have to act even quicker than he thought. He used to say that simple Lao perseverance and consciousness – not genius – was the best way to achieve LanXang unification. He drank his tea contemplatively and, as the sun grew hotter, I could sense his gathering thoughts. I asked him if there was anything he required or whether there was anything I could do. He replied with a bitter smile: 'Yes, raise an army to save our nation so that we can be the rulers of our own country and live a quiet life in ViengChan!' Then he leaned back in his couch, interlocked his fingers and rested them on his chest, closed his eyes and went silent. I quietly took a sip of my drink. 'For our independence,' he muttered to himself, "for our loved ones" land, for the sacred cause of our freedom.' Suddenly remembering these were his very words from the night before, I realised he'd perhaps not been under the influence of alcohol at all; just very upset. It grieved me to see him so worn down by his troubles.

In their pettiness Bangkok insisted on referring to him as Chao ViengChan – a mere prince of ViengChan – a junior royal title. They scornfully insulted him by calling him *Ai Anou* but he secretly revelled in the name. 'The truth is, Phia Jon, we are indeed *Ai*: the elders, their ancestors,' he said. Nevertheless he'd become a peripheral figure and wasn't the honours due to him as king of a larger country than Siam in terms of area and population. It implied the demotion of LanXang from a 'fraternal state' to a mere segment of Siam.

I suspected Chao Anouvong was far from amused that his honour had been abused in Bangkok. Nevertheless, for his peace of mind, he took the insults well. He understood and toed the line. He'd already mingled with his loyal subjects in the Nakhorn Phanom, Mukdahan, Udon and Khon Kaen regions. He'd gone out of his way to be charming although at first it had felt a little strange to sit amongst the less fortunate and the uneducated poor. I'd seen his hesitation in approaching the crowd in Khorat, but he'd soon got used to it. He accepted them for what they were. He even began to enjoy the experience so much that he'd shared food with the country people, even though they'd brought something of the whiff and manners of the wilderness with them and often forgot to wash their hands before eating. He'd probably have been the same under the circumstances. Hunger robbed man of his dignity, he said.

However, he fiercely defended the dignity of his charming and beautiful queen Nang Khampong. Descended from the royal house of Nakhorn Phanom, she was kind, highly amusing and sophisticated and did much to enliven him, blunting his witticisms when they might cause offence to ministers or foreign envoys. They'd been married for over thirty years; they rarely argued and when they did, they always showed each other mutual respect. They seemed to have lived a life of unalloyed happiness. Some found her demure, even flirtatious, but to most observers, myself included, she was a shy, simple and pious person by nature who had no interest in politics or history but would say precisely what she thought. Should any man have the nerve to ask her for a simple dance, she would smile graciously and draw back in horror. 'You're drunk and I must decline,' she would normally say, drawing a whoop of laughter because the Lao in general like to celebrate and have a good time: drinking, eating, having a singalong and dancing their traditional circle dance (*Fonh Lamvong*).

Chao Anouvong reminded me that Lao identity is as old as the Ai-Lao civilisation and culture and has conferred the greatest of benefits on us. He agreed when I added there could be no greater benefit for us than the freedom to enjoy a sense of patriotism. I said it was our intention to live our lives as nobly as our ancestors. But he replied we would accomplish nothing without freedom. After independence we would soon recover from the losses of war; our influence would be felt everywhere in the kingdom for the Lao people to embrace. We'd be able to partake of a well-deserved celebratory drink. The only alternative was for the Siamese to use sophistry and claim our identity, customs and culture as their own.

I can vouch that I was very active in those days. I often lay sleepless at night, brooding bitterly that the inhabitants of a once powerful kingdom had been reduced to such circumstances: without an army, political power or wealth. Now I understood why our weaker neighbours had resented and treated us with contempt when LanXang had been united, rich and powerful (1350–1690). By contrast, Siam's access to the seas had made it wealthy and powerful. Despite not being a natural entrepreneur, the Siamese king had easily become the richest man in the kingdom and his people had become obsessed with riches and materialism. It was not in our nature to envy anyone, but we took strong exception when the Siamese became abusive. Chao Anouvong was completely dejected, his dreams of returning the people to their homeland dashed.

Admittedly I was not entirely pleased with my kingdom's feudal past but what is human life worth unless it's woven into our ancestors' lives? I wished LanXang to rise again and I knew Chao Anouvong would use all his intelligence and resources to free his people. His patience had snapped and he was no longer interested in wasting his time in mingling and lobbying in the snobbish and unfriendly corridors of power in Bangkok. He found it demeaning. He believed the status quo was unjust and was determined to deliver change.

Without a doubt, Bangkok had shown him little or no respect. Nangklao's cronies had been conditioned to think of Chao Anouvong as a rotter or a downright opportunist. He was ignored or even downright teased by the most minor Siamese royals. They referred to him as the 'son of sticky rice' and a 'smelly *Padaek* eater'. A triviality, you might think, but Chao Anouvong claimed this was the moment his ambition hardened and took shape. His Lao pride was hurt because of his smallness in the eyes of the Rattanakosins. His responsibility – to protect the Lao nation – was onerous indeed.

Chao Anouvong realised that Bangkok's expansionist policies would persist as long as the Rattanakosins were in power. He'd no other option but to appeal directly to the Lao diaspora in Bangkok, Saraburi and the other cities in Siam scarred by the 1779 invasion and resentful at their exile from ViengChan. They were being oppressed and wished to return home. He was certain the Lao population throughout the Khorat Plateau, as well as in the north of Siam, would support him.

Bangkok's behaviour had destroyed the special relationship. No genuine 'Love and Friendship' would be achieved or maintained unless both kingdoms respected the promise – the sworn words (*Khaom Sabanh*) – made at the 1563 treaty at the That Si-SongHuck shrine. But the Siamese had broken their oath by invading ViengChan: a serious breach of trust and a total disgrace.

Before leaving Bangkok, Chao Anouvong wanted to pay homage to the Emerald Buddha. I wished it even more than he because I'd never seen it before. The Emerald Buddha and the golden Phrabang Buddha are the most revered of all holy artefacts and it's the dearest wish of every pious Lao to see them at least once in their lives. On the eve of our departure we tried our luck and made a discreet journey to the temple inside the palace grounds, which were encircled with armed soldiers in colourful uniforms, standing motionless and keeping a sharp lookout. When we reached the perimeter wall in the late afternoon, we weren't allowed into the Emerald Buddha chapel. Chao Anouvong was highly offended that none of the guards had heard of him, even though he grew up in Bangkok. I suspected they were just carrying out their orders and pretending not to know him. Well, let's be honest, no looter would want his loot spotted by its original owner. I'm not sure whether they were conspiring to pervert the course of justice or just being petty and difficult. Nevertheless we were determined to see it. I shamelessly approached another guard standing further away. I stepped forward to within touching distance, smiled and introduced myself in clear, polite Lao.

'*Nong Sai* (younger brother), sorry to bother you. We've come from far away in ViengChan; please do let us in to pay our respects and pray,' I pleaded sycophantically, 'and we'll be quick.'

The guard fell back a few steps and looked at us in surprise, his head tilting a little. He hesitated for a moment and then spoke in a strong ViengChan accent. 'I'm not supposed to, but you both seem all right. Of course you can go in.' He lowered his head in reverence and told us his father was from Nakhorn Phanom and his mother from Udon. 'I'm Lao. We're the same. Please be quick,' he whispered and rushed us in through the gate. We were lucky.

'Delighted to hear it but please don't forget your roots,' I said and thanked him as we walked into the courtyard, which was paved with white stone slabs.

'No. I won't forget. My grandparents told me not to,' he said defiantly.

We exchanged smiles and, without speaking, he put out his hand to help Chao Anouvong. As we scrambled up the few steps through the archway towards the entrance door with its gilded hinges I turned to whisper my thanks again and revealed our true identity.

'No need to thank me,' he said. His eyes gleamed in the shade. 'My respects. It's my duty and an honour,' he added and smiled broadly at us.

Chao Anouvong thanked him fulsomely before climbing the few steps towards the door of the prayer hall. I quickly followed him for I could hear loud voices approaching. With my heart racing, I turned round and looked at the guard. He put his finger to his lips and carefully tiptoed away. We stepped inside as the guard's footsteps faded. Then, we were alone.

To begin with, we were half blind. When my eyes had grown accustomed to the darkness I looked towards the Emerald Buddha, one of the spoils of

Siam, in admiration and awe. I could hardly conceal my delight. We gradually became used to the weak glow of the beeswax candlelight on the floor just in front of and immediately below the idol. Once we were inside, as a special sign of respect, Chao Anouvong knelt down and reverently crawled forward on his hands and knees. He sat down as close as possible to the Buddha statue, at the base of a pyramid decorated with dazzling trees of offerings made from silver and gold. I followed but kept my distance and sat with folded legs close to his side, occasionally glancing at him as he went through the rituals. Holding flowers and candles in a folded banana leaf, he made three deep obeisances to the green idol before lighting a candle. He then prostrated himself and prayed. I did the same, praying for a safe journey back to ViengChan and for all Chao Anouvong's wishes to come true. He lifted his hands in prayer and slowly looked up to see the Emerald Buddha in its golden summer costume, sitting atop the pyramid high above in the shadows of the lofty roof. My eyes began to moisten with tears when I saw his sad face, presumably wishing the statue was back in ViengChan.

I also lifted my hands in silent prayer to Lord Buddha and gazed at the revered, shiny-green figure, its diamond eyes sparkling in the dim light. 'Hear me, you who exist for ever as the unsleeping sacred idol, once happily housed in the Royal Chapel in ViengChan, respected and worshipped by the Lao people. You embody the heart of Lao LanXang. I burn a pure beeswax candle to honour you in this hall. Remember this offering and see how these Bangkok looters and tyrants have chained you up mercilessly to prevent you from returning home. They're besieging LanXang and thwarting our desire for independence at every opportunity. Please remember: your beautiful home in ViengChan awaits your return always.'

We continued to pray in silence, meditating and humming in sorrow at being so close to what had once been the treasure and protector of the Lao nation. I felt sad and resentful to see this wonderful object that had been in Viengchan until 1779. Chao Anouvong must have heard me swallowing a sob. The scent from the burning candles and sandalwood joss sticks wafted high across the face of the sacred green idol.

One wonders how the Rattanakosins had the nerve to claim the Buddha was Siamese. Surely deep down they knew the truth and felt guilty every time they changed the idol's golden dress. Nangklao had a passion for collecting bronze Buddha statues. Although he performed the rituals of kingship by placing

Buddha statues cast in the image of his grandfather and father beside the Emerald Buddha, he clearly didn't deserve the worshippers' prayers. Indeed, it became fashionable for sceptics to explain away his supposed divinity as merely a trick designed to impress the people.

When we solemnly left and were outside, Chao Anouvong reached into his trouser pocket and pulled out his soft white handkerchief to wipe his forehead and lips. I thought to myself that he too must have shed some tears. He told me later that tears were futile; like all Lao people he was sure that the Emerald Buddha, along with all the other looted treasures, would one day be returned to their rightful places. Saddened, we returned to our base before sunset.

During that last hot humid evening, even hotter than usual, we slipped through the gate unseen and went down to the banks of the Chaophraya river where we strolled along the path to catch the breeze. We could see the flickering lights from Wat Arun temple on the opposite bank. We stopped at a quiet spot where we stood for a time, smelling the breezes and looking at the moonlight striking the water. We turned to the sound of merry *Khaen* music brought to us by the wind from far away, along with the pungent smell of grilled meat and fish. In silence, I felt homesick and wanted to cry. I raised my eyes to the heavens to the northeast, watching the night sky filling with stars. I felt enormously fortunate when I saw shooting stars streaking across the sky. Chao Anouvong saw them too but was absorbed in thought; when he turned toward me, he'd changed. I don't exaggerate. I saw it in his eyes. His face glowed in the dim light and his expression seemed to say that the Rattanakosins could frolic, scold, humiliate and laugh at us until they ran out of air. Suddenly he said, 'Come, Phia Jon, time waits for no man. We have work to do.' I quickened my step to follow him back along the moonlit path, escaping from the whining insects and the moral darkness of a society governed by a lying boaster with no regard for the truth or idea how to run a country.

This experience, I'm inclined to say, was more valuable to me than if I'd been promoted to the rank of *Phraya* (Lord). Besides, I favoured human decency and respectability and firmly believed in the permanence of human relationships. From that day I made sure I was with Chao Anouvong every day: neither the palace doorkeeper, or his jealous relatives, nor my own sleep prevented me from seeing him and caring for him. I wanted him to triumph and was determined to play my part. I felt as strongly as he did. His dream had rooted itself in me. For the glory of the Lao nation and the unity of the LanXang kingdom, I wanted him to succeed more than anything else, but we were fighting against time. We forgot that leisure time even existed.

Each year in Lao LanXang, as in other Asian nations, is reckoned by the lunar calendar and has two names: one derived from an animal and the other from an element. The New Year festival (three days in the second week of April) is the greatest event of the year. Colourful bamboo flags on leaning bamboo poles are hoisted onto every temple. Religious texts are solemnly recited. The people bring offerings to the temple and worshippers reverently perform obeisance before the Buddha statues. Rich and poor alike, full of devotion and without misgivings lay their offerings before the gods and pray for their blessing. Although in Buddhism it is almost impossible to unravel the mysteries of life through meditation alone, it does at least allow you to contemplate the events of life with tranquillity rather than letting yourself be flung back and forth by circumstances in a world of doubt and chaos.

The journey back to ViengChan was memorable and significant. Chao Anouvong purposely delayed it by about a month, from March to April, to ensure we passed through as many cities as possible in the Khorat region during the Lao New Year (*Pi Mai Lao*) and the Rocket Festival (*Boun BangFai*). At this time all the smart *Chaomueangs* (chiefs), noblemen and important dignitaries were present, enjoying the festivities of the New Year and calling for rain to replenish the land.

Pi Mai is a major annual three-day-long festival to mark the passing of the old year and welcome in the new. On the first day of the New Year – which is also the last day of the old – houses are cleaned, and Buddha statues are brought out from their altars in houses and temples to be washed with flower-scented water to expel evils from the old year and gain merit for the new one ahead. The second day is a rest day for the elderly but of entertainment for the young, who participate high spiritedly in singing, dancing and water-throwing. The third day is New Year's Day, when the population gives alms to the monks in the temples to gain merit and pray for their future well-being. In the evening they pay ritual homage (*somma*) to parents and older relatives as a way of reaffirming and consolidating family ties.

Chao Anouvong objected to the unfairness of the fifty-year Siamese domination over LanXang and LanNa. The Bangkok establishment had become egotistical. He bemoaned their political arrogance; they seemed to care only for the customs of their own kingdom. It was so insulting when they called the Lao uncivilised. While everyone in LanNa and LanXang wanted to live in peace, Bangkok secretly pursued yet more territory with its repressive policies. Nangklao ensured there would be no punishment for the monsters Phromphakdy and Suriyaphakdy. When I remarked we lacked the power to stop their crimes, Chao Anouvong recovered his old fight. Nothing roused him more than the thought of standing up to Bangkok's unholy policies. If we lost then at least we would have gone down with a fight, he would say. He often stayed up late thinking how best to deliver results. Bangkok was not the place for a peaceful sleep. While the world slept under a dark sky of tropical heat he paced around, gazing through the windows at the white moon and the stars and wondering what made him care so much in the first place. Sometimes he was too exhausted and anxious to think but gradually his plan became clearer. Only then would he release me, shattered, to get some sleep. I think it was still some time before he saw his own bed.

At dawn Chao Anouvong, like myself, washed in cold water to revive himself and dressed carefully. When I went to him just before we set off on our journey he was as restless and anxious as a top kickboxer (*Muay Lao*), limbering up and raring to go. Suddenly he picked up his war sword. I pulled back and stood well out of the way with my back flat against the wall, my heart thumping. I was petrified at the sight of the naked sword, worried he might use me as a target. He stood motionless, composing himself and flushed with concentration. After a short pause he started to swing the shiny, sharp blade, dancing to the art of sword fighting. His movements became ever more violent. He yelled to the sound of every swing and stab as the sword cut though the still air. Then he brought himself to a standstill by stabbing the point of the sword into the floor. I heaved a sigh of relief and walked towards him cautiously, trying to conceal my anxiety. He could be very playful sometimes.

'We must be on our guard, Phia Jon,' he said, wiping the sweat from his forehead.

'Yes, indeed, Your Majesty. Our safety is in our own hands,' I said and fetched him a small towel.

While he was getting ready, I slipped back to my room. I was on the veranda looking at Bangkok for the last time when I noticed a horse-drawn carriage, accompanied by two horsemen fore and aft, appearing around the corner along the lane. My immediate thought was that Nangklao had come to arrest us.

I hurried back to alert Chao Anouvong, who was putting on his shoes when I found him. We looked at each other nervously at the sound of the horses outside. We rushed to the window and the horsemen were already clattering outside our door. They dismounted and opened the carriage door. He smiled with joy and hastened to make himself look presentable.

His sister, Princess KaeoYhodFah Kanlayani, known to him privately and lovingly as 'Kieokhom', had come to say goodbye. Leaving her attendants outside in the street she came inside to see us alone. She was slim and tall and her face embodied all the traditional Lao qualities of decency and honour. Despite her sadness, she looked beautiful and virtuous with her clear forehead and long brows arching over brilliant brown eyes. She always liked to look her best. She was wearing the formal Lao LanXang dress of flat golden shoes, long brocaded red silk skirt (*sinh*) embroidered with a dragon pattern in neat gold thread and a splendid gold belt around her slim waist. Her double-breasted flower-patterned high neckband and elbow-length cream silk shirt was matched with a long gold chain on top of a woven red shawl (*pha biaeng*) draped slantwise over her left shoulder. Her dress accentuated her fair skin. Her long black hair had been skilfully arranged into a pointed bun surmounted by a gold hairpin, wound around with a chain of gold beads and a gold chain. She wore gold necklaces and gold bead chains around her long, slender neck and delicate gold earrings which made her look taller. She looked like a figure from mythology and was amazingly adorable, truly a pearl of light. I was mesmerised by her beauty – a beauty she seemed completely unaware of.

Chao Anouvong, whose manners were reserved as always, was overjoyed and dashed downstairs. I followed. He made straight for her and threw his gentle arms around her, hugging her tenderly. Eventually he reluctantly broke the embrace and gave her a clean white handkerchief to wipe her running tears. He ushered her to a soft chair in the sitting room. When he questioned her, she avoided his eye and turned away. One could see she was in a state of despair; she felt repulsion rather than honour or lust towards the Siamese king and all she wanted to do was run away. But what could she do, as a woman? Not even Chao Anouvong, for all his brotherly perception, could do anything. I was instructed to pour some tea.

'My darling sister, I'm so sorry,' I heard him whisper as I made my way to the tea tray.

'Please don't worry,' she said between sobs. 'I cannot stay long. I have strict orders to be back at the palace within the hour. The guards outside warned me not to be late.' There was a short pause, and then she said, 'Please give my love to everyone in ViengChan.'

I obediently went off to fetch the tea and didn't look back. After bustling around I eagerly returned with the drink. I placed a small cup of fresh ginger and mint tea with a thin piece of lime on a small, low table next to her, but not a drop, I noticed, touched her soft, kind lips. She stayed with him as long as she could to offer her support and say a last farewell. I suspected she knew she might not live long enough to ever see him or attend the traditional prayers at the That Luang and That Phanom stupas again. She didn't linger long as she'd strict orders to be escorted back to the palace. She made no attempt to conceal her emotions. I saw her red, sad eyes and the tears running down her soft white cheeks as she rose from her seat to go. After a brief parting embrace, she sobbingly bade farewell to Chao Anouvong and left quickly. We followed her out and he momentarily held on to the carriage's door as it pulled away. It was a very sad moment for all of us. I shared their pain.

We rushed upstairs and he stuck his head out of the windows, raised his hand, called farewell to her and waved to the moving carriage. She didn't look back but waved her delicate hand, still holding his handkerchief, out of the carriage window in valediction. He stood in silence for a while and listened to the sound of the trotting horses fading into the distance. He was as controlled and calm as anyone could be in the heat of Bangkok, but at that moment he simply couldn't work out what sort of man Nangklao was. He came hoping to be rewarded with fraternal friendship and kindness but instead found himself torn to pieces in humiliation. He took a deep breath and then turned his thoughts to our departure.

All kinds of rumours were circulating, including that Princess Kanlayani was happy and had become popular, which I found difficult to believe. I was certain that she was being held against her will. Forced to join Nangklao's harem, her royal Lao blood inevitably spread throughout the Siamese court.

'Let's go, Phia Jon,' he announced impatiently. 'Any delay might lead to complications. I can't stand this place any longer. We need pure air and fresh streams to wash away the dirt of Siamese politics. We must get back to our more straightforward, minimalistic world.'

I too had had more than enough of smelly Bangkok and seedy Siam. I wanted to go back to the fresh, clean air of ViengChan and live a healthy life in austere simplicity. For me it was a virtue to drift away from the world in search of privacy. ViengChan was more than world enough for me. I could feed the fish in the pond and the chickens and ducks in the barns and tend to the vegetable and herb gardens while listening to the tinkle of the bells on the buffaloes', goats' and cows' necks as they grazed in the fields. I could go into the forest searching for wild mushrooms, edible berries and sweet young bamboo shoots; checking my traps, listening to the harmonious birdsong under the cool shade of giant trees, fishing and swimming in the crystal-clear rivers and lakes and then returning home to watch the setting sun while having a jolly, simple dinner amongst dear friends before retiring to a comfortable bed.

Our departure brought about a change in our circumstances. Hard-faced security men dressed in threatening dark uniforms, looking more like professional assassins or released prisoners than well-trained officers, escorted us when we left our residence. They'd probably been picked for their strength and easy cruelty. We didn't care for them at all.

An immense throng of local people, mostly of Lao origin, had already gathered. The cramped courtyard was packed by this time and Chao Anouvong's appearance brought a loud cheer. He waved to the noisy crowd of well-wishers from the stairway as we slowly descended to greet them; many of them had been waiting to see him off since dawn. The noise grew and the crowd cheered, although he seemed very preoccupied. He looked oddly nervous and told me to be on my guard. Naturally, my first concern was for his safety. Despite my fears I acted as his bodyguard, watching out for danger. Without telling him I'd persuaded six strong local pro-Lao men to act not only as a human shield, three on each side, but also as a deterrent to any assassin. Tightly escorted, we slowly made our way. At the extraordinary spectacle of jostling and cheering supporters, Chao Anouvong soon relaxed. He showed remarkable powers of recuperation, a sure sign of fortitude and endurance. Watching him come down the stairs in a freshly laundered white shirt, his face washed and shaved, his moustache trimmed, his hair combed and scented, no one would have guessed he'd hardly slept. He carried himself well, a very handsome man in his Lao clothes, the image of a smooth Lao aristocrat with a free and easy manner and a firm step.

I instructed the security officers to be a little more polite and to go easy on the crowd. They would obey for a while but soon slipped back into their usual rough ways. They rather looked down on Chao Anouvong as a mere vassal head of state and probably saw him as a temporary ruler, here today and gone tomorrow. I watched in horrified awe as our struggling, elderly supporters were harshly pushed out of the way. When I begged the security officers to desist, they just glared at me. We hated it but there was nothing we could do. The oppressive heat, the contorted faces of the crowds lining the streets and the stinking air made a powerful impression on me.

'These Siamese officials,' Chao Anouvong warned me afterwards, 'show what would happen to our country if they were in charge. They would soon see themselves as our masters. They would make us second-class citizens.'

The day was getting hot. He walked purposefully, occasionally raising his hand in greeting and holding his head high down an avenue of people who were laying colourful flowers in his path. He glanced around, nodding from side to side at the watchful crowd as though trying to spot an assassin. Suddenly, to everyone's delight, he grabbed hold of a pretty baby boy and lifted the infant up; he looked at him tenderly and hugged and tickled him gently before returning him to his adoring mother. There was plenty of happy laughter and tremendously loud cheers. The infant started crying as we made our way through the crowd towards the waiting transport. I was immensely impressed but it seemed he couldn't wait to get out of Bangkok.

Chao Anouvong was primed for the journey, playing the true patriot, armed only with his conviction and his voice; confronting the most despicable crimes committed by Siamese officials in his kingdom. The crowd quickly swelled in number and by the time we reached our elephants, a few thousand were there to see us off.

I looked back and there it was: the Rattanakosin Island fortress, the imposing Grand Palace, the colourful multi-tiered temple roofs and golden spires, sparkling under the white sky. I turned to the northeast and shut my eyes from the bright sun. Even now I can see the crowd's unhappy faces in the late morning light. Some of them seemed astonishingly sad; they'd accompanied Chao Anouvong from ViengChan, and we were now leaving them behind. Chao Anouvong ascended the elephant howdah with a happy heart; there he sat, never closing his eyes in sleep but keeping them fixed on the route ahead or looking out for friendly crowds.

We were looking forward to returning to our home, a land of peace and beauty and were beginning our journey in a state of euphoric freedom and happiness. The moment we passed through the city gate and were on our way we breathed a sigh of relief. Our spirits were up. Chao Anouvong warned me they might still try to assassinate him. A few days earlier, during the meeting, his life had been in the palm of Nangklao's hand; he could have crushed it like an egg. I could feel my heart thumping for I knew we weren't yet out of danger and had to be even more vigilant. Suddenly he looked back in anger and bitterness and let Nangklao have a piece of his mind. He struck his right fist into his left palm and let out a cry of frustration.

'Nangklao, you tyrant… you criminal blackmailer,' he said aloud, shaking his head in frustration, 'who thinks he's a god amongst men.'

We made drink offerings and poured libations from our howdah to our ancestors and the gods for a safe journey. We moved on with heavy hearts, for the joy we felt at our departure was tempered by grief for the compatriots we'd left behind.

Although Nangklao saw himself as above politics, he was rolling around in the muck as much as the rest of them. By indulging in the crude business of politics, they'd succumbed to corruption, learning from the notoriously venal overseas traders. Chao Anouvong stressed that the Rattanakosin administration must recognise that the continued occupation of Lao LanNa and LanXang was counterproductive to peace and security. An independent LanXang kingdom had been enshrined under the 1563 That Si-SongHuck shrine demarcation treaty. The Lao people must have the right to freedom in their own land and the Siamese people should deplore the Rattanakosins' shameful policies that deprived the Lao of their fundamental rights.

'What do you make of Nangklao?' he asked me abruptly when my elephant was alongside his. I replied noncommittally that he seemed an undesirable and untrustworthy character, a complex personality with a ruthless ambition for power and wealth. I added that I couldn't fathom why he didn't look much like an aristocrat at close quarters even though his golden clothes had been specially made for him. 'He certainly didn't behave like one. He is very cunning though and always seeks to dominate,' said Chao Anouvong. He thought a number of consequences had arisen from the meeting: Bangkok had been forced to reassess its policy towards LanXang and the Siamese elite had been forced to reconsider their moral authority. 'Political domination using manipulation and trickery is a major aspect of the Rattanakosins' make up,' he continued. 'Nangklao's authoritarian regime allows him to command his little world on Rattanakosin Island. He persistently and ruthlessly bends other people to his will, as if he has a constant need to impress and to always be the centre of attention. He's always looking to exploit other people's weaknesses to achieve his own ends. There were times during the meeting when he not only seemed to want our support, our allegiance and our loyalty but, more than that, I think he wants to absorb all Lao people into his Siamese kingdom. Bangkok will always be after more power, always itching to enforce its superiority over others.'

He looked away, full of thought, and went quiet for a while. I knew what he was thinking. Concerned, I asked, 'What if it really happens?'

He turned round and gazed at me. 'Phia Jon,' he said, lowering his eyes, 'we know that the ultimate purpose of the 1779 invasion was the complete annexation of our kingdom. They wanted to swallow us whole. I only want to save our people from misery and keep our Lao nation alive, but we don't have much power at our disposal.'

'May I tell you what I think?' I said eagerly, for I thought I'd perceived something.

'Please speak. It might cheer me up,' he said after I'd joined him on his howdah.

'Your Majesty, we pursue benevolence and morality,' I said, staring ahead and holding onto my seat. 'That's the difference between the peace-loving Lao and the villainous Rattanakosin Siamese.'

'Quite so,' he said, looking sideways at me.

'Since they disagree with us, the only way forward is for us to do what we think is right,' I continued. 'We're the masters of our own souls. LanXang has been in chaos since 1779. Our culture is withering away and our people live in fear. We may suffer beyond endurance, but we'll never yield. We'll never give in.' I took a deep breath and continued. 'You represent the ruling family of Lao LanXang. As a scion of the ViengChan LanXang rulers, you have a mandate to uphold the honour of the Lao. I know your heart pains you every time you gaze across the Mekong to the southwest, as does mine and the hearts of all Lao people. But pain often leads to inspiration. You're in distress, but even if heaven and earth collapse, we would never even think of surrendering.'

He nodded, thinking silently.

'LanXang has existed for over 1,000 years,' I went on. 'For the greater good we prefer peace, out of concern for our people and out of loyalty to and consideration for the lasting survival of our country. We never intimidate the weak, nor are we afraid of death. Peace ensures preservation whereas war leads to destruction. We hold a great ambition in our hearts: the revival of the Lao nation. We yearn for unity. However, if we want to release LanXang from Siam's yoke and let our names live on in history, we need an enlightened ruler to win the people's hearts and trust. We must ally with Lao LanNa and others to hold Siam at bay. We must adopt a strategy of patience. We must devise a plan to repel the Siamese and achieve LanXang unification in gradual steps. We may be heavily outnumbered in men and firepower, but we can overcome this disadvantage and defeat the many with the few. We must also cement diplomatic relations with all our friendly neighbouring countries, including faraway Malaya, although they'll probably only offer moral support. Equally, they might well help us to restore LanXang and save us from destruction.'

'Rightly so. A friend in need is a friend indeed,' he interjected, adding in despair that although neighbouring countries tended to take advantage of LanXang's weakness, friendly relations with all the nations under heaven would indeed be beneficial. Gazing at me he said, 'Whether we like it or not, the Siamese want to eat us up. That is the real problem.'

'The Khorat Plateau,' I continued, 'is vast, accessible and strategically important to us, a land of abundance and critical to the Lao population. It mustn't be ceded to Siam. LanXang would be desperately weak without it. We know that anyone who strives against Bangkok faces death but because of bribery and corruption, some of our feudal lords and educated elite – even some of the common folk in the region – have become docile and incompetent. Some have even adopted Siamese names and customs and no longer have the courage to proclaim they're Lao. They've lost their confidence and lack leadership. They cover their eyes and ears, pretending not to see or hear anything. Their morale has been truly shaken. They have no stomach for a fight.'

He listened with intense concentration.

'Nevertheless,' I pressed on, 'it is true that those who dwell in LanXang and LanNa and in many parts of Siam are Lao people who share the same language, customs and culture. In the face of such misery they'll turn to their closest family. Loyalty is the most basic principle for everyone living in this world. We've always been committed to caring for people and this could earn us the dedication of the entire Lao nation. We must educate them and seek the learned men of the land. If we abandon them we'll live on only in disgrace. I do believe our best days are ahead of us, but I won't pretend it'll be easy for us to unite LanXang. Disunity is as much a danger as losing in battle. If

Luang Phrabang favours submission to Siam and ViengChan favours war, then our country will remain divided. We must persuade Luang Phrabang to unite with us; we must also be of one heart and one mind with LanNa. With the people's support, LanXang on both banks of the Mekong will come together eventually. Perhaps it could even exist as separate entities, east and west. Who knows? Our success or failure will depend on them. If we can secure their trust we'll be able to forge an alliance with the LanNa princes and repel Bangkok. There is no other way for the two kingdoms to survive. It's only a matter of time before both are subjugated by Siam. Winning people's hearts and minds is therefore vital to our cause: as important as self-preservation, in fact. The situation will change rapidly and we must be able to react and adjust accordingly. Under heaven an opportunity will come to lead an expedition to seize the Khorat Plateau. We will be victorious and vanquish the tyrants of Bangkok; the Lao will rise again. If we follow our plans carefully, we might be able to succeed in our greatest endeavour: the unification of Lao LanXang. And of course the people of LanNa can do what they like: join with us or be independent.'

I paused and waited for him to share his thoughts and feelings.

'Phia Jon, what you have said is very sound and shows remarkable foresight. Your words are truly enlightening. I will forever respect you as my boon companion and friend.' He paused and, his spirits somewhat revived, continued. 'My one desire in life is to save our Lao nation. If I succeed, I will die without regret. We must be able to achieve our sovereignty through peaceful means. Let's hope we're worthy of heaven's command. Perhaps heaven won't agree with us. Perhaps we won't live to see a united Lao. It's so sad that the very people we love most – the Siamese – seek our destruction.'

He paused again, slowly shutting his eyes as if seeing ViengChan in ruins, its streets strewn with dead bodies, the Mother Mekong red with blood. 'The Rattanakosins are simply greedy and blatantly disregard the rights and well-being of others. Everything is possible in politics, but Bangkok would be insane to give up the name "Siam". Any fancy name they invent for their country – born of breathtaking selfishness and arrogance – would be a fraud. It would be a lament upon every wise man's lip because LanXang and LanNa have never been part of Siam. It would be sheer folly to even make such an attempt. The nation would exist in name only and the Lao population would be subservient to Siamese interests. It's essential our Emerald Buddha is returned to us and not a parcel of Lao land should be stolen. Otherwise, resentment will increase and a Siamese revolution would become inevitable. Lao LanNa and LanXang would want to break away. There'd be chaos!'

I could see he wasn't joking. He may have been right, I fear, for he stressed that things in the north and northeast or even in the south of Siam would always feel different. He understood exactly what it meant. I remarked that Siam's opportunism had contributed to the weakening of LanNa and LanXang. I began to fear that war was inevitable.

Chao Anouvong said that King Uthong had sought to expand Ayutthaya by trying to subjugate the northern kingdoms of Sukhotai and LanNa. The third Ayutthaya king, Borommaracha, continued this expansionist policy in 1371. LanNa and LanXang had been at war with Siam since 1775 and 1779 respectively and this would continue until justice was done. Both kingdoms were fighting for their freedom. Lao LanXang – the larger of the two – was struggling to protect itself from odious tyranny and to expel the oppressors from its territory. The Lao Xieng saw XiengMai LanNa as the centre of their culture, but for the Lao Vieng people in the Khorat Plateau (and in Siam itself), it would always be ViengChan. The struggle would continue until the Lao gained independence from Bangkok but no matter what happened, the Lao would always see the Siamese as their brothers. By contrast, the Siamese would always think the Lao dirty rustics, even idiots. This would sadden Lord Buddha and the gods because both peoples were descended from legendary Khoun Borom of the Ai-Lao race. Plainly speaking, the Siamese were descended from the Lao, not the other way round. The Tai race simply doesn't exist. But wealth and material possessions had made the Siamese arrogant and snobbish.

The Lao dwelled in the LanNa and LanXang kingdoms with the mighty Mekong flowing through the middle – Lao space – while the Siamese lived in the kingdom of Siam on the central plain of the Chaophraya river – Siamese space. There have always been three separate kingdoms.

XII

Hopeful Return

That was the end of our stay in Bangkok, Krung Thep – the City of Angels. We went, we saw, we (I) did not want to stay, or to conquer it as Phra Ajarn Khoon had suggested. We just wanted our land and independence back. Nangklao, I'm sure, would have liked to have locked Chao Anouvong up, or at least prevented him from returning to ViengChan. Fortunately we didn't have to activate the hazardous emergency escape plan we'd drawn up before leaving ViengChan. Our people were meticulously briefed on the details, such as the rendezvous point in the north-east corner of Bangkok and the route for escaping back to the Mekong. The great weight of responsibility had made me nervously bite my fingernails down to the quick. The plan had remained primed and we were ready to trigger it as a last resort.

As the ruler of ViengChan LanXang, Chao Anouvong had attended King Naphalai's funeral out of personal respect and to show support but Nangklao persisted in viewing him as a threat. Despite the difficult meeting, however, he'd the right to return to ViengChan. Nangklao's real intention was to use the Burmese to eliminate him – going to LanNa and dying in battle against them was a better plan than retaining him in Bangkok. Besides, Nangklao clearly needed Chao Anouvong's bravery and experience to win the war and then claim it as his own triumph. Chao Anouvong himself believed that Nangklao wouldn't have allowed him to leave Bangkok had it not been for his usefulness and ability to fight the war on Siam's behalf. However, he now had plenty of followers amongst both the Siamese and Lao communities in Bangkok. If he'd been seized, it would have caused further tension.

In a show of strength Chao Anouvong had requested leave to travel on the finest gilded howdah carried by the finest bull elephant so he could enter every city on the journey in style. When we were completely out of Bangkok's perimeter, we made a brief stop to change his howdah. He defiantly put on a pair of gold-edged shoes with slightly turned-up pointed toes, a decorated cream silk jacket and dark blue trousers (*Phahthong*). He was hesitant about my advice to be careful with political rhetoric and not to wear anything too elaborate on his head in case it further upset Bangkok.

'Nonsense, Phia Jon,' he retorted. 'We may be a vassal state of Siam but when travelling in our own country we're entitled to say what we want and wear a real crown if we so wish.'

'Your Majesty, you're the true king of Lao LanXang and you should let the people see what you really look like,' I reasoned, reminding him that he didn't really exist until his people had seen him in the flesh and heard what he had to say. 'Besides, it'll be too hot to wear a crown.'

'Very well, Phia Jon, if you say so,' he agreed reluctantly, complaining that I was right as usual. I heaved a sigh of relief, smiling to myself.

Shaded by a large white parasol (*Homkao*) as a symbol of the peaceful Lao kingdom of LanXang, he rode in an open elephant howdah on the back of a massive, strong young bull with frighteningly long pointed white tusks and a powerful trunk that gave a gentle trumpeting sound. Its head was covered with red and gold silk tapestry tapering down towards its trunk, which was draped in red flowers to ward off evil. The mahout wearing his red headdress sat on its neck. The beast was well trained and well controlled. Should it disobey, the sharp pointed ankus would fall gently on its head. It would give an ear-shattering trumpet in objection. I shared the poor creature's suffering.

How important is appearance in political campaigning and how superbly Chao Anouvong had been fashioned by nature to possess a look of greatness! As his kingly figure riding high on the plodding giant elephant came into view, Lao followers and well-wishers lining the routes gave him the most tremendous cheer. The mahout steadied the elephant and Chao Anouvong sat there as solid as a full-grown bull elephant himself. His round, strong head tilted back a little on his broad shoulders as he smilingly looked down on the upturned faces to acknowledge the applause.

I was given a smaller bull elephant to ride. I stayed closely behind but occasionally came alongside him to chat and receive orders. The journey was a torment. Even reading was impossible, let alone writing, eating and drinking in that rattling, swaying, and lurching rattan seat, high above the ground. I don't have a head for heights and as with the earlier journey I felt very sick at first. But what a glorious stirring sight! Oh my! Oh my! It was the only way to travel. It was blissful to be leaving Bangkok and a bonus not having to walk. Nevertheless, I managed a few rudimentary jottings.

Chao Anouvong needed money for the expedition. Bangkok had prevented him from making much income, even in the form of donations from the Lao community and his supporters: any type of direct contribution was prohibited. So he'd no ready cash for presents to show his kindness and gain him more support. His allowance from Siam was never enough and he objected to this kind of treatment because it was designed to humiliate him. It was the beginning of his increasing preoccupation with money, a subject that had never previously interested him in the least. He was beholden to the powerful man of Bangkok – a most unwelcome obligation – and he wanted rid of it.

The root of the problem was that Bangkok was not only unjust but also hungry for wealth and power, its ruler wanting to be the richest of them all. The regime there was worthy of contempt because it had set Siam at odds with its neighbouring states. It was unbelievable that they could pass such cruel decrees harming other human beings just for the sake of a Greater Siam; in doing so, they would become enemies of the gods, the Lord Buddha and all just men. Nangklao himself liked to extravagantly reward support and loyalty but fiercely punish any opposition, as if he intended to live in a bygone age by repressing his subjects. He demonstrated his enmity towards Chao Anouvong by cutting him dead in public and bad-mouthing him behind his back. I thought that if Chao Anouvong had been more submissive Nangklao might have shown more sympathy during their meeting, but my master thought this most unlikely.

Unfortunately, as I mentioned before, the two men found it difficult even to be together in the same room. The rivalry between them was to harm the two kingdoms for a generation, the inhabitants of the Khorat Plateau in particular. Chao Anouvong pointed out that injustice caused people to quarrel and hate each other, but Bangkok, out of spite, did nothing to prevent it. It was a most disturbing situation.

It was clear that the Rattanakosins had Chao Anouvong and the Lao people exactly where they wanted them. The rich were getting richer, but the rural poor were getting poorer, tortured by a burning sense of alienation from a system that enriched only a small minority in Bangkok but ensured a lifetime of poverty for the rest of Siam. It was an inequitable distribution at best. Bangkok's miserliness made things much worse in the vassal states of LanXang and LanNa. Even the well-educated Siamese elite who had a chance of a decent life were getting fed up. The great mass of people, especially the children, were kept in ignorance: their only education, the Siamese culture of indoctrination. They were taught only a gilded version of Siamese history; they didn't even know that the territories in the north and northeast of Siam were in fact two separate states.

Before our convoy reached the town of Saraburi north of Bangkok two days later, Chao Anouvong exultantly told me he had a few gifts to hand out, albeit less generous than he would have liked: his allowance from Bangkok was too miserly. The high spirits that had sustained him all the way from the Siamese capital seemed to have visibly deflated. He'd hoped to meet his people on the way and readily hand out gifts to show his generosity, but it was impossible with Nangklao in charge of the purse strings. He didn't want to waste time or cause trouble discussing money and had no choice but to make do with what he had.

When we arrived in Saraburi on the Lao New Year's Eve, a large crowd was waiting. Chao Anouvong excitedly stepped down from his elephant. We met with Lao families who had been exiled from ViengChan during the 1779 invasion or in the years afterwards. Most of them were out bartering or buying provisions for the New Year. He happily talked to them in plain Lao, straight from the heart. The crowd gave a patriotic whoop and nostalgia took over. It was as if their wishes of returning home had come true. He looked reborn and basked in the cheering and smiling crowds. He abandoned the obscure, high-pitched, pretentious accent of Siam for his simple deep-timbred Lao voice as he handed out gifts to the city officials and nobilities that he'd instructed the servants to purchase in Bangkok. I followed and kept a close watch.

'Happy Lao New Year! (*Sabaidee Pi Mai*) It's from the heart, it's nothing much but it's from the heart,' he said to the kneeling crowd.

'*Sabaidee Pi Mai*, Chao Anou, our humble respects to you,' the courteous, excited crowd responded reverently. 'Thank you very much (*Kobjai Lai Lai*) for our New Year presents. You're much too kind and you shouldn't have troubled yourself. We're just so happy to see you!'

It was all they could think of saying, but their expression of intense loyalty and the happiness on their faces was more impressive than the gifts, which were readily accepted. They praised his kind heart and revealed that despite making offerings and prayers to gain merit in the temple and working extra hard, they had become poorer because of high taxes and had received no help from Bangkok.

For a moment he looked at a loss, but he was doing his best. Even in his darkest visions he'd never contemplated such an occasion. I still hold the image of him frozen in my mind as he smiled triumphantly, his face transformed. I saw at that moment how the Lao people, for all their complaints about their treatment, relished his pledges. He confidently went up and down the lines of people, expressing sympathy and canvassing support, touching their hands lovingly and gently pinching the babies' soft cheeks. It was marvellous and without any prompting he asked the crowd not to waste time kneeling in reverence before him. He told them to stand up and be counted. The crowd hesitantly rose to their feet, waved and smiled at him as though he were their favourite *Khaen* player, opera singer (*Morlum*) or country singer.

'My beloved countrymen, warm greetings to you all (*Sabaidee, Pheeh-Nong Lao Thi HuckPhaeng*),' he said boisterously, in a clear ViengChan accent. 'I know I carry the hopes of your freedom. In so far as it lies within my power, and with your support, I shall not let you down.'

'*Sou, sou* (fight on), Chao Anou. Don't give up!' they bellowed and cheered loudly. They claimed to be a mixture of Lao Vieng, Lao Khrung, Lao Phuan, Lao Ngiao, Lao Songdam and others. 'We're all Lao (*SaeuZard Lao*). We'll always be Lao!' they roared.

Looking down at his loyal audience, he thanked them for the trust they'd placed in him. He beseeched them to be patient, though he was fighting against time. He knew all too well he was getting old and his vigour was fast deserting him. He told the crowd that the time for celebration would come when LanXang was a united and independent state. He was quite capable of showing his emotion and was genuinely concerned for them. He asked them to pray to Lord Buddha and their gods that before too long, great honour would descend upon Lao LanXang. 'But gods alone aren't enough. We must act together,' he roared. He then turned on his heels and sprang up to stand on the platform; fresh sweat like tears appeared to be shining on his cheeks. His feelings were unfeigned, I tell you.

One wonders, looking back, if he knew he would never see them again. I certainly thought so. I can see him now, standing on the ceremonial stage along the front of the temple, straining his eyes in the bright April sunlight, scanning the sorry crowd kneeling in front of him. At that moment a few of them, admiring his freshly gleaming robes of kingship, spoke of the hardship they'd endured since being forced to leave their homes in ViengChan. He looked surprised to see so many people advancing towards him, their arms harshly marked with crude census numbers. Some of the wounds hadn't yet healed from the burns because of infection and flies were buzzing around the rotting flesh. It was a sad and upsetting sight.

This showed beyond doubt that Siam's crimes were monstrous and on a vastly bigger scale than anything even Chao Anouvong had imagined. I really thought I was going to be sick. I'd come a long way from the peaceful environment and fresh air of ViengChan to find myself looking at these fly-infested people with their blood-oozing wounds: tell-tale markings that subjected them to discrimination and humiliation for life as second-class citizens or slaves. These went far deeper than mere physical scars. He promised he would try to rid them of cruelty and injustice. He waved and smiled at the crowd but there was anxiety in his eyes as he stood to address them. He appreciated the severity of their psychological wounds, the invisible damage from being forced to leave their homes. Their eyes, popping out of their sockets, seemed fixed and dead. Gazing at them I felt Nangklao's image still looming malevolently before my eyes. The incident continued to trouble my thoughts, as if his long arm had reached out for me from Bangkok, taken me away and kept me as a slave in his palace.

A moment later I was most relieved when an anxious little man kneeling at the front of the crowd made a deep obeisance. With his head bowed and his praying hands respectfully lifted to his chest, he asked, 'What news from ViengChan, Your Majesty?'

Chao Anouvong's (and my) shoulders drooped, and he was momentarily lost for words but he somehow managed to maintain his cheerfulness. He calmly leaned forward in his seat said, 'We've not come from there, my countrymen. We're returning from Bangkok to our capital ViengChan (*MueangLuang ViengChan*).' The usual decisiveness was back in his voice.

The crowd stirred and looked sideways at each other with gladness and excitement. Thoroughly unnerved, they said, 'Returning to ViengChan? Really?' in various degrees of nervous enthusiasm, eagerly wanting to hear more. They began to jostle for position to get closer to him. Some of them were teenagers and children who had never heard of Chao Anouvong, never mind actually seeing him or hearing him speak in their mother tongue. The air filled with happy, cheerful voices. Many older people who had been forced to settle in Saraburi in 1779 asked him questions. He gladly answered whilst seated and looking directly at them. He worked hard on his memory to soothe their plight, thanking them and making promises, particularly to those who hadn't made it to the gathering. Standing so close to such an eminent, revered figure, they applauded him joyfully. His presence was reflected in every Lao; their worth, their hopes and their self-esteem increased with his. Some women with babies rushed forward, throwing themselves down in despair and crawling towards him. 'Chao Anou!' they cried out, stretching out their arms, tears spurting from their eyes with pain and grief. Some of them had damp patches of leaking milk over their heavy breasts as they begged him for help. They sat on their heels, tears rolling down their cheeks, wailing like a high wind in the trees. They said they'd been forced to leave their homes and parents behind and were desperately homesick. They didn't want to be humiliated anymore and wished to return to ViengChan. Their words startled me.

I reviewed the records and asked for the names of all leading citizens, the familiar Lao faces, the sad, homesick, thin faces that offered us hospitality. We'd need their support in the forthcoming struggle and decided that if they had Lao names and wished to return home, then they should be allowed to speak up. The ground was soon filled with an anxious crowd, mostly thirty years old or older, all seeking a piece of Chao Anouvong's time and begging to be allowed to follow our convoy back to ViengChan.

I kept a close watch by his side. I was just stepping back when a skeletal figure that had slowly moved to the front suddenly lurched forward. He'd the stained, dusty clothes, straggling hair and uncut goatee beard of a man in mourning. He gave me a fright. He could have been a Siamese agent or assassin for all I knew. I was ready to act as Chao Anouvong's bodyguard and wrestle the man to the ground.

'Chao Anou!' the man cried out suddenly. The crowd jumped and turned to look at him as he sank to the floor close to Chao Anouvong. The king looked uneasy and concerned but turned calmly to ask the man's name. 'My name is Korn, Your Majesty,' he replied and started to cry aloud as if at the sudden appearance of a long-lost son. 'We've been waiting for you to come our way,' he announced between his sobs. 'Thanks to the Lord Buddha! I believed you were coming to take us back to our homes in ViengChan. We're so relieved; it's as if our feet already rest on LanXang soil.' His cloudy, pale, small eyes were wide open with excitement, his pupils darting from side to side and peering out at Chao Anouvong. He went on to say that he already knew our intended route back to ViengChan. Chao Anouvong pretended to be surprised but was unfazed: he knew the people liked their king to be well informed. Gradually, despite his condition, Korn shifted closer, held out his praying hands and was about to touch Chao Anouvong's feet. The king quickly got up and started pacing about the platform before returning to sympathise with Korn, who'd retreated a little. Chao Anouvong rested his chin on his hand and scrutinised this poor follower: the ragged hair, the filthy, bare feet and the cotton *Phasalong* (sarong) he probably hadn't washed for months.

It was not my place to comment on his appearance or ask what he was doing so far away from home and in such obvious distress. Chao Anouvong held out his hand, patted the man's shoulder and invited him to speak freely. There was a sudden pause in the crowd's wailing, like a storm wind dropping to silence. 'Come and sit down closer and let's hear what you have to say,' he said sympathetically, revealing he'd only been twelve years old at the time of the invasion. 'You surprise me. You must have been quite a little boy when you came to Siam,' he went on. 'Won't you tell me what happened? Were you abducted from the street when the Siamese sacked the city?'

The man, after a little hesitation, started to claw slowly forward on his hands and knees before sitting on his heels on the bare ground. His eyes were still flickering wildly back and forth like a blind man. With his praying hands lifted to his chest he said he was partially blind from cataracts, but the sight of Chao Anouvong up close made him happy and relaxed. After that, he spoke incessantly and hardly paused to draw breath. As his story poured out Chao Anouvong gestured to me to note it all down. He gently interrupted and asked the man to take his time and go back a long way, almost forty-six years, to the day his family had been forced to leave ViengChan, and to explain where the rest of his father's group had been sent. He said that he'd been born in 1774 so he was too young to remember everything. His eyes were wet with tears of anguish when he said that his father Thao Bounma used to be a caretaker at the Emerald Buddha temple. The only precious thing his father had with him was his *Khaen*, which he played when he wished to recall this eventful period of his life and to cheer the hearts of his friends. He died of hunger and exhaustion on the journey to exile. Chao Anouvong expressed his commiseration and praised him for his father's good service. The kneeling crowd began to wail in sympathy.

'It was his life, and this is the very *Khaen* my father brought with him,' Korn said hoarsely, sobbing in torment as he lifted the instrument up to Chao Anouvong who took it and looked at it admiringly. 'That's how I first came to Siam with my father. Many of our people were sent to Suphanbury.' He was so choked up that he started swallowing and almost bursting into tears, dabbing his eyes in silence.

'Your father didn't try to escape?' Chao Anouvong said pointedly.

'Where to?' he replied quickly. 'No. I'm afraid he didn't. We hated the Siamese for their cruelty but feared death more than slavery. We all wanted to stay alive so we might return home one day. That's why I'm still here.' He was clearly angry and upset at his treatment, adding that it was no shame to be poor and living in a hut in ViengChan, albeit with plenty to eat, unlike in Siam, where he was constantly hungry, laughed at, humiliated and treated like a slave by loyalist thugs. Meanwhile Siamese officials demanded bribes from the Lao exiles and threatened to imprison or kill them if they didn't pay. Inevitably many Lao people in the north and northeast of Siam became debt slaves: property of the plutocrats and ruling classes in Bangkok.

Back then Korn was just a scared five-year-old, but now, at fifty-one, all his vigour and hope had gone; he was a scrap of humanity, as thin as a stray dog. He swallowed hard and gathered his energy and courage to ask Chao Anouvong for guidance, as if it were his last hope. His life was in terrible danger for refusing to obey the Siamese governor and trying to return to his father's home in the north of the hills of That Luang.

'Chao Anou, we miss ViengChan too, very much!' lamented the crowd, making themselves heard like a badly trained chorus. 'We want to return to ViengChan and see the That Luang stupa again,' they added, begging to be allowed to follow him. But they became dejected and burst into tears when he told them that they could not. He thanked them and said that the vivid accounts of their misfortunes had moved him deeply. It was a very traumatic occasion.

Chao Anouvong personified loving kindness and compassion; it radiated from his eyes and his people realised it. They were overwhelmed by his natural ability to chat in a relaxed fashion with them and were charmed and surprised by him. They worshipped him as if he were a saint (*Arhut*). His studies at the That Phanom temple had clearly helped. He'd gained both merit and wisdom and was able to undertake any task satisfactorily. He spoke wisely and the people readily accepted his words. I sensed that he intended to raise Lao awareness to advance his political principles. I quietly recommended caution while the crowd looked on.

'I beg you, please be careful,' I whispered.

'Oh yes, be careful!' he muttered mockingly and winked with irrepressible mischief. Tapping me on the head with his fingers he said he needed to transform his ideas into genuine, practical power to ensure these people would follow him. 'Besides, we have certain rights, do we not, Phia Jon?'

'Yes, we certainly have,' I said, 'but please remember Siam is a country of prohibition. It's extremely dangerous to criticise the royal family and we're still a long way from safety.'

'Phia Jon, we aren't trying to influence the Siamese,' he countered. 'We're just telling the truth to our own Lao people.'

I didn't reply for I knew his mind was made up.

Consequently, far from worrying that Saraburi was too close to Bangkok, he went ahead with his speeches at the welcoming ceremonies, which were masterpieces of diplomacy. He took a great interest in conversing directly with the inhabitants and expressing his concern for their suffering. They appreciated it but he often had to deliver disappointing news, blaming himself for failing to obtain permission from Nangklao to take them back with him. He was visibly choked and almost lost his voice as he spoke to the people with solemnity and regret. Their cheering faces dejectedly dropped like stones as they cried in grief and disappointment. It was a truly sad moment. The poor people knew they couldn't really change anything, but they still seemed so hopeful at the sight of him as they stood in the heat and shuffled for a better position. I choked and held back my anger when I saw these sad people, most of whom had already packed what few belongings they had. Some were in great distress, ravaged by humiliation and illness, but they kept their dignity, standing about like deaf and bewildered people. Some women had very young babies held to their waists with cotton shawls across their chests and knotted over their shoulders. They jostled to get in line, crooning to their infants and ready to follow him.

Most of his speeches were spontaneous. Learning much from Phra Ajarn Khoon at the That Phanom temple, he delivered many of them by heart, without notes. Although his memory was phenomenal, I often feared he might stumble over his words so made sure I always had a copy to hand. Sometimes I'd catch his eye and would be just about to take out a piece of paper from my shirt pocket when he would tell me to save myself the trouble. 'I have the speech up here well enough,' he would whisper and tap the side of his head.

On one occasion he stared straight ahead and raised his right palm for silence but to no avail. He merely shrugged, stood up and looked around, and the noise gradually died down.

'Ladies and gentlemen, happy greetings to you all,' he began respectfully, adding that he assumed people might be surprised to see him on the platform as he'd never before sought to make a speech. He didn't really want to but he'd news for them.

He was devastated that his plea to Nangklao had failed. He took the view that the people had the right under the sacred, ancient (*Duekdamban*) laws of Khoun Borom to see justice done as he flung himself into the business of preparing his expedition back to ViengChan.

'My countrymen,' he continued, looking very solemn. 'What I am about to say is for our sake and for the sake of our kingdom.' The crowd went completely quiet. 'There is a human of unparalleled greed, impudence and wickedness in Bangkok. Who could possibly blame us for seeking justice in our lives? Tell me in the name of the Lord Buddha, what better service could we offer our kingdom at the present time? As you know, during these past two years the Siamese governors and their men have laid waste to our provinces. They've plundered Lao communities, stripped our homes and temples of treasures and marked our people with numbers.' He went on to say that if the Lao people could speak with a single voice they would say, 'The Emerald Buddha and other sacred Buddha statues, all the gold, the silver and all the beautiful things that belong in our cities, palaces, houses and temples; all these things that you, my Siamese friends, have stolen from us, we ask you to return them in the name of peace and friendship.' After a pause he lifted his index finger and said, 'These are the words that all Lao would utter.'

His words stirred the crowd; they looked and nodded at each other.

'Be patient, my countrymen,' he continued in a slightly choked voice. 'One day you'll be able to eat the fragrant new rice (*Khaow Horm*) in the land of your birth and in your beloved capital city of ViengChan.' As if unable to speak further he stood solemnly, his head raised slightly and staring meaningfully at the blue sky. After a brief silence he raised his arms and asked the crowd to relax. However, every time he mentioned ViengChan the crowd sighed with longing. Without taking their eyes off him they turned and began whispering excitedly to each other. He meanwhile was hitting his stride and by using a little mimicry, a variety of comic voices, a change of accent from Lao to Siamese or a simple gesture, he populated his speeches with the characters to whom he referred. He clearly wanted to bring some life back to these sad people who smiled, giggled with delight and howled with laughter. He waited, smiling, for the noise to die down.

'Ladies and gentlemen,' he began again. 'Today I come to offer my life in service to all Lao people. I intend to seek your freedom so that you may lead dignified lives. I do this not out of any desire for personal gain but for the glory of LanXang. Our nation demands that honest men stand up for justice and freedom. I have long been keeping an eye on the Siamese ruler and commissioners and officials. My intention, with your help, is to bring them to justice for the crimes they've committed against our people.' He extracted a murmur of approval and a few nervous cheers. He paused a little before raising his voice to attract more attention. 'We have a long, hard battle ahead of us. Your allegiance and support will count for everything. We will act together in the firm conviction that right will prevail.'

He waved to acknowledge the gathering, swung round and then unexpectedly descended a few steps to the kneeling, bemused crowd. He touched them gently on their outstretched hands and they responded by giving him small white and red bouquets of *Dork Champa* flowers. He sniffed them with delight and handed them over to me quicker than I could pass them on to the staff. Then he mounted the few steps back up onto the platform, turned round and raised his hands for calm. Soon the muttering faded away. With no sign of nerves he said, 'Let's pray to Theravada and the other gods to bear witness to our wishes.' He slowly sat down on his chair and pressed his hands together in prayer, looking upwards beyond the clouds. The crowd jostled to do the same. I could feel the wind dropping in the silent crowd as they solemnly prayed. Soon afterwards he rose to his feet and said, 'My dear countrymen, our identity and dignity are critically endangered. Our offerings and prayers alone will not be enough to satisfy Theravada and the other gods. So, whoever you are, please see to LanXang unification.' The happy, cheering crowd rose as a single, seething mass, chanting ecstatically and glorying in their nation despite still being imprisoned on Siamese soil.

I felt a tightening in my chest for I saw at once what Chao Anouvong meant. He announced that the Lao would no longer put up with the arrogance of Bangkok's autocratic rule and expansionist policies. He reminded the people that Legendary Khoun Borom had taught us to focus on the country, to know ourselves and never act to excess. Cleverly, tentatively, obliquely, he was preparing at last to challenge Bangkok. For that he had the Lao people's eternal admiration. He left them with the hope they might one day return to their homes entirely resting on him. A gigantic battle loomed in their hearts. We wished them good luck, good health and bade them farewell.

Chao Anouvong believed Bangkok wouldn't rest until it had broken him. He insisted the Lao had been a culturally distinct nation until the illegitimate Siamese invasion; indoctrination then followed. He firmly believed that fruits not only don't fall far from the tree but will also spread. Before long the inevitable would happen: when humans are forced to act in fear like a flock of sheep, the weakest amongst them will turn towards the safety of the conqueror and become Siamese puppets. They would reject their heritage through shame and prejudice.

The Rattanakosin Siam, he said, had corrupted the social fabric of LanXang and had no respect for the Buddhist belief in the diversity of humans. Bangkok's intention was to erase ethnically, historically and demographically the disparate peoples living in Siam by referring to them as 'Tai Siamese' or simply 'Tai'. Those living on the Khorat Plateau would be subject to particularly intense indoctrination, taught to reject their history and origins and cowed into submission by a process of 'Siamification'. Lao children would be brainwashed into believing the Siamese version of history from a young and tender age, taught only of Ayutthaya, Bangkok and Siam to mould their beliefs and characters before they had a chance to grow up and make their own minds up. They would never know they were the children of Lao LanXang. Siam would always be glorified as a fount of goodness, never of evil. The Siamese king would never be seen as less than perfect. To say anything else would be a crime. These are the tactics Bangkok would shamelessly deploy to cover for a man revelling in ignorance, arrogance, cruelty and authoritarianism.

While there's never been a serious language barrier between the two kingdoms, political barriers will always exist. At first the Lao people deeply resented Siamese indoctrination but were powerless to resist. They tried to hold on to their tradition but were effectively in thrall to Bangkok's vicious policies. The authoritarian regime would gradually have broken them, their minds deceived into believing falsehoods. Keen to be Lao but unable to alienate the Rattanakosin Siam, they would become ignorant of the truth.

Some of the young Lao on the Khorat Plateau would have turned against their own kind. They would even forget their origins: not necessarily the first generation, but certainly the second and later generations. Their loyalty to Bangkok would solidify, while all thoughts of fighting for the right to be Lao would be banished from their minds.

Those who wished to get anywhere in life would have to assimilate, to speak the official Siamese language and adopt Siamese culture. They might enjoy equal rights under the law in theory, but in practice they would always be subject to discrimination. Some of those born in Siam might have a serious identity problem: weak enough to be tainted by Bangkok doctrine but with a strong enough parental influence to prevent it happening. Some would end up considering themselves Siamese and become reluctant and ashamed to speak Lao in public. They would end up admiring the Bangkok ruler until their heritage was truly forgotten. The Siamese, however, would sneeringly continue to make derogatory remarks about them and use the word 'Lao' as a synonym for inferiority, disrespectfully regarding the Lao as second-class citizens and slaves.

The truth would ultimately prevail. Feeling foolish and hurt, the Lao would recall their true Lao upbringing and way of life. The Lao in Siam whose ancestors dwelt in old LanXang would wonder what Bangkok had done for them. Emboldened by learning and a growing realisation of the need to be Lao, they would bravely begin to express their Lao consciousness and no longer put up with falsehoods. They would tell the world they were Lao, not Tai Siamese of Siam. Sick of speaking Siamese they would dress in traditional Lao style, sing (*Lum*) and dance to the sound of the *Khaen* and speak their own Lao language, not a mere north-eastern provincial dialect of Siam as Bangkok would have it. Everything they said or sang would be in its original form. Bangkok would be unable to stop it. In turn, any honest and truthful Siamese, themselves of the Ai-Lao race, would simply have to accept the truth and learn to appreciate and enjoy Lao things.

This was Chao Anouvong's own analysis of the future, but it was reasonable enough to agree with.

We were to move on to a real test the following day but there was no great hurry. Chao Anouvong wanted to see for himself what was happening in the provincial city of Nakhorn Ratsasima, otherwise known as Khorat. Geographically and historically Khorat was LanXang's most south-westerly city, closer to Bangkok than ViengChan, so was hotly contested by the

Siamese. They settled around the city, keeping a close watch and hoping to take over. If you'd just arrived from Bangkok, as we had, it was clear why the city was so important to Bangkok. It stood on the south side of the Mun river but everything about it – the people, the traditions, customs, food, music, art, politics and so on – suggested an intermingling of mostly Lao with only a few Siamese people. Given its long history as a disputed frontier post (*Dan Nah*) between the two kingdoms, it remained an important bridging point: the gate to LanXang for Siam. This well-known province in the far southwest of LanXang, once part of the Khmer Empire, had been peopled with Lao citizens since King Fah Ngum's day; it was also where many Lao people had been forced to settle after the 1779 invasion. Most of the population saw themselves as Lao, the rest as Siamese, with some claiming to be both or neither. It could not cohere around race, religion or language because Lao and Siamese were so close to each other in all three. It was a tricky situation given the city's history of exploitation and slavery. While the Lao valued respect and preferred equality and liberty, Khorat hardly knew where it stood after forty-six years of Siamese rule. Nevertheless, the people were becoming more rebellious towards Bangkok.

Interestingly, unlike LanXang's, Siamese stupas were rounded. The architectural style of four-cornered stupas, previously confined to LanXang, stopped in Khorat, but due to forced migration, spread to other parts of Siam. The city was near enough to Bangkok to acquire Siamese tastes and habits, but the people strove to safeguard Lao LanXang's culture and traditions. The native people were not too elaborate and flowery – they perhaps used a few pompous Siamese phrases with their tinkling rhythms – but they were otherwise straightforward in conversation. The ancient Lao dialects and pronunciations made Khorat seem more like Viengchan than Ayutthaya or Bangkok. But being close to Siam, they were in thrall to the rapidly worsening purging policies of Bangkok.

When we arrived in Khorat Chao Anouvong was under no illusions. He made no secret of his profound patriotism and openly expressed his distaste for the un-Lao elements of some of the population. We'd obtained lists of the hundreds of Siamese supporters there, some of whom had probably been turned by Siamese flattery and bribery. The Siamese governor Phromphakdy resided in a high-walled and tightly guarded house in the city centre. We feared a hostile reception might await us but despite the danger of being seized and killed, Chao Anouvong made a point of seeking out Siamese friends and mentors: the city mayors, nobles and other influential men.

In fact, the opposite was the case. A group of people quickly realised who Chao Anouvong was and word was passed. Soon a large crowd appeared. Youths and young girls carrying flowers stood or knelt in reverence, waving, smiling and calling his name. 'They're for us!' I called out to Chao Anouvong in great excitement. With his eyes half closed, he smiled, raised his hand in acknowledgement and turned this way and that so everyone could see him. Nowhere was the population's devotion more evident than when we arrived at the city gate. News of Chao Anouvong's arrival had preceded him, and a crowd of cheering Lao citizens hailed him '*Somdet* (Majesty) *Phrachao* (King) Anourutharaja' and escorted us through the famous city gate. Towering wooden *Khaen* monuments stood on either side to signify Lao heritage. It felt as if we were being hugged to the heart of a dear long-lost brother.

One reason for his popularity was that most of the inhabitants regarded the Lao LanXang dynasty, not the Rattanakosins of Siam, as their rightful rulers. In terms of status and renown Chao Anouvong was undeniably the pre-eminent figure. He was a Lao like them and they hadn't forgotten his past generosity and respect, which had reaped great rewards for him. They perhaps cheered him more as a protest against Bangkok's oppressive regime than an expression of Lao LanXang independence.

Soon after our arrival, a procession of heavily laden men trooped towards us. To show their gratitude, farmers, grain merchants and Phraya Xayakane – a headman – presented a gift of the best fragrant rice (*Khaow Jaow Horm*) and glutinous rice (*Khaow Neow*). When Chao Anouvong tried to thank them they all modestly disclaimed the credit, unwilling to own up to their generosity. He expressed his regret that he possessed nothing of worth to give them as a token of his gratitude. He was even more immune to bribery than was a holy monk or superhuman to sword wounds. He was also shrewd enough to ensure that donations were shared around, passing them on to be distributed amongst the head monks of various temples who were respected by the community. In return, many pledged their allegiance out of gratitude. He also knew that the city was full of Lao nationalists, but they were keeping their heads below the parapet for fear of persecution. We suspected those who refused to offer their support had been bribed by being exempted from taxes throughout Phromphakdy's two years as governor.

We headed directly towards the governor's house along an avenue of a golden cascade of *Dork Khoon* ດອກຄູນ (Cassia Fistula) flowers intermingled with a cloud of white and red *Dork Champa* blossoms. I urged the mahout to bring my elephant alongside Chao Anouvong's. Then, as we approached, we realised that what we'd thought were guesthouses in front of the more elaborate governor's residence were actually prisons to detain those to be marked with numbers during the census, a blatant act of expansionist aggression and Rattanakosin Siam gangsterism.

'Those houses look flimsy but quite new, Phia Jon,' Chao Anouvong said suspiciously, wiping the sweat from his eyes and looking at a row of newly built, mysterious, long thatched houses. The citizens of Khorat were uncertain how to receive him. Some cautiously greeted him in high-pitched voices, the harsh tones of the plebeian Siamese which he and I found unpleasant (*Bor mouan*). He answered gently but emphatically in Lao, leaving them in no doubt as to his personal preference of language. Despite the hostility of a small group of people, most Lao citizens who'd been waiting to greet us bravely offered him typical Lao hospitality. He greeted them in a loud voice from high on the elephant's back. As he looked down on their upturned faces, they happily welcomed him with bright, happy and welcoming smiles.

'Happy Lao New Year (*Sabaidee Pi Mai Lao*) to you all,' he said cheerfully, wishing them good luck and good health.

'*Sabaidee Pi Mai Lao* and our respects to you Chao Anou, and good luck and good health to you too,' they responded affectionately, lifting their praying hands high above their heads and waving in euphoric excitement as they hurried along both sides of our procession. Their greetings echoed all around them.

The moment he stepped down from his elephant, Chao Anouvong asked them apprehensively about the long houses. They told him that the city governor was away and showed him the burn marks on their arms, begging to be excused from answering until they felt they were safe. He expressed his deep sympathy for their sufferings but didn't press them for an answer.

We were informed later that Phromphakdy spent his days living in the governor's residence, supervising the safe keeping of his loot and taking the census, sadistically abusing people with impunity as if it were all an entertainment. Lao citizens had been dragged from their homes; some had been stripped naked before being branded with hot irons which were still hooked to a pole next to the embers as a reminder to anyone who felt tempted to escape. No one knew why the Siamese officials had picked on the Lao. It was shocking.

There were deputations in the city from all over the Khorat Plateau. It swarmed with citizens who'd arrived both for the census and to greet our arrival. Groups of impoverished people gathered: fathers bewailing their teenage sons and daughters who'd been kidnapped into slavery; children mourning their parents who'd been tortured or even killed at the hands of Siamese officials. However, our arrival lifted the crowd's morale to a new height; I swayed back and forth in astonishment at the wall of faces and hands waving flowers. Chao Anouvong made a short sombre speech about liberty and listened to complaints. He could do nothing to help at that time but praised them for their vigilance and courage.

'Citizens of Khorat, greetings to you all,' he began. 'Shall I speak, or shall I hold my tongue? No, I feel I must speak because I care about the truth and our future.' There was a short pause while the crowd looked at him excitedly. 'You're all courageous people... and ladies, you're looking beautiful in your Lao silk skirts (*Sinh*). Our noble elder Pu Chan would have been very proud of you.' The crowd cheered with delight. 'You all know that the Bangkok elite understand – in fact, they've said it themselves – that your city is Siam's 'gateway' to the wealth of LanXang in the northeast. The truth is that their officials and soldiers have been in our country since 1779, causing destruction, injury and death to our democracy and freedom. Now they're plundering, taking a violent census of our people and plotting revenge on anyone who refused to conform to their policies. Ladies and gentlemen, boys and girls, believe me, Bangkok is wrong: you all know only too well that this city and others on the Khorat Plateau do not belong to Siam. They are part of Lao LanXang!' He paused to gather his breath. 'LanXang belongs to you... to all the Lao people!' he roared, pointing his finger at the cheering crowd who rose in acclamation. They gave him a tremendous ovation and it was quite a while before they quietened down.

Having been with him for so long I sometimes forgot how impressive a man he was. Now in his fifty-eighth year, he stood tall, with his powerful torso, strong arms and those famous long eyebrows, trimmed moustache and thick, straight, black hair, lying neatly like silk on his compassionate, friendly and handsome face.

'You therefore deserve the protection you're seeking,' he continued, his voice becoming louder and his outstretched finger jabbing the air, 'not merely from corruption but from that highly revered man in Bangkok who's supposed to punish corrupt governors and officials. There shouldn't be one rule for the Siamese aristocrats and another for ordinary citizens, especially the Lao. One cup of their bloodline and privilege isn't worth a drop of our merit.'

That raised the temperature well enough, I can tell you. The people roared approvingly. I was thrilled with the effect of his speech. Even so, I noticed that not everyone was pleased. A large group of hostile Siamese were scattered here and there at the back, scornfully standing with arms folded, their faces solemn, scowling at us, muttering angrily and disgustingly spitting on the ground. I pretended not to notice.

We'd decided that anyone who turned up would be granted an audience, so an anxious crowd had gathered, some holding flowers in their hands, all seeking advice and help. Chao Anouvong had spent some time patiently deciding whether they were likely to be on his side when the time came, until at last he felt he had their confidence. He steered well clear of those who'd been bribed by Siamese officials or who'd been victims of Bangkok indoctrination and propaganda, brainwashed into believing anything Siam told them or frightened into submission by force. He wouldn't waste any time trying to persuade them to protect their rights. 'It's up to them to decide what's right,' he muttered.

The crowd, which had been following us since the early morning, lingered around the city gate and was growing larger by the minute. It had been joined by all the distinguished citizens of the city, among them the chief monk Phra Ajarn Thongsa, who requested that Chao Anouvong should accompany him immediately to the temple hall, where the elders were waiting to welcome him with a formal *Baci* ceremony and a banquet. He was in two minds. He wanted to visit more cities on his journey, but it was undoubtedly a wonderful opportunity to increase his popularity and secure the city's loyalty. He raised his eyebrows and looked at me. With a nod I recommended we should accept the offer. After a brief hesitation he agreed to go, and we duly set off on foot, accompanied by a huge escort of happy citizens. The chief monk Thongsa and Chao Anouvong walked and conversed side by side while I followed closely behind and listened to them. Wings of chattering and immensely excited attendants crowded on either side and the curious crowd at the rear sent up clouds of dust.

The temple hall was packed. The city's most senior monks from various temples, nine in all, were sitting in a row on the upper tier. Phra Ajarn Thongsa sat in the middle and welcomed us in soft Lao, apologising for offering us no assistance up to now. Chao Anouvong – who insisted on being seated amongst the people lower down so as not to emphasise his royal birth – also spoke in Lao. He looked relaxed and fired up by the warm hospitality. He proceeded to make a most remarkable unprepared speech, roaring in his mother tongue that he would dedicate his life to righting the injustices done to the Lao people throughout LanXang and LanNa. The people, normally so reserved, praised him and clapped their hands in delight. It was a very poignant moment. Some were overcome by his kind words and started to weep, lifting their praying hands to their foreheads and saying, 'Let it be true! (*Sathu anumothami!*).' He patiently listened to their complaints. They sobbed and said that the Siamese officials, governors and commissioners had seized their family heirlooms. Most had similar tales to tell. Finally the elders unanimously voiced their commitment to ViengChan and retracted their praise for Bangkok. Although they feared repression and persecution, they were happy to calmly accept the consequences for their desire to remain Lao and for offering open support for ViengChan.

Once we'd all settled down, some of us holding long, white cotton threads in our praying hands, sitting around the grand, nine-tier stupa-shaped centrepiece (*PhaKhuan*), made from banana leaves and decorated with candles and flowers, a highly respected master of ceremonies (*MorPhon*), well versed in the Pali religious language and Lao proverbs, performed the ceremony for renewing spiritual ties (*Baci SouKhuan*). He invoked the spirits to bring good fortune and called upon them to protect Chao Anouvong and his party as they travelled home, wishing all of us good luck, good health and a prosperous future. After the ceremony, the *MorPhon* tied the knotted white threads around Chao Anouvong's wrists to honour and bless him. Everyone then lined up to do the same and then also to each other. Each thread had a single, mystical knot at the centre that had been made and blessed by the monks. The white threads now covering our wrists proved very useful in wiping the sweat from my forehead before I untied, rather than cut, them three or so days later. By noon the monks had finished their lunch and had given their blessings. Then, huge trays packed with a variety of food in small bowls were brought out for us to share: baskets of freshly steamed sticky rice, spicy green papaya salad, cooked bamboo shoots, red ant egg soup and *larb* (freshly chopped cooked meat or fish), all complemented with lots of vegetables and fresh herbs from the garden or collected from the forest. I smiled discreetly and hungrily rubbed my hands together with pleasure at the sight of all that food!

When a special tray was presented to Chao Anouvong to emphasise his royal birth, he politely refused, saying that food tasted better when eaten in company. He also had a pathological dislike of being served and insisted on helping himself. When he called myself and four other guests to join him, I sat next to him. Before eating, we poured libations to the ancestors' spirits and praised the welcome food. He told the gathering that their hearts were brimming with heavenly gold given them for eternity by the Lord Buddha. Once he started to eat, we followed and happy conversation flowed. Chao Anouvong announced that after three months in Bangkok it was so good to be eating Lao proper food again; he said everything was delicious (*Saeb Lai*). The crowd cheered and smiled with delight and urged him to eat his fill. You couldn't help but recognise the happiness lighting up their faces. They all wished him long life, poured libations of water and drank to his health. He thanked them fulsomely and told them to be strong, to keep calm, stay healthy and be happy.

Phra Ajarn Thongsa and the other monks had played their part, generating much enthusiasm in the hall, with people calling out to Chao Anouvong to save them from the menace of the Siamese officials. He put out feelers to ascertain whether he could count on their loyalty and support or whether he'd be met with hostility. He looked at me and told the crowd, only half in jest, that if any harm came to us, they should, as a matter of justice and duty, find out exactly what had happened and tell the whole world about it. The crowd unanimously told him to fight for LanXang and not to be fearful, for justice would prevail. They gave him a round of applause when he said he wasn't afraid and would continue to struggle on behalf of the Lao nation.

Chao Anouvong used to say the real business of the kingdom could be achieved only with his feet as he walked dutifully from one city to the next, talking to the common people, the real backbone of the nation. Observing him threading his way amongst them was like watching a craftsman working his teak to make furniture: a hand gently touching a poor peasant's bony shoulder, a cordial greeting, a word of sympathy followed by an earthy joke (*Talok*). Even when detained by a group of tedious men, he gave the impression of having all the time in the world to listen to their dreary stories; he would then turn gracefully away with a backward glance of apology. Whenever I suggested it was time to move on, he whispered to me that without these farmers – people of integrity with a wonderful work ethic, he called them – there would be no rice. These were his trademark beliefs. They all admired him.

As usual he stood tall outside the hall to show himself to the restless crowd, before making a speech to a prolonged silence that he allowed to grow. This was his habitual trick to increase tension: speaking very quietly and hesitantly at first, forcing his audience to strain their ears in anticipation, then waking them with an outpouring of patriotic words. Emboldened by his popularity and in an attempt to heighten Lao consciousness, he would usually give a resounding speech before leaving.

'My countrymen,' he began confidently, 'compared to the stirring accounts of our master in Bangkok whose orders we've obeyed up to now, what I'm about to say will sound very paltry indeed.' The crowd reacted strongly to the word 'master'. 'But the moment has come,' he raised his voice, 'when we no longer have ears for Bangkok's harsh rules; all your courageous deeds will be priceless, and we shall not bleed in vain.' There was a short pause and then he roared, 'Ladies and gentlemen, Bangkok reaps the crops you grow, steals the riches you find and takes the silk you weave. Your city should have been forbidden to them by right, yet still they came. It is your duty to stand up for your rights. Good and kind people in the world should always be made welcome. But we should stop pandering to Bangkok's desire to create an empire. I implore you to prevent the unruly Siamese using your city to reach ViengChan, the very heart of our Lao kingdom of LanXang.' The hearts and spirits of the crowd were clearly being lifted: they looked and nodded at each other, agreeing with his words. 'We mustn't succumb to the temptation of their dubious riches,' he continued, 'when they deliberately place temptation in our way. We should strengthen our will against their malpractices and treachery. We are honest, peace-loving and easy-going people; our treatment by these Siamese governors as they carry out Bangkok's barbaric decrees has been nothing short of shameful, so monstrous and cruel that the gods, the Lord Buddha and the Theravada themselves must have wept to hear of it. Now, for your freedom and LanXang unification, whose side will you be on? Siam's or LanXang's? Will you betray your Lao ancestors? Be honest to yourself and tell me truthfully which way your true feelings should lie.'

Well, as you can imagine, the crowd responded favourably but Chao

Anouvong could do nothing at that precise moment because he was far from ready. They nodded and broke into spontaneous applause. The younger members jumped up and down, waving their hands and applauding him enthusiastically in a show of support, cheering loudly and punching the air with their fists. 'Lao LanXang! Lao LanXang! Lao LanXang!' they screamed, before streaming forward to present him with flowers and sprinkling him with scented water – a symbol of felicity and blessing in the Lao New Year. He thanked them profusely.

I really think war would have started then and there if he'd told them to pick up their swords and guns. Though they didn't realise it, I believe this was their first glimpse of socio-political activity. Lao consciousness doesn't simply inspire enthusiasm: it gave them a sense of purpose, an identity and a focus, and they increasingly turned against Bangkok's malpractices and abuses of power.

'Ladies and gentlemen make your drink offerings now and see us safely off. For those we leave behind, may the gods bring happiness to you and your families and keep you all from harm. Have faith and be optimistic. Patience is a virtue. Work hard and stay healthy by eating half as much as usual, walking twice as much, laughing three times as much… and loving plenty!' The crowd smiled and roared with laughter. 'Happy New Year! Good luck! We shall meet again. Thank you all.'

I thought the poor people might die of gratitude. They thanked him, roaring in appreciation. Some dropped to their knees or prostrated themselves and prayed for their wishes to come true. '*Sathu Anumothami!*' they said loudly and looked to heaven. He told them to save their thanks until he'd actually achieved something. They implored him to act and pleaded with him to deliver them from terror. 'Chao Anou,' they called, 'may what you say come true. Our fate is in your hands, and we beseech you, please do something.'

'We've already pleaded with Bangkok on your behalf,' he responded. 'I'm saddened that my request to take some of you back to ViengChan with us has been refused. You can rest assured we now have no choice but to act. They'll ignore us at their peril.'

He pledged to send more petitions to Bangkok for their repatriation. As we made ready to go he told them to keep well and be happy. With a final wave we started to move away from the cheering crowd, who called out and wished him a safe journey.

Indeed, Chao Anouvong kept his promise, but his personal pleas were deliberately ignored by Bangkok. He wasn't surprised because Bangkok saw a larger population as a means of increasing its wealth. Nangklao's greatest sins, like his grandfathers before him, were covetousness and a lust for wealth and power. This extravagance ensured Nangklao retained Phraya Phromphakdy as governor of Khorat. Under his command Siamese officials were sent out to take the census. Nangklao revelled in power and luxury, showering his governors and officials with rewards; in return, they earned much ill-gotten wealth to fund his opulent lifestyle.

Phraya Phromphakdy's contemptuous behaviour had caught Chao Anouvong off guard. He'd really convinced himself that Bangkok would safeguard his people from further cruelty. A storm raged in his mind but once he realised he'd achieve nothing by begging for sympathy, he calmed down. The only way forward was to fight for LanXang.

Chao Anouvong walked away from the ceremonial ground like a man in a dream, weaving through the hopeful crowd, touching them reassuringly, waving eloquently to those standing at the back, out to our waiting elephants, without once looking back. I struggled along behind him carrying as many gifts as I could manage. I finally understood why he'd trained me to be strong twenty-nine years ago. Even my well-formed arms were struggling to cope with the weight. To begin with his steps were slow and thoughtful but once we'd bidden the main crowd farewell and left them to ponder, he suddenly turned on his heels and stepped onto the rough path, leaving clouds of choking brown dust behind him. I followed him closely, holding my breath and breathing gently through my fingers. When I finally caught up with him, he turned to look at me.

'That's the kind of treatment the Rattanakosins dish out to our people!' he muttered. 'What treasures do you think they've gathered in their palace?' I didn't reply. He gradually picked up speed and strode angrily, as if he couldn't wait any longer to be back in ViengChan. I had great difficulty in breathing and keeping up. Nangklao had allowed some of Chao Anouvong's more elderly followers, no longer useful for hard labour, to leave Bangkok. Some of the older noblemen, overweight from hardly ever walking in their lives, fell behind. They had great difficulty in catching up with us. I looked back and saw them struggling and out of breath. I slowed down for them to catch up.

'Please wait for us!' they cried in distress.

I paused to wipe away sweat and dust from my face and urged them to hurry. 'Let's be on our way before the sun leaves us!' I yelled, my hands cupped around my mouth. When they finally caught up with us, panting and sweating, they didn't have time to rest because Chao Anouvong was already on his elephant. We left amidst loud cheers and went on our way through the Khorat Plateau, further away from the prying eyes of Siamese spies, heading back north-eastward to our proud capital city of ViengChan.

I couldn't resist asking him why Nangklao was preventing the Lao people from returning to their homes in ViengChan. He looked thoughtful and nodded slowly from his howdah. 'Now that is a good question,' he mused. He sniffed the air and his thoughts deepened with the rising heat, recalling the multi-coloured shapes of the kneeling crowds, almost motionless in the April dust, like a field of statues before us. I remarked that Phromphakdy wasn't the only one to deliberately commit injustices against the Lao people. 'No,' he said and turned his thoughts to Bangkok. 'I think you're right.' I realised something important had just occurred to him. 'They're all in it together aren't they Phia Jon?'

I didn't respond. I simply couldn't think of a useful reply. 'The true Siamese aristocrats, or shall we say the Bangkok plutocrats,' he added, 'have no sense of fairness and will never lift a finger to help our cause unless it benefits them.' He also recognised that Phromphakdy and his chief officer Suriyaphakdy were protected by the Rattanakosins. The whole pack of them were intent on decimating the Lao, to the point of spreading the lie there were no Lao in ViengChan, Luang Phrabang and Champasak – only Siamese (*Tai Sayam* or *Tai* for short) and causing great offence by claiming other ethnic groups – such as the Zhuang, Lue and Nung – were all '*Tai*'. To say the least it was quite ludicrous, laughable and unbelievable! Even the academic world knew the Tai race didn't exist. Only the self-serving Siamese thought they could get away with it.

Chao Anouvong, usually so careful and diplomatic in his speech, often mischievously added that the Bangkok monarchy had always been a two-faced monster because of its trickery and broken promises. They were happy to give way when threatened and blatantly abandoned their promises whenever it suited them, just as they'd revoked the oath they swore in 1563 at the That Si-SongHuck shrine. This policy had so far prevented their colonisation by the Western powers.

Chao Anouvong was well within his rights to foment hostility towards any oppressors in LanXang: it surely wasn't treason for Lao citizens to criticise the injustices of the Siamese government. Because of his bravery and moral courage, he took risks that no one else dared to. He was the ruler of a once independent kingdom, addressing his people in their own native tongue. His resentment was directed towards the Siamese governors and officials who carried out Nangklao's decrees without compunction rather than the Rattanakosin dynasty itself, but he saw the governors' crimes as an opportunity to advance his cause. For this, Bangkok insolently referred to him as '*Buck Anou*': the little disloyal Lao.

Such intimidation was entirely unjustified in any language, and he was clearly disappointed by their impertinence. Besides, the 1779 destruction of ViengChan and his subsequent exile were still fresh in his memory, if not fresher than ever.

After Khorat, we picked up the ancient route and headed north, further away from the sea and into the central Khorat Plateau, where we could feel the less humid heat of summer. As the sun went down below Phetsabun Mountain and the Dong Phraya Yen range, which has divided Siam in the west and LanXang in the east since 1563, a black shadow rose to our left. It grew darker as cloud swirled round the hidden summits. To our right the diminishing evening light shone on the brown flood plain of the Chi and Mun rivers and the green forest that stretched out towards the great Mekong on the horizon. We hadn't gone far when we encountered another large throng clamouring for the opportunity to see Chao Anouvong, who always greeted well-wishers along the route before resuming his journey. Word was passed and news of our journey had spread throughout the Khorat Plateau. Huge crowds gathered outside every city gate to meet us.

By the time we'd crossed the Chi River and reached the principal city of Khon Kaen, known as Ban Nonhtan in ancient times, the crowds of predominantly Lao people from nearby villages and towns were in their thousands. Chao Anouvong was deeply touched by their loyalty and support. They all wanted to greet him and wish him well and had good reason for wanting to see this noble and charming figure. For the whole day long till sundown we sat amongst the noblemen inside the hospitality hall and banqueted on a rich supply of food washed down by some alcohol (*Lauw Lao*) and green coconut juice. Before the sun went down and it grew dark, the whole town was fragrant with the grilling of meat and fish, which they served piping hot, and the houses echoed to the sounds of joyful banqueting within. We were glad of our rest and held important conversations about Lao consciousness as well as mingling with the inhabitants and enjoying the performances of musicians and a group of beautiful young girl dancers.

The telling of tales in song and poetry was important for the agrarian way of life in LanXang. Drink was served in the early evening, adding to the cheerfulness of the gathering. The talented bards and balladeers (*Morlum*) with their beautiful clear voices were summoned to recite poems and sing traditional mournful ballads and epics at the welcoming party. These songs had been preserved for their usefulness, and inspired by the guests and enthusiastic audience members, the balladeers sang divinely to the tuneful *Khaen* and danced together to the music. We sat and listened in silence late into the night.

They sang about the demarcation line between Siam and LanXang, from the Phetsabun Mountain range down to Don Phraya Fai, calling on the Lao in Siam to return to LanXang. Then followed a patriotic ballad extolling the glory of ViengChan LanXang, retracing how the capital city of the kingdom was born and affirming that all Lao on both banks of the Mekong and on the Khorat Plateau were children of the legendary Pu Chan. They then sang a well-known passage about the downfall of ViengChan: the forced migration and the people's suffering. They sang the tale as powerfully as if they'd been there themselves. They followed this up with a very traumatic song called '*Lao Phaen*' describing the terrible anguish of the Lao people under the stony-hearted Rattanakosin Siamese. As they sang, their passions rose; they broke down and their eyes were wet with tears of resentment. A wave of sorrow swept through the gathering. Both the guests and the welcoming party of elderly noblemen and women wept. Nor could I keep my eyes dry when I thought of my loved ones who'd died. It was very sad, even more so when sung by a beautiful female voice. It never failed to upset Chao Anouvong, for no one had been dealt a heavier blow than when he lost his father, King Bounyasan. Thinking about his beloved sister Princess Kanlayani in Bangkok would also have saddened him terribly. He almost broke down but just about nerved himself to listen, because the song was not only about the destruction of ViengChan but the loss of the Emerald Buddha, the end of his father and the loyal brave city defenders and the people who were made to suffer afterwards. Some in the crowd caught the sad words of the stirring ballad – a poignant reminder of the passing of time – and wept profusely. They were probably tears of bitterness.

The bards brought the curtain down with the famous song '*Champa Mueang Lao*', a patriotic anthem which helped to stoke up the sort of nationalistic fervour that was needed to endure the horrors of the destruction of ViengChan. The song told of the Lao people who, when forced to migrate to Siam, planted *Dork Champa* flowers in their garden as a reminder of their homes in LanXang. The Siamese elite considered the flower suitable only for growing in cemeteries. Most of the audience sang along with great enthusiasm and feeling. Even Chao Anouvong and I were visibly moving our lips but neither of us could really sing.

Before retiring to bed Chao Anouvong thanked his hosts for their hospitality and praised the bards as highly as possible for their heavenly gift of voice and song. He told the crowd to forget their tears and turn their thoughts to celebration and the future. He felt there was nothing more pleasing than when a festive mood reigns in people's hearts. I wished I had a medicine with the power to rob grief and anger of their sting and to banish all painful memories, but the Lao could never forget how Bangkok had robbed ViengChan.

Although we were lodged in surprisingly comfortable quarters, my sleep was disturbed by sorrow for the people we'd left behind in Bangkok and my anxiety to be back in ViengChan. When the new dawn had scarcely flecked the eastern sky with red, I slipped out of bed. Chao Anouvong must also have seen the lovely dawn for he'd already gone outside to greet the people who'd gathered for breakfast. After a cup of coffee, fruit and a friendly chat, he stood tall in the morning sunshine and gave a speech.

'My good countrymen,' he said as he rose. 'Good morning to you all and thank you again for your company and your kind hospitality. We'd love to linger but we have work to do. Make your drink offerings now and see us safely off. And may every blessing of yours come true and may Lord Buddha permit me to enjoy them. Meanwhile, please remember this: grow plenty of rice and find wealth, but don't let a tyrant reap what you sow. We don't know from where the sun rises in the east to light our lands and where it sinks to in the west to bring darkness. But we do know that the east and west banks of the Mekong belong to the Lao people. So, the sooner we decide on a plan to reclaim our rights the better, or else Bangkok will continue to make free with our property. As for all of you that we leave behind, may the gods bring happiness and prosperity and keep everyone from harm. We take our leave of you all now.'

The crowd were so moved they all stood up and loudly applauded him. Some wept happy tears at his words. They told him between their sobs that they were as delighted to see him return one day as they would be to remain forever Lao. With this we left, accompanied by some of our noble hosts who led us into the morning sun and out of town.

The journey was easier than expected. It was the beginning of May by then but there was still no sign of rain and the ground of the Khorat Plain was still firm and welcoming. We didn't have much time to admire the scenery or enjoy the enchanting sound of birdsong or the sweet fragrance of the flowers. Chao Anouvong worked relentlessly, propped up and swaying about on his elephant's howdah, probably assembling the outline of his plans to move against Bangkok. I brought my elephant alongside his and quietly watched him with admiration before venturing into LanXang's affairs.

Chao Anouvong was unquestionably the greatest of patriots. From the day I became his private secretary I yearned to see him king of an independent country. I was honoured and delighted that he saw fit to appoint me as his confidant. The plan he revealed to me was to first unite the Lao principalities as one LanXang kingdom before separating the army into three main parts. Luang Phrabang and XiengKhuang would act as support units in charge of the Lao army's resources and supplies. ViengChan would provide the main fighting force and Champasak would help evacuate the people to ViengChan. He struggled to convince himself to trust Luang Phrabang. He also had doubts about the reliability of XiengKhuang and the support of the princes of LanNa.

'But then they are Lao,' he said. 'Surely we can trust them, can't we Phia Jon?'

I smiled at him as if to say that we could, for if Lao people couldn't unite like the sticky rice they were so fond of, then who would? 'Whom could we rely on if not the Lao?' I affirmed, for I too longed to believe right would prevail. Then again, I took nothing for granted.

He looked at me but said nothing before returning to his own thoughts. He'd done a vast amount of thinking while swaying about on the elephant, as though by a huge effort of will he'd been training his mind and body to carry the weight of his ambition. The journey therefore became a pilgrimage of enjoyment, albeit with a serious purpose, and the Lao people, especially those living on the Khorat Plateau, later named it 'Chao Anou's Route' (*Sen Thang Chao Anou*) in his honour.

We moved on from Khon Kaen, rattling up north through well-used paths and often fighting our way through rough tracks in the mountains before heading for NongBuaLamphu and then to Udon. Along the route Chao Anouvong gave his usual greetings from his elephant's howdah. He looked down on the upturned faces of the people we came across, gazing in awe at him.

'*Sabaidee!*' he called out cheerfully and enquired after their health, always following this with the same question: 'Don't you want to go to ViengChan and eat the new fragrant rice?' After a while I got to know his words so well that I'd quickly lick my dry lips and move them in time with his. He would have found this rather amusing if he'd known. He probably did! The people said they hoped to pray at the That Luang and That Phanom stupas before they died. That would surpass everything else in their lives.

LanXang's land had been created entirely by prehistoric geographical forces. The ancient village of BanXieng (BangChiang) near Udon, famous for its pottery, had been established thousands of years before. By the fourteenth century the Lao people were claiming land on the Khorat Plateau, establishing towns, villages, farmland and paddy fields scattered with grazing livestock. Meanwhile, the Siamese (*Khon Tai Sayam*) restricted themselves to the central plain of the Chaophraya river and minded their own business.

The whole of the Khorat Plateau right up to the ViengChan plain had been the rice bowl of LanXang. Soft green from July to September and golden brown from October to November, the paddy fields became the colour of Lao contentment. Rice was as vital to the people as the root is to the plant. Chao Anouvong pointed out that if Bangkok succeeded in annexing Lao territories, Siam would become a major rice grower, paying nothing for the crop and raising taxes to enrich the country while the farmers sweating their guts out remained poor. This class divide would open into a chasm between the unsympathetic and idle rich in Bangkok and the long-suffering poor Lao people in the north and northeast. You would be a fool to discount the importance of a people whose wealth had been generated by centuries of rice growing and trading.

We came across dilapidated farmhouses, deserted huts and the brown stubble of untended rice fields, depopulated and barren due to nature rather than the neglect and idleness of the people. During the census, Phromphakdy and his henchman, Suriyaphakdy, had acted not just as governors but as Siamese-appointed commissioners (*Khaluang*), fanning out across the region like a ravaging army, commandeering rice and livestock for a tiny percentage of their true value and raising taxes far beyond what most could afford. They behaved like a pestilence in the Lao LanXang provinces. The people were terrified of them and wished they could be brought to justice, but under Bangkok's protection they acted with impunity. They openly boasted of their rapidly increasing wealth. No wonder the people held such vociferously low opinions of Bangkok.

There was a tale of one farmer with nine children who'd tried to escape the census but had been captured some weeks later. On the orders of a Siamese official he was dragged into a detention house one morning, summarily denounced as a tax evader and tortured to death, despite the pleadings of his family and friends who'd come running when they heard what was happening. Most people ran away as far as they could and stayed with friends and relatives. Such stories enraged Chao Anouvong and spurred him on to work even harder for his country.

We passed through many villages and towns after we left Khorat city and Khon Kaen. To drum up support we stayed one night in each, accepting hospitality and enjoying some much-needed rest. It was often hot and humid when we headed off in the morning, but we pushed on along mostly shady tracks. The dreary, dry landscape often wore out my patience, for we were still days from ViengChan. However, we were happy to be far from Bangkok. The very name of the place upset Chao Anouvong… and me. I wondered how LanXang could ever have bowed before the haughty rulers of Siam. There was only one place on our minds, especially before the rain started, and that was ViengChan.

Chao Anouvong warned the people of Bangkok's impudent and insane plan to place heavy taxes on glutinous rice and to destroy the written Lao language in the temples and replace it with Siamese, all designed to change the Lao people's eating habits and force them to learn Siamese instead. Upon hearing this, the crowd rustled and roared, gesticulating angrily towards Bangkok.

At NongBuaLamphu towards the end of May we enjoyed the spectacle of some of the traditional Rocket Festivals (*Boun BangFai*), celebrated annually by the Lao people, but we didn't participate fully because some serious drinking was normally involved. The Lao drink deep on celebration, wedding and festival days. The Rocket Festivals were colourful occasions when drunkenness and mischievous behaviour in public was acceptable. Competitors came from near and far around NongBuaLamphu to compete for the best dancing team and best decorated rocket. A group of young choral dance girls wearing bright, traditional Lao costumes lined up to take their positions. They danced in unison to the music of the *Phin* and *Khaen* throughout the procession. As their feet moved expertly on the ground, they lifted their arms up and down, twisting and turning their hands and bending their long fingers with scintillating movements. We watched it from the stands, bobbing our heads, tapping our feet and musing on the pretty dancers. Chao Anouvong was appointed judge, but he hadn't a clue which team was the best. With great humour he announced that all were worthy winners, winning him a huge round of applause from the crowd.

Chao Anouvong responded to the dignitaries' welcoming ceremony with a light-hearted speech full of jokes and witticisms which brought plenty of happy laughter. I'd never seen him so lively. Everyone laughed aloud from sheer joy but the laughter hid a deep shadow of anxiety. He wished the participants well and prayed that the rockets would shoot high into heaven and bring plenty of rain to replenish the land. The festivals held throughout LanXang were important for preserving ancient traditions of song and story and for generating a sense of pride and unity amongst the scattered communities of the Lao-speaking people.

The top prize for the highest firing rocket – which left a trail of smoke followed by a 'WHOOOOSH' as it soared into the sky – was a jolly stiff drink of *Lauw Lao* and a prime bull buffalo. But the unfortunate owner of a less successful rocket – it gave out a few sparks and a puff of smoke before blowing up on the launching pad – was also given a cup of strong Lao wine before being thrown into a muddy pond as punishment.

The Rocket Festivals are a worthy reminder of the ancient love story of Thao Phadaeng and Nang Ay of NongHan Lake, made famous in one of the best Lao operatic arias. In short, Nang Ay's father, the king, offered her as the ultimate prize for the best firing rocket that would bring rain from heaven. Unfortunately, when Thao Phadaeng's rocket failed to leave the launching pad, he ended up losing his kingdom in a bet with the king instead of acquiring his lover, the beautiful Nang Ay. Well now, Nang Ay was also the love of Phaya Nark's life: the spirit king of dragons, who lived in the depths of the Mekong. He transformed himself into an albino squirrel and perched on a tree close by her. She fell for his charm and wanted him as a pet, but the servants couldn't catch him alive. Before he died, he placed a curse on her. The lovers – Phadaeng and Nang Ay – jumped on a horse and galloped away together but Phaya Nark pursued her until she drowned. Her spirit then joined him in his subterranean world of NongHan Lake, which still exists today.

The humid air was unbearable, the land and sky sweltering. We even sweated in the shade and our clothes were permanently soaked. With no safety precautions, each rocket, big and small, was lifted onto a steep launching pad high above the ground. We sat mute and gripped by the excitement while the fuse was lit. From time to time, when the rockets were fired into the air, storms miraculously lit up the horizon with multiple flashes and rumblings of thunder mixed with the noise of hailstorms, reverberating a thousand times around the distant mountains. Suddenly a thunderstorm flared in the inky sky above our heads, lightning rippled, and the temperature dropped by a few degrees. It was as if the dragon had soared to the skies and brought the rain clouds. The people jumped with joy at the sight of the dark sky. A moment later the heavens gaped, and it poured with rain, quite literally. The people started singing and dancing in harmony to the sound of lightning and thunder, but hard work in the paddy fields awaited them.

Every nation has its dream of happiness. For the laid-back landlocked LanXang, apart from the quintessentially Lao sticky rice, the people were filled with joy at the mighty Mekong, the Super Moon (when the moon hangs low and huge on the horizon) and the *Khaen* music. Nothing could compare the breath-taking romance with the magic of the Mekong on the full moon and the heart-rending sound of the *Khaen*. They have always been part of the Lao way of life. But more important at that time was the desire for independence and an end to Bangkok's expansion. What more could a proud and peaceful nation have wanted?

Chao Anouvong and his people absolutely opposed Siam's enlargement. Bangkok supported the supposedly civilised population of central Siam along the Chaophraya river, but ignored the alleged barbarians in the north and north-east of Siam. How could such an attitude, such discrimination, exist in a mild-mannered Buddhist society? The true paragon of barbarism was in fact the Rattanakosin institution. Nangklao and his appointees favoured extending Siamese citizenship to the Lao population. Bangkok clearly wanted to hold on to its vassal states and, cosseted in their homes and palaces, the regime used repression in pursuit of a Greater Siam.

From NongBuaLamphu we took a small detour instead of heading directly for Udon. Chao Anouvong wished to visit the city of Dan Sai in Loei province to pray at the That Si-SongHuck stupa. We dispatched a messenger well in advance. I guess it was around a three-day journey to Loei, running almost straight up along the plateau and up into the mountainous northernmost part of the Dong Phraya Yen range and then through narrow valleys to Dan Sai. However, with a favourably dry route and eager minds, we made it in less.

The That Si-SongHuck temple, which had fallen into neglect after Siam's 1779 invasion of LanXang, owed its creation to traditional Lao ideas and architecture, ideas which exist to this day. The way in which the exterior of the stupa embraced ideals of peace and friendship had a profound impact on the very nature of Lao LanXang. Even today the artistic culture of the Khorat Plateau differentiates itself with ease from Rattanakosin Siam. The great majority of the Lao population lived in towns but the true essence of LanXang could be found in the countryside throughout the twenty provinces of the Khorat Plateau and elsewhere in Siam where, despite living in poverty and dreaming of a better future, the people produced enough to eat and never went seriously hungry. The 1779 invasion had seriously scarred Lao life, but you could sense the fightback gathering pace as LanXang ached for self-rule and happier times.

When we reached Dan Sai in the early hours of the morning an immense horde came out to meet us. The city's nobles and elders rallied to offer Chao Anouvong their alliance and friendship, promising to obey his commands. He asked to be taken to the That Si-SongHuck temple – a symbol of peace, love, friendship and allegiance between the Siam and LanXang Kingdoms – to pray for justice and invoke the sacred words sworn by the two sides in 1563. A moment later, monks in their simple saffron robes, followed by a throng of people wearing elaborate Lao-style clothes and carrying silver bowls filled with flowers and beeswax candles, came out to greet us and escorted us to the shrine. With the monks in the lead we followed a path leading uphill.

On the high point of the hill was the temple itself, almost hidden from view. We climbed about twenty steps and took off our shoes before entering the sacred temple's perimeter, where the monks ceremonially welcomed us and where the main four-sided stupa (*That*) stands, facing north, south, east and west. Around its base were bouquets of mostly white and yellow flowers and small wax castles made of banana bark, decorated with beeswax flowers and lighted candles. Red was not allowed in the perimeter because it signified war and blood. Our appearance had clearly been noticed and was causing quite a stir but most of the people were happy to perform the ceremonial prayer with us. After Chao Anouvong had performed the customary ceremonies by lighting candles and making obeisance and prayer, he poured libations at the foot of the stupa. We then moved away from the holy ground to the temple courtyard down below.

Chao Anouvong spoke to the people on his journey whenever he could and Dan Sai city was no exception, although the inhabitants spoke in the Luang Phrabang dialect. Once we were outside the temple's sacred perimeter, he tilted his face upwards and stared towards the top of the stupa. He swung round to face the crowd and gave thanks to the welcoming party, who began to stir. He condemned the Siamese royal family's hostility, advising the Lao people to search their souls and never neglect their Lao consciousness.

'My countrymen,' he said, raising his awe-inspiring voice and pointing towards the sparkling stupa's golden top, 'it was at this very site that the Siamese royal family swore love and friendship with us in 1563 and accepted a permanent demarcation treaty between our two kingdoms. And if ever we should question whether they revoked their promises by invading ViengChan in 1779 and seeking domination over us, we should always remember what we see here in this sacred stupa in your city of Dan Sai. They broke their vows by sending their army across this sacred boundary.' The crowd loudly cheered in agreement and some were visibly moved.

'Remember. You know why this monument was built?' he continued. 'The name "Si-Song-Huck", or "Si-Song-Ruck" to the Siamese (Sacred-Two-Love) should never escape your memory. But it appears that Bangkok has forgotten!' He raised his head and pointed at the sun reflecting on the golden spire of the shrine. He explained that the sun – the source of light and life – never discriminates. 'We revere the sun,' he said, 'because the earth would be dead without it. It shines on all men, rich and poor, virtuous and immoral, and a sudden downpour doesn't distinguish between us – we all get soaked while the rest of the world laughs.' The crowd chuckled.

'At the moment,' he went on, 'the Siamese care only for themselves yet we still behave honourably towards them. They discriminate against us because they think they're more righteous than us, but they're not so different. If they've any honour left they should come here and renew their vows. We can no longer trust them. Our homes are still burning to remind us of that mistake. They're now trying to expand their territory and reduce us to second-class citizens. Think of who you are and what you want.' There was a short pause while the bewildered crowd looked at each other and waited anxiously.

'You and I, ladies and gentlemen, are Lao,' he said, looking and nodding at the crowd. 'I know what we want.' Then he roared, 'We want respect and justice! We don't want to belong to Siam or to become Siamese. We want to be Lao!' There was a spontaneous, deafening roar of approval from the crowd as they jostled to see him. He went on to tell the people that their struggle for freedom (*Itsarapharp* ອິສະຣະພາພ) would be a difficult undertaking. 'Your voice and your memory are all the power we need to achieve justice,' he continued. 'You all possess the intelligence and ability to overcome hardship. If I can convince you I'm right, then together we cannot fail in our struggle. Otherwise we'll count for nothing.' Then he roared again. 'We must stand up before Bangkok destroys us! Let us believe in ourselves and make sure they'll never take away that which is dearest to us. They may use their wealth and power to weaken us but they'll never crush us!'

The crowd applauded loudly, their faces flushing vengefully in the bright sunlight. He went on to say that if the Lao people decided to fight for unification, Bangkok would never again be able to buy Lao royalty with their bribes and threats. The effect of his words was obvious amongst the cheering crowd. He'd succeeded in rallying the people's support with his voice alone. Some of the younger supporters took a more robust view and began to remove Siamese flags along the route, tossing them to the ground and burning them. No one tried to stop them. We bade them a fond farewell and left them to contemplate the future as we slowly headed back to our convoy.

He told me afterwards that he'd prayed for LanXang unification and for the invocation of the 1563 accord at the That Si-SongHuck shrine. I congratulated him on his speech and told him I was praying for his wishes to come true. 'Let's hope the Lord Buddha and the gods care more for us than for those unjust people in Bangkok,' he muttered.

By now the sun had almost passed its zenith. We followed our tracks downhill back to NongBuaLamphu. To begin with our journey was somewhat slow and we were tired by late afternoon. After travelling for nearly a day we came across a small peaceful village and its industrious inhabitants near Phu KaoSan hill where we decided to stay for the night. The village consisted of about sixty houses dominated by the gentle hill, where a temple stood with its six monks and two nuns in residence. The monks, who performed no manual labour and occupied themselves solely with spiritual matters, were supported by the local community. They lived in strict celibacy and were forbidden to have anything to do with women but could ask to be released from their vows if they fell in love and wished to marry. As in the rest of LanXang the houses were built on stilts and were crowded together, each with its own vegetable and herb garden. Some owned domestic livestock, with the cultivated lands and paddy fields close by. The villagers used every minute of daylight for their agricultural work. The women wove their own cloth, and all their clothes were home-made.

It was customary in LanXang never to refuse the hospitality of a host. This might suggest there was often not enough food and drink, or space and blankets, for host and guests to sleep in comfort! Entertainment is in the Lao people's character. They are big-hearted optimists. Therefore, after a performance of *Khaen* and *Phin* music and a light welcoming meal of steamed fish and vegetables, young bamboo shoot soup, red ant egg broth, chilli sauce and steaming hot sticky rice, Chao Anouvong slept in the house of the village headman (*Tasaeng*), a subordinate of the governor (*Chaomueang*). The rest of us collapsed in exhaustion and slept inside mosquito nets in the guests' quarters and in the temple's donation hall. I slept well and happily dreamt that I flew like a bird over the mountains to ViengChan.

When I went to see Chao Anouvong just before the new dawn had touched the east with pink, he was already dressed. When the highest peak glowed like fire, he was keen to discover what the day would bring. As soon as it was light our convoy set off. Our route was announced in advance as usual. I was expecting we would head north-eastward towards Udon in the direction of ViengChan but instead we performed an abrupt about-turn and marched south-eastward around the northern edge of NongBuaLamphu Lake. I looked at Chao Anouvong in puzzlement but said nothing. When the sun broke through, the distant forest seemed to rise and drift high amongst the mountains into the cloud in the east. We could see the silhouettes of local fishermen standing in their pirogues and lifting their fishing nets from the glittering waters. By mid-morning we'd turned northeast and passed through a narrow passage of imposing trees, their rope-like climbers winding their way up high and through knee-high thick shrubs beneath. The impression was of an untouched and vast natural forest.

'This is our country (*Ban Mueang*),' Chao Anouvong murmured, inhaling deeply. 'This land, our beautiful land. One can feel, smell and see our country. And talk about it.' He went on to say that each plant, each animal and each man had a secret life as hidden as the depths of a lake (*Nong/Bueng*) or river (*Nam Xe*); the streams (*Huai*) mingle with the rivers and then with the ocean (*Thalay*); the winds (*Lom*) merge forever with the sky (*Tong Fah*) and nothing in the world can separate them. Each country, ruler and individual are subject to the land and has to learn when to take and when to give. LanXang is bound to the earth and to nature; it underpins its life and symbolises its traditions, connecting the people to the past and to the present. The mighty Mother Mekong (*Mae Nam Kong*) is the Lao people's spine. It should never become a mere boundary, dividing people from each other. It was unthinkable for the Lao to be ruled by the haughty Siamese: in Bangkok or anywhere else.

Finally, as soon as we emerged from the forest and arrived at the narrow valley of the Phou KhaoSan pass, Chao Anouvong stepped down from his elephant, setting foot on his motherland with a happy heart. In silence, he took a deep breath and kissed his native earth. I watched, my eyes wet with tears. It was a momentous and moving moment. Then, without any hesitation he made straight for the high ground as if he were a young man. It was astonishing. As soon as my elephant knelt, I jumped off my howdah and followed.

He pulled himself up steep slopes amongst small trees and walked through knee-high bushes, occasionally turning round to look at the scenery, me at his tail panting and sweating. Then he stopped at a vantage point, his left hand holding on to a small tree trunk. I stood at his side so I could pass him anything he needed. There was a sudden quietness, a silent quiver in the hot, still air. Ignoring the shouts of encouragement and warning from our followers below, he turned and shielded his eyes against the bright sunlight. He then scanned the vast surroundings, squinting to right and left, as a general might check the lie of the land and the position of the clouds hanging over mountain passes before giving the order for battle to commence. I watched him closely, never taking my eyes from him – not even the slightest blink of his eyes escaped me. He seemed tense and his concentration made him look very serious. He turned round and whispered to me, 'This could be it, Phia Jon. This could be the battleground, and perhaps this could be our last bastion.'

I gasped. Turning my head from the direct sunlight I scanned the view below. For almost the first time ever I found myself unable to see what was in his mind, the beautiful, narrow valley landscape scattered with forest trees and intermittent plantations stretching as far as the eye could see. I saw coconut trees in the distance swaying in the wind like brooms and the lifeless, sunburnt straw of the paddy fields shimmering in the sun, while the gibbons' song vibrated from the gigantic trees above. With my heart thumping I looked harder until I strained my eyes. Then I glanced up to find him climbing higher, away from me. I didn't follow and continued to study the landscape as carefully as possible. When he descended, he rushed straight past me, muttering to himself like a man on a mission. 'This KhaoSan pass will be a vital place for our defence,' he said. I took no notice and, without looking at the land again, followed him down carefully. We both got down safely. After dusting himself off he dispatched a messenger to ViengChan to inform the palace of our arrival. We climbed back on our howdahs and continued our journey at a speedy pace.

Three years later, in 1828, this was to be a major battleground.

XIII

Gathering Thoughts

O ur journey was exhilarating, thrilling and punishing but Chao Anouvong's calmness never wavered. And if our efforts to attend King Naphalai's funeral in Bangkok failed to deliver rich rewards, then our expedition through the Khorat Plateau back to ViengChan certainly did. Although, it had clearly exhausted him as well as me, it had really felt like a journey of discovery. His direct experience of the social and political unrest in Siam had provided ammunition for his speeches. I suspected he'd be denounced as a traitor in Bangkok, yet his rhetoric must have stirred the people's patriotism. The sentiments he evoked resonated with all the Lao people who'd been suffering from humiliation and who shared his ideology of sovereignty, homeland, family, work, honour, security, justice and common sense. On top of secretly promising to provide granaries and to fight for ViengChan, they'd been unreservedly hospitable, welcoming us with that inimitable Lao spirit and enthusiasm, showering us with unforgettable generosity and kind-heartedness. Their faces had been so happy whenever they saw us, and we'd felt very sad saying goodbye to them. Chao Anouvong was confident of popular support as he hastened towards a showdown with Bangkok, though he still favoured a peaceful resolution.

The diversion to Dan Sai slowed our return by two days, but after nearly two months of arduous travel through the provinces and stopping in Saraburi, Khorat, Khon Kaen, NongBuaLamphu, Dan Sai and Udon to name but a few, we at least reached the outskirts of Mueang Si-Xiengmai city unannounced. The crowds soon appeared, however. It was late afternoon and we headed straight for the port. As if the gods had dispersed the mists, ViengChan was clearly in view under a clear sky across the Mekong. The sight of the long line of shining, slender temple roofs and the golden palace's spires was an overwhelming sight for our exhausted bodies. We were in a state of euphoric happiness as we made drink offerings and gratefully looked up to heaven. Our tired elephants and horses were excited too and were taken straight down to the river to drink. Some of our horses' hooves were nearly worn down to the frogs. Nangklao could have detained Chao Anouvong, all of us, in Bangkok, but now, fuelled by the sight of our capital city, the sparkling river and the thoughts of the distant That Luang stupa, we sought to squeeze the last drops of energy out of our bodies. We excitedly waited to board the boats to cross over to our waiting families. It was blissful.

The people of ViengChan had gathered in large numbers to greet our return. With my tired eyes I could just see them sheltering under the shade and excitedly waving their colourful parasols and flags at us. The children were jumping up and down and running along the riverbank. The Mekong was at its lowest. The mighty muddy river, over a mile wide in the rainy season, was now a mere channel of clear blue water between the right bank and the sandy island of Donchan. Most of us couldn't resist jumping in to cool ourselves. Some plunged in with a splash and then swam about with joy.

Chao Anouvong hid his weariness well. I just about mastered mine. He appeared to gain immense relief from the spectacle of the people. With his morale lifted, as if he'd just solved a thorny problem, he smiled in satisfaction. Now and then he strode about to stretch his legs while the vessel was being prepared. Standing under a tree and looking across to ViengChan, he momentarily shut his eyes and took a deep breath. As soon as the staff informed us that everything was ready, he hurriedly went down to board the boat, but before joyfully urging everyone to hurry along, he unexpectedly jumped into the water fully clothed. I simply couldn't resist either and dived in immediately after him. It was indeed a moment of total joy! Everyone laughed heartily.

As our boat was drawing closer to the port in the Souantan district in the north of the city, he turned towards me with great pride. 'Isn't it good to be back,' he said. 'Oh bliss! There's no place like it.'

'Yes, it is indeed, Your Majesty,' I said softly, trying to hide my excitement. He smiled, nodding gently at my words.

As we approached the dock, he held up his hand to the excited welcoming party. Many people, children included, careered along the bank, cheerfully shouting and calling to each other. The sound of the murmuring crowd vibrated in the humid air.

'The king has arrived. Long live the king!' they cried out.

Chao Anouvong raised his hand to acknowledge the gathering, who responded with applause. We disembarked amidst cheers and jubilation. The moment he reached the top of the riverbank he was greeted by roaring crowds.

'*Sabaidee* everyone. Thank you for coming to meet us,' he said, smiling.

'Our humble respects, Chao Anou,' the crowd responded affectionately, raising a greeting of joy, stretching their praying hands to heaven, many even shedding tears. 'We're so happy to see you. Welcome back, Your Majesty!' He lifted his hand in acknowledgement. The courtiers soon brought a horse-drawn carriage to take him to the palace but he told them he was relieved to be back and full of energy.

'We need to stretch our legs, thank you,' he said and started to stroll along through the gazing throng. They praised him with pious words and threw flowers in his path, applauding him all the way to the palace.

Much to our relief, we happily and exhaustedly arrived back in the bosom of our capital ViengChan at the end of May – before the rainy season properly began – full of anecdotes. Frankly, after enduring three months of humiliation in Bangkok, trapped in a system that seemed to enjoy intimidation, we were elated to be back. Alone in the library I performed an ungainly dance of jubilation and then rebelliously blasted out the national anthem. The king must have heard it, for he mischievously suggested later that the two of us should take singing lessons.

With the approach of the monsoon it was getting hot and humid, and our lives were more and more frequently interrupted. Even the quiet garden and sheltered corners of the palace courtyard felt the breath of the coming storm. I turned my attention to the upkeep of the library. After five months of neglect the dust had multiplied into a coat of ash over the furniture and books. And then there were the archives to be written and properly kept in order. I tried to rest my tired body and to dispel the unpleasant experience of Bangkok, to wipe it from my mind. I kept myself very busy, visiting my mother, socialising and catching up with friends. I suspected that Chao Anouvong was giving serious consideration to the next stage of his reign, aware of the difficult challenges ahead. In fact, I was certain that his mind had been so permanently immersed in important thoughts that he'd very little time to do anything other than rest his aging body.

Over a week later he asked to see me. Admittedly I'd been happy in my own company, but I'd been pondering and anticipating the important business of the kingdom, which I knew had been gathering in his mind. One hot and humid late evening in early June, the rain arrived in earnest. Insects were rising from the ground in great numbers, filling the air as they flew about looking for mates. While I sat reading to the sound of the pouring rain, the moths and insects whirled like flakes of ash around the torches, throwing themselves at the flame, shrivelling and falling dead. The stars were above our heads when Chao Anouvong's face, flushed in the firelight, turned to me.

'Do you agree, Phia Jon,' he said, 'that independence is as important to our existence as food and water?'

'Very much so, Your Majesty,' I replied, closing my book.

'Well, LanXang mustn't forget how to live,' he said. 'People will remember who we are by our achievements. All my life, some great longing has possessed me, a deed I simply had to accomplish. I wish to fulfil my destiny. We must live courageously and die leaving everlasting fame. Our independence is vital and we must try to reclaim it. If it's not to be me, then I pray for another, future Lao hero. I fear terribly that our country might be overrun by the avaricious Siamese from Bangkok.'

'LanXang is entirely in your hands and the people depend on you to free them,' I said.

He went silent, shutting his eyes and nodding.

During our long journey back from Bangkok He'd complained bitterly about Siam's expansionist policies and condemned its governors' actions on the Khorat Plateau. His speeches not only marked the opening of his campaign against Bangkok but were a means of gathering support. He was convinced the Lao nation must be saved at all costs and he regarded himself as her champion. The people supported him. Up to now he'd always been quite passive politically, preferring peace and reconciliation because of his philosophical views. But now he was king he would become the personification of Lao resistance against Bangkok's tyranny.

What had caused this transformation? Well, internally, he was in turmoil. After nearly three tiresome months in Bangkok and almost two months' journey through the Khorat Plateau, exposing the full horror of the Rattanakosin regime, his dislike for Siam had increased. Back in ViengChan his dismay at Bangkok's arrogance, hypocrisy and injustice had deepened. His own subconscious sense of patriotism propelled him to fight for justice and freedom for his country. He felt obliged to oppose Bangkok.

The meeting with Nangklao, a tyrant whose government invoked fear and absolute subservience, prompted all these strands of a long-brewing rebellion to come together. The nearest parallel to Chao Anouvong's actions may be the Siamese King Naresuan the Great, who denounced Burmese domination. Chao Anouvong must have concluded that the Siamese had become insensitive, self-opinionated and egotistical bullies. With no sense of fair play or decorum, Bangkok sat on its hands and looked the other way while its governors and officials stepped up their campaign of intimidation and branding. Saddened, he was convinced Siam would never compromise over LanXang independence. He was determined not to waste the little time left to him and was prepared to go to war if necessary to save the Lao nation.

His words warmed the air, then travelled down my neck and along my spine like fire. With the experiences of Bangkok and our journey through the Khorat Plateau still fresh in our minds, I listened to his pain, the pain of responsibility and duty. He was faced with magnificent opportunities cleverly disguised as impossible situations. I sensed renewed hopes and plans. His confidence had increased and the memories of the 1779 Siamese invasion and his humiliation in Bangkok were as vivid as if they'd happened yesterday. Patience was still the order of the day, but the mood had changed since our return; feelings against Bangkok had unsurprisingly hardened and become more widespread. He was right to point out we were only human beings; that it was within the Lao people's right to want revenge, though they understandably feared for the safety of their families. His policy had always been to simply stay alive in the hope Bangkok would one day face payback. His upbringing in Bangkok had made him cautious but he was now willing to act, in spite of his fear.

'Phia Jon, do you realise it's impossible to know whether we'll succeed or fail?' he said thoughtfully, not looking at me but fixing his gaze across the Mekong.

'Yes, that's very true,' I said softly, putting my book away and listening to him.

'What would you attempt if you knew for sure you couldn't fail?' he asked.

I didn't respond immediately, though I knew what he meant. I suggested that one should only try one's best, without fear of failure. He said nothing but continued to fix his stare on the opposite side of the Mekong, tapping his foot. He took a deep breath and his face flushed slightly. He didn't normally show much emotion but at that moment it was impossible to hide it.

'Our long history has taught us that the Siamese have the very same origins as us,' he said. 'Why do they treat us like this? They refuse to tell their people the truth about LanXang. Instead they claim everyone's descended from them, with Bangkok as the centre of the Siamese world. For some unknown reason they've forgotten the sacred laws of Legendary King Khoun Borom: trust, respect, loyalty and peaceful co-existence. Perhaps their vanity has convinced them they're different from us; why else would they go about destroying our towns and cities and burning our temples? They tried to weaken us even further by taking away and enslaving our people, especially the intellectuals. I tell you, Phia Jon, the Lao people in Bangkok, Saraburi and Khorat we've just visited are painful reminders of this. Bangkok seems unaware that our willpower would never die. We might one day learn to forgive, but because of their injustices, we'll never forget.'

There was a long pause. I kept silent and held my breath in anticipation. I begged him to tell me more about the invasion of ViengChan.

'According to the lucky few,' he explained, 'who managed to escape and return home, the cruelty was unimaginable. They brought despairing messages from the captives, who said they were being hurried mercilessly along, many weighed down by burdens strapped to their backs. Men without wives or children who might be tempted to escape were tied together with ropes threaded through wooden collars. Those with families were allowed to walk freely. The sick and the weak were flung down to die miserably in the jungle. Many died from sickness, starvation and exhaustion en route.'

I was deeply moved by this story but just couldn't understand how such cruelty could exist; I was horrified at the scale of the atrocities and was haunted by the memory of Korn, the thin, partially blind old man in Saraburi with his *Khaen*; to think I'd nearly kicked him for getting too close to Chao Anouvong! His awful sufferings prompted me to ask myself how such closely related people could do such dreadful things to each other. The Siamese officials and soldiers were of course carrying out Bangkok's orders, but Chao Anouvong conceded that some of our own Lao rulers hadn't been particularly thoughtful and kind to their people in the past.

'It's so hard to believe that the Siamese, our blood brothers, could be so heartless,' he added. He paused to take a sip of water before denouncing as nonsense Bangkok's insistence that the Lao living in the northern and north-eastern provinces amongst the water buffaloes and the rice fields were rustic and uneducated, whereas the citizens of Bangkok – a mixture of Chinese migrants and Siamese under the influence of Western colonists – were civilised. 'They're quite wrong,' he said, 'to cast doubt on our intelligence. It's natural, of course, to want to spend most of your time with wise people but surely they would hang their heads in shame if those wise men realised how badly the Siamese behave. Our shared language makes us equal in many respects but how could we have anything in common with such an arrogant, untrustworthy, snobbish, boastful, slanderous, self-serving bunch?'

He stressed further that LanXang wasn't defined merely by its rivers or mountains, or even by its blood, race or religion. The land was the very embodiment of Legendary Khoun Borom's sacred laws of freedom, shared between Siamese and Lao alike since our ancestors migrated from China. Therefore Lao citizens in Siam should affirm their rights and privileges based on historic relations with their compatriots in LanXang.

He pointed across the Mekong and said that the Siamese and the Lao mustn't become enemies. 'We're descended from one of King Khoun Borom's seven sons. They all swore to abide by their father's doctrines before leaving to rule in different lands. The Siamese as much part of the Ai-Lao race as we are. Instead of simply discussing any differences between us, they thought fit to invade and dominate us, betraying those sacred laws. Let me tell you Phia Jon, from now on we'll fight to preserve our liberty and identity. We are a simple, laid-back, easy-going and peaceful people who deserve to live freely in our own beloved country. We will challenge them.'

Surely you can't argue with that!

Six months had passed since our return. As far as we were concerned, Bangkok was history: out of sight, out of mind. Chao Anouvong had recovered a little but still felt only contempt towards Nangklao. Unsurprisingly, Prince Rathsavong Ngao's plight upset him the most. It is every man's duty to protect his son, but he was powerless to do so. He was proud of all his children, but he loved Rathsavong Ngao with a silent intensity. His mind was weighed down with worry: the Lao people on the Khorat Plateau continued to suffer despite his pleas for Bangkok to end their cruel census. He passionately desired justice and freedom for the people and all his worries about LanXang's future came crowding back into his mind. His greatest concern was for Prince Ngao and his followers, forced to dig canals in Bangkok. I often found him on the balcony outside his study leaning on the balustrade, gazing across the Mekong as if he could see all the way to Bangkok where he would like to seize Nangklao by the throat. Alas there was nothing he could do but wait.

During dinner one evening he asked, as expected, to see the transcripts of the meeting with Nangklao. I fetched the bundle from my room before retiring to bed. When I attended the next morning's briefing, he said that my observations on Nangklao's appearance and character were rather unflattering, but marvellously put. He jokingly advised me to lock the papers away for fear they might rouse Bangkok's fury. I thanked him for defending me at the meeting, telling him that I'd thought his confrontational attitude towards Nangklao to be terribly risky. He readily admitted that his behaviour had demonstrated a certain degree of stupidity; he'd been close to signing his own death warrant. But he cheerfully claimed that his display of sycophancy and submission had got us safely out of Bangkok in the end. We heaved a sigh of relief and smiled at each other in satisfaction.

While we were waiting patiently for the prince and his followers to return from Bangkok, life in the palace almost paused, like the calm before a storm. We envisaged a time when the Siamese might visit our small cities, escaping from the cult of ugliness that dominated life in their rough, smelly and overcrowded capital. They would be more than welcome to sit in our shaded gardens, sipping cold drinks while listening to birdsong and watching the sun setting when the glowing ball retreated below the bank of the Mekong, throwing a pure, translucent pinkish light upon the twilit sky. It would perhaps be one of the most beautiful and moving visions they'd ever experienced. Tourists are one thing, but they should never see themselves as missionaries, spreading their values around the world and claiming everywhere as their own. They should value our shared histories but different destinies.

Rathsavong Ngao finally arrived back from Bangkok in late November, an angry man. It brought great happiness to all of us but we were told of the unimaginable physical and mental suffering inflicted on the Lao slave labourers: segregation, starvation and exhaustion. The eventful meeting with Nangklao and the stench of Bangkok came rushing back to my mind. The prince reported that hundreds of Laomen had died dragging a giant tree to build a huge ceremonial boat for Nangklao. He urged his father to declare war on Siam, but Chao Anouvong told him, after a *Baci SouKhuan* ceremony to recall his spirit and welcome him back, that food, drink and rest must come first. He looked old for twenty-five and had lost so much weight he seemed half the man he used to be.

A week later, a healthier looking Rathsavong Ngao came to see the king. He tapped softly at his door and walked into the study where Chao Anouvong was working at his desk. I rose to my feet, bowed in reverence and offered him a chair, but he stood facing his father anxiously.

'My respect to you, Your Majesty' he said and bowed. 'I'm sorry to disturb you, but may I please have a word?'

'Yes, of course, Ngao,' Chao Anouvong said, half turning but not looking up. 'What's troubling you?'

At first Rathsavong Ngao casually mentioned that Nangklao wanted Chao Anouvong to go and help him in Bangkok, before handing him a letter from the Siamese king. Chao Anouvong looked at the handwriting and quickly opened the envelope. He browsed through the letter before throwing it on his desk as though it wasn't important. Prince Ngao then told us of his unhappy experiences, a grim and angry expression on his face. He'd been bruised by the humiliation; despite managing to leave Bangkok alive, his dignity and moral character had been systematically abused. I noticed his anger furrowed his brow as if it physically pained him.

'We have to do something to restore LanXang,' he insisted, adding that he wanted to show the arrogant Siamese what a rustic Lao was really capable of.

There was a long pause while Chao Anouvong, who looked upset, folded the letter and dropped it into a silver tray before swinging round to face his son and saying, 'Nangklao's letter confirms what you've just told me. I'll certainly never go to that polluted and accursed city again. But did I hear you correctly: you and others were forced to work like slave labourers?'

'Yes, father.'

'Digging canals, finding your own food and water, some dying of exhaustion?'

'That's correct. They were so cruel and many of our people died needlessly. It was just terrible.'

'They insulted you and abused you when you complained about their inhumanity?'

'Yes, they kicked and flogged us… slapped our faces… called us names.'

'Did you complain to that bully Nangklao?'

'I certainly did. What else could I have done?'

'You confronted him – that brute of a mixed tribe – in his palace, that house of fear of his?'

'Yes, I did father. I had no choice!'

'Good for you, my son. Your courage is unrivalled. Oh my son! You make us all proud to be Lao!!'

'Here, here!' I said approvingly. I simply couldn't help it. 'If I may add, it was indeed a very commendable act of bravery, and we should make a drink offering for it.'

Chao Anouvong rushed forward and gave his son a congratulatory hug. They agreed to work together towards the liberation of LanXang. His humiliation and his inability to bring his sister back to ViengChan, as well as Nangklao's mercurial behaviour during their fateful encounter, were all sources of deep frustration for him. This was in fact the tipping point that provoked him to fight for the Lao nation. The situation had become intolerable and a Lao popular revolt against the Rattanakosins' regime began.

In late October 1826, the end of Buddhist Lent (*Boun Ork Phansa*) was nigh. It was well over a year since our return from Bangkok and any news that reached us was sketchy and out of date. We kept ourselves busy and were seldom disturbed when we worked together in Chao Anouvong's study. Then, for the first time, an important dispatch arrived from Bangkok. A footman threw himself to the floor in homage, drew his breath and delivered a letter sealed with a Garuda crest (a mythical eagle: the Siamese royal symbol) before withdrawing and closing the door silently behind him. Chao Anouvong hastily broke the seal and let out a shout of surprise.

'*Phachao Euyh*! (Good god!). We've received a letter from the king of Siam... plus a copy of the English Treaty. I think I'd better be seated, Phia Jon,' he announced. Chao Anouvong didn't sit but carried on reading quietly, his eyes rapidly scanning the dispatch. 'Would you believe it: we're being invited to go and rest by the pleasure lake! What have I done to deserve this?' he groaned, casting his eyes heavenwards and dropping the letter on his desk. You could tell he wasn't in the least interested in the invitation. 'You'd better have a look at it. Please study the English Treaty very carefully.'

The dispatch, which had come directly from Nangklao, contained a personal invitation to attend the opening of the newly enlarged pleasure lake. (King Naphalai had built the original lake in 1820 as a tribute to the close friendship between him and Chao Anouvong.) We weren't aware of the lake enlargement project or the outcome of the Burney Treaty (which Chao Anouvong referred to as the English Treaty). As the bureaucracy of both kingdoms ground along at a tediously slow pace, it was impossible to conduct a preliminary inquiry into these matters, but the invitation needed to be acknowledged without delay.

He found the invitation flattering at first but didn't consider it seriously. It certainly unsettled us and aroused our suspicions. I sensed a trap but stayed silent. Chao Anouvong was plunged into anxiety and became deadly serious. He began to worry even more about his faithful followers in Siam. I loathed Bangkok and declared that nothing would induce me to go there again. I was concerned how best to respond, but the Burney Treaty frantically stirred my thoughts.

'How will you reply, Your Majesty?' I asked anxiously while scanning the treaty; it was a huge blow to our morale. We both understood what it really meant for LanXang. The 1826 treaty ensured Siam wouldn't interfere with British interests in Burma.

'How else can one reply to a god, Phia Jon? A refusal would be seen as a snub. We'll have to say yes, of course,' he said, turning away. 'Well, let's not worry too much about it,' he added and calmly carried on with his work, composing political speeches and poems or writing short stories, mainly about nature, in prose and verse, which he rather enjoyed. It was his way of relaxing. My form of relaxation was reading them. It was such a pleasure, though his poetry was evanescent, and it wouldn't be easy to cajole people into reading it.

Chao Anouvong couldn't grasp Nangklao's real reasons for inviting him, so the letter was left untouched under a pile of books on his desk for a few days. He knew that if he fell victim to Bangkok's tricks his reign would be over; it would mean his destruction. And if he refused to accept, Nangklao would see it as an affront and condemn him as disloyal and traitorous. He saw Nangklao as an enemy of the Lao people, a tyrant who should be removed.

When he read the message properly many days later, he groaned and stared across the Mekong, realising the situation was even more complicated than he first thought. He wondered if he were worrying unnecessarily, but he feared there'd be no escape from Bangkok this time. He would suffer the same fate as his brother Nanthasene. He therefore decided to stay put in ViengChan. 'Perhaps it's a dereliction of duty, but frankly it would be a waste of time,' he said, but he continued to ponder. As did I, wondering if he were wasting a golden opportunity to negotiate for LanXang's future.

He reluctantly decided to compose a letter to Bangkok soon afterwards. In a panic, whenever he thought he'd successfully phrased suitably diplomatic phrases, the words he'd composed to praise the under-serving Siamese king ended up annoying him and became confused in his mind. He screwed the first draft into a ball and threw it into the bin. His relationship with Nangklao was becoming increasingly onerous. There was nothing to admire in the Siamese king, no subtlety of intellect, witty repartee or sharp observations that might then spin off into a profound discussion on the nature of human affairs.

I later discovered he even reminded Nangklao of his invitation to visit ViengChan in one of his discarded letters. When I said it had been a clever idea, he quipped that Nangklao would probably arrive with a large army, destroy the city and steal even more treasure.

Whatever the truth, Nangklao was inept and confused; he usually got one of his advisers to write his speeches and had no idea what he was going to say until the text was placed in front of him. How he could have become a statesman defeated me. Apparently, he would hold forth without interruption before sitting back to bask in the flattery of his mistresses, companions and guests, carousing with them and finishing the evening with endless monologues. The foreign emissaries and tradesmen encouraged his dreams of empire by suggesting he invade neighbouring countries. He became addicted to the gifts they deliberately plied him with. Lacking any talent for literary composition, he could only watch and listen in a stew of jealousy, rambling on about matters he knew nothing about. Being a king with the name Nangklao (which means 'sitting at the head'), he could do no wrong: one of the many perks of life at the top. He was easily impressed by wealthy foreign businessmen and diplomats, and he no longer cared about ordinary people. He took pleasure only in enriching himself and his associates. Like an impostor he seemed to be merely keeping the throne warm for a more suitable king: Mongkut, who'd become a monk during the power struggle to gain merit and build support.

Buddhist Lent ended a week or so later with an early morning offering to the monks at the temples. The Buddhist devotees built up merit for themselves, which they believed benefitted the spirits of their ancestors. At night the soft light of the early November full moon lent a new charm to the calm, fast-flowing river, but nearby everyone stayed awake. The people, mostly the lively youth, made their way to the Mekong to celebrate the annual Festival of light, which involved the launching of fire boats (*Lai Heua Fai* ໄຫຼເຮືອໄຟ) created by the monks, who would light candles and pray before launching them. Most of the smaller boats were made from banana stems, but the really tiny ones were carefully fashioned from folded banana leaves in the shape of lotus flowers, boats and pagodas, and were decorated with blossoms, incense sticks and lumps of sticky rice. To pay homage and respect to the Lord Buddha and the river spirit (*Phraya Nark Naga*) and to dispel bad luck, the people lit small candles on the miniature craft (*katong*) before setting them adrift (*Loy katong*). The flotilla of floating illuminations gradually grew and coalesced into a continuous stream of dotted, flickering lights as far as the eye could see. Then, quite suddenly, the mighty Mekong was transformed into a most spectacular mirror by the boats of fire, all ablaze with light in the shape of dragons and many other shapes and sizes. It was magical. The moon glowed and the darkness vibrated with joyful cheers, smiling crowds and happy laughter. The spectacle was wholly satisfying from start to finish, with the dark red floodlit temple roofs in the background and the foreground of fireworks reflected in the river. All night and day the streets along the Mekong were as crowded as on market day, with families happily buying gifts for loved ones and strangers chatting to each other and to the locals.

Lent (*Ork Phansa*) ended with the highly entertaining boat race festival (*Boun Suang Heua*) along the stretch of the Mekong north of the palace. The people made offerings to the gods and the vendors did a roaring trade. After three months of abstinence, the competitors' spirits were vociferously high with alcohol. They danced, sang and drank under the benevolent eyes of the monks. Groups of both old and young people from near and far wearing bright fancy clothes paraded around, singing and dancing joyfully. The lively gestures and harmonious rhythms of the performers and the improvised lyrics of their chants were complemented by the sound of the *Khaen* (bamboo pipes), the *Phin* or *kachapi* (guitars), the *ranart* (xylophones), the *khui* (flutes), the *vod* (oboes), the *kong* (drums) and the gongs, while the spectators performed a traditional circle dance (*Fonh Lamvong*). Men and women, boys and girls moved their legs and arms, bending and twisting their fingers as they danced in a circle to the music. Meanwhile the mighty, peaceful, muddy Mekong became crowded with long boats and hundreds of competing oarsmen. It was a magnificent sporting event in the true spirit of the end of Lent. By nightfall, calm had returned to the river, but on the banks the party went on late into the night.

Three weeks later, when the annual That Luang stupa celebration was also behind us, Chao Anouvong announced at a hastily convened dinner one evening that he'd received an invitation to visit Bangkok. The surprised guests turned to look at him. He produced the letter and laid it on the table before him for all to see. He gazed at it suspiciously before beckoning me to his side and handing it over to me. All the guests exchanged glances. While they were busy talking, I read it to him quietly and he heard it through. It was respectfully phrased:

From: Phra Nangklao Chao Yuhua in Bangkok.
To: Chao Anouvong in ViengChan.

'It is with the greatest pleasure that we inform Your Majesty that we have finally finished the enlargement of the pleasure pool… we request the pleasure of Your Majesty's company in Bangkok for a visit and to enable you to relax your mind and to share the mark of our esteem. We would advise you to bring along your family, musicians and artists, and exotic birds of paradise. We can assure Your Majesty that you will enjoy yourself.'

The letter was similar to that written by Naphalai to Chao Anouvong when the lake was first built. I handed it back to him and quietly told him that, although peremptory, the letter was at least polite. I reminded him that the Burney Treaty was a non-aggression pact ensuring that Siam wouldn't get involved in the Anglo-Burmese war but was free to do as it liked in LanXang, providing it didn't interfere with British interests in Malaya and Burma. I pictured his thoughts running ahead as water runs on dusty ground, first forwards then spreading everywhere, widening and branching out to consider possibilities and implications. In fact his real enmity towards Bangkok had been sparked off by Nangklao's refusal to enter into a dialogue with him concerning taking his sister, the court dancers and musicians and the Lao people back with him to ViengChan; forcing his followers to dig canals in Bangkok and to cut palm trees to build forts in Samud Pakan; the vicious census of the Lao population; and Siam's persistent designs on expansion. Nangklao's snub had hurt and humiliated him, provoking not only him but all freedom-loving Lao people to take up arms and fight for their rights.

Shortly afterwards he read the letter again, more slowly this time, and the pleasure seemed to have drained from his face. He rose and excused himself, taking his sons Rathsavong Ngao and Suthisan Poh aside and gesturing to Chief Registrar Phraya Sanon to follow him. 'I'm sorry to spoil such a pleasant evening,' he said before telling them about Nangklao's letter. They looked at each other in horror and astonishment. Phraya Sanon was not only an aristocrat by birth but had the airs of a true nobleman and a powerful voice to express his thoughts. He always spoke with authority and vigour when he'd important matters to impart. He made no secret of his intense opposition to Bangkok. He simply couldn't hide his hatred of the Rattanakosins. He tutted disapprovingly and cast his eyes upwards.

'It's a petty honey trap scheme, something they're particularly good at!' he declared. 'Bangkok's trying to soften and confuse you. For what it's worth, Siam may have a reputation as a visitors' paradise, but this is a dangerous trap. Not to mention they always use well-trained, beautiful girls as bait. Bangkok is full of seedy places and pretty young things.' The two princes gazed at each other as if to say, 'How does he know all about that?' but kept quiet. 'It's a city of the underworld riddled with corruption and the abuse of power. A malevolent atmosphere hangs over it,' he went on, looking at Chao Anouvong. 'Can't you see the wicked plot hidden in that letter? If you fall into temptation, you'll lose everything, including your life. Once you enter the gates of that smelly, polluted and immoral city, you'll never get out again. You'll be at his mercy and he's an autocrat, so he has none!'

Most of the guests went quiet and watched Chao Anouvong with concern.

'I think so, too,' Chao Anouvong said, adding that Nangklao was his own worst enemy.

'Not while I'm alive, he isn't,' Phraya Sanon said. 'You once said he's mixed race, but the Tai-Siamese exist in name only because they're Ai-Lao. Bluntly speaking he seems like a mixture of Mon and Persian to me! What a rogue!' The Mon were people from western Siam and south-eastern Burma. He spat out the Rattanakosin ruler's name as if it were poison. 'Nangklao! His very name pollutes my mouth. He's a detestable and oppressive ruler who seeks only to cement his place in Siamese history. Eliminating him would be a pleasure… a public service.' He moved a step closer. 'Your Majesty, please hear me. For LanXang's sake and to save the Lao nation, we must not embrace Bangkok. We must have the stomach to get rid of the Rattanakosins.' From the expression on his face it looked like he really meant it. 'I can't stand the whole Bangkok gang for their wicked desire for an empire at the expense of LanNa and LanXang,' he went on. 'Nangklao is the third and blackest scoundrel of them all. He's a chip off the old block, a tyrant. I see him not only as a two-faced brute but a deliberate illusionist. He deceives us with his duplicity, and like his grandfather and father before him, he believes he has the right to punish or kill anyone who stands in his way. He and his gang are a bunch of patronising snobs who think we don't know what we want for our nation. They're prejudiced against the Lao. Nothing will induce me to trust them, not even if they prostrated themselves before me and swore a solemn oath that they had no mischief in store for us. As a duty to the Lao nation, we must remove the evil villains of Bangkok who want to destroy us.' He paused to take a sip of his drink, but nobody spoke. 'In fact,' he continued thoughtfully, 'Nangklao could easily have prevented you leaving Bangkok after your meeting with him last year, for all I know. You're a genius who can speak so persuasively, but him and his men still loathe you and everything you stand for. He could have locked you up. How did you manage to persuade him to let you leave?'

Chao Anouvong winced and pondered. 'Well,' he said reluctantly, 'I did have to agree to provide military support in LanNa and...'

'Why, Your Majesty?' Phraya Sanon interrupted, amazed at how close to disaster his friend had come.

'I did try to get on good terms with him, but trust him, never,' Chao Anouvong said, beckoning the guests to sit. Everyone turned to look at him as he sat down. He gazed at Phraya Sanon and said, 'I had no choice but to pledge our loyalty and our military support.'

'For all I know,' persisted Phraya Sanon, 'they're vain and boastful, but when it comes down to it, moral and physical cowards. They show real political class and are sublime at sweet-talking, but none of these attributes have anything to do with genuine friendship. This has always been their policy towards us, forever twisting this way and that. They always manage to get someone else, young Laomen, to die for them. Their army is mostly composed of conscripts from poor Lao families on the Khorat Plateau. The Siamese pay the money and the Lao die. You could have been killed fighting for them in LanNa many years ago. Nevertheless, I must confess that no one is more pleased than I to see you back from Bangkok. I congratulate you for giving yourself a chance to fight another day. You have my full admiration.'

The other guests nodded and gave loud murmurs of assent.

'That was my only intention,' Chao Anouvong said and thanked Phraya

Sanon for his kind words, adding that convincing Nangklao to let him return to ViengChan was his greatest achievement, greater even than surviving the LanNa expeditions. He looked at his two sons, but their faces froze slightly.

'So, what are we going to do?' Rathsavong Ngao asked anxiously, adding that they were lucky to all be together again.

'Well,' said Chao Anouvong, wincing, 'if we refuse, Nangklao will turn against us. But if we accept and go to Bangkok, they'd probably lock me up and have me killed, just as they did to my dear brother Nanthasene.'

'And that Your Majesty simply mustn't happen. You must not accept the invitation,' insisted Phraya Sanon.

'But how will our goal ever be achieved?' Prince Ngao ventured.

'How?' repeated Chao Anouvong, turning to his son on his right-hand side. 'I think we've already wasted too much time rallying support to our cause.' He moved forward and clasped Prince Ngao's shoulder. 'I believe we should take the war to the enemy.'

'I agree,' said Phraya Sanon. 'The question is: how?'

Chao Anouvong glanced around and said that LanXang sought a peaceful solution and couldn't afford war. He turned to peer at the night sky across the Mekong and then swung round to glare at Phraya Sanon and all of us. Suddenly he slammed his fist on the table with a bang that made everyone jump.

'We should hit them with speed and take them by surprise,' he said loudly. 'We shall carry out a raid, a pre-emptive strike, to bring our people back from Saraburi and those other cities.'

Everyone listened intently. Phraya Sanon agreed nervously. A long march to within striking distance of Bangkok and an attempt to repatriate the tens of thousands of exiled Lao people was about the most provocative action Chao Anouvong could take. He knew this was a dicey strategy but wouldn't be dissuaded, for the sweat and tears of the Lao people in Saraburi was making Bangkok rich. The lack of manpower in ViengChan had made Chao Anouvong's position extremely, almost impossibly weak. Without the exiles, he was simply unable to restore LanXang to her former glory. It was clear that he was ready to fight.

'Remember,' Chao Anouvong roared, 'King Fah Ngum once said that where there are people, there also will be power and wealth.' He added that Bangkok's dark heart beat with hatred towards every Lao citizen.

As my heartbeat quickened, I found myself breaking into an anxious sweat. The raid would be sure to provoke Nangklao, and there was always the risk that some people might side with Bangkok and stage a rebellion. We all agreed there should be no middle ground: if any Lao people took up arms against their own countrymen, they would be condemned as traitors and enemies.

Chao Anouvong conceded that the raid was desperately risky but, after a short pause, he spoke with a firmness that was designed to settle the debate. 'He who controls the land controls the people,' he said. He was convinced the people were behind him and he invested all his hopes in their loyalty. Those hundreds of thousands, millions even, of Lao citizens across the Khorat Plateau were the solid foundation on which his popularity had been built. He was convinced they would never let him down.

Anyone could see he was right. King Fah Ngum the Great, after successfully uniting the Lao people, warned that the country couldn't develop without people. There was no denying that LanXang was large enough for a multitude of occupations: doctors, tutors, engineers, sculptors, painters, musicians, poets, actors, farmers, hunters, fishermen and so on, all of whom would continue to thrive in the kingdom. However, having lost vast numbers of people through forced migration to Siam in 1779, LanXang was unable to compete. It would take years to rebuild her to her former glory. There could be no power without wealth. What was more, without self-rule, the people's confidence and spirits would remain at their lowest ebb. Yet Chao Anouvong had demonstrated that he had a people and a kingdom to fight for and it would take more than mere words to deter him.

He feared the Lao identity would be eaten up or made to disappear from the earth. He found himself in a precarious situation: his kingdom faced imminent destruction. Should he declare war on Siam or wait and hope? He would initially adopt a patient but firm approach in an attempt to contain Bangkok's expansionist goals. But he realised that if left unchallenged, the Siamese had the capacity to dominate everyone. Charm alone would never persuade them to change their minds. LanXang might well end up with something far worse than the mendacious, autocratic Rattanakosin dynasty: a plague of jealousy and greed and a culture obsessed with the infectious pursuit of wealth.

The guests soon made their excuses and left into the night, bursting with food and thought. No doubt they had learned a lot about politics from Chao Anouvong.

To stage a pre-emptive strike on Siamese positions near Bangkok would no doubt make a villain of Chao Anouvong and hasten ambitions for a Greater Siam, but he only wanted to bring his people home. He didn't want war but knew that Bangkok would be jumping up and down like angry baboons. However, he felt strongly that the Siamese establishment would one day lose all its legitimacy with the urban poor. An uprising against Bangkok was imminent. Nevertheless, he still saw the military option as a last resort. While he continued to search for a peaceful solution, he kept war firmly in mind. Unless he fought for it, he believed the quest for LanXang unification would forever remain a mere silent dream.

XIV

Council of War

W hen I became Chao Anouvong's private and confidential secretary (*Laykar*) I began each morning, after being briefed by him and holding a private conversation with him, by gathering my thoughts. Assisted by good fortune and coincidence I felt I was very close to the centre of power. I had access to his desk, often littered with an assortment of official papers, classified documents and a bundle of his literary works. I devoted my time to summarising and arranging the most important of them according to subjects and particulars. He wrote poetry but very rarely anything about himself.

High-ranking officials, senior monks and many fair-minded intellectuals in both kingdoms sensed an increasingly bitter power struggle was brewing between Bangkok and ViengChan, which would only intensify until Bangkok either respected the That Si-SongHuck demarcation treaty and retreated to the Chaophraya river, or the Lao nation disappeared from the world forever. LanXang had been sensible enough to avoid outright confrontation up to then, but tension over the scale of Siam's controversial domineering policies had given way to mistrust in ViengChan, with the vicious census-taking proving the last straw for Chao Anouvong. ViengChan believed Bangkok was no longer fit to run a decent and balanced policy. Most Lao people felt dissatisfied at the prospect of a life that would neither make them prosperous nor provide any hope for the future.

The Lao nation had been held in low esteem since 1779, and Lao nationalism had been supplanted by Bangkok domination as an animating impulse. The Lao were fed up to the teeth with Siamese myths and glory. Very few of the educated Siamese elite were competent enough to realise both the advantages and disadvantages of a Greater Siam. Chao Anouvong was not a believer in this foolish, domineering system that required absolute subservience. He was no longer prepared to obey orders from Bangkok but was still willing to hear any reasonable suggestions. The Lao found it intolerable that Bangkok should even see fit to dictate the content of their food and culture. They tried to cope but increasingly found themselves forced to renounce more and more of their rights. They hated confrontation but their awareness of these absurdities only added strength to Bangkok's elbows. Siam's petty regulations had such an adverse effect on them that most Lao people felt dissatisfied at the prospect of a life that would neither make them prosperous nor provide any hope for the future. They increasingly distanced themselves from Bangkok and began to see the Rattanakosin Siamese as their enemies. They simply could not remain quiet and lay down their arms but were prepared to defend their honour against all slights. The Lao nationalist movement grew in strength, and, in the end, war became inevitable.

Privately I hold very ambivalent views about rulers and politicians, who seem to think they know everything there is to know about politics. Nobody does. I could never understand politics completely even if I stayed up all night thinking, analysing and solving problems or writing inspiring speeches for the king to deliver the following day. Nevertheless, while the world slept, I frequently sat by moonlight or lay in bed wondering what made these people want to be at the epicentre of politics in the first place. Frequently my mind would cease to have any coherent understanding of political matters. Then, somehow, under intense pressure, my thoughts became clear and I was able to commit any insights to memory. I was more of an ideas man, but I threw myself into politics at that time because I wanted to help Chao Anouvong achieve his goals for LanXang. I was ready to sacrifice everything for him and urged my compatriots to do likewise.

One observation of mine concerned the division of humans into different nations. On a basic level we are all human beings with the propensity to kill each other and to destroy the environment, but quite frankly the Lao could never be Siamese, and vice versa. It is impossible to make a leopard change its spots. The Lao became belligerent in the face of Bangkok's fraudulent policies. In my exhausted mind I often felt as if I were a wise man who appeared a fool in my wisdom. After spending many miserable, sleepless nights pondering, I finally came up with an idea and understood the geo-political history of the situation. You might well disagree with my theories, of course. Please feel free to make suggestions. I'm sure everyone would thank you for it.

Well now, bluntly speaking, the destruction of the Siamese capital Si-Ayutthaya by the Burmese in 1750 was the root cause of all this dissension. I believe the Siamese hated the Burmese: they were arch enemies, in a state of perpetual distrust and hostility because of territorial disputes. Burma at that time was being colonised by the British, who also wanted to gain a foothold in Siam. Influenced by greed, power and prosperity, Bangkok gladly welcomed colonisation as an opportunity to seal trading contacts with overseas investors, leading inexorably to moral bankruptcy through the accumulation for wealth, lack of concern for others and rampant consumerism.

The ethnically and linguistically different Malays were most certainly unhappy at the prospect of losing their northern lands to Siam, but their fate was in British hands.

The Khmers also disliked the Siamese intensely for invading, sacking and destroying their capital, Angkor Thom, three times: in 1352 by King Uthong; in 1393 by Uthong's son King Ramesuan; and finally by King Boromarachathirat in 1431. It was obvious Siam wanted to annex all Khmer land. After repelling a Siamese invasion in 1549, King Ong Chan (1516–1566) named one of his cities Siem Reap – literally the 'Defeat of Siam'. I've heard recently that Mongkut ordered the stone Khmer temple at Prasat Ta Prohm to be relocated stone by stone to Bangkok but failed in this endeavour. No wonder the Khmer people hated the Siamese.

Miraculously the Khmers and the Lao have never been to war with each other and have been allies since the fourteenth-century reign of King Fah Ngum of LanXang. Long may this be the case.

It's fair to say that the Vietnamese and the Burmese haven't played fair with LanXang either. In what has become known as the White Elephant War, King Le Thanh Tong of Vietnam demanded a sacred albino elephant from the Lao king, but when only its faeces was delivered, it drove him insane. He invaded Mueang Swa (Luang Phrabang) during the reigns of King Xay-Chakkhapat and his son Thaenkham in 1479. The Burmese King Bayin Naung the Great invaded ViengChan during King Xay-Setthathirath's reign in 1571. However, on both occasions the Lao successfully fought back and defeated them. They – the Vietnamese and the Burmese – did not remain in LanXang territory or establish any sort of power over the Lao. In fact they left without much destruction and looting and all was forgotten.

(For the sake of argument, one might add that Tang China was also an empire builder in ancient times. They invaded and conquered the Ai-Lao NanChao kingdom in Yunnan, but that's too long ago to even think about!)

For all its might, between 1350 (King Fah Ngum) and 1690 (Souriyavongsa), Lao LanXang refrained from invading any neighbouring countries because her people favoured peace, tranquillity, stability and reconciliation. Unfortunately the tripartition of LanXang in 1703 was the result of Siamese expansion and intrusion into the kingdom's affairs; this worsened considerably after the fall of ViengChan in 1779. Since then, Chao Anouvong not only urged his people to commemorate the heroism and sacrifice of the noble fighters and city defenders but used the events as a stark reminder of the oppression the Lao have suffered under Siam. ViengChan had been burnt to the ground and the Lao language had been suppressed. A poisonous distrust had festered between the two kingdoms. Rather than even attempting to understand the Siamese, all Lao could do was to have faith in themselves. The days of Lao–Siamese brotherhood were long gone, as the frequent Siamese references to Lao LanXang as the 'Rustic Buffalo' and the inhumane behaviour of their army attested to.

The Lao, with all their tolerance and charisma, and despite considerable effort, failed to persuade the arrogant and domineering Siamese to pull back to their own lands because of their insatiable desire for a Greater Siam. The situation was incredibly infuriating, but the Lao had courage, merit, dhamma and determination to aid them in their fight for justice against the Rattanakosins. With their pride, free spirit and easy manners, the Lao people, like any proud nation in the world, could be very forgiving, but they hated oppressors of any sort. Perhaps patriotism is written in our genes: all the Lao really wanted was to save their nation and to achieve their independence, but they faced alone a hostile Siam and its bestial, autocratic ruler. Meanwhile Lao nationalism surged to new levels. Nurtured by Bangkok's abusive policies, it fuelled the drive for LanXang autonomy.

Who do you think Chao Anouvong and the Lao people found most oppressive in 1826? Any fair-minded person would answer: the Rattanakosin government in Bangkok of course, for their villainy, their interfering expansionism and their growing arrogance and untrustworthiness, all in the name of an empire built at the expense of LanXang and LanNa, part of the Siamese conspiracy to eliminate both countries.

The Siamese government, fearful of an invasion by colonial powers, instead sold the kingdom to the highest bidder instead. Gangsterism grew and the traditional Siamese world gradually fell apart. Originally colonised by wealthy Chinese traders, Siam became a buffer zone between the British and the French. Both powers were happy to share the spoils.

Alas a landlocked Lao LanXang, deprived of her vast Lao population on the Khorat Plateau, was unable to compete economically, politically or militarily. Her people (comparable in number to the Siamese) became a poor and backward minority in their own land. No help came from neighbouring countries or the colonial powers. Chao Anouvong spoke with grief about how his kingdom had been abandoned. He felt something had to be done in the name of justice and peace to balance the power in the region.

Chao Anouvong realised making money was the colonists' primary motive but selling arms to Siam would only bring more conflict to the region. Nothing would ever make the Lao forget the terrible events of 1779, except perhaps the chance to win back their sovereignty and regain their territory. His plans to take advantage of British pressure on Siam from the south had been dashed by the Burney Treaty in which LanXang had been carved up between Siam and the colonial powers. He recognised that the Lao army had the will to fight but was very poorly equipped. Nevertheless, the time was right for revolt. He'd hoped not to go to war, but the sheer scale of Siamese cruelty made it inevitable. Rather than serving the foolish, he wished to peacefully coexist with the wise. He clearly expressed his final decision during a private debate over dinner one evening.

'Phia Jon, the wise know the future by observing the present,' he said. 'I'm aware of the horrors of the past but I believe it must be "Rise up Lao LanXang" now or never.'

We'd started to draw up rough contingency plans on how to face the Siamese in the event of war. I told him that though I might be devoid of talent, I wished to help in the preservation LanXang, in ridding our land of her illegal occupiers. In silence, I anxiously awaited his decision.

Then, one early morning at the beginning of December 1826, I was routinely busying myself with a few things in Chao Anouvong's study, straightening the desk and dusting the books. Meanwhile he remained motionless on his couch, murmuring inaudibly whenever he opened his eyes. I sensed something important was on his mind, as if he were hatching some sort of plot. I left him well alone and went outside to sit under a shady tree in the garden of tranquillity. I meditated for a while in an attempt to clear my head, but my mind was in disarray and I couldn't find a solution to anything. When I went back inside he was pacing about back and forth as if summoning his courage. Suddenly, a serious expression came over his face as he stared across the Mekong. His lips were moving as thoughts formed in his mind. I had faith in him, so I decided to ask, 'Please, may I share your thoughts?'

He calmly turned round and told me to leave everything alone before sighing and telling me about his dream. 'King Fah Ngum the Great wielding a sword and King Xay-Setthathirath holding the Emerald Buddha statue appeared to me. They recited lines from the doctrines of Legendary Khoun Borom and declared that the Rattanakosin Siamese had broken his sacred laws. They commanded me to rescue LanXang and save the Lao nation from Siam.'

He looked at me as though an apparition had appeared to him. I felt the hair standing up on the back of my head.

'Now, I have a task for you, Phia Jon,' he said. 'A rather important one.'

'I am at Your Majesty's disposal,' I said alertly.

He asked me to sit at the desk and write invitations to a secret meeting, similar to the series of letters he'd sent to the provincial governors and loyal rulers throughout LanXang the month before. Then he handed me a list of the important mandarins he wished to attend the meeting, most of whom lived outside the inner-city wall in the That Luang area. He commanded me to go round and inform each of them privately.

'And tell nobody what you're doing. Understood?' he ordered, warning me to be civil.

'Yes, fully,' I said, nodding my understanding.

He momentarily returned his gaze across the Mekong as if he could see the enemy in Bangkok.

'Now, are you ready to get to work, Anoujon?' he said.

'Certainly, Your Majesty,' I replied tentatively.

'What are you waiting for?' he said in an impatient voice when he saw me hesitating. He shooed me away with a flick of his fingers. 'Please go now, Anoujon. Go!'

Well, after so many years in his service, thirty-one years in fact, I'd got used to all sorts of bewildering commands. He knew danger didn't deter me. Obeying him was a matter of honour and I couldn't possibly decline, even if it meant risking my own life. I bowed to him and left the room in haste. Once I'd picked up a parasol to shelter myself against the blazing sun, and with only slippers on my feet instead of sandals or shoes, I set off through the inner-city gate to deliver the messages. It was indeed a very hot but exhilarating day for me.

Chao Anouvong used to say you could live in ViengChan without caring about what the lofty Siamese thought or said. Since 1779, thanks to the talent and determination of its people, ViengChan had been rebuilt. The houses were crowded close together and domestic livestock such as cows, pigs, goats and chickens were scattered all over the place. Everywhere herb gardens mingled with marigold. Birds flew and squirrels dashed from one fruit tree to the next – coconut, mango, jackfruit, banana, papaya, orange and lime trees intermingled with isolated big trees and bamboo bushes. You could smell burning beeswax candles and incense stones from the beautiful temples, hundreds of them. You could also hear the temple bells (*Kading*), some hanging high under the gables where they would catch the wind from all directions, jangling melodiously, competing with the chorus of birdsong. You could also see the shimmering golden spires (*Sorfah*) elegantly perched at the centre of the rising, tiered *Sim*'s roof in all directions. That might give you some idea of how fine ViengChan was.

For safety, I occasionally looked over my shoulder; when I glanced back towards the palace, I realised what a relief it would be for Chao Anouvong and all concerned when self-rule was finally restored to LanXang. I couldn't help but wonder how much longer he could endure.

He'd been emphatic about the need for secrecy because Bangkok was keeping a close watch on him. He wished to invite only the most important and trusted ministers as a matter of national security. I'd signed the official secrets act and was loyal to my country. I was delighted with the assignment and did as I was told. Each time I reached one of the minister's houses, I quietly repeated the same message. The Chief Registrar Phraya Sanon's high-walled residence behind the Wat That Luang temple was the first. The elegant, well-weathered teak house standing solidly in the shade of mango and coconut trees had been in his family for many generations. By the time he'd inherited it, a few smaller houses belonging to his close relatives had sprung up around it. I approached it tentatively and looked around before knocking nervously at the gate. After a while the servant, a small, friendly-looking young man in bare feet, appeared and came hastily towards me.

'*Sabaidee*. What brings you here?' he asked in a jovial manner, smoothing down his hair.

'*Sabaidee*. Sorry for disturbing you,' I said tactfully, looking around and asking him to come closer. 'Is this Phraya Sanon's house?'

'It may be Phraya Sanon's house,' he protested, adding mysteriously, 'but he's not receiving any visitors, so what do you want?'

'He'll see *me*,' I said firmly, giving him a sharp look over his shoulder. 'Listen, young fellow, I have an urgent message for Phraya Sanon. He's at home, isn't he?'

'Sorry, he gave me strict instructions that he wasn't to be disturbed,' he countered. 'I could give it to him later if you like. You can trust me.'

'But forgive me, I have a personal message for him from the king,' I whispered.

For a moment he stared at me, his mouth falling open. Then he raised his eyebrows and said, 'What did you say?'

Most of the servants were stunned at first and asked me to repeat what I'd said. I reiterated that I had a sealed letter from King Anouvong which had to be delivered personally. On hearing it for a second time, an exquisite expression of overwhelming surprise came across his face at the mention of the king's name. He rushed me through the gate and guided me to the cool shade of the garden.

'Please wait here, sir,' he said unctuously, placing a rattan stool under a mango tree for me and disappearing into the house. I sat and glanced nervously at the gate that he'd forgotten to close. He soon hurried back and gave me a glass of water. I thanked him and pointed at the open gate.

'Phraya Sanon will be with you shortly. Please keep cool,' he said and rushed to shut it.

Soon the elegant but rather pale and sleepy-looking Phraya Sanon appeared from his midday slumber. He was taller than I expected and most distinguished. He could have been a boxer with his big, strong chest and broad shoulders. I'd seen him many times before but had never plucked up the courage to introduce myself. In fact I'd never even got close enough to speak to him, yet I felt I knew him intimately. His presence was overwhelming. He was understandably huffy at first because of my intrusion but still managed to flicker a faint smile. I rose, raised my praying hands chest high and bowed respectfully.

'*Sabaidee*, my humble respects to you, Phraya Sanon,' I said affably with a smile, but trying not to be too familiar. With a hint of shyness I apologised for disturbing his rest, adding that it was an honour to meet him face to face at last. He smiled and chuckled with delight.

'Well, *Sabaidee*, and welcome,' he replied. 'It must be something frightfully important for you to come all this way to see me.' He paused to mop his brow, complained about the heat and gazed at me. 'Before we go any further, what am I to call you?'

'Well, sir, as you know, officially I was Khoun Jon but now I'm Phia Jon,' I said humbly. 'Although my given name is Goh Jon, but please call me Jon.'

'Goh Jon! That's an unusual but rather nice name,' he quipped, drawing a short breath.

'Thank you, sir,' I said with downcast eyes.

'Good. Now Jon,' he continued keenly, 'I apologise for keeping you waiting and do forgive my servant for his rudeness. I understand you have something important for me from the king.'

'Yes, indeed I have,' I said pleasantly and bowed again before giving him the king's letter sealed with the royal crest in the shape of a dragon's head, which he recognised immediately. While I waited in anticipation, he turned to one side, impatiently broke the seal open and read the message in silence. I knew what was in it because I'd written it: '*The King requests your company for an urgent meeting at the palace on…*'

I was under strict instructions to disclose the date and time from memory. Phraya Sanon gave me a sharp look with his widening eyes.

'Thank you, Jon, but I'm rather puzzled. Am I to know when?' he said with gentle irony.

I smiled and tried to stay calm, but my body was trembling, and my tight lips were struggling to speak. I felt as if my heart would break the bones of my thin breast. I instinctively glanced around to make sure I hadn't been followed. Only then would I disclose the date and time.

'But of course, sir,' I replied and moved a step closer to him. 'In two days' time, in the morning, at nine o'clock,' I whispered and reminded him not to tell anyone else. 'For security reasons. I'm afraid it's a strict order, sir.'

'Of course. I understand,' he said and reread the letter, looking flushed, as if he'd been injected with enthusiasm.

I could tell Phraya Sanon was intrigued, although he was too restrained to show it. He was generally a very relaxed and composed man. We chatted amicably in the shade. He kindly offered me some more drink, my one desire at that moment. I was thirsty and accepted it gladly. The servant took the order and shortly brought me fresh green coconut juice. Once I'd quenched my thirst, I thanked him and made my excuses to go. He didn't ask which other houses I was calling on. He knew I wouldn't tell. He said I was doing a good job, and since he wasn't renowned for dishing out compliments, I was flattered. I liked and admired him: he seemed sympathetic, intelligent and unpretentious, despite his wealth. I believed he liked me too, partly because he'd once wanted to marry his daughter off to me. I was sorry to take my leave and carried on to the next house and repeated the procedure.

Viceroy Tissah's residence, just inside the inner-city wall, was my last call. It was entirely my idea to leave him until last as his house was on the way back. I thought he was a risk to Lao national security because of his opposition to Chao Anouvong's resolve to fight for LanXang at that dinner party in 1824.

As usual I looked around before peering through the gate. A servant in a garden chair sat up with a start from his slumber when I pounded my fist on the thick wooden gate. He came bouncing over to me and guard dogs dashed forward, barking and snarling ferociously, but stopped after being shouted at. As he opened the gate, I eyed a big, fierce, brown one with distaste and fright. I edged past it through the garden and then followed the servant up the stairs into the house, where I waited nervously in a well-furnished room. A moment later Tissah, wearing a casual outfit, his face a little purplish, came hastily to greet me. He was consumed, as expected, with curiosity. He knew me well enough.

'Sabaidee, Phia Jon! Good to see you but what's this all about?' he said excitedly.

'Sabaidee, Viceroy, my respects to you,' I said as I rose and bowed. 'I apologise for troubling you and I'll be quick.' I handed him the king's sealed letter which he quickly opened and read, breathing fumes of alcohol, eager to know more and then gazing at me as if to say, 'Well, when?' I stepped forward and repeated the message '… in two days… at 9 a.m.'

'How interesting! Thank you,' he pondered, nodding thoughtfully with a thin smile.

Amusingly, while I was in Tissah's house he opened his well-stocked drinks cabinet. He explained its contents at inordinate length, claiming it was good for one's health and offering me one of his favourite medicinal alcoholic drinks. Out of politeness I reluctantly accepted the pickled root drink. He poured liberally into a slender crystal wine glass that I'd never seen before; he revealed it came from Bangkok and I took it with care and looked at it admiringly. After a first sip of the red-coloured liquid I closed my eyes and winced, swallowing it like medicine. He crooned about beauty, claiming that the liquor would boost your energy and inflame your carnal desires. 'Drink it up. It'll make you strong and randy!' he joked coarsely. I blushed and squirmed a little but chortled politely. I forced myself to toss the drink down and thanked him. He looked at me gleefully. I felt its effects soon after. I tingled and felt as if I were floating on a cloud of herbal medicine. 'I say, how do you feel?' he whispered, staring mesmerisingly at my red face. I managed to smile with an air of detached insouciance. Then he pressed me to tell him about the meeting by enticing me with more of his rare liquor. When I tactfully asked whether he was trying to corrupt me, he said, 'Of course not,' with a wry smile. I was loyal to my king and country and shrewd enough not to fall for bribery. I declined any more drink otherwise I would have begun babbling interminably to him. I vaguely told him that the meeting was crucial but refused point-blank to provide any more detail. I rose to my feet and hurriedly left him to brood.

When I'd finished delivering the messages by the late afternoon, I felt I'd done a significant job – my contribution to the country. And my first impulse was to hurry back to the palace. I hastened along the same rough, dusty paths, my black parasol over my head to block the blazing sun. I still had time to kill when the palace gate came into view so decided to make a brief visit to the Wat Sisaketh temple. The *Sim* still looked fresh. Its murals depicting the life of Buddha were beautifully painted. It was dark but welcoming. The cool air was moist with perfumed beeswax candles and sandalwood joss sticks burning on a metal rod attached to a gilded wooden candleholder placed strategically in front of the Buddha statues. The Phra OngSaen statue was the largest. The scented air and the weight of my tiredness from the heat made me feel drowsy. My feelings became strangely detached from the real concerns of the world. However, as my heart raced faster, it came to me that in two days' time the most important meeting would be well under way, and we would know whether Chao Anouvong had decided to march against Siam or not.

Incidentally, since the temple had been completed two years before, Chao Anouvong and his dignitaries had displayed their defiance against Siam many times there by praying with their backs to Bangkok.

I lingered and watched other people praying. The ancestors' words of wisdom came to my mind: if you think of a year, grow seeds; of ten years, plant trees; and of 100 years, teach your children to desire only what is right.

I wondered what it would be like to live amongst nature in an independent country, in tranquillity, eating sticky rice, drinking fresh green coconut juice from the trees our grandparents had planted decades ago, listening and dancing to the subtle sound of the *Khaen* and the *Phin*, never giving a damn about the world of politics – least of all not caring what the Siamese in Bangkok or anyone else in the world for that matter were doing and thinking. I looked at the Buddha statues sitting motionless high up above. Their mercifulness, I believed, would support my prayer for help in guiding us towards freedom. I simply couldn't imagine a catastrophe for LanXang. 'Lord Buddha,' I whispered. 'Please don't neglect a man whose heart is set on justice.'

It was almost dark when I finally arrived back at the palace to be told by the doorman to go and see Chao Anouvong immediately. I realised he'd been longing for my return. Head pounding, I hastened to see him. He was waiting for me in his study which had been patriotically decorated: painted white walls, ruby lacquered wooden ceiling, fine red silk curtains with white lining and a blue silk settee with red silk cushions – glamorous décor without being ostentatious. He sprang up from his couch the moment I appeared. I lifted my praying hands, bowed in reverence and gave my respects. I noticed that his light evening meal, which he sometimes took while working, had been served and cleared away. He came towards me calmly, but I knew he was anxious to hear the news. I shall never forget how he greeted me with an expression that combined pleasure and anxiety.

'I've been waiting for you, Phia Jon. Where have you been all this time?' he said anxiously, with a touch of excitement. 'Never mind. How did it go?' When I smiled and nodded to signify the mission was accomplished and told him I'd stopped at the Wat Sisaketh temple and prayed for him and LanXang, he congratulated me. 'Excellent! You've done me and your country proud,' he said and declared me the bravest of patriots. Then suddenly, in a typically Lao way, he said, 'You must be tired and hungry. Come and sit down and we'll order some barbecued chicken, spicy papaya salad and plenty of vegetables and green coconut juice for you.'

Thanking him for his thoughtfulness, I told him I'd already accepted the kind hospitality of food and drink from some of the houses I'd visited.

'Good. We thought you might have,' he said. He sniffed at me and wrinkled his nose but made no comment. 'We've got your favourite green coconut juice ready though.'

I accepted it willingly, expressed my gratitude and made myself comfortable to enjoy the drink. We carried on with our conversation and then rested silently for a while. He lay on his couch, staring at the ceiling, twirling his moustache while I sat on a chair reading and sipping at the remainder of my drink. I occasionally gazed at him attentively or tiptoed quietly around him, for it was important to give him space to think. He was, I thought, not merely trying to devise some clever plan to outwit the enemy. Soon after, he revealed he'd found a solution he believed in. It was the core of his genius, both as a supreme commander and a king. He believed in his idea and his whole mind was set on making it a reality. He concluded that he was, first and foremost, a human being, a Buddhist, a fervent patriot, a Lao citizen and a king who was being assailed in his own country by the Rattanakosins. Whatever the rights and wrongs of the forthcoming war, it was only necessary because of Bangkok's injustice and treachery.

The night was still young but hot. I stayed quietly in my seat close to him while he sat with his right elbow on his desk and his thumb pressed to his temple, slowly rubbing his forehead, studying his notes and speeches as if memorising them. He was preoccupied with something. I felt sorry for him but was too tired to help. Perhaps I was still under the influence of the 'medicinal' ginseng drink I'd taken at Tissah's house earlier. It seemed Chao Anouvong knew me better than I did: when he saw me nodding a few times, he told me to go to bed and get some sleep. 'Phia Jon, you have an important task as my private secretary so you must always be at your best.' As I stood to take my leave, he settled back on his couch and into his thoughts. 'How will the world judge us?' he muttered under his breath. 'We must first know who we really are. LanXang must be united, independent, rich and powerful.' I quietly left him, lost in his thoughts.

Two days later, the meeting was convened in the palace to determine how best to prepare for a full-scale war. There could scarcely have been a worse day for such an important meeting. It was still very early in the morning yet it felt hotter than ever. The bright sun was rising and the heat was almost unbearable. A cool breeze wafted from the Mekong and swirled pleasantly around the palace courtyards and the Hor Phra Kaeo temple. I stood outside the hall's main entrance, trying to stay calm and keep cool while the attendees arrived; they seemed undeterred by the heat, yet curious, restless and bewildered. Some asked me the purpose of the meeting. I'd never been foolish enough to take bribes or to be coaxed into revealing secrets. Out of principle I stayed loyal to the king and looked at them blankly, shook my head, smiled and gave nothing away. It was an exciting time.

Among the chief officials I watched arriving were Viceroy (*Saen Mueang/ Ouphahat*) Tissah; Chao Anouvong's sons, the Princes Rathsavong Ngao, Rathsabud Yoh and Suthisan Poh; Phraya Mueang Chan (Lord of Chan city); Phraya Mueang Khua (Lord of the Right); Phraya Mueang Khang (Lord of the Centre); Phraya Mueang Sai (Lord of the Left); the Chief Registrar; and the palace mandarins and officials. Other important governors (*Chaomueang*) from major cities along both sides of the Mekong who'd received invitations, such as Nakhorn Phanom, Mukdahan, Savanaketh and Thakhek, also turned up. The ministers from every department arrived one by one. Many of the attendees would be seeing and hearing Chao Anouvong as king for the very first time. Their names were checked at the entrance, and they crammed into the palace's great hall, built of everlasting timber and adorned with gold leaf, where they greeted and chatted with each other.

I moved inside and stationed myself in the doorway overlooking the assembly hall, my eyes fixed at the main door. The Chief Registrar, Phraya Sanon, a very elegant gentleman and a confidant of the king, arrived early, when only the three princes and myself were present. I greeted him with a smile and alertly bowed in reverence from a distance. He acknowledged me with a nod and discreetly made his way to his seat.

Viceroy Tissah arrived next and briefly conferred with the others before retreating to his seat in the front row. He wasn't at ease and was smirking a little. He literally sniffed the air and peered around suspiciously, wiping his lips and nose with his shirtsleeve instead of his usual white handkerchief while scanning the chamber with his little eyes like a hawk.

Soon the semi-circular assembly hall was completely full, and some had to stand at the back. The attendees were desperate to find out why he'd summoned them. It was without doubt one of the most decisive moments in the history of the kingdom – indeed in the history of all Lao people everywhere. The committee stood in front of their chairs facing the empty, throne-like chair, waiting for a few minutes – which felt like an hour – for Chao Anouvong to arrive. It had been made clear to them that they could only sit when the king invited them to do so. It was a very tense but charming moment.

Suddenly there was a stir and they all turned towards the main door. Chao

Anouvong entered the assembly hall eagerly and the whispered conversations gradually ceased. He looked fit and keen. When he saw me standing in the doorway, I flashed him an excited smile, mouthed 'Your Majesty' and bowed. Two armed guards shut the door securely and stood either side of it on guard; no one was allowed in or out. He went straight to his seat of honour placed significantly higher than the others. I quickly moved to my position. Everyone stood to attention and made a deep obeisance to the king, who then turned to look at me and gestured to signal the beginning of the meeting.

For a moment, everyone simply looked and nodded at one another and exchanged friendly glances. They made a very colourful assembly in their ministerial dress. They looked clever and noble. Murmurs grew among them as they realised something important was about to be announced. The king, like a man on a mission, neatly placed his notes on his desk; when beckoned to be seated, the attendees declined, smiling and waiting for him to sit first. Their faces grew serious as they finally sat down after the king had made himself comfortable. He leaned forward slightly, smiled through his black moustache, purposefully scanned the row of faces and gave them a benign look. When the committee were all seated, the king calmly radiated authority amongst his ministers and mandarins, seeking their opinion. He looked as if he'd an immensely important decision to make.

As usual I sat discreetly to the side but in full view of Chao Anouvong, out of sight of the others and out of the debate. I anticipated something important would happen and didn't want to miss anything. For almost the first time before an important meeting, I had no idea what anyone was going to say. They sat upright and looked at the king in anticipation as he scanned the hall. As was his way, he commanded attention by talking. I stole a glance now and then and tried to stay calm, but my heart was thumping. I nervously glanced up to look at the king, whose gaze drifted around the hall before resting on the notes in front of him. After looking through them, he poured a libation, cleared his throat, gestured to me with a nod and started to speak. I picked up my pen and started to write.

I wrote everything down. Although my accounts were lost during the annihilation of ViengChan two years later, I can still remember what the king and the others said. How could I forget?

'Gentlemen and fellow citizens, *Sabaidee* to you all and thank you for coming,' he began confidently. He paused and looked at the assembly, who were listening attentively. 'This meeting, my noble friends,' he continued, 'comes not a moment too soon in my opinion. Your presence today will undoubtedly encourage our people to be strong. You certainly inspire me to defend LanXang and fill me with hope that we can restore it.'

The ministers looked excited and pleased, but also tense and mystified. The king reminded them that LanXang was a vassal state of Siam and went on to tell them the latest news about Bangkok's insatiable ambition to annex LanXang and LanNa. At the mere mention of the Rattanakosin Siamese king's name, there was a perceptible stirring of hostility in the hall.

'We are fighting, gentlemen, against an enemy with whom no peace terms are possible. Indeed, we've tried to negotiate sensible and generous terms, but all were rejected. I predict now that they plan to eliminate us and other Tai ethnic groups, as if they have the right to kill anyone who stands in their way. They've waged a war of oppression against our hearts and lives since 1779, when some of us were just boys.' When he paused, there was a sigh of excitement as the ministers turned to one another for consultation. 'The authorities in Bangkok aren't merely guilty and wicked,' he continued, 'but also atrocious and immoral. Remember that we were born to glory and liberty, so the real agenda of this meeting is whether we shall live or perish in torture and shame. I would rather fall with dignity and meet my end honourably than serve Bangkok in ignominy. Today, however, it is my belief that the fire of freedom burns within us more fiercely than ever, and we have it within us to save LanXang. All of us in this hall can give our people hope that their liberty will be restored, and their future generations will live in a free Lao nation.'

Chao Anouvong then gave details of the Lao cities in the Khorat Plateau that had offered their support. He informed the committee that ViengChan controlled seventy-nine major cities on the right bank of the Mekong. This was the first most of the ministers had heard of this and they looked up in puzzlement. He added that ViengChan was staunchly supported by an impressive list of city allies throughout the Khorat Plateau. In fact, all the principal cities along Chao Anouvong's routes had voiced their support during our journey back from Bangkok the year before. The major routes to the Siamese capital were clear. Besides, most of the experienced high-ranking officers in Bangkok were busy with the ongoing Anglo-Burmese war. Britain and Siam might turn against each other over Burmese territory, and there was a real possibility the British might invade Siam.

Nakhorn Phanom, Udon Thani, Khon Kaen, Roi-Et, Maha Sarakham, NongBuaLamphu, Loei, Phou Khiao, Sakol Nakhorn, Mukdahan, Ubon Ratchathani, Souvannaphum, Sisaketh and Khukan had declared themselves Lao and given their full support.

Chonnabot was in two minds because its ruler and his deputy had differing opinions. The latter had been bought by Siamese money and was an enemy.

Phou Viang, Kalasin, Khemmarat and Chaiyaphum were unsure whether ViengChan could win and were reluctant to give their full support. They'd probably been bribed by the Siamese and so for security reasons they'd been branded as enemies and traitors for not helping their own Lao countrymen against Siam.

Well, there were plenty of nodding heads from the committee. Everyone was held captive by the king, leaning forward, listening, sweating and squirming uncomfortably in their seats. Their noble minds were being worked to the limit. It became clear to them that the Lao nation was in their hands. They had to make a decision at the end of the meeting.

Meanwhile King Nangklao in Bangkok was under serious threat from the British. He'd no choice but to allow the Europeans to trade freely in his kingdom. Meanwhile the Persians not only controlled the royal family but had also taken over the entire country's finances, especially when it came to military and internal affairs. They openly traded with the Europeans and were making a huge amount of money. Siam was completely beholden to them. The royalty and aristocracy, reliant on foreign money in return for favours, had no idea how cut off they'd become from normal life. Wealth and power counted in Bangkok, but society had split down the middle between the rich and the poor. Political power was in the hands of the plutocrats, who cared little for the rule of law; the ruling classes slavishly followed their example while the poor had no share in any of it. Siam was governed by corrupt and vicious people, an oligarchy of avaricious and manipulative military types who surrounded the king. Furthermore, Nangklao feared that Mongkut would try to overthrow him. It was hardly surprising he needed so much money to buy arms and fund his lavish lifestyle.

We in ViengChan recognised that Siam had probably been investing heavily in arms from the European traders And we knew they'd been recruiting a professional army. We sensed that if war were to break out, it wouldn't be the sort we'd always expected, and might not even be entirely between LanXang and Siam. It would be an undeclared, secret war; the enemy would arrive with the body of a lion and the head of a Garuda bird. Not only would we be fighting a wealthy enemy, but also the European arms traders: professional, merciless mercenaries, the tools of Bangkok. We were also aware that the Siamese government always sent raw recruits and prisoners of war to do their fighting for them instead of their own professional soldiers.

Chao Anouvong personally conceded that the Siamese had far more firepower than us, but he was confident of the people's support – on whose knowledge everything else depended – and he was convinced his men would fight like highly trained soldiers. He'd hoped to win support from Chao Noi of XiengKhuang and the princes of LanNa. He also wished to embrace King Manthathurath of Luang Phrabang. He'd bombarded him with letters and gifts, beseeching him to forget past differences and see the bigger picture. He even tried to persuade him to come to ViengChan for a meeting to reaffirm their shared family history. In one of his letters, Chao Anouvong suggested to Manthathurath that:

'We should hold a traditional Baci SouKhuan ceremony, sit side by side in perfect harmony, to renew our kinship and spiritual ties; hold a feast of reconciliation; make libations to the gods and beg for blessings; drink from the loving cup with a whole heart and with profound satisfaction put to rest any hint of misunderstandings that might have arisen between our two houses.'

Sadly, it never took place. He was deeply saddened by Manthathurath's lack of patriotism, empathy, vision and commitment.

He told the committee that it would be a failure to ignore such an opportunity to rebel against Siam. The fault would lie with him, because in times of war the whole country is entrusted to the care of the king. Success could never be guaranteed, but they had to fight to preserve the Lao nation. He urged the country to meet the economic challenges posed by the increasing wealth of its neighbours. For forty-seven years, he said, LanXang had been lacking in colour and identity and had lost her sense of self-belief. This painful chapter of her history was in danger of being swept under the carpet. The people had been trampled upon and no longer felt they were at home in their own country. He was now more emphatic than ever about regaining full control of LanXang. He told the committee to be an advocate for self-rule, to remove the negative karma that had grown as high as PhouBia Mountain, the highest in LanXang.

'It is higher than 2,800 wingspans of a crane, if you must know,' he said, pointing out that the purpose of this meeting was, at the very least, to eliminate the possibility of such a fate. 'If we fail to act, that mountain will become too formidable for us to ever ascend, trapping us in an endless cycle of power and decline. We're a civilised people, but Bangkok is steering our minds towards anger. But we can't just wash away the seeds of our anger and replace them with loving kindness and equanimity. We can practise asceticism as much as we wish, but only when peace and tranquillity have returned to our independent kingdom.'

Everyone stiffened and fixed their gaze on him. 'Even then, gentlemen,' he continued, lifting his forefinger in the air, his voice rising, 'it'll be easier said than done, because we're all subject to the common ailments of greed, anger, ignorance, pride and doubt. Our hard-working, brave ancestors transformed this land into the wonderful kingdom of LanXang. We mustn't just pile up riches for ourselves and idle away our lives. We ought to care more for our country than for our own interests. The very existence of our nation is at stake. We must wake up while there's still time and win back our sovereignty, so that we can re-build LanXang and rediscover our true nature.' He went on to say that as Bangkok was already under pressure from the British, a pre-emptive strike might well bring victory. 'I hope that is so, but we can't take anything for granted. We must expect and overcome obstacles, for without them we will not make progress in this struggle.'

Well, as expected, this attracted opposing views from his viceroy, Tissah, who hadn't joined in with the debate beyond a grunt or two. He was an unprincipled man with dark skin, bat-like ears, lazy, small eyes, a short nose and cracked, thin lips. He was a spineless mediocrity and an addle-headed appeaser – a man not to be trusted. He was over a year younger than Chao Anouvong but suffered from tinnitus and was quite deaf. Sometimes he put his finger in his right ear and spoke loudly. He quickly rose to his feet and looked directly at the king.

'I don't wish to lecture anyone,' he said tactfully, 'but can I remind you and this committee that the arrogant Siamese regard their neighbours, especially us, as inferior. It seems that the gods have never told them to abandon their ego and their attitude of galling insolence. Although it's clearly untrue, they think of us as rustic and unintelligent. We've been running our country satisfactorily for over a thousand years. Alas we're now weak; a mere vassal state of Siam. If we went to war, we would only be humiliated further.' He turned the palms of his hand outwards to make 'what-would-you-do' gestures and sat down.

'On the contrary, we're already being humiliated,' retorted Chao Anouvong. 'In fact, I have a phrase about Siamese exceptionalism for you: "Don't be Siamese (*Tai Sayam*) to me!" Why should we accept their orders just because they think they know more than us about our own nation's interests? No outsiders have the right to interfere with our internal affairs. The only difference is that they were strong and took advantage of our weakness by invading us. We have been too prudent and cautious, devoting our attention more to good than to evil. As you know gentlemen, I've also had misgivings about this undertaking. But after witnessing the debacle in Bangkok last year when they forced my followers into slave labour, and after I'd met my people in Saraburi and the Khorat Plateau who'd had census numbers literally burned into their flesh, I have to tell you my doubts have vanished completely. We simply have to take action for our own sake, for the sake of our children and for the dignity and authority of all Lao people.' He paused for thought.

'The Bangkok regime,' he continued, 'is systematically destroying our freedom to be, say and do as we like, but we will not be silenced. We should retaliate by defending the rights of our valiant people, by showing them that they're not alone. We must glare at Bangkok, make them splutter. There can be no question of ever surrendering our peaceful Ai-Lao nation. We've had enough of their fallacious arguments. We must remember that King Khoun Borom united six major cities into the NanChao kingdom and fought against the Tang Chinese. His son Khoun Loh established LanXang in 757. King Fah Ngum unified it 595 years later and it was independent for 427 years, only to be invaded by our traitorous Siamese brothers in 1779. To be precise, LanXang has existed securely and peacefully for 1,022 years, as you so correctly said, Tissah.' He paused to take a sip of his drink; everyone was most impressed by his grasp of detail. 'The evil influence of the Siamese government, gentlemen, has been apparent to us ever since. We simply cannot remain a vassal state or a mere province of Siam or anyone else. It might sound pathetic and laughable, but believe me, the Rattanakosins must be purposely deficient in intelligence if they can shamelessly claim that LanXang is part of Siam. I'm sure they'll try to do just that.'

'Look, Your Majesty!' Tissah interrupted, his hands clenched into fists on his desk as he rose. 'I don't need to tell you or anyone else in this hall that Siam is our chief tormentor, and we haven't been independent since 1779. But if we fight, LanXang will be plunged into misery. I think that rather than going to war and fighting to our deaths, we should take a risk. We should look for an opportunity to restrain the Siamese instead. Perhaps we should follow the will of heaven. Why not send a peace envoy instead? Nangklao wants to make a name for himself. I also strongly oppose Bangkok's expansionist policies. So, if you're willing to entrust the task to me, I'll go and reason with them. I'm not a military man or a specialist on Siamese affairs but given the opportunity to negotiate directly with the Siamese, I'd ask them to restore LanXang to us and to refrain from any interference in the north and northeast of Siam. If I fail, we'll just have to resign ourselves to the will of heaven. Furthermore, I know it's impossible to retrieve a bone from the dog that stole it, but I might also ask or even demand the return of the Emerald Buddha. We might as well give it a try. What do you say?' He sat down heavily, his face twitching as usual, before leaning back in his chair and looking directly at Chao Anouvong.

With my great passion for LanXang's independent past, I found it dispiriting that my country was becoming an economic and ideological satellite of Siam – perish the thought! At first it made me cringe to hear Tissah's defeatism. He'd always been something of an enigma, a conundrum to Chao Anouvong's friends. Many, I'm sure, suspected treason in his heart. He was a downright incorrigible pessimist, but in his own way he was as much a patriot as any other Lao. Many people liked him. I can't say why – probably because he was cautious. Everyone was deeply engrossed in the king's words, but Tissah had expressed his own extraordinary views. I stiffened with horror while he hissed and scratched and tried every means to put Chao Anouvong off. He probably thought that by suggesting submission he'd find a way to protect LanXang and save lives. It wasn't as if he was alone in his opinions. I respected his views, even though they cut across most of Chao Anouvong's principles, and I hated traitors. His courage was clearly not as strong as his hate for the Siamese. As well as him, some of the Lao ruling class and noblemen, even artisans and labourers all over LanXang, especially the simple country folk on the Khorat Plateau, were incompetent, riddled with appeasers, displaying pro-Siamese sympathies. They even worshipped Nangklao outright and rather liked being bound hand and foot and kept as tools in the political pocket of the Siamese royalty. They'd either become oppressed and fearful of the threat of persecution or had been corrupted or indoctrinated into believing in the Rattanakosin myth.

'Your spirit is commendable, but tell me then,' Chao Anouvong said, fixing a disapproving gaze on Tissah. 'Our attempts to reason with Bangkok have failed. They just laughed at us. I think you're too naïve and simply fail to understand Siam's attitude towards LanXang.' Tissah shifted in his seat uncomfortably. 'So far we've said no to war and killing because it leads only to a vale of suffering and tears. But it would be fatal to allow our fellow countrymen to suspect that we put Siam's interests above them. Bangkok spreads disinformation about us all the time. They shook their heads in denial when I personally complained about our people's suffering under their governors. They have done us a lot of harm with their rumours and lies. We cannot simply give up and succumb to despair. We can only put things right if we win back our independence. Can you conceive what might happen if we don't act now? As a close ally, Siam should have guided us towards LanXang unity. They invaded us instead. Quite frankly Bangkok owes us an explanation.'

He paused to take a drink, still looking straight at Tissah, but no one spoke.

'Now our people can no longer put up with Bangkok's madness and arrogance. They're clamouring for us to do something. We're all getting old so we must act now. If we take no action now, perhaps someone else will in the future. But if we never act, I can tell you what will happen.' At this the ministers shifted in their seats. Chao Anouvong took a swift look at them and loudly said, 'Siam will claim all King Fah Ngum's Lao LanXang as its own! That is what they will do, gentlemen. Even now there's a strong rumour that Siam will become a "Tai" nation. How would you, Tissah, and all of you, my noble friends, be able to stop them? By submitting your own grievances to Bangkok? Impossible! If we send envoys, Bangkok will merely repudiate them with utter contempt. Our people are being numbered like slaves before our very eyes, yet you, Tissah, remain an appeaser, like someone who feeds a tiger and hopes it won't eat them. There's no better man than you, but surely you don't want to be an envoy to a tyrant? There's no point wallowing in your pedantic, short-sighted views with your associates in Bangkok. Can't you see an appeasing aggressor is more dangerous than opposing? I've no doubt you'll be bound, gagged and killed like the rest! I'm aware that all great undertakings are risky, but ours is worthwhile. We must never abandon the plight of our people. We have no choice but to resort to arms if they don't give us back what is rightfully ours. They owe us a debt. We shall fight for our rights and free our people from oppression.'

There was a round of applause and cheers. Chao Anouvong looked pleased. It was an inspiring debate, I tell you. The one thing certain to rouse him to pick up his sword and lead his people to war was the prospect of living under Bangkok's rule. He'd long favoured economic co-operation and had been a tireless advocate for reconciliation. No longer. The Lao nation was vital to him. He truly believed that Bangkok had been secretly colluding with foreign powers to annex Lao land. He drew himself up, thrust out his strong jaw and stared around with his sharp eyes. I noticed Phraya Sanon giving him gentle nods of encouragement. His sons, Prince Ngao, Yoh and Poh, looked at each other and lifted themselves from their chairs, turning towards their father, smiling and nodding enthusiastically.

'Siam has many big cities. Bangkok, or Krung Thep if you like, is a huge city,' Tissah retorted as he rose, hunched forward. 'It would be impossible to defend it once captured. Besides, it has become rather fashionable for some clever and thoughtless Lao people to adopt Siamese attitudes. In fact I'm sure that some of our people, not only in Bangkok but also on the Khorat Plateau, have become spoilt and are inclined to favour Siam, even thinking they're *Tai Sayam*. They might well resist us. I personally deplore the use of the word 'war', and Nangklao is well known for his brutality. I believe that karma and patience are the most honourable ways of achieving our goal. How would we handle a war without destroying ourselves? We must not underestimate our enemies. We must be clever enough to recognise the risks and consider the consequences. If we meet them with full force, we would pay a cruel price for the crimes we want to avenge.'

Tissah lifted his eyes at Chao Anouvong, bowed and sat down heavily.

'Gentlemen, we know that all life is a journey,' Chao Anouvong responded immediately. 'Our ancestors managed to overcome the difficult terrain of our country: mountains, rivers, forests, dangerous animals. We've shaped and nurtured the landscape and helped to feed and sustain our country; through hardship we've grown strong. Our priority now is to correct an injustice and to secure our future. No greater responsibility rests upon us than safeguarding our nation. I will strain every nerve and sinew to preserve all that we love and cherish, and resist those who would seek to destroy us. Politics and gentle negotiations have failed. What choice is left to us but to fight?'

They all looked at the king as he paused, but no one spoke.

'Gentlemen, our enemy is not straightforward but insatiable, crafty and unprincipled,' he continued. 'They have their own homeland, but they think they own the whole world. I believe the time for talking is over. Will you place yourselves entirely in my hands?' He put the question firmly and quickly scanned the hall for a show of support. Rathsavong Ngao was the first to raise his hand, followed by his brothers; soon, one after another, the ministers raised theirs. Tissah was silent and looked rather pale. The hall began to fill with noise. Then, quite suddenly, the Chief Registrar, Phraya Sanon, rose to his full height from his chair.

'Your Majesty, you are the king,' he said, looking around. 'I wholly agree with you that the moment for action has arrived. We must act. The fall of the Rattanakosins would be the best thing for us. I'm sure I'm speaking for all of us here. The people expect you to take the lead. You alone have the authority to galvanise our people and our potential allies into action. We want peace, but Bangkok is bent on annexing LanXang, or at least on taking the Khorat Plateau. No one here wishes you harm or dreams of having a different king. We all want one thing only: to protect our nation, and we are ready to follow you into war. To discover the means of winning a fight, you have to start it in the first place. Go for it. We must do battle and fight them to the death. Thank you for the opportunity to make a good name for ourselves. May I be so bold to say that if Your Majesty wants to restore LanXang, then you must seize this opportunity. Take it. We will stand by you, whatever might come of it.'

Phraya Sanon bowed and sat down. No one else said anything but directed their nods and glances of approval at Chao Anouvong.

'Thank you, Phraya Sanon, for your valuable suggestions, but let the debate continue,' said Chao Anouvong, looking around the hall again.

Some of those present may have opposed his ideas. Viceroy Tissah considered them too risky, but it was in Chao Anouvong's character, as an ambitious king, to appeal for his people's support and lead them in the fight than to comply with the Bangkok regime. He was not born for himself alone but for his country, and all the children of LanXang who shared his faith in the Lao nation. I felt immensely proud to be part of it.

They knew all too well that LanXang was now at war, and it was just a matter of where Chao Anouvong would choose to fight rather than when. I felt my blood begin to pulse faster at the thought. He was truly warming to the idea of defending ViengChan by setting up defensive posts along the enemy's routes and in the narrow valleys of NongBuaLamphu. He disclosed that he'd carefully inspected the landscape during the journey back from Bangkok. The enemies, he said, had a well-equipped and powerful army but they would find it very difficult to maintain their supplies of food and ammunition. Nevertheless, he wanted to hear more from the assembly. Still seated, he scanned the hall again, more carefully this time, and said, 'Come! Let's hear more from you. You have nothing to fear from me.' At this the ministers glanced at each other. There was a shifting and shuffling as they waited for someone to speak.

Chao Anouvong's encouraging words seemed to have roused others to speak. The governor (*Chaomueang*) of Ubon, a small, no-nonsense man, rose and bowed to the king. It was totally unexpected. Regrettably, I can't even remember his name.

'Your Majesty, my respects to you. I don't believe we should negotiate with them,' he said boldly. Everyone turned towards him and listened intently. 'It would only encourage them to become even haughtier. Frankly, our patience has snapped at the criminal acts of their officials towards our people during the census. If left unchecked they would become a pestilence, swarming over and wiping out our Lao identity. We might never again know peace and security. Unfortunately, whether we like it or not, LanXang is already a vassal state of Siam. We have no wealth, but we must be strong in resisting the bullying of our neighbours. While the self-interested British and French compete for supremacy in the region, our identity as a nation is under threat. We have only limited appeal to those on the international stage, but we'll have none at all if we remain subordinate to the Siamese. Bangkok will deploy only Siamese officials to lobby the colonial powers and persuade them to divide our land.'

'So what is your advice?' Chao Anouvong interrupted, which stirred a few tired bodies.

'Well, this meeting has my vote, and since the 1779 invasion, like Your Majesty, I've been devoting much careful study to the possibility of rebellion,' he said and paused to gather his thoughts. 'The way to achieve our goal is by uniting the country and appealing to the world,' he continued, licking his lips. 'We've been waiting for an opportune moment. This could be it. While their guard is lowered, a pre-emptive strike to bring our people back has a good chance of success!' His face flushed a little. 'Our strategy must be to first unify all our people: Luang Phrabang, XiengKhuang, even Lao LanNa, all Lao people everywhere in the world. This would enable us to combine our military and political spheres. Our only other hope is to take advantage of a British attack on Siam from Malaya. Let's hope this happens. If not, we would be terribly outnumbered and outgunned and our chance of winning would be very slim indeed. We might just as well consider suicide before they catch us, if we don't want to suffer scourging, sizzling with hot irons or the torment of the pole.' At this, everyone started to shift in their seats and there was a great collective sigh and groan, as if the whole hall had been holding its breath.

'Thank you,' Chao Anouvong said, cutting him off swiftly before he'd a chance to describe those torments in greater detail. He lifted his palms to appeal for calm and gestured to the Ubon lord to sit down. 'Gentlemen,' continued the king, 'I too have been saying no to fighting and killing. It's easy to say that by avoiding war, we all have a greater chance of living longer. The truth is, we're mortal men and we don't know the hour of our death, but we mustn't be cowards, the sort of people who die many times before their end finally comes. Valiant people like us should only taste death once. It's not wrong for us to fear and foresee death, but no man born to die can evade it. For the very existence of our nation, our end will be a heroic one when it comes. Take courage and be a man. So, let's go!'

Suddenly Phra Borom Mang, the ruler of Nakhon Phanom and a staunch supporter of ViengChan, stood up and bowed.

'Your Majesty, my humble respects,' he said. 'May I report that our people in the Khorat Plateau show unprecedented and deepening hostility towards Bangkok, which I hope will lead to self-rule in the region. Sooner or later the Siamese would have to admit that our peoples, for the sake of peace, should live in separate nations. We know that the Siamese and Lao are both descendants of the Ai-Lao. That's precisely why Bangkok wants to annex LanXang: to deny us our right to exist. Their actions break the five fundamental precepts of Buddhism that they claim to believe in. They only have eyes for ugly things and unjust acts. They fail to realise, even with several revered holy monks (*Luang Phor*) advising them, that their preoccupation with expanding their territory is totally unjustifiable. They've been dreaming of an empire but lack the intelligence to know it's mere folly. They might be upset with us for saying so, but they have no right to be annoyed by the truth. Nangklao is certainly not a philosopher, merely an opinionated man with little knowledge. He has no respect for others and none whatsoever for the truth. The Siamese idolise the mystical powers of holy men (*Bhumibun*), but no one, not even the most revered monks – never mind the gods or Lord Buddha – can win Nangklao over, as you found out last year.'

'That is true. I did make a request, even though I knew he would never agree,' Chao Anouvong affirmed. 'But it certainly made Bangkok feel uneasy.'

'What's more disturbing, Your Majesty,' Phra Borom Mang continued, 'is that Bangkok looks on our land with covetous eyes. They're determined to annex LanXang and to turn all the Lao people on the Khorat Plateau into their supplicants, dancing to their tune. Precisely for this reason I call on the people to rebel. It's sickening to think of those people in Bangkok maintaining that our Lao people, culture and territory are all part of Siam. In theory we have the right to appeal directly to Bangkok, as your brother Nanthasene did, but that avenue is now firmly closed to us. Perhaps other honourable friends here have some clever ideas.'

The king gave a nod of thanks as the Nakhorn Phanom ruler sat down. The hall went silent as men worked their brains. I held my breath, wondering who would speak next.

After a while the king, anxious to get moving, invited his close friend, the Chief Registrar, who was widely respected and regarded as the ablest of us all, to speak again. Phraya Sanon, a nobleman of old stock, bone-loyal to the king, beside whom he'd fought since youth, immediately stirred himself. He was dignified, not in the style of an old warrior but merely with a hint of someone who understands the nature of war. He'd served with devotion and loyalty. He stood up purposefully, his hands resting easily just outside the pockets of his jacket. He lifted his shoulders and paid obeisance to the king before looking around to acknowledge the committee. After taking a sip of water he coughed gently to clear his throat. He looked ahead and bowed again before speaking.

'Your Majesty and noble friends, please hear what I think,' he began. 'The Rattanakosins have been ostracising us and making things very difficult for us. What a deplorable thing it is that Bangkok should blame ViengChan and the Lao people for their troubles, when it's their own wickedness that has brought sufferings on their own people and on us! We know that since the 1563 treaty at the That Si-SongHuck shrine, we've had a special relationship with Siam; both kingdoms were supposed to be working towards a strategic partnership. Disappointingly for us, their 1779 invasion violated the principle of Ai-Lao brotherhood. They betrayed out trust. They might call it the 'Great Victory' but it has become the source of bitter discord between us, as well as an opportunity for Bangkok to create a false narrative to push for the annexation of LanXang and LanNa. It was a turning point in our history; it demonstrated undeniably that Siam was LanXang's enemy. I have long perceived that Bangkok harbours ambitions for a Greater Siam. There is much deep-seated animosity. The rice fields and the people in the Khorat Plateau are attractive to them. It makes them green with envy, and now the most envious of them all is none other than their king, who is capricious and avaricious by nature.'

Phraya Sanon raised his head, looked at the king and continued. 'Your Majesty, Nangklao views you as a thorn in his flesh, an uncontrollable and treacherous wild beast.' The king smiled and the committee looked at him in amused curiosity. 'While feigning friendliness, Bangkok has been attempting to foment dissent using all sorts of pretexts. Their aim is to wage war on LanXang, raze ViengChan to the ground and capture us… especially you. They've arrested and imprisoned our noblemen – many of whom have met violent deaths – and replaced them with nasty men from Bangkok. They forget all their vows and principles whenever they perceive an advantage, however small. They've mastered the art of deception; they know the best time to strike is when the enemy is weak. Nothing is too deceitful for them. How morality has degenerated that such despicable men can have their way! When LanXang was divided they took advantage of the situation. When incited ViengChan and Luang Phrabang to fight each other, both cities suffered heavy losses. They waited until they could use LanXang's weakness to their own advantage and turned the Khorat plateau into a crusade against us. We've now been under their thumb for nearly five decades.'

He paused to look around the hall and gave another gentle cough before continuing.

'Well now, let's suppose the Siamese realise there's no real need to dominate us. It would cost them nothing to consider us their close friends and relatives. We'd be well matched, at least linguistically, in our special relationship. Regrettably they've been showing contempt for our intelligence and have the barefaced effrontery to tell us we're uncivilised, rustic and dim. Again, if they really are civilised and honest, nothing about us should be foreign to them; our languages are so similar, different only in intonation and vocabulary. There are no great differences between them and us. Now, if we – the Lao people – tell them yes there is, and that we have the right to exist as a separate nation, then surely they should understand it would be a terrible mistake to call the Lao people living in Siam Siamese, despite the superficial cultural similarities. We'll never become Siamese by choice, but I'm afraid Bangkok isn't intelligent enough to know that. They scandalously looted our artefacts, such as the gold finial of the That Phanom stupa. They shamelessly sought to destroy our roots by burning all our manuscripts and manipulating history by erasing the word "*Lao* ລາວ" and replacing it with "Tai", purely for the purpose of negating us.'

'They'll eventually have to face the truth, but they'll be too ashamed to admit it. This behaviour is one of the many privileges of being Siamese.' His voice ran on, unforced and expertly timed. 'That's what we're most afraid of. They can't handle the truth because they don't actually want to know about it. Their national history blatantly values patriotism over plain facts. They have a vested interest in glorifying Siam, so the knowledge they committed crimes against us would be deeply harmful to them. They may dominate us now but imagine the damage to their reputation and the memory of their achievements once all is revealed! Once we win back our sovereignty, we'll reveal the truth to the world and make the gods smile.'

He paused and looked respectfully at the king, who gestured for him to carry on.

'Although Bangkok keeps you under constant surveillance you took the brave risk of offending your friend, the late King Naphalai, by holding a clandestine meeting with the British trade envoy, Lord Crawfurd, in 1822. He clearly admired your integrity of character. It doesn't require much imagination to recognise your value: you're a decent and honourable man who's seen the foul depths of Bangkok's policies and has the guts to do something about it. Despite the superiority of your birth, you even paid obeisance to Lord Crawfurd: an attempt to win his sympathy no doubt. You directly appealed to him not to sell weapons to Siam. You said he talked tough on Bangkok, but we know that Britain is complicit in the arms trade: money is vital to colonialism. You also told him the truth about LanXang's territories and desire for independence and then begged that supposedly fair-minded man – from the greatest empire where the sun never sets – for help. Yet your words were not heard or considered. Shame on the British government for their passivity.' He paused for thought before continuing. 'Now, if the Lord Buddha asks them – the Rattanakosins – What do you mortal Siamese hope to gain by invading Lao LanXang? Is it your objective to dominate them? You've laid waste to their lands, burnt their homes and temples, driven off their livestock, looted their towns and cities, murdered thousands of their men, enslaved their children and forced yourselves on their women. All men are dear to us gods, but you have angered us. What do you think you deserve?'

'We know what their answer would be. They think they can commit crimes and escape the consequences, deceiving both men and gods! They would be in denial to the very end. We must appeal to Lord Buddha and the gods to escape from Siam's clutches. We prefer to be Lao without any outside interference in our lives. So, by the gods, let's hope that their wickedness will lead to the disintegration of Siam. That would benefit everyone in the region.'

Phraya Sanon paused to take a drink, while the ministers nodded and murmured assent, probably feeling inadequate to the task but busy making notes and quietly waiting. Everyone seemed amazed. The king was most certainly impressed. Phraya Sanon lifted his head to look directly at him, put his drink down, cleared his throat and continued.

'Your Majesty, we are unable to prosecute Phromphakdy and Suriyaphakdy because, as serving governors appointed by Bangkok, they have absolute immunity, despite being involved in racketeering and bribery. Besides, the authorities in Bangkok profit directly from their criminal actions. Unfortunately talk is cheap, and if we submissively present yet another petition to Bangkok, we'll have the same outcome and face yet more humiliation. The Bangkok authorities are very capable of silencing their critics, both within and outside Siam. They're on a mission to cleanse our kingdom of subversives – shoot to kill and no questions asked. All of our lives will be in danger if we try to protect our people. LanXang will simply be unable to protect those who love her. We've practically exhausted our resources.'

With that some looked dejected and restless after hours of stillness. The king raised himself from his seat, frowning in concentration. Phraya Sanon's voice had the swell of a true orator. I lifted my head and felt cold sweat on my brow as I raked my fingers through my long hair. The king sat staring straight ahead, stroking his moustache. He nodded assent as if he couldn't have put it better himself. The three princes muttered between themselves. Tissah's eyes swivelled scornfully towards Phraya Sanon as his words gathered momentum. I should mention that remarkably he'd been speaking without notes. I liked him because he'd a mind for detail and took everything incredibly seriously. His words had grabbed everyone's attention.

'There's no doubt,' he continued, 'that the Siamese have set up various clandestine organisations in LanXang since the invasion. One of them spreads subversive propaganda. Having invaded us and taken advantage of our weakness, the Siamese now wish to eradicate our rites and wipe out our collective memory, traditions and identity. That is the simple truth. For us, the only route to happiness lies in fulfilling our desire to be an independent nation once again.'

The hall went quiet, but I knew it was a very rousing statement. The king turned to look at Phraya Sanon and said, 'Your analysis, if I may say so, strikes me as impeccable. However, in my opinion, it's not the size of an army that counts, but its skill. Strangely, as a boy hostage growing up in Bangkok, I idolised the Siamese royals; not because of their noble lineage but because they made me feel inferior and ashamed in comparison. Now I see this third Rattanakosin king as a heartless, cunning brute: outwardly bold but a coward at heart. He holds everyone, especially us, in utter contempt and is narrow-minded, ignorant, wilful and suspicious. Nevertheless, he feels confident enough to sanction any decree and press ahead with his ambitions. There is only one option left to us.'

'Which is, if I may interrupt?' Phraya Sanon asked.

'It could be war, as you rightly said,' Chao Anouvong responded, shooting an enthusiastic glance at Phraya Sanon. 'We're a peaceful nation, so perhaps we should again ask ourselves whether we want war or peace. If it's to be war, do we march at speed to Bangkok or take it slowly? If peace, do we offer it or plead for it? Does anyone know the best option? It's quite understandable that some of us want to avoid war and negotiate a truce instead. Nonetheless, we simply must act; we must at least try to rescue our people before they're dispersed to another province in Siam, even as far away as the border with Burma. This would make our task so much more difficult and our people might well end up simply as lost tribes.' The king paused to take his drink. Everyone looked on in silence.

'We will go to war if we have to,' he continued, putting his arms on his desk and leaning forward. His face flushed red he raised his voice. 'I am a Lao citizen! It will be a just war for the freedom of the Lao nation. I agree with you entirely Phraya Sanon, that first we must be united by our love of LanXang. In fact I have something prepared for that. Luang Phrabang and XiengKhuang must be brought in to fight for our common cause. We should divide our military into three groups. One, under my son Rathsavong Ngao, should go first to gather up all the Lao families in Saraburi, Suphanbury and bring them back to ViengChan. Our two main fighting forces will be under my command in ViengChan and under Rathsabud Yoh in Champasak. Well, let's hope Luang Phrabang and XiengKhuang and the princes of LanNa will swear their allegiance and send armies in support. Then we should march on Khorat and hit our enemy with everything if need be. Our mission should be to scour the kingdom clean of Siamese officials and then persuade the local rulers, governors and noblemen to negotiate treaties with us so that gangs in Bangkok never returnn to our land. Any governors who refuse to cooperate should be branded as traitors and enemies. Those who aren't with us are against us. All three units should, if you all agree, report to me as supreme commander. I only hope fate will not punish me for what I'm about to do but I believe it's better to be guilty of leading an uprising than to continue living under a fraudulent regime. It would be fair and just.'

Phraya Sanon chuckled, stood up and said good-humouredly, 'Your Majesty, if we are led into defeat by this war, we will exonerate you of all failure and absolve you of all wrong. We and all the Lao people will praise you forever.' This remark made the king and some of the committee members smile.

I'm unable to convey the effect of Chao Anouvong's words on those present. They were stunned. The silence around the room amplified his speech. Everyone sat up and looked straight at him. Suddenly, like a headmaster, he stood up, lifted his shoulders, waved to the gathering to remain seated and then scanned the hall to draw their attention. The tension was palpable, and I held my breath in anticipation. I couldn't even hear anyone breathing. After a few moments the king poured libations and spoke in an awe-inspiring voice.

'Gentlemen and honourable friends,' he began, raising his voice. 'Since 1779 we've kept a constant watch on our own transgressions, making sure we didn't stray from the right course of action. We've managed to untie ourselves from physical and mental distraction and pain; we've conducted our lives unobtrusively and abstained from both vexation and exultation. We understand the bitter misery of our lives and our perpetual desire for self-rule. Forbearance has been fundamental to our survival: it has helped us act morally and has forestalled any resentment. But instead of tying our lives solely to agreeable circumstances and putting up with a situation that is far from perfect, our minds should instead be full of ideas for our deliverance. Like you I'm a Lao citizen and I want to be free; that goes for all Lao citizens. They deserve our protection against Bangkok. If you were a victim of repression in Bangkok or in the remotest part of the Khorat Plateau and were being dragged off to prison or to execution, I ask you, the only truthful words you could utter would be to proudly proclaim yourself a Lao citizen. This would of course speed up the end of your life, certainly with Siamese officials in the judgement seat. I believe the time has come. It is time to act, to battle for LanXang unification and to fight for our rights!'

Well, Chao Anouvong's exhortation produced an immediate stir of unease, for any war which was inadequately prepared for and thought out would be utterly suicidal. Nevertheless he revealed that he'd checked the balance of power and strength of the Siamese by referring to the will of the Lao people. The Bangkok authorities, under pressure from the British, feared they would be stripped of their powers. Nangklao would no longer be able to make his own decisions.

Apart from the odd call of nature there'd been no break and the sun had moved to the west. Speaker after speaker urged the Lao people of LanNa and LanXang and everywhere in the world to unite, to lay claim to all their territory and rebel against Bangkok. I flicked my eyes from one speaker to another and listened intently as I tried to write everything down or commit everything they said to memory. The debate meandered on for hours, from grand military strategies to serious political tactics, punctuated by fierce arguments, exasperation and silence.

Suddenly, amidst heated discussion and much jabbing of fingers, Chao Anouvong became aware that I was looking up at him. He turned, raised his eyebrows and gestured to me, but by shaking my head from side to side and moving my lips gently, I told him I wouldn't say a word in the debate. He knew I supported the motion for war though I had my own private misgivings.

I told him later that I was concerned about the consequences but entirely agreed with him that deeds, not words, were the only way forward.

After a short pause, while some ministers were arguing noisily with each other, Phraya Sanon spoke again. His quick senses had revived. He looked at Chao Anouvong and sprang to his feet, leaning forward with his clenched fists pressing on the desk.

'Your Majesty, Lao LanXang is fortunate to have someone like you, with such experience and vision, to call on,' he said, and the hall quietened down.

'Your idea is certainly a bold one, but perhaps you might consider that such a concentration of power in a single pair of hands might hinder our progress.'

Chao Anouvong immediately gave a clear sign of understanding and Phraya Sanon sat down. I knew the king intended to provoke more debate but just then, like an evil spirit, Tissah rose to his full height. He always seemed to make a point of speaking, just as he had during that dinner party conversation back in 1824, although most people found his arguments rather disappointing. Chao Anouvong occasionally tried to remonstrate with him, but to little or no effect. This time, perhaps, Tissah was trying to be honest and to conduct himself well. Unfortunately, because of his deafness, the poor man seemed to speak much louder than before. I felt quite sorry for him though, as did the king.

'It seems that I'm the only one in this hall playing the role of the perennial contrarian,' Tissah said, almost shouting and looked straight at Chao Anouvong. 'Well, frankly, I don't share your enthusiasm, because I still fail to see what we can do about it. We can talk through the night, but I still don't think we'll win this war: it's vastly over-ambitious. The lack of support makes it extremely unlikely we would win. I'm also concerned we would end up fighting alongside our Vietnamese allies against some of our fellow Ai-Lao and then being sucked into the conflict between Hue and Bangkok. Furthermore, some of the city rulers under Bangkok's influence might offer fierce resistance against us. This war will not be an ordinary one. If we lose, destruction will befall our cities and more harm will certainly come to our people. The Rattanakosins might aim for total annihilation.'

There was a mixture of grunts and loud groans of shock from the assembly. I took Tissah's words very seriously: despite being Buddhists, the Siamese officials were notoriously unforgiving, capable of slaughtering people in cold blood and destroying holy temples with their monks inside. I was most concerned but kept my counsel. Although some ministers surely agreed with Tissah, most shook their heads disapprovingly.

'With respect, it sounds to me as though our honourable friend shouldn't be here,' said Phraya Sanon sneeringly as he rose. I really thought he was going to openly accuse Tissah of cowardice. He was also a little embarrassed by the volume of Tissah's voice and told him mildly not to shout. Sanon shook his head and rolled his eyes, glancing at the king and raising his eyebrows in silent apology before lowering himself back into his seat.

'Gentlemen, gentlemen! Please, let's move on,' Chao Anouvong cut in courteously, realising that the appeal to reason with Tissah had failed. 'We shall do our country and ourselves more harm than good by squabbling.' He waved the room to be silent and leant forward. 'As a matter of fact, I understand your concerns and your objections. But I believe that a show of power, which could lead to a full-scale war, I grant you, still gives us a chance, does it not?' The blank looks in the hall gave him obvious satisfaction. Many moved about in their seats, fixing their gaze on the king and looking rather serious, as if they were searching for answers. 'Surely, we have the right to protect our people against injustice? Our people would think much less of us if we failed to do so. Suicide and war, as we all know, go hand in hand. Where is the objection? We're all mortal, and death is only a matter of time. Brave men like us surely prefer death in battle to defeat and slavery. Why not make history and go out with honour?'

The king turned to Tissah and said, 'I agree with you, Viceroy Tissah, and all of you, about the danger we face if we go to war. The power in Bangkok lies in the hands of Nangklao and his ministers. They're the real culprits. Our strategy has always been to carefully build up our reputation. We've tirelessly lobbied sympathisers in the Siamese royal household. If I may add, I took a risk, as our noble friend Phraya Sanon said, in holding a secret meeting with the British trade envoy, Lord John Crawfurd, in 1822. I offered him my compliments in a rather sycophantic way. He seemed a very nice gentleman and the atmosphere was friendly from the start. In fact, I begged him to accept my obeisance, even though there was no need for me to do so. I told him I wasn't paying obeisance to him as a simple king of backward Lao LanXang to a European master, but one human to another. He was an extremely courteous individual, I must say. I told him the truth about our kingdom and our people and begged him for help. Crucially, I asked him whether he would file an account of our meeting back in London but beseeched him to keep Bangkok out of the loop. He only gave a hint of agreement in his reply. As a matter of interest, gentlemen, the British are generally decent people – very subtle and frightfully diplomatic. Unfortunately, I doubt we would win over the British government and of course, for us, the most potent of all were the Siamese king's silver-tongued mandarins. We'll clearly never be able to conquer Bangkok if we can't achieve unity amongst ourselves. We must win back our independence so our people can rule their own lives.'

Chao Anouvong believed that Bangkok planned to first seize control of LanXang and LanNa under the pretext of an agreement with the colonial powers. Secondly, Nangklao intended to lay claim to the fertile plains around Bangkok. The landowners and villagers would be callously evicted from their land and the aristocrats would then move in and become fat and smiling on the proceeds of the land, stroking their perfumed chins and watching their fortunes growing. Thirdly, Bangkok would allow Phromphakdy, Suriyaphakdy and the other governors to tax the conquered lands, demanding nothing less than the total annexation of all the vassal states. They would be nourished in perpetuity by extorting the rural poor. Chao Anouvong also foresaw that any future colonial treaty would merely make the honest, hard-working, peaceful and dignified Lao population second-class citizens, subservient to Siamese interests and desperately poor. The thought horrified him, and me.

'This is what Siam wants to do,' he said. 'We must regain our independence to prevent this happening. Support me, and together we shall try to win back King Fah Ngum's LanXang and give our people their freedom.'

The day wore on. Food was not on anybody's mind, but after a quick lunch break the debate went on much longer than I'd anticipated. Everyone began to feel tired, and their concentration weakened. My hand was beginning to hurt from so much writing. Fortunately, as I started to give my sleepy eyes a quick rub, the decision was reached for an immediate approach to war, no matter the consequences, but some of the attendees were too numb with misery and fear to have a coherent opinion on anything.

Nangklao's actions had clearly prompted Chao Anouvong to act. It was clear he wouldn't relent until all his compatriots were safe. Freedom must be won for the benefit of future generations in a united Lao kingdom of LanXang, with ViengChan as the capital. This was his ideal. He reminded the meeting that being Lao was not just about understanding that opinions can change, and hatred will pass. It was also about believing in the rights of responsibility, the rule of the legendary Khoun Borom's law and King Fah Ngum's legacy, keeping all Lao ethnic groups united instead of division by an undiscriminating international boundary. They should never be kept apart by mountains and rivers and the banks of the Mekong should never be separated. The Lao traditional ties of love (*HuckPhaeng*) are impossible to break. Our people would laugh at these artificial frontiers and patriotically raise a comradely cheer of delight whenever they met, sharing food and drink.

'If we fail to act, who will take our place?' Chao Anouvong then asked the gathering. 'It is surely within our rights to rule our own country.' He raised his voice and his face reddened. 'Certainly not the Rattanakosins, whose land-grabbing policies only create divisions between our people!'

Tissah raised his head as if he were about to speak. Through the corners of his eyes, he quickly swivelled round and looked for others' reactions. His chin resting on his hand, he turned to the right where the three princes were sitting, and then quickly twisted his head to look at Phraya Sanon on the left. They ignored him. He must have felt very lonely. He dropped his heavy hand on the table as if he'd lost the argument.

Chao Anouvong concluded that Bangkok would be furious when they learned of his decision. But public outcry at Nangklao's policy and the prospect of full-scale war might yet persuade Siam to see sense and accept it had no business in LanXang. Surely no man of honour could stand by while Siam's unfair trading practices and corruption went unchecked. He suspected Bangkok would produce fabricated documents to 'prove' to the ignorant colonial powers that LanNa and LanXang had always been part of Siam. The British and the French would simply believe him; after all, it was much easier to deal with one powerful state than several smaller ones. It was all quite ridiculous; the Lao people knew this and would never forget.

Chao Anouvong believed Siam's strategy was clear: to deceive the Westerners into forcing the Lao to become Siamese. Lao culture was already being severely restricted, and the Lao history and alphabet had been banned in schools. But the moment had come for the Lao people to say: enough of Siamese trickery (*Xiengmieng*), oppression and domination. The Lao, their fate entwined for decades under the selfish rule of Bangkok, now faced out-and-out conflict. Chao Anouvong had appealed to the emotions of the committee. He now had to win their support.

'Now that we know the facts, we have a duty to make them public. We must try to stop them!' he said loudly. 'Going to war is indeed a real risk, but, on balance, it's the only option worth taking. If all else fails in politics, all that's left is start a fight, even if you're not sure you can win. Once the fight is on, you hope you might be able to see a way through.'

The room began to stir; everyone was looking around and talking quietly with each other.

'War it is, then,' asserted Phraya Sanon, standing and shaking his fist. He looked around and tried to convince the committee that Bangkok was full of deceitful men who looked to LanXang merely as a source of plunder and slaves. 'Siam has wanted to eliminate LanXang since 1779!' he yelled, warning that Nangklao would be the most dangerous enemy simply because he'd acquired enough ill-gotten wealth to buy huge quantities of arms. Everyone, Chao Anouvong included, nodded knowingly. The Lao army had tried to buy more arms with the little money they had.

'We are ready to fight if it comes to war!' roared brave Rathsavong Ngao as he rose. 'We will embark upon it on the principle that no outsider should place themselves above the Lao people. In fact, Your Majesty can assume we're unanimous. We're here for a final decision, not idle speculation,' he announced, looking at his two brothers and urging them to show their fighting spirit. The rest followed suit and the room shook with the voices of brothers-in-arms. The king was overjoyed to find his sons united and embraced them afterwards. Without their support, his ambitions would have been very much in doubt. 'I agree with Phraya Sanon,' continued Rathsavong Ngao, looking at his father. 'Let us clear one obstacle at a time. Firstly, there is the question of the supreme commander's power.'

I noted that Chao Anouvong was struck by the confidence with which his son spoke. He shot him an approving look and nodded his understanding. He was fully prepared to relinquish some of his power as supreme commander. He'd grown a protective shell around himself while growing up as a teenager in Bangkok. But he was also capable of accepting reasonable advice. Suddenly, he jumped to his feet and raised his hands for attention.

'Very well,' said the king. 'Our main aim must be to win this war, but we have to accept that one kingdom might not survive. I am under no illusions about the impact this conflict will have on our lives. The winners can look forward to the future.' He paused. 'For the losers, there might not be a future at all.'

There was a groan followed by a lengthy silence. Chao Anouvong must have realised what was at stake and it made me shift in my seat. He lifted his broad shoulders, then scanned the hall before continuing with his astonishing oration. I recognised some of his old rhetoric. The crisis facing LanXang merited the exalted level of his speeches. He did not seem over the top or archaic in his manner, but he wanted to evoke ancient instincts – the deep desire to be Lao and to expel the invaders. These speeches were the most sublime he ever made, all in the name of the Lao nation. From where I sat he looked twice his size – an imposing man of great wisdom and nobility, on the most important mission of his life. After another quick look around the hall, he reached for a glass of water and poured libations; while taking a sip he raised his eyebrows and stared in my direction. I nodded my head to signify my understanding and stretched my wrists to relieve the cramp in my hands. I retrieved my pen as he rose and turned to face the committee.

'Gentlemen, dear noble friends and brothers (*Ai-Nong*),' he began expressively. 'Thank you again for attending this crucial meeting.' He paused. 'It is a great honour to stand before you in this hall and tell you without fear that I have thought carefully since my return from Bangkok last year whether it was part of my duty to proclaim independence. Justice and fairness are the noblest qualities that any human being can possess. Besides, I believe in dialogue and have considered further mediation with Bangkok, but the chances of LanXang being offered anything in return for peace are minimal. Nangklao, like his two predecessors and whoever comes after him will refuse to grant us anything. Bangkok has showed its true colours by occupying us and expecting us to lay down our arms. We would lose everything if we stopped fighting, but they would lose nothing by leaving. They would win over not only Lao public opinion but the whole world's if they returned to us what's rightfully ours.'

The committee nodded and murmured assent.

'It would harm their vanity to lose LanXang as a vassal state, but torture and murder have cast a pall of terror over our country. I'm tired of the very name of Siam and of seeing oppression wherever I go. How much longer am I going to live? I'm already past my prime and my enemies will denounce me whatever I do. I've suffered enough humiliation and have earned the right to some peace, as I'm sure all of us have. However, can I – and all of you for that matter – really stand back and do nothing with dignity and honour when every instinct tells us that the Lao nation is heading for extinction? It is a cold, hard fact. LanXang will rue the day it tied its destiny to Siam. I don't know how much of my life remains. I've dedicated all my energies for forty-seven years to trying to right this wrong. I'm convinced that our people, instead of blaming themselves, would never forgive us if we were to do nothing. I know we all want to live, but our desire for self-rule is overwhelming. I therefore passionately believe that if our Lao LanXang is to end, let it end only when all of us lie choking in our own blood upon the ground.'

There was a short pause. All the mandarins were so moved that they began to cheer. Chao Anouvong had the courage to see that thousands would die in the war but it would be unimaginable to lose the Lao nation. The sheer emotion of his rhetoric struck me and the vehemence of his awe-inspiring words rang throughout the hall. After taking a sip of drink he raised his hand for calm. The noise slowly died down. His voice became increasingly severe as he continued.

'Now allow me to tell you also what I honestly think. I believe that Bangkok is rotten from the top down. Yes, from the head down,' he said slowly, amidst weak smiles and chuckles from the committee. 'It is a Garuda's head, poisoned with corruption, swollen with insatiable greed and bloated with arrogance. Anyone will tell you that the only thing to do with such a head is to remove it. I can tell you we're not alone in wanting to get rid of it. We want to throw it out of LanXang! Mind you, we'll need a strong hand and steady nerves to wield a sword powerful enough to sever it. So, to the soft and haughty-living Rattanakosins, I say enough! The time will come when LanXang's power will be restored, however hard the struggle. This conflict, gentlemen, is about nothing less than fighting for the survival of our nation. So I beg and pray to all the gods and Lord Buddha to grant us their grace and favour. We must unite and be prepared to make sacrifices. To you and all the Lao people falls the great test of being worthy of the fight to secure our unity, identity and sovereignty! The time has come, brothers, for us to act. Show courage. Let us show the world that it's better to die courageously than to drag out our lives in humiliation and misery. Our actions are essential to the cause of the Lao nation. We must rise up with confidence in our ideas and an abiding belief in our people, who depend on us to take the lead. Our lives have not been our own since 1779. Nothing in the world is more pleasant than good health and there is no greater pleasure than relief from pain.'

There was much applause as he paused to take another sip of his drink. He went on to urge the committee to tell the Lao people to prepare themselves to revive their identity and challenge the Siamese. He suggested that all the people – from north to south, from east to west of the Mekong, all over LanXang – should draw more closely together in the future, perhaps even through marriage.

'We recognise that the Siamese share an equal history with the Lao,' he continued. 'From the day we migrated from Mueang Pah city in Sichuan

China to struggle to build a new homeland, our alliance has been ancient: our shared language and heritage has ensured a special relationship between our nations. But this was recklessly abused by their rulers; they became deceitful and domineering and imposed their unacceptable policies on us. We mustn't lose hope; we must see a better future before us. We must regain our land and our independence. The Siamese flag must no longer fly over our territory. Our grief will be tempered by the knowledge that our people died for freedom and justice: not only because they wanted to be part of the struggle but because they wanted to change their own lives and the lives of their fellow countrymen for the better.' Then he roared, 'They will die fighting for our Lao nation!'

After a short pause, he said solemnly, 'And as for Siam? Well, gentlemen, your guess is as good as mine. Telling the truth has never been official policy for them. We are now a nation longing to determine its own destiny. After suffering under such terrible oppression, we must fight for change. We must not lose our ability to resist and remain enslaved by them. We must regain the rights of our nation and the rights of our people. The longing for freedom and dignity will never leave our hearts. We must stand up, prepare to strike a blow against tyranny, free our people and rebuild our country.' He glanced at me before reaching out for a glass of water and pouring libations; he then raised it above his head. 'May our struggle end well and happily for our nation. May this day be the beginning of the full restoration of LanXang! We must try to preserve our country as a unified nation – of the people, by the people and for the people in the entire Lao-speaking world.' He paused, then said beseechingly, 'Gentlemen, only vigilance and action can achieve success. Please remember this: solidarity makes us strong. United we live and divided we die. Thank you, gentlemen.' Then he poured libations again before drinking more of his water, showing no signs of the sleepless night spent worrying about what he would say at the meeting.

With that, Chao Anouvong sat down and brought the meeting to a close. His speeches – they must have taken a prodigious mental effort to compose, with some of my recommendations, of course – galvanised the committee into action. The words 'Lao nation' were the ultimate link between him and the eternal world. He'd thrown his audience into a trance by mere words, stirring them to their depths and casting a spell over them, compelling them to realise that although they were a mass of imperfections, they were proud to be Lao and willing to sacrifice their lives with him.

I remained seated but there was a great deal of noise. The committee stood up and indicated their support by a show of hands. Clapping and cheering filled the hall and the room erupted in applause and foot stamping. My heart couldn't stay unmoved, and I behaved like the rest, cheering at the force of his words and the passion of his delivery. Chao Anouvong looked at me with a smile. I gave him a congratulatory nod and a grin of admiration. He rose to his feet and turned to face the gathering with an appreciative smile. The blast of applause was like the opening of a furnace door and the chants of 'LanXang! Anouvong! LanXang! Anouvong!' rose high above the palace roof. They poured libations and raised their glasses above their heads to acknowledge the king, calling his name, before taking their drinks.

I can state on oath that the power of his speech took my breath away. The effect his words and phrases had on me persists to this day. Whenever I think of him my heart starts to beat faster and tears sometimes run down my face. I have treasured his memory all my life and will continue to do so for what little remains of it. He really had the right stuff in him; he was the first amongst equals. He'd spoke passionately and eloquently as the king of Lao LanXang who wanted freedom for his subjects. Most of all he wanted those despicable Rattanakosin Siamese out of LanXang and brought to justice in the eyes of the world.

Soon after, Chao Anouvong took all of us into his private room. He'd dedicated it as his ancestors' shrine soon after his accession. I'd never really noticed what was inside. We followed him in through the tall door and carefully moved about for fear of knocking things over. The hot dazzling December sunlight came through the windows, mixed with cool air and the smell of ancient spices and mould. The magnolia walls around us were dusky but the exquisite bronze Buddhas shone out clearly; their eyes, inlaid with agate, sparkled in the dim light. When no one was watching I knelt before them and wiped the Buddhas' faces with my handkerchief. Their shiny eyes looked as if they could really see and their subtle, smiling lips looked like they could really speak. I rubbed their delicate, long fingers, smoother and brighter than the rest of the hands from many such rubbings. The whole room had once glistened with a patina of beeswax. Now, after so many years of neglect, it was yellowed with smoke and grime and exuded an antique smell of dirt and dust. Its timber floor creaked as we moved about, and stale air wafted from the dusty old drapes on the chairs.

I was curious about the smell of incense and the large, blurred, rectangular outlines on the walls where tapestries or pictures had once hung. Half circles and squares of dust on the floor marked the absence of statues and furniture. When I asked what had become of them, he whispered to me that they had been spirited away to Siam. I was upset, but he was far too cool a man to show any emotion.

An old portrait of King Xay-Setthathirath the Great, at the far end of the room fascinated me the most. I hadn't previously paid much attention to it but I now studied it closely. I thought I saw a strong resemblance to Chao Anouvong. They were, of course, both royal descendants of Lao LanXang. Like a flash of enlightenment, it struck me how alike they were, though Xay-Setthathirath's face was slightly fuller. They might have been father and son. The portrait showed a noble, sensitive face: smooth, unlined, ethereal, the representation of a soul rather than flesh and blood. Xay-Setthathirath stood slightly sideways, his shiny golden shoes pointing to the right; he was dressed in formal regal robes: royal purple silk trousers, a heavy gold-embroidered high-collared cream jacket, two huge gold chains hanging loosely across his shoulders and resting perfectly on his hips, his right hand resting securely on a long, golden ceremonial sword. He was flanked by the Emerald Buddha in summer dress high above on his right, a fierce-looking dragon guardian slightly lower on his left and a long-tusked albino bull elephant in the background. A gold-pointed high crown rested on his head.

It had been painted in 1560 – the year ViengChan became the capital of LanXang. Chao Anouvong stood gazing at the portrait with pride, as if he'd received instructions directly from Xay-Setthathirath to liberate and restore the kingdom to its former glory. Some of the ministers stared at the painting. They knew nothing about it, even though they worshipped King Xay-Setthathirath.

'Do you like it?' asked Chao Anouvong, turning to his sons standing close to him.

'It's a nice painting,' said Rathsabud Yoh. He was not a man of the arts.

'I think it's an excellent work of art,' Chao Anouvong countered.

'I agree with you, father. We're proud of our ancestors. It's an amazing painting,' said Rathsavong Ngao, nodding appreciatively as if he were an artist, though he'd barely noticed it before.

'You like art, Phraya Sanon,' said the king. 'What do you think of it?'

'I haven't seen it before. It is remarkable indeed. I like it very much!' he said admiringly, as if he also were an art expert.

Chao Anouvong turned round and, pointing at the portrait, announced, 'Gentlemen, that is our King Xay-Setthathirath I, the Great, who transferred our capital from Luang Phrabang to ViengChan, now the heart of our nation. He not only defeated the Burmese invasion but also risked his own life helping Ayutthaya Siam fight against Burma.' We were silent for a moment, fixing our gaze on the painting in admiration. Phraya Sanon stood silently with his hand covering his mouth to inspect it more thoroughly. I personally preferred landscape painting, but I must say that the portrait, apart from its great significance, was indeed fascinating: a masterpiece that you could also enjoy aesthetically. 'And by the way,' Chao Anouvong said abruptly. 'Can we remind ourselves none of this is to be repeated outside this room? It is in our national security that we must swear our allegiance to Khoun Loh, the founder of our kingdom, Fah Ngum the Great who unified our nations and Xay-Setthathirath, of course.'

We all stood rooted to the spot and no one spoke. I was certain some of the ministers mistrusted each other, fearing the plot might be betrayed. Chao Anouvong knew he was vulnerable to betrayal from within. Our plans for war would be shattered if there were a traitor on the committee. I instantly began whittling down the list of potential traitors in my mind, looking around and wondering. I had a strong suspicion the king suspected Tissah.

Then Chao Anouvong beckoned us all to stand around a huge table that he and I had prepared. I pulled away a white sheet to reveal a large-scale map of LanXang and her neighbours, along with a series of impressive sketches detailing his war strategies. Everyone gazed in awe. He explained that the main Lao army would march directly to Udon and Khon Kaen and then take Khorat. On and on he went with his plans while we leant forwards, our eyes eagerly following every movement of his long bamboo stick.

'NongBuaLamphu will most probably be the main site. An epic battle may well be fought here,' he said, tapping the map with his stick. 'It's in the path of the Siamese army. They will come through a narrow pass at KhaoSan further north. We can prepare an ambush in the hills and forests along the pass to block their routes and burn their provisions in the rear; this should plunge them into chaos because food supplies are the lifeblood of any army.' We all looked at him in puzzlement. 'Significantly,' he continued, 'I can confirm – and I hope you'll will agree – that I've decided to send fifty high-ranking mandarins, our pride and joy bull elephant with a gilded war saddle and my personal letter, of course, to our noble cousins in Luang Phrabang, imploring them to play their part. If they support us and we win this holy war of independence, I swear I will enter the monkhood, like Fah Ngum.'

Simplicity and humility were his natural strengths. I knew that this letter was his personal, desperate appeal.

From: Chao Anouvong King of LanXang ViengChan
To: Chao Manthathurath King of LanXang Luang Phrabang.

We send Your Majesty our humble respects and warm Greetings. We trust this letter finds Your Esteemed Majesty and the people of Luang Phrabang well.

    Many misunderstandings have unfortunately arisen between our two houses in the past, which had become roots of distrust. But, with all due respect, Your Majesty, if they still exist, I wish to dispel them. For certain, I have never doubted the qualities of Your Majesty's intelligence, patriotism and command. Neither of us are young men anymore with golden prospects ahead of us. My earthly time will soon be over, but before I am safely dead, I wish to restore our beloved Lao LanXang to its former glory as 'one country'.

    I feel that it is my patriotic duty to inform Your Majesty, in confidence, of the decision of a meeting held two days ago in the palace in the presence of Ouphahat Tissah, Chief Registrar Phraya Sanon, my sons and all the important ministers. I beseech you to forget our past differences for there is a common link between our two houses and Champasak. Responsibility for LanXang's unity rests on our shoulders. I believe that Your Majesty also aspires to unite the kingdom. We must first unite for the sake of our nation – I beg you to support me and together we can fight to regain independence for our motherland. The Lao nation's future is vital. Please consider the bigger picture. Give me the army and I will save our Lao kingdom of LanXang. If we win, I pledge to Your Majesty that I will enter monkhood like our King Fah Ngum, and a united LanXang will be at your disposal. On this Your Majesty may rest assured.

'Would you indeed shave your head, dress in saffron robes and become a monk?' asked Phraya Sanon sarcastically, looking sharply at Chao Anouvong. 'Quite bluntly they should come begging to us. The house of Luang Phrabang is feeble and incompetent and virtually exists in name only. Could I remind you that we lost in 1779 in the first place partly because they sent 3,000 men, grudgingly perhaps, in support of the invading Siamese. I really don't think it made them any the wiser. They may well think your letter's nothing more than a plan to grab all the power for yourself. I believe Your Majesty has sent many envoys and letters in the past, not to mention magnificent gifts, including two gilded pirogues; they were happy to accept them but cowardly refused to make any pledges. Well, let's hope they swear allegiance this time.'

This all showed that nothing was dearer to Chao Anouvong than his country. I recalled how he half-jokingly disclosed to me during our journey back from Bangkok that if LanXang regained independence, he would seek sanctuary in the temple or retire to the country. I knew he meant it and wasn't surprised when he pledged to do so. The letter took Luang Phrabang, his own family and indeed the people entirely by surprise. It did the trick: initially Luang Phrabang and XiengKhuang agreed to send an army of a few thousand in support, but they both failed to fulfil their promises when they were really needed during the war. He really felt betrayed by them and labelled them as traitors.

As the king of LanXang ViengChan, Chao Anouvong lived by the laws of Ai-Lao Khoun Borom and the ideals of King Fah Ngum. He regarded Fah Ngum as a hero and an idol to be emulated. He drew on the military history of LanXang, all the way back from Fah Ngum's time to his own. He wished to begin the impending war with a pilgrimage to the ancient royal capital of Luang Phrabang, to honour Fah Ngum's ashes, to offer sacrifices and ask the ghosts for help, calling all the spirits of Fah Ngum's soldiers to his side for the coming war. The visit would not only fulfil his glorious ambition to pay homage to Fah Ngum, but it also appealed more to his politics than to his personality.

He reminded the committee that as a proud nation it would be wrong to ask the Ho from Yunnan and the Dai Viets (Vietnamese) for help. He said again that all undertakings were risky and therefore he'd to ask not only able Lao men from Luang Phrabang for their help but also all the other ethnic groups, including the courageous Tai ethnic groups (Tai Dam, Daeng, Leu, Nung and so on) from the principality of Sipsong ChuTai, as well as the Dai, the Zhuang from Sipsong Panna and the Shan from Xieng Hung. If they were sane, he said, they would declare for the Ai-Lao ancestors. He hoped that as Luang Phrabang had lost its power to ViengChan and was now fearful of

Siamese domination, they would join in the fight in the interests of Lao unity. He added that he must take the lead to stop the Rattanakosins' ambitions, even if Luang Phrabang, XiengKhuang and the other cities in LanNa would do nothing to support him. He simply couldn't, with any honour, stand back and do nothing when the Lao nation was heading for disaster.

'For all the Lao people's sake,' Chao Anouvong said firmly, 'I sincerely hope Luang Phrabang won't send their men to support the enemy again. The Siamese invasion taught us the perils of treachery from within. We must disregard past differences, forget old feuds and send envoys to offer generous terms of alliance before they're corrupted by Nangklao's men. They must be persuaded to unite with us, however far away and busy they are, and to provide trained soldiers that are committed to serve LanXang and the people. Our survival as a nation is vital. If we fail to unite, gentlemen, our factions, squabbles, disagreements and mistrust will destroy LanXang, and we'll only have ourselves to blame. The crown belongs to the nation: it should be in our hearts, not on our heads. I'm willing to relinquish the throne to Luang Phrabang and become a monk for the sake of our independence!'

'Your Majesty,' Phraya Sanon said. 'I believe that Luang Phrabang will lose hope if they can't see a better future ahead for them. They want to find a way out, an off-ramp, if we lose this war. Of course if they decide not to back us at all, that monster in Bangkok will really be on our backs.'

'No, they won't,' Chao Anouvong countered. 'This should of course be a concern for us, but the Lao population will never want to live under Bangkok's power. If they do, well, what's the point in living? Us Lao have a long history: twenty-three kings since Khoun Loh and almost 600 years up to King Fah Ngum. Gentlemen, it would be unthinkable if we were to lose our national identity.'

Those present gratefully expressed their appreciation, and a few were visibly touched.

Over their thousands of years of history, there have been many periods when the Lao people fought to protect their national independence against outside domination. Chao Anouvong encouraged solidarity and instilled a spirit of patriotism. He recognised the importance of unity and amity and devoted his life to improving the fortunes of LanXang. An ardent patriot, he was confident the various Lao peoples would join forces against Bangkok.

'I am optimistic, but let's face facts,' said Phraya Sanon softly. 'Our noble cousins in Luang Phrabang used to run the whole kingdom before 1560 with absolute feudal authority. We can't realistically expect them to accept our orders; it would offend their dignity. Isn't that so?' He then urged caution and touched on the one question playing on everyone's mind. 'If Luang Phrabang mobilised for the war, would LanNa and the rest of the kingdom also come to ViengChan's support?' After a short pause Phraya Sanon smiled and said, 'However, I do appreciate what a clever move this is of yours.'

'Good, you've understood the logic of it,' Chao Anouvong interrupted with satisfaction. 'For the sake of our nation I have to make this sacrifice by offering the throne to our dear cousins in Luang Phrabang if we're to have a chance, however slim, of winning this war.'

'Yes, I think I understand,' said Phraya Sanon, nodding. 'Very well then. I hope you're right.'

Those ministers who still didn't get it looked confused; they shifted nervously in their seats and looked sideways at each another.

'Let's not forget they're also Lao,' said Chao Anouvong firmly, 'and that goes for LanNa as well. We should make an earnest plea for support from all our relations: the Shan, Dai, Zhuang and so on further north. We must also appeal to all other ethnic groups to join us; they're all part of King Fah Ngum's LanXang. We need every able fighting man on our side. I'm giving them a chance to become part of our history.'

I had very little idea what the others were thinking but was pleased when they murmured and nodded their approval. Chao Anouvong was prepared to sacrifice everything in the knowledge that only a unified Lao LanXang would win him the war. It was a brilliant stroke which had first come to him in that flash of insight as we stood in the moonlight on the banks of the Chaophraya river and he'd said, 'Let's go, Phia Jon, we have work to do.' He always repeated this phrase when new ideas came to him.

'Well, let's hope Your Majesty's sacrifice won't be in vain,' Phraya Sanon affirmed.

He told the assembly that when he was being held captive in Bangkok, he'd quietly sought the full restoration of LanXang. In recognition of his successful military campaigns in LanNa, King Chulaloke had allowed him to return to ViengChan in 1795 and then to become king in 1804. King Naphalai then allowed him to appoint his son Rathsabud Yoh as governor of Champasak in 1821. His hopes had been raised that LanXang's fortunes were finally turning.

Like their father, both Rathsabud Yoh and Rathsavong Ngao were very able leaders: the latter especially was a very sharp and brave fighter who routinely practised his sword-fighting skills to keep fit.

Despite all this, Chao Anouvong had all along preferred a peaceful approach. He'd witnessed first-hand the savageries of war and had worked to reach an agreement that would preserve the ancient bond between the two kingdoms but allow them to exist as separate entities. Being a pacifist I'd always agreed with him, but I reluctantly concurred with his acceptance that war was now inevitable: I wanted him to fight for LanXang, as did most other Laomen did.

As the ministers began to leave, I gently reminded him that I was against war on principle, explaining that on the whole, Lao people are non-belligerent and apolitical, simply preferring to leave in peace and enjoy themselves. He saw life as a struggle however and knew that tough choices had to be made to protect the Lao nation.

'I agree Phia Jon, I've had similar thoughts. You're quite right to remind me about perseverance and patience. But right now, what choice do we have?'

'We can still change our minds, Your Majesty,' I said persuasively.

'Oh, my dear Phia Jon,' he said, 'I believe that the biggest risk for LanXang would be to do nothing. We'd be saying farewell to our traditional Lao way of life. We must grab every opportunity we can. For our nation let's do it now. Let's not defer, for we may never have a better opportunity. We mustn't fear failure, otherwise we would be too afraid to do anything. It's now or never!'

'Yes, you're right Your Majesty,' I replied as I scrutinised the ministers' faces: some showing relief, others sneering in contempt. When we were completely alone, I said, 'I meant to tell Your Majesty this earlier, but didn't for fear you might get upset.'

'Go on, I'm listening,'

'Your Majesty, with respect and admiration, you have a deeper understanding than I of this situation. I'm cautious by nature and more often than not I worry about the smallest things. We have much information at our disposal but not a crystal ball to predict the future. Looking at the bigger picture, we're not ready for war. We can't fight battles based on personal feelings alone, but need clever strategies, careful planning and patience. We ought to ask ourselves: is the country united? Is our national security at stake? Are we acting in unison, with one mind and one purpose? Besides, LanXang's foundations aren't as solid as we would want. In comparison, Siam is rich and powerful; defeating it will be difficult, even if we catch it by surprise before the gates of Bangkok. Siam has an army of at least 100,000 men: they outnumber us ten to one. Fuelled by their poisonous politics, they've ruled us for nearly fifty years; they've long excelled in the dark arts of propaganda. Their undercover agents are all over the Khorat Plateau observing our movements. They might well have seen through our plans. Although Nangklao has appointed idle rich men to his court, he still has mercenaries, trained soldiers, weapons and foreign assistance. Morale is high amongst his men. The advantage clearly lies with Siam; if they win, we'll be destroyed. Thousands of our people will be dragged to slavery in Siam.' I suggested we should lie low to hide our true strength from Bangkok. 'We're clearly in the right for wanting to take back control of LanXang,' I added. 'Our army is valiant but most of our soldiers are unskilled raw recruits. I worry that if war breaks out, their sacrifice will be in vain. We'll be crushed.'

I advised him that Siam had planted highly trained saboteurs and undercover agents all over LanXang, especially on the Khorat Plateau, spreading disinformation and deluding the people into believing that Vietnam was LanXang's true enemy. We needed to be extremely wary of these tactics, which were intended to sow distrust and pit the opposite sides of the Mekong against each other. The Lao were honest folk, but still susceptible to certain forms of persuasion. While older people were pressured into feeling ashamed to be Lao, our children were being brainwashed at school into believing the Siamese version of history was the only one that mattered. We were witnessing a merciless campaign to wipe out our history and erase our values.

The Siamese had recently become even more brazen. They were actively cultivating and recruiting Lao informants who were then used to spread propaganda. They distributed false evidence suggesting there were no Lao in LanNa and LanXang, only Siamese. They shamelessly fabricated and altered historical truth by erasing the word *Lao* from texts, replacing it with *Tai* to connect the Lao LanNa ruling dynasty with the Rattanakosin regime. There were strong rumours that Siam was planning to hijack the word *Tai* for the Siamese nation, disregarding other ethnic groups and establishing the superiority of the Siamese language. They also sought to rename all twenty of LanXang's provinces on the Khorat Plateau Issan (Pali for northeast) so the rest of the world would think they were Siamese. Bangkok wanted to swallow the whole lot; they would then refer to the Lao inhabitants as the Issan people

(*Khon Issan*), and the Lao language as a mere provincial dialect: the 'Issan language.' As soon as their informers whispered in their ears, Bangkok set to work, sabotaging the Lao nationalist movement and rooting out dissent. The people there had no wish to be subservient to the Rattanakosins in their own country but were powerless to stop the cruel census. The time had come to discredit Bangkok's unfounded claims.

'Well said, Phia Jon,' said Chao Anouvong. 'Nangklao believes we would never dare fall out with him. We don't want war, but...' He paused, briefly uncertain, almost confused, but then said, 'I'm not scared of Bangkok. I spent many years observing the Siamese court. I know their inner workings and what they're thinking and planning. They assume all other people are liars: that's one of the many reasons for their hostility towards their neighbours. They make pledges and then blatantly do the opposite; they take oaths of allegiance but never kept their end of the bargain. In the end the sheer flamboyance of their criminality will lead to rebellion in the provinces. They'll always try to slander our good name, but we believe in diversity and our spirit has remained indomitable when confronted with their expansionist policies. But if they attack us, they won't stop until they've destroyed ViengChan.'

He paused and sighed before adding, 'They can't change the facts. If they dare to rename the Khorat Plateau "Issan", it will exist in name only. There's no such thing as the Issan people, only the Lao: a peaceful race sharing the same language, history, culture and customs: sticky rice, *Khaen* and *Phin* music, the rocket festival and our traditional customs and rules of law (*Heed Sipsong-Khong Sipsi*) to name but a few. The Lao people will always respect and love (*HuckPhaeng*) each other. Alas, we don't have the funds to win a propaganda war against Bangkok, but we could print posters (*Seu Muan Sonh*) with the slogan "Remember 1779" and distribute them to our men. This would give the impression we're still outraged by the Siamese invasion and the loss of the Emerald Buddha. We could stage protests and get the people to shout, "The Siamese must go!" To annoy them even more, we could switch to "Down with Bangkok". Our traditional balladeers (*Morlum*) and singers can sing from their heart and perform Lao ballads about ViengChan LanXang to the music of the *Khaen*, appealing to the people never to forget their Lao heritage and ancestors. They are the living embodiment of our country.'

A moment later he went quiet and turned his gaze across the Mekong. He revealed he hadn't been too confident of victory but now believed Lao

LanXang would conquer the hearts of the world with their righteousness. His mind was made up. It was now or never, but his animosity towards Bangkok and his desire for independence had blinded him to the facts. He stubbornly refused to heed warnings of danger. He even told the assembly they could stay in ViengChan, but he and his sons would go to face the Siamese. I entirely agreed with him. Though I wasn't a military man like him, I too was ready to fight for LanXang.

While we were all still in the private room viewing King Xay-Setthathirath's portrait, Phraya Sanon moved tentatively towards Chao Anouvong, quietly clasped his arm and pulled him to one side. I couldn't hear what he said, but Chao Anouvong later revealed to me that he accused Viceroy Tissah of being a two-faced fraud and a threat to national security, openly accusing him of cowardice. Far from being offended, Chao Anouvong confessed to his own serious doubts about Tissah's loyalty if it came to war and suspected he might have friends amongst the Siamese nobility. But to avoid damaging his ministers' unity he decided not to follow Phraya Sanon's advice. He ignored the fact that Tissah was veering off the rails. This was quite a risk as his hopes were so firmly set on the element of surprise.

News came to my ears that other ministers afterwards disagreed on strategy, their egos clashing and their tempers flaring. But Chao Anouvong knew they meant no real harm. He urged them to keep up their courage and to rely on each other because trust and morale were as important as talent if they were to win the war. Deep down he probably realised he'd left everything too late. Perhaps he was gripped by some inner demon tempting him to ignore the predictions of disaster.

Privately, however, I thought he was rushing things. He could have waited until the British army marched from Malaya to Bangkok, but sadly the Burney Treaty put a stop to that. He certainly underestimated menace. He should at least have made certain that Luang Phrabang and XiengKhuang took their oaths of allegiance and were entirely with him, and that LanNa would mobilise in support. But deep down we profoundly believed that if we couldn't rely on the Lao people, then who else could we trust? Therefore he must have sensed that the moment for action had finally arrived. Ever since we'd arrived back in ViengChan from King Naphalai's funeral, he'd known exactly what to do. No one could stop him. After nearly five decades of frustration, humiliation and resentment, Lao LanXang's first howls of uprising were heard.

There is probably no need to describe Chao Anouvong's time as king in any great detail but perhaps we should remind ourselves of his most notable achievements.

Firstly, he built a new palace and government offices in the capital in 1807: if he were to rule and rebuild the kingdom, he needed a place to work. The sight of the glittering palace roof inspired the people with confidence. He ordered the two ViengChan city walls to be repaired and added a new, outer one, beginning at the Pasak river north of the city, then running along the north side of the That Luang marsh and ending at DoneKoy on the Mekong in the south. They were named 'Chao Anou's walls' in his honour.

In 1808 he built the Wat Sibounheang temple in Nongkhai city as well as a new bridge at Nakhorn Phanom. He recognised its strategic importance, and its ruler's allegiance to LanXang was important to ViengChan's defence.

In 1810 he built a new, smaller Hor Phra Kaeo (Emerald Buddha shrine) in the Wat XangPheuak temple in Si-Xiengmai city, as well as a bridge linking the two banks of the Mekong there in 1812.

The foundations of the old Hor Phra Kaeo in ViengChan were raised and restored in 1816, The That Luang stupa was embellished by the addition of a cloister.

He began the construction of Wat Sisaketh in 1818, the most significant temple of all, and the only one with its ordination hall (*Sim*) facing the Mekong. When it was completed in 1824, an imposing and elaborate celebration was staged to mark the event.

LanXang was trying to reinvent itself and ViengChan was going through a staggering transformation. It was Chao Anouvong's laborious attention to humdrum detail as much as his soaring confidence that made him such a formidable ruler and gave his people so much pleasure and happiness. He was a good general, a supreme commander and a successful leader; he believed his building programme would generate energy and confidence amongst the people. His next step was to build an army way beyond the walls of ViengChan in distant provincial cities all over the kingdom. Despite his success and status he respected the aged, the disadvantaged and the marginalised. He appealed directly to his people for courage and support. Only then, he thought, would Bangkok think twice before objecting both to his kingship and to the restoration of LanXang, or risk causing permanent damage to the brotherly love between Bangkok and ViengChan. His insight was brilliant. Nonetheless the state of his army placed him in a desperately weak position: His men were ill equipped; their weapons were out of date. Some were homemade and fit only for hunting small animals in the forest. But he'd great confidence in the willpower of the Lao people.

Whenever LanXang's kings went to war it was always second nature to guard their backs. Despite Chao Anouvong's reservations, which probably didn't bode well for the chances of success, Tissah was duly appointed as a field commander and given the responsibility of raising an army before marching his men to Kalasin, Roi-Et, Khon Kaen and Chonnabot. His final stop was to be Souvannaphum, once a principality equal to Champasak in status but now reduced by the Siamese to a small town. His task was to guard the south-eastern flank, to intercept any advance by the Siamese army and to keep lines of communication open on the eastern edge of the Khorat Plateau.

A few days later, the courageous Rathsabud Yoh was sent back to Champasak to recruit much-needed fighting men; he was to head down to Ubon before making his way to Sisaketh and then up to Yasothon with the aim of conscripting as many fighting men as possible. 'We must raise an army in the name of the Lao nation,' said Chao Anouvong, instructing his son to train the new recruits before bringing them up towards ViengChan before marching to Khorat, where they would meet Tissah at Souvannaphum. Prince Yoh kept his father closely informed of developments and later resisted Phraya Phromphakdy's attempts to take control of Champasak city. Chao Anouvong was outraged when the news reached him.

Chao Anouvong waited anxiously for news from Luang Phrabang before moving against Bangkok. The fifty mandarins who'd presented his letter of reconciliation to King Manthathurath had finally returned safely. Disappointingly he didn't receive the sworn allegiance he'd been hoping for and he was left surprised and deeply frustrated. He thought that Manthathurath, despite the flattery, was too cautious and fearful for his own survival and perhaps still smarting from the transfer of power to ViengChan. He hedged his bets, agreeing to provide support for the war effort without showing open hostility towards Bangkok. The news gave Chao Anouvong some hope; he wasn't entirely downhearted because he believed Manthathurath had genuine sympathy for him and the Lao nation.

XV

The War

Let's consider the details of Chao Anouvong's kingship. I am sure you want to know what happened to him so let me continue to sing about him. I shall soon get to the climax of the story: the Lao LanXang rising, the war of independence itself.

I will try to elucidate the essential nature and true characteristics of the war before demonstrating its consequences.

It was the most difficult period in Chao Anouvong's life in so far as LanXang's future was concerned. Despite his ever-toughening stance towards Nangklao, Chao Anouvong was still an advocate of rapprochement with Siam. The Rattanakosins probably knew their misrule over LanXang and LanNa had bred resentment, but they'd done nothing to stop it.

We'd hoped struggle against Bangkok's ideology through peaceful rather than violent means. We weren't out to seek revenge, despite the huge suffering of the Lao people. Should we go to war, with the mass killings and violence that it entails, or negotiate some kind of deal that might save thousands of lives? We thought the indignity of having to deal with Bangkok was inevitable and a price worth paying for the preservation of the Lao nation. However, Chao Anouvong feared he'd made such an enemy of Nangklao that all trust between the two kings had been destroyed. Besides, whatever we decided, only a few outcomes were still possible, none of which were pleasant. Either Chao Anouvong remained as king in ViengChan and quietly continued to accept Bangkok's orders, or we would coexist as a vassal state (*Phateth Salath*) under Rattanakosin Siam. But we knew the Lao nation would be slowly strangled out of existence.

Generally most Lao people, identifying with the country of their birth and the language they speak, are quiet nationalists. They tend to be courteous, respectful and peaceful. Any Lao of decent breeding doesn't have time to be impolite, to argue or to brawl. Nevertheless, like any other nation, they sometimes disagree with one another, though rarely violently. But they disagreed fiercely with the deceit and arrogance of the Bangkok regime that had subjugated and humiliated them. Chao Anouvong had decided that the Lao people had wasted enough time being discriminated against, oppressed, frightened and excluded in their own country. After spending over twenty years pleading for self-rule without success, he finally called time on the Rattanakosin government. There'd been enough humiliation and repression and he hated the filth of Siam. He decided to fight.

But how to break away from Siam? A unilateral declaration of independence would lead to a Siamese invasion. Chao Anouvong's dream of an independent country would degenerate into a lengthy armed struggle.

The Rattanakosins' policies had created serious political problems that required a political dialogue, yet the mediocre politicians in Bangkok, were too arrogant to see the bigger picture. Chao Anouvong and his people were ready to stand up and fight.

Once the politics of gentle persuasion had failed, retaliation was the only justice that made sense. The question of who started the war was irrelevant: the insurrection was in the name of the Lao nation and their struggle for independence was legitimate. Territorial integrity, national unity and the fight for liberation were essential. The Lao people wanted their LanXang back, if not now, then tomorrow. Bangkok had managed to not only turn Chao Anouvong against them but the entire Lao people. There would be no end to the troubles until LanXang was united.

Bad omens – violent thunderstorms, lightning and an earthquake that caused damage to ViengChan – were interpreted as clear warnings by the palace oracle, astronomers, venerable holy monks and many lay people. But Chao Anouvong seemed to know his own fate; he said he wasn't afraid, even though he'd no place to hide. He thanked them for their concern but persistently derided auguries and omens as nonsense. As a man of action and conviction he was prepared to face the consequences. He wished that he'd the youth, as he'd the stomach, to go to Bangkok himself. He was prepared to fight and die by the sword in his own palace rather than be subjected to endless humiliation.

As a show of their belief in the dangers ahead, some of the grey-headed court nobles and oracles begged the gods to give them wise counsel. They shed tears, prostrated themselves and begged Chao Anouvong to think it over. Surely no sane man wanted war. Their prophecies were dark and didn't bode well for the future: one forecast that a powerful foe from the southwest would invade and destroy ViengChan. The predictions were spread by whispers and seeped through to the people. In the end, the whole city buzzed with dark rumours like a beehive. The people, under threat as much as their king, sought the counsel of the gods and ancestral spirits. The clever ones hid their treasures in remote places or left the city, but most believed that the gods and Lord Buddha would help them and that a miracle would save the kingdom from destruction.

Chao Anouvong acknowledged that if the people lost their superstitious nature, they might also lose their minds. Similarly, if evil portents paralysed them with fear, then good omens would surely inspire them with strength and confidence. He dismissed such apocalyptic talk as excessively gloomy and he desired to lead his people from the fog of murky superstition. He argued that LanXang had endured all manner of disasters in the past – civil war, famine and invasion – and would do so again. His strategy under attack, he told his people he was confident he would find enough brave men willing to fight for LanXang. As for those who wished to stay at home, they were welcome to do so, but they would live to tell their grandchildren only of the regret they felt for not fighting for their country. Therefore, despite these portents and the resulting dejection of his viceroy, Tissah, Chao Anouvong himself was far from alarmed or deterred, but grimly prepared for the coming conflict. He refused to allow his faith to be shattered by the problems of the present and the fears of the future. He urged the people to prepare and be ready. His whole mind set on restoring LanXang, he chose to ignore the omens and was prepared to risk war in defiance of Lord Buddha and the gods.

The governors, the noblemen of the cities and country people throughout LanXang, especially on the Khorat Plateau, showed their support. But what we really needed above all, in addition to our will and resolve, was a united LanXang kingdom as well a heroic, well-equipped army. The general mood was overwhelmingly in favour of the uprising. In fact Chao Anouvong's refusal to accept the invitation to celebrate the pleasure lake in Bangkok at the risk of offending Nangklao's feelings had burned all the bridges between them. They had officially declared themselves enemies. So, inevitably, war and bloodshed normally follow.

Chao Anouvong was loved by the masses and, as expected, the people didn't let him down. Lao citizens from all walks of life were prepared to fight for their freedom. The people of NongBuaLamphu, where Chao Anouvong's mother came from, were among the first to arrive, offering their lives unreservedly. Like most peace-loving Lao, they were chiefly governed by resentment over their pride being trampled on, blaming Bangkok for the collapse of LanXang. The Siamese had broken the vows they'd sworn at That Si-SongHuck.

Not only Laomen from all over LanXang but others closely related to LanXang from the mountains of Sipsong ChuTai and Shan volunteered. Brave, fit, young Lao from the countryside rushed to offer their services, enlisting in huge numbers. They came from near and far with their homemade guns, spears and swords. Some had walked for many days or even weeks: from the mountains of Phongsali, Huaphan, Xamneua, XiengKhuang, Luang Phrabang and Mahaxay; from as far as the Vietnamese border; from the highlands of XiengMai, XiengRai and XiengSaen; from the plateau of Xekong, Saravan and Attapeu; from the plains of Lamphun, Lampang, Phrae, Nan, Dan Sai, Sayabury and other cities. They came not only to do their duty as patriotic citizens but also because of the insolent behaviour of the Rattanakosin Siamese. They knew they would be fighting not only for their lives but for their priceless Lao national identity, eagerly volunteering to fight for LanXang and become part of history. They were willing to die. The oppressive regime in Bangkok had not only stoked the fire of rebellion but had thrown oil onto it. An everlasting storm erupted in Siam, especially on the Khorat Plateau.

When they arrived in their thousands it seemed to us that heaven favoured our cause. Chao Anouvong received them with charm and sympathy and listened to their tales of woe. They'd been oppressed; their children had been taken away and sold openly in the market as domestic servants to the Bangkok elites, working like galley slaves to no purpose. He knew how to make good use of everyone's talents; his wisdom was evident. They pledged to give their all and join this citizens' army; their desire for revenge was as strong as hunger or thirst. They were ready to march.

I knew Chao Anouvong would expect me to go with him, but I tried desperately to think of excuses to stay behind. I was dreaded the outcome of the war and feared ViengChan might be destroyed, but I kept all of this to myself. He knew I wasn't at all a military man and was in love with peace. The library had become my sanctuary and its books were part of my soul. It was my refuge, where I could learn about life without having to participate in it, where I could understand people without having to talk to them. I was the custodian, so I begged him to leave me behind in ViengChan to oversee the safety of these important documents.

'Don't worry,' he said. 'I know you're dreading it, but they won't dare cross the Mekong, and this could be your last service to your country and to me. Besides, if you want to find out what human beings can do to each other, you'd better come along. You'll deserve a knighthood (*Phraya*) after that.'

I certainly wasn't suited for life in the military: I hated the boneheaded discipline. Fighting off the enemy's forces is nothing like fixing a leaking roof, and I would rather be woken by the call of cocks than by trumpets or the tramp of soldiers' boots. I didn't care about promotion, but I could hardly refuse to go: I'd devoted my life to him and to the cause of LanXang independence. For all our faults we were within our rights for wanting to save the Lao nation. I anticipated a long campaign, not a quick march. War is war, but while I was alive, I wanted to be with him and to be part of history. The decision was easy to make, and I knew precisely what I had to do. I put aside my forebodings and got myself ready to chance my providence in war, even though my expectations of surviving it were low.

After long deliberation Chao Anouvong went ahead with preparations for his campaign. He made sure the new recruits received tough military training, instilling discipline and equipping them with a good understanding of war. The regular soldiers were put through their paces at the That Luang military hill headquarters. Mobilisation went smoothly and it was invigorating seeing the positive reaction of the public, which we'd been hoping for. Chao Anouvong was deeply moved by the people's support.

He became more willing to consider his position as supreme commander. It would surely tire him out doing two jobs and it was surely too risky to entrust the security of the entire kingdom to one man. Warfare was a dangerous affair: what would happen should this one king and supreme commander be killed? Who would take over? He was concerned his kingdom might perish under a weak leader, and while he accepted he was too old to go off soldiering, he decided it was best he commanded the army, believing that as physical health declines, so mental acuity sharpens. He kept himself fit and alert and was confident in the success of the war preparations.

From the beginning, things went rather better than expected. A few days after the meeting the king quietly reassured Tissah that he was needed and dispatched him with about 10,000 men to take the city of Kalasin. Tissah's main mission was to stop Suriyaphakdy, who'd been directing the census in the region, and, if possible, to capture and kill all Siamese agents. The noblemen from Sakon Nakhorn and Kalasin who'd taken refuge from the census in ViengChan joined him. Tissah took his time but was expected to reach Kalasin by late December 1826. His final destination was Souvannaphum, further south.

On 17 January 1827, Chao Anouvong told Rathsavong Ngao of a courtly letter – an official reply to Nangklao's invitation – that he'd sent to Bangkok two days earlier, saying he was ready to send an army to protect Nangklao and to assist him against foreign invasion. He then ordered the prince – a fair-skinned, strong, elegant and clever man who closely resembled his father – to lead 3,000 men, 400 elephants and 200 horses to Khorat as an advance guard to secure the route towards Bangkok.

'The time has come,' said the king as he tied a white thread on his son's wrists (*Phouk Khaen*) and blessed him. 'Now I command you, Rathsavong Ngao, to bring our suffering people in Saraburi and elsewhere back to ViengChan. If Bangkok wants war, then we will fight to protect our people. Even if I die, our struggle will continue.'

'Your Majesty, I've been waiting for this moment,' said the brave prince, acknowledging the order with a deep bow as the king gave him his blessing. 'Let's go forth and reclaim our priceless rights and freedoms,' the prince added resolutely before rising to his feet and leaving to carry out his duty.

So the war began with an attempt to stop Bangkok's barbaric tattooing campaign (*Sucklek*). Rathsavong Ngao penetrated deep into the southwest of the Khorat plateau seeking justice for the people; he'd no real intention of waging war and certainly had no plans to push beyond the LanXang frontier at Khorat city. His mission was to repatriate the people from Dong Phraya Fai, Saraburi, Lomsak and elsewhere back to ViengChan, but also partly to halt the Siamese, who were purposefully trekking north-eastwards into LanXang in search of new territory. Prince Ngao and his men demanded retribution.

A few days later, once he was satisfied that Ngao was safely on his way to Khorat, Chao Anouvong led his main army of about 9,000 elite fighting men out of ViengChan to cross the Mekong. Thus began his fateful expedition to Khorat. I joined the column soon after dawn and followed him on horseback. From the direction of That Luang hill to the south came the booming of drums. As if they were already in heaven and oblivious of the future, children scampered excitedly all around them, followed by nine columns of green-uniformed armed soldiers. A mass of noblemen, ordinary citizens and curious monks lined the route. They would come out in large numbers to show their support. The monks chanted prayers and sprinkled holy water over the soldiers with jasmine branches. Some young girls and schoolchildren handed out small bouquets of flowers and loudly cheered and applauded. Since 1779 Lao LanXang had been drowning in difficulty, but on that day it was bliss to be alive and everything seemed possible. The people came out in force to tell the soldiers to be brave and bring back victory, urging their king to take control of the kingdom's destiny. Their support made all the difference.

At the centre of all this activity was Chao Anouvong himself, proudly dressed in his freshly laundered supreme commander's uniform which had already seen him through many victories for Siam in LanNa. He'd jokingly pledged he wouldn't take it off until victory was won or he met his death. For the first time I watched him from a distance; I would normally tuck in safely behind him. I realised how much I appreciated his natural leadership. His thick brows, phoenix-like eyes, newly trimmed moustache perched like a moth on his upper lip and clear complexion exuded an aura of valour. I was no military man but still found it exhilarating and thought of the war without dread. However I couldn't erase the fear he would be killed from my mind. He was dauntless and unflappable. He said he would try to stay alive if he could, for he was much needed. He'd so many excellent human qualities: discipline, courage, breadth of vision, clarity, honesty and conviction, in addition to his good looks: all seemed personified in his solid frame and steady gaze, seated high on his elephant's back as it strode past me. You could tell by the way he looked that he felt detached from his karma and was unconcerned about his fate; that he was working himself into a warlike mood. His son Suthisan Poh, a tall, elegant, fair-skinned man in his late thirties, followed closely behind on a tall, black horse.

The legions of his infantry were in full marching order – thousands of well-trained patriotic fighting men carrying flags and banners. The crash of their feet seemed to shake the very earth and they roared at the tops of their voices, 'Lao LanXang. Lao LanXang. Lao LanXang!' I noticed that most of the soldiers were the newest of recruits: mostly young, innocent-looking peasants, farmers and pale-faced urban boys who could barely swing their arms or walk in time. Their real power, however, lay in their resentment towards Siam. They would rather fight and die in battle than be subject to slavery and humiliation.

The ViengChan people, families, old men and women with multiple-coloured sashes across their breasts lined up along the route. Some had set up stools or chairs and were sitting in the shade or under their colourful parasols; others were hanging out of their verandas to watch, giving their support. There were mothers, fathers, sons, daughters, brothers, sisters and children; sad, worried and cheerful faces combined, all busily engaged with the rest of the cheering crowd. They threw flowers or scattered petals onto the path as a final farewell to their loved ones, wishing them luck and waving the national flag, the royal ViengChan flag (yellow with one white elephant on a red background in the top left-hand corner) and a flag showing a three-headed white elephant on a red background signifying the three Lao LanXang principalities – ViengChan, Luang Phrabang and Champasak. The people's willpower urged Chao Anouvong and his soldiers on. It was incredible and magical.

'Good luck and victory to us!' the crowds shouted, wiping tears of farewell from their eyes.

The marching men did not look back, for any hint of emotion would be a sign of weakness. Chao Anouvong signalled his mahout to steady the impressive bull elephant. It stopped, lifting its powerful, long trunk into an S shape. He got up and stood tall. Suddenly he lifted the three-headed white elephant flag and the national flag high above his head. He waved them gently back and forth in each hand to the cheering crowd, before planting them back into their sockets. The crowd quickly went silent.

'People of ViengChan,' he began, speaking rather too quickly in a low voice. 'I am honoured to be your king. What pleases me more is to see you out in force to support our cause.' I could feel the hair standing up on the back of my neck. 'I care about our kingdom and will do my utmost to save our nation.' Then he looked lovingly at the two flags and told the people that although both were equally significant, it was most important of all that the Lao people were of one heart and mind. 'To survive,' he roared, 'LanXang must unite as one.' The crowd cheered rapturously. He then lifted the national flag and reminded the people of its significance. 'The full *white* moon,' he said, 'represents the heart of the Lao peoples; the *blue* of the sky is the mighty Mekong, with the Lao people in *red* on both banks. The flag stands for equality and freedom but above all it stands for the people of LanXang. We must protect it.'

The crowd went into fresh ecstasies, clapping their hands in excitement.

Schoolchildren cheered excitedly and vigorously waved their flags. Chao Anouvong concluded by promising to hold a celebration, dedicated to all Lao, if he returned victorious. The people raised their praying hands above their heads and said, '*Sathu* (amen)!' in unison. 'Go well, bring back victory,' they cried and called farewell to their king and soldiers.

With a final wave to the crowd, the king climbed down from the elephant and then mounted his beloved, well-trained tall, dark-brown horse (*Asanai mah*) which stood solidly like a bronze statue. He patted its neck then urged it forward. It pricked up its ears, threw up its head, whinnied loudly and slowly trotted on before breaking into a gentle canter to the front, leaving a smoky trail of choking dust. His troops followed on and the cheering slowly died away with the settling dust. The armed forces strove for glory, knowing that death was inescapable. Some people cheered and laughed through their tears, accepting their loved ones might not return from the battle. There was a palpable sense of anxiety and loss as people stood around wondering what to do next. The noise faded and the marching army soon disappeared. The people slowly dispersed to their homes with their hearts beating for their king and soldiers. Some went to the temples to pray for their loved ones. I hastened after the king. The army was heading for the crossing point of the Mekong to PhanPhao village, where the legendary seven-headed serpent guardian once told the ruler and his people to cross the Mekong and found the renowned city of ViengChan.

Once he was on board the royal boat, Chao Anouvong stood at the bow to pour libations from a silver cup into the river to his ancestors Fah Ngum and Xay-Setthathirath, to the lord Buddha and to the gods (*Phra Inh* and *Phra Phom*) to whom he frequently paid honour. He propitiated the spirits of the river with prayers and offerings and poured another libation into the water. He was not only wise but also generous in his offerings, calling upon the ancestral spirits (*Phi Fah and Phi Thaen*) in heaven and the mythical seven-headed dragon (*Phraya Nark*) guardian who lives in the depths of the Mekong. Then he gave an order for the boats, men and animals to cross. The crossing went successfully.

(According to an ancient legend, Phraya Nark's subterranean city *Mueang Bardan* lies beneath this area of the Mekong, connected by a subterranean tunnel to a large pond in ViengChan. In time of war the magic drum (*Kong Mak Khaeng*) would be struck to call upon Phraya Nark to come to the defence of the city and attack the enemy.)

When the gathering at PhanPhao village was completed a few days later, Chao Anouvong paraded the army and staged extensive military exercises to test the skill and strength of his troops. His face had gradually tanned and become more weathered. Standing on a platform he anxiously watched his troops perform, intense concentration on his face as he tried to look everywhere at once: straight ahead, left then right as the troops manoeuvred in an organised fashion. The weight of responsibility fell only on him. When I pulled out a white cloth and handed it over to him, he used it to dab at his face and wipe the back of his neck. When the drills ended, he stood up to address the soldiers, telling them to stand easy as they stood in straight lines, sweating in the heat. There was absolute silence as he stepped down from the platform to inspect them. I didn't follow him but watched in great admiration. I'd never seen so many soldiers before; they were a fine body of men, holding long spears and lances decorated with red pennants. They were lean and impassive in their pale green uniforms, standing nervously to attention, fixing their gaze straight ahead.

'*Sabaidee*. Good to meet you, well done,' he would say. 'Good work, well done, good to meet you.' Most soldiers had never got that close to him before. The light on their bronze-pointed spears dazzled as brightly as the sun and he had to shield his eyes. His noble face, no question about it, left them numb and made them swallow hard, but he was humble enough to treat them with respect. He climbed back onto the platform and presented himself to the army as their powerful, determined king. Having scanned their faces, he seized his chance and made a rallying cry. Bangkok, he told them, would always be dangerous; the name of its ruler might change but nothing else would: its ambition would always be to annex LanXang. He declared that they were the edges of Lao's blades, the heads of Lao's arrows and spears, and, most of all, a band of brothers with a duty to fight to protect the Lao nation. He gazed at them and said, 'You are all my kindred, every one of you. All those who are prepared to serve and sacrifice with me, to stand and fight the enemy, are my courageous brothers. We are men of arms, now and in the next life, ferocious as tigers and wolves. We shall brave the elements together. Now, please listen.'

He paused and then said, 'How should we treat the Siamese? Just think of it. They're supposed to be well off, well fed, well-educated and well connected with us. Yet they invaded us and looted our treasures. Now they want to dominate us. For this, brothers, we must get rid of them. This war will not only decide the fate of Lao LanXang but also decide between life and death as well as glory and dishonour. It will determine the history of our country; all depends on winning this war, otherwise the colonial powers will carve us up without a second thought. In the name of the Lao nation, we will fight the good fight to regain our territory and independence. I expect ultimate bravery from everyone. All commanders should lead their men into combat.' He paused and made libations. 'May the spirits of our ancestors protect us and grant us a glorious triumph. Let us go forth from here and let each of us resolve to do his duty for our country. To LanXang!'

You could somehow sense the soldiers' tears as they roared confidently at the top of their voices, 'Victory! Victory! Victory! LanXang! LanXang! LanXang!' They swore loyalty to his every word and vowed in silent fervour to wreak vengeance on their enemies. With full lungs they yelled together, 'Long Live Anouvong! Long Live Anouvong! Long Live Anouvong!'

He smiled and looked at them with fatherly affection. I suspected he too was close to tears.

While we were still in PhanPhao we heard reports that two days after leaving ViengChan, Prince Ngao made a detour to Lomsak city, where he gave orders to repatriate some of the people and to build a fortress, helping the governor and citizens to complete the construction before heading further south. They reached Khorat at the beginning of February. The prince hastily asked the city treasurer and deputy governor to supply him with food, pretending that the demand came from Nangklao, who'd supposedly ordered him to Bangkok to fight the British. Fortunately the governor was away, and it didn't take much to convince the treasurer. Rathsavong Ngao was neither in awe of nor contemptuous of the enemy: having collected provisions he sent his commander, Phraya Mueang Khua, ahead with scouts to spy on the enemy at Saraburi.

Rathsavong Ngao and his task force, their lances decorated with red feathers, followed the next day. They reached Saraburi two days later and set up camp at Ban Khaengkhua village as planned to await news. A few days later Phraya Mueang Khua brought the governor of Saraburi and other officials to see the prince, who informed them of the impending attack on Bangkok by the British.

'In view of the situation,' he said, 'it's essential to evacuate all Lao people back to ViengChan for their safety. You may remember my father, Chao Anouvong.'

The Saraburi nobles muttered and nodded with delight and said, 'How is His Majesty?'

'He is fine, thank you,' replied the prince. 'He sends his greetings and thanks for welcoming him when he passed through your city two years ago. He was very happy to see you but very sad he wasn't able to take you back with him. He also said you might one day eat your favourite meals in your beloved city of ViengChan again. Well, here's the opportunity to do so and there's no time to waste.'

There was a loud cheer: all the citizens of Saraburi – about 30,000 Lao, 300 Chinese and 50 Siamese – had been ordered to gather. Although some Chinese and Siamese took the opportunity to escape, the majority were ready to leave joyfully. They hastily gathered up their belongings and provisions, left their homes and marched towards Khorat. The evacuation went satisfactorily.

Meanwhile the 9,000 men led by Chao Anouvong and his son Suthisan Poh were now on the great south-west route. We could see on our right the peaks of Phetsabun in their greenish dark hues. On the Khorat plain between the great Mekong and the mountains lay the vast lands and rivers that fed the Lao people. No one could accuse us of marching into Siam! An avenue of tall, leafless Ceiba trees (*Kapok*) were in full bloom, dotted with songbirds amongst the bright red flowers known to the Lao as *Dork Ngiew*. As we tramped across the dry, sunny plain, I could see scarlet Kapok trees here and there, glowing like fire. We lumbered along the ground well-trodden by those before us. Far ahead the column sent up a cloud of brown dust, more than enough to choke you. The bronze-pointed spears and long swords on the elephants' pack saddles glittered in the sun.

We laboured along barren lands and scorched brown paddy fields. The soldiers learnt of Chao Anouvong's pride as he sat and shared food with them. To loosen up his muscles he often sweated it out with them, leading the column on foot at a slower pace. I tagged along. After nearly a month of untroubled yet slow travel, we arrived in Khorat on 17 February 1827, lean men on thin animals. Chao Anouvong had lost a great deal of weight too. His solid flesh had disappeared under his uniform and his Adam's apple had become as prominent as a pointed egg under his chin.

Chao Anouvong had taken the bold decision to catch his enemy unprepared by assaulting Khorat. He was daring even in his old age. Fortunately the city governor Phraya Phromphakdy, one of his mortal enemies, was involved in the Khmer rebellion at Khukan. Phraya Akharath, a staunch ViengChan man who had been taken prisoner in 1779, was whooping with joy and obligingly opened the city gate to Chao Anouvong. It was crucial to capture this city – a bastion of Bangkok – without a single shot being fired. A clash would have been inevitable if Phromphakdy had been present. As it was, Chao Anouvong was content and quickly set up his headquarters close to Beung Thale lake, a swampy area swarming with hostile insects. The army made camp just in front of his royal tent, the swarm of followers, grooms and mahouts, carpenters and engineers, cooks and dancers, spread all around him. I could hear the soldiers' footsteps, the women chattering, the chopping of fallen trees for firewood and the distant trumpeting of the elephants. The conditions in the camps were crude, short of comfort, but I was prepared to endure some hardship. Chao Anouvong never complained, standing still, wiping his forehead and cheeks with a red, sodden handkerchief. 'So much to do,' he muttered, watching the insects flying into the remnants of sunlight. While his troops rested and ate, he went about inspecting that all was well. He scarcely rested. He wanted to make sure they never felt abandoned by him.

He returned satisfied and made himself comfortable on a chair. All became quiet; nothing could be heard except the incessant whining of mosquitoes, the constant croaking of the frogs and the bothersome droning of bluebottles. Yet the Siamese army's presence could be felt from afar. I was too tired and irritated by the insects, fanning them off with my hand, to be edgy.

At the assembly in Khorat city centre a few days later, the governor of Khukan city, Phraya Kai Songkram, came hurriedly with 3,000 men to pledge their allegiance and asked to be armed. He also volunteered to capture Phromphakdy. Chao Anouvong thanked them again for the welcome they gave him in 1825 and presented himself as their liberator from Bangkok. They saw him as the guardian of the Lao against the Siamese menace, but when they cheered him on his way to Bangkok, he denied that was ever his plan: 'War is not our preference!' he declared. The crowd roared their approval. 'The governor of Khorat is the source of our problems,' he said, telling them he was only there to put an end to the notorious Siamese census and to help some of them return to their homes. He promptly gave orders for the people to be evacuated back to ViengChan. They were more than willing to go and the evacuation only took four days.

Meanwhile, in the second week of January, after capturing and executing

Kalasin's governor Phraya Sunthon for refusing to swear allegiance, Tissah left Kalasin for Roi-Et and moved on to Yasothon further south. In early February he reached his intended destination of Souvannaphum, north of the Mun river, and was responsible for organising the transfer of some of the Lao population from Souvannaphum, Ubon, Kalasin, Yasothon, Roi-Et and Khon Kaen to ViengChan. He was also supposed to halt the census, but met Phromphakdy's chief officer, Suriyaphakdy the brute, who was directing the census in the Yasothon region. After a long, persuasive talk, Tissah's discipline, authority, rules of security and adherence to principles evaporated. Foreseeing a probable Lao defeat, Tissah instead revealed Chao Anouvong's plans to station his army in Khorat, from where he might attack Bangkok. He was therefore acting as a double agent for both the Siamese and the Lao, but his loyalties ultimately lay with Siam. He then granted Suriyaphakdy safe passage on the understanding he (Tissah) be appointed ViengChan's ruler as a reward for his act of disloyalty to Chao Anouvong. Suriyaphakdy hurried to Bangkok.

When Suriyaphakdy reached Khorat, he was intercepted and interrogated by Lao soldiers. They escorted him to see Chao Anouvong, who was most surprised to see his permit of safe passage. Suriyaphakdy then deviously told Chao Anouvong he'd promised Tissah he would retrieve the Emerald Buddha for the Lao, repatriate the Lao population in Bangkok and urge pro-Lao factions to rise up. He also shrewdly begged to be allowed to fetch his family from Bangkok and take them to ViengChan. 'With this pass, Your Majesty,' Suriyaphakdy said confidently, 'please allow me to be on my way to collect my family so we can live happily in ViengChan.' To reinforce his plea he cunningly handed over as a hostage the Siamese third army commander, Phraya Anuchid Phithak, who claimed he wished to stay in Khorat to enjoy the hospitality and company of the Lao troops. Unaware of Tissah's true motives and despite his own doubts about Suriyaphakdy's wishes, Chao Anouvong decided to accept the validity of the pass, which indicated that Suriyaphakdy had surrendered voluntarily.

I suspect that Tissah had met Suriyaphakdy whilst working in Bangkok and had been in secret contact all along. He'd now sold Chao Anouvong's war plans to the enemy and was bargaining for his own head. This made Chao Anouvong feel a fool. He knew full well that Suriyaphakdy had a strong and malign influence and was guilty of directing Bangkok's orders. But in a desperate attempt to avoid arousing suspicion, he made it clear to Suriyaphakdy that he was not a rebel but was in fact on a goodwill mission; he implored him to convey his respects to Nangklao. 'Please also inform His Majesty that we are officially in Khorat merely to redress the people's complaints and unhappiness, as set forth in my courtly letter of the 15 January,' he said.

Suriyaphakdy accepted Chao Anouvong's assurances that he'd absolutely no plans against Siam and meant no harm to Bangkok. He even craftily promised Chao Anouvong he would place his head under Nangklao's feet and make a compassionate and heartfelt appeal to him for the villainous tattooing decree to be revoked.

This was indeed a grave mistake on Chao Anouvong's part. Having been to Bangkok in person and complained to Naphalai, the late king, about the Siamese governors' offences against the Lao people, he should have recognised the danger. I was angry with myself for not being forthright with my advice. He should have prevented Suriyaphakdy from leaving Khorat, regardless of the legitimacy of the pass. Understandably, he thought killing Suriyaphakdy would have meant a declaration of war, but by letting him go, Nangklao might accept his account and war might be averted. I gazed beyond the clouds in consternation.

'At this juncture, Your Majesty,' I said, 'I have no choice but to speak to you bluntly.'

'This is no time to be taciturn, let's hear it,' he said and sat down.

I told him that Suriyaphakdy's promise to retrieve the Emerald Buddha was an outright lie. Any Lao man would want to take it back. Quite frankly I seriously thought of trying it myself during our stay in Bangkok in 1825, but the Siamese royalty had chained it up, believing it might escape. 'Suriyaphakdy,' I said, 'instead of conveying our respects, would undoubtedly give a very different sort of report. Besides, Nangklao is deaf to any pleas and would use our move as a pretext to further his monstrous ambitions: to invade and destroy ViengChan, to annex LanXang and to label you a traitor.' At first Chao Anouvong was very annoyed and disappointed with himself, accepting he was a victim of his own foolishness. 'More worryingly,' I added, 'I'm afraid we've put the lives of the pro-Lao population and Lao partisans in Siam in mortal danger. Siam is willing to kill its critics in cold blood. Whether we like it or not there's going to be a war, and if we lose...'

'We know the answer well enough, Phia Jon,' he said, sighed and shrugged. 'There's still hope,' he added. He'd every reason to believe in the single-mindedness of the ethnic Lao citizens in Bangkok and other cities who were still loyal to LanXang, but it was too late to stop Suriyaphakdy, who couldn't believe his luck as he hurried down to Bangkok. Chao Anouvong decided not to pursue him, but for LanXang's sake he prayed that his son Ngao would exercise better judgement than himself.

Not many days after leaving Khorat, Suriyaphakdy came across Ngao and his army at Dong Phraya Fai where he was preparing to repatriate the people to ViengChan. He made a point of detaining Suriyaphakdy and wanted to behead him on the spot despite the apparent validity of the pass, but this would have meant ignoring his father's authority. After strong objections from one of his advisors, Phraya Xiengtai, he grudgingly decided to let Suriyaphakdy continue his journey.

We had ample supplies while in Khorat. I thought it crucial that all intelligence activities were focused on Bangkok and on winning the war. Chao Anouvong had championed his people against the Siamese elite but had insufficient troops to march on Bangkok. Instead, he intended to lure Nangklao into fighting at NongBuaLamphu. He was also prepared to use Khorat as a forward base to strike at the first opportunity, depriving Bangkok of any time to organise its defence. However, rhetoric, philosophy, empathy and eloquence were his forte, sadly not psychology and politics. As a Buddhist, he was more in tune with a philosophical approach. He'd lost his impetus and sense of direction. Pondering the situation further, I realised to my horror that it was ruinous economically, questionable economically and a liability politically. In fact, it was a total blunder. The whole situation was chaotic. He blinked in shock for he now realised he'd to do what he'd most wanted to avoid: to fight far away from ViengChan. He blamed himself and began to look for an alternative.

'No, no – you were right, Phia Jon,' he groaned, visibly annoyed with himself. 'If only I'd arrested that monster Suriyaphakdy and put him away there and then. But, for the sake of our glory and liberty, we must stand and fight.' I said nothing while the Lao army was instructing the population to leave Khorat.

Unfortunately it wasn't long before the Khorat governor Phromphakdy stripped off his uniform, disguised himself in civilian clothes and infiltrated himself into the crowd. His men had helped him to evade capture by Phraya Kai Songkram at Khukan city twice before. He turned up as a Siamese army officer at the Lao army's headquarters and succeeded in persuading Chao Anouvong to trust him. Not long after, his deputy-governor Phraya Plat and his men also surrendered, claiming they wished to supervise the movement of people to ViengChan. They requested knives, axes and firearms to hunt for food. It was all very convincing, but Chao Anouvong committed a grave error in trusting them.

Whatever the truth, Phromphakdy and Plat ordered a rest camp to be set up when the evacuees reached the Samrid Plains. It was a very hot day. At this point both the people and their Lao military escorts led by Phraya Ramphixay were tired and welcomed some rest. While the guards fell asleep in the heat, some of the evacuees who were reluctant to go to ViengChan took the chance to hide themselves. The Lao soldiers fell into a trap, and most were killed when Phromphakdy and his men staged their own mutiny. The surviving Lao soldiers escaped and reported the massacre to Chao Anouvong at his camp.

Upon hearing the news, Chao Anouvong instructed his eldest son Suthisan Poh to ascertain the exact facts of the incident. This was the prince's first real experience of war, and he was in an unknown country. Rousing his troops from their slumber, he rushed 3,000 men to attack the mutineers. They put up strong resistance and he failed to crush them. Thinking the Siamese army had arrived, he hurried back to update his father. It was devastating news. The war of independence, originally intended to repatriate the Lao people to ViengChan and to destroy the core of Siamese oppression in Khorat rather than encroaching into Siamese territory, was now in full swing. Events were turning against the Lao side and the inhabitants were beginning to feel nervous.

The rumours were spreading rapidly that Bangkok was about to be invaded by a Lao army of 80,000 men, so the city emptied its prisons in panic and sent out a huge army to fight. Chao Anouvong, with only 20,000 men, had no time for speculation and was forced to rely on his military instincts; he knew that Nangklao would launch an offensive against him. He estimated that the enemy had a superiority of ten to one in every battalion. He'd two alternatives in mind: either confront the Siamese directly at Khorat city or move to NongBuaLamphu, destroying or hiding the harvests along the route to deprive the Siamese of provisions. He didn't appear to lose confidence and there was no panic. He maintained his faith and his belief and waited for his son. It was late February, hot during the day and cool at night.

Early in the morning, Rathsavong Ngao arrived back at Khorat with all the evacuees from Saraburi, but also with the alarming news that British mercenaries were fighting alongside the Siamese. They readily admitted that it had been a terrible mistake not to have detained and executed Suriyaphakdy. After briefly greeting his son, Chao Anouvong held a conference in his tent to decide whether to stay at Khorat or move to NongBuaLamphu where they would try to hold the Siamese army. The second option was not entirely to Prince Rathsavong Ngao's liking: he argued that retreat would sow disorder amongst the soldiers. He was for marching on Bangkok in the hope of bringing it down, without realising in his folly how implacable the Siamese would prove. Some competent, tough commanders agreed with him, but Chao Anouvong thought it unwise, as the already superior Siamese army could easily be reinforced by foreign fighters. Equally, he said, it would be too difficult to set up and defend fortifications along the Khorat plain. On the other hand, fighting at NongBuaLamphu was a more tactically sound option. The Siamese army would be tired after travelling and fighting their way north. Meanwhile, the Lao army would be rested and prepared; they would also hold a geographical advantage as NongBuaLamphu was their backyard.

'Let's engage them at NongBuaLamphu,' Chao Anouvong said, 'where King Naresuan the Great famously went to observe the outcome of our King Xay-Sethathirath's war with the Burmese in ViengChan in the 1570s. It's our main stronghold where we can also rally our people to fight.'

The committee showed their servility to the king, unanimously roaring their approval as they hastily rose to leave and get themselves ready.

Soon afterwards we were again amongst the buzzing insects that refused to leave us alone: the whining and bite of mosquitoes was enough to drive some people insane, though I hurried about gathering our belongings. Having dipped my water flask in the tank, I stood up and gazed at Chao Anouvong, who was ready to go. But before leaving the royal tent for his elephant howdah, he became silent and my heart thudded in my chest. He was having second thoughts.

'Phia Jon,' he said as he rose and came towards me. 'Neither of us want war,' he continued, 'but why not make Khorat or Bangkok our tomb?' He paused. 'Tell me, do you think retreat is a bad idea? Perhaps we should fight them here or march on Bangkok?'

'I don't know, Your Majesty,' I said in panic. 'Perhaps withdrawal is bad for morale and may well invite contempt, but I'm afraid I haven't thought about it at all.'

'Well, now's your chance. Come on. Think about it… quickly. Why are we retreating?'

'Because of Nangklao the tyrant… and his power, perhaps,' I replied without much thought. I really wanted to contradict him but didn't have a clear answer. However, at that instant, I felt that he should fight the Siamese there in the hope that the Lao people on the Khorat Plateau would rally behind him. I even resisted the temptation to suggest we should march on Bangkok. If we lost and died there, ViengChan might well be spared destruction. If we won, the Rattanakosins would be eliminated, and the Emerald Buddha would return to LanXang for certain.

'Now, understand this Phia Jon. Nangklao is powerful because he's under the influence of overseas traders: colonial powers who provide him with generous financial and military aid in return for using Siam for trade.' He paused. 'I can guarantee the foreigners will fight for him to protect their interests.' I understood his logic and nodded like a donkey to the chaotic sound of men, elephants and horses outside, while the mosquitoes and flies irritatingly whined in my ears. Whenever I tried to kill them, all I managed was to smack myself on the head and face a few times. He carried on his unceasing struggle with the enemy while I made do with the insects. I never got the better of them, but the view over the lake and the forest made up for my discomfort. 'That monstrous man of war,' he groaned, 'has probably emptied his prisons and dispatched his armies and foreign mercenaries to fight us. The courtly letter I sent before leaving ViengChan, and the goodwill and respects I conveyed via Suriyaphakdy won't work. Our potential allies haven't arrived and we're no match for him as we are. Phia Jon, there's no time to lose. Let's move.'

The retreat was a huge issue: he must have thought that withdrawing was cowardly, even though it seemed the only sensible manoeuvre, but it had at least broadened his options. He knew the Siamese army would pursue him and he planned to fight them at NongBuaLamphu. Rathsavong Ngao was ordered to march ten days north-westwards with about 3,000 men to join up with the very committed governor of Lomsak, Phraya Suriyavongsa, who had around 1,000 men. He was a determined advocate of Lao LanNa and LanXang independence and was eagerly awaiting developments.

We moved from our Beung Thale headquarters in Khorat without delay. Each day Chao Anouvong announced his route in advance, but he sometimes decided to explore new routes with only the hard core of his army accompanying him. The bulk of his army – the elephants, horses and other infantry units – were free to march by an easier route to the chosen defensive lines in NongBuaLamphu.

The retreat was a disappointment but not a disgrace, and his officers and men remained loyal to him. They wanted to fight no matter what.

Meanwhile, upon arriving in Bangkok, Suriyaphakdy hastily went to inform Nangklao of Chao Anouvong's presence in Khorat. Nangklao must have gone pale with shock. The news sparked him into announcing that the Lao had rebelled against Bangkok and were about to attack the city. He provoked hysteria by telling his court that the enemy could be at the gates within a day, conveniently allowing him to raise taxes, mobilise the troops and inflame their passions. He rallied his men by pledging with his blood to destroy ViengChan once and for all. Bangkok was abuzz with speculation. In a panic, his court hurriedly ordered the defence of the city. Once the forces under Nangklao's command, including the foreign mercenaries, had been assembled and were standing ready, he appointed his deputy, Bovon Sathanmongkhol, as commander-in-chief to lead the first army to Saraburi where his troops were stationed and waited for more troops from Bangkok to arrive at Phuthabath Hill. The Siamese units prepared for battle and marched off to Khorat a few days later, intending to fight their way along the Mun river towards Ubon before heading north to ViengChan.

It was reported that Phraya Cha Senyakorn and Phraya Kalahom Rajasena led the Siamese vanguard; the second unit was led by Phraya NaretYothi and Phraya SeniBorirak. Krom Mun Senithep led the centre units, Krom Mun Naranusit commanded the left and Krom Mun Swatvisai the right. Krom Mun Issareth and Krom Mun Thibetbovon oversaw the supply troops. Commander in chief Bovon appointed Phraya Surind Therarak and Phraya Raja Suphawady to lead the second army. When all the troops had reached Khorat in late April, Bovon instructed Suphawady to lead 6,000 men towards Champasak in the east to destroy the Lao troops commanded by Rathsabud Yoh and Tissah, while the Siamese main army commanded directly by Bovon headed north for Khon Kaen. The Lao capital of ViengChan was their ultimate goal.

The first battle of Chao Anouvong's war began in earnest when the Siamese army led by Phraya Suphawady first clashed with Phraya Thong's troops at Phimai, just to the east of Khorat. Both sides suffered heavy losses and many injuries, but the battle was inconclusive and the Siamese offensive temporarily ground to a halt. Unfortunately, Phraya Thong's army of about 3,000 men were heavily outnumbered and outgunned, and after several days' fierce fighting he'd little choice but to pull back. He led his one hundred elephants, thirty horses and men to link up with Tissah at Souvannaphum. Tissah's troops, who were supposed to intercept the Siamese advance, failed to commit themselves to the fight as planned.

Suddenly there was news of the most unwelcome sort. The Siamese commander Phraya Suphawady sent a letter to Tissah at Souvannaphum, acknowledging receipt of the vice king's information about Chao Anouvong's plan to attack Bangkok. He urged Tissah to march on ViengChan to show his true allegiance to Siam and to pave the way for the advance of the Siamese army. Similarly, Tissah wanted to place Suphawady under an obligation to himself: he replied that he would march north forthwith, but soon after, he forwarded Suphawady's message to Chao Anouvong at Phou KhaoSan hill in NongBuaLamphu. Tissah then moved his men far away to the north.

Meanwhile Rathsabud Yoh was unaware of Tissah's movements. He fought on in the cities of Sisaketh and Ubon before retreating to Champasak. Unfortunately, Phraya Suphawady's forces defeated Rathsabud Yoh's men when Phraya Hui, the governor of Champasak, betrayed him by shutting the city gates and refusing him entry. Suphawady's men later captured Yoh and his associates and they were sent down to Bangkok. Alas, that was the end of them.

As Tissah had already moved from Souvannaphum to the north and pointlessly stationed his troops in NongHan, east of Udon, the Lao troops at Yasothon, north of Ubon, were left pitifully exposed to Suphawady's attack. After a brief, fierce battle, Yasothon was captured and all of the city governor's family and relatives were rounded up and burnt on the banks of the River Chi. The Siamese troops were then able to move north with ease to attack Nakhorn Phanom.

Meanwhile an easy passage had opened up for the Siamese commander-in-chief Bovon from Souvannaphum towards the northeast. They waded across the River Chi to take Khon Kaen city, a mainly Lao stronghold in the heart of the Khorat Plateau. Despite brave resistance, thousands of its inhabitants were slaughtered or captured. Some were pursued to the death for trying to escape. Those able Lao men who were captured were forced into conscription before being sent out to plunder. On their return they gathered secretly at night and resentfully discussed the rumours of what lay in store for them. By pledging loyalty to Bangkok they'd betrayed their own country and become fools. Most Lao nobles were too embarrassed to obey and kept quiet, but those who dared to put their feelings into words were mercilessly put down and hacked to pieces – the Siamese soldiers were not chivalrous.

One could easily imagine the thousands of Siamese soldiers spreading all over the forsaken lands of the Khorat region, as if the paddy fields grew men instead of rice, marching north towards ViengChan. Bovon's real prey was Chao Anouvong.

Meanwhile, Chao Anouvong had arrived at the pre-selected battlefield at Phou KhaoSan in NongBuaLamphu in late March 1827 with more recruits. He immediately rode out to inspect the field. He scrambled up the hill and scanned the landscape even more thoroughly than two years before, working out how best to deploy his troops, marking out sites for the garrison fort and defences. I studied the scenery with him but could see no solution. The men prepared to sacrifice their lives with him there came from all over the Khorat Plateau: primarily from Saraburi, Khorat, Maha Sarakham, Udon and Khon Kaen. There was hardly time to think, yet he designed a fortress with moats to withstand a siege and assigned Phraya Narinh and Suthisan Poh to supervise the construction. Chao Anouvong then detailed his battle instructions.

Phraya Narinh, a solid man unparalleled in loyalty and courage, was instructed to line up his troops at Ban NongBua village outside NongBuaLamphu city with roughly 3,000 skilled men.

Phraya Xiengsa, a diminutive but brave leader and his troops were to be stationed at Ban Snom village, with Phraya Khongkham's men at Ban NgoiTak village just to the south of KhaoSan hill.

Minister of War Phraya Sanon and Chief of Staff Phraya Supho established the garrison of around 20,000 men and entrenched themselves on Phou KhaoSan hill, immediately overlooking a narrow pass where the road split in two. They prepared for ambushes in the hills and forests along the pass to burn the enemy's provisions and equipment.

The Lao army began a vast programme of construction at Phou KhaoSan – felling trees, building watchtowers and wooden forts, digging trenches and ditches to construct an earthen wall and setting traps. They put their whole souls into it, all day long. There was plenty of good food and water, so nobody sat down hungry or thirsty. The labour went on for days until they'd completed a one-mile-long fortified line that ran across the narrow KhaoSan pass. I was amazed how quickly it was all completed.

As the sun rose above the treetops, the distant NongBuaLamphu Lake, the nearby rivers and streams and the cobwebs sparkled in the light of the clear sky. While the men were hard at work, Chao Anouvong scaled the hill and paced around, working out the deployment of his troops. Below him spread his chosen battleground: the plain of SomPoi, into which the KhaoSan pass opened. He was sure the enemy would take this route. The Lao battalion positioned themselves on the rising hills to control the pass from the heights; they would be able to see the approaching enemy on the distant slopes below them. Chao Anouvong expected the Siamese to arrive with an army many times larger than his own. He gazed in deep concentration, narrowing his eyes at the pass below, going over his battle plan in his mind. His troops could ambush the enemy and deploy rapidly to block the invading force and cut off its supply route.

As usual, he occasionally asked for my views. And, as I'd often made clear to him, I told him I had no brain for warfare. This time, however, I was so flattered he was asking my opinion that I let loose a flood of garrulity: 'Your Majesty, we must consolidate our forces and defend the KhaoSan pass at all costs because of its strategic position. Our nation's survival depends on this battle.' I also reminded him that battles should not be fought on personal feelings alone but should follow proper rules and procedures; on and on I went, explaining my view. In silence, he gently nodded, staring at the pass.

The fortress at the main Phou KhaoSan camp was impressively and skilfully built to withstand the enemy's onslaught. The fortified line was ramparted with excavated earth. The outer slopes of the ramparts bristled with thousands of sharpened wooden and bamboo poles. Wherever I looked inside the camp I saw signs of war: carts full of weapons and armour, soldiers armed with swords, guns and rifles. The war elephants, cavalry horses and buffaloes waiting in harness were kept well fed. They stood placidly, flicking their ears and tails and their heads in clouds of swarming flies.

The troops were busy tending to their weapons, meticulously cleaning their rifles, sharpening their knives, spears and swords and preparing their lances while anxiously waiting for battle to commence. The fires were lit just before dusk and a wonderful scent of cooking rose into the darkening sky. They grilled steak, chickens and fish and steamed sticky rice and vegetables over the evening fires. The smoke rose with the flames flaring across the plain and their faces glowed in the firelight. They talked about their families and friends, life and death, reincarnation and making merit. They chiefly discussed the war and the hateful enemy they were about to fight while the dogs chewed contentedly at bones to reach the marrow, the domestic animals slept, the snakes slithered across the forest floors, the insects sang and the gibbons hooted raucously before bedding down in the trees for the night. Most of the soldiers were very young: some merely like boys, not yet past eighteen, who'd killed animals for food but never other human beings. Now they behaved like grown men and told each other not to be afraid. Their hearts were full of hatred and contempt for the haughty Siamese. The battle loomed and all was set, but there was no complacency.

We patiently waited for news. It was a very tense time.

Meanwhile there were cheers and jubilation when Rathsavong Ngao arrived unexpectedly at NongBuaLamphu. He really caught everyone by surprise. He hastily went to see his father at the camp. The king was working at his desk as usual, with me sitting nearby. When Prince Ngao reached his father's large wooden hut just before sunset, his tall, broad shape darkened the doorway. I rose and bowed to him. His brown and weathered face was stained with dirt. With his eyes half closed from lack of sleep, he blinked with exhaustion, made obeisance with his praying hands and knelt to greet his father.

'I pay my respects to you, Your Majesty,' said the exhausted prince and smiled.

'Well, well, what a pleasant surprise! How are you, my son? Come in, come in my prince,' said Chao Anouvong joyfully, leaving his desk. 'I'm relieved to see you, but where have you come from, Ngao?'

'Loei city, father,' he replied as he rose.

'Loei?' repeated Chao Anouvong anxiously, taking a deep breath. 'I'm delighted by your presence, but what happened to Lomsak?'

Rathsavong Ngao's face dropped. He licked his cracked, dry lips and said, 'I regret to say that we had to withdraw from Lomsak, father.'

Chao Anouvong sighed and shook his head in despair as he moved towards his son. After a brief embrace, they took a step back and inspected each other's faces by the lantern light.

'You look dead tired and much thinner,' said Chao Anouvong.

'More importantly, I hope you're in good health, father?' The king smiled but said nothing. 'Look! I've brought you a bag of exotic fruit from Loei,' continued the prince. 'They're very good and I hope you like them.'

'How thoughtful of you, thank you,' said the king, inspecting the dry, sweet tamarinds. 'They look very good indeed. Now, come and be seated. We'll call for food but have some of this drink first to pick you up, then you must eat.' The prince remained standing. 'Some NongBuaLamphu nobles kindly brought it to us a few days ago,' continued the king, handing over the jug. 'Now, drink it.'

Rathsavong Ngao sniffed at the drink and poured libations into the ground, calling on the ancestry spirit (*Phi Fah*) and the spirits of the surrounding area. After the first swallow he shut his eyes and shook his head. He ate some dry buffalo meat that had been grilled over the cooking fires, vegetables from the forest and steamed sticky rice flavoured with the famous strong chilli paste from Luang Phrabang. He scooped up the red paste with more rice and ate it hungrily. He turned the wine jug in his hands and then gulped down more of the cloudy liquid, smacked his lips and sucked the air through his teeth to cool his mouth. I'd broken into a sweat when I'd first tasted the hot stuff. Finally he thirstily emptied the jug of weak, filtered rice wine, drank some more water, washed his hands and wiped his fingers on his thighs. Chao Anouvong watched him with tender and steadfast eyes.

'That wine is very refreshing, father. Thank you,' said the prince cheerfully. 'I'm not too tired and feel much better already. One should be resilient in war.'

Chao Anouvong's face warmed. He said, 'That's better,' and gripped his son's arm lovingly. They sat down to business, talking about the battle. The king said he'd diverted him to Lomsak to intercept the Siamese army moving north from Sukhotai and to protect the lines of communication: this had given him time to prepare his fortress at the KhaoSan pass. The prince knelt and said they would fight the war together. His father clapped him on the shoulder.

Prince Ngao reported that the Siamese third army from Bangkok had sailed up the Pasak river from their headquarters in Phetsabun and Phitsanuloke led by the Prime Minister, Phraya Aphaiphuthon; armed with British and American weapons, they'd attacked his camp at Lomsak. His troops had been overwhelmed, cut off and forced to fight with little food, but they didn't give up. During the fighting he refused to leave the wounded behind and succeeded in rescuing them. He called on his men not to be downhearted and assured them he wouldn't desert them. He'd even crossed swords with the Siamese commander, Phraya Khraikosa, and had held the enemy at bay for many days before deciding to pull back. Lomsak's loyal governor Phraya Suriyavongsa was the last to leave, his town in flames around him. They retreated north and erected a fortress at Paeng Hak in Loei city, intending to join up with the main troops at Phou KhaoSan camp. The Siamese army were in pursuit.

'Very sorry, father. I had to abandon Lomsak,' said Rathsavong Ngao dejectedly.

'Well, how many do you think attacked your post there?'

'About 8,000. Our scouts thought 10,000 including the mercenaries, if not more.' He paused and then added, 'I did what I could to defend Lomsak, father, but we were heavily outnumbered.'

'How many men have we lost?' said the king.

'I estimate 600… perhaps 1,000. Lomsak has been reduced to ashes.'

There was a groan of dismay from Chao Anouvong. 'I'm proud of you, Ngao,' he said, firmly holding his kneeling son's shoulders. 'We may have lost many battles, but the war can still be won, for we're aligned with the will of heaven. You know how glad I am to have you with me, and I count my blessings in having you as a son to entrust the country to.' Rathsavong Ngao opened his mouth and breathed deeply. 'But you're a good field commander,' continued Chao Anouvong, 'and a true Rathsavong, my brave son; only you are capable of taking on this great responsibility. You know how to gain valour from failure. Go back and fight them. We need to ambush them to hold the frontier. We must attack them from the rear and burn their supplies and provisions.'

The prince raised his head a little but then gazed downwards and asked for reinforcements. 'I need a few thousand more men,' he said. He informed the king he'd commended his men for their courage, but if he lost Loei city they might never trust him again.

Chao Anouvong jumped to his feet, hands behind his back, pacing back and forth in thought. He stopped and turned to the prince. 'Well, let's see,' he said, running through figures, 'a thousand, maybe more.' The prince leaned forward to listen. 'How many troops exactly would you need?' the king asked.

'Also, if we lose this war,' said the prince, looking at his father, 'ViengChan will blaze up like a forest fire. They'll blot her from the earth. They've always said so. No more ViengChan, only annihilation, and we might well perish with her. Our people will be enslaved, and I'll never be king.'

'As a king I can reward you with many things Ngao, but as a father I can't reward you enough. I don't want to disappoint you, my son, but we're in desperate need of reinforcements. Morale is not too good. Our friends in LanNa and Luang Phrabang haven't come to our aid. Perhaps you could tell me why?'

I could feel Chao Anouvong's anguish; he was almost weeping in frustration over the lack of support. Luang Phrabang continued to appease Bangkok and had no intention of coming to his aid. We were intensely disappointed.

'I doubt they'll come,' Rathsavong Ngao said dejectedly. 'I suspect the LanNa princes and Luang Phrabang are probably working out what's best for themselves. I'm certain neither will come, father. They're cowards. We mustn't lose heart for we have no alternative but to fight on. We have to derive valour from failure.'

Prince Ngao was not entirely disappointed. He'd almost 2,000 extra men to add to his 3,000 remaining soldiers. He was told to find the rest himself. The king had done his best. The next day Rathsavong asked the king leave to depart, and with his father's blessing he returned to Loei city.

The Siamese army soon caught up with him and the Loei battle lasted for many days and nights. The Lao soldiers would rather die than be humiliated. They met the assault in strength and often went on the attack, but superior Siamese firepower forced the heroic Rathsavong Ngao and his courageous soldiers to abandon their positions. He marched north and took up a new position at Xiengkharn east of the Mekong, before finally joining up with his father at KhaoSan camp as planned. One sensed how brilliant a commander Prince Ngao was, safely leading his army through the mountain passes to link up with his father.

Meanwhile, by early April, Phraya Suphawady's letter that had been forwarded by Tissah from Souvannaphum had reached Chao Anouvong. After he'd finished reading it, he breathed heavily and blinked his eyes to hide the bad news. He passed the letter over to me.

From Phraya Suphawady to Phraya Tissah:
We have long been friends. When you were in Bangkok you warned us that Chao Anouvong was preparing to embark on a war against Siam. We apologise for not taking it seriously. Now, as a show of your true allegiance to Siam, I have one request to make of you. I urge you to march on ViengChan to pave an easy advance for my army. If you join us, you can keep your rank and honour and more reward awaits you.

'Well, Your Majesty,' I said in annoyance, but his face lit up as if he sought some word of comfort. I continued: 'We were unwise to put our faith in Tissah but let's hope his men have more sense and will refuse to follow his orders. Clearly, he's disobeyed you because of his relationship with Suphawady. He's put Siam before LanXang.'

I could understand why Chao Anouvong looked so upset. He realised that his military campaign was under extreme peril. He feared that Tissah had joined forces with the enemy, but the news came as no surprise because it had long been suspected and dreaded. The real shock was Tissah's impudence in assuming Chao Anouvong to be so stupid. 'Why turn against me?' he muttered. I said that, as a half-brother, Tissah should at least have made an honest enemy. He was apoplectic with rage and simply couldn't believe Tissah had betrayed him. He thought there must be some mistake. He'd shown leniency to Tissah when none was asked for and hadn't even received any thanks. He condemned Tissah's cowardice and treachery as a crime and cursed himself for not having seen it coming. He was truly in despair, but decided the letter was a trick to break the morale and unity of the Lao troops. He stayed put in KhaoSan hill camp and ordered his army to prepare for battle. Paralysed with anger, I had no comfort to offer him and feared the outcome of the war.

To make matters worse – though not known to us at the time – Tissah was by now encamped with his army at NongHan, east of Udon. We were still under the assumption that Tissah was carrying out Chao Anouvong's orders to intercept the advancing enemy at Souvannaphum.

The first fighting came on 1 May 1827 when the Siamese sent more than 8,400 prisoners, mostly made up of Mon slaves and Paguers from Burma in their traditional clothes, along with foreign mercenaries, to attack the first Lao defensive line outside NongBuaLamphu city. The loyal Lao troops under Rathsavong Ngao refused to capitulate. The fortress was engulfed in a sea of fire and the two sides fought on. The battle raged for four days until Prince Rathsavong retreated to join his father at Phou KhaoSan camp further north. The Siamese troops then marched north to SomPoi plain, not far from the KhaoSan pass.

Meanwhile, after taken Khon Kaen, the advancing main Siamese army led by Bovon encountered many Lao advance posts before taking Phou Khiao and then Phou Vieng further north. They then took the Lao army by surprise by entering the NongBuaLamphu region from the rear (the north). Soon after, a further five Siamese army units gathered to attack the Lao army at Ban NongBua. Despite his shock, Phraya Narinh quickly positioned his men and ordered them to defend the fortress to the death. 'Brothers,' he said, 'we fight for our country, our liberty and our lives. Our enemies are greater in number, but our spirit is incomparable; we will prevail.' He paused and honoured his brave men to the ancestors' spirits (*Phi Fah*) in the skies. Then he cried, 'Now, every man do his duty to LanXang!' The Lao troops rallied and offered stiff resistance. They fought ferociously, inflicting heavy casualties on the Siamese, many of whom died when they were caught in the traps. Their dead and injured soldiers littered the battlefield. Phraya Narinh was in the thick of the carnage and, during hand-to-hand fighting, he killed the Siamese commander Phraya Kiet with his sword. Only when fresh Siamese reinforcements arrived, including some European professional soldiers and mercenaries, did the heavily outnumbered Lao army begin to collapse. The fortress's gate was broken, and the Siamese were able to break through the Lao lines without too much resistance on 4 May 1827.

Unfortunately, Phraya Narinh, a proud, intelligent and honourable man from Chonnabot, armed with a courageous heart and a long spear, was captured, but refused to admit defeat while he still drew breath. Even after torture he rejected the terms of surrender and chose to die like a soldier, declaring that he welcomed death. A Lao nationalist, he refused to be a subject of the Siamese king. Losing face was not for him. Bovon, surprised by his decision, angrily ordered Narinh and his nephew to be tusked and then crushed to death by a war elephant while their hands were tied behind their backs.

Meanwhile the losses on the Khorat Plateau mounted. The news of Phraya Narinh's death reached Rathsavong Ngao, who by now had positioned his troops on KhaoSan hill. He was in shock and the morale in the Lao camps plummeted, but he ordered his men to prepare for battle. They were ready to fight to the death. He hastily provided his father with more details about the situation between Lomsak and Loie and the defensive line at NongBuaLamphu, as well as Phraya Narinh's demise. He recommended they should regroup for a better chance of defending the main defensive line at the Phou KhaoSan pass.

At first Chao Anouvong refused to accept: he seemed dazed by the news of Phraya Narinh's death. It was a serious blow. He was conscious of how close he'd come to negotiate reasonably or even to surrender, because the news was unbelievably bad and there seemed no hope of reinforcements. The prospect of battle was daunting: the enemy's numbers were reported to be immense. The Siamese forces were pumped up and lunging towards ViengChan, buffeting aside the Lao defences with almost contemptuous ease. Some of the Lao forces had been surrounded; others were scattered around the Khorat Plateau. They had managed to regroup and briefly counter-attack but had again been repulsed. Every day that went by, more Lao forces surrendered – sometimes after resistance of almost insane bravery, sometimes with a despairing and fatalistic ease.

Chao Anouvong sat by the lantern light deep in thought until the small hours of the morning, pondering his tactics. There was no realistic prospect of help, and without it the war was as good as over. He was alone, staring at the most shameful humiliation of his life. The Vietnamese were keeping quiet, perhaps because of the French. The Malayans and Burmese were firmly under British control; the British themselves looked the other way as long as Bangkok didn't meddle in their affairs. The Khmer had been subdued by Siam.

The call of cocks intensified at dawn, the cows mooed, the pigs screamed, and the birds perched on the trees sang loudly, but Chao Anouvong slept on, as if there was no price on his head. The morning sun grew hotter by the minute. I sat outside waiting in the shade, wondering whether he was ill but listening in case he should summon me, but I heard nothing. I was desperately worried, but somehow kept myself calm. Soon after, Phraya Sanon, the king's two sons Ngao and Poh and other chief commanders came hurriedly and wanted to rouse him from his bed, but I stopped them, explaining he'd hardly slept. We sat in silence drinking warm mint tea while Phraya Sanon stood, slurping noisily his drink, coughing, talking noisily and impatiently pacing about.

When Chao Anouvong emerged from his wooden hut, he seemed relaxed and calm. In fact he seemed entirely himself and was rather pleased to find us gathered outside. He promptly summoned us inside for a meeting to decide what should be done next. The critical problem was support. I took up a discreet position standing at the side. The king said that the Lao army had suffered a setback but wasn't yet defeated: there were still allies loyal to LanXang all over the world, especially King Minh Mang in Vietnam. He reminded us that LanXang was under threat and that it was our right and our duty to compel every citizen to support our cause. However, since LanNa had reluctantly sided with the enemy and help from Luang Phrabang and XiengKhuang hadn't arrived, he now agreed with his son Ngao. A motion for the regrouping and redeployment of the Lao troops at the main defensive line between SomPoi and the KhaoSan pass was approved.

After a short silence the congenitally unflappable Phraya Sanon said he'd no strong belief in omens or portentous nightmares but wished to share his dream with the rest of us. He'd witnessed a terrible battle on the SomPoi plain, with blood soaking into the dust and dying men groaning. He then saw ViengChan besieged and all of us fleeing into the forest, looking back and seeing the city in flames. In Lao LanXang it is believed dreams sometimes have the power to influence events, or that they are portents and should be taken seriously. Chao Anouvong would normally laugh at any sort of gloomy prophecy, but not this time. The others looked pensive, as if they hated the war or were unable to grasp the scale of their predicament. They all realised the Lao army faced insuperable odds and were probably convinced the war was lost, but there was no atmosphere of panic or despair. However, I believed Chao Anouvong knew in his heart that LanXang was lurching towards catastrophe but still placed all his hopes on the imminent and decisive battle, where the fate of the Lao nation would be decided. Perhaps he'd also foreseen his own fate, but he didn't reveal it for fear of destroying his men's morale. He willed them to fight while at the same time plotting for peace.

'Do you know how vital the KhaoSan pass is?' he asked, looking at his generals. No one spoke. 'This is our last stronghold: we can retreat no further. If we lose, the Siamese will charge straight to ViengChan; this will be the end of LanXang. We must fight them here and this is your chance to make history. If we win we'll preserve our homeland and the Lao nation. I will shave my head and live out a joyous life as a monk. Every one of you will be raised to the nobility and enjoy untold riches. But this is empty talk: we must prepare our troops well. We simply must win. It will be the greatest ever victory for us; otherwise the Siamese will achieve ultimate power, and I don't need to tell you what will then happen to LanNa and LanXang. Either way, we live in the most desperate times. We have nothing to lose so let's be brave and fight for our Lao nation.'

They gave him a round of applause and the meeting ended. The bonds of mutual confidence had been restored. After they'd gone, Chao Anouvong stood outside looking beyond the clouds to the heavens, conferring with Lord Buddha and the other gods before making offerings to the ancestors' spirits. I ventured to tell him with certainty that even if we could negotiate an early peace, Bangkok would now be able to dictate terms: the most cold-hearted terms ever.

'And if we lose,' he said, 'I'm certain the warmongers in Bangkok will destroy us!'

A few days later there was a breakthrough. Nine Lao conscripts from Khorat serving in the Siamese army at SomPoi managed to escape and came over to our side. They stank with sweat and looked scared. 'Water!' was the first word from their cracked, dry mouths. Our soldiers quickly brought them a large jug, spilling and dripping. Cheerfully welcomed at the camp by the war council outside Chao Anouvong's hut, they claimed they'd been deceived and conscripted into the Siamese army by force and had no choice but to feign loyalty to Bangkok. They then pledged themselves to Chao Anouvong so they could appease their ancestors in heaven. They reported that the Siamese troops were in a weak position because they didn't control the high ground, the rivers or the streams. The rain hadn't come. Their waterholes had silted up so water and food were rationed; their elephants and horses had fallen sick from dehydration and lack of fodder and their battle-weary men showed drastic signs of weakness. When Phraya Sanon warned them they would die the most terrible death if they were lying, they swore they were telling the truth, adding that they hated the Siamese for the destruction of their homes and the rape of their women. There was no reason for Chao Anouvong to doubt them, so an attack was approved for dawn the following day.

Phraya Sanon, one of the most reliable, decisive and intelligent of senior Lao commanders, and his counterpart, Phraya Supho, urgently sent messages to Phraya Xiengsa at Nong Snom village and Phraya Khongkham at Nong NgoiTak to join in with the attack on the Siamese troops on the SomPoi plain. The Lao troops began to gather, with no trumpets but much muttering. They moved stealthily, stumbling and clanking into position throughout the night.

I fretted sleeplessly about the battle and Chao Anouvong's safety but rose at dawn to prepare to accompany him to the waiting army.

Before dawn had painted the eastern sky with crimson, the king rose from his bed. He put on his uniform and shoes, picked up his long, sharp sword and strode from his quarters to his faithful old stallion which was waiting patiently for him. He mounted the tall, brown horse, surrounded by his officers and bodyguards. I didn't think anyone had slept much as they all stood there yawning. The sun had yet to show over the hills which still lay in shadow, and a cloudless, blood-red sky loomed over the far away mountains in the east. It was the 10th of May. With Rathsavong Ngao and Suthisan Poh at his side

Chao Anouvong, now sixty years old, seemed to have lost none of his strength and courage. He was still resolute, imaginative and supremely undaunted, but at that moment he hovered somewhere between life and death. His mind was as sharp as an arrow, and he seemed completely free from fear. He'd been amazingly brave during the wars in LanNa and had seen bloodshed at first hand. Perhaps in truth he was frightened out of his skin, but like a superhuman had managed to call upon a strength he never knew he'd. Regarded as a runt in Bangkok, he'd overcome many adversities and appalling treatment at the Rattanakosin court. Now, no grief could touch him. He was far cooler than I would have expected as he strutted in front of his soldiers with his head in the air. He was so extraordinary, both in his character and in his words, that I can think of no one who even comes close. He confidently cast sideways glances at his men before calmly observing the movements of the Siamese army lower down on the plain. There was no doubt our army was considerably smaller than the Siamese, but he worked up his courage and made it very clear he was prepared to fight if attacked. It promised to be a heavy battle.

At first light, Chao Anouvong rode up and down the lines and exhorted his men, who were mustering to fight. They urged him on, shouting to him to lead them against the Siamese army. He expertly steadied his horse to face the enemy, whose cavalry were cantering up and down in front of their war elephants. Then he looked across to me, his face fierce. I realised at once he was about to speak. He turned towards the plain below and, without blinking, read out a prayer: 'May the Lord Buddha and the gods bring this war to a successful end for the Lao people.' With that, he urged his men to fight bravely. He struck himself on the chest to steady his heart and raised his right arm to signal his courageous men to launch their attack at the enemy's positions. Rathsavong Ngao ordered and exhorted the Lao troops before marching them down into the plain against a foe three times larger.

My heart wanted to say that the Lao force would win but my head told me they could not. I turned to look at Chao Anouvong. 'May the gods bring Your Majesty a swift victory,' I whispered. He shut his eyes in prayer and nodded gently. As his two sons started to move, he lifted his hand and called farewell to them. The massive battle began in the early morning.

Rathsavong Ngao, who was said to have the courage of 1,000 men, led the troops in person, accompanied by his bodyguards and high-ranking officers. He galloped at the head of the cavalry charge. Flanked by ninety highly trained war elephants that were deeply attached to their mahouts, the cavalry spurred their horses forward and drove long-horned water buffaloes ahead of them, stampeding at the enemy. The thud of horses' and buffaloes' hooves and elephants' feet shook the earth and the trees, and a cloud of dust filled the plain like early morning fog. The charge set their adrenalin racing and they longed to kill as many enemies as they could. The roaring noise of the soldiers, the screaming of the horses and the trumpeting of the elephants vibrated through the hot, muggy air. The buffaloes lowered their heads and bellowed in a most unusual manner as they knocked and gored anyone in their path in their frenzy, causing carnage amongst the Siamese, who were caught by surprise.

The battle elephants that had been used since Khoun Borom's day were adorned with bells and scarlet coverlets. They fought with their tusks, trunks and feet, scaring off the foreign mercenaries, some of whom had probably never encountered them before. On seeing the mahouts shot or speared and falling to the ground, the elephants, trumpeting and spreading their ears, rushed to retrieve them, tramping on anyone in their path. The noise was deafening as officers roared orders and men screamed and yelled to one another or to the enemy with all the breath in their lungs, sweating, cursing, thrusting, panting and roaring. The air was darkened with clouds of flying arrows that sent men and horses screaming and crashing to the ground. The sound of explosions, gunfire and the crashing of swords echoed through the plain. The two sides slaughtered each other as they charged back and forth, their shields clashing as they shoved and pressed, stabbing with spears, hacking with swords. Their uniforms became ragged, bloodied and spattered like butchers' aprons. Phraya Konkaeo and Phraya Kongkham from Saraburi brought 8,000 brave men to join the Lao forces during this furious hand-to-hand combat, all tangled up as the victims fell to the blood-soaked ground.

Before long Rathsavong Ngao and his troops careered around into the enemy's rear. The shock of his charge so unsettled the Siamese that they scattered into the centre, looking for safety amongst their elephants, who were being goaded by the mahouts into retreat. But some of their elephants indignantly stampeded, tusking and trampling without any respect for the mahouts, friends or foe, seizing them in their trunks and smashing them against the ground. There were bodies everywhere, punctured with bullet wounds or pierced by arrows or spears.

It was a traumatic and terrible moment as I watched in horror from the high ground, trying to understand the meaning of the war while blood washed over the battlefield. I could hear the shrill cries of the wounded battle elephants and horses and the howling pain of dying men. I wished I could fill my countrymen's place. If I were Chao Anouvong, I would have accepted any truce and ended the war without further risk. But I was not. I prayed for his endeavours to end well but I knew that our brave men were heavily outgunned and outnumbered. By late morning the Lao troops had withdrawn to their camp, bringing their dead and injured comrades with them, some with horrible gaping wounds.

The scent of gunpowder from the battlefield, scarred with craters and scorch marks, mixed with the hot, humid afternoon air. The dust of combat had settled to hide the dried blood; crushed shrubs were scattered here and there. The fallen white and red *Dork Champa* flowers spread like feathers within our camp. The Lao army assembled and began to identify their dead. It was difficult to recognise each individual dead man, but the bloodstains and dust were washed away with clean water. As they read out names and wept warm tears, they silently piled the bodies of their comrades, still in their uniforms, on ceremonial pyres. After brief, solemn prayers they were quickly burned. The flames soon roared and fluttered in the wind, strongly stinking of burning death. All things must come to dust, but it was a scene and smell I couldn't easily forget.

The two sides were separated at nightfall. From our position on the hill the battlefield was dotted with smouldering fires where the Siamese troops were burning their dead or cooking their food. They were provoking us to battle with war drums and shouts of abuse. When the wind blew in our direction, we could hear them shouting at us. 'Ai-Lao you little rascal, eat shit!' they yelled. The sound clanged irritatingly in our heads, but our men didn't let them get away with such impudence. With full lungs they shouted back, 'Siamese, you son of a bitch, lick arse!' Under the cover of darkness our raiding parties crept across the lines and killed many enemies in the opposite trenches. The constant tension throughout the night preyed on my nerves. I hardly slept at all; neither did Chao Anouvong, I suspected.

I rose from my bed before dawn touched the east with red. At sunrise I followed Chao Anouvong and his sons as they went about inspecting the troops. One of the soldiers came running and informed us that Phraya Sanon had been slightly injured. Chao Anouvong was relieved it wasn't more serious.

We made our way slowly towards Phraya Sanon's tent. The morning mists and pure forest air eddied around the fortress at KhaoSan, mingling with the scents of war: woodsmoke, gunpowder, elephants, horses, buffaloes, cattle, chickens, rotten flesh, oozing wounds and thousands of unwashed men. I felt like a very tired, stiff old man. I was dirty too. I couldn't help but blow out my cheeks in disgust at my own smell. The king usually liked to have a wash before breakfast as well as before his evening meal. In the same way, he liked to wash himself both before and after battle. Like myself he really liked to be clean, but under the circumstances he'd only managed to rub or sponge himself down with damp cotton cloths.

I thought Chao Anouvong was going to scold Phraya Sanon for his recklessness. When he entered the tent everyone stood up and gave him a standing ovation, which he acknowledged by lifting his sword above his head. He went straight to sit on a wooden stool beside Phraya Sanon, who made light of a sword wound across his forearm. He seized Phraya Sanon's arm and inspected the bandage. Phraya Sanon explained that he'd been struck on the chest by a missile and knocked backwards but had got up and carried on fighting before being slashed and falling again during hand-to-hand fighting. One of his men had saved him, attacking the enemy before they could finish him off. The bleeding had been stopped with a strip of white cloth and the wound wasn't festering. The wound to his chest was painful, especially when he breathed deeply, but he was glad to still be on his feet. Chao Anouvong tenderly congratulated the brave soldier for saving his friend's life, but he was lucky to be alive and the king told him that, as one of the chief commanders, he shouldn't have exposed himself to danger. With a deep sigh of relief and a look of concern, he gave Phraya Sanon a caring smile and said, 'I know you're famously hard to kill but I dread being left without you.' There was a loud murmur of assent around the tent.

Apparently, Phraya Sanon didn't want to be a burden: an hour earlier he'd been visiting wounded soldiers and inspecting the enemy's positions. He reported that the Siamese had lost up to 2,000 men, with around 400 being taken prisoner, mostly sorry-looking young Lao recruits. He proposed that they should all be executed, otherwise their treasonous thoughts might well infect the Lao soldiers who were guarding them. Besides, he argued, they – the Lao conscripts – were traitors who'd fought against their own countrymen; an example must be made of them.

Chao Anouvong rightly objected, stressing we should be magnanimous because we were fighting for civilised values. He reminded those inside the tent that some of the prisoners were destitute young Lao just like them, who'd probably been indoctrinated. He was warmly cheered.

The fighting raged for several days. The Lao foot soldiers, once within range, expertly fired homemade rockets at the enemy positions. But other than burning down a few tents their projectiles had little effect: they were really designed for praying to heaven for rain during the rocket festivals. Rathsavong Ngao's battle lines poured into the enemy camp, surrounding the Siamese infantry who tried to make a stand. The Lao archers pinned down the Siamese forces at short range and surrounded them, cutting off their only source of water and inflicting heavy casualties every time they tried to break through the encirclement. Some of their injured soldiers were stranded and cut off, roasting in the heat. Those just about still alive crawled pathetically towards a stream. Many of their most battle-hardened men gave up the struggle and surrendered. Both sides fought on, but when a Lao officer called out that their lives would be spared if they surrendered, some of the Siamese troops, mostly Lao conscripts, laid down their arms and were marched off between the scattered bodies of the dying and the dead. They were made to sit amongst the other captives.

A few hundred to a thousand Lao soldiers were killed or injured. Phraya Kongkham was killed fighting alongside his Saraburi men. The Lao troops held on, but I despaired at the sight of so many dead soldiers. Some of our men were gasping with thirst due to loss of blood, their bodies covered in dust and sticky with darkened, dry blood. Their dying tongues lolled in their gaping mouths and their faces were set in grimaces of terrible agony. These memories would live long in the eye and the nostrils. The injured and the dead lay in their own blood on the ground. The dying, dripping with blood, moaned like wind in the thick forest and the groaning of the wounded rang mournfully in my ears. Blood was spattered over their sides and trickled from their mouths, their breath rattling in their chests. Limbs were blackened with clotted blood; others had slashes across their arms and cheeks, exposing the pale bones. I could do nothing to help. It broke my heart but I no longer had the power even to weep.

'It's war,' murmured Rathsavong Ngao. He seemed entirely indifferent to such sights, but then he was a military man. He and his brother helped to carry some of the corpses and lined them face up ready for burning on communal pyres. They washed the blood from their hands and shook them dry, then stood motionless with their heads down amongst the others. After a short prayer, incense was thrown upon the pyres and torches were put to the base, sending flames shooting up to dance in the breeze. The soldiers' strength was failing but their faces looked angry and vengeful in the firelight. Some of the younger ones were overcome with grief and wept like children.

Many of our war elephants and horses had been killed and injured. Buffalo killed by enemy weaponry became a feast for hungry soldiers on both sides. I could hear the squeals of the dying animals; some were lying on their sides twitching, others stiffened in death. A flock of grey vultures circled in the rising air over the SomPoi plain and then quickly descended one by one, swooping down on their targets. They danced around the corpses, bouncing up and down with partly opened wings, squawking, ripping at the dead remains and fighting one another with bloodied heads over the carcasses.

All my life I've never liked hunting expeditions, slaughtering animals or anything else that might remind me of mortality. I'm a coward, merely a man who's always sought freedom from physical and mental pain, doing my best to help others, especially the elderly. Seeking contentment I've always tried to avoid trouble and anxiety, although I realise this isn't always possible. Since the beginning of the campaign I'd stoically maintained a stiff upper lip and born hardships without complaint, but at that moment I was gripped by the pure misery of life, as was Prince Gohtama when he witnessed suffering and death. I had no inclination for a fight, but I could no longer bear the prissy self-righteousness of the Siamese. When Chao Anouvong noticed my expression, he told me to be optimistic and to fortify my spirit, for the war might soon be over. I made no reply but fixed my gaze on the battlefield, full of corpses and vultures. Despite being frightened of pain and terrified of death, I steeled my heart to be strong, for I detested Bangkok imperialism.

Whenever the Lao army began to lose the fight, and I saw my fellow countrymen falling under the gunfire and swords of the enemy, speared in their guts and chests or hit by bullets and falling like stones, I died many deaths and became convinced we were doomed. I closed my eyes and called upon the ancestors' spirits, praying to the Lord Buddha and all the gods for deliverance. I'd never killed anyone, but courageous men leave a lasting reputation when they die and I had a sudden impulse to be part of the battle. Most of all I wanted to save the Lao nation. I'd been fearless as a boy, so this represented an opportunity for me, as an adult, to be a man of action rather than a worthless observer. I was greatly tempted to ask the king if I could wear his spare uniform so the Siamese would think he'd entered the battle himself and try to single him out. On the other hand, many in the Siamese army were Lao by birth and might have pro-Lao sentiments. They might well follow him if they saw him on the battlefield.

I really wanted to say to him, 'Your Majesty, I'm not a trained soldier but I feel Lord Buddha will aid me in my fight against the enemy. I'm not afraid, and please don't put me to shame. Lend me your uniform and your sword. I promise I will endeavour to fight valiantly, and may heaven help our cause.' Oh, to mount my horse, armed with my gun and sword and protected by a shield, to go into battle and to die, never to return home to my dear mother and friends, never to grow old gracefully but to win everlasting fame! I knew only too well he would never allow this. As he stared beyond the clouds, probably recalling old hardships and old wounds, he turned his gaze to me.

'Phia Jon, we're renowned for our courage,' he said. 'Dignified and valiant men shed blood, not tears, for victory and defeat are equally universal in warfare.' I nodded thoughtfully. 'When you find yourself in the thick of battle, I'm sure I can rely on you not to shame your country.'

'Your Majesty,' I said, pulling my gaze away from the battlefield. 'We mustn't give up. I'll steel my heart to be courageous; in my present mood I won't put LanXang to shame.'

He shot a satisfied smile at me and said, 'Phia Jon, it's necessary to honour the gods and I praise your courage and sacrifice. Before us is the enemy; behind us the Mother Mekong. We have done all we can for now. The rest is up to heaven, who always seems to assist our enemies.' It was his moment of clarity. I sensed he knew the defensive line was lost: the enemy was just too strong. He heaved himself to his feet and gazed down at me. 'Come, let's not linger. Let's go back to our dear capital city to organise our defence and await our fate. We mustn't end up in a desperate situation.'

In silence I nodded assent, but thought his authority was vital at that critical moment: the situation would certainly become more volatile if he left. I quickly rose to my feet, stared at the distant battleground and very nearly suggested that if we were to be defeated, the land of his mother – NongBuaLamphu – should be our final resting place, not ViengChan. I decided not to say anything because I loved him and wished to protect him.

Chao Anouvong and Suthisan Poh decided to leave – they didn't flee – and hurried back to ViengChan to organise the capital's defence. We left our encampment at Phou KhaoSan in NongBuaLamphu to the sound of distant shooting, leaving Rathsavong Ngao and Phraya Sanon to face the Siamese army. Phraya Konkaeo and his loyal and brave Saraburi men were given the task of halting the Siamese advance at ViengKhuk city on the right bank of the Mekong. Although downhearted, we weren't without hope as we hastily crossed the river to find ViengChan strangely quiet.

I learned later that the 'Battle of SomPoi–KhaoSan Pass' – as it became known – was at first a success. On 23 May it was reported that the Lao troops had launched highly effective counterattacks and had been fighting with even more determination. They were greatly outnumbered but the Siamese troops proved no match for the disciplined, battle-hardened Lao troops. At one stage the Lao forces were deeply enmeshed in the battle. They had retrieved a hopeless position and were on the offensive, ready for a final assault to eliminate their enemy.

Whatever the truth, it was understood that the Siamese line was irretrievably broken, and they fell back. The Siamese army would have been totally defeated had it not been for their reinforcements, which sprang out of the ground like ghosts to attack the Lao forces from the rear. The first, led by Phraya NaretYothi, was repulsed and almost surrounded by Lao troops, although they didn't have enough men to surround them completely. When the second wave of reinforcements arrived by late afternoon, led by Phraya SeniBorirak – who'd gathered more men on the way – the Lao army of Rathsavong Ngao had to turn round and fight the battle on two fronts. Unable to risk a pitched battle against superior numbers, they reassembled in the face of the Siamese counterattack. The battle wasn't a fair one as the Lao forces were heavily outnumbered and hopelessly under-armed. Any Siamese troops still surrounded were able to break out. The tide had turned against the Lao troops but, with slavery the only other option, they were prepared to fight to the last man; they were infused with a new spirit and put up a desperate last fight as if their doom was at hand.

The Lao troops were at a critical juncture, but no one deserted or retreated without orders. Inevitably, they were forced to withdraw from the pass. Rathsavong Ngao rode about frantically, trying to direct his men's retreat. Some were overpowered and compelled to lay down their arms in ignominy. It was carnage. The battlefield was littered with wounded men and dead soldiers in the aftermath of the battle, the Lao commander Phraya Supho among them. They all died a heroic death. The Lao armed forces suffered massive losses and most of the soldiers barely escaped with their lives. They would have been annihilated, but when night fell the Siamese gave up the chase and tended to their dead and injured instead. Hundreds of Lao soldiers were taken prisoner and subjected to the enemy's mercy, of which there was none. They were massacred.

Every event during the battle was carefully recorded: the various points of attack, the position of the different troops, the execution of the Lao commander Phraya Narinh and the subsequent surrender of the pass. It was a massive defeat, a catastrophe for LanXang. All the cities in the Khorat Plateau, and those within the right bank of the Mekong, were severely affected.

The defeated Lao army took the opportunity to make their escape under the cover of darkness. Those able to walk underwent a forced march through the forest to safety and then on to ViengChan, leaving their pleading and dying comrades behind, crying out their names, hoping their friends would hear. The rest of the survivors just trudged on and continued to dodge their fate. There was no other choice. They marched to safety in utter dejection, their hearts heavy, for any joy they felt at their own escape was tempered by grief for the comrades-in-arms they'd lost. Rathsavong Ngao, Phraya Sanon, Phraya Xiengsa and the surviving soldiers escaped with their thirst for revenge intact. They scattered, before adopting similar guerrilla tactics to King Xay-Setthathirath. Many came to grief in the hazardous forests or died in their comrades' arms.

Panic-stricken soldiers are useless, no matter their number, but Phraya Xiengsa managed to regroup his men at Ban PhonXiengWang village on the banks of the HuaiLuang river near PhonPhisay city. They fought valiantly for weeks and defeated the troops of the Siamese commander Phraya Kaikosa. Kaikosa was ignominiously dismissed from his post and imprisoned by Commander-in-Chief Bovon for his failure. Kaikosa's loyal soldiers reviled Bovon for the way he'd treated their commander. The Lao army then engaged with another newly appointed Siamese commander, Phraya PhetPhisay.

A few isolated pockets of Lao troops remained encamped on the west bank of the Mekong and in forests throughout the Khorat Plateau. Furthermore, Phraya Khongkham's troops at Mueang Phen near Udon city were unaware of the fall of the KhaoSan pass. They refused to surrender, eventually regrouping with Xiengsa and fighting on at the HuaiLuang river, where Khongkham was killed. The Lao troops retreated to the mouth of the HuaiLuang at PhonPhisay city, aiming to follow the Mekong towards ViengChan.

Morale amongst the advancing Siamese troops was high. They wasted no time in taking advantage of the Lao retreat from KhaoSan. They quickly marched over the hills and through the narrow pass into the northern plains, heading directly towards Nongkhai, PhanPhao and then ViengKhuk, where Phraya Konkaeo's troops lay in waiting.

Well, the first news of this terrible defeat began to emerge from villages near the city of Udon. Hundreds of villagers had escaped, crossed the Mekong and taken shelter outside ViengChan. They claimed to have passed the survivors of Rathsavong Ngao's army, a group of desperate and starving soldiers encamped in the forest who'd escaped the pursuing Siamese army.

As for Chao Anouvong and myself, the nervous strain while waiting for news from NongBuaLamphu was indescribable. Neither of us slept well. What dire straits he must have been in. He'd sacrificed his life for the sake of his principles, for justice and the restoration of the Lao nation, but he was no match for the ambition and fraudulence of the Rattanakosins. When news of the fall of the Lao defensive line at the KhaoSan pass reached us officially, he was heartbroken and never quite the same again. The defeat must have pained him to the depths of his soul. I was in shock, scared and quite concerned about him. Convinced he'd committed a great error, he spent much of the crisis alone, brooding on the Siamese invasion and its implication for the kingdom and himself. It wasn't the retreat that worried him so much, but the shattering blow to the Lao people's psyche. It was hard not to feel sorry for him, quietly spending many hours in his study, either pacing about or sitting next to the window with his eyes fixed on the Mekong.

Whenever I looked in from time to time, he never sent me away. Some days he didn't seem to move from his couch, resting his locked hands on his stomach and staring at the ceiling with fixed eyes like a dead man. Sometimes he just sat and stared straight ahead through the window and across the Mekong as if presiding in judgement on himself, sitting shame-faced in his own presence. I shared food with him, but he ate little and hardly said a word. Each morning when I asked if he was all right, he merely smiled as if he'd an answer to the crisis. I put a plate of fruit, a small basket of freshly cooked sticky rice and a glass of coconut juice beside him. When he gulped it down I refilled it while he ate a handful of steamy rice. I told him I'd removed the most important papers and that the palace was now almost empty. It felt as if no one had lived in it for a long time. At night he often sat on the balcony outside his study, gazing at the brightly shining moon high up, but the stars were dimmed and forever beyond man's reach. He must have been wondering why his good fortune had deserted him. Some mornings it was difficult to rouse him from his bed. Without knowing exactly what had happened at SomPoi–KhaoSan, it was impossible to imagine the thoughts going through his mind. He must have thought all his friends had left him and he was a finished man, running out of soldiers to fight for his cause. He may even have been prepared to betray the world rather than let it betray him. Having lived by the principle that to lose face is a mortal sin, he may have wished to die when he saw his cause was hopeless. But he often said that when good men fail to act, then evil triumphs. Therefore he gathered his strength and organised his forces to continue the fight elsewhere.

Chao Anouvong realised there was now no chance of winning the war; all he could do was boost the morale of the people. He staked everything on the swift arrival of the Vietnamese army, now his only hope, but was left wondering whether they'd even heard his cry for help, and if so, why there was no response from Minh Mang. I too thought his hopes had been shattered, but perhaps not lost forever. He looked stunned by the scale of his defeat; he'd been trounced, his career ended, his enemies rewarded and his despotic nemesis in Bangkok elevated to new heights of power.

Knowing the Siamese reputation for forced marches and their eagerness to capture Chao Anouvong, I advised an immediate evacuation of ViengChan and the waging of a guerrilla war, just like King Xay-Setthathirath against the Burmese in 1571.

'Your Majesty, only the Mekong lies between us and the barbaric Siamese,' I said with great urgency. 'The enemy is coming. Life and death hang by a thread. All we have left is prayer; we must get you out of ViengChan.'

At first he shook his head emphatically and murmured, 'No!' He steadied his nerves and reminded me that good news often follows bad in times of war. Failure, he said, teaches us how to achieve ultimate victory. Battles can be won or lost, but there should be no fear of failure. Although we'd tasted bitter defeat at NongBuaLamphu, Lao foundations and traditions would remain unshaken. We still had the trust and loyalty of the Lao people. He remained optimistic, even though he was staring ruin in the face. No matter what, the war would continue endlessly in many forms long after he'd gone. He put his hand on my shoulder and asked if the villagers from Udon knew what had happened to Rathsavong Ngao and Phraya Sanon. I muttered that the surviving soldiers had told them that hundreds, perhaps thousands, had been slaughtered, but they hadn't actually seen Rathsavong Ngao or Phraya Sanon die. I added that if Prince Ngao were still alive the Siamese would be pursuing him for certain.

'I'm blessed to still have you by my side,' he said.

'Capturing you is their main goal,' I said firmly.

'Well, Phia Jon, I'm not afraid. I have faith in my people's courage. I will not leave the city and I dare the Siamese to do their worst. My death will be a price worth paying. Let them come,' he said defiantly and turned to look at the Mekong.

Our relationship was a unique amalgam of love, loyalty, trust and emotion, but my overriding priority was to look after him and save him; it was an unspoken commitment that his welfare and safety should come first. Losing him would be an act of personal betrayal and a cause for national lamentation.

'Your Majesty, you are a person of great importance. Condemnation for all this killing and destruction will fall on Bangkok, but you mustn't contemplate dying so easily. If any misfortune befalls you, I won't be able to live for the shame of it. I can't bear the thought of you being killed or captured, never mind seeing you leave, but I must beg you. For your own sake, if not mine, and for the sake of LanXang,' I pleaded.

'Nobody's indispensable,' he said and seemed momentarily dazed. 'Very well, Phia Jon. You're right. We must know when to hold on and when to let go. There is still hope if we manage to stay alive.' After a short pause he gripped my arm tightly and whispered, 'I know we have to escape, and we must make a dignified and valiant effort to save ourselves to fight another day.'

He promptly sent for his staff. When they arrived, they knelt before him with their heads bowed.

'You have all done your duty well, but we are at war and you can do no more for me,' said the king. 'Take this as my last command. I release all of you from your duty.'

They gave the sort of great wail you would normally only hear at the news of the death of a loved one. He told them to be brave and commanded them to save themselves while they still could. Overwhelmed with fear and grief, they left and wept for him.

It was my duty to be with Chao Anouvong and to share his sufferings, but I was in a quandary; in two minds. In the end I made a monumental self-sacrifice by deciding not to follow him. Knowing the mortal danger I was in, I couldn't face leaving ViengChan, although I knew he expected me to accompany him.

'And will you go to Vietnam?' I asked him.

'Yes, of course, to seek help from our friend Emperor Minh Mang,' he said and paused for thought. 'If LanXang is to be defended against Nangklao and his foreign army, then we have no choice but to rely on Vietnam. And if we draw strength from the spirit of our ancestors and the justice of our cause, we will triumph in the end.'

'That is indeed our only chance to save our nation. But will you be safe?'

'Well, I'll soon be sixty-one. I no longer fear death, though I still fear for LanXang's future.'

'The journey to Vietnam is treacherous. I'm worried some misfortune might befall you. Do you expect me to go with you?' Even asking the question made me feel sick, but I was determined not to change my mind.

'No, not at all. I know you would rather remain in ViengChan,' he said. In good spirits he told me to save what I could from the library. 'With armed men by my side your heart can rest easy,' he added and looked at me. 'Phia Jon, I know how intelligent you are and that you always put other people first. I understand your loyalty, but you must now think only of yourself. In comparison to the glory of the Lao nation, our personal ties – although unique – mean nothing.'

'Oh, Your Majesty, please forgive me. That's not why I'm staying,' I confessed. 'Someone has to stay behind to witness the fate of ViengChan.'

'I don't know when, but we will meet again,' he assured me. 'And your account of what happens to our city will be irreplaceable. But please take care.' He let go of my arm, nodding in acceptance of my decision, but with some apprehension at leaving me behind. As I turned to walk away, he called, 'Phia Jon, please keep that special place in your heart for me.'

I accepted our fate, hoping to see him again. But how his words rang in my ears!

'Your Majesty, my love (*Huck*) and respect for you is more precious than anything else. Your departure will separate us like earth is separated from heaven, but there'll always be a special place for you in my heart.' I knelt in reverence and signalled my pledge to him. He was dear to me, and I understood him. He looked into my face and smilingly thanked me with his eyes as I rose to leave.

There was no time to be wasted. I've always found goodbyes very difficult so I slipped away without a fuss, as he would probably have wanted. In fact our parting was a wrench to both of us. I left the palace soon afterwards without saying farewell and passed the outer walls, joining the stream of evacuees leaving the city.

ViengChan was in a state of panic. The people suffered from an atavistic and visceral fear of the invasion and hated the Siamese. They sensed the imminent collapse of the Lao nation as if it were a dark cloud hanging over them. So, as a symbol of destiny, some of the inhabitants sat down to a good-luck meal (*Larb*) of meat, chicken or fish, and clinked glasses. Many people, fearful of what the future might hold, recklessly abandoned their possessions, took deep breaths and fled. Groups formed and dispersed; men ran from one house to another; women rushed to gather their provisions and possessions while their children cried, and old people mournfully wept for fear of being left behind. It was the most pitiful scene – families with all the belongings they could take, including their cats, dogs and chickens. Before nightfall many vulnerable people made their way on ox or horse carts, but mostly on foot. The streets and paths were so congested with carts and people that it was quite a struggle to get out of the city. They fled through a cloud of dust to hide in the forest, where they lived off nature's bounties, praying for the fury to pass. Those who stayed behind were quiet and depressed, in fear of the future. Chao Anouvong's followers were finally deserting him. The vast majority had already fled to the cities of XiengMai, Lampang, Lamphun, Phrae, Nan and Luang Phrabang, a great exodus of people. I wonder what became of these people.

Towards the end of May 1827, King Anouvong sailed down the Mekong to Nakhorn Phanom where he disembarked on the left bank and then headed on to Mahaxay and Khamkheut city. Over forty high-ranking officials accompanied him, along with many of his numerous sons and daughters, including Prince Poh, Nuchine, Sayasan, Suea, Menh, Xang, Ungkham, Khattiyah, Phuthasad, Princess Ditsaphong and Suphan. Those who didn't accompany him were later captured and sent to Bangkok at the end of the war. What became of them all, I wonder?

I discovered later that having retreated from the KhaoSan pass, Rathsavong

Ngao hastened back to ViengChan, having convinced himself that the Lao army's ruin was entirely down to the treachery and cowardice of Tissah and others who did nothing to help. When he arrived he wasn't surprised to find the city virtually empty. He gathered the abandoned treasures in the palace and, under the cover of darkness, he too paddled down the Mekong to join his father in the south.

Meanwhile the Siamese troops fought their way to ViengChan. After fierce fighting, the Siamese took Nongkhai and PhanPhao and then defeated Phraya Konkaeo's troops at ViengKhuk. The Siamese army established their base at PhanPhao and prepared to cross the Mekong to ViengChan.

Meanwhile the news of Xiengsa's surrender at PhonPhisay reached the Siamese commander Suphawady at Nakhorn Phanom. He rushed his troops north to escort Xiengsa to the Siamese base at PhanPhao and ordered him to serve under his command. Xiengsa grudgingly agreed in order to save his life. Under the command of Phraya NaretYothi and Phraya SeniBorirak, the Siamese crossed the Mekong. As if any sane Siamese ruler would think of attacking a highly defended city!

Humbled by the thought of the hardships endured by our brave soldiers, I nevertheless somehow had to survive. All the survival skills I learnt from my parents came into play: I drank from streams or rivers and ate whatever I could find; wild fruits, berries, leaves and bamboo shoots were plentiful. Like most people, I tried to stay alive by moving between hiding places in the forest and derelict safehouses. When I got tired of hiding, I dressed in rags like an old beggar and ventured outside. I shook my head in dismay at the ease with which the timorous ViengChan population had been left defenceless, pitiably weak in the face of ruin, pathetically hoping their prayers for safety in the temples and shrines might prevail. Their ability to resist had gone and many had fled in confusion. The news was all bad.

Admittedly, the Lao aren't natural warriors. They'd enjoyed decades of peaceful living, but when memories were stirred of the plundering and burning of the 1779 invasion, brave city defenders and noble fighters gathered and fought back; hundreds were slaughtered.

Hours after overrunning ViengChan, the contemptible invaders, in defiance of all sacred laws and Buddhist precepts, set about destroying the city, including its temples. They rounded up the inhabitants, arrested them and then subjected them to merciless interrogations. One could scarcely believe that the Siamese ruler in Bangkok, fondly revered by his followers, could inflict such horrors – brutality, humiliation, deportation, rape, robbery, murder, starvation and torture. The Siamese officials' violence was to prove even worse than anyone had predicted. With murder in their hearts, they embarked upon a killing spree designed to rid the city of all potential enemies. Many prominent citizens were murdered, and their property seized. Temple assets, too, were confiscated, until enough treasure chests had been amassed to pay for their war. The Siamese considered gold the mother of their fighting force; that precious metal has caused death and ruin wherever it's been found. They greedily scraped the gilded Buddha statues and shrines of their gold and ransacked the city treasures, plundering as they went, cutting down all edible fruit trees and forcing local people to destroy the city walls. The main palace and important monuments were put to the torch. ViengChan and the surrounding villages were full of dead men's wives, mothers and fathers, and young families; the souls of the dead drifted upon the air. Blackened corpses with their sweet stench lay everywhere on the pale, withered grass. After a few days in the hot sun, the fallen city stank of charred buildings and rotting fresh.

Having learned that ViengChan had fallen and Chao Anouvong had escaped, the traitor Tissah hurried his troops from NongHan city to meet his Siamese counterpart Suphawady at PhanPhao. Instead of being rewarded, he was humiliated by being forced to take an oath of allegiance. He was then ordered to gather up Lao families for forced migration – himself and his family included – to Bangkok and nearby cities.

Chao Anouvong was horrified to learn that Luang Phrabang and LanNa had put their political principles ahead of their own wishes for nationhood and refused to send their armies to help. It was madness. When they half-heartedly sided with the Siamese army, Suphawady gave a bark of laughter and not only rejected and shamed them but had them collared and flogged, executing those who were unwilling to fight for Siam. The 20,000 remaining soldiers were made to reassemble at PhanPhao as prisoners of war and forced to take orders like sheep. One can imagine their humiliation as they realised they'd betrayed their Lao roots. They stood or sat about in the shade, aimlessly hanging their heads in shame as they waited for orders from the victorious Siamese commanders.

After capturing ViengChan, the Siamese commander-in-chief Bovon and his officials established their headquarters at the Wat Sisaketh temple:

a defilement, but at least it was spared from destruction. By occupying it and evicting the monks, they disrespected the temple's sanctity. Other temples were defiled and looted. The inhabitants had never seen anything so extremely troublesome and disgusting as the swarm of disrespectful Siamese soldiers infesting the streets and temples of ViengChan. Nangklao ordered the important bronze statues of Buddha to be removed: Phra Serm, Phra Suk, Phra Sai (named after the three daughters of King Xay-Setthathirath), Phra SaekKham, Phra KaenChan and many more. Some were just too heavy to be taken to Bangkok. Alas, Phra Suk sank in the Mekong during the crossing (a replica was later cast and housed in a purpose-built shrine at Wat Luang temple in PhanPhao). Phra Serm, Phra Sai and Phra SaekKham were considered worth taking to Bangkok: Phra Serm is now in the Wat Phatum Wanaramh temple and Phra SaekKham in Wat Kharuhabodi. Miraculously, the Phra Sai statue somehow ended up in the Wat Phonsay temple in Nongkhai.

Meanwhile my anxiety steadily mounted: had the king escaped or had he been caught? I patiently waited many weeks and months for news, hiding in the forest at what I thought was a safe distance from danger. The dread inside kept me alert. I wasn't suited to any sort of subterfuge but often climbed into my disguise, dressing up as a poor beggar to make clandestine visits to the city. I cut a bizarre figure as I slowly made my way down the ruined streets, a trickle of fear running down my back. Such was the state of the city: desperate, crippled elderly people held out trembling hands begging on the streets; drunken Siamese soldiers terrorised the starving and exhausted residents and moonless nights gave everyone the jitters. I tried not to look suspicious, but the sight of the Siamese soldiers made my stomach lurch and my horrified thoughts raced. Occasionally I glanced cursorily at them, but they raised no hue and cry. Perhaps they were watching me, perhaps not. The shadow of their brutality, by which thousands of innocent people had perished, lingered in my mind. I could have been arrested, interrogated, killed and dumped in the Mekong. I put my escape down to luck, but the many risks I took were worthwhile. Dead cats and dogs lay everywhere or were on the verge of dying from starvation; those still alive were so emaciated they staggered on their feet as they looked for scraps.

I picked up some news from the venerable old monks who refused to leave their badly damaged temples. The invaders had considered them harmless and had left them alone. They told me that vicious and boastful Siamese soldiers were rounding up local inhabitants, while one monk maintained that Chao

Anouvong was still alive. I disclosed my identity to him. He wasn't a soothsayer but when he ventured a prophecy that Chao Anouvong wouldn't be in exile for much longer, I was thrilled to hear it and made drink offerings in the temple, praying for the happy day of his return.

'But tell me, are you really his private secretary, as you said?' the old monk asked. 'Sadly I haven't seen him since the ceremony at Wat Sisaketh in 1824.'

I assured him I was indeed the king's confidant. I wished that his prophecy would come true, for I longed for Chao Anouvong's return. The monk told me to have faith.

I learned later that Chao Anouvong had waited on the eastern bank of the Mekong for nearly two months for more news about the war, before deciding to move on to Mahaxay-Kongkaeo, about halfway between Nakhorn Phanom and the Vietnamese border. Once there he constructed a fortress at Tha Sida town. Rathsavong Ngao joined him soon afterwards. They tried to gather the Lao troops scattered over the Khorat Plateau to prepare to recapture ViengChan. Meanwhile I took it upon myself to send a message to him, letting him know in confidence that I was still alive. I asked him not to respond because I was confident he would soon be back in ViengChan.

From Mahaxay city he decided to seek help from the Vietnamese Emperor Minh Mang in Hue, despite warnings from his mandarins that he couldn't be relied on. Much to Chao Anouvong's disappointment he at first showed no interest in supporting the Lao cause and there were even suspicions he might be colluding with Siam to carve up LanXang. As a word of warning, Lao elders used to say, 'If you listen to the Vietnamese, you lose the purity of your crop. If you listen to the Siamese, you bring fire to your house.' But surely at least some of them could be trusted.

Nevertheless, Chao Anouvong received a warm welcome in Vietnam and lived in exile in Vinh city in Nghe Anh province for a year. Emperor Minh Mang found the war between two brotherly countries offensive. He was appalled by the violence and intimidation unleashed by Bangkok, in which hundreds of thousands of people had been made homeless. His blood was up and he intended to do everything he could to get Chao Anouvong back in ViengChan, promptly ordering his general Ong Sam Khuan in Mueang Phousun to recruit troops to fight the Siamese. From his capital, Minh Mang also ordered his general Tien Yinh to send a stern message to the Siamese commander Suphawady at Nakhorn Phanom:

'…Return any number of the Lao population that you Siamese have removed and get out of LanXang and go back to your own Ayutthaya territory! Incidentally my commander in chief, Ong Kin Luak, has sent 20,000 men under my command to be stationed in Mueang Tam Dong. We are ready for war. If you do not heed our request, we shall throw in all our forces and turn the battlefield into a lake of blood. We might not stop until we reach Bangkok!'

Phraya Suphawady, no doubt feeling superior after his victory, simply ignored the message.

By July 1827, Bovon and the main Siamese army had left ViengChan with their loot. Suphawady was assigned the task of rounding up the ViengChan families and cleaning out any remaining Lao resistance. Bovon also appointed the Lao noble Phraya Mueang Chan to rule ViengChan, leaving only a small number of people, mostly poor farmers, for him to govern.

Before leaving ViengChan for Bangkok a few months later, Suphawady proceeded to round up 10,000 men and their families, about 50,000 people in all. Throughout LanXang the Lao population saw their menfolk murdered: hardly any were left alive to escape into the forest. The Siamese officials offered the women and children a deal: they would be spared, but only if they agreed to move to Siam. As tears poured down their cheeks, still begging for mercy, they were taken as hostages. Some were led off to Bangkok in chains to be sold into slavery.

The Lao families who were uprooted from ViengChan were scattered to the Siamese cities of Lopburi, Saraburi and Nakhorn Saisi, while those from Nakhorn Phanom and Luang Phrabang were sent to Phanatnikhom and Suphanbury respectively. The statue of the Phrabang Buddha was housed in Chakkawat Monastery. Many high-ranking officials and educated families, including Tissah's, were forced to migrate to Bangkok. Many Lao girls lost their good looks from pain and grief and stood shaking in the slave market hoping there was some sympathy in the world, while the bidders drank rice wine or tea out of porcelain cups and haggled over their price. Most were sold to brothels; some lucky ones caught the eye of rich men. The rest were enslaved, living a humdrum life as domestic servants. Some strong mountain-women made for better workers than the men and were sent to dig canals or to work in the paddy fields outside Bangkok.

There was no reward for viceroy Tissah. He was stripped of his rank and honour and later locked up in Bang Nhikhan prison. I never found out what happened to him after that, but assume he died through his own treachery and greed. The inhabitants of Luang Phrabang, including the vice-king UnKamo and other dignitaries, were taken down to Bangkok. Most of them never saw the daylight again and died without a trace.

Phraya Suphawady triumphantly hurried down to Bangkok with all his loot to be presented to King Nangklao. When he reached Yasothon he found the governor Thao Kham and his brother guilty of attempting to hide some families from ViengChan. Suphawady was as furious as a devil: the governor's families and associates were rounded up, packed into a cage and burnt alive.

Suphawady reached Bangkok on 3 February 1828 and was received by King Nangklao. Some say he – Nangklao – rose from his chair, punching the air with his fist in loud acclamation, declaring the glory to be his. He held himself as the living embodiment of Siamese virtue and spoke of 'my' this and that as if everything in Siam belonged to him, yet still he was unable to smile. His mandarins nodded cautiously, checked with their colleagues and applauded. Once the clamour died down, Nangklao announced a national almsgiving, to thunderous cheers from his mandarins. Nangklao must have been pleased with the loot. As an avid collector, he would have been charmed by the collection of authentic gold and bronze Buddha statues from ancient LanXang. Suphawady was duly awarded with the title of *Phraya Bodinthondecha*; he was entertained lavishly and rewarded generously with spoils of victory. But far from happy with the war reports, Nangklao remained dissatisfied that ViengChan had only been partly destroyed. Filled with anger, resentment and jealousy, he gave a blood-curdling oath and ordered Suphawady to go back, destroy it for good and not return to Bangkok until Chao Anouvong had been captured.

'I am the third Rattanakosin king,' he roared at Suphawady. 'If I were as responsible as my grandfather and father before me, I would have taken care of all Lao LanXang's rulers and we wouldn't be in the trouble we're in today.' Swelling with pride, he added, 'The problems with the Lao won't be over until their capital has been burned to the ground and left on the ash heap of history.' He paused, stared at Suphawady coldly and said, 'Let's hold a complete holocaust there. ViengChan's merely a paddy field on the Mekong. The city must be incinerated, reduced to ashes and sowed with salt so that traitor "Anouvong"' can never make use of it again.'

'Your Majesty, please hear me,' Suphawady said nervously. 'I don't mean to be presumptuous, but what I'm about to say is only out of loyalty. I might be an ignorant vassal, but I am loyal to my king.' He sighed, raised his head to look at Nangklao and said, 'Your Majesty, a man will give his life for anyone who values him and treats him with respect. Chao Anouvong is formidable, and a true scion of Lao LanXang and your late father treated him like a younger brother and a friend. It is difficult to handle a man who is both enemy and friend. His brave son Rathsavong Ngao is an accomplished and respected fighter. The people of the north and northeast are Lao and loyal to LanNa and LanXang. Our military campaign has caused them great suffering and bred much resentment amongst them. The war, whatever form it might take, will go on long after we're dead. If we sanction Chao Anouvong's execution, the Lao people – our trusted allies until our 1779 invasion – will forever brand us as guileful villains and enemies. They will simply never forgive Bangkok, and this may come back to haunt us. They will never stop fighting for LanXang liberation.'

'During my reign LanXang has proved an enemy of Siam, and Chao Anouvong is my nemesis,' Nangklao said, staring down at Suphawady. 'My hatred for him even surpasses our hatred for the Burmese. I know he wants to prevent us from subjugating LanNa and LanXang. We must cut him down now. He is merely a fish to be caught. I want nothing more than to cut his head off. If we spare him, he and his people will forever be a plague to Siam. Just make sure you capture him, dead or alive. You're my subordinate. I can assure you I will not be generous if you fail. Now go!'

Suphawady's head collapsed on his chest as if he'd been hypnotised and he threw himself down on the bare floor before Nangklao's feet. After performing another deep obeisance, he picked himself up and, his head lowered, he walked backwards as if a giant metal chain were hanging around his neck.

Meanwhile Nangklao's aunt, the patronising and self-entitled Princess Narinthonthewy, a turbulent, jealous and terrifying woman, had been dripping poison about Chao Anouvong in her nephew's ear. When she caught Suphawady on his way out of the palace, her dark brown eyes maliciously glaring, she screamed that the traitor (*Buk Lao Anou*) must be captured, tortured and executed for the glory and memory of Siam.

Having received his orders, Suphawady hastily left Bangkok and slowly headed back to ViengChan. In mid-July 1828 he reached NongBuaLamphu where he ordered 500 men to occupy PhanPhao. 300 men under the command of Phraya Phisai SongGram then crossed the Mekong to ViengChan and set up their headquarters at the Wat Kang temple, a little north of the palace.

Meanwhile, Phraya Sanon, Phraya Phet and their Lao army failed to retreat in time from the Khorat Plateau. On hearing that Chao Anouvong was still alive and would soon be returning to ViengChan from Vietnam, Phraya Sanon hurriedly mobilised his troops and, with 3,000 strong, brave men, marched towards the Mekong. They fought many tough battles against Siamese positions along the way before capturing Mukdahan and making it their headquarters. He then prepared his men to capture the Siamese posts at Khemmarat and Ubon before marching north to ViengChan.

When Suphawady heard the news, he contrived to lure Phraya Sanon and Phraya Phet to ViengChan by sending them a letter, sealed with Chao Anouvong's crest, requesting them to return urgently. It worked. Both Sanon and Phet believed the letter had been sent personally by their king and were delighted he'd returned to ViengChan. They headed back north overland to ViengChan instead of attacking the Siamese troops at Khemmarat and followed the Mekong upstream. As a security measure they avoided all major cities, which were heavily guarded by the Siamese army. He faced many obstacles: lacking provisions and with illness rife amongst his troops, it became even harder to maintain his men's confidence. Conditions in his camp deteriorated: short of supplies, many of his men were utterly exhausted and morale was at rock bottom. Sanon was forced to severely punish deserters as a warning to the others, but they marched tirelessly until their provisions ran low and their exhausted bodies fell victim to illness. They were forced to exchange valuable belongings, such as clothes and guns, for food until they were unable to go any further. Phraya Sanon had to abandon most of his troops with Phraya Phet and selected only the bravest and strongest to follow him to ViengChan, longing to meet up with Chao Anouvong..

My thoughts were with Chao Anouvong. We had such deep affection for each other. He was special. I honoured him, prayed for him and laughed and danced like a grateful child when he was around. Truly all the wealth in the world can't buy you a friend or compensate you for the loss of one. At the beginning, the want of him was hard to bear. Absence makes the heart grow fonder and it gradually became even more unbearable. I doted on him. I missed him and loved him. Missing him, I longed for him to be back in ViengChan; loving him, I wanted to see him alive and well. He wasn't just my lord but also a mentor, an inspiration and a dear friend. I was very happy to be part of him, or of his establishment rather. I was certain he would appreciate seeing me safe and well because of my service and loyalty to him and LanXang. I knew that if he somehow returned and continued to serve LanXang, his good name would be embellished.

It had been over a year since he'd escaped to Nghe Anh in Vietnam. I wasn't surprised he'd sought sanctuary there: in the late seventeenth century his grandfather Xay-OngVeh had been brought up in the Vietnamese imperial city of Hue and had later taken the throne of Lao LanXang under the name Xay-Setthathirath II. It was fitting, therefore, that Chao Anouvong ruled ViengChan under the kingly name of Xay-Setthathirath III. No one would have blamed him for escaping and carrying on living in Vietnam, but he was made of sterner stuff than that. While contemplating what to do next, he sought help, requesting men, weapons and financial support from the Vietnamese, but his appeals fell on deaf ears. The only soldiers left from the original 300 who'd been ordered by Emperor Minh Mang to escort him back from Mueang Phousun to XiengKhuang were eighty high-ranking Vietnamese officials, two of whom were able interpreters. The rest simply walked off, returning to Vietnam.

The Vietnamese, our friends and allies, Chao Anouvong said later, took the Siamese anger for granted. They thought that Minh Mang's letter sent to Nangklao on his behalf was enough in itself to bring peace, but they didn't even receive a reply.

Well, I tell you, when I heard that his banishment would soon be over, I felt a euphoric sense of happiness and freedom. The news brought me to tears, as I'd missed him terribly. I stopped mooning about in fear and started to gather my strength, collecting more information about Siamese positions and making discreet preparations for our rendezvous outside ViengChan. It seemed like ten years since we'd bade farewell. I'd trained my heart to endure hardship but longed for the happy day of his return.

Chao Anouvong resumed his campaign with a long, tiring march from XiengKhuang before heading southwest along the Nam Ngeum river valley towards ViengChan, accompanied by the eighty Vietnamese officials. When he reached Tha KhamXang, he dispatched a secret agent to gallop ahead to ViengChan to inform us of his impending arrival. He drummed up some support on the way, and about 2,600 able fighting men had joined him by the time he arrived in the northern suburbs of ViengChan a few weeks later, on

27 July 1828. The news of his arrival was truly an exciting time for me.

Hiding in the forest with little food for so many months, I was rather thin and quite weak, feeling old and infirm, in great distress in his absence. After making drink offerings to the forest that had become my friend, and saying farewell to the animals – the ants, birds, gibbons and insects who'd shared my environment – I hastened to meet Chao Anouvong and make my report. The guards at the gates of his camp guided me to his well-guarded quarters. I experienced a tremendous rush of joy and happiness. I was just blissed out – nothing in the world could compete with it, but the effort of hurrying towards him made me dizzy. He was at his desk in his tent. When he saw me he rose to his feet and came towards me, but seemed unable to speak. Despite my heart leaping for joy, even missing a beat, I got the first word in.

'Your Majesty, forgive me,' I said, kneeling in reverence at arm's length from him, wishing him to touch my head. 'How gracious of you to rush to welcome me. You do me too much honour. I'm truly overwhelmed, and you can't imagine how I've yearned for this moment.'

'Phia Jon!' he exclaimed, laying his hands on my shoulders. 'Seeing you has made me forget myself,' he whispered. 'Now, pull yourself together. There's no need for such courtesy. Please rise.' He grasped my arms, pulled me up and beckoned me closer.

'Oh Your Majesty, how I've missed you!' I said and moved a step forward. 'Isn't it a delightful thing to see each other again? I'm ecstatic – blissfully happy beyond words.'

'Come, let me hug a close friend I've also missed very much,' he said, throwing his arms wide open, clasping me to him and sighing blissfully. I could have been a son and Chao Anouvong my long-lost father, finally meeting after a long expedition. I'd forgotten how strong he was. The warmth of his embrace, the silent pounding on my back and the tears in my eyes (and in his) was truly surreal. Our eyes were wet with tears. He took a step back to examine me. At the sight of my astonished, gaunt face, he started smiling and laughing but couldn't disguise his shock at my appearance. I was equally staggered by how haggard he looked. In fact, I hardly recognised him: he looked half starved, certainly much gaunter, especially around the neck. With his straggling greyish hair, grey beard and the sunken eyes on his bony face, he looked like a corpse freshly emerged from the fog.

'Phia Jon, it is indeed delightful to see you and reunite with you,' he said, gazing at me. 'Now, I know a year in exile is a long time,' he added, feeling my bony shoulders and ribs, 'but there's no need to be so surprised or taken aback. Be quite certain I'm the same man you knew back in ViengChan. As for you, I command you to eat and recover your strength.' I could hardly conceal my excitement, but he stopped me with an anxious smile. 'Now, tell me, have the Siamese gone home with their plunder and left us in peace?'

'Your Majesty, I have no wish to put you off with ambiguous answers,' I said. 'On the contrary, I'll tell you everything without concealment.' I could see the mournful expression on his face when I told him about the violence of the Siamese and the destruction of ViengChan. 'It pains me to inform you that according to reliable intelligence,' I added, 'Nangklao is intent on bending us to his will. It looks like the Siamese are here to stay.'

'What tyranny!' he exclaimed. 'So many of our brave men have perished. The vanities and ambitions of the Rattanakosin Siam surely deserve the fullest scrutiny.'

'What's more, they plan to raze ViengChan to the ground and to capture you dead or alive... there is a good price on your head!'

'That doesn't inspire much confidence, Phia Jon. Must we be beholden to them forever?'

'I'm very sorry; we must take care for the sake of LanXang.'

He sighed, thought it over and then said, 'What do our people say about the war?'

'That our defeat at SomPoi – KhaoSan wasn't due to poor leadership. It was the will of heaven. We were heavily outnumbered and outgunned, but we fought to the death. Our men died fighting for our nation. Honest men are full of sorrow and regret about it all, but future generations will be so proud of us.'

'Do you think they still want me as king?' he ventured.

'Your Majesty, we live in hope, but...'

'No, Phia Jon, I don't expect to reclaim the throne until we've regained our independence and LanXang is united. Furthermore, while the Siamese are here, nowhere is safe for us. How are we to live? We might as well be dead!'

'Dead? No yet, Your Majesty,' I said, trying not to get upset. 'We mustn't contemplate it under any circumstances. You're back in the city you love surrounded by the affection of your people, so let's fight on and live our lives...' I couldn't say anymore because the words choked in my throat, and I had to turn away. He tried to console me.

Apart from his thinness, the Chao Anouvong who returned from Vietnam was indeed no different. His grasp on reality remained intact. He'd been defeated but his fighting spirit remained high, and he sought every opportunity to take on the invaders. He welcomed news of the 300 enemy troops under Phraya Phisai SongGram stationed at Wat Kang Monastery. I made no secret that I believed his days of political power were over, but he disagreed with me. He still clung to hope, doggedly believing he could find a way to win LanXang back. I doubt whether the notion of impossibility ever entered his head. He'd my admiration and I dearly wanted him to succeed.

'Remember, Phia Jon, we have work to do. We're still alive, and where there's life there's hope. Our hope is imbued in the way of truth and in the hearts of our people. But we must learn from our past and create the vision of an optimistic future.'

'Of course, let's fight on,' I said reassuringly.

The news of his return had been discreetly passed to people in the surrounding countryside and those who'd been hiding in the forests. Remarkably, a sizeable crowd soon appeared from nowhere to welcome him, along with their elephants and horses. They regarded him as a hero, made drink offerings in his honour and prayers of thanks for his safety. With silver trays of flowers and beeswax candles in their hands, they prostrated themselves in homage and begged him to take up the throne again and look to the future. He promised he wouldn't give his kingdom away to the Siamese like the charitable lord Phraweth Sandone, who gave his own son and daughter to a beggar. 'There's no time for complacency,' he said. 'LanXang independence and your freedom must come first.' They cheered him loudly.

At sunset we shared a meal of seared buffalo meat, spicy green papaya salad, a variety of edible vegetables from the surrounding forests and freshly steamed sticky rice, just like at Nakhorn Phanom thirty-two years earlier. I spooned a lean piece of meat onto his plate in token of my love and loyalty. He smiled fondly and gave me some of his in exchange. We ate our meal and tossed our drink down with obvious enjoyment, making drink offerings and toasting each other boisterously to renew our friendship. I was elated and devoured everything, even the rather unpalatable partially cooked steak, with gusto. We refrained from drinking to our hearts' content but chatted excitedly, talking more about the happy past than the war. Being of a jocular nature, we tended to succumb to the temptation of telling each other new (and old!) jokes.

'How do porcupines copulate?' he asked, smiling mischievously.

'Standing up!' I replied without thinking and chortled.

We laughed uproariously. Even the guards, who'd probably never heard the joke, started to chuckle. We poured libations and blissfully drank to our health. It was fascinating to hear him talking about his life in Vietnam; he said it had been a suitable place to recoup his strength, and the sea air had been perfect for recuperation. I told him he was always very much in my thoughts and prayers. He said that he'd missed me, especially when eating such wonderful seafood. He roused my appetite slightly when he said that prawn and crabs in Vietnam were big and delicious compared to the ones from the rivers or the paddy fields we were more used to. He loved Vietnamese food but wouldn't swap it for Lao food at any price. He lived, but not well, merely surviving. I was fascinated to hear that the sea was like a huge, greenish-blue lake with waves breaking on rocky and sandy beaches. He said the salty seawater had a sickly taste and he felt sick whenever he went out to sea on a boat. I didn't envy him. He told me that the slender Vietnamese ladies wore triangular hats, loose-fitting silk trousers and soft, semi-transparent outer dresses that floated in the wind, and they always walked as if they were in a hurry. He was very grateful to Emperor Minh Mang for giving him sanctuary. The people had been very welcoming there, but he'd longed to be back in LanXang. He'd felt deprived of his own country's history, society, culture and indeed of his own self. He was most happy to be back in ViengChan. When the dinner was ending, I brought out his old bamboo toothpick case and handed it to him.

'Ah, Phia Jon, my loyal friend, you've always been good to me. What would I do without you?' he said. While picking and sucking his stained teeth, he reminded me of the time we'd shared a meal in Nakhorn Phanom. 'My teeth are giving me a lot of trouble. You've saved my life!' he added with a sigh of satisfaction.

It was all I could do for him. I choked with emotion and struggled to find words as I turned a glass of water in my hands. He rested his hand on my shoulder, told me to remain positive and stressed I still had a job to do. I nodded assent and we retired for the night.

We woke up at sunrise next morning to find a group of happy and cheerful people waiting to escort us into the city. When he greeted them with enthusiasm and delight, they ecstatically declared their loyalty and love and began to shout his name. Soon after breakfast, we hastily boarded our elephants, and the crowd applauded him along the shady route. He sat aloft on his open howdah and raised his hand in acknowledgement. We moved slowly and cautiously towards the city.

Two days later we arrived close to the city's main northern gate but camped out of the enemy's sight outside the walls. Just before sunrise next morning, 31 July 1828, the air was balmy. We mounted our elephants and, with many euphoric followers on foot, gradually made our way through the deserted city to That Luang hill, where many great battles had been fought. With their soft, leather-like feet, our elephants walked gently side by side. As we marched out into the morning heat, Chao Anouvong seemed calm but was visibly upset at the state of ViengChan. Mystifyingly there was no sign of the Siamese army. I was worried they were waiting in ambush; my heart thumping, I apprehensively looked at him in puzzlement, but made no comment. The ruined and ghost-like city must have unnerved him as much as it did me.

By now the sun was hot as we moved slowly through the ruins. For the first time I inhaled that familiar scent of ViengChan, which should have filled me with the promise of happy days. Alas, the atmosphere of devastation and abandonment was palpable. It filled me with despair and misery, yet the birds were singing as if they were welcoming us home, oblivious of the future. Under dark rain clouds that were lifting, twisting and rising on the horizon, That Luang hill looked bleak and eerie ahead of us. The wind moaned hauntingly, shaking the trees, pushing into us, making us shiver; less from the wind perhaps than something else – maybe the spirits (*Phi*) of the thousands of soldiers who'd been killed. The hairs on the nape of my neck stirred and spiked. The elephants appeared to sense it too. They reluctantly moved forward with their trunks in the air, sensing and probing, making a great rumbling that went right through you, as if they were in a state of great agitation or even horror. Finally, with their ears extended fully forward, they came to a halt. We tried to urge them on but they trumpeted and moved backwards instead. They disobediently wheeled round and let out a loud, reverberating roar of real terror.

We turned round and made for the Hor Phra Kaeo temple. As we were approaching the undamaged Wat Sisaketh temple, shimmering in the sun, Chao Anouvong silently stared at it in astonishment. He'd assumed it was the first temple the Siamese had destroyed. The mahout ordered the elephant to kneel at the gate and Chao Anouvong gently climbed down, intending to prostrate himself in prayer in front of the Buddha statues inside the ordination hall (*Sim*). Suddenly one lonely, starved-looking monk in his tattered saffron robes, more hair on his bony head than permitted, bent with years and rich in wisdom, came out to greet us with a euphoric smile. Chao Anouvong knew the Siamese had made it their headquarters but was appalled by the damage to the cloisters – gold leaf and eyes inlaid with precious stones had been removed from the Buddha statues, some of which had been broken or decapitated. It was an unbelievably sinful act of vandalism!

On entering the *Sim*, Chao Anouvong touched the door in thankful amazement that he'd lived to see it once again. Many priceless bronze Buddha statues had disappeared or been damaged, but the scented, cool air inside felt sacred. He lit the candles, laid offerings of flowers and fruit in front of the idols and silently made a solemn prayer. It was a very moving occasion. When we emerged, the holy temple's perimeter was full of shaven-headed men in unwashed and shabby saffron robes. More monks had turned up unexpectedly from various temples around the city to welcome and shield Chao Anouvong from any attack. After a brief exchange of emotional and spiritual greetings, they blessed the white threads and tied them onto his wrists, calling for the return of his soul. They were inconsolable with grief for all the temples that had been lost.

'Chao Anouvong, our respects to you,' one venerable monk said. 'We mortal monks are not supposed to be political. We are very religious, preach toleration and think about other people more than ourselves. But there's no need for everyone to be religious. It is better to have empathy and be good, even though it is difficult and humbling. Your humility is powerful. We admire and support your noble cause. One day, we ourselves will become civilians and have families of our own. You have our blessing and may Lord Buddha and the gods reward you with your heart's desire!'

Their words comforted and encouraged Chao Anouvong as he lowered his head and lifted his praying hands to receive them. By now some local inhabitants had turned up as well, jostling to get a good view of him.

'Venerable monks and fellow countrymen,' he said solemnly, 'you should know the truth. I have no news from Bangkok. We lost our independence in 1779 and now we're fighting to win it back. War and the shedding of blood is extremely upsetting, but victory is vital for the survival of our nation. If we tolerate evil, it will only get worse. We must be able to see a better future, otherwise we'll lose hope.'

The monks and the people nodded and applauded passionately to show their support.

Soon after, accompanied by the monks, we moved across to the war-torn Hor Phra Kaeo temple, where we despondently inspected the damage. It looked haunted, empty, deserted and infinitely sad. Crows cawed from the broken roof. Every window had been removed, giving the building a dead, skeletal look. We were shocked by the smell of smoke, damp and human waste and wandered in dazzling sunlight amongst the ruins, where wild flowers and weeds had grown through the sacred stones of the temple. Inside the Hor Phra Kaeo, a royal chapel since 1566, bats hang in the dark corners of the roof; pigeons cooed on the broken beams; some sections of the roof and ceiling had come down; all the gilded furniture, bronze Buddha statues and artefacts were gone, and the silver floor had been prised up and carted away. The wind howled through the broken roof and from time to time a piece of debris became dislodged and tumbled down to join the rubble below. The garden was in ruins, but plants had rooted themselves and peacocks still strutted on the ground or perched on the trees, screeching tortuously. Weeds grew out of the broken stone floor, rabbits scampered, and rats scuttled about. It had stood there for 262 years. Chao Anouvong walked away silently, infinite revulsion on his face.

Outside, he mournfully stared at the badly burnt palace where we'd once slept, as if trying to reconstruct it in his mind. It must have had as powerful an effect on him as on me. I was terribly distraught but said nothing. The main palace building with its throne room had been completely burnt and demolished. We walked around in silence. It wasn't even possible to discern the original layout of the structure through the tangled weeds and rubble. Chao Anouvong stooped to pick up a charred piece of wood and a lump of brick from the ground. His voice was loaded with anger and regret as he flung the wood away. The brick crumbled in his shaking hand and a cloud of red dust trickled from his fingers. He turned to me. 'See this, Phia Jon,' he said with an expression of utter dejection. 'Perhaps it's my fault, but until our country is restored we're at their mercy.' He shook his hands forcefully before brushing them on some bushes to remove the dust. 'And whenever I think of this place, I'll be reminded of my humiliation, but we must never be broken by the weight of oppression.'

We returned to our camp outside the city for safety. We later spent many sad days and nights under the damaged roof of the Hor Phra Kaeo temple or inspecting the damaged palace, planning our next move. Armed men were stationed around the perimeter for our protection.

To begin with, Chao Anouvong was simply relieved to be back in ViengChan, but he gradually realised that he was in effect under house arrest, even though nothing stopped him leaving the Hor Phra Kaeo temple and moving around the city freely. We thought it would be too dangerous to go outside the gate: we were under an occupying force, after all. We decided not to venture outside during the day, but under the cover of darkness our men crept along the Mekong to spy on the Siamese headquarters at Wat Kang temple.

Although there'd been so much killing and many of the people were gone forever, Chao Anouvong insisted that LanXang was still worth fighting for. There was honour in the struggle. When we were alone he collapsed into agonies of guilt. He rubbed his temples, as he normally did when stressed, and said he would be blamed for his actions for many years to come. He always tried to steer a correct course by asking how history would judge him.

'Well, in this instance, Phia Jon,' he said, 'I believe history will agree our cause is just. If future generations scorn me for my follies, let them, but we must never give up fighting for the unity of the Lao nation. That desire must always be in our hearts.'

It occurred to me how selfless he'd been in the interests of LanXang. His strategy had been to appear as Siam's scapegoat to radicalise the Lao people, who normally preferred to avoid politics. He'd foreseen his humiliation, but for the greater good he was prepared to sacrifice his own reputation as a king and a man of intelligence in the knowledge he'd served his country well.

He disclosed to me that a few days before entering the city, he'd first tested the air by instructing his son Rathsavong Ngao to send a message to the Siamese general Phraya Phisai SongGram at PhanPhao, requesting a peaceful meeting in ViengChan on 2 August. This was accepted, but Phraya Suphawady was informed of it at his headquarters in NongBuaLamphu. The Siamese army therefore kept themselves quiet in their headquarters at Wat Kang temple. As a precaution, we also kept our distance. Suphawady offered a truce but insisted that any meeting should be held in PhanPhao, to where he then rushed his troops. Chao Anouvong was pleased at first but groaned at the prospect of having to cross the Mekong. He feared deception but after a sleepless night of hard thinking, he decided to go: it might be his last and most important meeting with the enemy.

'Is it wise to go, Your Majesty?' I asked worriedly. 'As things stand, there's money on your head and you're enemy number one. They might want to arrest you, torture you or even kill you.'

'Let them. I intend to show that we believe in dialogue and are ready to compromise on everything except LanXang independence. We want peace, not war.' He paused, looking thoughtful. 'Will you accompany me to the meeting?' He saw me hesitate. 'You'd better come along and act as a witness because they cannot be trusted. Besides, our agents reported that Suphawady likes to brutalise people. These Siamese villains are liars and quite capable of misrepresenting us. I'm aware they plan to arrest me. They might even want me dead, as you said. Well, if they kill me, there can be no better death than fighting for liberty. And if that happens,' he added with a wink, 'it would make for an excellent scene in your book.'

By coincidence Phraya Suphawady arrived and stationed his troops at PhanPhao on the same day Chao Anouvong entered ViengChan, 31 July. He wanted both to please Nangklao and to safeguard his own neck. On the other hand, although Chao Anouvong was now old, he believed he could still inspire his people. Bangkok had tried to undermine him, but he'd stood up for himself and earned respect: as opposed to Nangklao, who was too stiff-necked to inspire popularity.

The summit was scheduled to begin at dawn, so we had to cross the Mekong in partial darkness. Before crossing the river, Chao Anouvong told me he expected the Vietnamese and the Siamese to end up fighting each other. He believed that Bangkok's imperial ambitions extended not only to King Fah Ngum's LanXang but beyond the Annamite range (*Xai Phou Luang*) into Vietnamese territory to the south. They would become entangled in a bitter war. As a precaution he shrewdly selected two high-ranking Vietnamese officials to act as go-betweens so Suphawady wouldn't dare touch him. We confidently crossed the Mekong to PhanPhao. His plan was to surrender in the hope of being reinstated as king, but not before demanding LanXang sovereignty.

The meeting took place according to plan on 2 August 1828 and was held in the temple hall, supposedly as a symbol of peace and reconciliation.

Chao Anouvong and Prince Ngao entered the room with their go-betweens following behind. Two unarmed guards conducted us to our seats. Both sides greeted each other tensely, their hands extended in full supplication, but they eyed each other with curiosity, resentment, suspicion and some regret. Chao

Anouvong announced that the two Vietnamese envoys, who were seated either side of him, would act as chief mediators. However, their appearance provoked gasps of surprise amongst the impressive-looking Siamese officials, who looked at each other, their bodies tense with anger. Phraya Suphawady, a well-built man with a typical hard, pure-bred Siamese face, momentarily flushed with shock because he hadn't known in advance. With typical Siamese arrogance he could scarcely bring himself to greet the Vietnamese. There was no question of him detaining Chao Anouvong without harming the Vietnamese diplomats.

I sat slightly to one side next to Prince Ngao, who was immediately to Chao Anouvong's right at the back, amongst the anxious Lao officials. I felt myself turn cold at the sight of Suphawady, a man who'd outraged morality and caused so much anguish to the Lao people. With his hair cut close to his skull and his glaring dark eyes, he looked tough and disdainful, eminently capable of murder. It felt strange looking at him, a Siamese, who'd marched with thousands of soldiers, smashed LanXang to pieces and enslaved thousands of people. It was difficult to remain silent while inwardly vowing revenge. I noticed one of the Siamese guards glaring at Chao Anouvong with a devilish grin and I kept my eye on him. I feared he could be dangerous, so I whispered to Prince Ngao to keep watching out for assassins. It was nerve-racking and astonishing to see Chao Anouvong facing the enemy, barely an arm's length away. Sensing the meeting might well turn into a bloodbath, my heart thudded violently.

At first the atmosphere was surprisingly welcoming. Once everyone was seated, Chao Anouvong gestured to Suphawady to speak first. The Siamese commander quickly bowed, introduced himself and said he was pleased the meeting could take place. There was a short pause while Suphawady guardedly glanced around and asked Chao Anouvong whether he was concealing a knife. The king replied in the negative but said he would certainly have brought a large one if he thought Suphawady would refuse to guarantee his safety. Everyone smiled and laughed a little.

'But I've brought you this as a gift from XiengKhuang!' said Chao Anouvong pleasantly, handing a small, red silk wrapping to Suphawady. 'Please open it.'

Suphawady was pleasantly surprised and embarrassed. With a wry smile, he cast a suspicious look at the parcel before carefully unwrapping it like an eager child. He smiled broadly at the thumb-sized piece of rare horn from a rutting young deer: a well-known aphrodisiac to be ground into powder and mixed with drink. 'Well, what can I say?' he said, lost for words but managing to offer his thanks generously.

'I surmise by your expression that you have many young concubines,' Chao Anouvong teased, knowing that Suphawady was a great one for the women.

Suphawady seemed to have changed his attitude from deep suspicion and hostility to surprise that this enemy of Siam, whom he'd been ordered to capture or kill, was in fact a kind and thoughtful man. In his excitement he seemed oblivious to the laughter ringing around him.

'I am excited, but I'll go easy with it,' said Suphawady. 'But tell me, how shall I deal with you?'

'Like a king,' Chao Anouvong replied instantly. The hall fell silent.

'I shall try for my own sake. But for our king's…?' Suphawady took a deep breath and leant back in his seat.

'How is His Majesty, may I ask?' Chao Anouvong said graciously, charming Suphawady and trying to preserve a calm atmosphere. 'I do hope he's in good health,' he added, with an obsequiousness that could have earned him a reprieve from Bangkok.

'He is well, thank you, but very busy…and worried and most upset because of this war,' said Suphawady with an ironic stare, a tilt of the head and the thinnest of smiles.

'His Majesty, worried about me, with all his other worries, and upset? Really! That can't be good,' Chao Anouvong said and laughed. 'Oh no. I don't believe a word of it! He loves his vengeance. He wants to put an end to me for the glory of Siam. He's surely enjoying your amazing run of military success. Now please tell His Majesty that only when his heart is free of all desire – especially his ambition for total hegemony – will he have peace of mind.'

The meeting continued on friendly terms. Chao Anouvong willingly admitted he'd fled east but he played a clever political game by pointing out that while Vietnam was like a close friend who'd given him refuge, Siam was like a relative who'd reproached him over a difference of opinion and to whom he now wished to explain everything. He understood why Bangkok demanded he should beg for forgiveness. He also pointed out that King Minh Mang of Vietnam had already sent an explanatory message to King Nangklao on his behalf; from then onwards the Vietnamese felt it was their duty to take whatever action they deemed necessary. He closely studied Phraya Suphawady, who listened intently. He emphasised that the Lao and Siamese relationship had always been based on kinship and mutual love, but there had been times when Siam looked to LanXang for help in times of war. LanXang and Siam were like brotherly countries (*Ban Ai-Mueang Nong*): Village of Ai, the Lao; town of Nong, the Siamese.

Phraya Suphawady turned pale and leaned forwards, scowling at Chao Anouvong defiantly as if he hated the analogy. His presence filled the room, but he seemed shocked and bewildered by the comparison. His mouth set arrogantly in his chubby face and his thick black brows flared up like a Garuda bird's spread wings. It was obvious he'd no intention of compromising. He grinned devilishly and cunningly asked, in his thick raucous voice, about rumours of a conflict between Chao Anouvong and Minh Mang. The meeting was becoming confrontational.

Chao Anouvong was surprised at Nangklao's enquiries whether he'd been happy in Vietnam. It was Bangkok, he said, that didn't seem to want peace with ViengChan. However, he was prepared to wipe the slate clean and to start the reconciliation process. Wisely, he paused for a moment, sat back and then gestured with aplomb to the Vietnamese envoy and the interpreter to conduct most of the sensitive negotiations.

'Gentlemen, gentlemen!' the Vietnamese official stepped in. 'Let's be civilised to each other and get to the point.' He fixed his gaze on Suphawady, who was leaning back in his chair, thrusting his legs under the table and listening closely. 'Since I don't know your customs well enough, you must be wondering why I'm here.' The envoy then leaned forward with both hands resting on the table. 'Well, Phraya Suphawady, I carry a military order from my emperor, who believes that Chao Anouvong's objective in marching on Khorat was not to attack Bangkok or endanger others, but merely to protect the Lao people from wrong. I'm here to formally witness your king unjustifiably accusing a good man of being a rebel and a traitor, even though he isn't even Siamese.'

In his plodding but typical Vietnamese piping voice, the envoy determinedly portrayed King Nangklao as a tyrant addicted to war and bathed in blood and insisted the bullies of Bangkok were destroying peace in the region.

'The whole conflict arose from your government's hostile, cruel, and greed-stained idea of an empire, and those infamous census numbers tattooed on the Lao people. Our King Minh Mang is greatly offended by your king's lack of diplomacy, and by your arrogance for not responding to General Tien Yinh's demand you should pull out of LanXang. We are convinced of the legality of Chao Anouvong's struggle for LanXang independence; he never wronged your king intentionally. We believe he acted in accordance with heaven's will and his people's wishes. If you take our advice, you will spare him, but we suspect Nangklao wants to finish him off. We would regard this as a grave insult. We denounce your invasion of LanXang as illegal and immoral. Besides, Siam took an oath of "love and friendship" with LanXang in Dan Sai in 1563 and again in 1760… and we know of the existence of the That Si-SongHuck treaty. We'll take whatever action we think necessary. We feel strongly it was a great mistake to let Nangklao drive Chao Anouvong out of ViengChan.' He paused to take a drink. 'We want you Siamese out of the Khorat Plateau,' he continued staunchly, 'out of LanXang entirely, back to your own lands without delay. We want Chao Anouvong back in ViengChan, even though you've senselessly destroyed so much of it. Vietnam believes that if you restore His Majesty King Anouvong to an independent LanXang, he will pledge his loyalty and devotion, binding the Rattanakosins and their children to a lasting friendship with the Lao people. Vietnam will promise not to interfere. Now, what would His Majesty King Nangklao say to that?'

Phraya Suphawady shifted slightly in his chair, looking embarrassed and lost. 'That would be up to Chao Anouvong to settle with His Majesty our king,' he said, adding that Nangklao was magnanimous in victory and was willing to take pity on an old man by allowing him to live peacefully in exile, but not as king of LanXang.

Nangklao had completed his conquest of ViengChan and was now insisting his enemy must surrender or live in exile, that LanXang would be annexed to Siam and the Lao would be forced to become Siamese. What was Chao Anouvong to do? He believed he'd done nothing wrong, but he was unable to convince Suphawady. He insisted he only wanted to right all wrongs and was entitled to return to ViengChan, while the Siamese should keep themselves to the central plain of the Chaophraya river.

Chao Anouvong, though depressed in spirit, looked a little less ragged after trimming his hair and moustache and shaving his beard. He still had confidence and faith; he knew that the Lao nation must come first and surrender and exile was simply not an option. In effect he'd become an exile in his own country. Calming himself down, he picked up his drink, poured libations and took a sip of water, as he often did when preparing to speak, but this time he stayed silent. He nodded at the Vietnamese envoy to continue.

'I see. Your king Nangklao,' said the envoy, leaning forward with squared shoulders, 'wants reconciliation with Chao Anouvong. On what terms?'

'That is for Chao Anouvong,' said Suphawady, his arms on the table. 'But His Majesty needs something in writing before he can even think about it… and Chao Anouvong must consent to Bangkok's demands.' Suphawady gazed at Chao Anouvong and sneered. 'Look at him! He's a condemned man, but if he agrees to surrender and live in exile, my king will see that no harm befalls his family and relatives in Bangkok.'

'On whose authority, may I ask? And how long will the Lao be subjected to your king's rule?' the Vietnamese envoy said firmly.

'You have no right to be at this meeting!' Phraya Suphawady shouted insolently, his hands bunched into fists and his eyes narrowed, infused with vitriol and devilish hate. 'But since you ask, it is on his authority.' Suphawady pointed to a small portrait of King Nangklao in a golden cloak wielding a sword at the head of the negotiating table. 'LanXang's future rests on his sword. Nothing will happen without His Majesty's approval. Obey or else there will be no reconciliation.'

Chao Anouvong ignored the portrait but fixed his gaze on Suphawady. I feared the Siamese were about to pick up hidden weapons and kill us. Although I'm sure he was greatly agitated, my master looked oddly serene.

'Haven't enough good men died to satisfy your Rattanakosin king's vanity and insatiable ambition?' the Vietnamese retorted. 'Your king is said to be bright, obedient to the will of heaven and acquainted with the ways of the world, but his authority is blocking out the sun over LanXang. His warlords soar like vultures and his armies swarm like frenzied wasps, destroying everything under the sky! His actions are surely in defiance of heaven and are without just cause. Even if your king declares himself a god, he still has no right to interfere in all aspects of life in Lao LanXang. Please allow me to tell you that our neighbour, the Lao kingdom of LanXang with the Mekong flowing through the middle, deserves her independence. Vietnam simply will not desert her.'

Suphawady, still leaning forward, silently looked down at the table as if he'd lost the plot, or perhaps trying to hide his monstrous displeasure. But he boldly said that Bangkok's orders to destroy the rebels and take LanXang under Siamese control were just.

Chao Anouvong sat through the meeting with barely concealed annoyance that he would never achieve his ultimate ambition: independence for LanXang. He had barely drunk anything and I couldn't make out his expression clearly, but I was conscious of the buzz of cicadas and the occasional dog barking outside. The air seemed suddenly to be ferociously hot. I began to sweat. At a nod from the Vietnamese envoy, Chao Anouvong said that although Nangklao despised him, he was delighted at the Siamese king's desire for reconciliation. Everyone sat up and listened attentively. My heart was thumping but I tried to keep calm.

'Phraya Suphawady, I think you secretly hate me too,' said Chao Anouvong calmly. 'Are you supposed to take the document back to Bangkok?'

'No,' Suphawady replied, grinning and glaring at me with glittering eyes. He said sarcastically, 'but you might like to send your handsome and trusted secretary to deliver it personally into His Majesty's hands.'

The Siamese officials stared at me; no one spoke.

I was dumbfounded he recognised me with a mop of grey hair on my head. I lifted my eyes to heaven, thinking hard, and recalled that Suphawady had read out Chao Anouvong's written request to Nangklao during the fateful meeting in 1825. I realised it certainly wasn't a compliment and I felt my hostility growing. I was astonished at the audacity of his proposal. I shifted in my chair and the sweat ran copiously down my back. I knew Chao Anouvong would never accept such terms; there was no way he'd send me.

Chao Anouvong calmly told Suphawady that, in the interests of peace and friendship, this meeting was being held for the sake of compromise, not revenge. He profoundly wished events had turned out differently: the Lao and Siamese were brothers, after all. But he loved his country more than he loved his brothers, if such a thing is possible. And he hoped the future would be guided by justice and would be beneficial to both countries. He paused to pour libations, took a sip of water, looked straight ahead and coughed discreetly.

'Phraya Suphawady,' he said, glancing and nodding courteously at the other Siamese officials. 'Please allow me to say that you are, I believe, a patriot like us, but you are Siamese of Siam and the Chaophraya is your river; we are Ai-Lao or Lao of LanXang, and we have the Mekong. We're more than willing to forget the wrongs you Siamese have done to us since 1779. We're casting away the memory of our suffering and forgetting your cruelty towards us. After the misery and violence of the past fifty years, we're prepared to set aside past grievances and bitterness and to let bygones be bygones. We've put up with your brutality because we've never had the power to stop you, but we beg you to refrain from such outrages. If only my death will satisfy your king, well, I could accept that as long as you leave us in peace.' He paused and then said, 'Now, please listen carefully. There should be no revenge; let's sign a treaty of peace and reconciliation which honours me as king of LanXang in perpetuity; let the mutual goodwill of the old days be restored; let our special relationship, based on bonds of history, kinship and common interest, be preserved and let peace and plenty prevail. We truly respect His Majesty, yet also fear him. We want dialogue and a truce, right here in ViengChan, so the Siamese and Lao remain sworn brothers. Is this not sensible? So, please tell His Majesty that, in the agony of our grief and regret, we wish for only two things: LanXang independence and an end to the fighting. But I ask you this, if your king wants to build an empire at LanXang's expense, surely I'll be accused of consorting with him, and becoming corrupted and seduced by him?'

The Siamese delegation looked on while Chao Anouvong took another sip of his drink. The price of fighting for his principles had been banishment, hardship and powerlessness. But the terms offered by Suphawady would have made him Nangklao's dog. This must have been as infuriating to him as it was to me. He poured more libations but lapsed into silence. Everyone waited for him to continue, and the subsequent silence became uncomfortable. Eventually he glanced at me and then turned to the motionless Suphawady, who was as still as if he'd been turned to stone.

'Phraya Suphawady,' Chao Anouvong continued, licking his lips, 'I fear your noble nature has blinded you to the true intentions of your king, who has always wanted to get rid of me so he could annex LanXang. We're victims of Siam's envy and intimidation. King Nangklao knows full well that my private secretary is not part of these negotiations and that I have dedicated my life to the restoration of LanXang. If we cede ViengChan and LanXang, where would you Siamese have us call home and country? Living in Bangkok for nearly two decades is more than enough for anyone. I will never live in exile; I'll stay right here in ViengChan LanXang and continue to struggle against my fate. LanXang is for the Lao, not for the Siamese or anyone else. We want to remain Lao and therefore we simply cannot accept such terms. Never!'

Suddenly Phraya Suphawady lifted his gaze as if he'd just woken up, his face flushed red with anger. He saw fit to insult Chao Anouvong face to face, accusing him of being disloyal and as headstrong and vain as a wild buffalo. He said that Nangklao never expected he would become a fool and a traitor.

Well, at sixty-one, Chao Anouvong had no lack of wisdom in judging people and insults no longer bothered him. But in Lao LanXang, disrespect for others, especially for the elderly, is a serious matter.

'Please be silent and listen,' said Chao Anouvong, trying to stay calm. 'There's no need to bandy words, to show off your petty ideas or behave like a swaggering braggart with the heart of a bully. Words fix problems and we're merely telling you the truth. You should know the words of love and friendship sworn between our two royal families at the That Si-SongHuck shrine in 1563. Let's treat each other with civility and respect. To be frank, you need to be a little more courteous. Now, may I ask, how can you call me a traitor when your government is meddling in LanXang like a blundering child? Your king, of course, is never wrong, never confers favour, never forgives mistakes, never feels pity, never regrets anything. However, if he's wise, he should realise that Siam belongs to the Siamese people, not just to him. He should know how to strike a balance between crime and punishment; he should know how to be kind. God help you Siamese, ruled by an autocratic who believes he's immortal.'

'As a peace-loving nation, we don't hold violent or extreme views,' Chao Anouvong continued after a pause. 'We would refuse to be loyal to any Rattanakosin king who wanted to annex LanXang. As a Siamese man, you'll never better yourself while you live in fear of a king who rules by decree. You're a prime example of the Siamese species, a commander grovelling at the feet of your king, an obedient lacky stunted by repression. But underneath, you're fearful, horrified and most probably gnawed by guilt. Please tell me: will your king promote you, look after you and generously pension you off for your military successes? And what about the ordinary Siamese population? Don't you realise how pitiless and selfish he is? Does Nangklao really believe that LanXang wants to be part of Siam? If so, he must be an even greater fool than I thought. I might be a fool as well, but I'll have no truck with you Siamese who've so wronged my country.'

The Siamese delegation went red and looked daggers at Chao Anouvong, but held their tongues in disbelief, leaving it to Suphawady to speak. He blinked in disbelief, thrust his head forward and directed a storm of insults and derision at Chao Anouvong.

'Don't tempt me, you buffalo Lao fool,' he snapped, his face flushing redder, his eyes wide open like a devil. He scowled at Chao Anouvong and stamped his foot. He then leant forwards and pressed his clenched hands on the table. 'My king (*Nai Luang*) is no fool. He is highly revered. He is a god!' Suphawady exclaimed. 'No one can speak ill of him on pain of prison or death. His Majesty can do anything.' He leant back in his chair, throwing his arms in the air. 'He can do whatever he wants with a stupid, crazy fool like you!'

'Phraya Suphawady, you surprise me,' retorted Chao Anouvong. 'You seem a thoroughly decent fellow who conducts himself well, but that was an ugly and uncivilised remark. I'd never have imagined a gentleman like you could utter such foul words. It goes to show that it's impossible to have good looks, brains and eloquence, all at the same time. As they say, blood is thicker than water. You're cheerful enough when you sing your king's praises, not really because he's so wonderful but to save your own neck. You'll find out soon enough what sort of man he is. You and your officials, if you have a shred of conscience, please implore Bangkok to uphold the independence of Lao LanXang. Nangklao may look as handsome as a god in his golden cloak but he's certainly not immune from old age and will die like anyone else. You, if I might say so, present a very distinguished exterior, but you behave like a dolt and you've vexed us with your inept comments. You don't even know your country's history is a forgery, fabricated to present a view of events favourable only to Bangkok. It does you no good when you stir people into a fury with your Siamese superiority complex. I won't deny that all the misfortunes and hardships we've endured in our struggle weigh heavily upon me. Nevertheless, we will continue to struggle for our territory and independence.'

The room went completely quiet. I held my breath. With a blacker look than I'd ever seen before, Chao Anouvong leant forward.

'Now Phraya Suphawady, please do me a favour. Don't be "Siamese" to me or to anyone else. Enough of that! There's no need to be disrespectful; kindly spare me your insults and malice, your hard words and your threats of violence. It will only add fuel to our anger, so please listen to what I have to say.' After a pause he said, 'Peaceful LanXang, as you Siamese should know, is a land of elephants, buffaloes and rice: not sheep, goats, wheat and barley. It has rivers, timber and paddy fields; not oceans, mangroves and sandy beaches like Siam: the land of women and wine. You may sneer at us, but that's how we differ from our neighbours. LanXang is by no mean a poor country; we're just lagging behind slightly in development, perhaps. She's rich in natural resources and yields rich crops in their due seasons. Our food isn't scanty, our garments are silky smooth, our drink comes from natural streams and wells and when we sleep we rest our tired limbs on firm mats. Now, when you attend a banquet in your king's palace and talk turns to the achievements of the Lao people, please be kind enough to tell your noble, influential guests and colleagues that we too have had a fair degree of success over the years.'

'As a matter of fact, Phraya Suphawady,' he pressed on, awe-inspiringly, 'the Lao character and identity have, over time, been moulded by our mountains, valleys, forests and rivers. Our environment has allowed us to play a major role in one of the world's favourite pastimes: relaxation. We might be poor, but we're also free. You may marvel at our easy-going attitude, humour and contentment; to be fair, they're not beyond criticism. But you're only speaking the truth when you say that the Lao are more laid-back – although not necessarily lazier – than their neighbours. It is a deeper part of our personality than you might think. Furthermore, we take constant delight in peaceful co-existence with nature, a friendly smile, parties, banquets of non-fried food, the tuneful *Khaen* and *Phin*, songs, circle dances, literature, poetry, almsgiving to make merit, wallowing in cool, clear rivers and streams and sleeping happily in our comfortable beds.'

'Besides, Phraya Suphawady, we don't waste time being impolite and we therefore avoid war,' he continued after taking a sip of water. 'Your words haven't really offended me and I'm not demanding an apology for your discourtesy. But frankly you and your regime in Bangkok seem to take great satisfaction in provoking us. We've always tried to get on with you, not only because we respect the laws that Khoun Borom passed down to us all, but because we respect you as brothers. And still you arrogantly turn your noses up at us! For now, may I remind you that you're not an invited guest in LanXang? You're here because of your king's mistaken fantasy of conquering other countries, and his misguided belief we pose a threat to him. This is totally unacceptable, but I insist we talk in a civilised manner for the sake of peace and reconciliation. Now, please tell me honestly, what has King Nangklao decided to do about LanXang and me?'

'Very well, I'll tell you,' Suphawady scowled, adding, 'His Majesty is eagerly awaiting your letter of apology begging his pardon and promising to always obey him. Failing that, the consequences will be extremely unpleasant.' He sat back in his seat, smirking.

'Have you finished?' asked Chao Anouvong coolly.

'No, not quite,' Suphawady said menacingly, leaning forwards with one arm across the table and staring at Chao Anouvong. 'I have the king's order and I can tell you that if you don't comply, he'll put you all to the sword.' Suphawady snarled, showing his yellow teeth, and warned, 'I will no longer be able to guarantee you and your family's safety.'

'Then, please listen to me,' Chao Anouvong retorted, still trying to speak calmly but feeling he'd been reprimanded. He sat up, put his arms on the table and stared back at Suphawady. 'Phraya Suphawady, I do believe you Siamese want to torture me and cut my throat; you're very thirsty for my blood. Perhaps you intend to finish me off with poison. You should know we don't tolerate any encroachment on our territory. LanXang was a peaceful, independent country, but you Siamese under Phraya Kasatseuk invaded us in 1779, destroyed our temples and cities, looted our treasures and took me as a hostage. Remember?' Suphawady blinked in puzzlement. 'Now you want to repay King Xay-Setthathirath's loyalty by stealing his three revered Buddha statues: Phra Serm, Phra Suk and Phra Sai. You've not only broken our faith but placed a burden on us that we want to be rid of. Mind you, we have no quarrel with you personally. It's your king in Bangkok devoting his days to oppression who really stirs our resentment. All this time, despite promising to safeguard our rights, you've plundered LanXang and dominated her people. But now they're wise enough to know what really happened. They won't rest until they've let hell loose upon you. The truth is, Suphawady, we didn't invade Siam. We crossed the Khorat Plateau – our land, not yours – to Khorat city, in the interest of our peoples. What harm have you Siamese ever suffered at our hands that you now harass, plunder, brand and torture us so brutally? What pleasure can your king get out of seeing people being torn to pieces by his own ambition? We ask you: have you no shame? Where's your conscience?'

Phraya Suphawady, already sweating with anxiety, flushed even redder and started to stammer, as if he hadn't even heard of the 1779 invasion. He'd been taught that the Lao had sent an army into Siam. The Siamese had resented the Lao ever since.

Chao Anouvong cast his eyes to heaven, threw up his hands and sat back in disbelief. 'Come now Phraya Suphawady, you must know about it. It wasn't that long ago. For your information, the Emerald Buddha was taken away to Bangkok and ViengChan was burned to the ground! You're young enough to be my son; it seems they don't teach proper history in Siamese schools. It's about time they did because it will set all of you free. Surely your government can't be lying to you?! Or perhaps you're deliberately refusing to admit you were indoctrinated as a child. Your misguided beliefs are insulting to all Lao people. Shame on you!'

Phraya Suphawady listened attentively and didn't respond immediately. He looked terribly embarrassed and squirmed in his chair as if showing remorse.

'Well then, King Nangklao himself, if king he is, is the grandson of Phraya Kasatseuk. He must know the truth,' Chao Anouvong exclaimed. He warned that he wouldn't be the last Laoman to lead the fight for the rights and identity of the Lao nation.

A sudden change came over Suphawady. He looked pale, stopped fidgeting and went completely quiet. At that moment he realised he'd been in denial all his life.

'Phraya Suphawady,' Chao Anouvong continued crossly, 'You must understand that my countrymen would be ashamed of me if I went into exile. If your king has any shame, then he should return the Emerald Buddha, respect the 1563 That Si-SongHuck demarcation treaty and order his men to quit LanXang. I will personally send a formal letter apologising to him, and you must send one confirming the withdrawal of your troops. LanXang never asked his grandfather to wage a bitter war of occupation against us, and we're not asking now. But if you're here as friends or brothers, then we must ask you to respect Khoun Borom's laws and not interfere in our affairs. It would be dishonourable for you to stay in a city your king intended to obliterate. You should go back to where you belong and stay there, and never cross the frontier at Khorat city again, otherwise we'll pray to the immortal gods for a day of reckoning. We don't want to be part of Siam. There is so much land under the heavens. If building an empire is your ultimate goal, then look elsewhere and leave LanNa and LanXang alone. We can then empty the bitterness from our hearts. We prefer death to servitude. If the Lao people lose LanXang, I promise you disgrace will fall upon the kingdom of Siam. I call our Vietnamese friends as witnesses to this agreement. If you break it we'll accuse Siam of the illegal occupation of our lands, and demand justice.'

There was a long silence, with only the flies buzzing about. The Siamese delegation, although still smirking in victory, were lost for words. Rathsavong Ngao stood quietly in the background, turning to his father and nodding in support. Chao Anouvong rose from his chair a little and said in an unsettling manner, 'May I please ask you one last thing?'

'Go ahead. Ask anything you like,' said Suphawady, sitting back in his chair.

'Did my viceroy Tissah reply to the letter you wrote to him at Souvannaphum?'

'I didn't expect it, but yes, he did,' replied Suphawady. 'I was surprised, of course. In fact I can show it to you now if you wish.' Suphawady reached into his pocket and handed over the letter with a sneaky grin. 'And you can keep it. As far as we're concerned, it has served its purpose.'

Chao Anouvong nodded and read it with a stunned expression on his face. He gestured to me to have a look.

From: Viceroy Tissah.
To: Phraya Suphawady.

My feelings for you as a friend are the same. No apology is necessary. I shall move north to NongHan forthwith to pave the way for your easy advance. As for the reward I will count on you.

After so many harsh words the two sides were beginning to feel tired: as was I. Eventually, at least some of the negotiations were successful. Under the Vietnamese envoys' patient eyes, Chao Anouvong gave a symbolic nod of acceptance. Rathsavong Ngao looked angry and moved quickly to guard the rear as Chao Anouvong slapped his hands on the armrests of his chair to signal the end of the meeting.

'Tell me one thing,' Suphawady said suddenly. 'It makes no difference, but His Majesty our king would like to know. Would you really attack Bangkok and destroy it?'

'Well now, that's an interesting question,' Chao Anouvong said, stroking his chin and looking Phraya Suphawady in the eyes. 'Let me tell you that Lao patriotism is alive and kicking. Recently it has become more warlike. However, as I said, it wasn't ever our plan to raise our flag over Bangkok or anywhere else in Siam. We're simply not interested. Unlike you, we respect other people's territory. We also respect Buddhist precepts: we have no wish to do anything sinful because we know the wheel will eventually turn full circle. Had we captured Bangkok, we would of course have taken back what belonged to us, but we wouldn't have touched your holy temples or pillaged your riches.' He paused, narrowing his eyes in thought. 'You Siamese should be ashamed of yourselves, for what you did to ViengChan. Your Rattanakosin rulers should have known better.'

Suphawady said nothing and sank back unapologetically in his chair. The room went silent. We quietly watched the Siamese officials gaze remorsefully downwards, twiddling their hands as if they were mortified, worried they would pay for their sins with some future disaster.

A moment later Chao Anouvong courteously thanked Suphawady for his part in honouring peace and guaranteeing his safety. He pushed himself up onto his feet, smiled and calmly proffered his hand. At first Suphawady hesitated but then stood up, bowed in reverence and extended his praying hands. Chao Anouvong took them warmly before slowly turning and walking out of the room, the smile fading from his face. We followed closely behind to deter any sudden attack and didn't look back. Once we were standing outside the temple perimeter, Rathsavong Ngao spoke first.

'What tyrants these Siamese are, but at least now we know Nangklao's price.'

'No, it isn't Nangklao's price… far from it,' Chao Anouvong said. 'He is an oppressor. He wants me dead. Bangkok will never give anything in return, however much we give them. They are planning a far greater and more heinous crime. They want to eliminate the Lao nation. By Lord Buddha and the gods, may they never succeed and end up destroying themselves instead.'

'What is Your Majesty going to do?' I interrupted anxiously.

'Well, Phia Jon, I'm afraid that if we beg Nangklao's pardon, I'll become his creature; if we send a letter accepting his terms, LanXang is finished; if we reject it out of hand, he'll hunt me – us – down. If I were captured he would torture me to death in Bangkok. Whatever we do, we lose. Right now, we must maintain our guard and return home safely.' My poor knees seemed to shake underneath me when I heard this. He raised his eyes to heaven and said, 'I thank the Lord Buddha for allowing me to live and to fight on.' We headed straight for the Mekong to cross back to ViengChan. The moment he settled in our boat he growled, 'What an utter villain Suphawady is… and that narcissistic man in Bangkok. Can you believe it?'

It was clear that under Bangkok's terms, LanXang's independence would be denied. Chao Anouvong was deeply disappointed, but he went on to say that not being arrested or killed by Suphawady made this the greatest day of his life: even more significant and exhilarating than when Nangklao allowed him to return to ViengChan in 1825.

Unfortunately, while still at PhanPhao, we learned from the loyal inhabitants that the Siamese commander-in-chief Bovon had built a memorial with an impertinent inscription aimed personally at Chao Anouvong, labelling him a traitor. We were furious. In their attempt to disgrace his name forever and to humiliate the Lao nation, the Siamese named the monument 'Quelling of the ViengChan Revolt'. This offensive inscription, which served as a warning against further revolt, was far from edifying and an insult to all the people of LanXang, who felt strongly they were innocent of treason against Siam's oppressive regime.

On his return to ViengChan, Chao Anouvong sank into the usual chair in his study. After a moment of contemplation he immediately ordered his army to surround the 300 Siamese troops stationed at Wat Kang Monastery. At sunset the Siamese, in their usual self-assured way, were enjoying themselves with drink and dinner. Here and there in the temple's courtyard, fires were lit to cook their food and the smoke drifting in the early evening heat added to the confusion. The Lao army moved in stealthily. The sound of gunfire and groaning men lasted for half an hour. Later I went with Prince Ngao and his bodyguards to inspect the aftermath. I counted twenty, fifty, a hundred bodies, perhaps more. I couldn't tell whether they were dead or merely injured but there was blood everywhere.

Somehow, forty Siamese soldiers managed to escape. They reported back to Suphawady, who was completely shocked at the news. Unable to decide on the best course of action, he held an emergency meeting with the other generals. After a fierce debate they decided it was impracticable to make a stand at PhanPhao city, while a retreat to the frontier city of Khorat was too far. Nangklao would most certainly punish them for their cowardice and their failure to annihilate ViengChan or capture Chao Anouvong. They somehow agreed to the renegade Lao commander Xiengsa's recommendation that Yasothon, closer to Bangkok than ViengChan, should be chosen. But Phraya Suphawady insisted on staying put until everything was ready. By mid-October the Siamese eventually retreated under the cover of darkness, slowly heading back towards Yasothon. ViengChan was in a state of readiness for Siamese retaliation. It was a very tense time.

Upon hearing that the Siamese had withdrawn from PhanPhao, Chao

Anouvong promptly ordered Prince Ngao and his robust men to cross the Mekong before dawn on 18 October to destroy the offensive monument before it became a festering wound that might never heal. Young Rathsavong Ngao, who was nursing his loathing against the Siamese for humiliating him and degrading his father, was out to exact revenge.

Rathsavong Ngao and his men returned to ViengChan the next afternoon, bringing the Phra Serm Buddha statue back with them. Ngao limped into the study and gave a full report to his concerned father. He blurted out the news that he'd almost succeeded in killing Suphawady. Having successfully destroyed the shine in the morning, Ngao had mounted his black velvet horse and headed off in pursuit. They eventually caught up with the Siamese army at Ban Bokwanh village, south of Nongkhai city, and plunged straight into a hand-to-hand battle. Racial taunts and recriminations and a roar of abuse and curses flew between the two sides. With Suphawady on the field, Rathsavong Ngao clearly had something to prove. From his battle-charger he called to his men in his rich and deep voice. 'Get Suphawady! Dead or alive.' His horse reared in panic and charged furiously into the thick of the enemy. Prince Ngao hurled his bronze-pointed spear on the off chance of hitting Suphawady and covering himself with glory. It hit the Siamese commander on his side, knocking him from his saddle. He crashed poleaxed to the ground.

The two sides were fighting hand-to-hand, steel hitting steel, hacking at each other. The battle-frenzied Ngao was like a jungle tiger who'd felled the best stag. Wanting to make sure his prey was dead, he turned quickly and charging back to finish Suphawady off. With his sword firmly in his hand he dismounted and dashed over to the Siamese commander, who was screaming and clutching at the shaft of the spear with both hands, his white uniform crimson with blood. When Suphawady's brother Phraya Phisit tried to intercept him, Ngao stabbed his exposed throat. Phisit reeled back, his bloodied fingers clawing at his windpipe. Rathsavong Ngao then turned his attention to Suphawady once more, but he went too far. His luck left him. A bullet hit him in the leg and he fell to the ground. 'Prince Ngao has been shot! Prince Ngao has been shot!' his men shouted, rushing in to save him and helping him to climb back onto his horse.

Meanwhile Suphawady, surrounded by his men, had the spear pulled from his ribs. He was in a fit of anger. He picked himself up, groaning, cursing and yelling at his men in his high, sharp voice. 'Catch Rathsavong Ngao! Take him alive!' His men screamed and rushed forward, falling, stumbling over each other, crashing into Suphawady and sending him sprawling to the ground. He pushed himself up with both hands before finding his feet and reeling like a drunk. His lungs full of dust, he roared at the top of his voice, 'I want him to be led in chains through Bangkok. Catch him! Catch him!'

The fighting continued but the Lao were outnumbered three to one. Despairing of victory, Rathsavong Ngao yelled to his men, 'Back to ViengChan if you wish to save your skins!' A Lao soldier fired a small bamboo rocket into the sky to signal the retreat. With the fear of death upon them, they dashed away in panic and escaped by the skin of their teeth. They spurred their horses and with a sigh of relief galloped away from the chasing enemy.

'Fortunately, father, we were too far away for them to give chase,' said Rathsavong Ngao. His bullet wound wasn't serious. He limped about now and then when he forgot not to, but soon stopped himself.

Chao Anouvong was relieved to have the prince back but showed no signs of pleasure at the news. His face was set. He nodded slowly, told his son he did well and then smiled grimly because he anticipated more fighting and he was certain the Siamese would come after them. After analysing the situation, he ordered his wounded son to hobble down to the Mekong and board a boat with his bodyguards. They paddled downstream, aiming for Mueang Mahaxay and Khamkheut.

Meanwhile, after receiving medical treatment, Suphawady rushed to ViengChan with 600 men. He thought of chasing after Chao Anouvong and Rathsavong Ngao to prevent them from escaping, but realising he'd be unable to catch them, he continued to loot and destroy ViengChan.

Strangely, there was no more trace of Rathsavong Ngao after that, I'm afraid. It was another cruel blow for me. He completely disappeared. All sorts of rumours swirled around: many believed he was dead or had gone underground with the rest of the Lao army to evade capture. I'd seen him in quite a different context, a credit not only to his father but to the whole country. He nobly and impartially rewarded and punished his men. He toiled the hardest and undertook the most, standing at the forefront of all the battles at Lomsak-Loei, where he fought the third Siamese army with great determination before withdrawing to regroup with the main troops on KhaoSan hill, the last bastion in NongBuaLamphu. In the final retreat he calmly marched back to ViengChan to set up a defence, only to find his father had left. He earned the respect of LanXang's elders and the admiration of the young. I assure you, had LanNa, Luang Phrabang and XiengKhuang supported ViengChan, and had Tissah's troops fought the Siamese at Souvannaphum, Lao history would have been very different – ViengChan would have held its head high and never suffered such a terrible fall. Mind you, the Siamese were simply brutal and had no respect for anything.

I was deeply concerned for the fate of those sons and daughters of Chao Anouvong who'd managed to escape. A darkness had descended over LanXang under Nangklao's shadow and the Siamese flag floating in the wind. Perhaps some friendly souls were keeping them safe and well somewhere in the vastness of the forests or in a safe house in a remote village. Who knows whether some day they, or perhaps their heirs and successors, may reappear. The struggle for LanXang unity is certain to continue.

Perhaps Rathsavong Ngao himself sought sanctuary in the temple as a monk. The Siamese authorities scoured the country in search of his whereabouts, but most people didn't even know who he was, let alone what he'd achieved in the war. I'm quite sure the Siamese death squads never stopped looking for him or anyone else connected with the ViengChan royal family. Rathsavong Ngao's fate remains wrapped up in utter mystery: no one knows whether he'd been captured, killed, or had fled into exile. I was as mystified as everyone else and prayed he hadn't committed suicide. I pleaded with people to tell the truth about his unhappy end, if by some faint chance they'd witnessed it or someone who had – all to no avail. I would have preferred to live in hardship and fight on rather than surrender and die a violent death, but let us speak no more of these cruel and painful matters.

XVI

Catastrophe

It was most distressing for me to see Chao Anouvong leaving the city for a second time, especially as it was only three months since I'd had the pleasure of welcoming him back to his beloved city. I was greatly honoured to renew my service to him but we didn't have much time to talk. Once Prince Ngao had gone safely on his way down the Mekong, the king prepared to leave. While we were strolling in the derelict palace garden, I told him that my dear mother had unexpectedly gone to a better world. I was enveloped by grief; I shunned all human company, hiding myself under the thick shade of the bamboo bushes, with only the cries of the birds to disturb my peace. He was very upset to hear it. With sadness, he patted me sympathetically on the shoulder and gave me his condolences. I welcomed them. He helped me to forget my sorrow. When we stopped and stood still in the shade, I turned to look at him with a sad smile and expressed my concern for his safety. He gave a sigh of resignation as if he were a broken man trying to reconcile himself to his fate.

'Phia Jon, my dear friend,' he whispered, both hands clutching my bony shoulders, 'I'm afraid we have to leave ViengChan again, and soon.' There was only one place he could go: Vietnam. The risk of being captured was now greater than before. A terrible realisation gripped me. The thought of his departure was bitter, but he'd to go. Perhaps not for the last time I was inclined to rely upon good fortune rather than give way to despair. I begged him to leave without delay but hoped I would see him again.

'I understand, but we must get you out of the city at once,' I said anxiously, adding that ViengChan belonged to the Siamese, and Suphawady the monster was in command.

He also saw the end was imminent. He'd given up the fight and decided to set off to Vietnam once more, to seek refuge with Emperor Minh Mang,

Nangklao's enemy in the east. He didn't intend to live in exile permanently: his temperament wasn't really equipped for it. To thrive and to be happy he needed to be in ViengChan, surrounded by the people: family, friends, Lao food, jokes, Lao music and songs, circle dances (*Fonh Lamvong*), singalongs, conversation, news, politics, books, writing poetry, Lao culture and beautiful temples. It was a terrible agony for him, but he simply had no other choice. He was always terribly wracked by homesickness.

After long and hard thinking and with a mixture of regret and a profound sense of duty, I again reluctantly told him I'd decided to stay behind: I wanted to witness what the Siamese would do next. It was an extremely sad time; we knew we might never see each other again. We stood close and just looked at each other, unable to utter a word, I knelt on one knee and lowered my head for him to touch. I dared not take his hand unbidden. He pulled me up and briefly held me a little closer as a father would with his son. For an instant I stood rigid, but soon softened and was glad to feel the strength of his arms. He broke the embrace and took a step back.

'Your Majesty, you mustn't linger,' I said with great urgency. 'The Siamese are coming!'

'Yes, I know. I'm planning as best I can,' he said. He was unsure which route to take. Siamese troops were patrolling the Mekong and it was too dangerous to sail down to Nakhorn Phanom, though a few armed loyal soldiers would at least give him some protection. When he saw how worried I was, he laid a reassuring hand on my arm. 'Phia Jon, I'm not afraid of death but there's so much I would like to do for LanXang,' he said solemnly, looking at the Mekong as if he were saying goodbye. 'We'll be all right. We'll be protected by robust, dependable armed men and we'll be gone by nightfall.' He paused. 'I know only too well how much they hate me in Siam, but it's probably not in Siam's interest for any harm to befall me. They want me alive not dead so they can make an entertainment out of torturing me to death in Bangkok.' I looked at him with grave concern; I suspected he was predicting his own fate but said nothing. 'Besides, Phia Jon,' he whispered, 'we're friends with the Vietnamese king, and what better guarantee of safe passage is there than travelling in our own kingdom? Let's think of you now. It distresses me to leave you behind with no prospects and I'll be at a loss without you. My time here is over for now, but you have important work to do. Moreover, you must keep our lines of communication open. I know our country is passing through the most strenuous times, but we'll come through them, as we always have. You have a serious responsibility, but please stay safe and alive to see the events in our city. You are one of the guardians of Thammalong – 'The Ring' – remember? No more despair. The Lao nation must not die with us.'

'Yes, I know. I'll make sure you won't regret your decision. Please ensure the armed guards are always with you. I shall pray I'll meet you again – if not in this life, then the next.' I knew he would rather have me with him but I understood what he meant. I said nothing further and walked away with a heavy heart to gather my belongings before bidding him farewell.

On this fateful day – 19 October 1828 – his second, fatal escape, Chao Anouvong clasped my shoulders and was unable to conceal his pain as he sighed from the depths of his heart, looking deeply into my eyes before saying his last farewell. His words resonate in my ears to this day.

'My dear Phia Jon,' he said solemnly, 'you are so dear to me, more a younger brother and a loyal best friend than my private secretary, and have been so ever since we sat and learned and discussed philosophy and shared jokes together at Nakhorn Phanom thirty-three years ago – do you remember?' He paused and turned his thoughts over in his mind.

'Yes, indeed. I remember it very well,' I said sentimentally. 'How could I forget?'

'Ah, I wish I were still as young and strong as I was then,' he continued. 'Now Phia Jon, you have remarkable intelligence and organising skills; your sense of loyalty is truly unrivalled. I trust you totally. I shall forever respect you as my confidant – my right-hand man in everything I do. My gratitude towards you cannot be expressed in words. Your services to the country and to me are incalculable, not only in ViengChan and the provinces but also in private and public affairs, in my study and in the library. You've been exceptional, you've been with me through thick and thin, through fire and water. Now we're at war with the Siamese and there's no time left for talking. I should have awarded you the honourable title of Lord (*Phraya*) before now, but there was always something else to distract me. So, let me tell you now that it has long been my ambition to give our people independence and liberty; yes, that simple life in our peaceful country that we've long desired. I see a day when we shall ride our elephants (*Xang*) over ViengChan to Nongkhai and down to Udon and Khon Kaen, visiting every province on the Khorat Plateau... all the way to Khorat city. We'll eat the same kind of food, speak the same Lao language, make merit in temples and sit under the mango trees in our people's gardens. And then, as we watch the sun go down, we'll listen to the subtle tune of the *Khaen* and quietly examine the kingdom's affairs together. This desire of mine, Phia Jon, is for the good of our nation, so let me make it very clear we've earned the right to fight for our freedom. I would never order you, or anyone else, to endanger yourself. Now, once again, I take my leave, but you must do whatever you think best.'

While he paused, I revealed I'd already pieced together my story about him and LanXang.

'Ah, how pleased I am to hear it. I hope Lao LanXang will be as proud of you as I am.' He put his hands on my shoulders and looked at me, as if for the last time, before finally saying, 'If and when we meet again, Phia Jon, the destiny of all of us Lao people of LanXang might have changed for ever. Like the sacred crystal ring (*Thammalong*) hidden in the cave, you must bring our true history out into the light, polish it and show it to the world. There's no need to worry when I'm gone. The younger generation will take over; there'll always be someone else. Just don't forget to keep reminding our people on both banks of the Mekong to love each other and believe in the unity of the Lao nation. We must always seek to unite our country.'

He turned to me after a short pause and said, 'Do please remember me whenever anyone, strangers, come to our land and ask of you, "Who is Anouvong?" Then tell them in a clear voice, 'He was a man of kindness and justice and his heroic struggle for the Lao nation against Rattanakosin Siam deserves recognition." And please recite my name, and then it'll be as if I'm always with you.'

How could anyone forget these words? Most people can quote them from memory. As for the Lao, they should always celebrate his fame.

By this time most people had left the city for the safety of the jungle or elsewhere. Only a few people and animals were left. ViengChan was like a ghost city. The escape was planned for nightfall. As the sun began to splash the west with red and turn the Mekong gold, and a shadow was cast over That Luang hill, I looked down sadly and bade farewell to the king.

'Your Majesty, our parting desperately saddens me, but I must take my leave of you,' I said and begged him to go.

'Just a moment, Phia Jon,' he called and came towards me as I was about to leave for the last time. 'You've been a faithful servant of LanXang – loyal and true. You're a prince among men. In accordance with heaven's will you deserve to be marked with honour. I bestow on you forthwith the title of *Phraya* (Lord),' he said. I instantly went down on one knee and lowered my head. He gave me a tap on the shoulder and told me to rise. 'More importantly, there will always be a place in my heart for you, Phraya Jon. For a keepsake I give you this handsome silver cup with its rim of gold round the top, to remind you of me all your life whenever you make libations or drink offerings to the Lord Buddha and the other gods.'

'Your Majesty's kindness to me is as great as PhouBia Mountain,' I said, 'but I dare not accept such an honour.' Without him beside me, it meant nothing.

'And one last thing,' he said, 'let future generations mock and condemn me for my failures as they please, but they must stay optimistic for LanXang's future. I may have lost but we can still win in the future. Bangkok will condemn me, but please remember to tell the truth to the world about our LanXang and about me; but try not to portray me as a saint.'

Those were his final words to me. I made my pledge, turned and walked away with a heavy heart. I knew he hadn't moved so I raised my hand in acknowledgement and farewell but didn't look back. Clutching my personal belongings, I strode across the rubble-strewn courtyard and through the palace's main Luang Gate (*Patu Luang*) and out of the inner-city wall in the direction of my late mother's house. Halfway there I had a disturbing feeling that I would never see him alive in ViengChan again. For how could I, or Chao Anouvong himself for that matter, know the Siamese wouldn't capture him or obliterate the city again? I turned round and walked back quickly, breaking into a run towards the Luang Gate facing the Wat Sisaketh temple, in the hope I would glimpse him one last time. I discreetly stayed out of sight behind the library pavilion (*Hor Tay*) which he'd built in 1813 to house the *Tripikata* (the sacred canon of Buddhism). With my heart thumping, I waited anxiously and said a prayer for him.

After a while there was a clatter of hooves as the horses started to move. I held my breath and a moment later the gate was flung open and I watched him coming through in a plain, open carriage. He turned and took a last look around as if saying farewell to the badly damaged Hor Phra Kaeo, the palace and everything in it. Then he draped his head with a fine blue-and-white checked cotton cloth to avoid being recognised, more by the enemy than by the crowd. But I'm certain he took it off once he left the city, upset to be leaving ViengChan again. A guard sat at the front next to the driver while he and his family sat in the back. The carriage sped out into the street, but instead of heading south towards the That Luang stupa and on to the ancient escape route to Mueang Mahaxay, it turned north towards the Khua Luang Bridge over the Pasak river, joining the stream of people leaving the city for the safety of the forest. I knew at once he was heading for XiengKhuang, where he'd set up his headquarters before returning to ViengChan previously. The sound of galloping horses faded and then, as his carriage was almost out of sight, I ran after him in desperation until I could go no further. With my lungs bursting, I stopped to recover and held on to a huge, ancient *Dork Champa* tree, its roots embedded underneath an enormous rock as if they'd started life together. My eyes were wet with tears of anguish. The fast-setting sun was still hot, beating down on my back. My head was confused, awhirl with conflicting thoughts and anxiety. I tried to imagine life without him. Searching for guidance, I heard two commanding voices. *You must follow him.* I wanted to. I was responsible for him. *You must stay behind.* I had to. I'd promised to witness the fall of ViengChan. Recognising my fate, I decided on the latter.

I shook my head in disbelief and was left in perplexity and distress, in a state of utter shock that I was still in ViengChan, and he'd gone. I was no longer part of his life and might never see him again and stood staring at his fast-disappearing carriage. 'Farewell Chao Anouvong, my friend, my king,' I muttered solemnly. 'Oh, Lao LanXang, why couldn't you unite to protect those who love you?' My eyes blurred with tears, I hastened to a forested hill north of the city for safety from where I looked back mournfully at ViengChan. The smoke rising in the distance filled my mind with solemn thoughts.

All his family members who didn't accompany him, including his sons Princes Poh, Ban and Teh and his daughter Nang Khamvan were taken prisoner and sent to Bangkok on 23 October 1828. I wondered what became of them. Perhaps they'd forgotten their roots and fallen under their conqueror's sway.

I walked around the edge of the forbidding forest and peered in, listening to the birds and the wind rustling the trees, sniffing at the invigorating smell of wildflowers. I contemplated the wide expanse of deserted paddy fields and felt utterly isolated. I wondered whether I should have gone with the king. Perhaps I should have gone to ground in ViengChan, but then I would be living in fear and trembling every time there was a bang at the gate.

Perhaps I really should have gone after him, but I would almost certainly have been captured by the Siamese and met my end without anyone else knowing about it. Even if I dared paddle down the treacherous shallow stretches of water along the meanders of the river, my boat would most certainly have crashed against the rocks and sunk, carrying me to my death in the vast flowing, dark depths. Besides, I have a lasting fear of deep, mucky water.

I could recall an occasion when I was with him in 1796 and the bow of our boat came close to being smashed against the rocks by the fury of the river, rising and crashing down and soaking us. It wasn't easy to fight our way down between rocks against the turbulent, white water. My oar was torn from my hands. Had we been tossed off the boat, all our bones would have been broken and we would have come to a terrible end. The hull began to fill and our vessel sank dangerously low in the water. With the fear of death upon us, I frantically scooped up the water with a wooden bucket and tipped it over the side to stop us sinking; only then did we find deliverance.

Feeling marooned, I took counsel with my indomitable soul and asked myself with a groan what I should do. I decided it was too dangerous to follow him: I would never reach him alive. All I could do was stay alive and put up with the discomfort and distress. I was drawn to the gentle light of sunrise and sunset, the tall trees, the sweet melody of birdsong, the breath of cool, fresh air and fleeting meals of wild fruits, nuts and vegetables. I patiently stayed hidden in the jungle, roaming for food like a shy deer, feeding ravenously on whatever I could find. I passed each day practising transcendental meditation in absolute silence, my nerves jangling amongst the strange sounds of nature. I realised that a forest without its wild animals and birds was like a city without its people. Like most of the population, I sheltered high up in the trees and went to sleep as soon as the sun set.

It seemed that Phraya Sanon's prophetic dream had come true: ViengChan was besieged, with most of its inhabitants fleeing to the forested hills and mountains and looking back in shock at the city in flames, an immense red glow and smoke in the sky. It made them weep to see it.

It was during this time, towards the end of October 1828, Buddhist Lent, when monks are confined to their temples, that ViengChan was completely reduced to ashes. In the name of Nangklao – a Buddhist – a terrible vengeance was wreaked on the heart of LanXang. Under Suphawady's command the vengeful invaders spread over the city, frenzied and wild-eyed armies with yellow ribbons on their arms, seething with arrogance and loathing. They scattered through the streets leaving ruin in their wake. Armed with guns and swords and purple with drink and fury, they shouted orders at groups of terrified, kneeling inhabitants, who looked as though the air had been sucked from their lungs, forcing them to destroy their own city.

The victorious Suphawady and his officials behaved as if they were the city's new owners, without regard for human life. They slaughtered the fat livestock by the Mekong to hold a feast, sitting in luxury celebrating and enjoying the spoils of their victory, caring no more for the people than they feared the baleful eyes of the gods. Many drank themselves into unconsciousness and fell asleep under the trees. Most of them bragged of the campaign, of the women they'd raped and the temples they'd looted. Alcohol exacerbated their audacity and aggression. Their revenge was blind and their anger was irrational. They pelted the inhabitants with bones from their feast. They bayed for vengeance and threatened to kill anyone who refused to acknowledge portraits of their king they'd set up at various junctions. The Lao public looked on resignedly, silently condemning their conduct. Those less tolerant felt utter revulsion.

Soon after nightfall, the glow of fires wavered throughout the city. Clouds of smoke obscured the moon and the stars. Dogs ran around in panic, barking in anger and howling in distress at the sound of the thundering war drums. Violent bangs echoed on the inhabitants' gates and doors; the invaders smashed their way in through the wooden doors and began to plunder. They took all LanXang's finest treasures and loaded their carts with indiscriminate loot. With booze in their heads and torches in their hands, they set fire to the holy temples and beautiful timber houses and anything else that was left standing, as if Nangklao had ordered the total social and political annihilation of the city. They dragged out desks, tables, sofas, chairs and stools and threw them onto a great pyre. For their final act of vandalism, and much to my horror, they also carried out chests full of books (*Bai Larn*) and most were burnt. I felt as if they'd taken away our soul. It was sickening. I watched on with utter hopelessness and disbelief while the population grieved and the city went up in flames. The noise of their crying, wailing and screaming crawled and surged in my blood like a fever. It disturbed my sleep for months. I can still hear it now.

The burning of ViengChan filled the night sky with a red glow, turning the giant, full moon into a gold coin and the Mother Mekong into a river of fire. The mighty orange flames and scraps of burning books and leaves whirled against the sky. The wind sent the smoke high, filling the heavens like a volcanic eruption, lifting, twisting and rising across the face of the moon, casting dark shadows on the ground like ghosts. The animals – dogs, cats, pigs, monkeys, gibbons, squirrels, lizards, bats, birds and insects – took fright and tried to escape as the fire raged across the city. A fountain of black smoke and the scattering dust and ashes lingered over ViengChan for many days, weeks even, until the rain came and washed them away. Most of the population had long since disappeared into the nearby forest like ants. The jungle rumbled and shook at their cries of grief.

It was a catastrophe. Once renowned for its magnificence and beauty, ancient ViengChan was left with absolutely nothing; all had been reduced to dust, a scene of destruction and ruin by the time the Siamese left at the end of 1828. Other important relics – such as That Phanom's gold-and-gem encrusted summit – were also destroyed; the Siamese pretended to despise Lao workmanship and thus all concealed treasures were looted. If the full details of the fall of ViengChan ever becomes more widely known, it will surely rank as Siam's foulest deed.

The Siamese army moved quickly through LanXang, burning and destroying rebellious towns and villages. Supplicants were sometimes spared but irritated by his failure to capture Chao Anouvong and his own painful wound, Suphawady had become more savage.

The Lao people, especially those on the Khorat Plateau, had risen in revolt because they were in fear of their lives. Some hard-line groups took to the forest and offered guerrilla-style resistance, a holy vendetta in which they relied on their knowledge of poisoned arrows to kill the enemy. Those who gave themselves up were taken as slaves, but many fought to the death. However, the Siamese ended Lao resistance by killing all the leaders and obliterating all troublesome communities. No one could escape the long arm of Siamese revenge. Amiable and ill-equipped Lao patriots were massacred; captives were treated brutally. No mercy or forgiveness was shown.

The best Lao word to describe the Lao people's feelings after all this horror is probably *Khiad* ຂຽດ, which means both 'insult' and 'resentment'. Chao Anouvong was the embodiment of it.

Rattanakosin Siam achieved the destruction of ViengChan and struck a chord of terror in the hearts of the Lao people. Nangklao would forever be remembered as an oppressive ruler and these disgraceful events would stick to his name forever. He became the most feared and hated figure of his time, but in the depths of his villainy he condemned not only himself but the entire Siamese race for all time to come, earning them the everlasting enmity of the Lao people. A defeated LanXang awaited its fate.

The Lao, who'd never feared anything or anyone, now faced two terrible prospects: losing their national identity and becoming Siamese. Their dreams of freedom had gone, but in their endless optimism they still believed it would come true. Nevertheless, the seeds of bitterness had been truly sown, and the bad blood grew. The Lao would never fully forgive or trust the Siamese government again.

For a long time, there was no news of Chao Anouvong: hardly surprising, as his escape route was remote and almost inaccessible. I worried myself to death imagining he and his family struggling through narrow jungle paths while the Siamese raced to catch him.

The exact direction he took was a mystery. I later discovered that he planned initially to reach XiengKhuang and then move on to Nhge Anh in Vietnam. He didn't get far. Left to his own devices, he took the usual escape route north, travelling towards Ban NaNga and Ban Hai before heading for XiengKhuang. They had plenty of provisions but crossing the Annamite range – a cultural and a territorial border – to reach Vietnam would take some time. After nearly a month of marching and resting, he reached a cave at the foot of PhouBia Mountain, where his company camped. It was here that he was unable to escape the dragnet and his luck ran out. His fate was sealed by two separate acts of treason.

Initially, Chao Anouvong's son-in-law (Princess Kham's husband), Chao Noi of XiengKhuang, obeyed his orders, but the Siamese stratagem of daily arrests and killings finally broke his will. He made a deal with the Siamese in VppiengChan, agreeing to block the king's escape route in return for his people's lives and his city being spared from destruction. He sent fifty men to surround Chao Anouvong before rushing a report back to Suphawady in ViengChan revealing his father-in-law's hiding place. King Nangklao ordered Suphawady to spare no effort in capturing him dead or alive. He hurriedly dispatched Phraya Intharadeth with 300 conscripts from LanNa in hot pursuit, for a severed head alone might not be enough to convince Nangklao that Chao Anouvong had been killed.

At the same time, Manthathurath of Luang Phrabang, who'd refrained from supporting Chao Anouvong's crusade, also agreed to play his part to spare his people and city from Siamese brutality. It was not without shame and regret that he sent his representative Phraya Mahaphom to assist in the hunt.

Chao Anouvong was trapped. After tense negotiations during the night, while bats circled and flew in and out of the cave's narrow ledges, he simply couldn't persuade Phraya Mahaphom to let him go. He'd no choice but to surrender. Suphawady would have been severely punished if he'd let Chao Anouvong escape to Vietnam, and the top honours would have belonged to Emperor Minh Mang.

When Chao Anouvong struggled to his feet and emerged from hiding, he was not only calm but serene. He stepped out of the cave into the dawning light and stared at the rising sun. There was a glow in his eyes, as if he'd received enlightenment. As far as he was concerned, he'd followed his conscience and was at peace. He understood and was fully resigned to his fate. Although his bodyguards were ready to fight and die, he ordered them to stand down. If blood needed to be shed, it should be his alone. They gave him a look of agonised incomprehension but obediently dropped their weapons. He praised and thanked them for their devotion. He was compelled by his adversaries to go to Bangkok and face Nangklao, but before he departed, he called upon those Lao nobles present to act as witnesses so Bangkok would be held accountable for its actions. After making offerings and pouring libations he said: 'Please tell the people that Chao Anouvong died because he was deceived by the Siamese, not because his own countrymen betrayed him. If this should be my fate, then I will die without remorse.' Those were his words.

I must tell you I was heartbroken and shed tears of anguish when I first heard about this. The cave was renamed 'Chao Anouvong's Cave' in his honour.

Phraya Mahaphom brought him, together with other members of his family, down to Hat Duei, where they were handed over to Phraya Intharadeth. They were escorted back to ViengChan and presented to a triumphant Suphawady on 21 December 1828. Chao Anouvong presented himself with dignity. Suphawady ordered 300 men to escort them down the Siamese capital without delay in a common transport cart. The people stared after him, unbelieving, helpless and dumb. Suphawady's achievement was incomparable.

Meanwhile Emperor Minh Mang, after sending a message of explanation on Chao Anouvong's behalf to Nangklao in Bangkok, did nothing to assist his escape. Nevertheless, once news of his capture reached Hue, he went ballistic.

For his cowardice and thoughtless, petty ambitions, Chao Noi was arrested and taken to Vietnam and later executed in January 1830. Determined to make his feelings known, Minh Mang later sent two messages to Nangklao in October and December 1829. A bitter war began between Siam and Vietnam over LanXang, as Chao Anouvong had predicted. But the Vietnamese tactic in 1833 of establishing a military base in the area of the Bangfai and Banghiang rivers opposite Nakhorn Phanom as a decoy came too late. The Siamese had already cut the Vietnamese supply routes by burning towns and villages, leaving the people starving, homeless and desolate. The war was to last until the age of western colonisation.

Upon arriving in ViengChan after his tireless, eventful march from Mukdahan, Phraya Sanon was devastated by the news that Chao Anouvong had been captured and sent down to Bangkok. He realised the king hadn't sent a sealed letter to ask him to come to ViengChan after all. He refused to dwell on such sad and heart-breaking news but was determined to lead his trusted veterans to rescue his friend. After he'd shed manly tears, he jumped on his horse and set off in the hope he might catch up with the king. They were born apart but were like partners in death. Phraya Sanon had committed himself to King Anouvong's fate: if the king were to die in a strange land, he would perform his final rites and die with him if need be. Their fate was bound together like blood running through the same veins.

Unfortunately, Phraya Sanon's luck deserted him. After many nights and days he arrived in Bangkok, searching desperately for Chao Anouvong and hoping he was still alive. Alas, in his desperation, he made no attempt to evade arrest himself. He was captured and told that his friend and king was already dead. It was too late. The frail and devastated Phraya Sanon was held in custody and suffered the same fate as Chao Anouvong.

For me, this was an apocalyptic period in LanXang's history and in my life. Losing Chao Anouvong was devastating; I emitted a wail of grief when I heard the news of his capture. My mind was in turmoil, my knees shook and my heart grew faint. I collapsed and sat broken hearted under a shady tree and wept as if I had no further use for life. It seemed as if he stood before me day and night. To think that he, once my refuge in trouble, should now be so tormented! I didn't care who'd captured him, but the news came as a terrible shock. By now I'd built a simple tree house for myself on the high ground and stayed most of the time hiding out of reach, nosing around for food in the forest. I spread a thin reed mat over a humble bed of fallen leaves and lay there in misery, nursing my grief and yearning to see him alive. The war had robbed me of my comfort, but I lived and survived mostly on wild fruit and vegetables. Separation from him was an unbearable hardship, but not beyond endurance. Although the forest was my fortress, I lived in constant fear of tigers, black bears and snakes and being discovered by the Siamese. My provisions were beginning to run dangerously low and I was unable to think properly. I panicked and began to see things: day as night, elephant as pig, bird as mosquito and green as yellow. I muttered to myself in the hot, humid air. When I grew tired of tears, I began to walk about in a blind panic, but I no longer feared for my own life. As a loyal confidant of Chao Anouvong, I simply couldn't watch from afar. I had to follow him to smelly Bangkok in the hope I might hear rumours about him, even if it meant dying a terrible death myself.

After hurriedly packing my shoulder bag with a small pumpkin flask of water, steamed sticky rice, salt, pre-cooked dried buffalo meat and chilli paste, I tied a rather old but fine blue-and-white-checked sash round my waist. Without it I would have looked too Siamese: one should never look like a foreigner in one's own country. Then I picked up my sandals, bound them on my feet and grabbed the solid black walking stick with a silver cap on both ends that Chao Anouvong had given me as a parting present. I jumped on my lean old horse and headed off at a canter. I could feel its bones through the saddlecloth. Soon after, I gave him a flick of the whip to urge him on. I rode out past the haunted ruins of ViengChan before galloping at speed and then crossing the Mekong to Nongkhai and ghosting into the wide plain of Khorat. I was no horseman and I believe I unkindly cracked my whip rather too harshly and too often as I galloped after him. Shocked at this, he would have reprimanded me.

I'd never travelled so far on my own. I feared drowning less than being arrested and tortured by the Siamese, but I was truly afraid of the unfamiliar territory of the thick, forbidding forest (*Pa Himmapanh*) full of wild beasts at night. Most wild animals depend on the acuteness of their nose or tongue for their safety or sustenance. I was also conscious that a big, rapacious python that could easily have slithered over the forest floor undetected and attacked me while I was asleep, constricting and asphyxiating and then swallowing me whole. At night the jungle was full of dangerous animals: tigers, and venomous snakes such as cobras; it was clearly no place for a lonely, faint-hearted old man. The growling of the tigers in the forests of the night made my hairs stand up and tingle on my neck and arms. At fifty-three, my tired, ageing body was even older in spirit, and sometimes everything seemed colourless and unimportant. I thought of death: from a snakebite or being eaten by a tiger while resting in the jungle. My horse was unused to small, narrow bridges and jibbed vigorously whenever he'd to cross one. I could only get him across by pulling him. Many days passed with scant food and I survived mostly on fruit. Each day I made drink offerings, poured libations and started my journey at dawn; instead of breakfast I ate a sparse early lunch and a light supper, and following it with a prayer for my own safety and for Chao Anouvong before going to sleep.

For first time ever, I had no official business to concern myself with. I relinquished all aspirations for worldly personal gain. There was nothing in the world I was reluctant to part with. I've always trained my mind to try to abstain from trivial attachments. In fact, since the fall of ViengChan, I'd been consuming only plain food and clothing myself simply and devoting myself to the task of staying alive. I kept my mind solely on Chao Anouvong as I gazed at the tranquil landscape with its coconut trees, paddy fields and buffalo herds; the villages and towns with their temples and houses. I made no attempt to contact him and always tried to stay out of sight. I constantly reminded myself not to take any risks; during our final farewell he'd ordered me to stay alive to reveal his story – to bring the ring (*Thammalong*) out of the cave. I feared the worst for him and was almost in a state of mourning, but I had to think of future generations. He was surely surrounded by armed guards: it would be impossible to see him, even from a distance, without risking my own life. Fortunately I had plenty of help on the way in terms of transport, food, water and accommodation in temples. The people were still more than willing to help Chao Anouvong's cause.

North of Khon Kaen city I stayed the night in the guest quarter (*Sala*) of the temple, and slept very deeply despite my anxieties, such was my tiredness. I learned from the chief monk that the city's nobles had been forcibly scattered to other parts of Siam to prevent them waging war on Bangkok. I continued my journey at dawn and went past the odd group of Siamese soldiers standing idly in the shade, yawning and joking amongst themselves, but they made no attempt to stop me or ask my business. Sighing with relief, I rode on, up and down the hills, at a gallop most of the way. I fell off a few times but without damaging much more than my pride. Alas, soon after, my poor horse, as luck would have it, became ill and ran out of wind. I reluctantly gave him away in exchange for some provisions and continued my journey on foot, which slowed my pace considerably. At one point luck deserted me again: after losing my footing I fell down a steep, hilly slope, tumbling over some rocks, I was bruised black and blue and covered with bloody grazes. With a swollen foot which could hardly bear my weight, I tried to get along using my stick, occasionally sitting down on a fallen tree trunk for a break. Sometimes, in my anxiety to get to Bangkok, I barely rested. I was utterly exhausted and extremely worried that my allotted time might soon expire.

I have always been sensitive to the charm of handsome, giant forest trees that look like homes to nature spirits. Whenever the sun was going down and with no settlement in sight, I selected and took refuge under a giant, forbidden tree that seemed to have the physical characteristics of a mysterious being, very intimidating with its enormous roots and straight, towering trunk, but the grandeur of it smote my heart. I made drink offerings to the Lord Buddha and poured libations from the silver cup that Chao Anouvong had given me as a memento. I called upon the guardian of the tree and the ancestors' spirits (*Phi Fah* and *Phi Thaen*) for protection. Then I prayed, 'Please hear me, noble tree that men respect. You are the pillar and the framework of my roof, the bed in which I sleep, the warmth in the cold night and the flower of beauty. Under your closely intertwined majestic branches and thick green leaves high above, I find shelter from the burning sun. Take pity on me. Do not rebuff me, a poor soul who seeks the sanctuary of your handsome trunk for the night.' I was too exhausted by my journey to notice anything else. I bent my knees and sturdy arms and crept into a gap between the exposed roots and made up a bed of leaves. I was overwhelmed with exhaustion and anxiety gnawed at my heart; I was too weak to stir and wondered whether I might become a meal for wild beasts of prey. There I lay in a state of delectable hibernation, conquered by sleep through the wretched, moonless night.

Yet before the pink glow in the sky gave rise to a sunny day, I came to life. I waited for the blessed light of day and reflected on my dreams. I'd dreamt I was in a land of savage Siamese tribes, but the growls echoed in my ears as if tigers were prowling nearby. I knew I was far from any help. I quickly rose from my leafy bed, made drink offerings, threw my feeble arms to thankfully embrace the tree trunk and gave it a farewell kiss.

Fortunately, groups of travellers with a pony and trap or ox cart, seeing an elderly man struggling along, often kindly offered me a lift. I would gladly accept it but simply sat with my chin in my hand, staring at the passing country, retracing the same route along which Chao Anouvong had been transported. I gave them my heartfelt thanks, blessing them like a holy man when they dropped me off and put me back on the path.

Once, a friendly dog took pity on me, not barking at me but greeting me with his tail wagging. I threw a ball of sticky rice to the poor, scruffy creature. It took a stranger as its master and happily walked with me until I reached the next village at midday, when it disappeared. It was very comforting while it lasted. Sometimes noisy, unfriendly dogs caught sight of me and flew at me, growling and yapping loudly. I had the presence of mind to ignore them before sending them flying with my walking stick and a shower of stones. Incidentally the dogs, usually obstreperous, not only didn't bark at me but even ran away whimpering in fright whenever I snarled back at them.

By now I hadn't washed or changed for days; my badly torn clothes exposed my wrinkled, grimy and stinking old body. With dusty, long greyish hair, wispy beard and tattered shoulder bag, I struggled along with my walking stick that had become my useful companion. Some people shrank from me in disgust and took me for a vagabond, but generally I was treated with kindness and compassion. Although I never caused any trouble, some onlookers weren't particularly sympathetic. I must have made a gruesome sight, egregiously unattractive, for one look at me sent children scuttling in all directions, running up the steep stairs of their houses and then laughing at me from the veranda. I took no notice of them. Oh well, perhaps I hadn't fostered much of an affinity with them in a previous life. I must have cut a sorry figure, looking nothing more than a poor, gaunt old man. I didn't beg but some kind people caught sight of me and gave me a pitying look. They offered me food and drink, as one might expect in LanXang, which I willingly accepted, thanking them effusively. As it happened, I was invited to take a break and eat lunch at a village after leaving Khon Kaen city. Normally people wouldn't look at me twice, but I must have roused this particular lady's sympathy when she saw me staggering on my feet.

'Sabaidee, Phor! (Senior)' a polite, kind, smiling face called from the balcony. 'Our respects to you. Where have you come from? Don't you want to take a rest?'

'*Sabaidee*, thank you for asking,' I said, catching my breath.

'Please (*Xeurn*) come upstairs and join us for a meal and try our best green coconut juice. When you've satisfied your hunger and thirst, you must tell us your name and what brings you here.' She came down hurriedly and took me by the arm. 'I'm Kaeo,' she said, her complexion soft, with beautiful brown eyes, 'and my husband's name is Sone. Now, please come with me.'

After a brief hesitation and with her lending me a hand, I went up to her house. One couldn't possibly refuse. Her husband, a short but well-built man of noble birth, came speedily up to me, proffered his hand and greeted me with warmth. 'A welcome to you, gentleman,' he said with a broad smile. He ushered me in and bade me be seated on a soft reed cushion next to a big rattan tray of food. Kaeo brought a bowl filled with water for me to rinse my hands. They made me feel thoroughly at home and gave me the hospitality their house could afford. I was delighted by such a welcome and showed my pleasure.

'You're such kind hosts,' I said softly. 'I hope Lord Buddha and the other gods will reward both of you with your heart's desire for receiving me so kindly.'

'With respect, Phor,' she said, 'our conscience and the customs of LanXang won't allow us to turn away strangers or wanderers in need of help. Besides, we don't suffer from parsimony. When I saw you coming along, sweat broke out and my eyes filled with tears. You remind me in some indefinable way of my father, who died a month ago. You seem down on your luck, but you have the bearing of a nobleman. Our land is in the hands of those rogues and embezzlers from Bangkok who have no fear of the wrath to come and no compassion in their hearts. They took some of our best rice and fatted livestock. If there are still gods in heaven, they should make sure these Siamese suffer the pangs of shame and pay the price for their behaviour, but let's not waste our energy talking about them. For now, please help yourself to what food we can offer you.'

They said it with such conviction that I almost sobbed into my handkerchief. I, of course, felt at home next to no time due to their kind-heartedness. I was ravenous and ate greedily in silence, but my brain was teeming with thoughts of what I might have to do in Bangkok. Once I was there, I would have to depend on my own resources. However, I dreaded that hunger and thirst might force me to wander about in the open hoping someone would give me food and water. I had to stay alive to give myself any chance of seeing Chao Anouvong again.

After I'd eaten my fill, I was able to satisfy my kind hosts' curiosity by telling them about myself and the purpose of my journey. I was glad to provide genuine news about ViengChan and Chao Anouvong, whose misfortunes I'd shared. I could have talked for a whole week without coming to the end of all the hardships I'd endured. Alas, there was no time to linger. There is no past, no future: only the present. Time waits for no one.

'Poor you!' they exclaimed. 'You've certainly touched our hearts with your suffering,' said Sone. 'We dread to think what might happen to Chao Anouvong now. The news of the annihilation of ViengChan is shocking and unforgivable. We're doomed to slave away as second-class citizens of Siam. Never mind, Phor, we're pleased to help you.'

'Kind hosts,' I said, 'I hope Lord Buddha and other gods will look on you as kindly as I do for helping a poor stranger like me.'

'Thank you, Phor. May your wishes come true,' said Kaeo, lifting her hands to heaven.

'Dear hosts, a guest never forgets a host who treats him well. I shall remember you. If you ever come to my land, I'll return your hospitality, as is right and proper when such a fine example has been set. But if I stay too long you might find me a nuisance, and I don't want to be a burden on you or anyone. I must say goodbye now. I very much hope we'll meet again.'

'You've suffered much,' said Sone. 'We hope you reach Bangkok safely and find Chao Anouvong without too much trouble.' They gave me some more provisions before sending me on my way. 'Good luck, Phor,' they called as I was walking away. I turned round and lifted my hand in appreciation.

I hurried along, racing through many towns and villages, paying respect to their spirit guardians with drink offerings. I stayed only one night each in temples or friendly houses in Udon, Khon Kaen, Phon and Nakhorn Ratsasima to name but a few.

When I finally reached Saraburi in the late afternoon of 15 January 1829, I was hoping I would catch up with Chao Anouvong's convoy. I approached some women wearing traditional Lao silk Sinh dress (as taught by legendary Pu Chan, who urged his people to preserve their traditions and customs). On hearing my tale and realising their hopes of returning to ViengChan had been dashed, they burst into floods of tears. They guided me to the temple, where I was told by a sad-faced elderly Lao monk that Chao Anouvong and the other captives had been sent floating down the Chaophraya river at dawn two days before. My heart ached with sadness and I sank into despair. 'They should have arrived in Bangkok today, but some of his entourage have been distributed among the Siamese nobles as slaves, or have been forced into their harems,' he added. My heart was stirred. I groaned heavily and muttered to myself. Although I'd often thought on my travels that only sudden death awaited me in Bangkok, my heart now leapt up and I revelled in the knowledge he was still alive. I made a drink offering and prayed to the gods for a chance to see him alive again. There was no time for tears and lamentations. After a quick wash at the temple's well and with help from the monk I hastened down to Bangkok on a horse-drawn cart.

Well now, I'm sorry to have to tell you that things were very different in Bangkok when I reached it two days later. I had no idea where to find Chao Anouvong and was left wandering about the city, my heart stricken. I hobbled along with my walking stick and dirty clothes like a wretched old beggar. I walked into various temples and casually asked the monks, but they hardly knew about the war, let alone Chao Anouvong's fate.

In my desperation, like a secret agent, I covertly listened to gossip in the streets, but to no avail. Standing on the pavement outside a teahouse next to a food shop, I realised I was being watched, so pretended to rummage in my tatty shoulder bag. A group of men – who appeared to be cheerful, civilised and highly intelligent – let out a derisive whistle and burst into a torrent of vulgar abuse as soon as they saw me.

'Tell me, you poor, miserable, nauseating, stinking old beggar, where did you escape from?' one said viciously. 'Why don't you just clear out of here and go touting for alms to fill your greedy belly somewhere else!' said another.

As the world progresses, so the quality of life improves, but a man can never conceal the utter curse of his ravening belly; it causes so much trouble, bringing death and destruction to mankind. I had neither money nor anything else worth bartering for a meal. If I were to wander about begging for scraps, I might find some charitable souls willing to provide food and water, but I would have to learn to distinguish between the good from the bad. I knew most Siamese were Buddhists, but sadly they worshipped and feared their king as if he were a god. Perhaps I would be lucky enough to encounter some generosity, but everyone seemed so unwelcoming. Anyway, their words roused me to fury. I was unsure whether to tell them politely that I was neither a beggar nor poor, or to lash out at them with strong words and my walking stick. But they would probably retaliate and there were more of them than me. With no one lifting a finger to save me, I might well meet my end. Nevertheless, I didn't want to starve, so I decided to test their charity, though I was acutely aware that wealth had inured people to hardship, and decency was in decline in Bangkok.

'Please, kind gentlemen,' I reasoned, 'there's no need to set upon me, even though I look dirty and I'm wearing shabby clothes.' They looked down at me sneeringly. 'I would rather deliver rice to someone in need than beg for it. I used to have a nice house; I've shared dinner with great noblemen and given alms to beggars such as myself. You might be surprised to know I once lived in a palatial house with plenty of servants; I took my place in society as a scholarly, wealthy man. But god, it seems, has stripped me of all I had.' They narrowed their eyes at me in malice and laughed at me sarcastically. I steeled myself to remain calm; with my face downcast, I stretched my hand out to them and said, 'Your alms, kind sir... please... and I will sing your praises the world over and wish you the blessing of a long life.' Surely no one could resist this?!

'Stop pestering around here, you vagabond, do you hear?' growled one, 'and keep out of our sight. Go back to where you came from...go elsewhere, or we'll blow your head off!'

'Ah, good sir. Sorry, I was wrong in thinking your hearts might match your noble looks,' I retorted, knowing straightaway it was a mistake. When they shot black looks at me, I let them have a piece of my mind. 'Lord Buddha grant me my wish,' I cried, raising my eyes to heaven and my praying hands in earnest prayer. 'Whenever I make drink offerings, hear my wish that honest, sensible, kind men be granted healthy lives, but unjust, nasty, selfish ones be dragged to hell.'

This roused them to a real fury. Their wrath boiled over. With their dark malevolent eyes and glowering faces, they rounded on me and could easily have biffed me in the face. I was terrified but buoyed up with rage born of fear, I parried their blows with my deadly black walking stick. I avoided a missile by ducking to one side. They snarled and spat at me then walked away laughing when a crowd of onlookers intervened. Unsettled and wounded by their inhumanity, I tried to calm my anger but ended up feeling sad instead: my thoughts were with Chao Anouvong.

Until then luck seemed to have deserted me, but in an extraordinary dispensation of spirituality, I witnessed his last day and the very last moment of his cruel end in the City of Angels. His death was uncivilised and inhuman;

it was no way to treat a king. The Rattanakosin Siamese were extremely imaginative in enacting death sentences: people were tortured, and their severed heads impaled on poles as a warning to other potential traitors. Chao Anouvong suffered unspeakable horror and pain before his death. I still see those awful images in my mind as clear as anything and they'll stay with me for the rest of my life. I'll tell all and keep nothing back, because I would simply hate the Siamese or anyone else to suppose I wasn't appalled and upset. Your tears will flow soon enough before I've finished my tale.

Upon reaching Saraburi, the very city where he'd made an emotional speech urging the people not to forget their Lao roots, the city governor Phraya Saivari locked Chao Anouvong in a cage and labelled him as a common beast, placed on board an open boat for all to see, attracting attention with the thunder of drums and the blast of trumpets. Boats packed with prisoners of war sailed slowly down the Chaophraya river to Bangkok. Lured by the noise, curious crowds rushed to the riverbank in droves. The procession stopped at every town and village; he must have suffered terribly, subjected to humiliation all the way from ViengChan to Bangkok, where his arrival as a prisoner was awaited with jubilation and excitement.

The boats eventually reached Rachini pier in Bangkok on 15 January 1829, where much harsher treatment followed. Chao Anouvong and the others were chained and locked up in Bang Nhikhan prison. He knew full well he'd be horribly tortured before his execution, unless by some miracle Nangklao pardoned him. At night the prisoners were locked away and would have wallowed in a mire of filth. It's impossible to conceive of a more unpleasant and execrable system of punishment. I've never heard before or since of such depravity and un-Buddhist-like cruelty.

They spent the first few days of their imprisonment being whipped, cut and burnt. They were locked in small, iron-barred cells equipped with all kinds of torturing devices: mortars, hooks, boiling oil, hot sand, spears and sharp blades. The cages allowed minimum movement and maximum pain; decorated with slogans and insults, they were placed strategically in open fields, exposed to the burning sun. Officials went round the city with bells, inviting or ordering people to go and see, urging them to call the prisoners every name under the sun and throw rubbish at them.

Bangkok was in the power of a mob that vengefully spat and threw stones at Chao Anouvong and his family, some of whom were tortured and executed.

It goes without saying that his good nature failed to attract the sympathy of the vindictive Siamese officials but worse was to come. Before parading him through the streets, he was placed on his own in an iron cage like an animal – which must have enraged all of heaven – a sign reading 'Traitor of ViengChan' hanging round his neck. Bangkok has been known ever since as the City of the Cage (*Bangkok khorknarm* ບາງກອກ ຄອກນຫາມ) to the Lao.

His family suffered just as badly. Some of his grandsons were mere children, wailing with fright in the dust as they trudged at their mothers' skirts. They were slapped on the face as they cried and screamed in pain and fear. It is said one of his young grandsons escaped and ran for his life like a wild boar trying to escape from a pack of hungry predators. The guards set off in chase like rip-fanged wolves that had sighted a piglet. The poor boy was eventually cornered and stood in terror in front of the raised swords of the chasing guards, gibbering in tears. He knew what was coming and begged for his life, kneeling with his hands pressed together pleading for clemency. 'Please sir, have mercy and let me live,' he was heard to cry. The merciless guards struck him down with their swords and his body crashed to the dust. They vaulted over his blood-gushing and dying body, which was still crying and speaking, impiously exulting over the slain boy, calling him the son of a Lao fool but telling the world of their own and their Rattanakosin king's excellence.

Chao Anouvong and his family were escorted from Bang Nhikhan prison by armed guards, their loaded muskets pointed at his head, a brace of loaded pistols in their belts. With the armed soldiers leading the way, a sinuous line of people moved along slowly. Following behind were the arms and insignia – the three-headed white elephant and parasol representing the three divided LanXang kingdoms. Then came the chained prisoners and Chao Anouvong's followers, bearing burdens, driven forward under the lash, shuffling along as orders were barked and their bodies were whipped with canes. I followed closely after the soldiers in the line. I saw bodies tied to trees with placards round their necks reading 'Traitors'. I'd never witnessed such brutality before. It was the most traumatic, humiliating and disgusting sight I'd ever beheld. It took about half the morning for the procession to end as it wound through the rough streets of Bangkok towards the main camp, to face Nangklao at Sanamluang field.

The most awful torture of all was inflicted on Chao Anouvong. Horrific arrays of instruments of torture were placed near his cage. He was singled out, mentally and physically subjected to terrible ordeals. They mauled him limb by limb. His body was cut and slashed with knives before hot oil was poured over the wounds. I was in shock, my eyes wet with tears and I shook my head in disbelief. I felt the pain stabbing at my own heart but watched in silence and steeled myself to calm my vindictive thoughts. He was gagged and, his hands tied behind his back, hooked by the chin and pulled up until he was hanging by a chain from the top of a tripod. He gestured to his grieving family with his eyes. Despite the trauma, they watched and cried in horror, calling and extending their hands through their cages to him, tenderly reminding him of his good fortune in living such a long, contented life.

Meanwhile, Nangklao piously ascended the steps of his palace ten days after Chao Anouvong's arrival in Bangkok (25 January) to light candles and throw flowers into a sacrificial fire before the temple of his ancestors inside the Suthaisawan Hall. He'd decreed that every public almsgiving festival should henceforth include a prayer in his honour to celebrate his triumph over LanXang. Most people wouldn't have agreed that the annihilation of thousands of fellow human beings was something to glory in.

Nevertheless, at Suthaisawan Hall, built as an offering to heaven, he held his splendid victory celebration. Not even King Naresuan the Great had ever equalled such an epic of self-glorification. Tables were loaded with food and drinks and seats were filled with invited guests from all over Siam. It made earlier feasts seem mere family dinner parties, a show of sycophancy unparalleled in Siamese history. Dignitaries prostrated themselves in fear as much as in praise and thanked him, hoping to be rewarded. All the important Lao feudal lords and princes were summoned to attend: the ambitious lickspittles were more than willing to be in the thick of it, but those who pleaded old age and ill health as an excuse not to attend were threatened with violence. However, there were still plenty of empty seats, a sign that some Lao dignitaries on the Khorat Plateau didn't support Rattanakosin Siam and remained loyal to LanXang in their hearts. Nevertheless, those from the north and northeast knew the intricacies of politics. They looked glum and took care of their Siamese accent, not daring to ask any questions or to express their true feelings. It was better they kept their mouths shut; it meant death to air any objection or show displeasure.

Nangklao exulted and declared it was a most glorious occasion; claiming the victory as his, he arrogantly styled himself 'ViengChan Conqueror'. He talked mostly of himself and his plans for the territories, warning his frightened guests not to cause any trouble. 'Let LanXang ViengChan be an example,' he roared, loving to intimidate people despite the danger of fuelling long-term resentment. His obediently prostrating mandarins raised their praying hands above their heads and cheered in acclamation. They then made offerings and pleaded with the gods to comfort Nangklao throughout his reign. The king raucously told all the guests to look to him to lead them; their sons would then look to his son and heir as a god. Thirsting to settle scores, he brought legal proceedings against Chao Anouvong using trumped-up treason charges and accusing him of insurrection. Such were the severity of the charges that he called for the death penalty. The buzz of thunderous applause and shouts of approval drowned out the music playing in the background, but most of the Lao noble guests sat solemnly at the back, some muttering angrily that Bangkok would inevitably rob them of their nationhood. If they lost their rights, their children and grandchildren would lose their future.

As if there hadn't been enough bloodshed, Nangklao announced he planned to send his soldiers to liquidate the renegades and wipe out Chao Anouvong's bloodline, murdering anyone who criticised him and refused to submit to his rule. Chao Anouvong's fate had a salutary effect on the Lao nobles: they knew what to expect if they were accused of disloyalty to Bangkok, but it also strengthened their determination in their struggle for the Lao nation. They wanted to be Lao, but they were stunned and fearful of persecution.

One after another, eight Siamese dignitaries obsequiously applauded and praised Nangklao. Finally an unknown, elderly nobleman from Khon Kaen who had nothing but contempt for the Rattanakosins jumped to his feet. He was rather stiff in the knees and didn't try to hide his infirmities. He stood up as best he could, stooping and sticking out his backside a little. Someone guffawed loudly, but he didn't stumble and managed to keep his dignity. He was courageous, intelligent, resourceful and articulate. He probably wanted to declare his loyalty to LanXang and test whether Nangklao was broadminded enough to treat honest and talented men with respect. He spoke with equanimity and without rancour and fear. Instead of enthusiastically praising and extolling Nangklao's victory and the glory of Siam, he daringly upbraided the Siamese king, courageous enough not to lie like the rest of them. 'Honourable friends, surely honesty is more important in friendship than cheating,' he said loudly. 'You must be aware that Bangkok has behaved most unjustly and brutally towards ViengChan.' He paused, looked around and then roared, 'It seems that none of my noble friends in this gathering dare to tell the truth about this ghastly war, but show blind obedience to the cruel Rattanakosins. By their own account they've merely defeated a weaker country, annihilated its capital, looted its riches, slaughtered thousands of men, women and children and forced thousands more to leave their homes – the very Lao people whom they regarded as their own. This is absolutely nothing to boast about.'

He added that the sack of ViengChan was the worst crime ever committed by Bangkok. As long as the Lao people drew breath, they would never stop believing in their rights and trying to broadcast the truth to the world. As for Chao Anouvong's death sentence and the fate of ViengChan, the Siamese should know that the Lao people might learn to forgive but they would never forget, even if they died a thousand deaths. 'No secret can be kept hidden forever,' he said. 'You, my Siamese friends, shouldn't make fun of the truth. You can boast and lie all you want, but Lao blood is on your hands.' He defiantly told the gathering that instead of celebrating and gloating, they should condemn the invasion of ViengChan as a crime against humanity, make drink offerings to the Lord Buddha and pray to the gods to turn their wrath on Nangklao. His comments triggered a fracas: they were greeted with demonic laughter followed by an almighty storm of insults and derision. 'I fear losing my Lao nation, but I'm not afraid to die,' he said fiercely.

King Nangklao rose to his full height as if possessed by a bloodthirsty devil. He gave the Khon Kaen noble a tongue-lashing, vehemently calling him a traitor, a ViengChan lover and a stupid Lao. The loyal Siamese nobles, purple with drink and rage, jumped to their feet and accused him of being a retard who wanted to cut the king's throat. The shouts of fury and profanities exploded like howls of pain, but amid the disturbances the old man remained unperturbed. He reaffirmed that he was born a Lao in the kingdom of LanXang. He and his fellow Lao citizens feared for their lives, and he knew his fate. 'Kill him!' someone yelled and other angry faces followed. 'Kill him! Kill him! Off with his head!' They rounded on him like a pack of wild dogs, tearing into him and shoving him back and forth, but he stood his ground like an elephant (*Xang* ຊ້າງ) and pushed them back. They jumped on him and overpowered him. He was kicked, punched and dragged away, condemned for his supposedly treacherous opinions. In truth he was a just man who had the courage not to pledge allegiance to the Rattanakosins and to tell the truth with the transparency of a holy monk. That was the end of him. Most of his noble colleagues from the northeast of Siam, sadly, were too cowed to follow his example. They sat rigid as if they were embalmed corpses. Later, those who refused to pledge loyalty to Bangkok were threatened with violence.

Meanwhile, King Nangklao's most eminent prisoner – the condemned Lao king – and his followers were slowly herded from the main Sanamluang camp to the execution ground in front of Suthaisawan Hall. It was to be a fitting spectacle: Nangklao the conqueror ending the life of Chao Anouvong, the conquered. You could hear the distant cheering echoing through the thick, hot, smelly air. But before joining the crowd I delayed the horror by hanging around outside the perimeter fence for a while, imagining Chao Anouvong entering the scene of his ultimate humiliation: death.

The sight of Chao Anouvong being taken out of his cage in a tumbril and led amongst the captives was truly sad and humiliating, I can tell you. His wrists and ankles were covered in raw, bloody sores from the rubbing of the bracelets and chains. He made the best of it and kept his dignity, though he must have resented it mightily as he was made to walk, his hands bound, picking his way through the horse shit and elephant dung left behind by the procession. I joined in with some Lao citizens amongst the throng. We made a gallant effort, pleading for mercy for our king's life, reminding the officials that Siamese and Lao came from the same ancient Ai-Lao race. Lao supporters, who'd turned up in large numbers, cried out courageously. Then all of them, myself included, fell as one to our knees, performed a deep prostration and begged for clemency. Nangklao's hardened men weren't even touched by our entreaties. Bangkok – Krung Thep – was renowned as the City of Angels, but none of them heard our prayers for leniency. The Angel of Death stalked the accursed Suthaisawan Hall instead. The Siamese scornfully laughed and sneered at us. I looked at the wicked Bangkok partisans' faces in dismay. Siam was supposed to be the land of smiles, but here were angry, sinful men who'd forgotten the meaning of humanity and philosophy. They flung him back into the cage. The golden Garuda and Siamese national flags flew menacingly next to the ubiquitous portraits of Nangklao.

As the procession went by, I checked my own pain and anger. It was utterly hopeless, but I'd secretly thought of appealing for clemency and telling Nangklao that the entire fault rested with the Lao people... and with me.

I briefly considered running to Chao Anouvong to share his suffering but decided to follow the procession closely and kept my eyes on his cage until it was finally placed in front of Nangklao at Suthaisawan Hall. I fixed my stare on my king and said solemnly to myself, 'No.' There was nothing I could do. How could a man who'd sacrificed so much and who wanted only to bring justice to the world die so alone? He didn't move or even blink. I couldn't collect myself sufficiently to look at him, but neither could I tear myself away. I needed to witness it all so I could tell others, but I couldn't rid myself of the knowledge that an unimaginable horror was being inflicted on him, an old man at the very end of his life.

I wished I were superhuman, like the legendary Sin-Xay who shoots invisible arrows and can change into a tiger or dragon at will. 'Let me unburden my heart,' I muttered to myself and asked the Lord Buddha and the gods to stand at my side and imbue me with their spirit. I had no more tears to shed but thoughts of revenge grew stronger by the minute until I turned away from the crowd and felt for the knife I'd tucked securely across my chest. I gripped the handle tightly and made ready to make a dash for Nangklao and take him hostage, but then I heard Chao Anouvong's words – 'stay alive' – ringing in my ears. I'd promised him I would live to tell the tale. He knew I was no warrior and would have wanted me to be safe rather than risk death. I stared down at the dirty ground and released my vengeful hand from the knife's handle. Among the cheering, spiteful crowds, I watched him suffering before his painful death. After such a torturous life as a captive, he'd lost the will to live and was pitifully curled up in exhaustion, awaiting his fate. 'May Theravada have mercy on those who see fit to end his life in such a cruel and undignified way,' I mumbled and looked to heaven. Nangklao's name flooded my mind like a tsunami.

As to how he was finally executed, I must confess to concealing a secret all these years. I'm now happy to unburden myself. I don't know why I've kept it all to myself. I'm sure you can appreciate how deeply his death grieved me, what a huge loss it was to me. He gave me all the pleasure and friendship I could ever hope to receive from another human being.

For the glory of Siam, all just men should remember that the Rattanakosin king's followers pointed their fingers at the prisoners of war, scolding them as they knelt on the hard ground, begging for mercy until their knees bled. The Bangkok partisans roared that these acts of supreme cruelty should teach the Lao rebels a lesson.

Nangklao delivered a tirade of abuse and launched into a flood of self-justification, blaming everything on Chao Anouvong, stripping him of all his titles and labelling him a rebel and a traitor. There was only one legal penalty for treason: 'Death'. The crowd looked at each other in puzzlement as the terrible word was spoken. 'Death to the traitor!' Nangklao roared out of his pitiless heart and the torture to continue.

It was, without doubt, a monstrously perverse accusation, so utterly devoid of the truth that it passed into the realms of the ridiculous. To accuse Chao Anouvong of being a traitor was to consign him to the lowest circle of hell. The Rattanakosins' compulsive narcissism had led to a reign of terror in Bangkok and the invasion of LanXang. Chao Anouvong simply wanted to free his people from oppression and to preserve the Lao nation. Yet he was being condemned to death for his love of LanXang rather than for anything he'd done to Siam. It was hard to imagine such inhumanity. Not caring a jot for Lord Buddha and the gods, Bangkok continued to plot the destruction of the Lao nation.

Chao Anouvong was a stubborn man, but no one can survive such brutality. He was scourged and scorched with flame, in severe pain and short of breath, probably trying to bear the inevitable as well as he could. He refused to buckle under Nangklao's hostility and condemnation. Faced with death, his spirit remained steadfast and he held the bars of his cage, still wearing his badly torn commander's uniform, and slowly pulled himself up to his full height. Crying out with pain he swore he was innocent and begged for time to plead his case. With his remaining energy he stared at Nangklao before turning slowly towards the crowd. He spoke softly of his innocence, coughing, trying to breathe steadily to gather his strength. Then he turned back to Nangklao and swore he was innocent of all charges.

'I'm not your traitor!' he cried out. 'Rattanakosin Siam was founded by traitors, the loyal subjects of the usurper King TakSin of Thonburi, just like your grandfather who became the first king of Bangkok in 1782: another traitor. The throne of Siam will always be stained with treachery. I am a Lao. I am a former commander in chief of the Lao army who fought Siam's enemies on your behalf. I was a close friend of your late father, for whom I fought heroically for the love of Siam. Now, tell me then, do the sacrifices that I and my men made for Siam in the mountains of LanNa awake no compassion in your Siamese heart? Why so much malice against me and the Lao people?'

After a short pause he announced as clearly as he could, 'I fight for justice and for independence for LanXang, just as your king Naresuan the Great did for Ayutthaya Siam.' He paused again to gather his energy before roaring in defiance, 'I am not a traitor!' He then collapsed to the floor and passed out, prompting some of the crowd to break down and sob like children.

Nangklao's ears were deaf. Absorbed in his 'don't care' attitude, he pretended not to have heard and took no notice. His heart and mind remained unapproachably fierce. With the eyes of a devil and full of loathing he turned to his sentry and ordered the execution to begin.

Neither gods nor men helped Chao Anouvong or took him to their hearts. His heroic willpower seemed to have gone and the darkness of death clouded his eyes, yet by some superhuman effort, he woke and managed to sit with his knees drawn up. He summoned up a final spark of defiance and lifted his head and screamed, pointing his finger at Nangklao.

'I am not Siamese and therefore I am not a liar and cannot be a traitor to Siam. I will die a Laoman and ascended to the uncorrupted heavens; you, a Siamese, will live and rule in this accursed and corrupted land, but which of us has the happier prospects is unknown to anyone but god and Theravada's trinity: *Phra Phud* (the Buddha), *Phra Tham* (Buddhist teaching) and *Phra Song* (Buddhist disciples). I put a curse on you. Your palace will be smashed down and destroyed. You will pay for your misdeeds with utter disaster. You will die in mortal sin because of your greediness, cruelty and tyranny. You may bathe in your ill-gotten riches and in the glory of Siam, but my torture and death will never be forgotten. This portion of the Sanamluang field of Bangkok will be forever Lao LanXang.'

His words were scarcely audible but a bitter reproach to the dictatorial and spiteful Rattanakosin king. The hush among the crowd seemed to amplify his words, but they did nothing to change Nangklao's mind.

'Let this be a lesson to all of you traitors. Traitors!' Nangklao repeated angrily, and his followers gave a loud murmur of assent as if they relished the sight of torture and execution. Very quickly the chant was taken up all around us. With arms flashing out they bellowed, 'Traitor! Traitor! Death to the traitor!'

Well, no one's perfect. Our faults are many, but the shouts of the Siamese crowd were particularly sinful. Some Lao supporters, I felt sure, thirsted for murder in their hearts and were desperate to pay the Siamese back. But god never granted them their wish. My heart sank.

By this time Chao Anouvong was probably dying; to my utter horror, Nangklao then ordered his eyes to be gouged out with hot irons. The crowd gasped in disbelief. The sentries dragged his cage inside the building and out of sight. I heard his face being slapped violently and stood frozen in anticipation. The Lao in the crowd shut their eyes and closed their ears. A moment later they jumped up and shrank back as his scream of pain vibrated in the thick, heavy air. Even god must have heard it. He must have suffered from pain so unimaginable that only death could take it away. From inside came a moaning that was too terrible to hear; the blood drained from my cheeks and tears started to my eyes. I can still hear it now.

The rest of the Lao captives stayed calm and retained their dignity, saying nothing, but I sensed the crowd were unprepared for what was to follow. They brought the cage back out. In severe pain, Chao Anouvong covered his eyes with one hand and fumbled about. It was a truly heart-rending sight and the crowd were overcome with grief. To prolong his agony they tortured him with hot irons, while a group of innocent boys were engrossed with their colourful kites, which screamed in the murky air; a hot gust blew across the ground.

Sanamluang was thronged with a hate-filled mob, mostly royalists and hard-line local Siamese partisans, some clearly drunk. They lined up with their arms around each other's shoulders on a patch of grass on the bare, dusty ground. Patriotism in Siam is seriously loud and boastful. Some of them even disgustingly performed a little triumphant dance at the prospect of the execution. I pitied them but it grieved me to do nothing while they mocked my king. It was not a good time to be a Lao. We could hardly have been more unpopular, but my revulsion prompted me to act. I was fearful, but I decided I would pretend to be Siamese and ask them whether beneath their smiles they felt any compassion for Chao Anouvong, an old man who'd fought for Siam and had never threatened Bangkok. With a fixed smile I daringly wandered over to where one unkempt but sensible-looking younger man was standing. I approached him carefully but stumbled and accidentally knocked into him.

'Oh, sorry brother, forgive me,' I said smiling and quickly regaining my composure. He seemed calm enough so I gently took him by the arm and asked, 'As a matter of great concern and interest, do you approve of all this?'

'Approve?' He frowned and his brows lifted in surprise, gawping at me and giving off a rather ripe, unwashed smell. 'We may have no business in LanXang, but we're patriots. We've won the war. It's the greatest deed in

Siamese history.' He hissed and turned away to shout at the top of his voice, 'Death to the traitor!'

'Traitor? Really?' I said, letting go of his arm. I glanced around furtively and whispered, 'But brother, isn't Chao Anouvong a Lao?'

'Well, he might be a Lao but he's a traitor to us!' he countered, scornfully spitting sideways and seizing my wrist.

'Listen brother,' I said mildly, snatching my hand away, casting such a look of hatred and indignation at him that he was obliged to notice and he frowned in irritation. 'I'm old enough to know that Bangkok only tells you what it wants you to hear,' I continued. 'For a start, you've been misled. Don't be so ignorant. You Siamese would do well to pay attention to reality or at least listen to someone who can tell you the truth. Perhaps you should pray to Lord Buddha and the other gods to open your king's eyes. For the rest, just take my word.'

'We're the victors! Woe to the conquered!' he said smugly and snarled at me.

'It will do Siam no good in the end, you know,' I said in a voice of doom. 'I swear to Lord Buddha before all the other gods and your good heart; this surely shouldn't happen in Buddhist Siam.' He seemed momentarily paralysed with confusion. 'What's more,' I pressed on, 'will your government tell the truth once this "traitor" has been executed? What about his veterans and followers who've pledged revenge for his death? All Lao people will want to right this wrong. They might wish to appease his spirit in heaven. If this "traitor" of yours is executed, it will leave a stain on Rattanakosin Siam – on Bangkok. Your king will be forever known as a figure of terror. For this act of barbarity – which you seem to find rather entertaining – the chickens will come home to roost. There'll be irreconcilable distrust between Bangkok and ViengChan. The Lao people on both banks of the Mekong who've paid the price for opposing your king will be united in grief and may well swear to avenge Chao Anouvong. The genie of Lao nationalism will rise with a vengeance.'

He was truly vexed by my words. His brow narrowed and his eyelids fluttered as if he were about to stamp me underfoot, but he didn't reply. I lapsed into silence and returned to my agony of grief. Fearing my voice might have carried, I turned away as if I'd agreed with him and we parted company. I laughed and smiled through my tears.

Sadly the Siamese in their ignorance failed to understand what sort of message Chao Anouvong's execution would send to the world, especially to the Lao people and his loyal veterans.

Fearsome-looking armed soldiers in black uniforms fenced the spectators off, allowing no one through, while plain-clothed officers had infiltrated themselves into the crowd. The Lao supporters stood out in this sea of hatred by chanting, 'The Siamese and Lao are brothers!' at the soldiers. They could hardly disguise their distress at seeing a man who possessed such kindness waiting to meet his end like a common criminal. They looked shocked, bewildered and fearful. I didn't want to become a target for vengeance, but I plucked up courage to join them anyway. When I sensed I was putting myself in mortal danger, I dropped my shoulders and stopped chanting.

On hearing the commotion, a group of anxious people heaved and swayed to get a better view. Some had arrived late and didn't know what was going on. They jostled at the back and pushed forwards. I soon lost my position at the front and craned my neck to catch a glimpse of Chao Anouvong over the forest of heads. When I anxiously asked a man in front of me what was happening, he glanced sharply over his shoulder and muttered that the traitor was being tortured. A moment later a voice next to me cried out that the execution was imminent. The crowd surged forward and some people tumbled to the ground. Suddenly, as if a spell had been broken, pandemonium erupted. The benches or stools the crowd were standing on toppled over. There was a scream and a crash. The crowd burst into profanity and clambered over one another in their panic to get to their feet. I was almost trampled in the chaos and lost sight of him for a while but ducked and twisted my way through the bodies and scrambled to one side as several hundred anxious spectators continued to jostle and push forwards. I somehow regained my balance and got to the front again but couldn't quite bring myself to look. The wind suddenly stiffened and began to howl across the Chaophraya river; ominous dark clouds gathered, twisting like a cyclone over Bangkok. Most of Chao Anouvong's sympathisers wept in desperate fear and sorrow.

His capturer, Nangklao, known for his cruelty and extravagance, who'd pursued Chao Anouvong with relentless malice, could now do what he wanted to him, his captive. He was the most merciless of beings; he'd abandoned all Buddhist precepts and the law of karma and had become so hardened to cruelty he didn't even realise that the pang of death, the scream of misery and resentment, would lead to a vicious cycle of killing and revenge. He stood triumphantly in front of Suthaisawan Hall holding a feathery, red silk cloth between his fingers high in the humid air. His face grew red, bitter and angry; so angry that he fired a final, devilish glare towards Chao Anouvong, who had collapsed and was breathing his last. How I wished I could hold his hand and say goodbye. Nangklao looked to both sides; when his gaze finally rested on his victim, he released the red cloth, which dropped like blood onto the dusty ground.

A moment later I witnessed the last terrible moments of this magnificent man. With hardly a cloth covering his body, he was dragged out of the cage backwards, his chin drooping on his chest, his lower body scraping the floor. But he, the poor, grey-headed king, was already dead – the common destiny of all human beings. It was a traumatic, pitiful sight. I looked up to heaven and muttered, 'Why let me see this?' He wasn't breathing, as dead as earth. He died broken-hearted. When they tried to close his eyes, they found the lids wouldn't shut because his hopes hadn't yet been fulfilled. His eyeless face had the agonised expression of a man who'd died in terrible pain and despair, but his immortal soul had left his body for a better world. I could do nothing but lift my hands to Lord Buddha in horror at the ghastly sight, paralysed by a sense of utter helplessness. Although there was no need to weep over his dead body – tears are worthless – some people in the crowd who'd managed to restrain their tears now wept hysterically when they saw he was dead, bursting into such a storm of weeping. How I wished I could have embraced his body and caught his departing soul. I wanted to prostrate myself before Nangklao, press my hands on his feet, throw my arms round his knees in supplication, kiss those terrible hands that were stained with so much Lao blood and tell him about the virtue of ViengChan; to beg him for the body of my lord so I could rest him on the royal pyre and cremate him with dignity in the Wat Sisaketh temple. I didn't want him to feel lonely in the netherworld, so I planned to keep a hundred days' vigil for him and burn incense stones as offerings. When I'm gone I want my ashes to me mingled with his so not even heaven can separate us.

For an instant I contemplated killing myself at the gate of Nangklao's palace in full view of the crowd to make him die in shame, but he was clearly a man without virtue or morality; he'd no sense of shame. He was no more affected by the death of a man than he was by the death of a fly. I would probably be arrested before I could set fire to myself and be tortured to death.

Not satisfied with his death, Nangklao rose from his seat and looked at the gaping mouth and white face, already becoming discoloured. He stood tall and, with an acerbic tilt of his head, he gloated over his death. To his right, the gilded wooden Garuda looked down in disdain. Calling a sentry over, he tried the edge of his naked sword on his thumb like a butcher and yelled 'Off with the traitor's head!' The soldier briefly hesitated but, sword in hand, he obediently moved forward and towered over the corpse. Nangklao laughed and swore.

The crowd cringed, shut their eyes and turned away. The sentry forced himself to keep his eyes open and doggedly struck at the neck bone, spattering himself with blood, until the head rolled free. He stabbed the sticky, slimy and raw-smelling sword into the ground, then grasped a handful of grey hair and held the eyeless head up. With his eyes shut, the guard swallowed and fought to keep from vomiting as he placed it on a silver tray. He lifted the tray to his forehead and cautiously presented it as a trophy to Nangklao, who acknowledged the livid head with a condescending nod. Before retreating to his palace he ordered it to be impaled atop a long pole and erected on public ground near the Rachini (Queen) pier close to the Chaophraya river, to serve as a warning to the Lao people that they would suffer the same fate if they dared to speak openly of autonomy and freedom. Hungry flies enjoyed the sight and smell of the severed, silent head; they have no respect for death but eagerly buzz and feast on corpses and blood-soaked ground.

Suddenly the clear sky began to fill with immense, thick, black clouds rolling in from nowhere, pressing down on the roof of the Suthaisawan Hall, drifting and whirling ferociously in the howling wind, and followed by thunder and lightning. It was as if the Lord Buddha or Mother Siam disapproved of Nangklao's evil deeds and were showing their anger.

A moment later, a shaft of bright sunlight pierced the dark clouds and then quickly faded back up into the sky. Some claimed it was Chao Anouvong ascending to heaven. It eased my heart to know he was going to the gods.

Nangklao the divine, who feared no one, retreated nervously to the safety of his palace like a mere mortal. Chao Anouvong's killing probably made the Rattanakosins even more tyrannical, but at that moment his demeanour was grim, showing none of the jubilation you would expect at the death of his enemy. The news of Chao Anouvong's demise spread like wildfire among the people.

In war one expects many casualties, but the manner of Chao Anouvong's death was appalling. Those accustomed to the death of a king would have been shocked and surprised at its brutality. A just man had been imprisoned, humiliated, scourged, tortured, blinded and finally executed. The sight of his severed head dripping blood down the pole, buzzing with flies, was beyond belief.

While it drew loud cheers from Siamese nationalists, most of the crowd averted their eyes, covered their mouths with their hands and cried in disbelief. It was unbelievably traumatic for the Lao people, who were overcome with grief and wept. Some standing nearby began tearing at their hair and clothes in frustration. A group of curious onlookers looked as if they'd been shaken by an earthquake. Soon the crowd, exhausted by grief, started to leave, but most of the Lao supporters were in a state of shock and unable to move. They collapsed on their knees and remained motionless, covering their faces with their trembling hands. Some shook their heads up and down as if their sadness had driven them mad.

Chao Anouvong, king of the Lao kingdom of LanXang, was gone! His headless body was taken away and hidden somewhere in the accursed city of Bangkok, where the Angel of Death and the guardian angel fight for supremacy. In silence I laid a bunch of flowers, bowed my head in respectful farewell and slowly walked away in a daze. I looked at no one and heard nothing, seeking solitude and wandering the streets. Eventually god guided me to a quiet spot in a distant temple. Chao Anouvong's passing felt as if it were just a bad dream. I washed my hands and face at the temple's well to wake my mind then fell to my knees beneath a shady *Dork Champa* tree nearby to light a beeswax candle. I looked up in prayer to the Lord Buddha and suddenly a blossom fell from high above. I caught it gently without thinking, and the thought of Chao Anouvong's soul flickered in my mind. I smelt the gentle fragrance of the white flower with its yellow centre and put it in my shirt pocket for safekeeping as if it were a piece of gold. Then I lit a candle, lifted my hands and solemnly prayed for his soul.

'Chao Anouvong,' I said softly, choking back my sorrow, 'you are my friend, my lord, the king of Lao LanXang, and you gave your life for our nation. With immense anguish in my heart, I light this candle for you with my hands, which are still free, in acknowledgment of your death. No one else, family or friends, can pay their respects. Now, with a grief-torn heart, I perform the prostrating ritual and pour libations for you as a king. This will be the last honour from me as your confidant and servant. You, the king, a heaven-born noble, was tortured to death here in Bangkok while I and the Lao people live on. I only wish you could still hear me; I wish you had never been without love and that you find it waiting for you wherever you've gone. With your death, the people of LanXang have been deprived of their pillar of strength. It's so cruel of heaven to take you away. I've lost a kindred spirit; we shall now be as eternally separated as heaven from earth. Oh Chao Anouvong, we part forever. In the name of justice, I will never abandon your cause. I humbly mourn your death, the passing of a martyr. I kneel before you, my king, on behalf of the Lao people. With my own heart I thank you for leading us and for giving us hope for the future. May your spirit go to heaven and rest in peace. It won't be heaven for me if you're not there. Now you're gone I'll invoke your power and support. We will meet again, but not yet. The memories of your virtue will never fade into obscurity. You will forever be respectfully remembered.'

I already knew what it was to mourn the dead. For my father and mother, I wept my heart out. For Chao Anouvong, I plunged into an abyss of grief; my eyes were wet with weeping as if my life were ebbing away in the tears I shed. His death was so hard to accept: if only I could have met the same fate and died in Bangkok with him. I was truly inconsolable and wretched; it felt like part of me was draining away with him, as though we were one. I sat with arms folded around my legs in the shade and used my bony knees to wipe away my tears. I was alone but I was sure he hadn't forsaken me. Part of his soul was in mine.

My spirit failed me and I had half a mind to climb a tall Bo tree and jump to my death. I felt sick with sadness, grieving, torturing myself with tears and heartache, thinking I was doomed to end my days in Bangkok, away from my loyal friends and my beloved city. When I looked up with streaming eyes beyond the clouds to heaven, the thought pierced me that there was still hope. Miraculously, I somehow managed to steel myself to bear it, although I couldn't find the courage or the means to get home. My provisions were running out and I may well have starved if one of the monks hadn't taken pity on me. The sight of me, a forlorn figure sitting under the mango trees, must have roused his compassion.

As soon as he'd finished his lunch the monk approached, stood in front of me and greeted me amiably. I knelt down and raised my hands above my head in supplication. He took them in his and tended to me with sympathy. I was in such anguish that I could scarcely utter a single word, my rising sobs sticking in my throat. When I looked up and saw his eyes twinkling, hope returned to me. I introduced myself and begged him to help me.

'Sabaidee, venerable monk (*Phra Ajarn*). My respects to you,' I said between my sobs. 'I'm not a common vagabond, despite my shabby, dirty clothes. I'm merely taking refuge in your holy temple as a suppliant, in the hope you may grant me a friendly welcome or even go further with your kindness and generosity. I beseech you to fit me out with new clothes, give me some provisions and please don't banish me.'

'*PhorOrk* (layman), relax! I welcome you with open arms,' he said pleasantly. 'We monks lead holy lives and must always be kind and reasonable. We don't assume any stranger to be an enemy, for no man on earth would dare to set hostile feet on this holy ground. One mustn't judge a man by his clothes. On the contrary, you look more like a gentleman of royal blood, the sort of person who enjoys the finer things in life, has a long bath, gets dressed then drinks and dines and sleeps on a big, firm bed. But you look worn out and depressed, as if you've forgotten what it is to have a merry heart. You must tell me the cause of your troubles, which I hope won't intensify your grief. I can assure you that monks, who themselves live easy lives, do not like to see anyone in distress.' After a short pause he sighed heavily, squeezing my shoulder in sympathy and said in a low voice, 'What's your name? Where are you from? And what evil power is to blame for making you so unhappy?'

'Oh venerable monk, it would be too tiresome to tell you everything,' I replied guardedly. 'I beg you not to insist on finding out, for it'll bring fresh sorrow to my heart. I shall confine myself to answering your questions instead.' I paused for thought. 'You can see I'm not immune from age, and, as one mortal to another, I'll speak frankly. Lest anyone assumes I'm a nobody, I can tell you that my lineage is an old one. My name is Jon; I'm the son of a dignified feudal lord, from a race that eats sticky rice, lives mostly on fish and vegetables and respects nature and human values. My father died because he kept faith with King Bounyasan against King TakSin. I'm now trapped in sorrow, cut off from hope and heartbroken for the loss of a dear friend, the best and bravest of men, for whom I grieve even more deeply than for my own parents. He was not only mistreated but tortured. His death is a terrible blow to me. I'm frail and old before my time. I feel I have no further use for life and certainly have no wish to see the sunshine in Siam anymore. I don't know a soul in this city; I know no sweeter sight than my motherland, which may well no longer exist. But I still want to return to the heaven-fed waters of the Mekong.'

'Ah, yes, I know the peace-loving kingdom of LanXang and her easy-going, kind-hearted and hospitable people,' he said, his voice seeming to come from far away. 'You talk like a man of sense and goodwill. I'm deeply sorry for you.

We're not used to seeing people in distress from as far away as you. Who is this unfortunate friend of yours, and what city is your home?'

'My home, your holiness, is under the clear sky of ViengChan, the city of the full moon, where the Siamese army not only set foot on sacred ground but burnt our temples and looted our treasures. My noble-hearted friend is Chao Anouvong, the ill-fated king, to whom I was private secretary and confidant, and whose head has been brutally impaled atop a pole at Sanamluang field near the Rachini pier. I never thought his life would end as brutally as it did. But why would the gods want to punish him for his most desired wish? His death has brought terrible grief to Lao LanXang, and above all to me. The birds must by now have torn the flesh from his bones.'

'Really! How terrible?' he groaned. 'I'm shocked to hear it; that is unforgivable. May your king's spirit go to heaven,' he added, looking up to the sky in earnest prayer. 'Well now,' he said quietly, 'my parents were forced to leave ViengChan in 1779. They now live in Saraburi, where I was born over thirty years ago.' I wasn't entirely surprised to hear it. He then tried to speak to me in Lao. He thought I was weak in the head to be stuck in Bangkok and that I was upsetting myself unnecessarily with my incontinent grief. 'There's no need to prolong your miseries. I'm wondering what I would do if I found myself in your plight. Surely it's better to get back to ViengChan as quickly as possible, or you may well die like your noble friend. If you wander about in the city, you'll be courting sudden death. There are too many rich and powerful men in Bangkok devoted to tyranny. I advise you not to go out, for their brutality knows no bounds. Their recklessness and violence have outraged both man and heaven. They would arrest you and lock you up in their crowded pigsty-like prison; you would never see your home again.'

For that whole afternoon I was able to satisfy his thirst for news by giving a full account of the annihilation of ViengChan. He was no less obliging when I asked whether he knew anything of the war. Monks play no part in politics – you're not supposed to wear religious robes and enter the political arena – but he willingly gave his opinion.

'*PhorOrk*, I'm aware of the conflict,' he said disapprovingly. 'But do you know, of all the creatures that breathe and creep about on Mother Earth, man is the most cruel. He kills his own kind. War robs people of comfort and feeds them only with bitterness. Now, hear what I think. Siam was totally wrong to invade LanXang, to remove the Emerald Buddha, to destroy ViengChan and to force people to leave their homes and enslave them. It was an act of evil. I'm sickened by the barbarities and iniquities of this war. Bangkok is at fault for wanting to annex LanXang. Nangklao is undeniably at fault for having Chao Anouvong tortured and executed. But let's not be vengeful: let the gods be the judge of such wickedness.'

His words warmed my heart. I replied, 'Phra Ajarn, I have no wish to linger in Bangkok, which I detest more and more every passing hour. I long to be home. I don't want to be a burden to you but should be glad of your advice. I beg you, in the Lord Buddha's name, to enlighten me and please find me some transport and help me out of the city. Please tell me how to get home across the wide expanse of the Khorat Plateau. Once I'm on my way, I'll wander about in the hope someone will give me a cup of water and a handful of rice. In return, I'll raise my voice in prayer for their health.'

'Don't worry, *PhorOrk*,' the monk said with a pitying look. 'I'll give you clothing and some money to send you on your way along the route of your king, but you must get moving as soon as possible. On the other hand, we seem to be like-minded and I would wish for nothing better than for you to stay longer, if you're willing to become a monk and settle here. For now, I suggest you eat and drink plenty to regain your strength and spend the night here. I'll catch up with you in the morning. After breakfast, you can start this journey you're so eager to make and take some tasty provisions, so you'll have no fear of starvation. However, before embarking, you should make an offering and pray to the Lord Buddha and the other gods.'

My heart was filled with happiness as I listened to him. By then I was worn out with anguish and the sun was setting. It grew dark and night soon descended on me. After satisfying my hunger and thirst, I lay on a thin mattress in the guest quarters, curled up and tried to sleep. When the stars had passed their zenith, I woke up and then couldn't get back to sleep because of the anxiety of the journey. When the rosy light of dawn had scarcely touched the east, I rose from my bed, washed and dressed. At breakfast I ate and drank hungrily from the monks' leftovers; it had been a long time since I'd tasted proper food. Soon after, the venerable monk returned eagerly with a bundle of clothing; to my delight, he greeted me in Lao.

'*Sabaidee, PhorOrk*, and how are you today?' he said cheerfully, standing in front of me.

'*Sabaidee*. My respects to you, Phra Ajarn. I'm feeling better, thank you,' I said with a smile and made my reverence.

'I see you're looking better than yesterday and are still determined to leave for your beloved home. I would rather keep you in our temple, but I respect your wishes,' he said, handing over the clothes.

'It is indeed my never-failing wish to reach ViengChan,' I asserted, thanking him. 'Phra Ajarn, you'll agree with me that even though people live far from home, they still love their motherland and their parents above all else. I'm eager now to be gone. If you don't mind, I would like to get changed for the journey and be off.'

'I fully understand,' he said with a look of acquiescence and turned away. After I'd excused myself and put on new shirt and trousers, the monk gave me a formal cummerbund – a fine silk red-and-white checked sash – which I wound round my waist with great care. '*PhorOrk*, you've shown your true intentions,' he said. 'It wouldn't be right to keep you here any longer. It's my earnest hope that Lord Buddha will grant you a safe journey. You've suffered much, but now you've set foot on holy ground, I feel assured you'll safely reach your pleasant home.' He then sprinkled holy water on my head and sent me on my way with his blessing. 'Go home now and I wish you good luck. I hope you'll remember me sometimes when you're there.'

'My heartfelt thanks, your holiness, for treating me so well,' I said. 'Our life is short enough. A mean person with no idea of hospitality earns ill will while he lives and contempt when he's dead, whereas a kind-hearted and generous man will have no lack of loyal friends to sing his praises. I pray to the Lord Buddha and the other gods to let me reach my home. If I escape the cruel hand of fate, I will indeed remember you for the rest of my days, however far away I live. But for now, may the Lord Buddha grant you your heart's desire, as a joyful life never seems to last long enough.'

After I'd made drink offerings, poured libations and prayed, he walked me to the gate, where a small grey horse was waiting out of sight. The amount of money he gave me was a fortune beyond the dreams of avarice for a peasant in Siam. I was doubly happy with my transport and thanked him profusely. Before mounting, I gave the horse a handful of grass and stroked his neck; he nudged me gently. I reverently said farewell (*Lahkorn*) to the monk and he lifted his hand in affirmation. I moved as fast as a young man longing to see the happy day of his return.

I had started my journey north-eastwards in a state of happiness and rode away slowly, mournfully saluting every temple that came to view. When I passed Sanamluang field, which seemed like a haunted burial ground, I jumped off, snatched my hat from my head, clasped it to my chest and fell on my knees in sorrow, sobbing at the sad reminder of my ill-fated king and friend. I had a sense of trepidation, as if the city of angels still had evil intentions towards me. I resisted the temptation to provoke the packs of savage men prowling about as I rode away at a canter, but when I was safely out of the city gates, my blood was up. I stopped, turned my horse round, looked towards the palace with contempt and let the Rattanakosin king have a piece of my mind. 'Nangklao,' I cried, 'you tyrant who thinks that you're a god amongst men and style yourself the conqueror of ViengChan. You took the life of a just man and brought grief upon his family, friends and countrymen. Your crimes will come home to roost one day. You didn't even have the decency to refrain from annihilating ViengChan. The five curses that had been prophesied when your grandfather looted the Emerald Buddha will fall on Siam with vengeance.' With this, I made drink offerings and lifted my hands to the heavens that hold the stars. I prayed (*Sathu Der*), 'Hear me, Lord Buddha and the other gods. Let there be no revenge, but restore the mutual goodwill of the old days, as Chao Anouvong would have wished. But if justice is a pillar of your divine law, then let the Lao nation live on so history records that the real "traitors" were Nangklao and his men; let strife tear accursed Siam apart!' I turned my back on Bangkok, poured libations and then cantered away with a heavy heart, for the joy I felt at going home was tempered by grief for a fair-minded king and a dear friend whom I'd loved beyond all others and had lost. It remained my dominant emotion as I tried to survive and followed the rough paths leading up into the northeast, and patiently trampled along Chao Anouvong's route towards ViengChan and home.

I actually believed Chao Anouvong's spirit was accompanying and protecting me through the wide plain of Khorat as a companion and an ally, his soul living on as a disembodied ghost. On one occasion, while sleeping under the shade of an ancient tree, I saw him as a mighty king among his men. In measured tones, he greeted me with the title of *Phraya* (Lord) that he'd bestowed on me and asked me anxiously whether his dear son Rathsavong Ngao was still leading his men and fighting on. He rejoiced in the news I gave him of his son's renown. In my heart's desire I dearly wanted to embrace him. I started forward with outstretched hands to clasp him to me, but like a shadow he slipped through my arms. The dream was unbelievably real, but when I woke up and found myself alone, tears of joy rolled down my cheeks. I was blessed by the thought that his spirit had allowed me to travel unseen and had guided me on my way home: I wasn't meant to die just yet. I often slept in my new outfit; it looked much like the old one I'd left behind with the monk in Bangkok. I occasionally lashed at my horse's rump and galloped towards ViengChan, for I longed to get back. A month later, I arrived; my beloved city was still in ruins, looking haunted and sad. I dismounted with a happy heart and stepped under the roof of my damaged home and saw my friends again. I stayed out of trouble, remembered Chao Anouvong's merits and tried to forget my grief. I clung on to life and hope for LanXang.

Despite having lived in Bangkok for many years, I still believed Chao Anouvong would have wanted to be taken back to his beloved city of ViengChan. He always wanted his ashes to be interred in the Wat Sisaketh temple that he'd ordered to be built. He said, 'Phia Jon, make sure my ashes face southwest in the stupa. And should I be honoured or commemorated with a bronze statue, please make sure it faces the Mekong in the direction of Bangkok. Whenever they look at it, the Siamese royalty and government will feel faint with guilt and unease.'

Well now, I must confess I have no idea what happened to Chao Anouvong's remains. I'm certain they stayed in Bangkok, but where exactly? No trace of them has ever been found and it remains one of the strangest mysteries in the history of Siam, providing food for thought for future generations. I dare say Bangkok is too ashamed to tell the truth: it would prove their guilt and arouse Lao patriotism.

Soon after his death, his victorious rival King Nangklao ordered all images and records of Chao Anouvong to be destroyed. A nondescript red brick wall is all that remains of his residence (*Wang Lao*) in Bangkok. Nangklao's subjects were forced to comply, but the order caused great offence all over LanXang, and especially on the Khorat Plateau. But there was nothing the people could do; anyone caught in possession of his image was severely punished.

After a good rest, many days later I braced myself for a walk to inspect what was left of ViengChan. I felt lost at the sight of such total devastation; the undamaged Wat Sisaketh stood hauntingly alone amongst the windswept ruins, amid a cloud of dust and ash. I went inside the ordination hall to make offerings, to pray, to contemplate mortality and to parley with destiny. I lit a candle and placed it on the candleholder which was flanked by two of Chao Anouvong's life-size bronze Buddhas. Then I carefully rested the dried *Dork Champa* blossom (*Malah*) I'd brought back from Bangkok on the floor in front of the largest Buddha. I burned some incense to honour his memory and gazed at his portrait – a magnificent creation bathed in flickering candlelight – and prayed for justice. Perhaps his soul had returned to ViengChan and wouldn't rest until LanXang had been fully united. I was suddenly overcome, and tears pricked my eyes as I thought of happier days and how much I missed him. His death was a reminder that the Lao people in Siam were LanXang's children. They believed in Chao Anouvong and still looked back with nostalgia.

Although not born in Rattanakosin Siam, Chao Anouvong was shaped by it, loved by it, twisted, damaged and finally destroyed by it. He underwent a profound ideological conversion and probably never imagined he might one day rebel. He first arrived in Bangkok at the age of twelve, living as a hostage and growing up amongst the Siamese elite in a palace reserved for Lao royals (*Wang Lao*) in Bang Yi Khan. He belonged to Siam but had the heart and mind of a Lao. He never seriously contemplated being anything else. In his twenties he took part in a military campaign on Siam's behalf against the Burmese in LanNa, earning him admiration and respect in Bangkok. His ideological dependability was thoroughly examined before he was allowed to return to ViengChan. One of his most endearing qualities was that rather than expressing bitterness, he preferred to laugh at the absurdity of the Siamese obsession with their kings and their politics of repression. When LanXang was besieged by Siam, Chao Anouvong transformed himself into an unquestioning Lao patriot with a rigid belief in Lao sovereignty. He persevered in a peaceful struggle for LanXang independence, but Siam's harsh policies and his personal humiliation in Bangkok forced him to fight for it instead.

Chao Anouvong regarded me as a great servant, a loyal confidant and a true companion. Fate had chosen him to be my lord. I respected him enormously and was always happy in his presence. He was full of the joys of living, receiving and giving, a great dining companion when old thoughts stirred and new ones came to mind; he possessed such a wealth of knowledge. I truly loved him; I'd spent my life with one of the most tireless and intelligent people. I always hoped to protect him from danger, even at the expense of my own life, but I knew he'd want me to keep on living. Sometimes I was frightened of him: out of respect, I never forgot to take my hat off, lowering my head and stepping aside to make way for him and standing to attention whenever we chanced to meet, an attention to detail he never allowed to pass unacknowledged. I always fetched his shoes as a sign of filial affection. Now it had all ended: henceforth I would only have my own soul to listen to.

King Anouvong was sixty-two years old at his death on 25 January 1829, the Year of the Bull. This tragic loss marked the end of the ViengChan royal family, although some ended up serving Siam in Bangkok. There was no state funeral, no pomp, no pageantry for the executed king. Siam won the war and Chao Anouvong was not only mistreated but tortured and executed and even mentioning his name became a crime. His death and the annihilation of ViengChan tore the two nations apart. The sun had truly set, not only on LanXang but also on the Siamese special relationship with the Lao people. It can only be retrieved if Bangkok admits its guilt and returns what rightfully belongs to LanXang

The subsequent course of events showed what a huge gap Chao Anouvong's death had left. The shock of his execution paralysed everyone at first and LanXang swirled with rumours, while the mass deportation of the Lao population to Siam continued. In this chaotic situation most of the Lao nobility, especially on the Khorat Plateau, continued to peacefully plead with Siam for their rights, despite the ongoing repression and killings. But Bangkok's selfish, stony heart was unmoved.

With Chao Anouvong's death the fabric of the Lao kingdom was irreparably torn. The country was plunged into horrified despair and mourning, the women wailing and the men escaping into temples or forests. It was a time of hopelessness. The Lao world had changed but there was still hope for the future. LanXang, once independent, prosperous and respected, had lost everything except its people's hearts and minds. Chao Anouvong sought to take back control and unite the country. His sacrifice made him a martyr. It was the end of an era and a new beginning.

Epilogue

The Lao people's hurt, humiliation and shock turned to disappointment and anger before, finally, a palpable sense of loss, defiance and a burning desire to make up for their defeat. The Lao care little for material values and are highly self-sufficient, so the loss of property was of less concern to them. However, the destruction of ViengChan and the death of Chao Anouvong – the by-product of Bangkok's treacherous ambition for a Greater Siam – proved a calamity for Lao LanXang. The good feelings had gone and they trembled with rage and thirsted for revenge. His memory became sacred and many mourned him for the rest of their lives. They were hammered into despair by it all, unable to understand why there was so much injustice in the world. They had seen their loved ones and fellow countrymen fall under the swords of the enemy and now their king was dead, but after his death came hope. They still had their unconquerable cheerfulness to help them endure the bitterest of afflictions with serenity and obliterate the painful memory from their minds. Sorrow for their departed king was relieved by the prospect of reincarnation. Despite being under foreign dominance, they fearlessly expressed their revulsion at his torture and execution and were united in grieving his death. There was scarcely a family that hadn't been touched by sorrow. They gathered at Wat Sisaketh temple to mourn a son of ViengChan – a man as Lao as the country he spent his childhood in, a man proud and fond of his country yet so hated in Bangkok that even his remains were secretly interred and refused permission to return home. His people wanted to build a shrine for him and accord him all proper funeral rites.

In time of great distress and hardship, the Lao traditionally seek comfort in spiritual sanctuary and making merit in the temples as a way to end their anguish. They said solemn prayers and lit candles in commemoration of Chao

Anouvong's death. Many men went into spiritual retreat, shaving their heads, dressing in white and silently lamenting the passing of their ill-fated and fair-minded king. One hundred days after his passing, in the agony of their grief many entered the monkhood and performed almsgiving services. The people would never forget the debt they owed him. He will be forever remembered. Even widows and orphans, who could barely support themselves, made offerings in their local temples and shrines, more in grief than in expectation. They longed to know when the world would bring them justice. The light had gone out of LanXang but will always shine for Chao Anouvong and all those who sacrificed their lives. They deserve to be honoured. How could we possibly let those who'd spilled their blood for their nation be forgotten? Alas, in Bangkok, Chao Anouvong is an eternally vexed spirit. Bangkok overlooked how deeply wounded the Lao people were at the news of his death

It is widely accepted that victors in war mostly write their own glorious history. The Siamese are extremely good at it but in war there are always two sides to the story. Although LanXang's past has been suppressed by Bangkok it is impossible to forever deny the truth. The Lao people on the Khorat Plateau spent their lives knowing they'd committed a historic crime by keeping their silence under Bangkok's act of supremacy.

Siam started the war by invading LanXang in 1779 and characterised the 1828 war as 'Chao Anouvong's war', astonishingly accusing ViengChan of invading their land. In fact Chao Anouvong and his men kept to LanXang territory as they marched to Khorat; he didn't need Bangkok's permission for this. There's no evidence he planned to move on the Siamese capital. The biased and zealous Siamese historians painted Siam and its ruler in a praiseworthy and sympathetic light – that's what they want you to remember. But any honest king would have flung that particular history book away as a work of fiction. The Siamese owe the world an acknowledgment of the truth. In an attempt to exonerate themselves from the plundering and annihilation of ViengChan, they heaped the blame on to Chao Anouvong and the Lao people. It would be a terrible mistake to misunderstand the true reasons behind the Lao uprising against Siam, no matter what the Siamese might teach their children.

The conquest of ViengChan was Siam's finest hour: the kingdom was barely brushed by the horrors of war. Her cities escaped unscathed; her treasures were not looted, her citizens weren't rounded up, massacred and enslaved. Bangkok congratulated itself for having won the war, triumphantly transforming it into a righteous drama, the subject of history books, plays, grand monuments and memorials.

The Lao LanXang people fought for their identity and livelihood during the 1779 invasion. They watched the Siamese soldiers burning ViengChan, refusing to surrender but ending up crushed in the dust. Despite losing everything except their hearts and minds and living under the most brutal tyranny, they still behaved with courage, dignity and restraint. They then had to face it all over again in 1828 in a desperate attempt to survive as a nation. Alas, Chao Anouvong failed in his bid for independence and the war ended in devastation; ViengChan was brought to her knees by Siam's army of foreign mercenaries; her armed forces were destroyed, her kingdom dismembered.

Nangklao was guilty of savagely suppressing the Lao people and executing Chao Anouvong without any due process of law. The colonial powers in turn were guilty of supplying Siam with military aid. History has the case prepared and will one day bring Siam's rulers to book by exposing them as villains. Their doom will be well deserved, for in their madness they twice invaded and annihilated their cousins' capital city and betrayed the Ai-Lao brotherhood.

The memory of their victory has influenced the ruling class's behaviour ever since: their children were never allowed to grow up in the light of truth for fear of rebelling against the Rattanakosins, conditioned into believing only in the glory of Siam and that LanXang was the aggressor. The degree of human suffering was never acknowledged. Perhaps they have no decency, no shame and no regard for the truth, but they surely know that nothing can stay hidden forever.

The Rattanakosins can't even handle their own kingdom's affairs, let alone govern their vassal states fairly. The peaceful Lao people felt no bitterness or enmity towards anybody, but Bangkok made conflict unavoidable. When ViengChan was sacked for the second time, memories of the first invasion's cruelty made many Lao people too frightened to act: the risk of being discovered floating face down in the Mekong or ending up amongst the fly-ridden, severed heads paraded on pirogues for the terrified population to see was too much. Yet many were brave enough to take up arms in spite of their fear and died fighting for LanXang.

Many people wondered what motivated Chao Anouvong to rebel: why be so foolish as to put LanXang and his own life at risk? Perhaps he was paranoid or just wanted revenge. No: in truth all he wanted was to protect the Lao nation and he didn't deserve his awful fate. The obvious question to ask is: why did

Chao Anouvong become a nationalist (*Phu HuckZard*)? Perhaps if he'd chosen a different path, the Lao people wouldn't have rallied to his cause. His struggle was a struggle for civilisation (*Ariyatham*); by executing him Bangkok made him a martyr. His death helped to create an enduring association with the Lao youth. He became an ethereal, national prodigy and an ineffable hero, despite his ultimate failure. He succeeded in implanting his brave principles in all Lao people. LanXang owes him a debt far greater than he would ever have claimed for himself. I hope we see his like again.

Bangkok has been arrogant and condescending to the Lao, viewing LanXang as backward and uncivilised. To compensate for their inglorious past they've shown contempt for Lao territorial integrity, national identity and the livelihoods of ordinary Lao people, purging a simple, yet respected and well-run independent country.

Well, it's been over three decades since Chao Anouvong's death – the death of a conscientious and decent man who feared for the Lao nation. Yet the Rattanakosins scornfully judged him a traitor. He was contemptuous of tyrants but indifferent to the insults that Bangkok heaped upon him; he was vigilant in his nation's interests, a defender of decency and freedom and a patriot who was willing to die rather than submit to an oppressor. The nature of his passing has a particular religious meaning: one day it will bring down the wrath of the Lord Buddha and the gods on Siam. Some of the Siamese elite have at least a grudging respect for Chao Anouvong; others openly revere him for his bravery and patriotism, like their former king Naresuan the Great.

When I was Chao Anouvong's confidant, I dreamt that he met with the Siamese kings Naphalai and Nangklao, speaking passionately to persuade them that Lao LanXang was a separate ethnic nation with its own language and deserved to exist and remain independent. He reminded them of the 1350 boundary agreement between King Fah Ngum and King Uthong and the 1563 That Si-SongHuck demarcation treaty between Siam and LanXang. None of these hopes and dreams were fulfilled. His end was a real tragedy, one of the saddest of fates; whenever I think of it my eyes blur with tears and my heart aches, but I continue to dream of him and live with his memory.

With his emollient approach to the conflict Chao Anouvong sincerely believed that the future could be put right if Bangkok respected previous agreements. He wanted peace and love for everybody, agreeing with scholars that the two nations were so similar genetically, culturally and linguistically.

They should bond and live peacefully as one and the same, albeit in separate countries. They shouldn't be blind to their differences but use them as a guide towards a common good where these differences could be resolved. They would do well to settle their historical and territorial disputes so that peace, trust and love could return. Most people wanted the 1563 treaty to be respected: wishful thinking perhaps, because the Bangkok political elite had become cynical, grasping and duplicitous. Sadly it'll never happen now: domineering policies and colonial fantasies have destroyed our sacred bond forever.

After many years of contemplation since the war ended, one day, as the sun climbed over the treetops, I had a disturbing premonition. As I sat, sipping cool, green coconut juice, watching the flaming sun set across the Mekong, I realised the Lao people were living in a dream, for how could anyone in the whole of LanXang ever have hoped the Siamese government would admit their guilt and return the property they'd stolen? But losing their land through violence and fraud rather than negotiation was never going to be easy for the Lao to forget. They cling to a belief in their nation's territorial integrity and yearn to restore their country to its rightful size with the Mekong running through its middle as if it were the blood and nerves running through their spine: their axis.

Chao Anouvong used to say that maintaining peace and security was indispensable for every kingdom's prosperity. Every neighbouring country should be friends, rooted in an enduring combination of amity and hostility: a mixture of envy, admiration, shared values and high regard. He wanted to devise a strategy to keep Siam close to LanXang and maximise the benefits. Perhaps ViengChan could have made a gesture of reconciliation to Bangkok. Reconciliation is imperative, but the only true way forward is for Siam to return to LanXang what's rightfully hers.

Perhaps you think we should just move on and let things take their course. What goes up must come down; the wheel will turn full circle; the sword of justice will punish the wicked; humanity is as capable of development as devastation; man can rise and fall in the blink of an eye; no one will become too powerful if they follow their goals within their own limits.

The Lao believed they were fighting to protect their nation, but Bangkok ludicrously condemned them as traitors, not only denying their misdeeds but refusing to even mention them. Bangkok will sit in an eternal nightmare, growing like a cancer in their hearts, haunting them with fear. The presence of the Emerald Buddha will always unnerve them; they will live their lives in shame and guilt in its shadow. For Siamese children Chao Anouvong will become merely a fictional character, a name to jeer at. Who can blame them? They weren't around in the 1820s. But do the Siamese have to brainwash their children with books? Why not let them see the truth; it might make them think. Bangkok should restore the role of the noble elders; their ancient knowledge might overrule the demands of power and the greed of the Rattanakosins.

Perhaps not everyone in LanXang is as troubled as you would expect them to be, certainly not the ordinary people. Time is a great healer, so this is quite understandable. I doubt whether anyone apart from Chao Anouvong tried to look so far into the future. The past can't be changed but the Lao still yearn for the restoration of LanXang.

The Lao people lived in fear after the 1779 invasion and the ensuing Siamese occupation, but even then you could still detect the influence of their more relaxed, Buddhist faith. The chief characteristics of the Lao are cheerfulness, generosity, sincerity and an earthy sense of humour, which, when it's not erupting in moments of sheer delight, is usually bubbling beneath the surface of every conversation, every glance and every communication. The Lao possess an ancient heritage of great courtesy, spirituality and brotherly existence.

LanXang was a land where all fellow beings, rich and poor, were equal in terms of their respect for each other. The gulf between the ruling class and its subjects was insignificant; it was more important for the Lao identity to remain intact. Lao culture was never based on money; it is more a meaningful and carefree way of life in which each person respects those around them and takes care of elders, family members and guests. They prefer to count the blessings of money rather than wallow in the love of it. Health, openness and simplicity are important but deep human values are prized above all else. I hope this never changes.

More than eighty years of subjugation have left LanXang deeply suspicious of Siam. A love-hate relationship has developed between the two nations; it will continue to exist until Bangkok comes to terms with the truth. The bond between the Lao and Siamese is similar to that between brothers: close but competitive, mutually supportive but liable to squabbles, a complicated mixture of fondness and resentment, jealousy and loyalty. After all both are descended from King Khoun Borom, all Ai-Lao before becoming LanXang and LanPhya (Siam) with their respective capitals of ViengChan and Bangkok. But the violent events I've described will remain etched in memory, the basis of a mistrust that has long bedevilled relations between Bangkok and ViengChan. It might be hard for the Siamese to say sorry but leaving LanXang territory should be easy: its residents are ethnic Lao. They should be allowed to decide their own future and manage their own lives.

Chao Anouvong indeed accepted that the past couldn't be changed, but the future is a different matter. Bangkok should be obliged to put things right so that wounds can be healed. It is strange how history never fails to return to haunt the minds of future generations.

Logically speaking, the land under the heavens belongs to those who nurture it and live in it. The Lao people in the north and northeast of Siam have remained closely connected, despite being forced to live under Siam's rule. Most of them have friends and relatives on both sides of the mighty Mekong, which has never been a geographical or political boundary but always of great social and economic importance. It has nevertheless been a struggle to retain LanXang unity: Chao Anouvong's most desired wish.

While the Siamese believed they were reclaiming lost lands, they were in fact destroying the Lao nation's existence. The vast Khorat Plateau and LanNa, trophies of Siamese imperialism, should be returned to their rightful owner at once, otherwise the Lao will never trust Bangkok. A Greater Siam might sound impressive, but it will forever cast a long shadow. Throughout LanXang and LanNa the people are historically and culturally distinct, highly patriotic and protective of their native language. They should be as far away from Bangkok's rule as possible, learning what it means to be Lao and maintaining the Lao traditions and laws which provide variety, joy and inspiration in their lives.

After the war most Lao people who loved and revered Chao Anouvong, especially those on the Khorat Plateau, daringly declared themselves his soldiers. He'd earned himself a deep reservoir of respect. They accepted he was gone forever, but while his memory remained fresh in their minds he would live for as long as they did. They cherished his memory and many cling to the hope he'll come again. They bitterly begrudge Bangkok's policies of oppressing the Lao culture and exterminating the Lao ruling class. Many attempts have been made to make Bangkok see sense, but any Lao noble who's peacefully protested has been imprisoned or killed or has simply disappeared without trace.

Elite Siamese army units likely operated as secret agents, seeking revenge, silencing any Lao nobles whose views were judged offensive. They became a malign and disruptive force that behaved just like criminals, assassinating their victims in an attempt to hide their crimes. The Siamese were determined to erase all trace of Lao opposition. Any army commander, holder of high office or close companion to King Anouvong were marked men. All of LanXang – the Khorat Plateau and ViengChan in particular – became hunting grounds where Lao nationalists were tracked down. Well-bred members of the Lao nobility who'd had the temerity to attack the Siamese ruler were lured to Bangkok. Members of the Lao educated class and ruling elite who disobeyed orders were also tricked into going to the capital by bribery or being told that the king wanted to hear their complaints in person. None of them even got close to Bangkok. They were either killed or imprisoned and such actions were condoned and even encouraged. Far from being the city of angels, Bangkok became the city of the underworld.

For devotees of the truth, the past is LanXang and LanNa's best friend. An impulse for nostalgia could well lead them back to their former selves. There seem to be two forces at play in Lao LanXang life: one seeks unity: looking to the future but also recognising the importance of preserving the past. The other is unconcerned about history and identity and avoids confrontation, priding itself on peaceful living, missing the bigger picture and losing hope. 'Keep calm, carry on, never mind, the future can wait, all will be well,' has become its rallying cry.

A fair and impartial observer might well ask whether Siam should renounce its annexation of Lao land. You would probably cover your mouth with your hand to stifle your laughter. No problem. Then you might well ask what leads me to believe Siam would give back the land. Well, if I may speak frankly, Bangkok drew an arbitrary map of Siam and plucked a name out of thin air for this new, enlarged country. But they were wrong to encroach on our territory. The Lao language is the very identity of the Lao people, not a mere north-east provincial dialect of Siam. ViengChan is geographically and culturally central to the Lao world, which should always straddle both banks of the Mekong. The Siamese would be better off sticking to the central plain of the Chaophraya river: the closer they get to the Mekong, the bigger the problem.

A reconciliation between Siam and LanXang would be a godsend: it would allow the Lao people to stop looking backwards and finally get on with their lives. Bangkok should see the bigger picture and, in the name of justice, the rest of the world should do all it can to help. No doubt the Siamese would be angry at such a suggestion; I daresay they would dispute my point of view that their insatiable desire for empire-building created enormous vanity in Bangkok and made them the enemy of all their neighbours. But I merely articulate my own opinion. What could be fairer than that?

The people in the north and northeast of Siam were made to look like second-class citizens, impoverished by Bangkok expansionism. The Rattanakosin ruler ruled the land like a despot and refused to allow any condemnation. Protected by the constitution, the Bangkok elite become unpredictable and self-interested aristocrats who regarded criticism as treason. Most of their decrees were opposed to democracy and freedom, betraying their people, the backbone of the nation. Behind the gilded gates of the Rattanakosins' palace, the ruler and his officials wined and dined on ill-gotten gains while the bones of the starved lay scattered outside.

Many educated people believe Siam can never survive in its present form, with Bangkok flourishing at the expense of the impoverished north and northeast. Perhaps the whole kingdom should be broken up, pulled down and rebuilt from scratch. It will only get worse with time. While the elite in Bangkok, under the patronage of the royal family, live the high life and walk around toffee-nosed, the rest of the country suffers under Siamese commissioners and governors who stop at nothing to protect and enrich the monarchy. Bangkok discriminates against the underprivileged majority with higher taxes and has excluded its best educated citizens from important posts in government. Critics who believe in equal opportunity, justice and freedom are labelled as traitors, ignored and persecuted and sometimes even murdered with impunity. ViengChan has always been critical of the assimilation of Lao citizens in Siam and has raised many grievances over their unfair treatment by Siamese society.

LanXang has a burning distrust of Siam. Whatever Siam calls itself, it'll always be portrayed as something greater than a mere expression of its political and economic success: it will be defined by its supposed 'triumphs'. It has little history as a nation state worthy of note: hardly surprising, as it was only able to expand by aggressively invading LanXang and LanNa. Perhaps it won't last much longer because of the resentment between the easy-going Lao and the domineering Siamese. By heavily taxing sticky rice, the Bangkok authorities offended the Lao principles of a decent and honourable way of life and then preferred to turn a blind eye to the problems they'd created. Alas Siam remained so intent on its annexation of LanXang and LanNa that it failed to see where its power would lead. Truth is the first casualty in a war of occupation, but it will always prevail in the end. Despite the damage caused by their lies and ignorance, Bangkok still refuses to tell the truth to their people or to the world at large. They refuse to mention the annihilation of ViengChan and the mass deportation of the Lao people to Siam in their historical narrative. Siam cannot force its vassal kingdoms to remain part of a unified kingdom based on a capital – Bangkok – that is only eighty-three years old. ViengChan, on the contrary, has been LanXang's capital for more than 300 years.

It is important once again to mention Siam's two invasions of LanXang. By eliminating the Lao royal family, Bangkok hoped to achieve complete dominance over its neighbours. Firstly, in 1779, on the unjustifiable pretext that the Lao had sided with Burma, King TakSin dispatched his friend Phraya Kasatseuk the warlord with 30,000 men to invade the peaceful LanXang kingdom; they captured ViengChan and seized the Emerald Buddha. In the past, the Lao people had sacrificed themselves to help the Ayutthaya Siamese fight the Burmese whenever they were asked, especially during the reigns of the Siamese King Chakraphat and the Lao King Xay-Setthathirath I. It's highly likely Bangkok would not have triumphed over Burmese rule in LanNa without Chao Anouvong's bravery.

The second invasion was based on the false pretext that Chao Anouvong was a danger to Siam. It was pure folly for Bangkok to dominate LanXang and LanNa. As if insane, they adopted deliberately harsh policies and aimed to eliminate both kingdoms. Nangklao, his demeanour haughty and imperious, seemed isolated from reality, ignorant of the relations between the Siamese and the Lao, surrounded by yes men. Rather than oblige the Lao, Bangkok portrayed them as traitors and saw Chao Anouvong as a threat to be eliminated, because they selfishly believed the future belonged to Siam alone. This was a fundamental misreading of who Chao Anouvong really was and why he acted the way he did. His uprising against the oppressive Bangkok regime in the name of the Lao nation was surely justifiable in the eyes of both man and god, but the 1828 annihilation of ViengChan – in which thousands of people lost their lives and many more were forced to migrate to Siam – was undeniably a crime against humanity, a betrayal of the centuries-long relationship between the Siamese and Lao people.

No narration of LanXang's history can omit the Siamese invasions – especially the sacking and massacres of ViengChan – which had enormous consequences for Lao civilization, beyond even the unimaginable number of people who were indiscriminately killed and the survivors who were forced to leave their homes. One may never find a satisfactory answer to why any of this happened, but for the sake of argument it's safe to say it was caused by Bangkok's jealousy, insanity, insecurity, suspicion and expansionist desires. Without the increased manpower and natural resources they gained from the invasions, the Siamese might not have achieved the prosperity they enjoy today.

It was hard in the face of such a catastrophe to imagine any sort of future for Lao LanXang. What sort of god could inflict such a tragedy on a peaceful nation? Nevertheless, Siam will never entirely exterminate LanXang and force the Lao and Siamese people to assimilate. Perhaps the Lao migration to Siam was a blessing in disguise. No one can ever destroy Lao LanXang: the *Khaen* and *Phin* music; the poetry, opera, singing, dancing and communal singalongs; the villages and towns on the rivers; the houses on stilts; the temples for making merit, the laid-back peaceful living; the sticky rice; the rocket festivals; the circle dance (*Lamvong*) and so on... now *that* is Lao LanXang. No one can take it away. Lao culture and personality will endure forever. Lao will be Lao. Bangkok's purging policies will fail.

Having heard my story perhaps you'll now realise Chao Anouvong's war was completely justified. All he wanted was justice for the Lao nation. Lao has always been peace-loving and war was never his preferred option, but we must remember all those whose lives were affected by the Siamese invasions, which simply tore the people apart. The fault lies squarely with our Siamese 'brothers, friends and partners' who wanted to eat LanXang up. The That Si-SongHuck shrine in the city of Dan Sai stands for all to see as evidence of Siamese duplicity.

Surely some truthful Siamese secretly recognise their nation's crimes, though they would never admit them openly. They probably wish to forget the 1779 and 1828 invasions or, on the other hand, celebrate them as Siamese victories. A great country accepts its wrongs, apologises for them and tries to correct them, but the Rattanakosin government seems incapable of change, of reconciliation, of love or of understanding. These events will certainly come back to haunt them.

Siam's solution to the problems they themselves created was to blame Chao Anouvong and to execute him. The documents written by Siamese court historians, obstinately and obsessively gilding Siam's image, contemptuously labelled him as a traitor and provided a template for future academics and teachers. Although appearing on the surface to satisfy the Siamese world, in reality it fractured the country politically. He was never a traitor (*Khaboad* ກະບົດ). He was Lao, not Siamese; how could he betray a state he owed no allegiance to? He was not only innocent of the charge but was horribly tortured, kept in a cage in squalor, deprived of care and subject to a savage and lingering death.

To the Lao people he became a martyr, the hero who never really died but who continues to fight for justice and for their rights. It must only be a matter of time before the Lao citizens rebel against Bangkok. Chao Anouvong lit the flame of self-rule and nothing – not even the wicked Rattanakosins – can extinguish it. What goes round comes round, one presumes. Could the cycle of death and revenge continue? I exaggerate of course, but only to make the point.

After his death the Siamese authorities were determined to erase even the memory of Chao Anouvong. They confiscated all his portraits, and anything written about him and burnt it all. Secret files on him were put to the torch unread: presumably their contents would have only irritated Bangkok or contradicted the accepted history that the Rattanakosin king was a genius and a god, and all who opposed him were traitors, idiots, ingrates and diehards. Bangkok would rather remain ignorant than be obliged to face the truth. Even the Wang Lao palace in Bang Yi Khan where Chao Anouvong stayed was pulled down, leaving only ruined heaps of red brick. It became dangerous to even discuss his death and Bangkok banned all mention of the gruesome details of his execution because they knew how much they stood to lose if it became public. Their secrecy bred rumours; soon they were quarrelling amongst themselves and blaming each other without any respect for the truth.

Now that Chao Anouvong was gone from the world and no longer posed a threat, Siam ought to have acknowledged him as the bravest and greatest Laoman. If heaven looked upon justice as a virtue, it would surely not have favoured the coterie of dunces and scoundrels who formed a confederacy against him. Unfortunately, during his lifetime, the Bangkok elite became inflated with egotism, selfishness, brutality, arrogance and deceitfulness. In the meantime the Lao people passionately believed the Siamese would one day return their lost possessions to them. How marvellous that would be: they would rejoice even though they would only be receiving what should never have been taken away in the first place. Still, they have reason to be positive because their karma fills them with hope and optimism.

During Chao Anouvong's war the Lao people suffered terrible violence. It's a pity Bangkok didn't pause for thought before trying to destroy a nation, killing and uprooting innocent people, destabilising an entire country and breeding eternal resentment, all in the name of a Greater Siam. The Siamese officials and soldiers brutally put down Lao resistance for refusing to accept Bangkok's rule. Hundreds of high-ranking Lao nobles and captives were the victims of grave acts of brutality. During the forced migration they were subjected to Siam-sponsored violence, including torture, sexual assault, systematic beatings and barbaric executions.

Bangkok has been trying to evade an uncomfortable truth. The way forward should be obvious, but their unwillingness to make amends is blatantly out of step with Buddhist doctrine. Intending to erase Lao LanXang from the world, they build memorials and monuments to the past and forge their history to make them feel superior. They could never excuse their unwarranted behaviour without admitting responsibility. They should show sorrow and regret for not keeping their word and failing to respect the wisdom of Legendary Khoun Borom. But it would be absurd to blame the Siamese people; it was their narcissistic and autocratic rulers who decided to invade LanXang.

Despite appearances the people wallowing in luxury in their palatial houses and palaces in Bangkok are far from happy: an appetite for wealth and power still dominates their souls and they're still intent on acquiring as much money as possible, giving no thought to the truth and to their own consciences. They'll suffer eventually for their misdeeds, either later in this life or in the next. They're already living in a hell of their own making.

Bangkok claimed the Lao LanXang 'problem' wouldn't be solved until ViengChan was destroyed. Well, it had been prophesied that wild foxes would build their homes in the ruins of the Lao capital, but will there be anywhere for rabbits to dig their holes when Bangkok is ruined? I suspect all civilisations end in ruins: the question is when. Perhaps the 'problem' with Siam and the Siamese won't be over until Bangkok disappears beneath the waves, but let's leave that to nature: god's justice.

Since King Fah Ngum's time, LanXang had always got on well with her neighbours. Historically and culturally, the Lao people have always possessed their own, distinct identity, eating sticky rice and playing the *Khaen*. Chao Anouvong couldn't have been more right in his attempt to save the Lao nation from Siam. Lao blood will always flow and never run dry. There will always be a generation of Lao children who know the true history of Chao Anouvong and the Siamese annihilation of ViengChan. The majority of Lao people in LanNa and the Khorat Plateau and those who were forced like slaves to settle all over Siam – the Lao Vieng, the Lao Krung, the Lao Ngiao, the Lao Tai Dam, the Lao Phuan and many more – will surely remember. They will strive to right the wrongs that have been perpetrated against them. The time will come for those who wait. Where there's a will there's a way. Siam may well be at the dawn of a new age.

The memory of Chao Anouvong's death in Bangkok, his head stuck on a pole at Sanamluang field, is a desperately sad one. ViengChan was completely laid waste and burned to the ground, a city of ruins where scattered mountains of stones, bricks and rubble disfigured the city. Acres of fruit trees were uprooted and burnt. Both the inner and outer city walls were knocked down. The palaces, the Hor Phra Kaeo and other holy temples were dismantled and burnt. The badly damaged That Luang stupa, the symbolic heart of the city and of the entire Lao nation, stood in no man's land at the end of a once-magnificent tree-lined avenue where glittering temples and houses had been reduced to roofless and precarious ruin. The heart of ViengChan – once a great capital – had been ripped out by Siamese savagery. This was the lowest point in LanXang's history, but the city still stood as a memorial to the Lao people's heroic past.

How could Bangkok derive any satisfaction from using all its resources to reduce a well-established, beautiful city to ashes? Jealousy and selfishness may have made them irrational, but why destroy their own ancestors? I honestly will never know, for I am neither a military nor a political man. The Lao people have a simple rebuttal to Bangkok's denials that it ever depopulated LanXang or annihilated the holy temples in ViengChan: 'The Siamese are lying,' they say. Bangkok will continue to lie, because these lies unite Siam's political classes and encourage people to demonstrate their loyalty by believing in them.

When the That Luang stupa fell, ViengChan fell. When ViengChan fell, the entire Lao world fell, but it was a world worth fighting for. Physically devastated, LanXang became poverty stricken, a land of wrack and ruin decorated with painful reminders of what it once had been. The ruined temples were sad, evocative reminders of the storm of violence, symbols of an abiding strand in Lao life, reminders not only of the disappearance of the ViengChan dynasty but also happy, awe-inspiring memories of Chao Anouvong's reign. Alas the depopulation led to a widespread loss of skills, including writing. Civilisation was pushed backward, tearing apart not only individual lives and livelihoods but whole villages, ecosystems centuries in the making. The scale of the destruction, which deserved a 'Made in Siam' label, truly shocked the Lao world and beyond. The Lao tried valiantly to forget but it proved impossible to overlook a period of such oppression when the Lao people lost their freedom and suffered a terrible physical and moral degeneration. The whole kingdom lived in fear and suspense, a nation with a great past but no future. LanXang was broken, its very history rapidly disappearing, no longer even a vassal state, adrift from the family of nations in South-East Asia. It was a daunting time.

As a restrained and reserved little man growing old in the 1860s, my lasting memory of the Siamese invasion is the news of Nangklao's death in April 1851. Many tales of him are best left out – the truths are already known to the world, while there are more than enough falsehoods. Nangklao was a figure of terror, a tyrant and the foremost enemy of the Lao people. When he died it felt as if a shadow had been lifted from the Lao kingdom, yet all too quickly I became aware of another ghost lurking about: the Rattanakosin line would continue with Mongkut and then another male king after him. The prophesy that nine dynastic kings would rule Siam might well be true: if so there'll be five after Mongkut and that will be it. I will continue to observe the hearts of the people. For now, Lao LanNa and LanXang belong to Siam. They must surely demand independence at some stage, otherwise Siam will be riven with endless conflicts and toxic political tribalism. By the will of heaven, dynasties rise and fall or just fade into irrelevance. The universe is forever changing, and nature renews itself, but the truth can never be overturned. I paid my respects to Nangklao and patiently continued to wait in dignified silence, mourning Chao Anouvong's death at the same time. It was the only thing I could do: hide my true feelings and wait for an opportunity.

A long way from Siam stands the holy That Luang and That Phanom stupas where the mighty Mekong flows through ViengChan, all emblems of Lao LanXang but claimed by the Rattanakosin regime. The annihilation of ViengChan occurred nearly forty years ago; the ashes have settled; the plants and trees have replanted themselves everywhere. New settlers have gradually moved in but fear still grips them that they'll see the end of their nation in their lifetime. The pain and anger remain fresh and will continue to do so. The way things are going the Lao might have to get used to it: what had initially seemed merely the illegal removal of the Emerald Buddha has become more like a total occupation, not by King TakSin but by the dark, charismatic Bangkok dynasty. The corrupt King TakSin of Thonburi and the Rattanakosins of Bangkok can well claim to be the most influential rulers in Siamese history. Their country has thrived since dominating LanXang and LanNa, but the Lao people would have been happier if they'd never been born. Siam would have been restricted to the central plain of the Chaophraya river and the two nations would have remained truthful to each other: a genuine testament of requited love.

It could be argued that Siam's invasion was actually beneficial to human development and the Rattanakosins weren't necessarily all bad, not embittered narcissists but behaving only according to the prevailing ethics of the time and to moral impulses rooted deep in their history. We are all a combination of good and bad, after all. Perhaps this should be open to discussion, but then again what has proved beneficial for Siam has caused immense suffering for the Lao. Although there should be a willingness to understand those who think differently from us, the fact remains that if Siam had behaved honestly and not fallen under the sway of colonial powers, King Fah Ngum's LanXang would still be a happy country for everyone.

Since 1779, Siam has always responded with contempt to Lao LanXang's desire for freedom. Only an unprincipled nation could prepare its people to be so contemptuous of others. Bangkok owes the world honesty and should be obliged to speak the truth, yet they persist in claiming that the language spoken in the north and northeast of Siam is a mere provincial dialect rather than the language of a separate Lao nation. It is impossible to conceal the truth forever. If the Siamese continue to do so they should expect no mercy from international scholars, or from any honest man for that matter.

Deep, dark secrets weigh heavily. Perhaps we should then feel sorry for the innocent Siamese people, taught only lies about their history from the day they're born, fed works of notorious imagination, compiled, altered, elaborated and expanded many years after Chao Anouvong's death. But surely history should always be subject to re-evaluation rather than old lies being endlessly celebrated. The Rattanakosins adopted a calculated policy merely to inculcate and woo their people, refusing to hold themselves accountable for capturing, pillaging and destroying ViengChan. They aimed only to put Siam in the most positive light, hoping no one would know enough to contradict them. Amidst all the sensational accounts, only one thing, perhaps, was certain: the guilty didn't want their names to appear in the public eye; a cover-up culture developed, protecting the elite from any suggestion they were to blame. But there are still intelligent people in Siam and the rest of the world who believe in justice; they will soon learn the truth and draw their own conclusions. They're not ignoramuses.

One could justifiably argue that Chao Anouvong provoked Siam into war, but then again provocation is generally a characteristic of the oppressor.

Nangklao was in fact the real provocateur; his decrees provoked a storm of protest as much from the Siamese people as the Lao. He made no pretence that through marginalisation and re-education, he wished to force the Lao to think like and actually become Siamese. Now, perhaps the question should be asked: did the Siamese public know the truth about their king's actions, and if they did, were they too frightened to act? Many would surely have taken the view that such a decree was a crime against humanity and would bring Siam into disrepute. Any ruler capable of such behaviour should have been condemned and deposed.

Everything changes and no one can live in the past, but we always look back to find answers. The flaws of the Siamese conquest of ViengChan should be debated without fear or self-censorship because the discovery of the truth is in the interests of the future. Bangkok should be able to accept opposing views and frank discussion. The younger generation should be allowed to express themselves and to openly challenge the status quo and should be protected for doing so. Such a sensitive subject merits an unfettered debate and the more provocative a story, the more it should be told. It should no longer be controversial to condemn the ambition of Rattanakosin Siam rather than merely mentioning it in passing. It's shameful that Chao Anouvong's memory has been publicly dishonoured by Bangkok's insinuations he was a traitor.

Rather than a genuine threat, Chao Anouvong was a paper tiger as far as Siam was concerned. Their identification of him as a double-crosser and a traitor chimed in with the glorious tales of splendour and glory they taught their children in the absence of accurate history. On the contrary, he was a patriotic and proud Lao nobleman and a man of principle. Chao Anouvong himself once said that if the price of being gentlemanly was to be oppressed, trampled upon or even killed, then he would rather be a crafty rebel. He remained true to himself and didn't worry about others misjudging him.

Please listen to what Chao Anouvong said: 'The Rattanakosin Siamese are full of arrogance and vanity, boasting and lies, discord and disunity, presumption and haughtiness. They love bragging about their wealth and arguing over their place in society; so much so that they'll seek vengeance or stage coups. They would murder each other, kill their own brothers, to acquire power. Siam will continue to tremble on the brink of civil unrest until it breaks down completely.'

Siamese society is like a rigid 'tree' rooted in snobbery and exceptionalism. At its base are the million-strong commoners who create wealth and the peasants who tend the lands, all paying onerous taxes to the crown. In the middle and near the top are the army and the politicians, the racketeering, influential nobles and the aristocrats. They're the real power behind the throne and they fight for riches and power. But set above all in venerable seclusion is the autocratic king, sitting on his golden throne like a god amongst men, distant, lonely and often insecure, barely human in his elusiveness, only accessible through an elite group of noblemen. During an audience with him the people fall to their knees, bringing their praying hands to their chests, lifting them above their heads and then prostrating themselves with respectful, submissive gestures. Without the common sense to live their lives according to Buddhist doctrines, Siamese society has become deceitful (*Kohoke-Torlae*). The path to genuine peace and happiness has been lost. There will be no end to the kingdom's troubles until a just or caring man becomes leader. Finally, when that rigid tree falls down, the masses will scatter, and chaos and destruction will follow. The realm will die.

Bangkok should let the Lao kingdom of LanXang be, but being fond only of the glory of Siam, their obsession was so extreme they became a laughingstock, even going so far as to suggest their military success was a divine expression of racial supremacy. Siamese racial theorists argued they were superior to their neighbours, a grim argument that fires anti-Siamese resentment to this day.

The Lao know what's good for them. They maintain a dignified silence, though they'll keep on striving until a united Lao kingdom of LanXang with the great Mekong flowing through the middle reappears on the map. The time will come when the people, not only in the north and northeast of Siam but elsewhere, will decide to form an autonomous region, thus confirming their loyalty to the historic truth. Bangkok has become so hardened to brutality that it doesn't even occur to them that human beings have the right to protest, but a culture of political protest will ultimately be formed. Siam's out-dated moral and social ideals will completely disintegrate. Siam's intentions, as Chao Anouvong said, will never be realised; her dark past will be a festering wound becoming poisonous. Chao Anouvong's ghost will hover over Bangkok as the regime continues to use repression to thwart the rebels. The people on the other hand will see things quite differently. They will want a return to reality, the chance to exist with purpose and to live the life they once dreamt of. They will have their own sense of nationhood, not slavishly believe the false patriotism that Bangkok tries to impose on them. It might take Lao LanXang 150 years or more to escape from Siamese domination, but it will happen.

It was never going to be an easy task to rescue LanNa and LanXang from Siam's yoke, but an eternal existence under Bangkok's power is simply not an option. Eventually the silent majority – the talented sleeping dragons (*Phraya Nark*) – will be galvanised into action. In Bangkok, ethnic Lao labourers and the educated elite will become confrontational. Not even guns will be able to stop them, and the Siamese government will be unable to simply arrest all of them. Siam will rightly shrink back into the central plain of the Chaophraya river. There is a strong whiff of anxiety in Bangkok.

During many restless nights in ViengChan I see Chao Anouvong's face in dreams, as though he's arrived on tropical moonbeams. He instructs me to tell the people not to seek vengeance against those who brutally ended his life; they'll meet the death they deserve in the end. He tells me he wishes to come home to ViengChan, but evil people are holding him against his will in Bangkok. His voice still rings in my ears when I wake, brushing away my tears and gazing up at the stars. I know he's gone. Life is but a dream and seems futile if you can't share it with the right person. How can it be possible for two people to share their lives for so long and then never see each other again. I miss him dearly.

You will forgive me, I feel sure, for complaining about the past. Time passes quickly. I've waited thirty-six years for the chance to tell the whole world. Not everyone knew who Chao Anouvong was until he was gone. His true worth at last became clear, but the poor king we once knew and loved ended his life in a cage, tortured and executed. How will the Lao world speak his name in years to come? Certainly not as a traitor, as in Bangkok, where the politics of repression forced him to act the way he did. He demonstrated the strength of his will and his contempt for Nangklao. Countless Lao people in Siam both secretly and openly see Chao Anouvong's life as a role model for their own. Indeed, thrusting young Lao, especially males in the Khorat Plateau, regard Chao Anouvong as a sort of heaven-sent hero whose ambitions will one day be fulfilled. These courageous and honest fellows will remember and talk about him everywhere. They may even claim to have served in his army in a previous life, hoping to receive some psychic charge before heroically claiming the return of the Emerald Buddha and LanXang territory.

Siam – the victor – with more land and people, enjoys peace and prosperity while LanXang – the loser – suffers endless misery. Sadly Chao Anouvong left no obvious successor to come forward and claim the right to rule the kingdom. His sons who escaped capture are lying low, but perhaps his grandsons or great grandsons might emerge one day. It's been a shocking spectacle to see LanXang in such an incoherent state, its ruling class divided and weak, with no idea who they really were. Chao Anouvong, on the other hand, believed in the awakening of national conscience, a foundation for the resurrection of the Lao.

Whatever the truth, it was reported later that Luang Phrabang's King Manthathurath repaid Chao Anouvong's generosity by dispatching a delegation – including his son Prince Sukhaseum – down to Bangkok as soon as ViengChan's mandarins had left the city. Determined to side with the victors, Manthathurath demonstrated his loyalty to Bangkok by pledging to make fighting men available in return for his city being spared. Once these delegates reached Bangkok, there is no doubt Chao Anouvong's secret war plans would have been betrayed.

The Siamese threatened to invade Luang Phrabang and kill its inhabitants unless they showed their loyalty. King Manthathurath, perhaps not fully realising the consequences, half-heartedly dispatched 5,000 fighting men to support the Siamese, abdicating his responsibility as a Lao citizen at the worst possible time: a colossal and shameful act of treachery. Chao Anouvong must have been filled with utter horror.

After the war, Manthathurath's pride at having supported the Siamese was coupled with a soul-crushing guilt. Most of his subjects were forced to migrate to Siam while a Siam-style kingdom was declared in Luang Phrabang. Unkmo, the vice king, was taken to Bangkok where he died in prison. When Manthathurath died in 1836, Bangkok appointed Sukhaseum to rule. After his demise in 1850 his brother Tiantharath took over; Luang Phrabang's Buddha statue was restored to the city in 1867. When Tiantharath died in 1870, he was succeeded by Manthathurath's fourth son, Ounkham, but they were all mere puppets of Siam and Bangkok demanded absolute subservience from them. They did nothing to restore LanXang.

Naturally I was delighted to hear that a Frenchman (*Farang*), Henri Mouhot, turned up in Luang Phrabang in 1861 but unfortunately died from malaria the same year. I'd hoped Tiantharath would tell Mouhot the truth about Chao Anouvong's war and ask him for help in restoring LanXang and preventing the extinction of the Lao identity. However, the French government's main interest was the Mekong, which Francis Garnier explored in 1866. Thinking it would provide economic opportunities, they were soon disabused by the raging waterfalls and rapids at Khone Phapheng in Champasak. I prayed for them to subdue the Siamese and stand up for LanXang.

I can do nothing but hope that some clever young Lao will find a way to revive the Lao nation, to restore what has been torn away. Since I brought the ring '*Thammalong*' out of the cave as Chao Anouvong requested, someone must be prepared to pick up the power that's been left lying in the dust. That was his hope. A peaceful settlement was always the Lao people's preference, but when I look out the window and see Siamese flags, soldiers and officials, I ask myself how the Lao-speaking people will ever gain their liberty. It must arouse a sense of smouldering resentment in them. I fear a bloodbath unless Bangkok comes to its senses. What else can they do if they fail to restore Lao LanXang by peaceful means?

As Chao Anouvong predicted, LanXang territory has been signed away illegitimately, but in the interests of justice, the world should step in to help us. I hope the oppressors' menace will be banished as dawn vanquishes the darkness of night. LanXang will recall the valiant deeds of her past. The day will come when LanXang will face the future with pride and cry out to the world that she has cast off the fetters of Siam and slavery. Lao LanXang territory should at least extend to the land that King Fah Ngum unified in 1352. This will undo the injustice done to the Lao and level out the balance of power in the region. There must be over twenty million Lao citizens in the LanXang territories alone. But I'll be long gone by then.

Now, if I close my eyes, I can still see King Anouvong's face in the golden light of that last evening before he left ViengChan at nightfall. 'My goal is simple,' he declared. 'A complete restoration of Lao LanXang as a nation in the world.' Alas, his objective was as unachievable as it was glorious; his final day in Bangkok marked the end of an era and was the saddest time of my life. It will remain in my mind forever. It is so hard to believe that he and his ambitions, even ViengChan and the very palaces with which we were so intimately associated, are now nothing but ash.

Chao Anouvong was truly an outstanding monarch, a philosopher who acted justly and behaved honourably, who said that which benefits us is fair and that which harms us shameful. He was ready to live a quiet and steady life, unmoved by war. He was a genuine man of wisdom and honour who had a natural tendency to strive for good. He was a remarkable and successful king, not a failure or a traitor as some people in Siam sneeringly declare. He was born in an era of chaos; his kingdom was in a state of disarray, yet he strove to be like King Fah Ngum. He became a bold and visionary man as well as a virtuous one. He suffered many hardships in his struggles to preserve the Lao nation. He knew himself and he knew his enemies. Perhaps he lost the war, despite all his efforts, through miscalculation, misfortune, lack of manpower and deficient military skills, or simply because he underestimated Nangklao's brutality. Besides, there was discord amongst his ministers and he'd no army, power or wealth to fight the war with, but still the burden fell upon him. He'd to do it. He sacrificed himself for the sake of us all.

I don't think anyone could have done any better. One can only do one's best and leave the rest to heaven. Having succeeded in becoming king, he then had to overcome insurmountable odds to keep the Rattanakosins at bay. He failed to ensure Lao LanXang's independence but should never be accused of failure against mighty Siam, with its foreign aid and mercenaries. He, like any ruler, had his faults – most significantly in placing too much trust in King Naphalai's friendship, too much faith in his viceroy Tissah and for allowing the notorious governor Suriyaphakdy to reach Bangkok. It will be forever unpleasant for a Lao nationalist to travel through the Khorat Plateau and feel ashamed for the loss of his country but remember that Chao Anouvong lost his life trying to reclaim LanXang. It's questionable whether he should have marched on Khorat in the first place; once he'd taken the city, perhaps he should have had the guts, no matter what, to go all the way to Bangkok and catch his enemy cold. The usually mild-mannered Lao people were solidly behind him on that momentous occasion. History would have been so different if the war had been won.

He was always fighting a losing battle: LanXang was fractured and her people were not of one mind. Some in the Khorat Plateau and Luang Phrabang were disloyal to ViengChan. Burma (the Shan state) had been neutralised by the British so was unable to march into Siam if asked. For the British, Siam was a valuable source of soldiers and grain and a viable commercial partner, so they would never assist the Lao. The French were too busy to help as they were competing politically and commercially with the British. The Vietnamese emperor Minh Mang was incompetent and unreliable. All these factors were fundamental to Chao Anouvong's defeat. His abilities were not beneath Nangklao's. He failed only because his friends and allies were weaker and less able than his enemies. Nevertheless, his endeavour remains a lasting inspiration.

No one would ever dare ask the Rattanakosins whether annexing LanXang for the sake of Greater Siam was worth the cost in blood, yet Chao Anouvong didn't want war but preferred peaceful negotiations. He loved his country and was uncompromising and principled in his beliefs. His triumph would have been the highest achievement for the Lao nation.

Chao Anouvong was a Laoman to his fingertips. Bangkok might denounce him as a warmonger and a traitor and heap scorn and insult upon him but because of him, we – the Lao – live our lives in the full knowledge we are Lao people. You, my young fellow countrymen, if I may say so, must be as brave as he. You are the future, and you should ensure that such a fate will never again befall the Lao nation. Future generations will then sing your praises. We must not repeat the mistakes of the past, but – please remember – actions speak louder than words. We should wholeheartedly commit ourselves to the defence of our country, to the last drop of blood. We should follow the can-do spirit of King Fah Ngum: not sitting back and doing nothing but ready to fight to protect our people (*Paxaxon*) and territory. We must unite to revive our shattered country. The mountains may collapse, and the rivers may run dry, but we should be ready to draw on Chao Anouvong's spirit and pick up his sleeping sword to defend our nation. Never again will we be divided and defeated!

Do you know whom we should hold a feast in honour of and drink to? May I propose we dedicate our offerings, make libations and drink a toast in respect of the ancestors, and to commemorate the heroic sacrifice made by our dear King Anouvong. In remembering him and his gallantry we should celebrate by performing customary almsgiving in honour of his immortality. We should also remember our brave fighters who gave their blood to defend our country. They deserve respect. But before taking your drink, please don't forget to make offerings and pour libations to the Lord Buddha and the other gods. Perhaps we should make a pilgrimage to the site and kneel on the spot where he was executed. Similarly, whenever you're in Bangkok, you might like to lay a wreath at Sanamluang field in commemoration of Chao Anouvong. We should unite and anchor ourselves in the past, offer our services to our country and turn his death into the celebration of a national hero.

As a human being, Chao Anouvong's bravery and principles should be appreciated. One can't help but admire him in every respect. He didn't deserve to lose and die the way he did. Despite his failure, he is still a true Lao hero. He was in no way responsible for Siam's brutality. He profoundly believed that all wrongdoing was the result of ignorance. He was a patriotic Lao man, an example of the very best in human nature, a lover of justice and freedom, certainly not a 'rebel' or 'traitor' to Siam. Never! He was executed by the wicked ambition of an unjust ruler in Bangkok. He simply recognised the importance of the Lao nation and made the supreme sacrifice in pursuit of his desire to save the Lao people from injustice and to help the younger generation to grow and flourish into the people they deserved to be.

Therefore, as a nation, it is our duty to thank Chao Anouvong for guiding us, inspiring us and making us proud to be Lao with his selfless duty and sacrifice. He alone stood against Bangkok's domination and injustice. We should make a deep obeisance and then raise our praying hands in a triumphant salute to his spirit. And let us pray also to the gods and the Lord Buddha that before too many years have passed, fresh and greater honour will descend upon our country.

I am going to be bold enough to risk saying that although Chao Anouvong got things wrong, his struggle to preserve the Lao national identity was justified. If only the Lao people live up to his ideals of excellence and do their best to match him in both words and deeds, we can unite the Lao nation with the Mekong running through the middle. This can still be achieved if Lao all around the world unite and share the same hopes and dreams. His desire for Lao LanXang will never be snuffed out by the insatiable ambition of Siam.

King Anouvong believed he'd a duty to save the Lao nation from Bangkok, to regain national sovereignty and leave the kingdom a better place than the one he'd inherited: a kingdom where everyone felt part of a shared endeavour and destiny. Sadly, he paid for it with his own life: a great tragedy for Lao LanXang.

This reverential attitude to LanXang's past opened the way for another powerful national habit: a nostalgic preoccupation with history. It has become an undeniable fact of Lao life, an impulse that has given rise to the Lao Development Front, drawing strength from Chao Anouvong and his son Rathsavong Ngao and their love for the Lao nation.

It's worth repeating that until Bangkok accepts responsibility for its shameful deeds, the Lao will remain wary of even the friendliest Siamese.

King Mongkut passed away three years ago. Apart from paying respects, I have nothing more to say about him but am delighted to have glimpsed him in Bangkok in 1825. King Khoun Borom (750) was the legendary progenitor of the Ai-Lao people: his son Khoun Loh founded LanXang in 757 while King Fah Ngum united it in 1352. His successors fought hard to maintain its independence until 1779. Alas, a vast amount of territory and people have been unacceptably and unjustifiably placed under Siam control (*Ananikom* of Siam). Nevertheless, Lao names and the Lao language and culture persist to this day throughout Siam, predominantly in the north and northeast. It would make sense if the lost Lao – the Phu Tai, the Tai Phuan, the Tai Dam, Tai Daeng, Tai Lue, Tai Nung and the Lao of Siam, Burma, China, Vietnam, Cambodia and elsewhere throughout the world – with their culture and common language, turn to the historical truth.

It is quite a thought. How different King Fah Ngum's Lao LanXang with both banks of the mighty Mekong would have been if Siam had respected the That Si-SongHuck shrine treaty: one Lao nation sharing habits, thoughts, feelings, formed by the same breeding, fed by the same foods and governed by the same rule of laws (*Heed Sipsong-Khong Sipsi*). This was truly what Chao Anouvong and indeed the Lao people wanted, only to be thwarted by Bangkok.

Fortunately LanXang is like a giant, ancient tree growing on a hilltop with deep, strong roots and thick foliage, surrounded by a forest with the wind blowing at it from every direction. Although badly damaged by a nasty south-westerly storm, LanXang, her wealth hidden away underground, is safe and sound. Bangkok thought they'd put her to death because she stooped and drooped and became dull and lifeless. But she is very much alive in root and trunk and ready to shoot. Should the world come dancing, she will grow strong again. One neither knows the will of heaven nor the fortunes of the world, but misery is often followed by good fortune.

You may well ask why I wrote about Lao LanXang and her ill-fated king. It was purely from a desire to establish some facts, not because I sought to be special but because I wanted to delve deeper into the truth. I was fully aware of the social and political significance. Please understand that I'm telling a story, not recording history. As far as I'm concerned, I couldn't do the story justice without making Chao Anouvong immortal – a legend. Bangkok knows all about him but remains silent for fear of losing face. How he lived in comparison with how he died does matter. He was both courageous and patriotic; he may have failed courageously but his death will never be forgotten. His story unquestionably shows that Bangkok was guilty of annihilating ViengChan, of pillaging, of forcing people to leave their homes, of annexing territory from LanNa and LanXang, of marking people with numbers, of torturing and killing a just man.

Had Chao Anouvong's LanXang been equipped with enough weaponry to compete militarily with the Siamese, then he might well have claimed victory. He would have been lauded and feted and held up as an example of good triumphing over evil. Nevertheless, despite his ultimate failure, his endeavours laid the foundations for a resurgence of Lao consciousness.

The purpose of this story is to set the record straight for LanXang and to do justice to the reputation of a man who was, without any doubt, a most engaging being of the highest integrity. I am investigating the truth, not propagating untruths. This is not only a moral proclamation but a worthwhile study for anyone who wishes to share it. It took me many years and on some occasions I could almost feel Chao Anouvong's hand taking mine, helping me to write about all the memorable years I spent in his company. It didn't fill me with depression because he'd prepared himself for his fate. I was sometimes conscious of the presence of his spirit; very often he appeared in my sleep, advising me what to say and even scolding me if my writing became too political or emotional. 'Your Majesty, forgive me,' I would answer. 'I apologise unreservedly in advance for any offence caused, but my opinions on Siam and other countries are perhaps not without merit. Perhaps I shouldn't have written what I did but the Siamese gave us a glorious excuse. The truth should really come from those who invaded, colonised and carved up Lao LanXang and caused widespread suffering.' I had to calm down when I woke up, I tell you. Truly, many times I think he's still alive; if that were so and his dreams were to come true, I would be the happiest man on earth. There would be unbelievable scenes of jubilation in LanXang.

Now I'm an infirm old man of nearly a hundred; physically weak but mentally sound. I exert every muscle and limb to move about, for staying still is a killer and most people die in their beds. I have no interests except for the love of a dear friend and happy memories to keep me going in this world, to which I am indifferent. I sit alone most of the time and vegetate, utterly feeble, dispirited and downhearted after breaking both hips in a series of bad falls. I can hardly walk without a friend's support or the aid of a stick. I'm fit only to keep books, distant seas, mountains and rivers company. I keep myself busy trying to lessen my follies, prejudices and false opinions. My days are numbered, but for the prosperity of future generations I devote them to the past. One of the saddest things about my advanced age is that relatives smile, laugh inwardly and show no charity towards you. Despite the power in their hands, they can't be bothered with the very old and decrepit, who need love and attention but hate the world which has left them behind and have no future to look forward to. You don't want to change anything, but because of their love of money, they betray you; they wanted you out! My infirmities are now obvious but knowing Chao Anouvong for so long and having a close, trustworthy friend who really cared and looked after me has added years to my life, enough to see many wheels come full circle. They will continue to turn, long after I'm gone.

At the beginning I really thought I would never recover from his death and the harsh realities of life in losing him and the Lao identity. Despite bouts of depression, time kills grief and I've said enough now. Soon I'll be dead too and these words will be all that remains of me, enough I hope to make Chao Anouvong and his followers rejoice in the afterlife. The thought of mortality has induced a frantic determination in me to finish the story before my power fades. That, my noble friends, is all I have to say in honour of LanXang and King Anouvong the Great (*Maharath*). One of the truisms about his reign is that we can see his failures and not his successes. I apologise if I have over-emphasised, over-pontificated and over-praised him. Equally, I am sorry about anything boring in my narrative! I rest my case. At any rate, writing about him and LanXang has been my humble salvation. It has meant a lot to me. It has comforted me in my loneliness. I hope the story has cheered you. My deeds don't count. The credit belongs to the man who sacrificed himself for his country. He and his followers were martyrs to the worthy cause of the Lao Kingdom of LanXang. It is done.

Now I'm free but quite concerned by the thought I may have woken Chao Anouvong's ghost. We can only look back to this remarkable man and recognise in his bravery and sacrifice a quality that more than merits a narrative history. As you wander around beneath the pale sky of Bangkok, the Rattanakosin Island's dark past, if the truth were told, would make rather a chilling walk. You might even sense where he was tortured and killed. His spirit must be watching over the Lao people's fate. He'll be overjoyed when LanXang reunification is achieved, even in that other world. He would be reborn!

I don't mind if people say excoriating things or make disparaging remarks about me. I don't mean to offend, though the Siamese should be in absolutely no doubt where Lao LanXang stands on this issue. They should laugh at the truth instead of wanting to harm me. I really hope they don't take it too seriously. However, there could be hissing voices and uproar and moral outrage in Siam as a result of my book, but it will pass. Besides, only people with guilty consciences would be overwhelmed by feelings of hate and revenge and seek retaliation. One shouldn't be surprised by the speed of reaction and the degree of hatred of the Siamese, but how good would it be if they channelled their outrage into a fight against prejudice. For the noblest of reasons some people might turn against Siam, become disaffected with the Rattanakosins and do their level best to unearth the truth now that I have started. However, a true Buddhist should never seek to harm another being, not even an insect. Yet Bangkok has a long reach: you may never intend harm against others but beware of their intentions towards you. I can steel myself to bear the thought of death and my body going up in flames, but the thought of Siamese academics, scholars and royalists burning my book without even reading it makes me tremble. Some still dare to deny the truth to the very end. I wouldn't be surprised, even in my grand and silly old age, if nasty people in Siam come after me with weapons and poison and do something terrible to me: kidnap me, torture me and make me vanish without trace. I sincerely hope not. Perhaps they regard me as radioactive and won't come near! But I hope sympathetic friends, those who believe in peace and justice, and my country – Lao LanXang – will protect me. Surely Lord Buddha (*Phra Buddhachao*) and the gods won't punish me for my most desired wish.

I declare that King Anouvong, the last monarch of ViengChan, is utterly unforgettable.

He invigorated the Lao people and for his glorious deeds he became immortalised in history.

Beyond doubt he is an immortal.

Lest we forget.

Thank you (*Kobjai* ຂອບໃຈ) for listening.

Xanouvong